AF528832

The yellowbacks... classics of popular fiction

The yellowjackets or yellowbacks were a great series of bestselling adventure and crime thrillers that had its origins in the mid to late 19th century following on from the 'penny dreadfuls'. They virtually began the mass market revolution of the early 20th century with a clear standard format and imprint/series livery (what would today be called branding). Hodder & Stoughton published the yellowjackets in two main series with series run dates of: 1923-1939 and later 1949-1957.

As the tagline ('where thrillers really began') on the back cover implies, the imprint and series focused on thrillers that were the bestsellers of their time. This current reissue or retro revival if you will, brings back many of these masterpieces, now classics in their own way and extends it further by including key titles from that period that were either great crime or thriller or even general commercial fiction (including sub-genres of noir, horror, gothic, romance, westerns, etc.) influences of their time. There are some perennial favourites and many rarities either lost or not easily available being revived in the current series. Writers and characters ranged from adventure heroes like Bulldog Drummond, Allan Quatermain, Richard Hannay or the Saint through thriller grandmasters Edgar Wallace and E. Phillips Oppenheim, crime and mystery maestros like Patricia Wentworth, GK Chesterton, Agatha Christie and the Detection club, to western and swashbucklers like Zane Grey, Max Brand, Captain Blood and even romance or general fiction classics like Hermina Black, Denise Robins, Marie Corelli or Stella Morton. These were books that had storytelling at their heart and always entertained.

The yellowbacks had both hardback (with varying design elements) and paperback (which built the series look) versions with the latter still carrying the imprint 'yellowjacket'. The current reissues pay tribute to both and use an amalgam of elements from both editions while retaining the complete yellow (or 'mustard-plaster') livery with the author's name in blue beveled type with a 'simulated emboss' effect and a white outer 'outline', and the book title in black. These reissues retain the distinctive size of the original mass market paperback and follow the three main category variations—the thrillers (crime, westerns, mystery, adventure) had blue lettering for the author's name, while Romance and softer general fiction had red; and other categories like humour had green.

For more detail and a full list of titles visit https://www.hachetteindia.com/home/yellowbacks

THE COMPLETE CONTINENTAL OP

VOLUME I

THE COMPLETE CONTINENTAL OP

Dashiell Hammett, (1894-1961), was an American writer who created the hard-boiled school of detective fiction. Hammett left school at 13 and worked at a variety of low-paying jobs before working eight years as a detective for the Pinkerton agency. He served in World War I, contracted tuberculosis, and spent the immediate postwar years in army hospitals. He began to publish short stories and novelettes in pulp magazines and wrote two novels—*Red Harvest* and *The Dain Curse* (both published in 1929)—before writing *The Maltese Falcon* (1930), generally considered his finest work. It introduced Sam Spade, Hammett's fictional detective creation, played by Humphrey Bogart in the film version directed by John Huston (1941), which became a classic of its genre. He also wrote *The Glass Key* (1931) and *The Thin Man* (1934), which initiated a motion picture and later a television series built around his detecting couple, Nick and Nora Charles. Nora was based on the playwright Lillian Hellman, with whom he formed a romantic alliance in 1930 that lasted until his death. Her *Pentimento* (1973) has an account of their life together.

After 1934, Hammett devoted his time to left-wing political activities and to the defense of civil liberties. He served in World War II as an enlisted man. In 1951, he went to jail for six months because he refused to reveal the names of the contributors to the bail bond fund of the Civil Rights Congress, of which he was a trustee.

THE COMPLETE CONTINENTAL OP

Dashiell Hammett

VOLUME I

Section One: The Sutton Years
Section Two: The Cody Years

hachette

The Complete Continental Op
The Continental Op's first appearance was in 1923. This collection across 2 volumes includes all 37 stories featuring the Op - comprising the 28 short stories, the unfinished story and the eight parts of the two serialized novels, *The Cleansing of Poisonville (Red Harvest)* and *The Dain Curse* as they first appeared in the pulp magazines. See contents pages for detailed publishing history.

1

The texts in these editions in most cases have been reprinted as is, with minimal editorial changes and by and large no bowdlerizing for political correctness; though in some editions, a few words and phrases considered archaic, or those considered offensive now, along with archaic punctuation may have been modified in places to make the text more accessible to today's readers. The narratives, language, beliefs, social mores and/or cultural depictions in these volumes are a reflection of their times and must be viewed as such. They may also contain certain cultural, racial and gender prejudices and stereotypes that may be outdated or clearly wrong then and wrong today; but their removal would be tantamount to claiming these prejudices never existed. The Publisher does not endorse or support those depictions or stereotypes; and these books have been made available for a discerning audience that will read it for entertainment value and a chronicle/record of popular fiction of past times.

Cover design by Priya Singh adapted from the original classic yellowjacket by Hodder & Stoughton.

Cover illustration by Ishan Trivedi.

Series note: Some of the books in the series (unless otherwise credited) may have cover or inside illustrations from the original yellowbacks or early editions, and while full restoration has been attempted, some images may be grainy or faded due to the condition of the original material. The endnotes or bonus material or blurb details may have been sourced from the public domain or free use publications such as Wikipedia and attribution is hereby made also allowing similar free use reproduction from here. Sources requiring further specific attribution may write in and further detailing and/or corrections shall be made in subsequent printings/editions.

Reprint specifications may be subject to change including but not limited to finishes, paper, colour sections.

ISBN: 978-93-5731-224-0

Hachette Book Publishing India Pvt. Ltd.
4th & 5th Floors, Corporate Centre,
Plot No. 94, Sector 44, Gurugram - 122 003, India

Typeset in Electra LT STD 10/12.5 pt by Manipal Technologies Limited, Manipal

Printed and bound in India by Manipal Technologies Limited, Manipal

CONTENTS

Sections One and Two (the Sutton and Cody years) are in Vol 1. Section Three (the Shaw years), the unfinished story and the Novels *Red Harvest* and *The Dain Curse* are in Vol 2.

Section One: The Sutton years

(Hammett's output was classified under the editorial reigns of Black mask. The Sutton years refers to the stewardship of George Sutton)

Publication history

1. 'Arson Plus' (Black Mask, October 1, 1923) (as Peter Collinson)
2. 'Crooked Souls' ('The Gatewood Caper') (Black Mask, October 1, 1923)
3. 'Slippery Fingers' (Black Mask, October 15, 1923) (as Peter Collinson)
4. 'It' ('The Black Hat That Wasn't There') (Black Mask, November 1, 1923)
5. 'Bodies Piled Up' (:The House Dick') (Black Mask, December 1, 1923)
6. 'The Tenth Clew' ('The Tenth Clue') (Black Mask, January 1, 1924)
7. 'Night Shots' (Black Mask, February 1924)
8. 'Zigzags of Treachery' (Black Mask, March 1, 1924)
9. 'One Hour' (Black Mask, April 1924)

Section Two : The Cody Years (stories in the Black Mask)

(The Cody years refers to the stewardship of Phillip C. Cody who became the editor of *Black Mask* in 1924)
Joseph T. Shaw

Publication history

10. 'The House in Turk Street' (Black Mask, April 15, 1924)
11. 'The Girl with Silver Eyes' (Black Mask, June 1924)
12. 'Women, Politics and Murder' ('Death on Pine Street') (Black Mask, September 1924)
13. 'The Golden Horseshoe' (Black Mask, November 1924)
14. 'Who Killed Bob Teal?' (True Detective Stories, November 1924)
15. 'Mike, Alec or Rufus?' ('Tom, Dick or Harry') (Black Mask, January 1925)
16. 'The Whosis Kid' (Black Mask, March 1925)
17. 'The Scorched Face' (Black Mask, May 1925)
18. 'Corkscrew' (Black Mask, September 1925)
19. 'Dead Yellow Women' (Black Mask, November 1925)
20. The Gutting of Couffignal (Black Mask, December 1925)
21. 'Creeping Siamese' (Black Mask, March 1926)

Section One: The Sutton Years

CONTENTS

1

ARSON PLUS

BLACK MASK, OCTOBER 1, 1923

This is a detective story you'll have a hard time solving before the end. Form your ideas of the outcome as you go along and then see how near you guessed it.

Jim Tarr picked up the cigar I rolled across his desk, looked at the band, bit off an end, and reached for a match.

"Fifteen cents straight," he said. "You must want me to break a *couple* of laws for you this time."

I had been doing business with this fat sheriff of Sacramento County for four or five years—ever since I came to the Continental Detective Agency's San Francisco office—and I had never known him to miss an opening for a sour crack; but it didn't mean anything.

"Wrong both times," I told him. "I get two of them for a quarter; and I'm here to do you a favor instead of asking for one. The company that insured Thornburgh's house thinks somebody touched it off."

"That's right enough, according to the fire department. They tell me the lower part of the house was soaked with gasoline, but God knows how they could tell—there wasn't a stick left standing. I've got McClump working on it, but he hasn't found anything to get excited about yet."

"What's the layout? All I know is that there was a fire."

Tarr leaned back in his chair, turned his red face to the ceiling, and bellowed:

"Hey; Mac!"

The pearl push-buttons on his desk are ornaments as far as he is concerned. Deputy sheriffs McHale, McClump and Macklin came to the door together—MacNab apparently wasn't within hearing.

"What's the idea?" the sheriff demanded of McClump. "Are you carrying a bodyguard around with you?"

The two other deputies, thus informed as to who "Mac" referred to this time, went back to their cribbage game.

"We got a city slicker here to catch our firebug for us," Tarr told his deputy. "But we got to tell him what it's all about first."

McClump and I had worked together on an express robbery, several months before. He's a rangy, towheaded youngster of twenty-five or six, with all the nerve in the world—and most of the laziness.

"Ain't the Lord good to us?"

He had himself draped across a chair by now—always his first objective when he comes into a room.

"Well, here's how she stands: This fellow Thornburgh's house was a couple miles out of town, on the old county road—an old frame house. About midnight, night before last, Jeff Pringle—the nearest neighbor, a half-mile or so to the east—saw a glare in the sky from over that way, and phoned in the alarm; but by the time the fire wagons got there, there wasn't enough of the house left to bother about. Pringle was the first of the neighbors to get to the house, and the roof had already fell in then.

"Nobody saw anything suspicious—no strangers hanging around or nothing. Thornburgh's help just managed to save themselves, and that was all. They don't know much about what happened—too scared, I reckon. But they did see Thornburgh at his window just before the fire got him. A fellow here in town—name of Handerson—saw that part of it too. He was driving home from Wayton, and got to the house just before the roof caved in.

"The fire department people say they found signs of gasoline. The Coonses, Thornburgh's help, say they didn't have no gas on the place. So there you are."

"Thornburgh have any relatives?"

"Yeah. A niece in San Francisco—a Mrs Evelyn Trowbridge. She was up yesterday, but there wasn't nothing she could do, and she couldn't tell us nothing much, so she went back home."

"Where are the servants now?"

"Here in town. Staying at a hotel on I Street. I told 'em to stick around for a few days."

"Thornburgh own the house?"

"Uh-huh. Bought it from Newning & Weed a couple months ago."

"You got anything to do this morning?"

"Nothing but this."

"Good! Let's get out and dig around."

We found the Coonses in their room at the hotel on I Street. Mr Coons was a small-boned, plump man with the smooth, meaningless face, and the suavity of the typical male house-servant.

His wife was a tall, stringy woman, perhaps five years older than her husband—say, forty—with a mouth and chin that seemed shaped for gossiping. But he did all the talking, while she nodded her agreement to every second or third word.

"We went to work for Mr Thornburgh on the fifteenth of June, I think," he said, in reply to my first question. "We came to Sacramento, around the first of the month, and put in applications at the Allis Employment Bureau. A couple of weeks later they sent us out to see Mr Thornburgh, and he took us on."

"Where were you before you came here?"

"In Seattle, sir, with a Mrs Comerford; but the climate there didn't agree with my wife—she has bronchial trouble—so we decided to come to California. We most likely would have stayed in Seattle, though, if Mrs Comerford hadn't given up her house."

"What do you know about Thornburgh?"

"Very little, sir. He wasn't a talkative gentleman. He hadn't any business that I know of. I think he was a retired seafaring man. He never said he was, but he had that manner and look. He never went out or had anybody in to see him, except his niece once, and he didn't write or get any mail. He had a room next to his bedroom fixed up as a sort of workshop. He spent most of his time in there. I always thought he was working on some kind of invention, but he kept the door locked, and wouldn't let us go near it."

"Haven't you any idea at all what it was?"

"No, sir. We never heard any hammering or noises from it, and never smelt anything either. And none of his clothes were ever the least bit soiled, even when they were ready to go out to the laundry. They would have been if he had been working on anything like machinery."

"Was he an old man?"

"He couldn't have been over fifty, sir. He was very erect, and his hair and beard were thick, with no gray hairs."

"Ever have any trouble with him?"

"Oh, no, sir! He was, if I may say it, a very peculiar gentleman in a way; and he didn't care about anything except having his meals fixed right, having his clothes taken care of—he was very particular about them—and not being disturbed. Except early in the morning and at night, we'd hardly see him all day."

"Now about the fire. Tell us the whole thing—everything you remember."

"Well, sir, I and my wife had gone to bed about ten o'clock, our regular time, and had gone to sleep. Our room was on the second floor, in the rear. Sometime later—I never did exactly know what time it was—I woke up, coughing. The room was all full of smoke, and my wife was sort of strangling. I jumped up, and dragged her down the back stairs and out the back door, not thinking of anything but getting her out of there.

"When I had her safe in the yard, I thought of Mr Thornburgh, and tried to get back in the house; but the whole first floor was just flames. I ran around front then, to see if he had got out, but didn't see anything of him. The whole yard was as light as day by then. Then I heard him scream—a horrible scream, sir—I can hear it yet! And I looked up at his window—that was the front second-storey room—and saw him there, trying to get out the window. But all the woodwork was burning, and he screamed again and fell back, and right after that the roof over his room fell in.

"There wasn't a ladder or anything that I could have put up to the window for him—there wasn't anything I could have done.

"In the meantime, a gentleman had left his automobile in the road, and come up to where I was standing; but there wasn't anything we could do—the house was burning everywhere and falling in here and there. So we went back to where I had left my wife, and carried her farther away from the fire, and brought her to—she had fainted. And that's all I know about it, sir."

"Hear any noises earlier that night? Or see anybody hanging around?"

"No, sir."

"Have any gasoline around the place?"

"No, sir. Mr Thornburgh didn't have a car."

"No gasoline for cleaning?"

"No, sir, none at all, unless Mr Thornburgh had it in his workshop. When his clothes needed cleaning, I took them to town, and all his laundry was taken by the grocer's man, when he brought our provisions."

"Don't know anything that might have some bearing on the fire?"

"No, sir. I was surprised when I heard that somebody had set the house afire. I could hardly believe it. I don't know why anybody should want to do that."

"What do you think of them?" I asked McClump, as we left the hotel.

"They might pad the bills, or even go South with some of the silver, but they don't figure as killers in my mind."

That was my opinion, too; but they were the only persons known to have been there when the fire started except the man who had died. We went around to the Allis Employment Bureau and talked to the manager.

He told us that the Coonses had come into his office on June second, looking for work; and had given Mrs Edward Comerford, 45 Woodmansee Terrace, Seattle, Washington, as reference. In reply to a letter—he always checked up the references of servants—

Mrs Comerford had written that the Coonses had been in her employ for a number of years, and had been "extremely satisfactory in every respect." On June thirteenth, Thornburgh had telephoned the bureau, asking that a man and his wife be sent out to keep house for him; and Allis had sent two couples that he had listed. Neither had been employed by Thornburgh, though Allis considered them more desirable than the Coonses, who were finally hired by Thornburgh.

All that would certainly seem to indicate that the Coonses hadn't deliberately maneuvered themselves into the place, unless they were the luckiest people in the world—and a detective can't afford to believe in luck or coincidence, unless he has unquestionable proof of it.

At the office of the real estate agents, through whom Thornburgh had bought the house—Newning & Weed—we were told that Thornburgh had come in on the eleventh of June, and had said that he had been told that the house was for sale, had looked it over, and wanted to know the price. The deal had been closed the next morning, and he had paid for the house with a check for $4,500 on the Seamen's Bank of San Francisco. The house was already furnished.

After luncheon, McClump and I called on Howard Handerson—the man who had seen the fire while driving home from Wayton. He had an office in the Empire Building, with his name and the title "Northern California Agent, Instant-Sheen Cleanser Company," on the door. He was a big, careless-looking man of forty-five or so, with the professionally jovial smile that belongs to the salesman.

He had been in Wayton on business the day of the fire, he said, and had stayed there until rather late, going to dinner and afterward playing pool with a grocer named Hammersmith—one of his customers. He had left Wayton in his machine, at about ten-thirty, and set out for Sacramento. At Tavender he had stopped at the garage for oil and gas and to have one of his tires blown up.

Just as he was about to leave the garage, the garage-man had called his attention to a red glare in the sky, and had told him that it was probably from a fire somewhere along the old county road that paralleled the State Road into Sacramento; so Handerson had taken the county road, and had arrived at the burning house just in time to see Thornburgh try to fight his way through the flames that enveloped him.

It was too late to make any attempt to put out the fire, and the man upstairs was beyond saving by then—undoubtedly dead even before the roof collapsed; so Handerson had helped

Coons revive his wife, and stayed there watching the fire until it had burned itself out. He had seen no one on that county road while driving to the fire.

"What do you know about Handerson?" I asked McClump, when we were on the street.

"Came here, from somewhere in the East, I think, early in the summer to open that Cleanser agency. Lives at the Garden Hotel. Where do we go next?"

"We get a machine, and take a look at what's left of the Thornburgh house."

An enterprising incendiary couldn't have found a lovelier spot in which to turn himself loose, if he looked the whole county over. Tree-topped hills hid it from the rest of the world, on three sides; while away from the fourth, an uninhabited plain rolled down to the river. The county road that passed the front gate was shunned by automobiles, so McClump said, in favor of the State Highway to the north.

Where the house had been, was now a mound of blackened ruins. We poked around in the ashes for a few minutes—not that we expected to find anything, but because it's the nature of man to poke around in ruins.

A garage in the rear, whose interior gave no evidence of recent occupation, had a badly scorched roof and front, but was otherwise undamaged. A shed behind it, sheltering an ax, a shovel, and various odds and ends of gardening tools, had escaped the fire altogether. The lawn in front of the house, and the garden behind the shed—about an acre in all—had been pretty thoroughly cut and trampled by wagon wheels, and the feet of the firemen and the spectators.

Having ruined our shoe-shines, McClump and I got back in our machine and swung off in a circle around the place, calling at all the houses within a mile radius, and getting little besides jolts for our trouble.

The nearest house was that of Pringle, the man who had turned in the alarm; but he not only knew nothing about the dead man, but said he had never seen him. In fact, only one of the neighbors had ever seen him: a Mrs Jabine, who lived about a mile to the south.

She had taken care of the key to the house while it was vacant; and a day or two before he bought it, Thornburgh had come to her house, inquiring about the vacant one. She had gone over there with him and showed him through it, and he had told her that he intended buying it, if the price, of which neither of them knew anything, wasn't too high.

He had been alone, except for the chauffeur of the hired car in which he had come from Sacramento, and, save that he had no family, he had told her nothing about himself.

Hearing that he had moved in, she went over to call on him several days later—"just a neighborly visit"—but had been told by Mrs Coons that he was not at home. Most of the neighbors had talked to the Coonses, and had got the impression that Thornburgh did not care for visitors, so they had let him alone. The Coonses were described as "pleasant enough to talk to when you meet them," but reflecting their employer's desire not to make friends.

McClump summarized what the afternoon had taught us as we pointed our machine toward Tavender: "Any of these folks could have touched off the place, but we got nothing to show that any of 'em even knew Thornburgh, let alone had a bone to pick with him."

Tavender turned out to be a crossroads settlement of a general store and post office, a garage, a church, and six dwellings, about two miles from Thornburgh's place. McClump knew the storekeeper and postmaster, a scrawny little man named Philo, who stuttered moistly.

"I n-n-never s-saw Th-thornburgh," he said, "and I n-n-never had any m-mail for him. C-coons"—it sounded like one of these things butterflies come out of—"used to c-come in once a week t-to order groceries—they d-didn't have a phone. He used to walk in, and I'd s-send the stuff over in my c-c-car. Th-then I'd s-see him once in a while, waiting f-for the stage to S-s-sacramento."

"Who drove the stuff out to Thornburgh's?"

"M-m-my b-boy. Want to t-talk to him?"

The boy was a juvenile edition of the old man, but without the stutter. He had never seen Thornburgh on any of his visits, but his business had taken him only as far as the kitchen. He hadn't noticed anything peculiar about the place.

"Who's the night man at the garage?" I asked him, after we had listened to the little he had to tell.

"Billy Luce. I think you can catch him there now. I saw him go in a few minutes ago."

We crossed the road and found Luce.

"Night before last—the night of the fire down the road—was there a man here talking to you when you first saw it?"

He turned his eyes upward in that vacant stare which people use to aid their memory.

"Yes, I remember now! He was going to town, and I told him that if he took the county road instead of the State Road he'd see the fire on his way in."

"What kind of looking man was he?"

"Middle-aged—a big man, but sort of slouchy. I think he had on a brown suit, baggy and wrinkled."

"Medium complexion?"

"Yes."

"Smile when he talked?"

"Yes, a pleasant sort of fellow."

"Curly brown hair?"

"Have a heart!" Luce laughed. "I didn't put him under a magnifying glass."

From Tavender, we drove over to Wayton. Luce's description had fit Handerson all right; but while we were at it, we thought we might as well check up to make sure that he had been coming from Wayton.

We spent exactly twenty-five minutes in Wayton; ten of them finding Hammersmith, the grocer with whom Handerson had said he dined and played pool; five minutes finding the proprietor of the pool-room; and ten verifying Handerson's story.

"What do you think of it now, Mac?" I asked, as we rolled back toward Sacramento.

Mac's too lazy to express an opinion, or even form one, unless he's driven to it; but that doesn't mean they aren't worth listening to, if you can get them.

"There ain't a hell of a lot to think," he said cheerfully. "Handerson is out of it, if he ever was in it. There's nothing to show that anybody but the Coonses and Thornburgh were there when the fire started—but there may have been a regiment there. Them Coonses ain't too honest looking, maybe, but they ain't killers, or I miss my guess. But the fact remains that they're the only bet we got so far. Maybe we ought to try to get a line on them."

"All right," I agreed. "I'll get a wire off to our Seattle office asking them to interview Mrs Comerford, and see what she can tell about them as soon as we get back in town. Then I'm going to catch a train for San Francisco, and sec Thornburgh's niece in the morning."

Next morning, at the address McClump had given me—a rather elaborate apartment building on California Street—I had to wait three-quarters of an hour for Mrs Evelyn Trowbridge to dress. If I had been younger, or a social caller, I suppose I'd have felt amply rewarded when she finally came in—a tall, slender woman of less than thirty; in some sort of clinging black affair;

with a lot of black hair over a very white face, strikingly set off by a small red mouth and big hazel eyes that looked black until you got close to them.

But I was a busy, middle-aged detective, who was fuming over having his time wasted; and I was a lot more interested in finding the bird who struck the match than I was in feminine beauty. However, I smothered my grouch, apologized for disturbing her at such an early hour, and got down to business.

"I want you to tell me all you know about your uncle—his family, friends, enemies, business connections, everything."

I had scribbled on the back of the card I had sent into her what my business was.

"He hadn't any family;" she said; "unless I might be it. He was my mother's brother, and I am the only one of that family now living."

"Where was he born?"

"Here in San Francisco. I don't know the date, but he was about fifty years old, I think—three years older than my mother."

"What was his business?"

"He went to sea when he was a boy, and, so far as I know, always followed it until a few months ago."

"Captain?"

"I don't know' Sometimes I wouldn't see or hear from him for several years, and he never talked about what he was doing; though he would mention some of the places he had visited—Rio de Janeiro, Madagascar, Tobago, Christiania. Then, about three months ago—sometime in May—he came here and told me that he was through with wandering; that he was going to take a house in some quiet place where he could work undisturbed on an invention in which he was interested.

"He lived at the Francisco Hotel while he was in San Francisco. After a couple of weeks, he suddenly disappeared. And then, about a month ago, I received a telegram from him, asking me to come to see him at his house near Sacramento. I went up the very next day, and I thought that he was acting very queerly—he seemed very excited over something. He gave me a will that he had just drawn up and some life insurance policies in which I was beneficiary.

"Immediately after that he insisted that I return home, and hinted rather plainly that he did not wish me to either visit him again or write until I heard from him. I thought all that rather peculiar, as he had always seemed fond of me. I never saw him again."

"What was this invention he was working on?"

"I really don't know. I asked him once, but he became so excited—even suspicious—that I changed the subject, and never mentioned it again."

"Are you sure that he really did follow the sea all those years?"

"No, I am not. I just took it for granted; but he may have been doing something altogether different."

"Was he ever married?"

"Not that I know of."

"Know any of his friends or enemies?"

"No, none."

"Remember anybody's name that he ever mentioned?"

"No."

"I don't want you to think this next question insulting, though I admit it is. But it has to be asked. Where were you the night of the fire?"

"At home; I had some friends here to dinner, and they stayed until about midnight. Mr and Mrs Walker Kellogg, Mrs John Dupree, and a Mr Killmer, who is a lawyer. I can give you their addresses, or you can get them from the phone book, if you want to question them."

From Mrs Trowbridge's apartment I went to the Francisco Hotel. Thornburgh had been registered there from May tenth to June thirteenth, and hadn't attracted much attention. He had been a tall, broad-shouldered, erect man of about fifty, with rather long brown hair brushed straight back; a short, pointed brown beard, and healthy, ruddy complexion—grave, quiet, punctilious in dress and manner; his hours had been regular and he had had no visitors that any of the hotel employees remembered.

At the Seamen's Bank—upon which Thornburgh's check, in payment of the house, had been drawn—I was told that he had opened an account there on May fifteenth, having been introduced by W. W. Jeffers & Sons, local stock brokers. A balance of a little more than four hundred dollars remained to his credit. The cancelled checks on hand were all to the order of various life insurance companies; and for amounts that, if they represented premiums, testified to rather large policies. I jotted down the names of the life insurance companies, and then went to the offices of W. W. Jeffers & Sons.

Thornburgh had come in, I was told, on the tenth of May with $84,000 worth of Liberty bonds that he wanted sold. During one of his conversations with Jeffers, he had asked the broker to recommend a bank, and Jeffers had given him a letter of introduction to the Seamen's Bank.

That was all Jeffers knew about him. He gave me the numbers of the bonds, but tracing Liberty bonds isn't the easiest thing in the world.

The reply to my Seattle telegram was waiting for me at the agency when I arrived.

MRS EDWARD COMERFORD RENTED APARTMENT AT ADDRESS YOU GIVE ON MAY TWENTY-FIVE GAVE IT UP JUNE SIX TRUNKS TO SAN FRANCISCO SAME DAY CHECK NUMBERS GN FOUR FIVE TWO FIVE EIGHT SEVEN AND EIGHT AND NINE

Tracing baggage is no trick at all, if you have the dates and check numbers to start with—as many a bird who is wearing somewhat similar numbers on his chest and back, because he overlooked that detail when making his getaway, can tell you—and twenty-five minutes in a baggage room at the Ferry and half an hour in the office of a transfer company gave me my answer.

The trunks had been delivered to Mrs Evelyn Trowbridge's apartment!

I got Jim Tarr on the phone and told him about it.

"Good shooting!" he said, forgetting for once to indulge his wit. "We'll grab the Coonses here and Mrs Trowbridge there, and that's the end of another mystery."

"Wait a minute!" I cautioned him. "It's not all straightened out yet! There's still a few kinks in the plot."

"It's straight enough for me. I'm satisfied."

"You're the boss, but I think you're being a little hasty. I'm going up and talk with the niece again. Give me a little time before you phone the police here to make the pinch. I'll hold her until they get there."

Evelyn Trowbridge let me in this time, instead of the maid who had opened the door for me in the morning, and she led me to the same room in which we had had our first talk. I let her pick out a seat, and then I selected one that was closer to either door than hers was.

On the way up I had planned a lot of innocent-sounding questions that would get her all snarled up; but after taking a good look at this woman sitting in front of me, leaning comfortably back in her chair, coolly waiting for me to speak my piece, I discarded the trick stuff and came out cold-turkey.

"Ever use the name Mrs Edward Comerford?"

"Oh, yes." As casual as a nod on the street.

"When?"

"Often. You see, I happen to have been married not so long ago to Mr Edward Comerford. So it's not really strange that I should have used the name."

"Use it in Seattle recently?"

"I would suggest," she said sweetly, "that if you are leading up to the references I gave Coons and his wife, you might save time by coming right to it?"

"That's fair enough," I said. "Let's do that."

There wasn't a half-tone, a shading, in voice, manner, or expression to indicate that she was talking about anything half so serious or important to her as a possibility of being charged with murder. She might have been talking about the weather, or a book that hadn't interested her particularly.

"During the time that Mr Comerford and I were married, we lived in Seattle, where he still lives. After the divorce, I left Seattle and resumed my maiden name. And the Coonses *were* in our employ, as you might learn if you care to look it up. You'll find my husband—or former husband—at the Chelsea apartments, I think.

"Last summer, or late spring, I decided to return to Seattle. The truth of it is—I suppose all my personal affairs will be aired anyhow—that I thought perhaps Edward and I might patch up our differences; so I went back and took an apartment on Woodmansee Terrace. As I was known in Seattle as Mrs Edward Comerford, and as I thought my using his name might influence him a little, perhaps, I used it while I was there.

"Also I telephoned the Coonses to make tentative arrangements in case Edward and I should open our house again; but Coons told me that they were going to California, and so I gladly gave them an excellent recommendation when, some days later, I received a letter of inquiry from an employment bureau in Sacramento. After I had been in Seattle for about two weeks, I changed my mind about the reconciliation—Edward's interest, I learned, was all centered elsewhere; so I returned to San Francisco."

"Very nice! But—"

"If you will permit me to finish," she interrupted. "When I went to see my uncle in response to his telegram, I was surprised to find the Coonses in his house. Knowing my uncle's peculiarities, and finding them now increased, and remembering his extreme secretiveness about his mysterious invention, I cautioned the Coonses not to tell him that they had been in my employ.

"He certainly would have discharged them, and just as certainly would have quarreled with me—he would have thought that I was having him spied upon. Then, when Coons telephoned me after the fire, I knew that to admit that the Coonses had been formerly in my employ, would, in view of the fact that I was my uncle's heir, cast suspicion on all three of us. So we foolishly agreed to say nothing about it and carry on the deception."

That didn't sound all wrong, but it didn't sound all right. I wished Tarr had taken it easier and let us get a better line on these people, before having them thrown in the coop.

"The coincidence of the Coonses stumbling into my uncle's house is, I fancy, too much for your detecting instincts," she went on, as I didn't say anything. "Am I to consider myself under arrest?"

I'm beginning to like this girl; she's a nice, cool piece of work.

"Not yet," I told her. "But I'm afraid it's going to happen pretty soon."

She smiled a little mocking smile at that, and another when the doorbell rang.

It was O'Hara from police headquarters. We turned the apartment upside down and inside out, but didn't find anything of importance except the will she had told me about, dated July eighth, and her uncle's life insurance policies. They were all dated between May fifteenth and June tenth, and added up to a little more than $200,000.

I spent an hour grilling the maid after O'Hara had taken Evelyn Trowbridge away, but she didn't know any more than I did. However, between her, the janitor, the manager of the apartments, and the names Mrs Trowbridge had given me, I learned that she had really been entertaining friends on the night of the fire—until after eleven o'clock, anyway—and that was late enough.

Half an hour later I was riding the Short Line back to Sacramento. I was getting to be one of the line's best customers, and my anatomy was on bouncing terms with every bump in the road; and the bumps, as "Rubber-head" Davis used to say about the flies and mosquitoes in Alberta in summer, "is freely plentiful."

Between bumps I tried to fit the pieces of this Thornburgh puzzle together. The niece and the Coonses fit in somewhere, but not just where we had them. We had been working on the job sort of lopsided, but it was the best we could do with it. In the beginning we had turned to the Coonses and Evelyn Trowbridge because there was no other direction to go; and now we had something on them—but a good lawyer could make hash of our case against them.

The Coonses were in the county jail when I got to Sacramento. After some questioning they had admitted their connection with the niece, and had come through with stories that matched hers in every detail.

Tarr, McClump, and I sat around the sheriff's desk and argued.

"Those yarns are pipe-dreams," the sheriff said. "We got all three of 'em cold, and there's nothing else to it. They're as good as convicted of murder!"

McClump grinned derisively at his superior, and then turned to me.

"Go on! You tell him about the holes in his little case. He ain't your boss, and can't take it out on you later for being smarter than he is!"

Tarr glared from one of us to the other.

"Spill it, you wise guys!" he ordered.

"Our dope is," I told him, figuring that McClump's view of it was the same as mine, "that there's nothing to show that even Thornburgh knew he was going to buy that house before the tenth of June, and that the Coonses were in town looking for work on the second. And besides, it was only by luck that they got the jobs. The employment office sent two couples out there ahead of them."

"We'll take a chance on letting the jury figure that out."

"Yes? You'll also take a chance on them figuring out that Thornburgh, who seems to have been a nut all right, might have touched off the place himself! We've got something on these people, Jim, but not enough to go into court with them! How are you going to prove that when the Coonses were planted in Thornburgh's house—if you can even prove they were—they and the Trowbridge woman knew he was going to load up with insurance policies?"

The sheriff spat disgustedly.

"You guys are the limit! You run around in circles, digging up the dope on these people until you get enough to hang 'em, and then you run around hunting for outs! What the hell's the matter with you now?"

I answered him from half-way to the door—the pieces were beginning to fit together under my skull.

"Going to run some more circles! Come on, Mac!"

McClump and I held a conference on the fly, and then I got a machine from the nearest garage and headed for Tavender. We made time going out, and got there before the general store had closed for the night. The stuttering Philo separated himself from the two men with whom he had been talking Hiram Johnson, and followed me to the rear of the store.

"Do you keep an itemized list of the laundry you handle?"

"N-n-no; just the amounts."

"Let's look at Thornburgh's."

He produced a begrimed and rumpled account book and we picked out the weekly items I wanted: $2.60, $3.10, $2.25, and so on.

"Got the last batch of laundry here?"

"Y-yes," he said. "It j-just c-c-came out from the city t-today."

I tore open the bundle—some sheets, pillowcases, tablecloths, towels, napkins; some feminine clothing; some shirts, collars, underwear, sox that were unmistakably Coons's. I thanked Philo while running back to my machine.

Back in Sacramento again, McClump was waiting for me at the garage where I had hired the car.

"Registered at the hotel on June fifteenth, rented the office on the sixteenth. I think he's in the hotel now," he greeted me.

We hurried around the block to the Garden Hotel.

"Mr Handerson went out a minute or two ago," the night clerk told us. "He seemed to be in a hurry."

"Know where he keeps his car?"

"In the hotel garage around the corner."

We were within two pavements of the garage, when Handerson's automobile shot out and turned up the street.

"Oh, Mr Handerson!" I cried, trying to keep my voice level and smooth.

He stepped on the gas and streaked away from us.

"Want him?" McClump asked; and, at my nod, stopped a passing roadster by the simple expedient of stepping in front of it.

We climbed aboard, McClump flashed his star at the bewildered driver, and pointed out Handerson's dwindling tail-light. After he had persuaded himself that he wasn't being boarded by a couple of bandits, the commandeered driver did his best, and we picked up Handerson's taillight after two or three turnings, and closed in on him—though his machine was going at a good clip.

By the time we reached the outskirts of the city, we had crawled up to within safe shooting distance, and I sent a bullet over the fleeing man's head. Thus encouraged, he managed to get a little more speed out of his car; but we were definitely overhauling him now.

Just at the wrong minute Handerson decided to look over his shoulder at us—an unevenness in the road twisted his wheels—his machine swayed—skidded—went over on its side. Almost immediately, from the heart of the tangle, came a flash and a bullet moaned past my ear. Another. And then, while I was still hunting for something to shoot at in the pile of junk we were drawing down upon, McClump's ancient and battered revolver roared in my other ear.

Handerson was dead when we got to him—McClump's bullet had taken him over one eye.

McClump spoke to me over the body.

"I ain't an inquisitive sort of fellow, but I hope you don't mind telling me why I shot this lad."

"Because he was Thornburgh."

He didn't say anything for about five minutes. Then: "I reckon that's right. How'd you guess it?"

We were sitting beside the wreckage now, waiting for the police that we had sent our commandeered chauffeur to phone for.

"He had to be," I said, "when you think it all over. Funny we didn't hit on it before! All that stuff we were told about Thornburgh had a fishy sound. Whiskers and an unknown profession, immaculate and working on a mysterious invention, very secretive and born in San Francisco—where the fire wiped out all the old records—just the sort of fake that could be cooked up easily.

"Then nobody but the Coonses, Evelyn Trowbridge and Handerson ever saw him except between the tenth of May and the middle of June, when he bought the house. The

Coonses and the Trowbridge woman were tied up together in this affair somehow, we knew—so that left only Handerson to consider. You had told me he came to Sacramento sometime early this summer—and the dates you got tonight show that he didn't come until after Thornburgh had bought his house. All right! Now compare Handerson with the descriptions we got of Thornburgh.

"Both are about the same size and age, and with the same color hair. The differences are all things that can be manufactured—clothes, a little sunburn, and a month's growth of beard, along with a little acting, would do the trick. Tonight I went out to Tavender and took a look at the last batch of laundry, and there wasn't any that didn't fit the Coonses—and none of the bills all the way back were large enough for Thornburgh to have been as careful about his clothes as we were told he was."

"It must be great to be a detective!" McClump grinned as the police ambulance came up and began disgorging policemen. "I reckon somebody must have tipped Handerson off that I was asking about him this evening." And then, regretfully: "So we ain't going to hang them folks for murder after all."

"No, but we oughtn't have any trouble convicting them of arson plus conspiracy to defraud, and anything else that the Prosecuting Attorney can think up."

BLACK MASK, OCTOBER 1, 1923

FROM THE AUTHOR OF "ARSON PLUS"

I'm glad you liked "Arson Plus"—it cost me gallons of sweat and acres of chewed finger nails! It went along nicely until I tried to bring it to an end—then it was hell-bent on running two or three thousand words further; but I finally fought it into reasonable length.

This detective of mine: I didn't deliberately keep him nameless, but he got through "Slippery Fingers" and "Arson Plus" without needing one, so I suppose I may as well let him run along that way. I'm not sure that he's entitled to a name, anyhow. He's more or less of a type: the private detective who oftenest is successful: neither the derby-hatted and broad-toed blockhead of one school of fiction, nor the all-knowing, infallible genius of another. I've worked with several of him.

Apropos of Charles Somerville's excellent article on capital punishment in the June 15th issue: under a law passed about two years ago, Nevada uses lethal gas for executions. The condemned man is placed in the lethal chamber during the week set by the court for his death. The gas is turned on while the condemned is asleep, the warden selecting the night of the week.

DASHIELL HAMMETT *San Francisco, Cal.*

2

CROOKED SOULS

BLACK MASK, OCTOBER 1, 1923

We've all seen the modern girl. She's a rare bird and here she is in all her glory—if that's what it is. A good detective yarn, this, with lots of action and some real people. Go to it.

Harvey Gatewood had issued orders that I was to be admitted as soon as I arrived, so it only took me a little less than fifteen minutes to thread my way past the door-keepers, office boys, and secretaries who filled up most of the space between the Gatewood Lumber Corporation's front door and the president's private office. His office was large, all mahogany and bronze and green plush, with a mahogany desk as big as a bed in the center of the floor.

Gatewood, leaning across the desk, began to bark at me as soon as the obsequious clerk who had bowed me in bowed himself out.

"My daughter was kidnapped last night! I want the... that did it if it takes every cent I got!"

"Tell me about it," I suggested, drawing up the chair that he hadn't thought to offer me.

But he wanted results, it seemed, and not questions, and so I wasted nearly an hour getting information that he could have given me in fifteen minutes.

He's a big bruiser of a man, something over two hundred pounds of hard red flesh, and a czar from the top of his bullet head to the toes of his shoes that would have been at least number twelves if they hadn't been made to measure.

He had made his several millions by sandbagging everybody that stood in his way, and the rage that he's burning up with now doesn't make him any easier to deal with.

His wicked jaw is sticking out like a knob of granite and his eyes are filmed with blood—he's in a lovely frame of mind. For a while it looks as if the Continental Detective Agency is going to lose a client; because I've made up my mind that he's going to tell me all I want to know, or I'm going to chuck up the job. But finally I got the story out of him.

His daughter Audrey had left their house on Clay street at about seven o'clock the preceding evening, telling her maid that she was going for a walk. She had not returned that night—though Gatewood had not known that until after he had read the letter that came this morning.

The letter had been from someone who said that she had been kidnapped. It demanded fifty thousand dollars for her release; and instructed Gatewood to get the money ready in hundred-dollar bills, so that there might be no delay when he is told in what manner it is to be paid over to his daughter's captors. As proof that the demand was not a hoax, a lock of the girl's hair, a ring she always wore, and a brief note from her, asking her father to comply with the demands, had been enclosed.

Gatewood had received the letter at his office, and had telephoned to his house immediately. He had been told that the girl's bed had not been slept in the previous night, and that none of the servants had seen her since she started out for her walk. He had then notified the police, turning the letter over to them; and, a few minutes later, he had decided to employ private detectives also.

"Now," he burst out, after I had wormed these things out of him, and he had told me that he knew nothing of his daughter's associates or habits, "go ahead and do something! I'm not paying you to sit around and talk about it!"

"What are you going to do?" I asked.

"Me? I'm going to put those... behind the bars if it takes every cent I've got in the world!"

"Sure! But first you can get that fifty thousand ready, so you can give it to them when they ask for it."

He clicked his jaw shut and thrust his face into mine.

"I've never been clubbed into doing anything in my life! And I'm too old to start now!" he said. "I'm going to call these people's bluff!"

"That's going to make it lovely for your daughter. But, aside from what it'll do to her, it's the wrong play. Fifty thousand isn't a whole lot to you, and paying it over will give us two chances that we haven't got now. One when the payment is made—a chance to either nab whoever comes for it or get a line on them. And the other when your daughter is returned. No matter how careful they are it's a cinch that she'll be able to tell us something that will help us grab them."

He shook his head angrily, and I was tired of arguing with him. So I left him, hoping that he'd see the wisdom of the course I had advised before too late.

At the Gatewood residence I found butlers, second men, chauffeurs, cooks, maids, upstairs girls, downstairs girls, and a raft of miscellaneous flunkies—he had enough servants to run a hotel.

What they told me amounted to this: The girl had not received a phone call, note by messenger, or telegram—the time-honored devices for luring a victim out to a murder or abduction—before she left the house. She had told her maid that she would be back within an hour or two; but the maid had not been alarmed when her mistress failed to return all that night.

Audrey was the only child, and since her mother's death she had come and gone to suit herself. She and her father didn't hit it off very well together—their natures were too much alike, I gathered—and he never knew where she was; and there was nothing unusual about her remaining away all night, as she seldom bothered to leave word when she was going to stay overnight with friends.

She was nineteen years old, but looked several years older; about five feet five inches tall, and slender. She had blue eyes, brown hair,—very thick and long,—was pale and very nervous. Her photographs, of which I took a handful, showed that her eyes were large, her nose small and regular, and her chin obstinately pointed.

She was not beautiful, but in the one photograph where a smile had wiped off the sullenness of her mouth, she was at least pretty.

When she left the house she had worn a light tweed skirt and jacket with a London tailor's labels in them, a buff silk shirtwaist with stripes a shade darker, brown wool stockings, low-heeled brown oxfords, and an untrimmed gray felt hat.

I went up to her rooms—she had three on the third floor—and looked through all her stuff. I found nearly a bushel of photographs of men, boys, and girls; and a great stack of letters of varying degrees of intimacy, signed with a wide assortment of names and nicknames. I made notes of all the addresses I found.

Nothing there seemed to have any bearing on her abduction, but there was a chance that one of the names and addresses might be of someone who had served as a decoy. Also, some of her friends might be able to tell us something of value.

I dropped in at the agency and distributed the names and addresses among the three operatives who were idle, sending them out to see what they could dig up.

Then I reached the police detectives who were working on the case—O'Gar and Thode—by telephone, and went down to the Hall of Justice to meet them. Lusk, a post office inspector, was also there. We turned the job around and around, looking at it from every angle, but not getting very far. We were all agreed, however, that we couldn't take a chance on any publicity, or work in the open, until the girl was safe.

They had had a worse time with Gatewood than I—he had wanted to put the whole thing in the newspapers, with the offer of a reward, photographs and all. Of course, Gatewood was right in claiming that this was the most effective way of catching the kidnappers—but it would have been tough on his daughter if her captors happened to be persons of sufficiently hardened character. And kidnappers as a rule aren't lambs.

I looked at the letter they had sent. It was printed with pencil on ruled paper of the kind that is sold in pads by every stationery dealer in the world. The envelope was just as common, also addressed in pencil, and post-marked "San Francisco, September 20, 9 P.M." That was the night she had been seized.

The letter reads:

"SIR:

WE HAVE YOUR CHARMING DAUGHTER AND PLACE A VALUE OF $50,000 UPON HER. YOU WILL GET THE MONEY READY IN $100 BILLS AT ONCE SO THERE WILL BE NO DELAY WHEN WE TELL YOU HOW IT IS TO BE PAID OVER TO US.

WE BEG TO ASSURE YOU THAT THINGS WILL GO BADLY WITH YOUR DAUGHTER SHOULD YOU NOT DO AS YOU ARE TOLD, OR SHOULD YOU BRING THE POLICE INTO THIS MATTER, OR SHOULD YOU DO ANYTHING FOOLISH.

$50,000 IS ONLY A SMALL FRACTION OF WHAT YOU STOLE WHILE WE WERE LIVING IN MUD AND BLOOD IN FRANCE FOR YOU, AND WE MEAN TO GET THAT MUCH OR .....!

THREE."

A peculiar note in several ways. They are usually written with a great pretense of partial illiterateness. Almost always there's an attempt to lead suspicion astray. Perhaps the ex-service stuff was there for that purpose ... or perhaps not.

Then there was a postscript:

"WE KNOW A CHINAMAN WHO WILL BUY HER EVEN AFTER WE ARE THROUGH WITH HER–IN CASE YOU WON'T LISTEN TO REASON."

The letter from the girl was written jerkily on the same kind of paper, apparently with the same pencil.

"Daddy—

Please do as they ask! I am so afraid—

Audrey"

A door at the other end of the room opened, and a head came through.

"O'Gar! Thode! Gatewood just called up. Get up to his office right away!"

The four of us tumbled out of the Hall of Justice and into a machine.

Gatewood was pacing his office like a maniac when we pushed aside enough hirelings to get to him. His face was hot with blood and his eyes had an insane glare in them.

"She just phoned me!" he cried thickly, when he saw us.

It took a minute or two to get him calm enough to tell us about it.

"She called me on the phone. Said, 'Oh, daddy! Do something! I can't stand this—they're killing me!' I asked her if she knew where she was, and she said, 'No, but I can see Twin Peaks from here. There's three men and a woman, and—' And then I heard a man curse, and a sound as if he had struck her, and the phone went dead. I tried to get central to give me the number, but she couldn't! It's a damned outrage the way the telephone system is run. We pay enough for service, God knows, and we ..."

O'Gar scratched his head and turned away from Gatewood.

"In sight of Twin Peaks! There are hundreds of houses that are!"

Gatewood meanwhile had finished denouncing the telephone company and was pounding on his desk with a paperweight to attract our attention.

"Have you people done anything at all?" he demanded.

I answered him with another question: "Have you got the money ready?"

"No," he said, "I won't be held up by anybody!"

But he said it mechanically, without his usual conviction—the talk with his daughter had shaken him out of some of his stubbornness. He was thinking of her safety a little now instead of altogether of his own fighting spirit.

We went at him hammer and tongs for a few minutes, and after a while he sent a clerk out for the money.

We split up the field then. Thode was to take some men from headquarters and see what he could find in the Twin Peaks end of town; but we weren't very optimistic over the prospects there—the territory was too large.

Lusk and O'Gar were to carefully mark the bills that the clerk brought from the bank, and then stick as close to Gatewood as they could without attracting attention. I was to go out to Gatewood's house and stay there.

The abductors had plainly instructed Gatewood to get the money ready immediately so that they could arrange to get it on short notice—not giving him time to communicate with anyone or make any plans.

Gatewood was to get hold of the newspapers, give them the whole story, with the $10,000 reward he was offering for the abductors' capture, to be published as soon as the girl was safe—so that we would get the help of publicity at the earliest moment possible without jeopardizing the girl.

The police in all the neighboring towns had already been notified—that had been done before the girl's phone message had assured us that she was held in San Francisco.

Nothing happened at the Gatewood residence all that evening. Harvey Gatewood came home early; and after dinner he paced his library floor and drank whiskey until bedtime, demanding every few minutes that we, the detectives in the case, do something besides sit around like a lot of damned mummies. O'Gar, Lusk and Thode were out in the street, keeping an eye on the house and neighborhood.

At midnight Harvey Gatewood went to bed. I declined a bed in favor of the library couch, which I dragged over beside the telephone, an extension of which was in Gatewood's bedroom.

At two-thirty the bell rang. I listened in while Gatewood talked from his bed.

A man's voice, crisp and curt: "Gatewood?"

"Yes."

"Got the dough?"

"Yes."

Gatewood's voice was thick and blurred—I could imagine the boiling that was going on inside him.

"Good!" came the brisk voice. "Put a piece of paper around it, and leave the house with it, right away! Walk down Clay street, keeping on the same side as your house. Don't walk too fast and keep walking. If everything's all right, and there's no elbows tagging along, somebody'll come up to you between your house and the waterfront. They'll have a handkerchief up to their face for a second, and then they'll let it fall to the ground.

"When you see that, you'll lay the money on the pavement, turn around and walk back to your house. If the money isn't marked, and you don't try any fancy tricks, you'll get your daughter back in an hour or two. If you try to pull anything—remember what we wrote you about the Chink! Got it straight?"

Gatewood sputtered something that was meant for an affirmative, and the telephone clicked silent.

I didn't waste any of my precious time tracing the call—it would be from a public telephone, I knew—but yelled up the stairs to Gatewood:

"You do as you were told, and don't try any foolishness!"

Then I ran out into the early morning air to find the police detectives and the post office inspector.

They had been joined by two plainclothes men, and had two automobiles waiting. I told them what the situation was, and we laid hurried plans.

O'Gar was to drive in one of the machines down Sacramento street, and Thode, in the other, down Washington street. These streets parallel Clay, one on each side. They were to drive slowly, keeping pace with Gatewood, and stopping at each cross street to see that he passed.

When he failed to cross within a reasonable time they were to turn up to Clay street—and their actions from then on would have to be guided by chance and their own wits.

Lusk was to wander along a block or two ahead of Gatewood, on the opposite side of the street, pretending to be mildly intoxicated, and keeping his eyes and ears open.

I was to shadow Gatewood down the street, with one of the plainclothes men behind me. The other plainclothes man was to turn in a call at headquarters for every available man to be sent to Clay street. They would arrive too late, of course, and as likely as not it would take them some time to find us; but we had no way of knowing what was going to turn up before the night was over.

Our plan was sketchy enough, but it was the best we could do—we were afraid to grab whoever got the money from Gatewood. The girl's talk with her father that afternoon had sounded too much as if her captors were desperate for us to take any chances on going after them roughshod until she was out of their hands.

We had hardly finished our plans when Gatewood, wearing a heavy overcoat, left his house and turned down the street.

Farther down, Lusk, weaving along, talking to himself, was almost invisible in the shadows. There was no one else in sight. That meant that I had to give Gatewood at least two blocks' lead, so that the man who came for the money wouldn't tumble to me. One of the plainclothes men was half a block behind me, on the other side of the street.

Two blocks down we walked, and then a little chunky man in a derby hat came into sight. He passed Gatewood, passed me, went on.

Three blocks more.

A touring-car, large, black, powerfully engined, and with lowered curtains, came from the rear, passed us, went on. Possibly a scout! I scrawled its license number down on my pad without taking my hand out of my overcoat pocket.

Another three blocks.

A policeman passed, strolling along in ignorance of the game being played under his nose; and then a taxicab with a single male passenger. I wrote down its license number.

Four blocks with no one in sight ahead of me but Gatewood—I couldn't see Lusk any more.

Just ahead of Gatewood a man stepped out of a black doorway—turned around—called up to a window for someone to come down and open the door for him.

We went on.

Coming from now here, a woman stood on the sidewalk fifty feet ahead of Gatewood, a handkerchief to her face. It fluttered to the pavement.

Gatewood stopped, standing stiff-legged. I could see his right hand come up, lifting the side of the overcoat in which it was pocketed—and I knew the hand was gripped around a pistol.

For perhaps half a minute he stood like a statue. Then his left hand came out of his pocket, and the bundle of money fell to the side-walk in front of him, where it made a bright blur in the darkness. Gatewood turned abruptly, and began to retrace his steps homeward.

The woman had recovered her handkerchief. Now she ran to the bundle, picked it up, and scuttled to the black mouth of an alley, a few feet distant—a rather tall woman, bent, and in dark clothes from head to feet.

In the black mouth of the alley she vanished.

I had been compelled to slow up while Gatewood and the woman stood facing each other, and I was more than a block away now. As soon as the woman disappeared I took a chance, and started pounding my rubber soles against the pavement.

The alley was empty when I reached it.

It ran all the way through to the next street, but I knew that the woman couldn't have reached the other end before I got to this one. I carry a lot of weight these days, but I can still step a block or two in good time. Along both sides of the alley were the rears of apartment buildings, each with its back door looking blankly, secretively at me.

The plainclothes man who had been trailing behind me came up, then O'Gar and Thode in their machines, and soon, Lusk. O'Gar and Thode rode off immediately to wind through the neighboring streets, hunting for the woman. Lusk and the plainclothes man each planted himself on a corner from which two of the streets enclosing the block could be watched.

I went through the alley, hunting vainly for an unlocked door, an open window, a fire-escape that would show recent use—any of the signs that a hurried departure from the alley might leave.

Nothing!

O'Gar came back shortly with some reinforcements from headquarters that he had picked up, and Gatewood.

Gatewood was burning.

"Bungled the damn thing again! I won't pay your agency a nickel, and I'll see that some of these so-called detectives get put back in a uniform and set to walking beats!"

"What'd the woman look like?" I asked him.

"I don't know! I thought you were hanging around to take care of her! She was old and bent, kind of, I guess, but I couldn't see her face for her veil. I don't know! What the hell were you men doing? It's a damned outrage the way..."

I finally got him quieted down and took him home, leaving the city men to keep the neighborhood under surveillance. There was fourteen or fifteen of them on the job now, and every shadow held at least one.

The girl would naturally head for home as soon as she was released and I wanted to be there to pump her. There was an excellent chance of catching her abductors before they got very far if she could tell us anything at all about them.

Home, Gatewood went up against the whiskey bottle again, while I kept one ear cocked at the telephone and the other at the front door. O'Gar or Thode phoned every half hour or so to ask if we'd heard from the girl. They had still found nothing.

At nine o'clock they, with Lusk, arrived at the house. The woman in black had turned out to be a man, and had gotten away.

In the rear of one of the apartment buildings that touched the alley—just a foot or so within the back-door—they found a woman's skirt, long coat, hat and veil—all black. Investigating the occupants of the house, they had learned that an apartment had been rented to a young man named Leighton three days before.

Leighton was not at home when they went up to his apartment. His rooms held a lot of cold cigarette butts, and an empty bottle, and nothing else that had not been there when he rented it.

The inference was clear: he had rented the apartment so that he might have access to the building. Wearing woman's clothes over his own, he had gone out of the back door—leaving it unlatched behind him—to meet Gatewood.

Then he had run back into the building, discarded his disguise, and hurried through the building, out the front door, and away before we had our feeble net around the block; perhaps dodging into dark doorways here and there to avoid O'Gar and Thode in their automobiles.

Leighton, it seemed, was a man of about thirty, slender, about five feet eight or nine inches tall, with dark hair and eyes; rather good-looking, and well-dressed, on the two occasions when people living in the building had seen him, in a brown suit and a light brown felt hat.

There was no possibility, according to the opinions of both of the detectives and the post office inspector, that the girl might have been held, even temporarily, in Leighton's apartment.

Ten o'clock came, and no word from the girl.

Gatewood had lost his domineering bull-headedness by now and was breaking up. The suspense was getting him, and the liquor he had put away wasn't helping him. I didn't like him either personally or by reputation, but at that I felt sorry for him this morning.

I talked to the agency over the phone and got the reports of the operatives who had been looking up Audrey's friends. The last person to see her had been an Agnes Dangerfield, who had seen her walking down Market street near Sixth, alone, on the night of her abduction—sometime between 8:15 and 8:45. Audrey had been too far away for the Dangerfield girl to speak to her.

For the rest, the boys had learned nothing except that Audrey was a wild, spoiled youngster who hadn't shown any great care in selecting her friends—just the sort of girl who could easily fall into the hands of a mob of highbinders!

Noon struck. No sign of the girl. We told the newspapers to turn loose the story, with the added developments of the past few hours.

Gatewood was broken; he sat with his head in his hands, looking at nothing. Just before I left to follow a hunch I had, he looked up at me, and I'd never have recognized him if I hadn't seen the change take place.

"What do you think is keeping her away?" he asked.

I didn't have the heart to tell him what I was beginning to suspect, now that the money had been paid and she had failed to show up. So I stalled with some vague assurances, and left.

I caught a street-car and dropped off down in the shopping district. I visited the five largest department stores, going to all the women's wear departments from shoes to hats, and trying to learn if a man—perhaps one answering Leighton's description—had been buying clothes that would fit Audrey Gatewood within the past couple days.

Failing to get any results, I turned the rest of the local stores over to one of the boys from the agency, and went across the bay to canvass the Oakland stores.

At the first one I got action. A man who might easily have been Leighton had been in the day before, buying clothes that could easily fit Audrey. He had bought lots of them, everything from lingerie to a cloak, and—my luck was hitting on all its cylinders—had had his purchases delivered to T. Offord, at an address on Fourteenth street.

At the Fourteenth street address, an apartment house, I found Mr and Mrs Theodore Offord's names under the vestibule telephone for apartment 202.

I had just found them when the front door opened and a stout, middle-aged woman in a gingham house-dress came out. She looked at me a bit curiously, so I asked:

"Do you know where I can find the manager?"

"I'm the manager," she said.

I handed her a card and stepped indoors with her.

"I'm from the bonding department of the North American Casualty Company"—a repetition of the lie that was printed on the card I had given her—"and a bond for Mr Offord has been applied for. Is he all right so far as you know?" With the slightly apologetic air of one going through with a necessary but not too important formality.

She frowned.

"A bond? That's funny! He is going away tomorrow."

"Well, I can't say what the bond is for," I said lightly. "We investigators just get the names and addresses. It may be for his present employer, or perhaps the man he is going to work for wherever he's going has applied for it. Or some firms have us look up prospective employees before they hire them, just to be safe."

"Mr Offord, so far as I know, is a very nice young man," she said, "but he has been here only a week."

"Not staying long, then?"

"No. They came here from Denver, intending to stay, but the low altitude doesn't agree with Mrs Offord, so they are going back."

"Are you sure they came from Denver?"

"Well," she said, "they told me they did."

"How many of them are there?"

"Only the two of them; they're young people."

"Well, how do they impress you?" I asked, trying to get the impression that I thought her a woman of shrewd judgment over.

"They seem to be a very nice young couple. You'd hardly know they were in their apartment most of the time, they are so quiet. I am sorry they can't stay."

"Do they go out much?"

"I really don't know. They have their keys, and unless I should happen to pass them going in or out I'd never see them."

"Then, as a matter of fact, you couldn't say whether they stayed away all night some nights or not. Could you?"

She eyed me doubtfully—I was stepping way over my pretext now, but I didn't think it mattered—and shook her head.

"No, I couldn't say."

"They have many visitors?"

"I don't know. Mr Offord is not—"

She broke off as a man came in quietly from the street, brushed past me, and started to mount the steps to the second floor.

"Oh, dear!" she whispered. "I hope he didn't hear me talking about him. That's Mr Offord."

A slender man in brown, with a light brown hat—Leighton perhaps.

I hadn't seen anything of him except his back, nor he anything except mine. I watched him as he climbed the stairs.

If he had heard the manager mention his name he would use the turn at the head of the stairs to sneak a look at me.

He did. I kept my face stolid, but I knew him. He was "Penny" Quayle, a con man who had been active in the East four or five years before. His face was as expressionless as mine. But he knew me.

A door on the second floor shut. I left the manager and started for the stairs.

"I think I'll go up and talk to him," I told her.

Coming silently to the door of apartment 202, I listened. Not a sound. This was no time for hesitation. I pressed the bell-button.

As close together as the tapping of three keys under the fingers of an expert typist, but a thousand times more vicious, came three pistol shots. And waist-high in the door of apartment 202 were three bullet holes.

The three bullets would have been in my fat carcass if I hadn't learned years ago to stand to one side of strange doors when making uninvited calls.

Inside the apartment sounded a man's voice, sharp, commanding.

"Cut it, kid! For God's sake, not that!"

A woman's voice, shrill, bitter, spiteful screaming blasphemies.

Two more bullets came through the door.

"Stop! No! No!" The man's voice had a note of fear in it now.

The woman's voice, cursing hotly. A scuffle. A shot that didn't hit the door.

I hurled my foot against the door, near the knob, and the lock broke away.

On the floor of the room, a man—Quayle—and a woman were tussling. He was bending over her, holding her wrists, trying to keep her down. A smoking automatic pistol was in one of her hands. I got to it in a jump and tore it loose.

"That's enough!" I called to them when I was planted. "Get up and receive company."

Quayle released his antagonist's wrists, whereupon she struck at his eyes with curved, sharp-nailed fingers, tearing his cheek open. He scrambled away from her on hands and knees, and both of them got to their feet.

He sat down on a chair immediately, panting and wiping his bleeding cheek with a handkerchief.

She stood, hands on hips, in the center of the room, glaring at me.

"I suppose," she spat, "you think you've raised hell!"

I laughed—I could afford to.

"If your father is in his right mind," I told her, "he'll do it with a razor strop when he gets you home again. A fine joke you picked out to play on him!"

"If *you'd* been tied to him as long as I have, and had been bullied and held down as much, I guess *you'd* do most anything to get enough money so that you could go away and live your own life."

I didn't say anything to that. Remembering some of the business methods Harvey Gatewood had used—particularly some of his war contracts that the Department of Justice was still investigating—I suppose the worst that could be said about Audrey was that she was her father's own daughter.

"How'd you rap to it?" Quayle asked me, politely.

"Several ways," I said. "First, I'm a little doubtful about grown persons being kidnapped in cities. Maybe it really happens sometimes, but at least nine-tenths of the cases you hear about are fakes. Second, one of Audrey's friends saw her on Market street between 8:15 and 8:45 the night she disappeared; and your letter to Gatewood was post-marked 9 P.M. Pretty fast work. You should have waited a while before mailing it, even if it had to miss the first morning delivery. I suppose she dropped it in the post office on her way over here?"

Quayle nodded.

"Then third," I went on, "there was that phone call of hers. She knew it took anywhere from ten to fifteen minutes to get her father on the wire at the office. If time had been as valuable as it would have been if she had gotten to a phone while imprisoned, she'd have told her story to the first person she got hold of—the phone girl, most likely. So that made it look as if, besides wanting to throw out that Twin Peaks line, she wanted to stir the old man out of his bullheadedness.

"When she failed to show up after the money was paid I figured it was a sure bet that she had kidnapped herself. I knew that if she came back home after faking this thing we'd find it out before we'd talked to her very long—and I figured she knew that too, and would stay away.

"The rest was easy, as I got some good breaks. We knew a man was working with her after we found the woman's clothes you left behind, and I took a chance on there being no one else in it. Then I figured she'd need clothes—she couldn't have taken any from home without tipping her mitt—and there was an even chance that she hadn't laid in a stock beforehand. She's got too many girl friends of the sort that do a lot of shopping to make it safe for her to risk showing herself in stores. Maybe, then, the man would buy what she needed for her. And it turned out that he did, and that he was too lazy to carry away his purchases, or perhaps there was too many of them, and so he had them sent out. That's the story."

Quayle nodded again.

"I was damned careless," he said, and then, jerking a contemptuous thumb toward the girl, "but what can you expect? She's had a skin full of hop ever since we started. Took all my time and attention keeping her from running wild and gumming the works. Just now was a sample—I told her you were coming up and she goes crazy and tries to add your corpse to the wreck!"

The Gatewood reunion took place in the office of the captain of inspectors, on the second floor of the Oakland City Hall, and it was a merry little party. For an hour it was a toss-up whether Harvey Gatewood would die of apoplexy, strangle his daughter, or send her off to the state reformatory until she was of age. But Audrey licked him. Besides being a chip off the old block, she was young enough to be careless of consequences, while her father, for all his bullheadedness, had had some caution hammered into him.

The card she beat him with was a threat of spilling everything she knew about him to the newspapers, and at least one of the San Francisco papers had been trying to get his scalp for years. I don't know what she had on him, and I don't think he was any too sure himself; but, with his war contracts even then being investigated by the Department of Justice, he couldn't afford to take a chance. There was no doubt at all that she would have done as she threatened.

And so, together, they left for home, sweating hate for each other at every pore.

We took Quayle upstairs and put him in a cell, but he was too experienced to let that worry him. He knew that if the girl was to be spared, he himself couldn't very easily be convicted of anything.

3

SLIPPERY FINGERS

BLACK MASK, OCTOBER 15, 1923

You'll have the time of your life trying to solve this crime before you get to the end of the story. You'll think some of the characters don't act logically, but when you figure it out afterward you'll decide they were all pretty wise.

"You are already familiar, of course, with the particulars of my father's—ah—death?"

"The papers are full of it, and have been for three days," I said, "and I've read them; but I'll have to have the whole story first-hand."

"There isn't very much to tell."

This Frederick Grover was a short, slender man of something under thirty years, and dressed like a picture out of *Vanity Fair*. His almost girlish features and voice did nothing to make him more impressive, but I began to forget these things after a few minutes. He wasn't a sap. I knew that downtown, where he was rapidly building up a large and lively business in stocks and bonds without calling for too much help from his father's millions, he was considered a shrewd article; and I wasn't surprised later when Benny Forman, who ought to know, told me that Frederick Grover was the best poker player west of Chicago. He was a cool, well-balanced, quick-thinking little man.

"Father has lived here alone with the servants since mother's death, two years ago," he went on. "I am married, you know, and live in town. Last Saturday evening he dismissed Barton—Barton was his butler-valet, and had been with father for quite a few years—at a little after nine, saying that he did not want to be disturbed during the evening.

"Father was here in the library at the time, looking through some papers. The servants' rooms are in the rear, and none of the servants seem to have heard anything during the night.

"At seven-thirty the following morning—Sunday—Barton found father lying on the floor, just to the right of where you are sitting, dead, stabbed in the throat with the brass paper-knife that was always kept on the table here. The front door was ajar.

"The police found bloody finger-prints on the knife, the table, and the front door; but so far they have not found the man who left the prints, which is why I am employing your agency. The physician who came with the police placed the time of father's death at between eleven o'clock and midnight.

"Later, on Monday, we learned that father had drawn $10,000 in hundred-dollar bills from the bank Saturday morning. No trace of the money has been found. My finger-prints, as well as the servants', were compared with the ones found by the police, but there was no similarity. I think that is all."

"Do you know of any enemies your father had?"

He shook his head.

"I know of none, though he may have had them. You see, I really didn't know my father very well. He was a very reticent man and, until his retirement, about five years ago, he spent most of his time in South America, where most of his mining interests were. He may have had dozens of enemies, though Barton—who probably knew more about him than anyone—seems to know of no one who hated father enough to kill him."

"How about relatives?"

"I was his heir and only child, if that is what you are getting at. So far as I know he had no other living relatives."

"I'll talk to the servants," I said.

The maid and the cook could tell me nothing, and I learned very little more from Barton. He had been with Henry Grover since 1912, had been with him in Yunnan, Peru, Mexico, and Central America, but apparently he knew little or nothing of his master's business or acquaintances.

He said that Grover had not seemed excited or worried on the night of the murder, and that nearly every night Grover dismissed him at about the same time, with orders that he be not disturbed; so no importance was to be attached to that part of it. He knew of no one with whom Grover had communicated during the day, and he had not seen the money Grover had drawn from the bank.

I made a quick inspection of the house and grounds, not expecting to find anything; and I didn't. Half the jobs that come to a private detective are like this one: three or four days—and often as many weeks—have passed since the crime was committed. The police work on the job until they are stumped; then the injured party calls in a private sleuth, dumps him down on a trail that is old and cold and badly trampled, and expects—Oh, well! I picked out this way of making a living, so...

I looked through Grover's papers—he had a safe and a desk full of them—but didn't find anything to get excited about. They were mostly columns of figures.

"I'm going to send an accountant out here to go over your father's books," I told Frederick Grover. "Give him everything he asks for, and fix it up with the bank so they'll help him."

I caught a street-car and went back to town, called at Ned Root's office, and headed him out toward Grover's. Ned is a human adding machine with educated eyes, ears, and nose. He can spot a kink in a set of books farther than I can see the covers.

"Keep digging until you find something, Ned, and you can charge Grover whatever you like. Give me something to work on—quick!"

The murder had all the earmarks of one that had grown out of blackmail, though there was—there always is—a chance that it might have been something else. But it didn't look like the work of an enemy or a burglar: either of them would have packed his weapon with him, would not have trusted to finding it on the grounds. Of course, if Frederick Grover, or one of the servants, had killed Henry Grover... but the finger-prints said "No."

Just to play safe, I put in a few hours getting a line on Frederick. He had been at a ball on the night of the murder; he had never, so far as I could learn, quarreled with his father; his father was liberal with him, giving him everything he wanted; and Frederick was taking in more money in his brokerage office than he was spending. No motive for a murder appeared on the surface there.

At the city detective bureau I hunted up the police sleuths who had been assigned to the murder; Marty O'Hara and George Dean. It didn't take them long to tell me what they knew about it. Whoever had made the bloody finger-prints was not known to the police here: they had not found the prints in their files. The classifications had been broadcast to every large city in the country, but with no results so far.

A house four blocks from Grover's had been robbed on the night of the murder, and there was a slim chance that the same man *might* have been responsible for both jobs. But the burglary had occurred after one o'clock in the morning, which made the connection look not so good. A burglar who had killed a man, and perhaps picked up $10,000 in the bargain, wouldn't be likely to turn his hand to another job right away.

I looked at the paper-knife with which Grover had been killed, and at the photographs of the bloody prints, but they couldn't help me much just now. There seemed to be nothing to do but get out and dig around until I turned up something somewhere.

Then the door opened, and Joseph Clane was ushered into the room where O'Hara, Dean and I were talking.

Clane was a hard-bitten citizen, for all his prosperous look; fifty or fifty-five, I'd say, with eyes, mouth and jaw that held plenty of humor but none of what is sometimes called the milk of human kindness.

He was a big man, beefy, and all dressed up in a tight-fitting checkered suit, fawn-colored hat, patent-leather shoes with buff uppers, and the rest of the things that go with that sort of combination. He had a harsh voice that was as empty of expression as his hard red face, and he held his body stiffly, as if he was afraid the buttons on his too-tight clothes were about to pop off. Even his arms hung woodenly at his sides, with thick fingers that were lifelessly motionless.

He came right to the point. He had been a friend of the murdered man's, and thought that perhaps what he could tell us would be of value.

He had met Henry Grover—he called him "Henny"—in 1894, in Ontario, where Grover was working a claim: the gold mine that had started the murdered man along the road to wealth. Clane had been employed by Grover as foreman, and the two men had become close friends. A man named Denis Waldeman had a claim adjoining Grover's and a dispute had arisen over their boundaries. The dispute ran on for some time—the men coming to blows once or twice—but finally

Grover seems to have triumphed, for Waldeman suddenly left the country.

Clane's idea was that if we could find Waldeman we might find Grover's murderer, for considerable money had been involved in the dispute, and Waldeman was "a mean cuss, for a fact," and not likely to have forgotten his defeat.

Clane and Grover had kept in touch with each other, corresponding or meeting at irregular intervals, but the murdered man had never said or written anything that would throw a light on his death. Clane, too, had given up mining, and now had a small string of race-horses which occupied all his time.

He was in the city for a rest between racing-meets, had arrived two days before the murder, but had been too busy with his own affairs—he had discharged his trainer and was trying to find another—to call upon his friend. Clane was staying at the Marquis hotel, and would be in the city for a week or ten days longer.

"How come you've waited three days before coming to tell us all this?" Dean asked him.

"I wasn't noways sure I had ought to do it. I wasn't never sure in my mind but what maybe Henny done for that fellow Waldeman—he disappeared sudden-like. And I didn't want to do nothing to dirty Henny's name. But finally I decided to do the right thing. And then there's another thing: you found some finger-prints in Henny's house, didn't you? The newspapers said so."

"We did."

"Well, I want you to take mine and match them up. I was out with a girl the night of the murder"—he leered suddenly, boastingly—"all night! And she's a good girl, got a husband and a lot of folks; and it wouldn't be right to drag her into this to prove that I wasn't in Henny's house when he was killed, in case you'd maybe think I killed him. So I thought I better come down here, tell you all about it, and get you to take my fingerprints, and have it all over with."

We went up to the identification bureau and had Clane's prints taken. They were not at all like the murderer's.

After we pumped Clane dry I went out and sent a telegram to our Toronto office, asking them to get a line on the Waldeman angle. Then I hunted up a couple of boys who eat, sleep, and breathe horse racing. They told me that Clane was well known in racing circles as the owner of a small string of near-horses that ran as irregularly as the stewards would permit.

At the Marquis hotel I got hold of the house detective, who is a helpful chap so long as his hand is kept greased. He verified my information about Clane's status in the sporting world, and told me that Clane had stayed at the hotel for several days at a time, off and on, within the past couple years.

He tried to trace Clane's telephone calls for me but—as usual when you want them—the records were jumbled. I arranged to have the girls on the switchboard listen in on any talking he did during the next few days.

Ned Root was waiting for me when I got down to the office the next morning. He had worked on Grover's accounts all night, and had found enough to give me a start. Within the past year—that was as far back as Ned had gone—Grover had drawn out of his bank-accounts nearly fifty thousand dollars that couldn't be accounted for; nearly fifty thousand exclusive of the ten thousand he had drawn the day of the murder. Ned gave me the amounts and the dates:

May 6, 1922, $15,000
June 10, 5,000
August 1, 5,000
October 10, 10,000
January 3, 1923, 12,500

Forty-seven thousand, five hundred dollars! Somebody was getting fat off him!

The local managers of the telegraph companies raised the usual howl about respecting their patrons' privacy, but I got an order from the Prosecuting Attorney and put a clerk at work on the files of each office.

Then I went back to the Marquis hotel and looked at the old registers. Clane had been there from May 4th to 7th, and from October 8th to 15th last year. That checked off two of the dates upon which Grover had made his withdrawals.

I had to wait until nearly six o'clock for my information from the telegraph companies, but it was worth waiting for. On the third of last January Henry Grover had telegraphed $12,500 to Joseph Clane in San Diego. The clerks hadn't found anything on the other dates I had given them, but I wasn't at all dissatisfied. I had Joseph Clane fixed as the man who had been getting fat off Grover.

I sent Dick Foley—he is the agency's shadow-ace—and Bob Teal—a youngster who will be a world-beater some day—over to Clane's hotel.

"Plant yourselves in the lobby," I told them. "I'll be over in a few minutes to talk to Clane, and I'll try to bring him down in the lobby where you can get a good look at him. Then I want him shadowed until he shows up at police headquarters tomorrow: I want to know where he goes and who he talks to. And if he spends much time talking to any one person, or their conversation seems very important, I want one of you boys to trail the other man, to see who he is and what he does. If Clane tries to blow town, grab him and have him thrown in the can, but I don't think he will."

I gave Dick and Bob time enough to get themselves placed, and then went to the hotel. Clane was out, so I waited. He came in a little after eleven and I went up to his room with him. I didn't hem-and-haw, but came out cold-turkey:

"All the signs point to Grover's having been blackmailed. Do you know anything about it?"

"No," he said.

"Grover drew a lot of money out of his banks at different times. You got some of it, I know, and I suppose you got most of it. What about it?"

He didn't pretend to be insulted, or even surprised by my talk. He smiled a little grimly, maybe, but as if he thought it the most natural thing in the world—and it was, at that—for me to suspect him.

"I told you that me and Henny were pretty chummy, didn't I? Well, you ought to know that all us fellows that fool with the bang-tails have our streaks of bad luck. Whenever I'd get up against it I'd hit Henny up for a stake; like at Tijuana last winter where I got into a flock of bad breaks. Henny lent me twelve or fifteen thousand and I got back on my feet again. I've done that often. He ought to have some of my letters and wires in his stuff. If you look through his things you'll find them."

I didn't pretend that I believed him.

"Suppose you drop into police headquarters at nine in the morning and we'll go over everything with the city dicks," I told him.

And then, to make my play stronger:

"I wouldn't make it much later than nine—they might be out looking for you."

"Uh-huh," was all the answer I got.

I went back to the agency and planted myself within reach of a telephone, waiting for word from Dick and Bob. I thought I was sitting pretty. Clane had been blackmailing Grover—I didn't have a single doubt of that—and I didn't think he had been very far away when Grover was killed. That woman alibi of his sounded all wrong!

But the bloody finger-prints were not Clane's—unless the police identification bureau had pulled an awful boner—and the man who had left the prints was the bird I was setting my cap for. Clane had let three days pass between the murder and his appearance at headquarters. The natural explanation for that would be that his partner, the actual murderer, had needed nearly that much time to put himself in the clear.

My present game was simple: I had stirred Clane up with the knowledge that he was still suspected, hoping that he would have to repeat whatever precautions were necessary to protect his accomplice in the first place.

He had taken three days then. I was giving him about nine hours now: time enough to do something, but not too much time, hoping that he would have to hurry things along and that in his haste he would give Dick and Bob a chance to turn up his partner: the owner of the fingers that had smeared blood on the knife, the table, and the door.

At a quarter to one in the morning Dick telephoned that Clane had left the hotel a few minutes behind me, had gone to an apartment house on Polk Street, and was still there.

I went up to Polk Street and joined Dick and Bob. They told me that Clane had gone in apartment number 27, and that the directory in the vestibule showed this apartment was occupied by George Farr. I stuck around with the boys until about two o'clock, when I went home for some sleep.

At seven I was with them again, and was told that our man had not appeared yet. It was a little after eight when he came out and turned down Geary Street, with the boys trailing him, while I went into the apartment house for a talk with the manager. She told me that Farr had been living there for four or five months, lived alone, and was a photographer by trade, with a studio on Market Street.

I went up and rang his bell. He was a husky of thirty or thirty-two with bleary eyes that looked as if they hadn't had much sleep that night. I didn't waste any time with him.

"I'm from the Continental Detective Agency and I am interested in Joseph Clane. What do you know about him?"

He was wide awake now.

"Nothing."

"Nothing at all?"

"No," sullenly.

"Do you know him?"

"No."

What can you do with a bird like that?

"Farr," I said, "I want you to go down to headquarters with me."

He moved like a streak and his sullen manner had me a little off my guard; but I turned my head in time to take the punch above my ear instead of on the chin. At that, it carried me off my feet and I wouldn't have bet a nickel that my skull wasn't dented; but luck was with me and I fell across the doorway, holding the door open, and managed to scramble up, stumble through some rooms, and catch one of his feet as it was going through the bathroom window to join its mate on the fire-escape. I got a split lip and a kicked shoulder in the scuffle, but he behaved after a while.

I didn't stop to look at his stuff—that could be done more regularly later—but put him in a taxicab and took him to the Hall of Justice. I was afraid that if I waited too long Clane would take a run-out on me.

Clane's mouth fell open when he saw Farr, but neither of them said anything.

I was feeling pretty chirp in spite of my bruises.

"Let's get this bird's finger-prints and get it over with," I said to O'Hara.

Dean was not in.

"And keep an eye on Clane. I think maybe he'll have another story to tell us in a few minutes."

We got in the elevator and took our men up to the identification bureau, where we put Farr's fingers on the pad. Phels—he is the department's expert—took one look at the results and turned to me.

"Well, what of it?"

"What of what?" I asked.

"This isn't the man who killed Henry Grover!"

Clane laughed, Farr laughed, O'Hara laughed, and Phels laughed. I didn't! I stood there and pretended to be thinking, trying to get myself in hand.

"Are you sure you haven't made a mistake?" I blurted, my face a nice, rosy red.

You can tell how badly upset I was by that: it's plain suicide to say a thing like that to a finger-print expert!

Phels didn't answer; just looked me up and down.

Clane laughed again, like a crow cawing, and turned his ugly face to me.

"Do you want to take my prints again, Mr Slick Private Detective?"

"Yeah," I said, "just that!"

I had to say something.

Clane held his hands out to Phels, who ignored them, speaking to me with heavy sarcasm.

"Better take them yourself this time, so you'll be sure it's been done right."

I was mad clean through—of course it was my own fault—but I was pig-headed enough to go through with anything, particularly anything that would hurt somebody's feelings; so I said:

"That's not a bad idea!"

I walked over and took hold of one of Clane's hands. I'd never taken a finger-print before, but I had seen it done often enough to throw a bluff. I started to ink Clane's fingers and found that I was holding them wrong—my own fingers were in the way.

Then I came back to earth. The balls of (Jane's fingers were too smooth—or rather, too slick—without the slight clinging feeling that belongs to flesh. I turned his hand over so fast that I nearly upset him and looked at the fingers. I don't know what I had expected to find but I didn't find anything—not anything that I could name.

"Phels," I called, "look here!"

He forgot his injured feelings and bent to look at Clane's hand.

"I'll be—" he began, and then the two of us were busy for a few minutes taking Clane down and sitting on him, while O'Hara quieted Farr, who had also gone suddenly into action.

When things were peaceful again Phels examined Clane's hands carefully, scratching the fingers with a finger-nail.

He jumped up, leaving me to hold Clane, and paying no attention to my, "What is it?" got a cloth and some liquid, and washed the fingers thoroughly. We took his prints again. They matched the bloody ones taken from Grover's house!

Then we all sat down and had a nice talk.

"I told you about the trouble Henny had with that fellow Waldeman," Clane began, after he and Farr had decided to come clean: there was nothing else they could do. "And how he won out in the argument because Waldeman disappeared. Well, Henny done for him—shot him one night and buried him—and I saw it. Grover was one bad actor in them days, a tough *hombre* to tangle with, so I didn't try to make nothing out of what I knew.

"But after he got older and richer he got soft—a lot of men go like that—and must have begun worrying over it; because when I ran into him in New York accidentally about four years ago it didn't take me long to learn that he was pretty well tamed, and he told me that he hadn't been able to forget the look on Waldeman's face when he drilled him.

"So I took a chance and braced Henny for a couple thousand. I got them easy, and after that, whenever I was flat I either went to him or sent him word, and he always came across. But I was careful not to crowd him too far. I knew what a terror he was in the old days, and I didn't want to push him into busting loose again.

"But that's what I did in the end. I 'phoned him Friday that I needed money and he said he'd call me up and let me know where to meet him the next night. He called up around half past nine Saturday night and told me to come out to the house. So I went out there and he was waiting for me on the porch and took me upstairs and gave me the ten thousand. I told him this was the last time I'd ever bother him—I always told him that—it had a good effect on him.

"Naturally I wanted to get away as soon as I had the money but he must have felt sort of talkative for a change, because he kept me there for half an hour or so, gassing about men we used to know up in the province.

"After a while I began to get nervous. He was getting a look in his eyes like he used to have when he was young. And then all of a sudden he flared up and tied into me. He had me by the throat and was bending me back across the table when my hand touched that brass knife. It was either me or him—so I let him have it where it would do the most good.

"I beat it then and went back to the hotel. The newspapers were full of it next day, and had a whole lot of stuff about bloody finger-prints. That gave me a jolt! I didn't know nothing about finger-prints, and here I'd left them all over the dump.

"And then I got to worrying over the whole thing, and it seemed like Henny must have my name written down somewheres among his papers, and maybe had saved some of my letters or telegrams—though *they* were wrote in careful enough language. Anyway I figured the police would want to be asking me some questions sooner or later; and there I'd be with fingers that fit the bloody prints, and nothing for what Farr calls a alibi.

"That's when I thought of Farr. I had his address and I knew he had been a finger-print sharp in the East, so I decided to take a chance on him. I went to him and told him the whole story and between us we figured out what to do.

"He said he'd dope my fingers, and I was to come here and tell the story we'd fixed up, and have my finger-prints taken, and then I'd be safe no matter what leaked out about me and Henny. So he smeared up the fingers and told me to be careful not to shake hands with anybody or touch anything, and I came down here and everything went like three of a kind.

"Then that little fat guy"—meaning me—"came around to the hotel last night and as good as told me that he thought I had done for Henny and that I better come down here this morning. I beat it for Farr's right away to see whether I ought to run for it or sit tight, and Farr said, 'Sit tight!' So I stayed there all night and he fixed up my hands this morning. That's my yarn!"

Phels turned to Farr.

"I've seen faked prints before, but never any this good. How'd you do it?"

These scientific birds are funny. Here was Farr looking a nice, long stretch in the face as "accessory after the fact," and yet he brightened up under the admiration in Phels's tone and answered with a voice that was chock-full of pride.

"It's simple! I got hold of a man whose prints I knew weren't in any police gallery—I didn't want any slip up there—and took his prints and put them on a copper plate, using the ordinary photo-engraving process, but etching it pretty deep. Then I coated Clane's fingers with gelatin—just enough to cover all his markings—and pressed them against the plates. That way I got everything, even to the pores, and..."

When I left the bureau ten minutes later Farr and Phels were still sitting knee to knee, jabbering away at each other as only a couple of birds who are cuckoo on the same subject can.

BLACK MASK, OCTOBER 15, 1923

FROM THE AUTHOR OF "SLIPPERY FINGERS"

Since writing "Slippery Fingers" I have read an article in the San Francisco *Chronicle* wherein August Vollmer, chief of police of Berkeley, California, and president of the International Association of Chiefs of Police, is quoted as saying that although it is possible successfully to transfer actual finger-prints from one place to another it is not possible to forge them—"Close inspection of any forged finger-print will soon cause detection."

It may be that what Farr does in my story would be considered by Mr Vollmer a transference rather than a forgery. But whichever it is, I think there is no longer reasonable room for doubt that finger-prints can be successfully forged. I have seen forged prints that to me seemed perfect, but not being even an amateur in that line, my opinion isn't worth much. I think, however, that quite a number of those qualified to speak on the subject will agree with me that it can be, and has been, done.

In the second Arbuckle trial, if my memory is correct, the defense introduced an expert from Los Angeles who testified that he had deceived an assembly of his colleagues with forged prints.

The method used in my story was not selected because it was the best, but because it was the simplest with which I was acquainted and the most easily described. Successful experiments were made with it by the experts at the Leavenworth federal prison.

Sincerely,
S. D. HAMMETT

BLACK MASK, JUNE 1925

FINGER-PRINTS

(A LETTER FROM DASHIELL HAMMETT)

Since this finger-print argument is to be a free-for-all, I should like to have my little say in reply to Mr Reeves' article in the April issue. This is really my second say; I used the juggling of prints as the basis for a story entitled "Slippery Fingers," published in BLACK MASK for October 15, 1923. Before I start, however, let me make it clear I am not an expert, not even one of Mr Reeves' "half-baked (half-boiled?) potatoes." What I am turning loose here is simply an opinion or two accumulated in a few years of dabbling in criminal affairs as private detective, writer, and idle spectator.

Mr Reeves says: "The infallibility of finger-prints as an *absolute means* of identification is based on the three following iron-clad facts: First, they never change. Second, they cannot be counterfeited. Third, no two are alike." Let us look at these facts.

They never change. This is still only probably true. Not enough proof has been piled up to convince a properly skeptical, that is to say a scientific, mind. It is certain that with the years the pattern areas become distorted, or may become distorted. How far this distortion may go without altering the patterns themselves is an open question. Then, too, the ridges disintegrate, as in the case of the prints of Sir William Herschel, whose prints (the first in 1856 and the second in 1914 or 1916) establish, I think, the longest record of persistence. Those prints are both recognizable as the prints of the same man. But what has been done to determine the effects an altogether new manner of living may have on a man's prints and because a hundred men may have this year the same patterns of ridges and pores they had twenty or fifty years ago, is that sufficient evidence to lay down laws purporting to include all the hundreds of millions of varying men in the world?

Experiments have been made to determine whether a person can change the patterns of his fingers. It has been definitely established that if the finger-ends are rubbed smooth, or cut, the old patterns grow out again, in every respect as they were originally. But these experiments have been, so far as I have knowledge of them, rather crude affairs, dealing with the surface of the fingers only. If, as is certain, these patterns to some government, perhaps of the nerves and glands, what might not be done in the way of alteration by tampering with these sources? Isn't it likely that a skillful surgeon might—and may someday actually—learn to alter the design of these ridges and pores by killing certain nerves, or otherwise manipulating them and the glands?

They cannot be counterfeited. Counterfeited is, like forgery, a tricky word in this connection. What Mr Reeves must mean, to support his contention, is that a finger-print put on any surface by any other means that the pressure of the finger to which it belongs will not deceive a man who has at his disposal the training and instruments of the modern finger-print expert. Certainly Mr Reeves is right when he says he can tell the difference between a print made by a finger and one made by a rubber stamp. About that degree of expertness is not quite all that is required. Personally, I am of the opinion that an engraver who gave the matter sufficient study could, with Mr

Reeves' microscope and a few simple tools, sit down to a fresh print and duplicate it, oil, pores, ridges and all. His counterfeit might not be philosophically accurate, but it would be exact enough to fool the very finite mind of the keenest expert who ever lived. I have never heard of anything so simple as a finger-print that could not be counterfeited.

But I am not an expert, so we will throw my opinion on that point out. There is a simpler and easier way of juggling prints than forging them—the transferring of the actual print from one place to another. I shall quote August Vollmer, one-time president of the International Association of Chiefs of Police, because he is known as a staunch believer in finger-print identification.

Discussing some experiments of E. O. Brown, a former secret service agent, later connected with the San Francisco post office, Chief Vollmer told W. T. Amis, of the San Francisco *Chronicle*, "Brown's method of transferring finger-prints will work only with a fresh print, and consists merely of the moving of the mark from one location to another. When a person's finger is placed on a smooth surface, such as glass or highly polished metals, there is an oily substance deposited, which is usually invisible to the eye, but can be developed by the use of chemicals. It is this fresh mark that is necessary for the transferring of the finger-print from one location to another. Brown has shown us that he is able to take this oily deposit and place it where he pleases.

"The greatest trouble to result in this discovery no doubt will be that a criminal, who knows the method employed, and wishes to cover up his crime, will be able to leave the print of another person around the place... and throw suspicion on the innocent man.... These finger-prints that the criminal might wish to use could very easily be obtained in an innocent manner and by means of the method be placed on a window of the place he has robbed... or on a safe or elsewhere as he chooses.

"Fortunately, however, the method is not known to more than half a dozen men at present, and all efforts will be made to keep it a secret of trusted police officials."

No two are alike. I have not gone into this angle very deeply. My understanding of the matter has always been that the most that finger-prints claimed was a ridiculously small likelihood of two men's prints being alike. I remember Wesley Turner, of the Spokane police identification bureau giving me the figures once: one chance in some enormous number of millions of two prints being alike. But I do not believe that there is, or that there ever can be, demonstrable grounds for saying, *no two are alike.* How could it possibly be proved? Think of all the people who now live, of all who lived before them in this old world, and of all who will someday live. No, honestly, don't you think Nature is going to run out of variations some day? And, erratic as Nature is, can we trust her to duplicate—when duplication becomes necessary—only the fingers of the long-dead? But, seriously, there is no proof that each man's pattern is peculiar to him, and there can be no proof until everybody, everywhere, has been examined. The chance of two men with identical proofs coming together is slight—ridiculously slight, perhaps—but if you have fooled around with crap games as much as I have, you know what chance can do to the laws of probabilities when it sets its mind to it.

Our three facts seem to be: (1) There is no proof that finger-prints change, and thus far experiments have not found a method *for* changing them; (2) there seems to be some confusion as to whether finger-prints can be actually forged, but they can be moved from place to place readily enough; and (3) there is nothing to show that two men with similar prints are likely to be in the same neighborhood at that same time.

Unfortunately, the most valuable data on this subject—and there seems to be a vast amount of it—is kept under cover, as is suggested in the last paragraph of my quotation from chief Vollmer. We would get a lot more truth out of our experts and police officials if it were not for their fear that confessions of fallibility will discredit the system, thus leaving the experts jobless and the police minus an effective weapon. These fears are, I think, groundless. The truth will put finger-print classification where it belongs: it is a valuable adjunct to the detective's and the prosecuting attorney's repertory, but it is not infallible when it stands alone, and it may then be dangerous.

The same thing holds true of all the devices of "scientific" detecting. Many of them are excellent when kept to their places, but when pushed forward as infallible methods, they become forms of quackery, and nothing else. The trouble is that criminals are so damned unscientific, and always will be so long as the most marked trait criminal is the childish desire for a short-cut to wealth. The chemist and the photographer and the rest make excellent assistants to our old friend, the flat-footed, low-browed gumshoe, but he's the boy who keeps the jails full of crooks in the long run. But, as I have said, these other things help him now and then. Take, for example, that species of nonsense which, in one shape or another, is commonly called the "lie detector." Usually it is attached somehow to the suspect, and purports to register his nervous glandular or heart reactions, on the naive theory that a congenital liar or a half-animal thug will get all worked up over having to tell a fib. Nevertheless, these machines are, in their small way not without value: sometimes a crook is picked up who really believes in them, thinks he can't beat them, and so tells the truth when the dingus is tied on him.

There is no doubt that finger-prints are a valuable part of the anti-criminal arsenal, but they are only a part of it. As evidence goes, I favor what is usually called "circumstantial evidence," as against the testimony of witnesses, but I haven't a very high opinion of a jury that will condemn a man on the unsupported evidence of finger-prints, if there is a reasonable—and I don't mean overwhelming—amount of contrary evidence. Neither have I much faith in experts who claim infallibility in any field except, perhaps, abstract mathematics.

Sincerely,

DASHIELL HAMMETT

San Francisco, March 28, 1925

4

IT

Calling a detective to solve a crime that turns out to be something quite different from the first diagnosis makes a very unusual story of this. You'll be surprised!

"Now listen, Mr Zumwalt, you're holding out on me; and it won't do! If I'm going to work on this for you I've got to have the whole story."

He looked thoughtfully at me for a moment through screwed-up blue eyes. Then he got up and went to the door of the outer office, opening it. Past him I could see the book-keeper and the stenographer sitting at their desks. Zumwalt closed the door and returned to his desk, leaning across it to speak in a husky undertone.

"You are right, I suppose. But what I am going to tell you must be held in the strictest confidence."

I nodded, and he went on:

"About two months ago one of our clients, Stanley Gorham, turned $100,000 worth of Liberty bonds over to us. He had to go to the Orient on business, and he had an idea that the bonds might go to par during his absence; so he left them with us to be sold if they did. Yesterday I had occasion to go to the safe deposit box where the bonds had been put—in the Golden Gate Trust Company's vault—and they were gone!"

"Anybody except you and your partner have access to the box?"

"No."

"When did you see the bonds last?"

"They were in the box the Saturday before Dan left. And one of the men on duty in the vault told me that Dan was there the following Monday."

"All right! Now let me see if I've got it all straight. Your partner, Daniel Rathbone, was supposed to leave for New York on the twenty-seventh of last month, Monday, to meet an R. W. DePuy. But Rathbone came into the office that day with his baggage and said that important personal affairs made it necessary for him to postpone his departure, that he had to be in San Francisco the following morning. But he didn't tell you what that personal business was.

"You and he had some words over the delay, as you thought it important that he keep the New York engagement on time. You weren't on the best of terms at the time, having quarreled a couple of days before that over a shady deal Rathbone had put over. And so you—"

"Don't misunderstand me," Zumwalt interrupted. "Dan had done nothing dishonest. It was simply that he had engineered several transactions that—well, I thought he had sacrificed ethics to profits."

"I see. Anyhow, starting with your argument over his not leaving for New York that day, you and he wound up by dragging in all of your differences, and practically decided to dissolve partnership as soon as it could be done. The argument was concluded in your house out on Fourteenth Avenue; and, as it was rather late by then and he had checked out of his hotel before he had changed his mind about going to New York, he stayed there with you that night."

"That's right," Zumwalt explained. "I have been living at a hotel since Mrs Zumwalt has been away, but Dan and I went out to the house because it gave us the utmost privacy for our talk; and when we finished it was so late that we remained there."

"Then the next morning you and Rathbone came down to the office and—"

"No," he corrected me. "That is, we didn't come down here together. I came here while Dan went to transact whatever it was that had held him in town. He came into the office a little after noon, and said he was going East on the evening train. He sent Quimby, the book-keeper, down to get his reservations and to check his baggage, which he had left in the office here overnight. Then Dan and I went to lunch together, came back to the office for a few minutes—he had some mail to sign—and then he left."

"I see. After that, you didn't hear from or of him until about ten days later, when DePuy wired to find out why Rathbone hadn't been to see him?"

"That's right! As soon as I got DePuy's wire I sent one to Dan's brother in Chicago, thinking perhaps Dan had stopped *over* with him, but Tom wired back that he hadn't seen his brother. Since then I've had two more wires from DePuy. I was sore with Dan for keeping DePuy waiting, but still I didn't worry a lot.

"Dan isn't a very reliable person, and if he suddenly took a notion to stop off somewhere between here and New York for a few days he'd do it. But yesterday, when I found that the bonds were gone from the safe deposit box and learned that Dan had been to the box the day before he left, I decided that I'd have to do something. But I don't want the police brought into it if it can be avoided.

"I feel sure that if I can find Dan and talk to him we can straighten the mess out somehow without scandal. We had our differences, but Dan's too decent a man, and I like him too well, for all his occasional wildness, to want to see him in jail. So I want him found with as much speed and as little noise as possible."

"Has he got a car?"

"Not now. He had one but he sold it five or six months ago."

"Where'd he bank? I mean his personal account?"

"At the Golden Gate Trust Company."

"Got any photos of him?"

"Yes."

He brought out two from a desk drawer—one full-face, and the other a three-quarter view. They showed a man in the middle of his life, with shrewd eyes set close together in a hatchet face, under dark, thin hair. But the face was rather pleasant for all its craftiness.

"How about his relatives, friends, and so on—particularly his feminine friends?"

"His only relative is the brother in Chicago. As to his friends: he probably has as many as any man in San Francisco. He was a wonderful mixer.

"Recently he has been on very good terms with a Mrs Earnshaw, the wife of a real estate agent. She lives on Pacific Street, I think. I don't know just how intimate they were, but he used to call her up on the phone frequently, and she called him here nearly every day. Then there is a girl named Eva Duthie, a cabaret entertainer, who lives in the 1100 block of Bush Street. There were probably others, too, but I know of only those two."

"Have you looked through his stuff, here?"

"Yes, but perhaps you'd like to look for yourself."

He led me into Rathbone's private office: a small box of a room, just large enough for a desk, a filing cabinet, and two chairs, with doors leading into the corridor, the outer office, and Zumwalt's.

"While I'm looking around you might get me a list of the serial numbers of the missing bonds," I said. "They probably won't help us right away, but we can get the Treasury Department to let us know when the coupons come in, and from where."

I didn't expect to find anything in Rathbone's office and I didn't.

Before I left I questioned the stenographer and the book-keeper. They already knew that Rathbone was missing, but they didn't know that the bonds were gone too.

The girl, Mildred Narbett was her name, said that Rathbone had dictated a couple of letters to her on the twenty-eighth—the day he left for New York—both of which had to do with the partner's business—and told her to send Quimby to check his baggage and make his reservations. When she returned from lunch she had typed the two letters and taken them in for him to sign, catching him just as he was about to leave.

John Quimby, the book-keeper, described the baggage he had checked: two large pigskin bags and a cordovan Gladstone bag. Having a book-keeper's mind, he had remembered the number of the berth he had secured for Rathbone on the evening train—lower 4, car 8. Quimby had returned with the checks and tickets while the partners were out at luncheon, and had put them on Rathbone's desk.

At Rathbone's hotel I was told that he had left on the morning of the twenty-seventh, giving up his room, but leaving his two trunks there, as he intended living there after his return from New York, in three or four weeks. The hotel people could tell me little worth listening to, except that he had left in a taxicab.

At the taxi stand outside I found the chauffeur who had carried Rathbone.

"Rathbone? Sure, I know him!" he told me around a limp cigarette. "Yeah, I guess it was about that date that I took him down to the Golden Gate Trust Company. He had a coupla big yellow bags and a little brown one. He busted into the bank, carrying the little one, and right out again, looking like somebody had kicked him on his corns. Had me take him to the Phelps Building"—the offices of Rathbone & Zumwalt were in that building—"and didn't give me a jit over my fare!"

At the Golden Gate Trust Company I had to plead and talk a lot, but they finally gave me what I wanted—Rathbone had drawn out his account, a little less than $5,000, on the twenty-fifth of the month, the Saturday before he left town.

From the trust company I went down to the Ferry Building baggage-rooms and cigared myself into a look at the records for the twenty-eighth. Only one lot of three bags had been checked to New York that day.

I telegraphed the numbers and Rathbone's description to the agency's New York office, instructing them to find the bags and, through them, find him.

Up in the Pullman Company's offices I was told that car "8" was a through car, and that they could let me know within a couple hours whether Rathbone had occupied his berth all the way to New York.

On my way up to the 1100 block of Bush Street I left one of Rathbone's photographs with a photographer, with a rush order for a dozen copies.

I found Eva Duthie's apartment after about five minutes of searching vestibule directories, and got her out of bed. She was an undersized blonde girl of somewhere between nineteen and twenty-nine, depending upon whether you judged by her eyes or by the rest of her face.

"I haven't seen or heard from Mr Rathbone for nearly a month," she said. "I called him up at his hotel the other night—had a party I wanted to ring him in on—but they told me that he was out of town and wouldn't be back for a week or two."

Then, in answer to another question:

"Yes, we were pretty good friends, but not especially thick. You know what I mean: we had a lot of fun together but neither of us meant anything to the other outside of that. Dan is a good sport—and so am I."

Mrs Earnshaw wasn't so frank. But she had a husband, and that makes a difference. She was a tall, slender woman, as dark as a gypsy, with a haughty air and a nervous trick of chewing her lower lip.

We sat in a stiffly furnished room and she stalled me for about fifteen minutes, until I came out flat-footed with her.

"It's like this, Mrs Earnshaw," I told her. "Mr Rathbone has disappeared, and we are going to find him. You're not helping me and you're not helping yourself. I came here to get what you know about him.

"I could have gone around asking a lot of questions among your friends; and if you don't tell me what I want to know that's what I'll have to do. And, while I'll be as careful as possible, still there's bound to be some curiosity aroused, some wild guesses, and some talk. I'm giving you a chance to avoid all that. It's up to you."

"You are assuming," she said coldly, "that I have something to hide."

"I'm not assuming anything. I'm hunting for information about Daniel Rathbone."

She bit her lip on that for a while, and then the story came out bit by bit, with a lot in it that wasn't any too true, but straight enough in the long run. Stripped of the stuff that wouldn't hold water, it went like this:

She and Rathbone had planned to run away together. She had left San Francisco on the twenty-sixth, going directly to New Orleans. He was to leave the next day, apparently for New York, but he was to change trains somewhere in the Middle West and meet her in New Orleans. From there they were to go by boat to Central America.

She pretended ignorance of his designs upon the bonds. Maybe she hadn't known. Anyhow, she had carried out her part of the plan, but Rathbone had failed to show up in New Orleans. She hadn't shown much care in covering her trail and private detectives employed by her husband had soon found her. Her husband had arrived in New Orleans and, apparently not knowing that there was another man in the deal, had persuaded her to return home.

She wasn't a woman to take kindly to the jilting Rathbone had handed her, so she hadn't tried to get in touch with him, or to learn what had kept him from joining her.

Her story rang true enough, but just to play safe, I put out a few feelers in the neighborhood, and what I learned seemed to verify what she had told me. I gathered that a few of the neighbors had made guesses that weren't a million miles away from the facts.

I got the Pullman Company on the telephone and was told that lower 4, car 8, leaving for New York on the twenty-eighth, hadn't been occupied at all.

Zumwalt was dressing for dinner when I went up to his room at the hotel where he was staying.

I told him all that I had learned that day, and what I thought of it.

"Everything makes sense up until Rathbone left the Golden Gate Trust Company vault on the twenty-seventh, and after that nothing does! He had planned to grab the bonds and elope with this Mrs Earnshaw, and he had already drawn out of the bank all his own money. That's all orderly. But why should he have gone back to the office? Why should he have stayed in town that night? What was the important business that held him? Why should he have ditched Mrs Earnshaw? Why didn't he use his reservations at least part of the way across the country, as he had planned? False trail, maybe, but a rotten one! There's nothing to do, Mr Zumwalt, but to call in the police and the newspapers, and see what publicity and a nation-wide search will do for us."

"But that means jail for Dan, with no chance to quietly straighten the matter up!" he protested.

"It does! But it can't be helped. And remember, you've got to protect yourself. You're his partner, and, while not criminally responsible, you are financially responsible for his actions. You've got to put yourself in the clear!"

He nodded reluctant agreement and I grabbed the telephone.

For two hours I was busy giving all the dope we had to the police, and as much as we wanted published to the newspapers, who luckily had photographs of Rathbone, taken a year before when he had been named as co-respondent in a divorce suit.

I sent off three telegrams. One to New York, asking that Rathbone's baggage be opened as soon as the necessary authority could be secured. (If he hadn't gone to New York the baggage should be waiting at the station.) One to Chicago, asking that Rathbone's brother be interviewed and then shadowed for a few days. And one to New' Orleans, to have the city searched for him. Then I headed for home and bed.

News was scarce, and the papers the next day had Rathbone spread out all over the front pages, with photographs and descriptions and wild guesses and wilder clews that had materialized somehow within the short space between the time the newspapers got the story and the time they went to press.

I spent the morning preparing circulars and plans for having the country covered; and arranging to have steamship records searched.

Just before noon a telegram came from New York, itemizing the things found in Rathbone's baggage. The contents of the two large bags didn't mean anything. They might have been packed for use or for a stall. But the things in the Gladstone bag, which had been found unlocked, were puzzling.

Here's the list:

> Two suits silk pajamas, 4 silk shirts, 8 linen collars, 4 suits underwear, 6 neckties, 6 pairs sox, 18 handkerchiefs, 1 pair military brushes, 1 comb, 1 safety razor, 1 tube shaving cream, 1 shaving brush, 1 tooth brush, 1 tube tooth paste, 1 can talcum powder, 1 bottle hair tonic, 1 cigar case holding 12 cigars, 1.32 Colt's revolver, 1 map of Honduras, 1 Spanish English dictionary, 2 books postage stamps, 1 pint Scotch whiskey, and 1 manicure set.

Zumwalt, his book-keeper, and his stenographer were watching two men from headquarters search Rathbone's office when I arrived there. After I showed them the telegram the detectives went back to their examination.

"What's the significance of that list?" Zumwalt asked.

"It shows that there's no sense to this thing the way it now stands," I said. "That Gladstone bag was packed to be carried. Checking it was all wrong—it wasn't even locked. And nobody ever checks Gladstone bags filled with toilet articles—so checking it for a stall would have been the bunk! Maybe he checked it as an afterthought—to get rid of it when he found he wasn't going to need it. But what could have made it unnecessary to him? Don't forget that it's apparently the same bag that he carried into the Golden Gate Trust Company vault when he went for the bonds. Damned if I can dope it!"

"Here's something else for you to dope," one of the city detectives said, getting up from his examination of the desk and holding out a sheet of paper. "I found it behind one of the drawers, where it had slipped down."

It was a letter, written with blue ink in a firm, angular and unmistakably feminine hand on heavy white note paper.

"Dear Danny boy:

If it isn't too late I've changed my mind about going. If you can wait another day, until Tuesday, I'll go. Call me up as soon as you get this, and if you still want me I'll pick you up in the roadster at the Shattuck Avenue station Tuesday afternoon.

More than ever yours,
Boots."

It was dated the twenty-sixth—the Sunday before Rathbone had disappeared.

"That's the thing that made him lay over another day, and made him change his plans," one of the police detectives said. "I guess we better run over to Berkeley and see what we can find at the Shattuck Avenue station."

"Mr Zumwalt," I said, when he and I were alone in his office, "how about this stenog of yours?"

He bounced up from his chair and his face turned red.

"What about her?"

"Is she—How friendly was she with Rathbone?"

"Miss Narbett," he said heavily, deliberately, as if to be sure that I caught every syllable, "is to be married to me as soon as my wife gets her divorce. That is why I canceled the order to sell my house. Now would you mind telling me just why you asked?"

"Just a random guess!" I lied, trying to soothe him. "I don't want to overlook any bets. But now that's out of the way."

"It is," he was still talking deliberately, "and it seems to me that most of your guesses have been random ones. If you will have your office send me a bill for your services to date, I think I can dispense with your help."

"Just as you say. But you'll have to pay for a full day today; so, if you don't mind, I'll keep on working at it until night."

"Very well! But I am busy, and you needn't bother about coming in with any reports."

"All right," I said, and bowed myself out of the office, but not out of the job.

That letter from "Boots" had *not* been in the desk when I searched it. I had taken every drawer out and even tilted the desk to look under it. The letter was a plant!

And then again: maybe Zumwalt had given me the air because he was dissatisfied with the work I had done and peeved at my question about the girl—and maybe not.

Suppose (I thought, walking up Market Street, bumping shoulders and stepping on people's feet) the two partners were in this thing together. One of them would have to be the goat, and that part had fallen to Rathbone. Zumwalt's manner and actions since his partner's disappearance fit that theory well enough.

Employing a private detective before calling in the police was a good play. In the first place it gave him the appearance of innocence. Then the private sleuth would tell him everything he learned, every step he took, giving Zumwalt an opportunity to correct any mistakes or oversights in the partners' plans before the police came into it; and if the private detective got on dangerous ground he could be called off.

And suppose Rathbone was found in some city where he was unknown—and that would be where he'd go. Zumwalt would volunteer to go forward to identify him. He would look at him and say, "No, that's not him," Rathbone would be turned loose, and that would be the end of that trail.

This theory left the sudden change in Rathbone's plans unaccounted for; but it made his return to the office on the afternoon of the twenty-seventh more plausible. He had come back to confer with his partner over that unknown necessity for the change, and they had decided to leave Mrs Earnshaw out of it. Then they had gone out to Zumwalt's house. For what? And why had Zumwalt decided not to sell the house? And why had he taken the trouble to give me an explanation? Could they have cached the bonds there?

A look at the house wouldn't be a bad idea!

I telephoned Bennett, at the Oakland Police Department.

"Do me a favor, Frank? Call Zumwalt on the phone. Tell him you've picked up a man who answers Rathbone's description to a T; and ask him to come over and take a look at him. When he gets there stall him as long as you can—pretending that the man is being finger-printed and measured, or something like that—and then tell him that you've found that the man isn't Rathbone, and that you are sorry to have brought him over there, and so on. If you only hold him for half or three-quarters of an hour it'll be enough—it'll take him more than half an hour traveling each way. Thanks!"

I stopped in at the office, stuck a flashlight in my pocket, and headed for Fourteenth Avenue.

Zumwalt's house was a two-storey, semi-detached one; and the lock on the front door held me up about four minutes. A burglar would have gone through it without checking his stride. This breaking into the house wasn't exactly according to the rules, but on the other hand, I was legally Zumwalt's agent until I discontinued work that night—so this crashing in couldn't be considered illegal.

I started at the top floor and worked down. Bureaus, dressers, tables, desks, chairs, walls, woodwork, pictures, carpets, plumbing—I looked at everything that was thick enough to hold paper. I didn't take things apart, but it's surprising how speedily and how thoroughly you can go through a house when you're in training.

I found nothing in the house itself, so I went down into the cellar.

It was a large cellar and divided in two. The front part was paved with cement, and held a full coal-bin, some furniture, some canned goods, and a lot of odds and ends of housekeeping accessories. The rear division, behind a plaster partition where the steps ran down from the kitchen, was without windows, and illuminated only by one swinging electric light, which I turned on.

A pile of lumber filled half the space; on the other side barrels and boxes were piled up to the ceiling; two sacks of cement lay beside them, and in another corner was a tangle of broken furniture. The floor was of hard dirt.

I turned to the lumber pile first. I wasn't in love with the job ahead of me—moving the pile away and then back again. But I needn't have worried.

A board rattled behind me, and I wheeled to see Zumwalt rising from behind a barrel and scowling at me over a black automatic pistol.

"Put your hands up," he said.

I put them up. I didn't have a pistol with me, not being in the habit of carrying one except when I thought I was going to need it; but it would have been all the same if I had had a pocket full of them. I don't mind taking chances, but there's no chance when you're looking into the muzzle of a gun that a determined man is holding on you.

So I put my hands up. And one of them brushed against the swinging light globe. I drove my knuckles into it. As the cellar went black I threw myself backward and to one side. Zumwalt's gun streaked fire.

Nothing happened for a while. I found that I had fallen across the doorway that gave to the stairs and the front cellar. I figured that I couldn't move without making a noise that would draw lead, so I lay still.

Then began a game that made up in tenseness what it lacked in action.

The part of the cellar where we were was about twenty by twenty feet and blacker than a new shoe. There were two doors.

One, on the opposite side, opened into the yard and was, I supposed, locked. I was lying on my back across the other, waiting for a pair of legs to grab. Zumwalt, with a gun out of which only one bullet had been spent, was somewhere in the blackness, and aware, from his silence, that I was still alive.

I figured I had the edge on him. I was closest to the only practicable exit; he didn't know that I was unarmed; he didn't know whether I had help close by or not; time was valuable to him, but not necessarily so to me. So I waited.

Time passed. How much I don't know. Maybe half an hour.

The floor was damp and hard and thoroughly uncomfortable. The electric light had cut my hand when I broke it, and I couldn't determine how badly I was bleeding. I thought of Tad's "blind man in a dark room hunting for a black hat that wasn't there," and knew how he felt.

A box or barrel fell over with a crash—knocked over by Zumwalt, no doubt, moving out from the hiding-place wherein he had awaited my arrival.

Silence for a while. And then I could hear him moving cautiously off to one side.

Without warning two streaks from his pistol sent bullets into the partition somewhere above my feet. I wasn't the only one who was feeling the strain.

Silence again, and I found that I was wet and dripping with perspiration.

Then I could hear his breathing, but couldn't determine whether he was nearer or was breathing more heavily.

A soft, sliding, dragging across the dirt floor! I pictured him crawling awkwardly on his knees and one hand, the other hand holding the pistol out ahead of him—the pistol that would spit fire as soon as its muzzle touched something soft. And I became uneasily aware of my bulk. I am thick through the waist; and there in the dark it seemed to me that my paunch must extend almost to the ceiling—a target that no bullet could miss.

I stretched my hands out toward him and held them there. If they touched him first I'd have a chance.

He was panting harshly now; and I was breathing through a mouth that was stretched as wide as it would go, so that there would be no rasping of the large quantities of air I was taking in and letting out.

Abruptly he came.

Hair brushed the fingers of my left hand. I closed them about it, pulling the head I couldn't see viciously toward me, driving my right fist beneath it. You may know that I put everything I had in that smack when I tell you that not until later, when I found that one of my cheeks was scorched, did I know that his gun had gone off.

He wiggled, and I hit him again.

Then I was sitting astride him, my flashlight hunting for his pistol. I found it, and yanked him to his feet.

As soon as his head cleared I herded him into the front cellar and got a globe to replace the one I had smashed.

"Now dig it up," I ordered.

That was a safe way of putting it. I wasn't sure what I wanted or where it would be, except that his selecting this part of the cellar to wait for me in made it look as if this was the right place.

"You'll do your own digging!" he growled.

"Maybe," I said, "but I'm going to do it now, and I haven't time to tie you up. So if I've got to do the digging, I'm going to crown you first, so you'll sleep peacefully until it's all over."

All smeared with blood and dirt and sweat, I must have looked capable of anything, for when I took a step toward him he gave in.

From behind the lumber pile he brought a spade, moved some of the barrels to one side, and started turning up the dirt.

When a hand—a man's hand—dead-yellow where the damp dirt didn't stick to it—came into sight I stopped him.

I had found "it," and I had no stomach for looking at "it" after three weeks of lying in the wet ground.

NOTE: In court, Lester Zumwalt's plea was that he had killed his partner in self-defense. Zumwalt testified that he had taken the Gorham bonds in a futile attempt to recover losses in the stock market; and that when Rathbone—who had intended taking them and going to Central America with Mrs Earnshaw—had visited the safe deposit box and found them gone, he had returned to the office and charged Zumwalt with the theft.

Zumwalt at that time had not suspected his partner's own dishonest plans, and had promised to restore the bonds. They had gone to Zumwalt's house to discuss the matter; and, Rathbone, dissatisfied with his partner's plan of restitution, had attacked Zumwalt, and had been killed in the ensuing struggle.

Then Zumwalt had told Mildred Narbett, his stenographer, the whole story and had persuaded her to help him. Between them they had made it appear that Rathbone had been in the office for a while the next day—the twenty-eighth—and had left for New York.

However, the jury seemed to think that Zumwalt had lured his partner out to the Fourteenth Avenue house for the purpose of killing him; so Zumwalt was found guilty of murder in the first degree.

The first jury before which Mildred Narbett was tried disagreed. The second jury acquitted her, holding that there was nothing to show that she had taken part in either the theft of the bonds or the murder, or that she had any knowledge of either crime until afterward; and that her later complicity was, in view of her love for Zumwalt, not altogether blameworthy.

5

BODIES PILED UP

BLACK MASK, DECEMBER 1, 1923

One of our best detectives is this nameless sleuth of Mr Hammett's. He's deductive, practical, and maybe a little unromantic. Probably that's why he runs into such wild adventures and takes such horrible chances, in this story he walks into a whirlwind of death. Go to it.

The Montgomery Hotel's regular detective had taken his last week's rake-off from the hotel bootlegger in merchandise instead of cash, had drunk it down, had fallen asleep in the lobby, and had been fired. I happened to be the only idle operative in the Continental Detective Agency's San Francisco branch at the time, and thus it came about that I had three days of hotel-coppering while a man was being found to take the job permanently.

The Montgomery is a quiet hotel of the better sort, and so I had a very restful time of it—until the third and last day.

Then things changed.

I came down into the lobby that afternoon to find Stacey, the assistant manager on duty at the time, hunting for me.

"One of the maids just phoned that there's something wrong up in 906," he said.

We went up to that room together. The door was open. In the center of the floor stood a maid, staring goggle-eyed at the closed door of the clothes press. From under it, extending perhaps a foot across the floor toward us, was a snake-shaped ribbon of blood.

I stepped past the maid and tried the door. It was unlocked. I opened it. Slowly, rigidly, a man pitched out into my arms—pitched out backward—and there was a six-inch slit down the back of his coat, and the coat was wet and sticky.

That wasn't altogether a surprise: the blood on the floor had prepared me for something of the sort. But when another followed him—facing me, this one, with a dark, distorted face—I dropped the one I had caught and jumped back.

And as I jumped a third man came tumbling out after the others.

From behind me came a scream and a thud as the maid fainted. I wasn't feeling any too steady myself. I'm no sensitive plant, and I've looked at a lot of unlovely sights in my time, but for weeks afterward I could see those three dead men coming out of that clothes press to pile up at my feet: coming out slowly—almost deliberately—in a ghastly game of "follow your leader."

Seeing them, you couldn't doubt that they were really dead. Every detail of their falling, every detail of the heap in which they now lay, had a horrible certainty of lifelessness in it.

I turned to Stacey, who, deathly white himself, was keeping on his feet only by clinging to the foot of the brass bed.

"Get the woman out! Get doctors—police!"

I pulled the three dead bodies apart, laying them out in a grim row, faces up. Then I made a hasty examination of the room.

A soft hat, which fitted one of the dead men, lay in the center of the unruffled bed. The room key was in the door, on the inside. There was no blood in the room except what had leaked out of the clothes press, and the room showed no signs of having been the scene of a struggle.

The door to the bathroom was open. In the bottom of the bath tub was a shattered gin bottle, which, from the strength of the odor and the dampness of the tub, had been nearly full when broken. In one corner of the bathroom I found a small whisky glass, and another under the tub. Both were dry, clean, and odorless.

The inside of the clothes press door was stained with blood from the height of my shoulder to the floor, and two hats lay in the puddle of blood on the closet floor. Each of the hats fitted one of the dead men.

That was all. Three dead men, a broken gin bottle, blood.

Stacey returned presently with a doctor, and while the doctor was examining the dead men, the police detectives arrived.

The doctor's work was soon done.

"This man," he said, pointing to one of them, "was struck on the back of the head with a small blunt instrument, and then strangled. This one," pointing to another, "was simply strangled. And the third was stabbed in the back with a blade perhaps five inches long. They have been dead for about two hours—since noon or a little after."

The assistant manager identified two of the bodies. The man who had been stabbed—the first to fall out of the clothes press—had arrived at the hotel three days before, registering as Tudor Ingraham of Washington, D. C., and had occupied room 915, three doors away.

The last man to fall out—the one who had been simply choked—was the occupant of this room. His name was Vincent Develyn. He was an insurance broker and had made the hotel his home since his wife's death, some four years before.

The third man had been seen in Develyn's company frequently, and one of the clerks remembered that they had come into the hotel together at about five minutes after twelve this day. Cards and letters in his pockets told us that he was Homer Ansley, a member of the law firm of Lankershim and Ansley, whose offices were in the Miles Building—next door to Develyn's office, in fact.

Develyn's pockets held between \$150 and \$200; Ansley's wallet contained more than \$100; Ingraham's pockets yielded nearly \$300, and in a money belt around his waist we found \$2200 and two medium-sized unset diamonds. All three had watches—Develyn's was a valuable one—in their pockets, and Ingraham wore two rings, both of which were expensive ones. Ingraham's room key was in his pocket.

Beyond this money—whose presence would seem to indicate that robbery hadn't been the motive behind the three killings—we found nothing on any of their persons to throw the slightest light on the crime. Nor did the most thorough examination of both Ingraham's and Develyn's rooms teach us anything.

In Ingraham's room we found a dozen or more packs of carefully marked cards, some crooked dice, and an immense amount of data on racehorses. Also we found that he had a wife who lived on East Delavan Avenue in Buffalo, and a brother on Crutcher Street in Dallas; as well as a list of names and addresses that we carried off to investigate later. But nothing in either room pointed, even indirectly, at murder.

Phels, the police department Bertillon man, found a number of finger-prints in Develyn's room, but we couldn't tell whether they would be of any value or not until he had worked them up. Though Develyn and Ansley had apparently been strangled by hands, Phels was unable to get prints from either their necks or their collars.

The maid who had discovered the blood said that she had straightened up Develyn's room between ten and eleven that morning, but had not put fresh towels in the bathroom. It was for this purpose that she had gone to the room in the afternoon. She had found the door unlocked, with the key on the inside, and, as soon as she entered, had seen the blood and telephoned Stacey. She had seen no one in the corridor nearby as she entered the room.

She had straightened up Ingraham's room, she said, at a few minutes after one. She had gone there earlier—between 10:20 and 10:45—for that purpose, but Ingraham had not then left it.

The elevator man who had carried Ansley and Develyn up from the lobby at a few minutes after twelve remembered that they had been laughingly discussing their golf scores of the previous day during the ride. No one had seen anything suspicious in the hotel around the time at which the doctor had placed the murders. But that was to be expected.

The murderer could have left the room, closing the door behind him, and walked away secure in the knowledge that at noon a man in the corridors of the Montgomery would attract little attention. If he was staying at the hotel he would simply have gone to his room; if not, he would have either walked all the way down to the street, or down a floor or two and then caught an elevator.

None of the hotel employees had ever seen Ingraham and Develyn together. There was nothing to show that they had even the slightest acquaintance. Ingraham habitually stayed in his room until noon, and did not return to it until very late at night. Nothing was known of his affairs.

At the Miles Building we—that is, Marty O'Hara and George Dean of the police department homicide detail, and I—questioned Ansley's partner and Develyn's employees. Both Develyn and Ansley, it seemed, were ordinary men who led ordinary lives: lives that held neither dark spots nor queer kinks. Ansley was married and had two children; he lived on Lake Street. Both men had a sprinkling of relatives and friends scattered here and there through the country; and, so far as we could learn, their affairs were in perfect order.

They had left their offices this day to go to luncheon together, intending to visit Develyn's room first for a drink apiece from a bottle of gin someone coming from Australia had smuggled in to him.

"Well," O'Hara said, when we were on the street again, "this much is clear. If they went up to Develyn's room for a drink, it's a cinch that they were killed almost as soon as they got in the room. Those whisky glasses you found were dry and clean. Whoever turned the trick must have been waiting for them. I wonder about this fellow Ingraham."

"I'm wondering, too," I said. "Figuring it out from the positions I found them in when I opened the closet door, Ingraham sizes up as the key to the whole thing. Develyn was back against the wall, with Ansley in front of him, both facing the door. Ingraham was facing them, with his back to the door. The clothes press was just large enough for them to be packed in it—too small for any of them to slip down while the door was closed.

"Then there was no blood in the room except what had come from the clothes press. Ingraham, with that gaping slit in his back, couldn't have been stabbed until he was inside the closet, or he'd have bled elsewhere. He was standing close to the other men when he was knifed, and whoever knifed him closed the door quickly afterward.

"Now, why should he have been standing in such a position? Do you dope it out that he and another killed the two friends, and that while he was stowing their bodies in the closet his accomplice finished him off?"

"Maybe," Dean said.

And that "maybe" was still as far as we had gone three days later.

We had sent and received bales of telegrams, having relatives and acquaintances of the dead men interviewed; and we had found nothing that seemed to have any bearing upon their deaths. Nor had we found the slightest connecting link between Ingraham and the other two. We had traced those other two back step by step almost to their cradles. We had accounted for every minute of their time since Ingraham had arrived in San Francisco—thoroughly enough to convince us that neither of them had met Ingraham.

Ingraham, we had learned, was a book-maker and all around crooked gambler. His wife and he had separated, but were on good terms. Some fifteen years before, he had been convicted of "assault with intent to kill" in Newark, N. J., and had served two years in the state prison. But the man he had assaulted—one John Pellow—had died of pneumonia in Omaha in 1914.

Ingraham had come to San Francisco for the purpose of opening a gambling club, and all our investigations had tended to show that his activities while in the city had been toward that end alone.

The finger-prints Phels had secured had all turned out to belong to Stacey, the maid, the police detectives, or myself. In short, we had found nothing!

So much for our attempts to learn the motive behind the three murders.

We now dropped that angle and settled down to the detail-studying, patience-taxing grind of picking up the murderer's trail. From any crime to its author there is a trail. It may be—as in this case—obscure; but, since matter cannot move without disturbing other matter along its path, there always is—there must be—a trail of some sort. And finding and following such trails is what a detective is paid to do.

In the case of a murder it is possible sometimes to take a short-cut to the end of the trail, by first finding the motive. A knowledge of the motive often reduces the field of possibilities; sometimes points directly to the guilty one. It is on this account that murderers are, as a rule, more easily apprehended than any other class of criminals.

But a knowledge of the motive isn't indispensable—quite a few murder mysteries are solved without its help. And in a fair proportion—say, ten to twenty per cent—of cases where men are convicted justly of murder, the motive isn't clearly shown even at the last, and sometimes is hardly guessed at.

So far, all we knew about the motive in the particular case we were dealing with was that it hadn't been robbery; unless something we didn't know about had been stolen—something of sufficient value to make the murderer scorn the money in his victims' pockets.

We hadn't altogether neglected the search for the murderer's trail, of course, but—being human—we had devoted most of our attention to trying to find a short-cut. Now we set out to find our man, or men, regardless of what had urged him or them to commit the crimes.

Of the people who had been registered at the hotel on the day of the killing there were nine men of whose innocence we hadn't found a reasonable amount of proof. Four of these were still at the hotel, and only one of that four interested us very strongly. That one—a big raw-boned man of forty-five or fifty, who had registered as J. J. Cooper of Anaconda, Montana—wasn't, we had definitely established, really a mining man, as he pretended to be. And our telegraphic communications with Anaconda failed to show that he was known there. Therefore we were having him shadowed—with few results.

Five men of the nine had departed since the murders; three of them leaving forwarding addresses with the mail clerk. Gilbert Jacquemart had occupied room 946 and had ordered his mail forwarded to him at a Los Angeles hotel. W. F. Salway, who had occupied room 1022, had given instructions that his mail be readdressed to a number on Clark Street in Chicago. Ross Orrett, room 609, had asked to have his mail sent to him care of General Delivery at the local post office.

Jacquemart had arrived at the hotel two days before, and had left on the afternoon of the murders. Salway had arrived the day before the murders and had left the day after them. Orrett had arrived on the day of the murders and had left the following day.

Sending telegrams to have the first two found and investigated, I went after Orrett myself. A musical comedy named "What For?" was being widely advertised just then with gaily printed plum-colored hand-bills. I got one of them and, at a stationery store, an envelope to match, and mailed it to Orrett at the Montgomery Hotel. There are concerns that make a practice of securing the names of arrivals at the principal hotels and mailing them advertisements. I trusted that Orrett, knowing this, wouldn't be suspicious when my gaudy envelope, forwarded from the hotel, reached him through the General Delivery window.

Dick Foley—the agency's shadow specialist—planted himself in the post office, to loiter around with an eye on the "O" window until he saw my plum-colored envelope passed out, and then to shadow the receiver.

I spent the next day trying to solve the mysterious J. J. Cooper's game, but he was still a puzzle when I knocked off that night.

At a little before five the following morning Dick Foley dropped into my room on his way home to wake me up and tell me what he had done for himself.

"This Orrett baby is our meat!" he said. "Picked him up when he got his mail yesterday afternoon. Got another letter besides yours. Got an apartment on Van Ness Avenue. Took it the day after the killing, under the name of B. T. Quinn. Packing a gun under his left arm—there's that sort of a bulge there. Just went home to bed. Been visiting all the dives in North Beach. Who do you think he's hunting for?"

"Who?"

"Guy Cudner."

That was news! This Guy Cudner, alias "The Darkman," was the most dangerous bird on the Coast, if not in the country. He had only been nailed once, but if he had been convicted of all the crimes that everybody knew he had committed he'd have needed half a dozen lives to crowd his sentences into, besides another half-dozen to carry to the gallows. However, he had decidedly the right sort of backing—enough to buy him everything he needed in the way of witnesses, alibis, even juries, and—so the talk went—an occasional judge.

I don't know what went wrong with his support that one time he was convicted up North and sent over for a one-to-fourteen-year hitch; but it adjusted itself promptly, for the ink was hardly dry on the press notices of his conviction before he was loose again on parole.

"Is Cudner in town?"

"Don't know," Dick said, "but this Orrett, or Quinn, or whatever his name is, is surely hunting for him. In Rick's place, at 'Wop' Healey's and at Pigatti's. 'Porky' Grout tipped me off. Says Orrett doesn't know Cudner by sight, but is trying to find him. Porky didn't know what he wants with him."

This Porky Grout was a dirty little rat who would sell out his family—if he ever had one—for the price of a flop. But with these lads who play both sides of the game it's always a question of which side they're playing when you think they're playing yours.

"Think Porky was coming clean?" I asked.

"Chances are—but you can't gamble on him."

"Is Orrett acquainted here?"

"Doesn't seem to be. Knows where he wants to go but has to ask how to get there. Hasn't spoken to anybody that seemed to know him."

"What's he like?"

"Not the kind of egg you'd want to tangle with off-hand, if you ask me. He and Cudner would make a good pair. They don't look alike. This egg is tall and slim, but he's built right—those fast, smooth muscles. Face is sharp without being thin, if you get me. I mean all the lines in it are straight. No curves. Chin, nose, mouth, eyes—all straight, sharp lines and angles. Looks like the kind of egg we know Cudner is. Make a good pair. Dresses well and doesn't look like a rowdy—but harder than hell! A big game hunter! Our meat, I bet you!"

"It doesn't look bad," I agreed. "He came to the hotel the morning of the day the men were killed, and checked out the next morning. He packs a rod, and changed his name after he left. And now he's paired off with The Darkman. It doesn't look bad at all!"

"I'm telling you," Dick said, "this fellow looks like three killings wouldn't disturb his rest any. I wonder where Cudner fits in."

"I can't guess. But, if he and Orrett haven't connected yet, then Cudner wasn't in on the murders; but he may give us the answer."

Then I jumped out of bed.

"I'm going to gamble on Porky's dope being on the level! How would you describe Cudner?"

"You know him better than I do."

"Yes, but how would you describe him to me if I didn't know him?"

"A little fat guy with a red forked scar on his left cheek. What's the idea?"

"It's a good one," I admitted. "That scar makes all the difference in the world. If he didn't have it and you were to describe him you'd go into all the details of his appearance. But he has it, so you simply say, 'A little fat guy with a red forked scar on his left cheek.' It's a ten to one that that's just how he has been described to Orrett. I don't look like Cudner, but I'm his size and build, and with a scar on my face Orrett will fall for me."

"What then?"

"There's no telling; but I ought to be able to learn a lot if I can get Orrett talking to me as Cudner. It's worth a try anyway."

"You can't get away with it—not in San Francisco. Cudner is too well known."

"What difference does that make, Dick? Orrett is the only one I want to fool. If he takes me for Cudner, well and good. If he doesn't, still well and good. I won't force myself on him."

"How are you going to fake the scar?"

"Easy! We have pictures of Cudner, showing the scar, in the criminal gallery. I'll get some collodion—it's sold in drug stores under several trade names for putting on cuts and scratches—color it, and imitate Cudner's scar on my cheek. It dries with a shiny surface and, put on thick, will stand out just enough to look like an old scar."

It was a little after eleven the following night when Dick telephoned me that Orrett was in Pigatti's place, on Pacific Street, and apparently settled there for some little while. My scar already painted on, I jumped into a taxi and within a few minutes was talking to Dick, around the corner from Pigatti's.

"He's sitting at the last table back on the left side. And he was alone when I came out. You can't miss him. He's the only egg in the joint with a clean collar."

"You better stick outside—half a block or so away—with the taxi," I told Dick. "Maybe brother Orrett and I will leave together and I'd just as leave have you standing by in case things break wrong."

Pigatti's place is a long, narrow, low-ceilinged cellar, always dim with smoke. Down the middle runs a narrow strip of bare floor for dancing. The rest of the floor is covered with closely packed tables, whose cloths are always soiled; and the management hasn't yet verified the rumor that the country has gone dry.

Most of the tables were occupied when I came in, and half a dozen couples were dancing. Few of the faces to be seen were strangers to the morning "line up" at police headquarters.

Peering through the smoke, I saw Orrett at once, seated alone in a far corner, looking at the dancers with the set blank face of one who masks an all-seeing watchfulness. I walked down the other side of the room and crossed the strip of dance-floor directly under a light, so that the scar might be clearly visible to him. Then I selected a vacant table not far from his, and sat down facing him.

Ten minutes passed while he pretended an interest in the dancers and I affected a thoughtful stare at the dirty cloth on my table; but neither of us missed so much as a flicker of the other's lids.

His eyes—gray eyes that were pale without being shallow, with black needle-point pupils—met mine after a while in a cold, steady, inscrutable stare; and, very slowly, he got to his feet. One hand—his right—in a side pocket of his dark coat, he walked straight across to my table and sat down opposite me.

"Cudner?"

"Looking for me, I hear," I replied, trying to match the icy smoothness of his voice, as I was matching the steadiness of his gaze.

He had sat down with his left side turned slightly toward me, which put his right arm in not too cramped a position for straight shooting from the pocket that still held his hand.

"You were looking for me, too."

I didn't know what the correct answer to that would be, so I just grinned. But the grin didn't come from my heart. I had, I realized, made a mistake—one that might cost me something before we were done. This bird wasn't hunting for Cudner as a friend, as I had carelessly assumed, but was on the war path.

I saw those three dead men falling out of the closet in room 906!

My gun was inside the waist-band of my trousers, where I could get it quickly, but his was in his hand. So I was careful to keep my own hands motionless on the edge of the table, while I widened my grin.

His eyes were changing now, and the more I looked at them the less I liked them. The gray in them had darkened and grown duller, and the pupils were larger, and white crescents were showing beneath the gray. Twice before I had looked into eyes such as these—and I hadn't forgotten what they meant—the eyes of the congenital killer!

"Suppose you speak your piece," I suggested after a while.

But he wasn't to be beguiled into conversation. He shook his head a mere fraction of an inch and the corners of his compressed mouth dropped down a trifle. The white crescents of eyeballs were growing broader, pushing the gray circles up under the upper lids.

It was coming! And there was no use waiting for it!

I drove a foot at his shins under the table, and at the same time pushed the table into his lap and threw myself across it. The bullet from his gun went off to one side. Another bullet—not from his gun—thudded into the table that was upended between us.

I had him by the shoulders when the second shot from behind took him in the left arm, just below my hand. I let go then and fell away, rolling over against the wall and twisting around to face the direction from which the bullets were coming.

I twisted around just in time to see—jerking out of sight behind a corner of the passage that gave to a small dining room—Guy Cudner's scarred face. And as it disappeared a bullet from Orrett's gun splattered the plaster from the wall where it had been.

I grinned at the thought of what must be going on in Orrett's head as he lay sprawled out on the floor confronted by two Cudners. But he took a shot at me just then and I stopped grinning. Luckily, he had to twist around to fire at me, putting his weight on his wounded arm, and the pain made him wince, spoiling his aim.

Before he had adjusted himself more comfortably I had scrambled on hands and knees to Pigatti's kitchen door—only a few feet away—and had myself safely tucked out of range around an angle in the wall; all but my eyes and the top of my head, which I risked so that I might see what went on.

Orrett was now ten or twelve feet from me, lying flat on the floor, facing Cudner, with a gun in his hand and another on the floor beside him.

Across the room, perhaps thirty feet away, Cudner was showing himself around his protecting corner at brief intervals to exchange shots with the man on the floor, occasionally sending one my way. We had the place to ourselves. There were four exits, and the rest of Pigatti's customers had used them all.

I had my gun out, but I was playing a waiting game. Cudner, I figured, had been tipped off to Orrett's search for him and had arrived on the scene with no mistaken idea of the other's attitude. Just what there was between them and what bearing it had on the Montgomery murders was a mystery to me, but I didn't try to solve it now. I kept away from the bullets that were flying around as best I could and waited.

They were firing in unison. Cudner would show around his corner, both men's weapons would spit, and he would duck out of sight again. Orrett was bleeding about the head now and one of his legs sprawled crookedly behind him. I couldn't determine whether Cudner had been hit or not.

Each had fired eight, or perhaps nine, shots when Cudner suddenly jumped out into full view, pumping the gun in his left hand as fast as its mechanism would go, the gun in his right hand hanging at his side. Orrett had changed guns, and was on his knees now, his fresh weapon keeping pace with his enemy's.

That couldn't last!

Cudner dropped his left-hand gun, and, as he raised the other, he sagged forward and went down on one knee. Orrett stopped firing abruptly and fell over on his back—spread out full-length. Cudner fired once more—wildly, into the ceiling—and pitched down on his face.

I sprang to Orrett's side and kicked both of his guns away. He was lying still but his eyes were open.

"Are you Cudner, or was he?"

"He."

"Good!" he said, and closed his eyes.

I crossed to where Cudner lay and turned him over on his back. His chest was literally shot to pieces.

His thick lips worked, and I put my ear down to them.

"I get him?"

"Yes," I lied, "he's already cold."

His dying face twisted into a triumphant grin.

"Sorry... three in hotel..." he gasped hoarsely. "Mistake... wrong room... got one... had to... other two... protect myself... I..."

He shuddered and died.

A week later the hospital people let me talk to Orrett. I told him what Cudner had said before he died.

"That's the way I doped it out," Orrett said from out of the depths of the bandages in which he was swathed. "That's why I moved and changed my name the next day."

"I suppose you've got it nearly figured out by now," he said after a while.

"No," I confessed, "I haven't. I've an idea what it was all about but I could stand having a few details cleared up."

"I'm sorry I can't clear them up for you, but I've got to cover myself up. I'll tell you a story, though, and it may help you. Once upon a time there was a high-class crook—what the newspapers call a Master Mind. Came a day when he found he had accumulated enough money to give up the game and settle down as an honest man.

"But he had two lieutenants—one in New York and one in San Francisco—and they were the only men in the world who knew he was a crook. And, besides that, he was afraid of both of them. So he thought he'd rest easier if they were out of the way. And it happened that neither of these lieutenants had ever seen the other.

"So this Master Mind convinced each of them that the other was double-crossing him and would have to be bumped off for the safety of all concerned. And both of them fell for it. The New Yorker went to San Francisco to get the other, and the San Franciscan was told that the New Yorker would arrive on such-and-such a day and would stay at such-and-such a hotel.

"The Master Mind figured that there was an even chance of both men passing out when they met—and he was nearly right at that. But he was sure that one would die, and then, even if the other missed hanging, there would only be one man left for him to dispose of later."

There weren't as many details in the story as I would have liked to have, but it explained a lot.

"How do you figure out Cudner's getting into the wrong room?" I asked.

"That was funny! Maybe it happened like this: My room was 609 and the killing was done in 906. Suppose Cudner went to the hotel on the day he knew I was due and took a quick slant at the register. He wouldn't want to be seen looking at it if he could avoid it, so he didn't turn it around, but flashed a look at it as it lay—facing the desk.

"When you read numbers of three figures upside-down you have to transpose them in your head to get them straight. Like 123. You'd get that 3-2-1, and then turn them around in your head. That's what Cudner did with mine. He was keyed up, of course, thinking of the job ahead of him, and he overlooked the fact that 609 upside-down still reads 609 just the same. So he turned it around and made it 906—Develyn's room."

"That's how I doped it," I said, "and I reckon it's about right. And then he looked at the key-rack and saw that 906 wasn't there. So he thought he might just as well get his job done right then, when he could roam the hotel corridors without attracting attention. Of course, he may have gone up to the room before Ansley and Develyn came in and waited for them, but I doubt it.

"I think it more likely that he simply happened to arrive at the hotel a few minutes after they had come in. Ansley was probably alone in the room when Cudner opened the unlocked door and came in—Develyn being in the bathroom getting the glasses.

"Ansley was about your size and age, and close enough in appearance to fit a rough description of you. Cudner went for him, and then Develyn, hearing the scuffle, dropped the bottle and glasses and rushed out, and got his.

"Cudner, being the sort he was, would figure that two murders were no worse than one, and he wouldn't want to leave any witnesses around.

"And that is probably how Ingraham got into it. He was passing on his way from his room to the elevator and perhaps heard the racket and investigated. And Cudner put a gun in his face and made him stow the two bodies in the clothes press.

And then he stuck his knife in Ingraham's back and slammed the door on him. That's about the—"

An indignant nurse descended on me from behind and ordered me out of the room, accusing me of getting her patient excited.

Orrett stopped me as I turned to go.

"Keep your eye on the New York dispatches," he said, "and maybe you'll get the rest of the story. It's not over yet. Nobody has anything on me out here. That shooting in Pigatti's was self-defense so far as I'm concerned. And as soon as I'm on my feet again and can get back East there's going to be a Master Mind holding a lot of lead. That's a promise!"

I believed him.

6

THE TENTH CLEW

BLACK MASK, JANUARY 1, 1924

There were enough clews in this crime to give Mr Hammett's nameless detective a year or so of work. But solving a mystery in that length of time didn't appeal to him. He wanted faster action—and he got it in good measure. So will you if you begin this entertaining novelette.

I

"DO YOU KNOW... EMIL BONFILS?"

"Mr Leopold Gantvoort is not at home," the servant who opened the door said, "but his son, Mr Charles, is—if you wish to see him."

"No. I had an appointment with Mr Leopold Gantvoort for nine or a little after. It's just nine now. No doubt he'll be back soon. I'll wait."

"Very well, sir."

He stepped aside for me to enter the house, took my overcoat and hat, guided me to a room on the second floor—Gantvoort's library—and left me. I picked up a magazine from the stack on the table, pulled an ash tray over beside me, and made myself comfortable.

An hour passed. I stopped reading and began to grow impatient. Another hour passed—and I was fidgeting.

A clock somewhere below had begun to strike eleven when a young man of twenty-five or -six, tall and slender, with remarkably white skin and very dark hair and eyes, came into the room.

"My father hasn't returned yet," he said. "It's too bad that you should have been kept waiting all this time. Isn't there anything I could do for you? I am Charles Gantvoort."

"No, thank you." I got up from my chair, accepting the courteous dismissal. "I'll get in touch with him tomorrow."

"I'm sorry," he murmured, and we moved toward the door together.

As we reached the hall an extension telephone in one corner of the room we were leaving buzzed softly, and I halted in the doorway while Charles Gantvoort went over to answer it.

His back was toward me as he spoke into the instrument.

"Yes. Yes. Yes!"—sharply—"*What?* Yes"—very weakly—"Yes."

He turned slowly around and faced me with a face that was gray and tortured, with wide shocked eyes and gaping mouth—the telephone still in his hand.

"Father," he gasped, "is dead—killed!"

"Where? How?"

"I don't know. That was the police. They want me to come down at once."

He straightened his shoulders with an effort, pulling himself together, put down the telephone, and his face fell into less strained lines.

"You will pardon my—"

"Mr Gantvoort," I interrupted his apology, "I am connected with the Continental Detective Agency. Your father called up this afternoon and asked that a detective be sent to see him tonight. He said his life had been threatened. He hadn't definitely engaged us, however, so unless you—"

"Certainly! You are employed! If the police haven't already caught the murderer I want you to do everything possible to catch him."

"All right! Let's get down to headquarters."

Neither of us spoke during the ride to the Hall of Justice. Gantvoort bent over the wheel of his car, sending it through the streets at a terrific speed. There were several questions that needed answers, but all his attention was required for his driving if he was to maintain the pace at which he was driving without piling us into something. So I didn't disturb him, but hung on and kept quiet.

Half a dozen police detectives were waiting for us when we reached the detective bureau. O'Gar—a bullet-headed detective-sergeant who dresses like the village constable in a movie, wide-brimmed black hat and all, but who isn't to be put out of the reckoning on that account—was in charge of the investigation. He and I had worked on two or three jobs together before, and hit it off excellently.

He led us into one of the small offices below the assembly room. Spread out on the flat top of a desk there were a dozen or more objects.

"I want you to look these things over carefully," the detective-sergeant told Gantvoort, "and pick out the ones that belonged to your father."

"But where is he?"

"Do this first," O'Gar insisted, "and then you can see him."

I looked at the things on the table while Charles Gantvoort made his selections. An empty jewel case; a memoranda book; three letters in slit envelopes that were addressed to the dead man; some other papers; a bunch of keys; a fountain pen; two white linen handkerchiefs; two pistol cartridges; a gold watch, with a gold knife and a gold pencil attached to it by a gold-and-platinum chain; two black leather wallets, one of them very new and the other worn; some money, both paper and silver; and a small portable typewriter, bent and twisted, and matted with hair and blood. Some of the other things were smeared with blood and some were clean.

Gantvoort picked out the watch and its attachments, the keys, the fountain pen, the memoranda book, the handkerchiefs, the letters and other papers, and the older wallet.

"These were father's," he told us. "I've never seen any of the others before. I don't know, of course, how much money he had with him tonight, so I can't say how much of this is his."

"You're sure none of the rest of this stuff was his?" O'Gar asked.

"I don't think so, but I'm not sure. Whipple could tell you." He turned to me. "He's the man who let you in tonight. He looked after father, and he'd know positively whether any of these other things belonged to him or not."

One of the police detectives went to the telephone to tell Whipple to come down immediately.

I resumed the questioning.

"Is anything that your father usually carried with him missing? Anything of value?"

"Not that I know of. All of the things that he might have been expected to have with him seem to be here."

"At what time tonight did he leave the house?"

"Before seven-thirty. Possibly as early as seven."

"Know where he was going?"

"He didn't tell me, but I supposed he was going to call on Miss Dexter."

The faces of the police detectives brightened, and their eyes grew sharp. I suppose mine did, too. There are many, many murders with never a woman in them anywhere; but seldom a very conspicuous killing.

"Who's this Miss Dexter?" O'Gar took up the inquiry.

"She's well—" Charles Gantvoort hesitated. "Well, father was on very friendly terms with her and her brother. He usually called on them—on her several evenings a week. In fact, I suspected that he intended marrying her."

"Who and what is she?"

"Father became acquainted with them six or seven months ago. I've met them several times, but don't know them very well. Miss Dexter—Creda is her given name—is about twenty-three years old, I should judge, and her brother Madden is four or five years older. He is in New York now, or on his way there, to transact some business for father."

"Did your father tell you he was going to marry her?" O'Gar hammered away at the woman angle.

"No; but it was pretty obvious that he was very much—ah—infatuated. We had some words over it a few days ago—last week. Not a quarrel, you understand, but words. From the way he talked I feared that he meant to marry her."

"What do you mean 'feared'?" O'Gar snapped at that word.

Charles Gantvoort's pale face flushed a little, and he cleared his throat embarrassedly.

"I don't want to put the Dexters in a bad light to you. I don't think—I'm sure they had nothing to do with father's—with this. But I didn't care especially for them—didn't like them. I thought they were—well—fortune hunters, perhaps. Father wasn't fabulously wealthy, but he had considerable means. And, while he wasn't feeble, still he was past fifty-seven, old enough for me to feel that Creda Dexter was more interested in his money than in him."

"How about your father's will?"

"The last one of which I have any knowledge—drawn up two or three years ago—left everything to my wife and me jointly.

Father's attorney, Mr Murray Abernathy, could tell you if there was a later will, but I hardly think there was."

"Your father had retired from business, hadn't he?"

"Yes; he turned his import and export business over to me about a year ago. He had quite a few investments scattered around, but he wasn't actively engaged in the management of any concern."

O'Gar tilted his village constable hat back and scratched his bullet head reflectively for a moment. Then he looked at me.

"Anything else you want to ask?"

"Yes. Mr Gantvoort, do you know, or did you ever hear your father or anyone else speak of an Emil Bonfils?"

"No."

"Did your father ever tell you that he had received a threatening letter? Or that he had been shot at on the street?"

"No."

"Was your father in Paris in 1902?"

"Very likely. He used to go abroad every year up until the time of his retirement from business."

II

"THAT'S SOMETHING!"

O'Gar and I took Gantvoort around to the morgue to see his father, then. The dead man wasn't pleasant to look at, even to O'Gar and me, who hadn't known him except by sight. I remembered him as a small wiry man, always smartly tailored, and with a brisk springiness that was far younger than his years.

He lay now with the top of his head beaten into a red and pulpy mess.

We left Gantvoort at the morgue and set out afoot for the Hall of Justice.

"What's this deep stuff you're pulling about Emil Bonfils and Paris in 1902?" the detective-sergeant asked as soon as we were out in the street.

"This: the dead man phoned the agency this afternoon and said he had received a threatening letter from an Emil Bonfils with whom he had had trouble in Paris in 1902. He also said that Bonfils had shot at him the previous evening, in the street. He wanted somebody to come around and see him about it tonight. And he said that under no circumstances were the police to be let in on it—that he'd rather have Bonfils get him than have the trouble made public. That's all he would say over the phone; and that's how I happened to be on hand when Charles Gantvoort was notified of his father's death."

O'Gar stopped in the middle of the sidewalk and whistled softly.

"That's something!" he exclaimed. "Wait till we get back to headquarters—I'll show you something."

Whipple was waiting in the assembly room when we arrived at headquarters. His face at first glance was as smooth and mask-like as when he had admitted me to the house on Russian Hill earlier in the evening. But beneath his perfect servant's manner he was twitching and trembling.

We took him into the little office where we had questioned Charles Gantvoort.

Whipple verified all that the dead man's son had told us. He was positive that neither the typewriter, the jewel case, the two cartridges, or the newer wallet had belonged to Gantvoort.

We couldn't get him to put his opinion of the Dexters in words, but that he disapproved of them was easily seen. Miss Dexter, he said, had called up on the telephone three times this night at about eight o'clock, at nine, and at nine-thirty. She had asked for Mr Leopold Gantvoort each time, but she had left no message. Whipple was of the opinion that she was expecting Gantvoort, and he had not arrived.

He knew nothing, he said, of Emil Bonfils or of any threatening letters. Gantvoort had been out the previous night from eight until midnight. Whipple had not seen him closely enough when he came home to say whether he seemed excited or not. Gantvoort usually carried about a hundred dollars in his pockets.

"Is there anything that you know of that Gantvoort had on his person tonight which isn't among these things on the desk?" O'Gar asked.

"No, sir. Everything seems to be here—watch and chain, money, memorandum book, wallet, keys, handkerchiefs, fountain pen—everything that I know of."

"Did Charles Gantvoort go out tonight?"

"No, sir. He and Mrs Gantvoort were at home all evening."

"Positive?"

Whipple thought a moment.

"Yes, sir, I'm fairly certain. But I know Mrs Gantvoort wasn't out. To tell the truth, I didn't see Mr Charles from about eight o'clock until he came downstairs with this gentleman"—pointing to me—"at eleven. But I'm fairly certain he was home all evening. I think Mrs Gantvoort said he was."

Then O'Gar put another question—one that puzzled me at the time.

"What kind of collar buttons did Mr Gantvoort wear?"

"You mean Mr Leopold?"

"Yes."

"Plain gold ones, made all in one piece. They had a London jeweler's mark on them."

"Would you know them if you saw them?"

"Yes, sir."

We let Whipple go home then.

"Don't you think," I suggested when O'Gar and I were alone with this desk-load of evidence that didn't mean anything at all to me yet, "it's time you were loosening up and telling me what's what?"

"I guess so—listen! A man named Lagerquist, a grocer, was driving through Golden Gate Park tonight, and passed a machine standing on a dark road, with its lights out. He thought there was something funny about the way the man in it was sitting at the wheel, so he told the first patrolman he met about it.

"The patrolman investigated and found Gantvoort sitting at the wheel—dead—with his head smashed in and this dingus"—putting one hand on the bloody typewriter—"on the seat beside him. That was at a quarter of ten. The doc says Gantvoort was killed—his skull crushed—with this typewriter.

"The dead man's pockets, we found, had all been turned inside out; and all this stuff on the desk, except this new wallet, was scattered about in the car—some of it on the floor and some on the seats. This money was there too—nearly a hundred dollars of it. Among the papers was this."

He handed me a sheet of white paper upon which the following had been typewritten:

"L F. G.—

I want what is mine. 6,000 miles and 21 years are not enough to hide you from the victim of your treachery. I mean to have what you stole.

E. B."

"L. F. G. could be Leopold F. Gantvoort," I said. "And E. B. could be Emil Bonfils. Twenty-one years is the time from 1902 to 1923, and 6,000 miles is, roughly, the distance between Paris and San Francisco."

I laid the letter down and picked up the jewel case. It was a black imitation leather one, lined with white satin, and unmarked in any way.

Then I examined the cartridges. There were two of them, S. W. .45-caliber, and deep crosses had been cut in their soft noses—an old trick that makes the bullet spread out like a saucer when it hits.

"These in the car, too?"

"Yep—and this."

From a vest pocket O'Gar produced a short tuft of blond hair—hairs between an inch and two inches in length. They had been cut off, not pulled out by the roots.

"Any more?"

There seemed to be an endless stream of things.

He picked up the new wallet from the desk—the one that both Whipple and Charles Gantvoort had said did not belong to the dead man—and slid it over to me.

"That was found in the road, three or four feet from the car."

It was of a cheap quality, and had neither manufacturer's name nor owner's initials on it. In it were two ten-dollar bills, three small newspaper clippings, and a typewritten list of six names and addresses, headed by Gantvoort's.

The three clippings were apparently from the Personal columns of three different newspapers—the type wasn't the same—and they read:

"GEORGE—

Everything is fixed. Don't wait too long.

D. D. D.

R. H. T.—

They do not answer.

FLO.

GAPPY.—

Twelve on the dot and look sharp.

BINGO."

The names and addresses on the typewritten list, under Gantvoort's, were:

> Quincy Heathcote, 1223 S. Jason Street, Denver; B. D. Thornton, 96 Hughes Circle, Dallas; Luther G. Randall, 615 Columbia Street, Portsmouth; J. H. Boyd Willis, 4544 Harvard Street, Boston; Hannah Hindmarsh, 218 E. 79th Street, Cleveland.

"What else?" I asked when I had studied these.

The detective-sergeant's supply hadn't been exhausted yet.

"The dead man's collar buttons—both front and back—had been taken out, though his collar and tie were still in place. And his left shoe was gone. We hunted high and low all around, but didn't find either shoe or collar buttons."

"Is that all?"

I was prepared for anything now.

"What the hell do you want?" he growled. "Ain't that enough?"

"How about finger-prints?"

"Nothing stirring! All we found belonged to the dead man."

"How about the machine he was found in?"

"A coupé belonging to a Doctor Wallace Girargo. He phoned in at six this evening that it had been stolen from near the corner of McAllister and Polk Streets. We're checking up on him—but I think he's all right."

The things that Whipple and Charles Gantvoort had identified as belonging to the dead man told us nothing. We went over them carefully, but to no advantage. The memoranda book contained many entries, but they all seemed totally foreign to the murder. The letters were quite as irrelevant.

The serial number of the typewriter with which the murder had been committed had been removed, we found—apparently filed out of the frame.

"Well, what do you think?" O'Gar asked when we had given up our examination of our clews and sat back burning tobacco.

"I think we want to find Monsieur Emil Bonfils."

"It wouldn't hurt to do that," he grunted. "I guess our best bet is to get in touch with these five people on the list with Gantvoort's name. Suppose that's a murder list? That this Bonfils is out to get all of them?"

"May be. We'll get hold of them anyway. Maybe we'll find that some of them have already been killed. But whether they have been killed or are to be killed or not, it's a cinch they have some connection with this affair. I'll get off a batch of telegrams to the agency's branches, having the names on the list taken care of. I'll try to have the three clippings traced, too."

O'Gar looked at his watch and yawned.

"It's after four. What say we knock off and get some sleep? I'll leave word for the department's expert to compare the typewriter with that letter signed E. B. and with that list to see if they were written on it. I guess they were, but we'll make sure. I'll have the park searched all around where we found Gantvoort as soon as it gets light enough to see, and maybe the missing shoe and the collar buttons will be found. And I'll have a couple of the boys out calling on all the typewriter shops in the city to see if they can get a line on this one."

I stopped at the nearest telegraph office and got off a wad of messages. Then I went home to dream of nothing even remotely connected with crime or the detecting business.

III

"A SLEEK KITTEN THAT DAME!"

At eleven o'clock that same morning, when, brisk and fresh with five hours sleep under my belt, I arrived at the police detective bureau, I found O'Gar slumped down at his desk, staring dazedly at a black shoe, half a dozen collar buttons, a rusty flat key, and a rumpled newspaper—all lined up before him.

"What's all this? Souvenir of your wedding?"

"Might as well be." His voice was heavy with disgust. "Listen to this: one of the porters of the Seamen's National Bank found a package in the vestibule when he started cleaning up this morning. It was this shoe—Gantvoort's missing one—wrapped in this sheet of a five-day-old *Philadelphia Record,* and with these collar buttons and this old key in it. The heel of the shoe, you'll notice, has been pried off, and is still missing. Whipple identifies it all right, as well as two of the collar buttons, but he never saw the key before. These other four collar buttons are new, and common gold-rolled ones. The key don't look like it had had much use for a long time. What do you make of all that?"

I couldn't make anything out of it.

"How did the porter happen to turn the stuff in?"

"Oh, the whole story was in the morning papers—all about the missing shoe and collar buttons and all."

"What did you learn about the typewriter?" I asked.

"The letter and the list were written with it, right enough; but we haven't been able to find where it came from yet. We checked up the doc who owns the coupé, and he's in the clear. We accounted for all his time last night. Lagerquist, the grocer who found Gantvoort, seems to be all right, too. What did you do?"

"Haven't had any answers to the wires I sent last night. I dropped in at the agency on my way down this morning, and got four operatives out covering the hotels and looking up all the people named Bonfils they can find—there are two or three families by that name listed in the directory. Also I sent our New York branch a wire to have the steamship records searched to see if an Emil Bonfils had arrived recently; and I put a cable through to our Paris correspondent to see what he could dig up over there."

"I guess we ought to see Gantvoort's lawyer—Abernathy—and that Dexter woman before we do anything else," the detective-sergeant said.

"I guess so," I agreed, "let's tackle the lawyer first. He's the most important one, the way things now stand."

Murray Abernathy, attorney-at-law, was a long, stringy, slow-spoken old gentleman who still clung to starched-bosom shirts. He was too full of what he thought were professional ethics to give us as much help as we had expected; but by letting him talk—letting him ramble along in his own way—we did get a little information from him. What we got amounted to this:

The dead man and Creda Dexter had intended being married the coming Wednesday. His son and her brother were both opposed to the marriage, it seemed, so Gantvoort and the woman had planned to be married secretly in Oakland, and catch a boat for the Orient that same afternoon; figuring that by the time their lengthy honeymoon was over they could return to a son and brother who had become resigned to the marriage.

A new will had been drawn up, leaving half of Gantvoort's estate to his new wife and half to his son and daughter-in-law. But the new will had not been signed yet, and Creda Dexter knew it had not been signed. She knew—and this was one of the few points upon which Abernathy would make a positive statement—that under the old will, still in force, everything went to Charles Gantvoort and his wife.

The Gantvoort estate, we estimated from Abernathy's roundabout statements and allusions, amounted to about a million and a half in cash value. The attorney had never heard of Emil Bonfils, he said, and had never heard of any threats or attempts at murder directed toward the dead man. He knew nothing—or would tell us nothing—that threw any light upon the nature of the thing that the threatening letter had accused the dead man of stealing.

From Abernathy's office we went to Creda Dexter's apartment, in a new and expensively elegant building only a few minutes' walk from the Gantvoort residence.

Creda Dexter was a small woman in her early twenties. The first thing you noticed about her were her eyes. They were large and deep and the color of amber, and their pupils were never at rest. Continuously they changed size, expanded and contracted—slowly at times, suddenly at others—ranging incessantly from the size of pinheads to an extent that threatened to blot out the amber irises.

With the eyes for a guide, you discovered that she was pronouncedly feline throughout. Her every movement was the slow, smooth, sure one of a cat; and the contours of her rather pretty face, the shape of her mouth, her small nose, the set of her eyes, the swelling of her brows, were all cat-like. And the effect was heightened by the way she wore her hair, which was thick and tawny.

"Mr Gantvoort and I," she told us after the preliminary explanations had been disposed of, "were to have been married the day after tomorrow. His son and daughter-in-law were both opposed to the marriage, as was my brother Madden. They all seemed to think that the difference between our ages was too great. So to avoid any unpleasantness, we had planned to be married quietly and then go abroad for a year or more, feeling sure that they would all have forgotten their grievances by the time we returned.

"That was why Mr Gantvoort persuaded Madden to go to New York. He had some business there—something to do with the disposal of his interest in a steel mill—so he used it as an excuse to get Madden out of the way until we were off on our wedding trip. Madden lived here with me, and it would have been nearly impossible for me to have made any preparations for the trip without him seeing them."

"Was Mr Gantvoort here last night?" I asked her.

"No. I expected him—we were going out. He usually walked over—it's only a few blocks. When eight o'clock came and he hadn't arrived, I telephoned his house, and Whipple told me that he had left nearly an hour before. I called up again, twice, after that. Then, this morning, I called up again before I had seen the papers, and I was told that he—"

She broke off with a catch in her voice—the only sign of sorrow she displayed throughout the interview. The impression of her we had received from Charles Gantvoort and Whipple had prepared us for a more or less elaborate display of grief on her part. But she disappointed us. There was nothing crude about her work—she didn't even turn on the tears for us.

"Was Mr Gantvoort here night before last?"

"Yes. He came over at a little after eight and stayed until nearly twelve. We didn't go out."

"Did he walk over and back?"

"Yes, so far as I know."

"Did he ever say anything to you about his life being threatened?"

"No."

She shook her head decisively.

"Do you know Emil Bonfils?"

"No."

"Ever hear Mr Gantvoort speak of him?"

"No."

"At what hotel is your brother staying in New York?"

The restless black pupils spread out abruptly, as if they were about to overflow into the white areas of her eyes. That was the first clear indication of fear I had seen. But, outside of those tell-tale pupils, her composure was undisturbed.

"I don't know."

"When did he leave San Francisco?"

"Thursday—four days ago."

O'Gar and I walked six or seven blocks in thoughtful silence after we left Creda Dexter's apartment, and then he spoke.

"A sleek kitten—that dame! Rub her the right way, and she'll purr pretty. Rub her the wrong way—and look out for the claws!"

"What did that flash of her eyes when I asked about her brother tell you?" I asked.

"Something—but I don't know what! It wouldn't hurt to look him up and see if he's really in New York. If he is there today it's a cinch he wasn't here last night—even the mail planes take twenty-six or twenty-eight hours for the trip."

"We'll do that," I agreed. "It looks like this Creda Dexter wasn't any too sure that her brother wasn't in on the killing. And there's nothing to show that Bonfils didn't have help. I can't figure Creda being in on the murder, though. She knew the new will hadn't been signed. There'd be no sense in her working herself out of that three-quarters of a million berries."

We sent a lengthy telegram to the Continental's New York branch, and then dropped in at the agency to see if any replies had come to the wires I had got off the night before.

They had.

None of the people whose names appeared on the typewritten list with Gantvoort's had been found; not the least trace had been found of any of them. Two of the addresses given were altogether wrong. There were no houses with those numbers on those streets—and there never had been.

IV

MAYBE THAT AIN'T SO FOOLISH!

What was left of the afternoon, O'Gar and I spent going over the street between Gantvoort's house on Russian Hill and the building in which the Dexters lived. We questioned everyone we could find—man, woman and child—who lived, worked, or played along any of the three routes the dead man could have taken.

We found nobody who had heard the shot that had been fired by Bonfils on the night before the murder. We found nobody who had seen anything suspicious on the night of the murder. Nobody who remembered having seen him picked up in a coupé.

Then we called at Gantvoort's house and questioned Charles Gantvoort again, his wife, and all the servants—and we learned nothing. So far as they knew, nothing belonging to the dead man was missing—nothing small enough to be concealed in the heel of a shoe.

The shoes he had worn the night he was killed were one of three pairs made in New York for him two months before. He could have removed the heel of the left one, hollowed it out sufficiently to hide a small object in it, and then nailed it on again; though Whipple insisted that he would have noticed the effects of any tampering with the shoe unless it had been done by an expert repairman.

This field exhausted, we returned to the agency. A telegram had just come from the New York branch, saying that none of the steamship companies' records showed the arrival of an Emil Bonfils from either England, France, or Germany within the past six months.

The operatives who had been searching the city for Bonfils had all come in empty-handed. They had found and investigated eleven persons named Bonfils in San Francisco, Oakland, Berkeley, and Alameda. Their investigations had definitely cleared all eleven. None of these Bonfilses knew an Emil Bonfils. Combing the hotels had yielded nothing.

O'Gar and I went to dinner together—a quiet, grouchy sort of meal during which we didn't speak six words apiece—and then came back to the agency to find that another wire had come in from New York.

> "Madden Dexter arrived McAlpin Hotel this morning with Power of Attorney to sell Gantvoort interest in B. F. and F. Iron Corporation. Denies knowledge of Emil Bonfils or of murder. Expects to finish business and leave for San Francisco tomorrow."

I let the sheet of paper upon which I had decoded the telegram slide out of my fingers, and we sat listlessly facing each other across my desk, looking vacantly each at the other, listening to the clatter of charwomen's buckets in the corridor.

"It's a funny one," O'Gar said softly to himself at last.

I nodded. It was.

"We got nine clews," he spoke again presently, "and none of them have got us a damned thing.

"Number one: the dead man called up you people and told you that he had been threatened and shot at by an Emil Bonfils that he'd had a run-in with in Paris a long time ago.

"Number two: the typewriter he was killed with and that the letter and list were written on. We're still trying to trace it, but with no breaks so far. What the hell kind of a weapon was that, anyway? It looks like this fellow Bonfils got hot and hit Gantvoort with the first thing he put his hand on. But what was the typewriter doing in a stolen car? And why were the numbers filed off it?"

I shook my head to signify that I couldn't guess the answer, and O'Gar went on enumerating our clews.

"Number three: the threatening letter, fitting in with what Gantvoort had said over the phone that afternoon.

"Number four: those two bullets with the crosses in their snoots.

"Number five: the jewel case.

"Number six: that bunch of yellow hair.

"Number seven: the fact that the dead man's shoe and collar buttons were carried away.

"Number eight: the wallet, with two ten-dollar bills, three clippings, and the list in it, found in the road.

"Number nine: finding the shoe next day, wrapped up in a five-day-old Philadelphia paper, and with the missing collar buttons, four more, and a rusty key in it.

"That's the list. If they mean anything at all, they mean that Emil Bonfils whoever he is—was flimflammed out of something by Gantvoort in Paris in 1902, and that Bonfils came to get it back. He picked Gantvoort up last night in a stolen car, bringing his typewriter with him—for God knows what reason! Gantvoort put up an argument, so Bonfils bashed in his noodle with the typewriter, and then went through his pockets, apparently not taking anything. He decided that what he was looking for was in Gantvoort's left shoe, so he took the shoe away with him. And then—but there's no sense to the collar button trick, or the phoney list, or—"

"Yes there is!" I cut in, sitting up, wide awake now. "That's our tenth clew—the one we're going to follow from now on. That list was, except for Gantvoort's name and address, a fake. Our people would have found at least one of the five people whose names were on it if it had been on the level. But they didn't find the least trace of any of them. And two of the addresses were of street numbers that didn't exist!

"That list was faked up, put in the wallet with the clippings and twenty dollars—to make the play stronger—and planted in the road near the car to throw us off-track. And if that's so, then it's a hundred to one that the rest of the things were cooked up too.

"From now on I'm considering all those nine lovely clews as nine bum steers. And I'm going just exactly contrary to them. I'm looking for a man whose name isn't Emil Bonfils, and whose initials aren't either E or B; who isn't French, and who wasn't in Paris in 1902. A man who hasn't light hair, doesn't carry a .45-caliber pistol, and has no interest in Personal advertisements in newspapers. A man who didn't kill Gantvoort to recover anything that could have been hidden in a shoe or on a collar button. That's the sort of a guy I'm hunting for now!"

The detective-sergeant screwed up his little green eyes reflectively and scratched his head.

"Maybe that ain't so foolish!" he said. "You might be right at that. Suppose you are—what then? That Dexter kitten didn't do it—it cost her three-quarters of a million. Her brother didn't do it—he's in New York. And, besides, you don't croak a guy just because you think he's too old to marry your sister. Charles Gantvoort? He and his wife are the only ones who make any money out of the old man dying before the new will was signed. We have only their word for it that Charles was home that night. The servants didn't see him between eight and eleven. You were there, and you didn't see him until eleven. But me and you both believe him when he says he *was* home all that evening. And neither of us think he bumped the old man off—though of course he might. Who then?"

"This Creda Dexter," I suggested, "was marrying Gantvoort for his money, wasn't she? You don't think she was in love with him, do you?"

"No. I figure, from what I saw of her, that she was in love with the million and a half."

"All right," I went on. "Now she isn't exactly homely—not by a long shot. Do you reckon Gantvoort was the only man who ever fell for her?"

"I got you! I got you!" O'Gar exclaimed. "You mean there might have been some young fellow in the running who didn't have any million and a half behind him, and who didn't take kindly to being nosed out by a man who did. Maybe—maybe."

"Well, suppose we bury all this stuff we've been working on and try out that angle."

"Suits me," he said. "Starting in the morning, then, we spend our time hunting for Gantvoort's rival for the paw of this Dexter kitten."

V

"MEET MR SMITH"

Right or wrong, that's what we did. We stowed all those lovely clews away in a drawer, locked the drawer, and forgot them. Then we set out to find Creda Dexter's masculine acquaintances and sift them for the murderer.

But it wasn't as simple as it sounded.

All our digging into her past failed to bring to light one man who could be considered a suitor. She and her brother had been in San Francisco three years. We traced them back the length of that period, from apartment to apartment. We questioned everyone we could find who even knew her by sight. And nobody could tell us of a single man who had shown an interest in her besides Gantvoort. Nobody, apparently, had ever seen her with any man except Gantvoort or her brother.

All of which, while not getting us ahead, at least convinced us that we were on the right trail. There must have been, we argued, at least one man in her life in those three years besides

Gantvoort. She wasn't—unless we were very much mistaken—the sort of woman who would discourage masculine attention; and she was certainly endowed by nature to attract it. And if there was another man, then the very fact that he had been kept so thoroughly under cover strengthened the probability of him having been mixed up in Gantvoort's death.

We were unsuccessful in learning where the Dexters had lived before they came to San Francisco, but we weren't so very interested in their earlier life. Of course it was possible that some old-time lover had come upon the scene again recently; but in that case it should have been easier to find the recent connection than the old one.

There was no doubt, our explorations showed, that Gantvoort's son had been correct in thinking the Dexters were fortune hunters. All their activities pointed to that, although there seemed to be nothing downright criminal in their pasts.

I went up against Creda Dexter again, spending an entire afternoon in her apartment, banging away with question after question, all directed toward her former love affairs. Who had she thrown over for Gantvoort and his million and a half? And the answer was always *nobody*—an answer that I didn't choose to believe.

We had Creda Dexter shadowed night and day—and it carried us ahead not an inch. Perhaps she suspected that she was being watched. Anyway, she seldom left her apartment, and then on only the most innocent of errands. We had her apartment watched whether she was in it or not. Nobody visited it. We tapped her telephone—and all our listening-in netted us nothing. We had her mail covered—and she didn't receive a single letter, not even an advertisement.

Meanwhile, we had learned where the three clippings found in the wallet had come from—from the Personal columns of a New York, a Chicago, and a Portland newspaper. The one in the Portland paper had appeared two days before the murder, the Chicago one four days before, and the New York one five days before. All three of those papers would have been on the San Francisco newsstands the day of the murder—ready to be purchased and cut out by anyone who was looking for material to confuse detectives with.

The agency's Paris correspondent had found no less than six Emil Bonfilses—all bloomers so far as our job was concerned—and had a line on three more.

But O'Gar and I weren't worrying over Emil Bonfils any more—that angle was dead and buried. We were plugging away at our new task—the finding of Gantvoort's rival.

Thus the days passed, and thus the matter stood when Madden Dexter was due to arrive home from New York.

Our New York branch had kept an eye on him until he left that city, and had advised us of his departure, so I knew what train he was coming on. I wanted to put a few questions to him before his sister saw him. He could tell me what I wanted to know, and he might be willing to if I could get to him before his sister had an opportunity to shut him up.

If I had known him by sight I could have picked him up when he left his train at Oakland, but I didn't know him; and I didn't want to carry Charles Gantvoort or anyone else along with me to pick him out for me.

So I went up to Sacramento that morning, and boarded his train there. I put my card in an envelope and gave it to a messenger boy in the station. Then I followed the boy through the train, while he called out:

"Mr Dexter! Mr Dexter!"

In the last car—the observation-club car—a slender, dark-haired man in well-made tweeds turned from watching the station platform through a window and held out his hand to the boy.

I studied him while he nervously tore open the envelope and read my card. His chin trembled slightly just now, emphasizing the weakness of a face that couldn't have been strong at its best. Between twenty-five and thirty, I placed him; with his hair parted in the middle and slicked down; large, too-expressive brown eyes; small well-shaped nose; neat brown mustache; very red, soft lips—that type.

I dropped into the vacant chair beside him when he looked up from the card.

"You are Mr Dexter?"

"Yes," he said. "I suppose it's about Mr Gantvoort's death that you want to see me?"

"Uh-huh. I wanted to ask you a few questions, and since I happened to be in Sacramento, I thought that by riding back on the train with you I could ask them without taking up too much of your time."

"If there's anything I can tell you," he assured me, "I'll be only too glad to do it. But I told the New York detectives all I knew, and they didn't seem to find it of much value."

"Well, the situation has changed some since you left New York." I watched his face closely as I spoke. "What we thought of no value then may be just what we want now."

I paused while he moistened his lips and avoided my eyes. He may not know anything, I thought, but he's certainly jumpy. I let him wait a few minutes while I pretended deep thoughtfulness. If I played him right, I was confident I could turn him inside out. He didn't seem to be made of very tough material.

We were sitting with our heads close together, so that the four or five other passengers in the car wouldn't overhear our talk; and that position was in my favor. One of the things that every detective knows is that it's often easy to get information—even a confession—out of a feeble nature simply by putting your face close to his and talking in a loud tone. I couldn't talk loud here, but the closeness of our faces was by itself an advantage.

"Of the men with whom your sister was acquainted," I came out with it at last, "who, outside of Mr Gantvoort, was the most attentive?"

He swallowed audibly, looked out of the window, fleetingly at me, and then out of the window again.

"Really, I couldn't say."

"All right. Let's get at it this way. Suppose we check off one by one all the men who were interested in her and in whom she was interested."

He continued to stare out of the window.

"Who's first?" I pressed him.

His gaze flickered around to meet mine for a second, with a sort of timid desperation in his eyes.

"I know it sounds foolish, but I, her brother, couldn't give you the name of even one man in whom Creda was interested before she met Gantvoort. She never, so far as I know, had the slightest feeling for any man before she met him. Of course it is possible that there may have been someone that I didn't know anything about, but—"

It did sound foolish, right enough! The Creda Dexter I had talked to—a sleek kitten, as O'Gar had put it—didn't impress me as being at all likely to go very long without having at least one man in tow. This pretty little guy in front of me was lying. There couldn't be any other explanation.

I went at him tooth and nail. But when he reached Oakland early that night he was still sticking to his original statement—that Gantvoort was the only one of his sister's suitors that he knew anything about. And I knew that I had blundered, had underrated Madden Dexter, had played my hand wrong in trying to shake him down too quickly—in driving too directly at the point I was interested in. He was either a lot stronger than I had figured him, or his interest in concealing Gantvoort's murderer was much greater than I had thought it would be.

But I had this much: if Dexter was lying—and there couldn't be much doubt of that—then Gantvoort *had* had a rival, and Madden Dexter believed or knew that this rival had killed Gantvoort.

When we left the train at Oakland I knew I was licked, that he wasn't going to tell me what I wanted to know—not this night, anyway. But I clung to him, stuck at his side when we boarded the ferry for San Francisco, in spite of the obviousness of his desire to get away from me. There's always a chance of something unexpected happening; so I continued to ply him with questions as our boat left the slip.

Presently a man came toward where we were sitting—a big burly man in a light overcoat, carrying a black bag.

"Hello, Madden!" he greeted my companion, striding over to him with outstretched hand. "Just got in and was trying to remember your phone number," he said, setting down his bag, as they shook hands warmly.

Madden Dexter turned to me.

"I want you to meet Mr Smith," he told me, and then gave my name to the big man, adding, "he's with the Continental Detective Agency here."

That tag—clearly a warning for Smith's benefit—brought me to my feet, all watchfulness. But the ferry was crowded—a hundred persons were within sight of us, all around us. I relaxed, smiled pleasantly, and shook hands with Smith. Whoever Smith was, and whatever connection he might have with the murder—and if he hadn't any, why should Dexter have been in such a hurry to tip him off to my identity?—he couldn't do anything here. The crowd around us was all to my advantage.

That was my second mistake of the day.

Smith's left hand had gone into his overcoat pocket—or rather, through one of those vertical slits that certain styles of overcoats have so that inside pockets may be reached without unbuttoning the overcoat. His hand had gone through that slit, and his coat had fallen away far enough for me to see a snub-nosed automatic in his hand—shielded from everyone's sight but mine—pointing at my waist-line.

"Shall we go on deck?" Smith asked—and it was an order.

I hesitated. I didn't like to leave all these people who were so blindly standing and sitting around us. But Smith's face wasn't the face of a cautious man. He had the look of one who might easily disregard the presence of a hundred witnesses.

I turned around and walked through the crowd. His right hand lay familiarly on my shoulder as he walked behind me; his left hand held his gun, under the overcoat, against my spine.

The deck was deserted. A heavy fog, wet as rain,—the fog of San Francisco Bay's winter nights,—lay over boat and water, and had driven everyone else inside. It hung about us, thick and impenetrable; I couldn't see so far as the end of the boat, in spite of the lights glowing overhead.

I stopped.

Smith prodded me in the back.

"Farther away, where we can talk," he rumbled in my ear.

I went on until I reached the rail.

The entire back of my head burned with sudden fire... tiny points of light glittered in the blackness before me... grew larger... came rushing toward me...

VI

"THOSE DAMNED HORNS!"

Semi-consciousness! I found myself mechanically keeping afloat somehow and trying to get out of my overcoat. The back of my head throbbed devilishly. My eyes burned. I felt heavy and logged, as if I had swallowed gallons of water.

The fog hung low and thick on the water—there was nothing else to be seen anywhere. By the time I had freed myself of the encumbering overcoat my head had cleared somewhat, but with returning consciousness came increased pain.

A light glimmered mistily off to my left, and then vanished. From out of the misty blanket, from every direction, in a dozen different keys, from near and far, fog-horns sounded. I stopped swimming and floated on my back, trying to determine my whereabouts.

After a while I picked out the moaning, evenly spaced blasts of the Alcatraz siren. But they told me nothing. They came to me out of the fog without direction—seemed to beat down upon me from straight above.

I was somewhere in San Francisco Bay, and that was all I knew, though I suspected the current was sweeping me out toward the Golden Gate.

A little while passed, and I knew that I had left the path of the Oakland ferries—no boat had passed close to me for some time. I was glad to be out of that track. In this fog a boat was a lot more likely to run me down than to pick me up.

The water was chilling me, so I turned over and began swimming, just vigorously enough to keep my blood circulating while I saved my strength until I had a definite goal to try for.

A horn began to repeat its roaring note nearer and nearer, and presently the lights of the boat upon which it was fixed came into sight. One of the Sausalito ferries, I thought.

It came quite close to me, and I halloed until I was breathless and my throat was raw. But the boat's siren, crying its warning, drowned my shouts.

The boat went on and the fog closed in behind it.

The current was stronger now, and my attempts to attract the attention of the Sausalito ferry had left me weaker. I floated, letting the water sweep me where it would, resting.

Another light appeared ahead of me suddenly—hung there for an instant—disappeared.

I began to yell, and worked my arms and legs madly, trying to drive myself through the water to where it had been.

I never saw it again.

Weariness settled upon me, and a sense of futility. The water was no longer cold. I was warm with a comfortable, soothing numbness. My head stopped throbbing; there was no feeling at all in it now. No lights, now, but the sound of fog-horns... fog-horns... fog-horns ahead of me, behind me, to either side; annoying me, irritating me.

But for the moaning horns I would have ceased all effort. They had become the only disagreeable detail of my situation—the water was pleasant, fatigue was pleasant. But the horns tormented me. I cursed them petulantly and decided to swim until I could no longer hear them, and then, in the quiet of the friendly fog, go to sleep....

Now and then I would doze, to be goaded into wakefulness by the wailing voice of a siren.

"Those damned horns! Those damned horns!" I complained aloud, again and again.

One of them, I found presently, was bearing down upon me from behind, growing louder and stronger. I turned and waited. Lights, dim and steaming, came into view.

With exaggerated caution to avoid making the least splash, I swam off to one side. When this nuisance was past I could go to sleep. I sniggered softly to myself as the lights drew abreast, feeling a foolish triumph in my cleverness in eluding the boat. Those damned horns....

Life—the hunger for life—all at once surged back into my being.

I screamed at the passing boat, and with every iota of my being struggled toward it. Between strokes I tilted up my head and screamed....

VII

"YOU HAVE A LOT OF FUN, DON'T YOU?"

When I returned to consciousness for the second time that evening, I was lying on my back on a baggage truck, which was moving. Men and women were crowding around, walking beside the truck, staring at me with curious eyes.

I sat up.

"Where are we?" I asked.

A little red-faced man in uniform answered my question.

"Just landing in Sausalito. Lay still. We'll take you over to the hospital."

I looked around.

"How long before this boat goes back to San Francisco?"

"Leaves right away."

I slid off the truck and started back aboard the boat.

"I'm going with it," I said.

Half an hour later, shivering and shaking in my wet clothes, keeping my mouth clamped tight so that my teeth wouldn't sound like a dice-game, I climbed into a taxi at the Ferry Building and went to my flat.

There, I swallowed half a pint of whisky, rubbed myself with a coarse towel until my skin was sore, and, except for an enormous weariness and a worse headache, I felt almost human again.

I reached O'Gar by phone, asked him to come up to my flat right away, and then called up Charles Gantvoort.

"Have you seen Madden Dexter yet?" I asked him.

"No, but I talked to him over the phone. He called me up as soon as he got in. I asked him to meet me in Mr Abernathy's office in the morning, so we could go over that business he transacted for father."

"Can you call him up now and tell him that you have been called out of town—will have to leave early in the morning—and that you'd like to run over to his apartment and see him tonight?"

"Why yes, if you wish."

"Good! Do that. I'll call for you in a little while and go over to see him with you."

"What is—"

"I'll tell you about it when I see you," I cut him off.

O'Gar arrived as I was finishing dressing.

"So he told you something?" he asked, knowing of my plan to meet Dexter on the train and question him.

"Yes," I said with sour sarcasm, "but I came near forgetting what it was. I grilled him all the way from Sacramento to Oakland, and couldn't get a whisper out of him. On the ferry coming over he introduces me to a man he calls Mr Smith, and he tells Mr Smith that I'm a gumshoe. This, mind you, all happens in the middle of a crowded ferry! Mr Smith puts a gun in my belly marches me out on deck, raps me across the back of the head, and dumps me into the bay"

"You have a lot of fun, don't you?" O'Gar grinned, and then wrinkled his forehead. "Looks like Smith would be the man we want then—the buddy who turned the Gantvoort trick. But what the hell did he want to give himself away by chucking you overboard for?"

"Too hard for me," I confessed, while trying to find which of my hats and caps would sit least heavily upon my bruised head. "Dexter knew I was hunting for one of his sister's former lovers, of course. And he must have thought I knew a whole lot more than I do, or he wouldn't have made that raw play—tipping my mitt to Smith right in front of me.

"It may be that after Dexter lost his head and made that break on the ferry, Smith figured that I'd be on to him soon, if not right away; and so he'd take a desperate chance on putting me out of the way. But we'll know all about it in a little while," I said, as we went down to the waiting taxi and set out for Gantvoort's.

"You ain't counting on Smith being in sight, are you?" the detective-sergeant asked.

"No. He'll be holed up somewhere until he sees how things are going. But Madden Dexter will have to be out in the open to protect himself. He has an alibi, so he's in the clear so far as the actual killing is concerned. And with me supposed to be dead, the more he stays in the open, the safer he is. But it's a cinch that he knows what this is all about, though he wasn't necessarily involved in it. As near as I could see, he didn't go out on deck with Smith and me tonight. Anyway he'll be home. And this time he's going to talk—he's going to tell his little story!"

Charles Gantvoort was standing on his front steps when we reached his house. He climbed into our taxi and we headed for the Dexters' apartment. We didn't have time to answer any of the questions that Gantvoort was firing at us with every turning of the wheels.

"He's home and expecting you?" I asked him.

"Yes."

Then we left the taxi and went into the apartment building.

"Mr Gantvoort to see Mr Dexter," he told the Philippine boy at the switchboard.

The boy spoke into the phone.

"Go right up," he told us.

At the Dexters' door I stepped past Gantvoort and pressed the button.

Creda Dexter opened the door. Her amber eyes widened and her smile faded as I stepped past her into the apartment.

I walked swiftly down the little hallway and turned into the first room through whose open door a light showed.

And came face to face with Smith!

We were both surprised, but his astonishment was a lot more profound than mine. Neither of us had expected to see the other; but I had known he was still alive, while he had every reason for thinking me at the bottom of the bay.

I took advantage of his greater bewilderment to the extent of two steps toward him before he went into action.

One of his hands swept down.

I threw my right fist at his face—threw it with every ounce of my 180 pounds behind it, re-enforced by the memory of every second I had spent in the water and every throb of my battered head.

His hand, already darting down for his pistol, came back up too late to fend off my punch.

Something clicked in my hand as it smashed into his face, and my hand went numb.

But he went down—and lay where he fell.

I jumped across his body to a door on the opposite side of the room, pulling my gun loose with my left hand.

"Dexter's somewhere around!" I called over my shoulder to O'Gar, who with Gantvoort and Creda, was coming through the door by which I had entered. "Keep your eyes open!"

I dashed through the four other rooms of the apartment, pulling closet doors open, looking everywhere—and I found nobody.

Then I returned to where Creda Dexter was trying to revive Smith, with the assistance of O'Gar and Gantvoort.

The detective-sergeant looked over his shoulder at me.

"Who do you think this joker is?" he asked.

"My friend Mr Smith."

"Gantvoort says he's Madden Dexter."

I looked at Charles Gantvoort, who nodded his head.

"This is Madden Dexter," he said.

VIII

"I HOPE YOU SWING!"

We worked upon Dexter for nearly ten minutes before he opened his eyes.

As soon as he sat up we began to shoot questions and accusations at him, hoping to get a confession out of him before he recovered from his shakiness—but he wasn't that shaky.

All we could get out of him was:

"Take me in if you want to. If I've got anything to say I'll say it to my lawyer, and to nobody else."

Creda Dexter, who had stepped back after her brother came to, and was standing a little way off, watching us, suddenly came forward and caught me by the arm.

"What have you got on him?" she demanded, imperatively.

"I wouldn't want to say," I countered, "but I don't mind telling you this much. We're going to give him a chance in a nice modern court-room to prove that he didn't kill Leopold Gantvoort."

"He was in New York!"

"He was not! He had a friend who went to New York as Madden Dexter and looked after Gantvoort's business under that name. But if this is the real Madden Dexter then the closest he got to New York was when he met his friend on the ferry to get from him the papers connected with the B. F. & F. Iron Corporation transaction; and learned that I had stumbled upon the truth about his alibi—even if I didn't know it myself at the time."

She jerked around to face her brother.

"Is that on the level?" she asked him.

He sneered at her, and went on feeling with the fingers of one hand the spot on his jaw where my fist had landed.

"I'll say all I've got to say to my lawyer," he repeated.

"You will?" she shot back at him. "Well, I'll say what I've got to say right now!"

She flung around to face me again.

"Madden is not my brother at all! My name is Ives. Madden and I met in St. Louis about four years ago, drifted around together for a year or so, and then came to Frisco. He was a con man—still is. He made

Mr Gantvoort's acquaintance six or seven months ago, and was getting him all ribbed up to unload a fake invention on him. He brought him here a couple of times, and introduced me to him as his sister. We usually posed as brother and sister.

"Then, after Mr Gantvoort had been here a couple times, Madden decided to change his game. He thought Mr Gantvoort liked me, and that we could get more money out of him by working a fancy sort of badger-game on him. I was to lead the old man on until I had him wrapped around my finger—until we had him tied up so tight he couldn't get away—had something on him—something good and strong. Then we were going to shake him down for plenty of money.

"Everything went along fine for a while. He fell for me—fell hard. And finally he asked me to marry him. We had never figured on that. Blackmail was our game. But when he asked me to marry him I tried to call Madden off. I admit the old man's money had something to do with it—it influenced me—but I had come to like him a little for himself. He was mighty fine in lots of ways—nicer than anybody I had ever known.

"So I told Madden all about it, and suggested that we drop the other plan, and that I marry Gantvoort. I promised to see that Madden was kept supplied with money—I knew I could get whatever I wanted from Mr Gantvoort. And I was on the level with Madden. I liked Mr Gantvoort, but Madden had found him and brought him around to me; and so I wasn't going to run out on Madden. I was willing to do all I could for him.

"But Madden wouldn't hear of it. He'd have got more money in the long run by doing as I suggested—but he wanted his little handful right away. And to make him more unreasonable he got one of his jealous streaks. He beat me one night!

"That settled it. I made up my mind to ditch him. I told Mr Gantvoort that my brother was bitterly opposed to our marrying, and he could see that Madden was carrying a grouch. So he arranged to send Madden East on that steel business, to get him out of the way until we were off on our wedding trip. And we thought Madden was completely deceived—but I should have known that he would see through our scheme. We planned to be gone about a year, and by that time I thought Madden would have forgotten me—or I'd be fixed to handle him if he tried to make any trouble.

"As soon as I heard that Mr Gantvoort had been killed I had a hunch that Madden had done it. But then it seemed like a certainty that he was in New York the next day, and I thought I had done him an injustice. And I was glad he was out of it. But now—"

She whirled around to her erstwhile confederate.

"Now I hope you swing, you big sap!"

She spun around to me again. No sleek kitten, this, but a furious, spitting cat, with claws and teeth bared.

"What kind of looking fellow was the one who went to New York for him?"

I described the man I had talked to on the train.

"Evan Felter," she said, after a moment of thought. "He used to work with Madden. You'll probably find him hiding in Los Angeles. Put the screws on him and he'll spill all he knows—he's a weak sister! The chances are he didn't know what Madden's game was until it was all over."

"How do you like that?" she spat at Madden Dexter. "How do you like that for a starter? You messed up my little party, did you? Well, I'm going to spend every minute of my time from now until they pop you off helping them pop you!"

And she did, too—with her assistance it was no trick at all to gather up the rest of the evidence we needed to hang him. And I don't believe her enjoyment of her three-quarters of a million dollars is spoiled a bit by any qualms over what she did to Madden. She's a very respectable woman *now*, and glad to be free of the con-man.

BLACK MASK, JANUARY 1, 1924

FROM THE AUTHOR OF "THE TENTH CLEW"

Thanks for the check for "The Tenth Clew."

And I want to plead guilty to a bit of cowardice in connection with the story. The original of *Creda Dexter* didn't resemble a kitten at all. She looked exactly like a bull-pup—and she was pretty in the bargain!

Except for her eyes, I never succeeded in determining just what was responsible for the resemblance, but it was a very real one.

When, however, it came to actually putting her down on paper, my nerve failed me. "Nobody will believe you if you write a thing like that," I told myself. "They'll think you're trying to spoof them." So, for the sake of plausibility, I lied about her!

Sincerely,

DASHIELL HAMMETT

San Francisco

7

NIGHT SHOTS

BLACK MASK, FEBRUARY 1, 1924

Mr Hammett's nameless detective is lured into a sweet little domestic mess with an outside mystery; as usual, he walks into a lot of excitement, not all of which comes from the muzzle of a gun.

I

The house was of red brick, large and square, with a green slate roof, whose wide overhang gave the building an appearance of being too squat for its two storeys; and it stood on a grassy hill, well away from the county road, upon which it turned its back to look down on the Mokelumne River.

The Ford that I had hired to bring me out from Knownburg carried me into the grounds through a high steel-meshed gate, followed the circling gravel drive, and set me down within a foot of the screen porch that ran all the way around the house's first floor.

"There's Exon's son-in-law now," the driver told me as he pocketed the bill I had given him, and prepared to drive away.

I turned to see a tall, loose-jointed man of thirty or so coming across the porch toward me—a carelessly dressed man, with a mop of rumpled brown hair over a handsome sunburned face. There was a hint of cruelty in the lips that were smiling lazily just now, and more than a hint of recklessness in his narrow gray eyes.

"Mr Gallaway?" I asked as he came down the steps.

"Yes." His voice was a drawling baritone. "You are—"

"From the Continental Detective Agency's San Francisco branch," I finished for him.

He nodded, and held the screen-door open for me.

"Just leave your bag there. I'll have it taken up to your room."

He guided me into the house and—after I had assured him that I had already eaten luncheon—gave me a soft chair and an excellent cigar. He sprawled on his spine in an armchair opposite me—all loose-jointed angles sticking out of it in every direction—and blew smoke at the ceiling for several thoughtful minutes.

"First off," he began presently, his words coming out languidly, "I may as well tell you that I don't expect very much in the way of results. I sent for you more for the soothing effect of your presence on the household than because I expect you to do anything. I don't believe there's anything to do. However, I'm not a detective. I may be wrong. You may find out all sorts of more or less important things. If you do—fine! But I don't insist upon it."

I didn't say anything, though this beginning wasn't much to my taste. He smoked in silence for a moment, and then went on:

"My father-in-law, Talbert Exon, is a man of fifty-seven, and ordinarily a tough, hard, active, and fiery old devil. But just now he's recovering from a rather serious attack of pneumonia, which has taken most of the starch out of him. He hasn't been able to leave his bed yet, and I understand that Dr Rench hopes to keep him on his back for another week at the very least.

"The old man has a room on the second floor—the front, right-hand corner room—just over where we are sitting. His nurse, Miss Caywood, occupies the next room, and there is a connecting door between. My room is the other front one, just across the hall from the old man's; and my wife's bedroom is next to mine—across the hall from the nurse's. I'll show you around later; I just want to make the situation clear to you first.

"Last night, or rather this morning, at about half-past one, somebody shot at Exon while he was sleeping—and missed. The bullet went into the frame of the door that leads to his nurse's room, about six inches above his body as he lay in bed. The course the bullet took in the woodwork would indicate that it had been fired from one of the windows—either through it or from just inside.

"Exon woke up, of course, but he saw nobody. The rest of us—my wife, Miss Caywood, the Figgs, and myself—were also awakened by the shot. We all rushed into his room, and we saw nothing either. There's no doubt that whoever fired it left by the window. Otherwise some of us would have seen him—we came from every other direction. However, we found nobody on the grounds, and no traces of anybody. That, I think, is all."

"Who are the Figgs, and who else is there on the place besides you and your wife, Mr Exon, and his nurse?"

"The Figgs are Adam and Emma; she is the housekeeper and he is a sort of handy-man about the place. Their room is in the extreme rear, on the second floor. Besides them, there is Gong Lim, the cook, who sleeps in a little room near the kitchen, and the three farm hands. Joe Natara and Felipe Fadelia are Italians, and have been here for possibly more than two years; Jesus Mesa, a Mexican, has been here a year or longer. The farm hands sleep in a little house near the barns. I think—

if my opinion is of any value—that none of these people had anything to do with the shooting."

"Did you dig the bullet out of the doorframe?"

"Yes. Shand, the deputy sheriff at Knownburg, dug it out. He says it is a .38-caliber bullet."

"Any guns of that caliber in the house?"

"No. A .22 and my .44—which I keep in the car—are the only pistols on the place. Then there are two shotguns and a .30-30 rifle. Shand made a thorough search, and found nothing else in the way of firearms."

"What does Mr Exon say?"

"Not much of anything, except that if we'll put a gun in bed with him he'll manage to take care of himself without bothering any policemen or detectives. I don't know whether he knows who shot at him or not—he's a close-mouthed old devil. From what I know of him, I imagine there are quite a few men who would think themselves justified in killing him. He was, I understand, far from being a lily in his youth—or in his mature years either, for that matter."

"Anything definite you know, or are you guessing?"

Gallaway grinned at me—a mocking grin that I was to see often before I was through with this Exon affair.

"Both," he drawled. "I know that his life has been rather more than sprinkled with swindled partners and betrayed friends; and that he saved himself from prison at least once by turning state's evidence and sending his associates there. And I know that his wife died under rather peculiar circumstances while heavily insured, and that he was for some time held on suspicion of having murdered her, but was finally released because of a lack of evidence against him. Those, I understand, are fair samples of the old boy's normal behavior; so there may be any number of people gunning for him."

"Suppose you give me a list of all the names you know of enemies he's made, and I'll have them cheeked up, and see what we can find that way."

He raised an indolent hand in protest.

"The names I could give you would be only a few in many, and it might take you months to check up those few. It isn't my intention to go to all that trouble and expense. As I told you, I'm not insisting upon results. My wife is very nervous, and for some peculiar reason she seems to like the old man. So, to soothe her, I agreed to employ a private detective when she asked me to. My idea is that you hang around for a couple of days, until things quiet down and she feels safe again. Meanwhile, if you should stumble upon anything—go to it! If you don't—well and good."

My face must have shown something of what I was thinking, for his eyes twinkled and he chuckled banteringly.

"Don't, please," he drawled, "get the idea that you aren't to find my father-in-law's would be assassin if you wish to. You're to have a free hand. Go as far as you like; except that I want you to be around the place as much as possible, so my wife will see you and feel that we are being adequately protected. Beyond that, I don't care what you do. You can apprehend criminals by the carload. As you may have gathered by now, I'm not exactly in love with my wife's father; and he's no more fond of me. To be frank, if hating weren't such an effort—if it didn't require so much energy—I think I should hate the old devil. But if you want to, and can, catch the man who shot at him, I'd be glad to have you do it. But—"

"All right," I said. "I don't like this job much; but since I'm up here I'll take it on. But, remember, I'm trying all the time."

"Sincerity and earnestness," he showed his teeth in a sardonic smile as we got to our feet, "are very praiseworthy traits."

"So I hear," I growled shortly. "Now let's take a look at Mr Exon's room."

Gallaway's wife and the nurse were with the invalid, but I examined the room before I asked the occupants any questions.

It was a large room, with three wide windows, opening over the porch; and two doors, one of which gave to the hall, and the other to the adjoining room, occupied by the nurse. This door stood open, with a green Japanese screen across it; and, I was told, was left that way at night, so that the nurse could hear readily if her patient was restless or if he wanted attention.

A man standing on the slate roof of the porch, I found, could have easily leaned across one of the window-sills (if he did not care to step over it into the room) and fired at the man in the bed. To get from the ground to the porch roof would have required but little effort; and the descent would be still easier—he could slide down the roof, let himself go feet-first over the edge, checking his speed with hands and arms spread out on the slate, and drop down to the gravel drive. No trick at all, either coming or going. The windows were unscreened.

The sick man's bed stood just beside the connecting doorway between his room and the nurse's, which, when he was lying down, placed him between the doorway and the window from which the shot had been fired. Outside, within long rifle range, there was no building, tree, or eminence of any character from which the bullet that had been dug out of the door-frame could have been fired.

I turned from the room to the occupants, questioning the invalid first. He had been a raw-boned man of considerable size in his health, but now he was wasted and stringy and dead-white. His face was thin and hollow; small beady eyes crowded together against the thin bridge of his nose; his mouth was a colorless gash above a bony projecting chin.

His statement was a marvel of petulant conciseness.

"The shot woke me. I didn't see anything. I don't know anything. I've got a million enemies, most of whose names I can't remember. That's all I can tell you."

He jerked this out crossly, turned his face away, closed his eyes, and refused to speak again.

Mrs Gallaway and the nurse followed me into the latter's room, where I questioned them. They were of as opposite type as you could find anywhere; and between them there was a certain coolness, an unmistakable hostility which I was able to account for later in the day.

Mrs Gallaway was perhaps five years older than her husband; dark, strikingly beautiful in a statuesque way, with a worried look in her dark eyes that was particularly noticeable when those eyes rested on her husband. There was no doubt that she was very much in love with him, and the anxiety that showed in her eyes at times—the pains she took to please him in each slight thing during my stay at the Exon house—convinced me that she struggled always with a fear that she would not be able to hold him, that she was about to lose him.

Mrs Gallaway could add nothing to what her husband had told me. She had been awakened by the shot, had run to her father's room, had seen nothing—knew nothing—suspected nothing.

The nurse—Barbra Caywood was her name—told the same story, in almost the same words. She had jumped out of bed when awakened by the shot, pushed the screen away from the connecting doorway, and rushed into her patient's room. She was the first one to arrive there, and she had seen nothing but the old man sitting up in bed, roaring and shaking his feeble fists at the window.

This Barbra Caywood was a girl of twenty-one or two, and just the sort that a man would pick to help him get well. A girl of a little under the average height, with an erect figure wherein slimness and roundness got an even break under the stiff white of her uniform; with soft golden hair above a face that was certainly made to be looked at. But she was businesslike and had an air of efficiency, for all her prettiness.

From the nurse's room, Gallaway led me to the kitchen, where I questioned the Chinese cook. Gong Lim was a sad-faced Oriental whose ever-present smile somehow made him look more gloomy than ever; and he bowed and smiled and yes-yes'd me from start to finish, and told me nothing.

Adam and Emma Figg—thin and stout, respectively, and both rheumatic—entertained a wide variety of suspicions, directed at the cook and the farm hands, individually and collectively, flitting momentarily from one to the other. They had nothing upon which to base these suspicions, however, except their firm belief that nearly all crimes of violence were committed by foreigners; which, while enough for them, didn't satisfy me.

The farm hands—two smiling middle-aged and heavily mustached Italians, and a soft-eyed Mexican youth—I found in one of the fields. I talked to them for nearly two hours, and I left with a reasonable amount of assurance that neither of the three had had any part in the shooting.

II

Dr Rench had just come down from a visit to his patient when Gallaway and I returned from the fields. He was a little wizened old man with mild manners and eyes, and a wonderful growth of hair on head, brows, cheeks, lips, chin, and nostrils.

The excitement, he said, had retarded Exon's recovery somewhat, but he did not think the setback would be serious. The invalid's temperature had gone up a little, but he seemed to be improving now.

I followed Dr Rench out to his machine after he left the others, for a few questions I wanted to put to him in privacy; but the questions might as well have gone unasked for all the good they did me. He could tell me nothing of any value. The nurse, Barbra Caywood, had been secured, he said, from San Francisco, through the usual channels, which made it seem unlikely that she had worked her way into the Exon house for any hidden purpose which might have some connection with the attempt upon Exon's life.

Returning from my talk with the doctor, I came upon Hilary Gallaway and the nurse in the hall, near the foot of the stairs. His arm was resting lightly across her shoulders, and he was smiling down at her. Just as I came through the door, she twisted away, so that his arm slid off, laughed elfishly up into his face, and went on up the stairs.

I did not know whether she had seen me approaching before she eluded the encircling arm or not; nor did I know how long the arm had been there; and both of those questions would make a difference in how their positions were to be construed.

Hilary Gallaway was certainly not a man to allow a girl as pretty as the nurse to lack attention, and he was just as certainly attractive enough in himself to make his advances not too unflattering. Nor did Barbra Caywood impress me as being a girl who would dislike his admiration. But, at that, it was more than likely that there was nothing very serious between them; nothing more than a playful sort of flirtation.

But, no matter what the situation might be in that quarter, it didn't have any direct bearing upon the shooting—none that I could see, any-way. But I understood now the strained relations between the nurse and Gallaway's wife.

Gallaway was grinning quizzically at me while I was chasing these thoughts around in my head.

"Nobody's safe with a detective around," he complained.

I grinned back at him. That was the only sort of an answer you could give this bird.

After dinner, Gallaway drove me to Knownburg in his roadster, and set me down on the door-step of the deputy sheriff's house. He offered to drive me back to the Exon house when I had finished my investigations in town, but I did not know how long those investigations would take, so I told him I would hire a car when I was ready to return.

Shand, the deputy sheriff, was a big, slow-spoken, slow-thinking, blond man of thirty or so—just the type best fitted for a deputy sheriff job in a San Joaquin County town—and he balanced a fat blond child on each knee while he talked to me.

"I went out to Exon's as soon as Gallaway called me up," he said. "About four-thirty in the morning, I reckon it was when I got there. I didn't find nothing. There weren't no marks on the porch roof, but that don't mean nothing. I tried climbing up and down it myself, and I didn't leave no marks neither. The ground around the house is too firm for footprints to be followed. I found a few; but they didn't lead nowhere; and everybody had run all over the place before I got there, so I couldn't tell who they belonged to.

"Far's I can learn, there ain't been no suspicious characters in the neighborhood lately. The only folks around here who have got any grudge against the old man are the Deemses—Exon beat 'em in a law suit a couple years back—but all of them—the father and both the boys—were at home when the shooting was done."

"How long has Exon been living here?"

"Four—five years, I reckon. Came in 1918 or '19."

"Nothing at all to work on, then?"

He shifted one of the kids around to keep from having an eye jabbed by a stubby finger, and shook his head.

"Nothing I know about."

"What do you know about the Exon family?" I asked.

Shand scratched his head thoughtfully and frowned.

"I reckon it's Hilary Gallaway you're meaning," he said slowly. "I thought of that. The Gallaways showed up here a couple of years after her father had bought the place, and Hilary seems to spend most of his evenings up in Ady's back room, teaching the boys how to play poker. I hear he's fitted to teach them a lot.

I don't know, myself. Ady runs a quiet game, so I let 'em alone. But naturally I don't never set in, myself. I just stay away so I won't see nothing.

"Outside of being a card-hound, and drinking pretty heavy, and making a lot of trips to the city, where he's supposed to have a girl on the string, I don't know nothing much about Hilary. But it's no secret that him and the old man don't hit it off together very well. And then Hilary's room is just across the hall from Exon's, and their windows open out on the porch roof just a little apart. But I don't know—"

Shand confirmed what Gallaway had told me about the bullet being .38-caliber; about the absence of any pistol of that caliber on the premises; and about the lack of any reason for suspecting the farm hands or servants.

I put in the next couple hours talking to whomever I could find to talk to in Knownburg; and I learned nothing worth putting down on paper. Then I got a car and driver from the garage, and was driven out to Exon's.

Gallaway had not yet returned from town. His wife and Barbra Caywood were just about to sit down to a light luncheon before retiring, so I joined them. Exon, the nurse, said, was asleep, and had spent a quiet evening. We talked for a while—until about half-past twelve—and then went to our rooms.

My room was next to the nurse's, on the same side of the hall that divided the second storey in half. I sat down and wrote my report for the day, smoked a cigar, and then—the house being quiet by this time—put a gun and a flashlight in my pockets, went downstairs, and let myself out of the kitchen door.

The moon was just coming up, lighting the grounds vaguely, except for the shadows cast by house, outbuildings, and the several clumps of shrubbery. Keeping in these shadows as much as possible, I explored the grounds, finding everything as it should be.

The lack of any evidence to the contrary pointed to last night's shot having been fired—either accidentally, or in fright at some fancied move of Exon's—by a burglar, who had been entering the sick man's room through a window. If that were so, then there wasn't one chance in a thousand of anything happening tonight. But I felt restless and ill at ease, nevertheless—possibly a result of my failure to learn the least thing of importance all day.

Gallaway's roadster was not in the garage. He had not returned from Knownburg. Beneath the farm hands' window I paused until snores in three distinct keys told me that they were all safely abed.

After an hour of this snooping around, I returned to the house. The luminous dial of my watch registered 2:35 as I stopped outside the Chinese cook's door to listen to his regular breathing.

Upstairs, I paused at the door of the Figgs' room, until my ear told me that they were sleeping. At Mrs Gallaway's door I had to wait several minutes before she sighed and turned in bed. Barbra Caywood was breathing deeply and strongly, with the regularity of a young animal whose sleep is without disturbing dreams. The invalid's breath came to me with the evenness of slumber and the rasping of the pneumonia convalescent.

This listening tour completed, I returned to my room.

Still feeling wide-awake and restless, I pulled a chair up to a window, and sat looking at the moonlight on the river—which twisted just below the house so as to be visible from this side—smoking another cigar, and turning things over in my mind—to no great advantage.

Outside there was no sound.

Suddenly down the hall came the heavy explosion of a gun being fired indoors!

I threw myself across the room, out into the hall.

A woman's voice filled the house with its shriek—high, frenzied.

Barbra Caywood's door was unlocked when I reached it. I slammed it open. By the light of the moonbeams that slanted past her window, I saw her sitting upright in the center of her bed. She wasn't beautiful now. Her face was distorted, twisted with terror. The scream was just dying in her throat.

All this I got in the flash of time that it took me to put a running foot across her sill.

Then another shot crashed out—in Exon's room.

The girl's face jerked up—so abruptly that it seemed her neck must snap—she clutched both hands to her breast—and fell face-down among the bedclothes.

I don't know whether I went through, over, or around the screen that stood in the connecting doorway. I was circling Exon's bed. He lay on the floor on his side, facing a window. I jumped over him—leaned out the window.

In the yard that was bright now under the moon, nothing moved. There was no sound of flight.

Presently, while my eyes still searched the surrounding country, the farm hands, in their underwear, came running bare-footed from the direction of their quarters. I called down to them, stationing them at points of vantage.

Meanwhile, behind me, Gong Lim and Adam Figg had put Exon back in his bed, while Mrs Gallaway and Emma Figg tried to check the blood that spurted from a hole in Barbra Caywood's side.

I sent Adam Figg to the telephone, to wake the doctor and the deputy sheriff, and then I hurried down to the grounds.

Stepping out of the door, I came face to face with Hilary Gallaway, coming from the direction of the garage. His face was flushed, and his breath was eloquent of the refreshments that had accompanied the game in Ady's back room; but his step was steady enough, and his smile was as lazy as ever. He had apparently arrived while I was sending Figg to the phone and running downstairs—otherwise I would have heard his car.

"What's the excitement?" he asked.

"Same as last night! Meet anybody on the road? Or see anybody leaving here?"

"No."

"All right. Get in that bus of yours, and burn up the road in the other direction. Stop anybody you meet going away from here or who looks wrong! Got a gun?"

He spun on his heel with nothing of indolence.

"One in my car," he called over his shoulder, as he broke into a run.

The farm hands still at their posts, I combed the grounds from east to west and from north to south. I realized that I was spoiling my chance of finding footprints when it would be light enough to see them; but I was banking on the man I wanted still being close at hand. And then Shand had told me that the ground was unfavorable for tracing prints, anyway.

On the gravel drive in front of the house I found the pistol from which the shots had been fired—a cheap .38-caliber revolver, slightly rusty, smelling freshly of burnt powder, with three empty shells and three that had not been fired in it.

Besides that I found nothing. The murderer—from what I had seen of the hole in the girl's side, I called him that—had vanished completely.

Shand and Dr Rench arrived together, just as I was finishing my fruitless search. A little later, Hilary Gallaway came back—empty-handed.

III

Breakfast that morning was a melancholy meal, except to Hilary Gallaway. He refrained from jesting openly about the night's excitement; but his eyes twinkled whenever they met mine, and I knew he thought it a tremendously good joke for the shooting to have taken place right under my nose. During his wife's presence at the table, however, he was almost grave, as if not to offend her.

Mrs Gallaway left the table shortly, and Dr Rench joined us. He said that both of his patients were in as good shape as could be expected, and he thought both would recover.

The bullet had barely grazed the girl's ribs and breast bone, going through the flesh and muscles of her chest, in on the right side and out again on the left. Except for the shock and the loss of blood, she was not in danger, although she was still unconscious.

Exon was sleeping, the doctor said; so Shand and I crept up into his room to examine it. The first bullet had gone into the door-frame, about four inches above the one that had been fired the night before. The second bullet had pierced the Japanese screen, and, after passing through the girl, had lodged in the plaster of the wall. We dug out both bullets—they were of .38-caliber. Both had been apparently fired from the vicinity of one of the windows—either just inside or just outside.

Shand and I grilled the Chinese cook, the farm hands, and the Figgs, unmercifully that day. Detectives are only human—or at least this one is—and I don't mind confessing that some of my humiliation and chagrin was worked off on these people. But they came through it standing up—there was nothing to fix the shooting on any of them.

And all day long that damned Hilary Gallaway followed me from pillar to post, with a mocking glint in his eyes that said plainer than words, "I'm the logical suspect. Why don't you put me through your little third degree?" But I grinned back, and asked him nothing.

Shand had to go to town that afternoon. He called me up on the telephone later, and told me that Gallaway had left

Knownburg early enough that morning to have arrived home fully half an hour before the shooting, if he had driven at his usual fast pace.

The day passed—too rapidly—and I found myself dreading the coming of night. Two nights in succession Exon's life had been attempted—and now the third night was coming.

At dinner Hilary Gallaway announced that he was going to stay home this evening. Knownburg, he said, was tame in comparison; and he grinned at me.

Dr Rench left after the meal, saying that he would return as soon as possible, but that he had two patients on the other side of town whom he must visit. Barbra Caywood had returned to consciousness, but had been extremely hysterical, and the doctor had given her an opiate. She was asleep now. Exon was resting easily except for a high temperature.

I went up to Exon's room for a few minutes after the meal, and tried him out with a gentle question or two. But he refused to answer them, and he was too sick for me to press him.

He asked how the girl was.

"The doc says she's in no particular danger. Just loss of blood and shock. If she doesn't rip her bandages off and bleed to death in one of her hysterical spells, he says, he'll have her on her feet in a couple weeks."

Mrs Gallaway came in then, and I went downstairs again, where I was seized by Gallaway, who insisted with bantering gravity that I tell him about some of the mysteries I had solved. He was enjoying my discomfort to the limit. He kidded me for about an hour, and had me burning up inside; but I managed to grin back with a fair pretense of indifference.

When his wife joined us presently—saying that both of the invalids were sleeping—I made my escape from her tormenting husband, saying that I had some writing to do. But I didn't go to my room.

Instead, I crept stealthily into the girl's room, crossed to a clothes press that I had noted earlier in the day, and planted myself in it. By leaving the door open the least fraction of an inch, I could see through the connecting doorway—from which the screen had been removed—across Exon's bed, and out of the window from which three bullets had already come, and the Lord only knew what else might come.

Time passed, and I was stiff from standing still. But I had expected that—had felt it before on somewhat similar occasions—and I knew it would pass. But whether it did or not, I meant to stay here until something happened—if it was only the rising of the sun. Nothing else was going to be pulled off in this corner of the house without my being in on it!

Twice Mrs Gallaway came up to look at her father and the nurse. Each time I shut my closet door entirely as soon as I heard her tip-toeing steps in the hall, I was hiding from *everybody*.

She had just gone from her second visit, when, before I had time to open my door again, I heard a faint rustling, and a soft padding on the floor. Not knowing what it was or where it was, I was afraid to push the door open.

In my narrow hiding-place I stood still and waited.

The padding was recognizable now—quiet footsteps, coming nearer. They passed not far from my clothes press door.

I waited.

An almost inaudible rustling. A pause. The softest and faintest of tearing sounds.

I came out of the closet—my gun in my hand.

Standing beside the girl's bed, leaning over her unconscious form, was old Talbert Exon, his face flushed with fever, his night shirt hanging limply around his wasted legs. One of his hands still rested upon the bedclothes he had turned down from her body. The other hand held a narrow strip of adhesive tape, with which her bandages had been fixed in place, and which he had just torn off.

He snarled at me, and both his hands went toward the girl's bandages.

The crazy, feverish glare of his eyes told me that the threat of the gun in my hand meant nothing to him. I jumped to his side, plucked his hands aside, picked him up in my arms, and carried him—kicking, clawing and swearing—back to his bed.

Then I called the others.

IV

Hilary Gallaway, Shand—who had come out from town again—and I sat over coffee and cigarettes in the kitchen, while the rest of the household helped Dr Rench battle for Exon's life. The old man had gone through enough excitement in the last three days to kill a healthy man, let alone a pneumonia convalescent.

"But why should the old devil want to kill her?" Gallaway asked me.

"Search me," I confessed, a little testily perhaps. "I don't know why he wanted to kill her, but it's a cinch that he did. The gun was found just about where he could have thrown it when he heard me coming. I was in the girl's room when she was shot, and I got to Exon's window without wasting much time, and I saw nothing. You, yourself, driving home from Knownburg, and arriving here right after the shooting, didn't see anybody leave by the road; and I'll take an oath that nobody could have left in any other direction without either one of the farm hands or me seeing them.

"And then, tonight, I told Exon that the girl would recover if she didn't tear off her bandages; which, while true enough, gave him the idea that she had been trying to tear them off.

And from that he built up a plan of tearing them off himself—knowing that she had been given an opiate, perhaps—and thinking that everybody would believe she had torn them off herself. And he was putting that plan in execution—had torn off one piece of tape—when I stopped him. He shot her intentionally, and that's flat. Maybe I couldn't prove it in court without knowing why; but I know he did. But the doc says he'll hardly live to be tried; he killed himself trying to kill the girl."

"Maybe you're right," and Gallaway's mocking grin flashed at me, "but you're a hell of a detective just the same. Why didn't you suspect me?"

"I did," I grinned back, "but not enough."

"Why not? You may be making a mistake," he drawled. "You know my room is just across the hall from his, and I could have left my window, crept across the porch, fired at him, and then run back to my room, on that first night.

"And on the second night—when you were here—you ought to know that I left Knownburg in plenty of time to have come out here, parked my car down the road a bit, fired those two shots, crept around in the shadow of the house, ran back to my car, and then come driving innocently up to the garage. You should know also that my reputation isn't any too good—that I'm supposed to be a bad egg; and you do know that I don't like the old man. And for a motive, there is the fact that my wife is Exon's only heir. What more do you want? I hope," he raised his eyebrows in burlesqued pain, "that you don't think I have any moral scruples against a well-placed murder now and then."

I laughed.

"I don't."

"Well, then?"

"If Exon had been killed that first night, and I had come up here, you'd be doing your joking behind bars long before this. And if he'd been killed the second night, even, I might have grabbed you. But I don't figure you as a man who'd bungle so easy a job—not twice, anyway. You wouldn't have missed, and then run away, leaving him alive."

He reached over for my hand and shook it gravely.

"It is comforting to have one's few virtues appreciated."

Before Talbert Exon died he sent for me. He wanted to die, he said, with his curiosity appeased; and so we traded information. I told him how I had come to suspect him—just about what I had told his son-in-law—and he told me why he had tried to kill Barbra Caywood.

Fourteen years ago he had killed his wife; not for the insurance, as he had been suspected of doing, but in a fit of jealousy. However, he had so thoroughly covered up the proofs of his guilt that he had never been brought to trial; but the murder had weighed upon him, to the extent of becoming an obsession.

He knew that he would never give himself away consciously—he was too shrewd for that—and he knew that proof of his guilt could never be found. But there was always the chance that some time, in delirium, in his sleep, or when drunk, he might tell enough to bring him to the gallows.

He thought upon this angle too often, until it became a morbid fear that always hounded him. He had given up drinking—that was easy—but there was no way of guarding against the other things.

And one of them, he said, had finally happened. He had got pneumonia, and for a week he had been out of his head, and he had talked. Coming out of that week's delirium, he had questioned the nurse. She had given him vague answers, would not tell him what he had talked about, what he had said. And then, in unguarded moments, he had discovered that her eyes rested upon him with loathing—with intense repulsion.

He knew then that he had babbled of his wife's murder; and he set about laying plans for removing the nurse before she repeated what she had heard. For so long as she remained in his house, he counted himself safe. She would not tell strangers, and it might be that for a while she would not tell anyone. Professional ethics would keep her quiet, perhaps; but he could not let her leave his house with her knowledge of his secret.

Daily and in secret, he had tested his strength, until he knew himself strong enough to walk about the room a little, and to hold a revolver steady. His bed was fortunately placed for his purpose—directly in line with one of the windows, the connecting door, and the girl's bed. In an old bond-box in his closet—and nobody but he had ever seen the things in that box—was a revolver; a revolver that could not possibly be traced to him.

On the first night, he had taken this gun out, stepped back from his bed a little, and fired a bullet into the door-frame. Then he had jumped back into bed, concealing the gun under the blankets—where none thought to look for it—until he could return it to its box.

That was all the preparation he had needed. He had established an attempted murder directed against himself; and he had shown that a bullet fired at him could easily go near—and therefore through—the connecting doorway.

On the second night, he had waited until the house had seemed quiet. Then he had peeped through one of the cracks in the Japanese screen at the girl, whom he could see in the reflected light from the moon. He had found, though, that when he stepped far enough back from the screen for it to escape powder marks, he could not see the girl, not while she was lying down. So he had fired first into the door-frame—near the previous night's bullet—to awaken her.

She had sat up in bed immediately, screaming, and he had shot her. He had intended firing another shot into her body—to make sure of her death—but my approach had made that impossible, and had made concealment of the gun impossible; so, with what strength he had left, he had thrown the revolver out of the window.

He died that afternoon, and I returned to San Francisco.

But that was not quite the end of the story.

In the ordinary course of business, the agency's book-keeping department sent Gallaway a bill for my services. With the check that he sent by return mail, he enclosed a letter to me, from which I quote a paragraph:

> I don't want to let you miss the cream of the whole affair. The lovely Caywood, when she recovered, denied that Exon had talked of murder or any other crime during his delirium. The cause of the distaste with which she might have looked at him afterward, and the reason she would not tell him what he had said, was that his entire conversation during that week of delirium had consisted of an uninterrupted stream of obscenities and blasphemies, which seem to have shocked the girl through and through.

8

ZIGZAGS OF TREACHERY

BLACK MASK, MARCH 1, 1924

Here is a detective story which we think will please all comers. It is a happy combination of deduction and swift action.

I

"All I Know about Dr Estep's death," I said, "is the stuff in the papers."

Vance Richmond's lean gray face took on an expression of distaste.

"The newspapers aren't always either thorough or accurate. I'll give you the salient points as I know them; though I suppose you'll want to go over the ground for yourself, and get your information first-hand."

I nodded, and the attorney went on, shaping each word precisely with his thin lips before giving it sound.

"Dr Estep came to San Francisco in '98 or '99—a young man of twenty-five, just through qualifying for his license. He opened an office here, and, as you probably know, became in time a rather excellent surgeon. He married two or three years after he came here. There were no children. He and his wife seem to have been a bit happier together than the average.

"Of his life before coming to San Francisco, nothing is known. He told his wife briefly that he had been born and raised in Parkersburg, W. Va., but that his home life had been so unpleasant that he was trying to forget it, and that he did not like to talk—or even think—about it. Bear that in mind.

"Two weeks ago—on the third of the month—a woman came to his office, in the afternoon. His office was in his residence on Pine Street. Lucy Coe, who was Dr Estep's nurse and assistant, showed the woman into his office, and then went back to her own desk in the reception room.

"She didn't hear anything the doctor said to the woman, but through the closed door she heard the woman's voice now and then—a high and anguished voice, apparently pleading. Most of the words were lost upon the nurse, but she heard one coherent sentence. 'Please! Please!' she heard the woman cry, 'Don't turn me away!' The woman was with Dr Estep for about fifteen minutes, and left sobbing into a handkerchief. Dr Estep said nothing about the caller either to his nurse or to his wife, who didn't learn of it until after his death.

"The next day, toward evening, while the nurse was putting on her hat and coat preparatory to leaving for home, Dr Estep came out of his office, with his hat on and a letter in his hand. The nurse saw that his face was pale—'white as my uniform,' she says—and he walked with the care of one who takes pains to keep from staggering.

"She asked him if he was ill. 'Oh, it's nothing!' he told her. 'I'll be all right in a very few minutes.' Then he went on out. The nurse left the house just behind him, and saw him drop the letter he had carried into the mail box on the corner, after which he returned to the house.

"Mrs Estep, coming downstairs ten minutes later,—it couldn't have been any later than that,—heard, just as she reached the first floor, the sound of a shot from her husband's office. She rushed into it, meeting nobody. Her husband stood by his desk, swaying, with a hole in his right temple and a smoking revolver in his hand. Just as she reached him and put her arms around him, he fell across the desk—dead."

"Anybody else—any of the servants, for instance—able to say that Mrs Estep didn't go to the office until after the shot?" I asked.

The attorney shook his head sharply.

"No, damn it! That's where the rub comes in!"

His voice, after this one flare of feeling, resumed its level, incisive tone, and he went on with his tale.

"The next day's papers had accounts of Dr Estep's death, and late that morning the woman who had called upon him the day before his death came to the house. She is Dr Estep's first wife—which is to say, his legal wife! There seems to be no reason—not the slightest—for doubting it, as much as I'd like to. They were married in Philadelphia in '96. She has a certified copy of the marriage record. I had the matter investigated in Philadelphia, and it's a certain fact that Dr Estep and this woman—Edna Fife was her maiden name—were really married.

"She says that Estep, after living with her in Philadelphia for two years, deserted her. That would have been in '98, or just before he came to San Francisco. She has sufficient proof of her identity—that she really is the Edna Fife who married him; and my agents in the East found positive proof that Estep had practiced for two years in Philadelphia.

"And here is another point. I told you that Estep had said he was born and raised in Parkersburg. I had inquiries made there, but found nothing to show that he had ever lived there, and found ample to show that he had never lived at the address he had given his wife. There is, then, nothing for us to believe except that his talk of an unhappy early life was a ruse to ward off embarrassing questions."

"Did you do anything toward finding out whether the doctor and his first wife had ever been divorced?" I asked.

"I'm having that taken care of now, but I hardly expect to learn that they had. That would be too crude. To get on with my story: This woman—the first Mrs Estep—said that she had just recently learned her husband's whereabouts, and had come to see him in an attempt to effect a reconciliation. When she called upon him the afternoon before his death, he asked for a little time to make up his mind what he should do. He promised to give her his decision in two days. My personal opinion, after talking to the woman several times, is that she had learned that he had accumulated some money, and that her interest was more in getting the money than in getting him. But that, of course, is neither here nor there.

"At first the authorities accepted the natural explanation of the doctor's death—suicide. But after the first wife's appearance, the second wife—my client—was arrested and charged with murder.

"The police theory is that after his first wife's visit, Dr Estep told his second wife the whole story; and that she, brooding over the knowledge that he had deceived her, that she was not his wife at all, finally worked herself up into a rage, went to the office after his nurse had left for the day, and shot him with the revolver that she knew he always kept in his desk.

"I don't know, of course, just what evidence the prosecution has, but from the newspapers I gather that the case against her will be built upon her finger prints on the revolver with which he was killed; an upset inkwell on his desk; splashes of ink on the dress she wore; and an inky print of her hand on a torn newspaper on his desk.

"Unfortunately, but perfectly naturally, one of the first things she did was to take the revolver out of her husband's hand.

That accounts for her prints on it. He fell—as I told you—just as she put her arms around him, and, though her memory isn't very clear on this point, the probabilities are that he dragged her with him when he fell across the desk. That accounts for the upset inkwell, the torn paper, and the splashes of ink. But the prosecution will try to persuade the jury that those things all happened before the shooting—that they are proofs of a struggle."

"Not so bad," I gave my opinion.

"Or pretty damned bad—depending on how you look at it. And this is the worst time imaginable for a thing like this to come up! Within the past few months there have been no less than five widely-advertised murders of men by women who were supposed to have been betrayed, or deceived, or one thing or another.

"Not one of those five women was convicted. As a result, we have the press, the public, and even the pulpit, howling for a stricter enforcement of justice. The newspapers are lined up against Mrs Estep as strongly as their fear of libel suits will permit. The woman's clubs are lined up against her. Everybody is clamoring for an example to be made of her.

"Then, as if all that isn't enough, the Prosecuting Attorney has lost his last two big cases, and he'll be out for blood this time—election day isn't far off."

The calm, even, precise voice was gone now. In its place was a passionate eloquence.

"I don't know what you think," Richmond cried. "You're a detective. This is an old story to you. You're more or less callous, I suppose, and skeptical of innocence in general. But I *know* that Mrs Estep didn't kill her husband. I don't say it because she's my client! I was Dr Estep's attorney, and his friend, and if I thought Mrs Estep guilty, I'd do everything in my power to help convict her. But I know as well as I know anything that she didn't kill him—couldn't have killed him.

"She's innocent. But I know too that if I go into court with no defense beyond what I now have, she'll be convicted! There has been too much leniency shown feminine criminals, public sentiment says. The pendulum will swing the other way—Mrs Estep, if convicted, will get the limit. I'm putting it up to you! Can you save her?"

"Our best mark is the letter he mailed just before he died," I said, ignoring everything he said that didn't have to do with the facts of the case. "It's good betting that when a man writes and mails a letter and then shoots himself, that the letter isn't altogether unconnected with the suicide. Did you ask the first wife about the letter?"

"I did, and she denies having received one."

"That wasn't right. If the doctor had been driven to suicide by her appearance, then according to all the rules there are, the letter should have been addressed to her. He might have written one to his second wife, but he would hardly have mailed *it*.

"Would she have any reason for lying about it?"

"Yes," the lawyer said slowly, "I think she would. His will leaves everything to the second wife. The first wife, being the only legal wife, will have no difficulty in breaking that will, of course; but if it is shown that the second wife had no knowledge of the first one's existence—that she really believed herself to be Dr Estep's legal wife—then I think that she will receive at least a portion of the estate. I don't think any court would, under the circumstances, take everything away from her. But if she should be found guilty of murdering Dr Estep, then no consideration will be shown her, and the first wife will get every penny."

"Did he leave enough to make half of it, say, worth sending an innocent person to the gallows for?"

"He left about half a million, roughly; $250,000 isn't a mean inducement."

"Do you think it would be enough for the first wife—from what you have seen of her?"

"Candidly, I do. She didn't impress me as being a person of many very active scruples."

"Where does this first wife live?" I asked.

"She's staying at the Montgomery Hotel now. Her home is in Louisville, I believe. I don't think you will gain anything by talking to her, however. She has retained Somerset, Somerset, and Quill to represent her—a very reputable firm, by the way—and she'll refer you to them. They will tell you nothing. But if there's anything dishonest about her affairs—such as the concealing of Dr Estep's letter—I'm confident that Somerset, Somerset and Quill know nothing of it."

"Can I talk to the second Mrs Estep—your client?"

"Not at present, I'm afraid; though perhaps in a day or two. She is on the verge of collapse just now. She has always been delicate; and the shock of her husband's death, followed by her own arrest and imprisonment, has been too much for her. She's in the city jail, you know, held without bail. I've tried to have her transferred to the prisoner's ward of the City Hospital, even; but the authorities seem to think that her illness is simply a ruse. I'm worried about her. She's really in a critical condition."

His voice was losing its calmness again, so I picked up my hat, said something about starting to work at once, and went out. I don't like eloquence: if it isn't effective enough to pierce your hide, it's tiresome; and if it is effective enough, then it muddles your thoughts.

II

I spent the next couple of hours questioning the Estep servants, to no great advantage. None of them had been near the front of the house at the time of the shooting, and none had seen Mrs Estep immediately prior to her husband's death.

After a lot of hunting, I located Lucy Coe, the nurse, in an apartment on Vallejo Street. She was a small, brisk, business-like woman of thirty or so. She repeated what Vance Richmond had told me, and could add nothing to it.

That cleaned up the Estep end of the job; and I set out for the Montgomery Hotel, satisfied that my only hope for success—barring miracles, which usually don't happen—lay in finding the letter that I believed Dr Estep had written to his first wife.

My drag with the Montgomery Hotel management was pretty strong—strong enough to get me anything I wanted that wasn't too far outside the law. So as soon as I got there, I hunted up Stacey, one of the assistant managers.

"This Mrs Estep who's registered here," I asked, "what do you know about her?"

"Nothing, myself, but if you'll wait a few minutes I'll see what I can learn."

The assistant manager was gone about ten minutes.

"No one seems to know much about her," he told me when he came back. "I've questioned the telephone girls, bell-boys, maids, clerks, and the house detective; but none of them could tell me much.

"She registered from Louisville, on the second of the month. She has never stopped here before, and she seems unfamiliar with the city—asks quite a few questions about how to get around. The mail clerks don't remember handling any mail for her, nor do the girls on the switchboard have any record of phone calls for her.

"She keeps regular hours—usually goes out at ten or later in the morning, and gets in before midnight. She doesn't seem to have any callers or friends."

"Will you have her mail watched—let me know what postmarks and return addresses are on any letters she gets?"

"Certainly."

"And have the girls on the switchboard put their ears up against any talking she does over the wire?"

"Yes."

"Is she in her room now?"

"No, she went out a little while ago."

"Fine! I'd like to go up and take a look at her stuff."

Stacey looked sharply at me, and cleared his throat.

"Is it as—ah—important as all that? I want to give you all the assistance I can, but—"

"It's this important," I assured him, "that another woman's life depends on what I can learn about this one."

"All right!" he said. "I'll tell the clerk to let us know if she comes in before we are through; and we'll go right up."

The woman's room held two valises and a trunk, all unlocked, and containing not the least thing of importance—no letters—nothing. So little, in fact, that I was more than half convinced that she had expected her things to be searched.

Downstairs again, I planted myself in a comfortable chair within sight of the key rack, and waited for a view of this first Mrs Estep.

She came in at 11:15 that night. A large woman of forty-five or fifty, well dressed, and carrying herself with an air of assurance. Her face was a little too hard as to mouth and chin, but not enough to be ugly. A capable looking woman—a woman who would get what she went after.

III

Eight o'clock was striking as I went into the Montgomery lobby the next morning and picked out a chair, this time, within eye-range of the elevators.

At 10:30 Mrs Estep left the hotel, with me in her wake. Her denial that a letter from her husband, written immediately before his death, had come to her didn't fit in with the possibilities as I saw them. And a good motto for the detective business is, "When in doubt—shadow 'em."

After eating breakfast at a restaurant on O'Farrell Street, she turned toward the shopping district; and for a long, long time—though I suppose it was a lot shorter than it seemed to me—she led me through the most densely packed portions of the most crowded department stores she could find.

She didn't buy anything, but she did a lot of thorough looking, with me muddling along behind her, trying to act like a little fat guy on an errand for his wife; while stout women bumped me and thin one's prodded me and all sorts got in my way and walked on my feet.

Finally, after I had sweated off a couple of pounds, she left the shopping district, and cut up through Union Square, walking along casually, as if out for a stroll.

Three-quarters way through, she turned abruptly, and retraced her steps, looking sharply at everyone she passed. I was on a bench, reading a stray page from a day-old newspaper, when she went by. She walked on down Post Street to Kearny, stopping every now and then to look—or to pretend to look—in store windows; while I ambled along sometimes beside her, sometimes almost by her side, and sometimes in front.

She was trying to check up the people around her, trying to determine whether she was being followed or not. But here, in the busy part of town, that gave me no cause for worry. On a less crowded street it might have been different, though not necessarily so.

There are four rules for shadowing: Keep behind your subject as much as possible; never try to hide from him; act in a natural manner no matter what happens; and never meet his eye. Obey them, and, except in unusual circumstances, shadowing is the easiest thing that a sleuth has to do.

Assured, after a while, that no one was following her, Mrs Estep turned back toward Powell Street, and got into a taxicab at the St. Francis stand. I picked out a modest touring car from the rank of hire-cars along the Geary Street side of Union Square, and set out after her.

Our route was out Post Street to Laguna, where the taxi presently swung into the curb and stopped. The woman got out, paid the driver, and went up the steps of an apartment building. With idling engine my own car had come to rest against the opposite curb in the block above.

As the taxicab disappeared around a corner, Mrs Estep came out of the apartment building doorway, went back to the sidewalk, and started down Laguna Street.

"Pass her," I told my chauffeur, and we drew down upon her.

As we came abreast, she went up the front steps of another building, and this time she rang a bell. These steps belonged to a building apparently occupied by four flats, each with its separate door, and the button she had pressed belonged to the right-hand second-storey flat.

Under cover of my car's rear curtains, I kept my eye on the doorway while my driver found a convenient place to park in the next block.

I kept my eye on the vestibule until 5:35 P.M., when she came out, walked to the Sutter Street car line, returned to the Montgomery, and went to her room.

I called up the Old Man—the Continental Detective Agency's San Francisco manager—and asked him to detail an operative to learn who and what were the occupants of the Laguna Street flat.

That night Mrs Estep ate dinner at her hotel, and went to a show afterward, and she displayed no interest in possible shadowers. She went to her room at a little after eleven, and I knocked off for the day.

IV

The following morning I turned the woman over to Dick Foley, and went back to the agency to wait for Bob Teale, the operative who had investigated the Laguna Street flat. He came in at a little after ten.

"A guy named Jacob Ledwich lives there," Bob said. "He's a crook of some sort, but I don't know just what. He and 'Wop' Healey are friendly, so he must be a crook! 'Porky' Grout says he's an ex-bunco man who is in with a gambling ring now; but 'Porky' would tell you a bishop was a safe-ripper if he thought it would mean five bucks for himself.

"This Ledwich goes out mostly at night, and he seems to be pretty prosperous. Probably a high-class worker of some sort. He's got a Buick—license number 645-221—that he keeps in a garage around the corner from his flat. But he doesn't seem to use the car much."

"What sort of looking fellow is he?"

"A big guy—six feet or better—and he'll weigh a couple hundred easy. He's got a funny mug on him. It's broad and heavy around the cheeks and jaw, but his mouth is a little one that looks like it was made for a smaller man. He's no youngster—middle-aged."

"Suppose you tail him around for a day or two, Bob, and see what he's up to. Try to get a room or apartment in the neighborhood—a place that you can cover his front door from."

V

Vance Richmond's lean face lighted up as soon as I mentioned Ledwich's name to him.

"Yes!" he exclaimed. "He was a friend, or atleast an acquaintance, of Dr Estep's. I met him once—a large man with a peculiarly inadequate mouth. I dropped in to see the doctor one day, and Ledwich was in the office. Dr Estep introduced us."

"What do you know about him?"

"Nothing."

"Don't you know whether he was intimate with the doctor, or just a casual acquaintance?"

"No. For all I know, he might have been a friend, a patient, or almost anything. The doctor never spoke of him to me, and nothing passed between them while I was there that afternoon. I simply gave the doctor some information he had asked for and left. Why?"

"Dr Estep's first wife—after going to a lot of trouble to see that she wasn't followed—connected with Ledwich yesterday afternoon. And from what we can learn, he seems to be a crook of some sort."

"What would that indicate?"

"I'm not sure what it means, but I can do a lot of guessing. Ledwich knew both the doctor and the doctor's first wife; then it's not a bad bet that *she* knew where her husband was all the time. If she did, then it's another good bet that she was getting money from him right along. Can you check up his accounts and see whether he was passing out any money that can't be otherwise accounted for?"

The attorney shook his head.

"No, his accounts are in rather bad shape, carelessly kept. He must have had more than a little difficulty with his income tax statements."

"I see. To get back to my guesses: If she knew where he was all the time, and was getting money from him, then why did his first wife finally come to see her husband? Perhaps because—"

"I think I can help you there," Richmond interrupted. "A fortunate investment in lumber nearly doubled Dr Estep's wealth two or three months ago."

"That's it, then! She learned of it through Ledwich. She demanded, either through Ledwich, or by letter, a rather large share of it—more than the doctor was willing to give. When he refused, she came to see him in person, to demand the money under threat—we'll say—of instant exposure. He thought she was in earnest. Either he couldn't raise the money she demanded, or he was tired of leading a double life. Anyway, he thought it all over, and decided to commit suicide. This is all a guess, or a series of guesses—but it sounds reasonable to me."

"To me, too," the attorney said. "What are you going to do now?"

"I'm still having both of them shadowed—there's no other way of tackling them just now; I'm having the woman looked up in Louisville. But, you understand, I might dig up a whole flock of things on them, and when I got through still be as far as ever from finding the letter Dr Estep wrote before he died.

"There are plenty of reasons for thinking that the woman destroyed the letter—that would have been her wisest play. But if I can get enough on her, even at that, I can squeeze her into admitting that the letter was written, and that it said something about suicide—if it did. And that will be enough to spring your client. How is she today—any better?"

His thin face lost the animation that had come to it during our discussion of Ledwich, and became bleak.

"She went completely to pieces last night, and was removed to the hospital, where she should have been taken in the first place. To tell you the truth, if she isn't liberated soon, she won't need our help. I've done my utmost to have her released on bail—pulled every wire I know—but there's little likelihood of success in that direction.

"Knowing that she is a prisoner—charged with murdering her husband—is killing her. She isn't young, and she has always been subject to nervous disorders. The bare shock of her husband's death was enough to prostrate her—but now—You've *got* to get her out—and quickly!"

He was striding up and down his office, his voice throbbing with feeling. I left quickly.

VI

From the attorney's office, I returned to the agency, where I was told that Bob Teale had phoned in the address of a furnished apartment he had rented on Laguna Street. I hopped on a street car, and went up to take a look at it.

But I didn't get that far.

Walking down Laguna Street, after leaving the car, I spied Bob Teale coming toward me. Between Bob and me—also coming toward me—was a big man whom I recognized as Jacob Ledwich: a big man with a big red face around a tiny mouth.

I walked on down the street, passing both Ledwich and Bob, without paying any apparent attention to either. At the next corner I stopped to roll a cigarette, and steal a look at the pair.

And then I came to life!

Ledwich had stopped at a vestibule cigar stand up the street to make a purchase. Bob Teale, knowing his stuff, had passed him and was walking steadily up the street.

He was figuring that Ledwich had either come out for the purpose of buying cigars or cigarettes, and would return to his flat with them; or that after making his purchase the big man would proceed to the car line, where, in either event, Bob would wait.

But as Ledwich had stopped before the cigar stand, a man across the street had stepped suddenly into a doorway, and stood there, back in the shadows. This man, I now remembered, had been on the opposite side of the street from Bob and Ledwich, and walking in the same direction.

He, too, was following Ledwich.

By the time Ledwich had finished his business at the stand, Bob had reached Sutter Street, the nearest car line. Ledwich started up the street in that direction. The man in the doorway stepped out and went after him. I followed that one.

A ferry-bound car came down Sutter Street just as I reached the corner. Ledwich and I got aboard together. The mysterious stranger fumbled with a shoe-string several pavements from the corner until the car was moving again, and then he likewise made a dash for it.

He stood beside me on the rear platform, hiding behind a large man in overalls, past whose shoulder he now and then peeped at Ledwich. Bob had gone to the corner above, and was already seated when Ledwich, this amateur detective,—there was no doubting his amateur status,—and I got on the car.

I sized up the amateur while he strained his neck peeping at Ledwich. He was small, this sleuth, and scrawny and frail. His most noticeable feature was his nose—a limp organ that twitched nervously all the time. His clothes were old and shabby, and he himself was somewhere in his fifties.

After studying him for a few minutes, I decided that he hadn't tumbled to Bob Teale's part in the game. His attention had been too firmly fixed upon Ledwich, and the distance had been too short thus far for him to discover that Bob was also tailing the big man.

So when the seat beside Bob was vacated presently, I chucked my cigarette away, went into the car, and sat down, my back toward the little man with the twitching nose.

"Drop off after a couple of blocks and go back to the apartment. Don't shadow Ledwich any more until I tell you. Just watch his place. There's a bird following him, and I want to see what he's up to," I told Bob in an undertone.

He grunted that he understood, and, after a few minutes, left the car.

At Stockton Street, Ledwich got off, the man with the twitching nose behind him, and me in the rear. In that formation we paraded around town all afternoon.

The big man had business in a number of pool rooms, cigar stores, and soft drink parlors—most of which I knew for places where you can get a bet down on any horse that's running in North America, whether at Tanforan, Tijuana, or Timonium.

Just what Ledwich did in these places, I didn't learn. I was bringing up the rear of the procession, and my interest was centered upon the mysterious little stranger. He didn't enter any of the places behind Ledwich, but loitered in their neighborhoods until Ledwich reappeared.

He had a rather strenuous time of it—laboring mightily to keep out of Ledwich's sight, and only succeeding because we were downtown, where you can get away with almost any sort of shadowing. He certainly made a lot of work for himself, dodging here and there.

After a while, Ledwich shook him.

The big man came out of a cigar store with another man. They got into an automobile that was standing beside the curb, and drove away; leaving my man standing on the edge of the sidewalk twitching his nose in chagrin. There was a taxi stand just around the corner, but he either didn't know it or didn't have enough money to pay the fare.

I expected him to return to Laguna Street then, but he didn't. He led me down Kearny Street to Portsmouth Street, where he stretched himself out on the grass, face down, lit a black pipe, and lay looking dejectedly at the Stevenson monument, probably without seeing it.

I sprawled on a comfortable piece of sod some distance away—between a Chinese woman with two perfectly round children and an ancient Portuguese in a gaily checkered suit—and we let the afternoon go by.

When the sun had gone low enough for the ground to become chilly, the little man got up, shook himself, and went back up Kearny Street to a cheap lunch-room, where he ate meagerly. Then he entered a hotel a few doors away, took a key from the row of hooks, and vanished down a dark corridor.

Running through the register, I found that the key he had taken belonged to a room whose occupant was "John Boyd, St. Louis, Mo.," and that he had arrived the day before.

This hotel wasn't of the sort where it is safe to make inquiries, so I went down to the street again, and came to rest on the least conspicuous nearby corner.

Twilight came, and the street and shop lights were turned on. It got dark. The night traffic of Kearny Street went up and down past me: Filipino boys in their too-dapper clothes, bound for the inevitable black-jack game; gaudy women still heavy-eyed from their day's sleep; plainclothes men on their way to headquarters, to report before going off duty; Chinese going to or from Chinatown; sailors in pairs, looking for action of any sort; hungry people making for the Italian and French restaurants; worried people going into the bail bond broker's office on the corner to arrange for the release of friends and relatives whom the police had nabbed; Italians on their homeward journeys from work; odds and ends of furtive-looking citizens on various shady errands.

Midnight came, and no John Boyd, and I called it a day, and went home.

Before going to bed, I talked with Dick Foley over the wire. He said that Mrs Estep had done nothing of any importance all day, and had received neither mail nor phone calls. I told him to stop shadowing her until I solved John Boyd's game.

I was afraid Boyd might turn his attention to the woman, and I didn't want him to discover that she was being shadowed. I had already-instructed Bob Teale to simply watch Ledwich's flat—to see when he came in and went out, and with whom—and now I told Dick to do the same with the woman.

My guess on this Boyd person was that he and the woman were working together—that she had him watching Ledwich for her, so that the big man couldn't double-cross her. But that was only a guess—and I don't gamble too much on my guesses.

VII

The next morning I dressed myself up in an army shirt and shoes, an old faded cap, and a suit that wasn't downright ragged, but was shabby enough not to stand out too noticeably beside John Boyd's old clothes.

It was a little after nine o'clock when Boyd left his hotel and had breakfast at the grease-joint where he had eaten the night before. Then he went up to Laguna Street, picked himself a corner, and waited for Jacob Ledwich.

He did a lot of waiting. He waited all day; because Ledwich didn't show until after dark. But the little man was well-stocked with patience—I'll say that for him. He fidgeted, and stood on one foot and then the other, and even tried sitting on the curb for awhile, but he stuck it out.

I took it easy, myself. The furnished apartment Bob Teale had rented to watch Ledwich's flat from was a ground floor one, across the street, and just a little above the corner where Boyd waited. So we could watch him and the flat with one eye.

Bob and I sat and smoked and talked all day, taking turns watching the fidgeting man on the corner and Ledwich's door.

Night had just definitely settled when Ledwich came out and started up toward the car line. I slid out into the street, and our parade was under way again—Ledwich leading, Boyd following him, and we following *him*.

Half a block of this, and I got an idea!

I'm not what you'd call a brilliant thinker—such results as I get are usually the fruits of patience, industry, and unimaginative plugging, helped out now and then, maybe, by a little luck—but I do have my flashes of intelligence. And this was one of them.

Ledwich was about a block ahead of me; Boyd half that distance. Speeding up, I passed Boyd, and caught up with Ledwich. Then I slackened my pace so as to walk beside him, though with no appearance from the rear of having any interest in him.

"Jake," I said, without turning my head, "there's a guy following you!"

The big man almost spoiled my little scheme by stopping dead still, but he caught himself in time, and, taking his cue from me, kept walking.

"Who the hell are you?" he growled.

"Don't get funny!" I snapped back, still looking and walking ahead. "It ain't my funeral. But I was coming up the street when you came out, and I seen this guy duck behind a pole until you was past, and then follow you up."

That got him.

"You sure?"

"Sure! All you got to do to prove it is turn the next corner and wait."

I was two or three steps ahead of him by this time, I turned the corner, and halted, with my back against the brick building front. Ledwich took up the same position at my side.

"Want any help?" I grinned at him—a reckless sort of grin, unless my acting was poor.

"No."

His little lumpy mouth was set ugly, and his blue eyes were hard as pebbles.

I flicked the tail of my coat aside to show him the butt of my gun.

"Want to borrow the rod?" I asked.

"No."

He was trying to figure me out, and small wonder.

"Don't mind if I stick around to see the fun, do you?" I asked, mockingly.

There wasn't time for him to answer that. Boyd had quickened his steps, and now he came hurrying around the corner, his nose twitching like a tracking dog's.

Ledwich stepped into the middle of the sidewalk, so suddenly that the little man thudded into him with a grunt. For a moment they stared at each other, and there was recognition between them.

Ledwich shot one big hand out and clamped the other by a shoulder.

"What are you snooping around me for, you rat? Didn't I tell you to keep away from Frisco?"

"Aw, Jake!" Boyd begged. "I didn't mean no harm. I just thought that—"

Ledwich silenced him with a shake that clicked his mouth shut, and turned to me.

"A friend of mine," he sneered.

His eyes grew suspicious and hard again, and ran up and down me from cap to shoes.

"How'd you know my name?" he demanded.

"A famous man like you?" I asked, in burlesque astonishment.

"Never mind the comedy!" He took a threatening step toward me. "How'd you know my name?"

"None of your damned business," I snapped.

My attitude seemed to reassure him. His face became less suspicious.

"Well," he said slowly, "I owe you something for this trick, and—How are you fixed?"

"I have been dirtier." Dirty is Pacific Coast argot for prosperous.

He looked speculatively from me to Boyd, and back.

"Know 'The Circle'?" he asked me.

I nodded. The underworld calls "Wop" Healey's joint "The Circle."

"If you'll meet me there tomorrow night, maybe I can put a piece of change your way."

"Nothing stirring!" I shook my head with emphasis. "I ain't circulating that prominent these days."

A fat chance I'd have of meeting him there! "Wop" Healey and half his customers knew me as a detective. So there was nothing to do but to try to get the impression over that I was a crook who had reasons for wanting to keep away from the more notorious hang-outs for a while. Apparently it got over. He thought a while, and then gave me his Laguna Street number.

"Drop in this time tomorrow and maybe I'll have a proposition to make you—if you've got the guts."

"I'll think it over," I said noncommittally, and turned as if to go down the street.

"Just a minute," he called, and I faced him again. "What's your name?"

"Wisher," I said, "Shine, if you want a front one."

"Shine Wisher," he repeated. "I don't remember ever hearing it before."

It would have surprised me if he had—I had made it up only about fifteen minutes before.

"You needn't yell it," I said sourly, "so that everybody in the burg *will* remember hearing it."

And with that I left him, not at all dissatisfied with myself. By tipping him off to Boyd, I had put him under obligations to me, and had led him to accept me, at least tentatively, as a fellow crook. And by making no apparent effort to gain his good graces, I had strengthened my hand that much more.

I had a date with him for the next day, when I was to be given a chance to earn—illegally, no doubt—"a piece of change."

There was a chance that this proposition he had in view for me had nothing to do with the Estep affair, but then again it might; and whether it did or not, I had my entering wedge at least a little way into Jake Ledwich's business.

I strolled around for about half an hour, and then went back to Bob Teale's apartment.

"Ledwich come back?"

"Yes," Bob said, "with that little guy of yours. They went in about half an hour ago."

"Good! Haven't seen a woman go in?"

"No."

I expected to see the first Mrs Estep arrive sometime during the evening, but she didn't. Bob and I sat around and talked and watched Ledwich's doorway, and the hours passed.

At one o'clock Ledwich came out alone.

"I'm going to tail him, just for luck," Bob said, and caught up his cap.

Ledwich vanished around a corner, and then Bob passed out of sight behind him.

Five minutes later Bob was with me again.

"He's getting his machine out of the garage."

I jumped for the telephone and put in a rush order for a fast touring car.

Bob, at the window, called out, "Here he is!"

I joined Bob in time to see Ledwich going into his vestibule. His car stood in front of the house. A very few minutes, and Boyd and Ledwich came out together. Boyd was leaning heavily on Ledwich, who was supporting the little man with an arm across his back. We couldn't see their faces in the dark, but the little man was plainly either sick, drunk, or drugged!

Ledwich helped his companion into the touring car. The red tail-lights laughed back at us for a few blocks, and then disappeared. The automobile I had ordered arrived twenty minutes later, so we sent it back unused.

At a little after three that morning, Ledwich, alone and afoot, returned from the direction of his garage. He had been gone exactly two hours.

VIII

Neither Bob nor I went home that night, but slept in the Laguna Street apartment.

Bob went down to the corner grocer's to get what we needed for breakfast in the morning, and he brought a morning paper back with him.

I cooked breakfast while he divided his attention between Ledwich's front door and the newspaper.

"Hey!" he called suddenly, "Look here!"

I ran out of the kitchen with a handful of bacon.

"What is it?"

"Listen! 'Park murder mystery!'" he read. "'Early this morning the body of an unidentified man was found near a driveway in Golden Gate Park. His neck had been broken, according to the police; who say that the absence of any considerable bruises on the body, as well as the orderly condition of the clothes and the ground nearby, show that he did not come to his death through falling, or being struck by an automobile. It is believed that he was killed and then carried to the Park in an automobile, to be left there.' "

"Boyd!" I said.

"I bet you!" Bob agreed.

And at the morgue a very little while later, we learned that we were correct. The dead man was John Boyd.

"He was dead when Ledwich brought him out of the house," Bob said.

I nodded.

"He was! He was a little man, and it wouldn't have been much of a stunt for a big bruiser like Ledwich to have dragged him along with one arm the short distance from the door to the curb, pretending to be holding him up, like you do with a drunk. Let's go over to the Hall of Justice and see what the police have got on it—if anything."

At the detective bureau we hunted up O'Gar, the detective-sergeant in charge of the Homicide Detail, and a good man to work with.

"This dead man found in the park," I asked, "know anything about him?"

O'Gar pushed back his village constable's hat—a big black hat with a floppy brim that belongs in vaudeville—scratched his bullet-head, and scowled at me as if he thought I had a joke up my sleeve.

"Not a damned thing except that he's dead!" he said at last.

"How 'd you like to know who he was last seen with?"

"It wouldn't hinder me any in finding out who bumped him off, and that's a fact."

"How do you like the sound of this?" I asked. "His name was John Boyd and he was living at a hotel down in the next block. The last person he was seen with was a guy who is tied up with Dr Estep's first wife. You know—the Dr Estep whose second wife is the woman you people are trying to prove a murder on. Does that sound interesting?"

"It does," he said. "Where do we go first?"

"This Ledwich—he's the fellow who was last seen with Boyd—is going to be a hard bird to shake down. We better try to crack the woman first—the first Mrs Estep. There's a chance that Boyd was a pal of hers, and in that case when she finds out that Ledwich rubbed him out, she may open up and spill the works to us.

"On the other hand, if she and Ledwich are stacked up against Boyd together, then we might as well get her safely placed before we tie into him. I don't want to pull him before night, anyway. I got a date with him, and I want to try to rope him first."

Bob Teale made for the door.

"I'm going up and keep my eye on him until you're ready for him," he called over his shoulder.

"Good," I said. "Don't let him get out of town on us. If he tries to blow have him chucked in the can."

In the lobby of the Montgomery Hotel, O'Gar and I talked to Dick Foley first. He told us that the woman was still in her room—had had her breakfast sent up. She had received neither letters, telegrams, or phone calls since we began to watch her.

I got hold of Stacey again.

"We're going up to talk to this Estep woman, and maybe we'll take her away with us. Will you send up a maid to find out whether she's up and dressed yet? We don't want to announce ourselves ahead of time, and we don't want to burst in on her while she's in bed, or only partly dressed."

He kept us waiting about fifteen minutes, and then told us that Mrs Estep was up and dressed.

We went up to her room, taking the maid with us.

The maid rapped on the door.

"What is it?" an irritable voice demanded.

"The maid; I want to—"

The key turned on the inside, and an angry Mrs Estep jerked the door open. O'Gar and I advanced, O'Gar flashing his "buzzer."

"From headquarters," he said. "We want to talk to you."

O'Gar's foot was where she couldn't slam the door on us, and we were both walking ahead, so there was nothing for her to do but to retreat into the room, admitting us—which she did with no pretense of graciousness.

We closed the door, and then I threw our big load at her.

"Mrs Estep, why did Jake Ledwich kill John Boyd?"

The expressions ran over her face like this: Alarm at Ledwich's name, fear at the word "kill," but the name John Boyd brought only bewilderment.

"Why did what?" she stammered meaninglessly, to gain time.

"Exactly," I said. "Why did Jake kill him last night in his flat, and then take him in the park and leave him?"

Another set of expressions: Increased bewilderment until I had almost finished the sentence, and then the sudden understanding of something, followed by the inevitable groping for poise. These things weren't as plain as billboards, you understand, but they were there to be read by anyone who had ever played poker—either with cards or people.

What I got out of them was that Boyd hadn't been working with or for her, and that, though she knew Ledwich had killed somebody at some time, it wasn't Boyd and it wasn't last night. Who, then? And when? Dr Estep? Hardly! There wasn't a chance in the world that—if he had been murdered—anybody except his wife had done it—his second wife. No possible reading of the evidence could bring any other answer.

Who, then, had Ledwich killed before Boyd? Was he a wholesale murderer?

These things are flitting through my head in flashes and odd scraps while Mrs Estep is saying:

"This is absurd! The idea of your coming up here and—"

She talked for five minutes straight, the words fairly sizzling from between her hard lips; but the words themselves didn't mean anything. She was talking for time—talking while she tried to hit upon the safest attitude to assume.

And before we could head her off, she had hit upon it—silence!

We got not another word out of her; and that is the only way in the world to beat the grilling game. The average suspect tries to talk himself out of being arrested; and it doesn't matter how shrewd a man is, or how good a liar, if he'll talk to you, and you play your cards right, you can hook him—can make him help you convict him. But if he won't talk you can't do a thing with him.

And that's how it was with this woman. She refused to pay any attention to our questions—she wouldn't speak, nod, grunt, or wave an arm in reply. She gave us a fine assortment of facial expressions, true enough, but we wanted verbal information—and we got none.

We weren't easily licked, however. Three beautiful hours of it we gave her without rest. We stormed, cajoled, threatened, and at times I think we danced; but it was no go. So in the end we took her away with us. We didn't have anything on her, but we couldn't afford to have her running around loose until we nailed Ledwich.

At the Hall of Justice we didn't book her; but simply held her as a material witness, putting her in an office with a matron and one of O'Gar's men, who were to see what they could do with her while we went after Ledwich. We had had her frisked as soon as she reached the Hall, of course; and, as we expected, she hadn't a thing of importance on her.

O'Gar and I went back to the Montgomery and gave her room a thorough overhauling—and found nothing.

"Are you sure you know what you're talking about?" the detective-sergeant asked as we left the hotel. "It's going to be a pretty joke on somebody if you're mistaken."

I let that go by without an answer.

"I'll meet you at 6:30," I said, "and we'll go up against Ledwich."

He grunted an approval, and I set out for Vance Richmond's office.

IX

The attorney sprang up from his desk as soon as his stenographer admitted me. His face was leaner and grayer than ever; its lines had deepened, and there was a hollowness around his eyes.

"You've *got* to do something!" he cried huskily. "I have just come from the hospital. Mrs Estep is on the point of death! A day more of this—two days at the most—and she will—"

I interrupted him, and swiftly gave him an account of the day's happenings, and what I expected, or hoped, to make out of them. But he received the news without brightening, and shook his head hopelessly.

"But don't you see," he exclaimed when I had finished, "that that won't do? I know you can find proof of her innocence in time. I'm not complaining—you've done all that could be expected, and more! But all that's no good! I've got to have—well—a miracle, perhaps.

"Suppose that you do finally get the truth out of Ledwich and the first Mrs Estep or it comes out during their trials for Boyd's murder? Or that you even get to the bottom of the matter in three or four days? That will be too late! If I can go to Mrs Estep and tell her she's free now, she may pull herself together, and come through. But another day of imprisonment—two days, or perhaps even two hours—and she won't need anybody to clear her. Death will have done it! I tell you, she's—"

I left Vance Richmond abruptly again. This lawyer was bound upon getting me worked up; and I like my jobs to be simply jobs—emotions are nuisances during business hours.

X

At a quarter to seven that evening, while O'Gar remained down the street, I rang Jacob Ledwich's bell. As I had stayed with Bob

Teale in our apartment the previous night, I was still wearing the clothes in which I had made Ledwich's acquaintance as Shine Wisher.

Ledwich opened the door.

"Hello, Wisher!" he said without enthusiasm, and led me upstairs.

His flat consisted of four rooms, I found, running the full length and half the breadth of the building, with both front and rear exits. It was furnished with the ordinary none-too-spotless appointments of the typical moderately priced furnished flat—alike the world over.

In his front room we sat down and talked and smoked and sized one another up. He seemed a little nervous. I thought he would have been just as well satisfied if I had forgotten to show up.

"About this job you mentioned?" I asked presently.

"Sorry," he said, moistening his little lumpy mouth, "but it's all off." And then he added, obviously as an afterthought, "for the present, at least."

I guessed from that that my job was to have taken care of Boyd—but Boyd had been taken care of for good.

He brought out some whisky after a while, and we talked over it for some time, to no purpose whatever. He was trying not to appear too anxious to get rid of me, and I was cautiously feeling him out.

Piecing together things he let fall here and there, I came to the conclusion that he was a former con man who had fallen into an easier game of late years. That was in line, too, with what "Porky" Grout had told Bob Teale.

I talked about myself with the evasiveness that would have been natural to a crook in my situation; and made one or two carefully planned slips that would lead him to believe that I had been tied up with the "Jimmy the Riveter" holdup mob, most of whom were doing long hitches at Walla Walla then.

He offered to lend me enough money to tide me over until I could get on my feet again. I told him I didn't need chicken feed so much as a chance to pick up some real jack.

The evening was going along, and we were getting nowhere.

"Jake," I said casually—outwardly casual, that is, "you took a big chance putting that guy out of the way like you did last night."

I meant to stir things up, and I succeeded.

His face went crazy.

A gun came out of his coat.

Firing from my pocket, I shot it out of his hand.

"Now behave!" I ordered.

He sat rubbing his benumbed hand and staring with wide eyes at the smouldering hole in my coat.

Looks like a great stunt—this shooting a gun out of a man's hand, but it's a thing that happens now and then. A man who is a fair shot (and that is exactly what I am—no more, no less), naturally and automatically shoots pretty close to the spot upon which his eyes are focused. When a man goes for his gun in front of you, you shoot at *him*—not at any particular part of him. There isn't time for that—you shoot at *him*. However, you are more than likely to be looking at his gun, and in that case it isn't altogether surprising if your bullet should hit his gun—as mine had done. But it looks impressive.

I beat out the fire around the bullet-hole in my coat, crossed the room to where his revolver had been knocked, and picked it up. I started to eject the bullets from it, but, instead, I snapped it shut again and stuck it in my pocket. Then I returned to my chair, opposite him.

"A man oughtn't to act like that," I kidded him, "he's likely to hurt somebody."

His little mouth curled up at me.

"An elbow, huh?" putting all the contempt he could in his voice; and somehow any synonym for detective seems able to hold a lot of contempt.

I might have tried to talk myself back into the Wisher role. It could have been done, but I doubted that it would be worth it; so I nodded my confession.

His brain was working now, and the passion left his face, while he sat rubbing his right hand, and his little mouth and eyes began to screw themselves up calculatingly.

I kept quiet, waiting to see what the outcome of his thinking would be. I knew he was trying to figure out just what my place in this game was. Since, to his knowledge, I had come into it no later than the previous evening, then the Boyd murder hadn't brought me in. That would leave the Estep affair—unless he was tied up in a lot of other crooked stuff that I didn't know anything about.

"You're not a city dick, are you?" he asked finally; and his voice was on the verge of friendliness now: the voice of one who wants to persuade you of something, or sell you something.

The truth, I thought, wouldn't hurt.

"No," I said, "I'm with the Continental."

He hitched his chair a little closer to the muzzle of my automatic.

"What are you after, then? Where do you come in on it?"

I tried the truth again.

"The second Mrs Estep. She didn't kill her husband."

"You're trying to dig up enough dope to spring her?"

"Yes."

I waved him back as he tried to hitch his chair still nearer.

"How do you expect to do it?" he asked, his voice going lower and more confidential with each word.

I took still another flier at the truth.

"He wrote a letter before he died."

"Well?"

But I called a halt for the time.

"Just that," I said.

He leaned back in his chair, and his eyes and mouth grew small in thought again.

"What's your interest in the man who died last night?" he asked slowly.

"It's something on you," I said, truthfully again. "It doesn't do the second Mrs Estep any direct good, maybe; but you and the first wife are stacked up together against her. Anything, therefore, that hurts you two will help her, somehow. I admit I'm wandering around in the dark; but I'm going ahead wherever I see a point of light—and I'll come through to daylight in the end. Nailing you for Boyd's murder is one point of light."

He leaned forward suddenly, his eyes and mouth popping open as far as they would go.

"You'll come out all right," he said very softly, "if you use a little judgment."

"What's that supposed to mean?"

"Do you think," he asked, still very softly, "that you can nail me for Boyd's murder—that you can convict me of murder?"

"I do."

But I wasn't any too sure. In the first place, though we were morally certain of it, neither Bob Teale nor I could swear that the man who had got in the machine with Ledwich was John Boyd.

We knew it was, of course, but the point is that it had been too dark for us to see his face. And, again, in the dark, we had thought him alive; it wasn't until later that we knew he had been dead when he came down the steps.

Little things, those, but a private detective on the witness stand—unless he is absolutely sure of every detail—has an unpleasant and ineffectual time of it.

"I do," I repeated, thinking these things over, "and I'm satisfied to go to the bat with what I've got on you and what I can collect between now and the time you and your accomplice go to trial."

"Accomplice?" he said, not very surprised. "That would be Edna. I suppose you've already grabbed her?"

"Yes."

He laughed.

"You'll have one sweet time getting anything out of her. In the first place, she doesn't know much, and in the second—well, I suppose you've tried, and have found out what a helpful sort she is! So don't try the old gag of pretending that she has talked!"

"I'm not pretending anything."

Silence between us for a few seconds, and then—"I'm going to make you a proposition," he said. "You can take it or leave it. The note Dr Estep wrote before he died was to me, and it is positive proof that he committed suicide. Give me a chance to get away—just a chance—a half-hour start—and I'll give you my word of honor to send you the letter."

"I know I can trust you," I said sarcastically.

"I'll trust you, then!" he shot back at me. "I'll turn the note over to you if you'll give me your word that I'm to have half an hour's start."

"For what?" I demanded. "Why shouldn't I take both you and the note?"

"If you can get them! But do I look like the kind of sap who would leave the note where it would be found? Do you think it's here in the room maybe?"

I didn't, but neither did I think that because he had hidden it, it couldn't be found.

"I can't think of any reason why I should bargain with you," I told him. "I've got you cold, and that's enough."

"If I can show you that your only chance of freeing the second Mrs Estep is through my voluntary assistance, will you bargain with me?"

"Maybe—I'll listen to your persuasion, anyway."

"All right," he said, "I'm going to come clean with you. But most of the things I'm going to tell you can't be proven in court without my help; and if you turn my offer down I'll have plenty of evidence to convince the jury that these things are all false, that I never said them, and that you are trying to frame me."

That part was plausible enough. I've testified before juries all the way from the City of Washington to the State of Washington, and I've never seen one yet that wasn't anxious to believe that a private detective is a double-crossing specialist who goes around with a cold deck in one pocket, a complete forger's outfit in another, and who counts that day lost in which he railroads no innocent to the hoosegow.

XI

"There was once a young doctor in a town a long way from here," Ledwich began. "He got mixed up in a scandal—a pretty rotten one—and escaped the pen only by the skin of his teeth. The state medical board revoked his license.

"In a large city not far away, this young doc, one night when he was drunk,—as he usually was in those days,—told his troubles to a man he had met in a dive. The friend was a resourceful sort; and he offered, for a price, to fix the doc up with a fake diploma, so he could set up in practice in some other state.

"The young doctor took him up, and the friend got the diploma for him. The doc was the man you know as Dr Estep, and I was the friend. The real Dr Estep was found dead in the park this morning!"

That was news—if true!

"You see," the big man went on, "when I offered to get the phoney diploma for the young doc—whose real name doesn't matter—I had in mind a forged one. Nowadays they're easy to get—there's a regular business in them,—but twenty-five years ago, while you could manage it, they were hard to get. While I was trying to get one, I ran across a woman I used to work with—Edna Fife. That's the woman you know as the first Mrs Estep.

"Edna had married a doctor—the real Dr Humbert Estep. He was a hell of a doctor, though; and after starving with him in Philadelphia for a couple of years, she made him close up his office, and she went back to the bunko game, taking him with her. She was good at it, I'm telling you—a real cleaned—and, keeping him under her thumb all the time, she made him a pretty good worker himself.

"It was shortly after that that I met her, and when she told me all this, I offered to buy her husband's medical diploma and other credentials. I don't know whether he wanted to sell them or not—but he did what she told him, and I got the papers.

"I turned them over to the young doc, who came to San Francisco and opened an office under the name of Humbert Estep. The real Esteps promised not to use that name any more—not much of an inconvenience for them, as they changed names every time they changed addresses.

"I kept in touch with the young doctor, of course, getting my regular rake-off from him. I had him by the neck, and I wasn't foolish enough to pass up any easy money. After a year or so, I learned that he had pulled himself together and was making good. So I jumped on a train and came to San Francisco. He was doing fine; so I camped here, where I could keep my eye on him and watch out for my own interests.

"He got married about then, and, between his practice and his investments, he began to accumulate a roll. But he tightened up on me—damn him! He wouldn't be bled. I got a regular percentage of what he made, and that was all.

"For nearly twenty-five years I got it—but not a nickel over the percentage. He knew I wouldn't kill the goose that laid the golden eggs, so no matter how much I threatened to expose him, he sat tight, and I couldn't budge him. I got my regular cut, and not a nickel more.

"That went along, as I say, for years. I was getting a living out of him, but I wan't getting any big money. A few months ago I learned that he had cleaned up heavily in a lumber deal so I made up my mind to take him for what he had.

"During all these years I had got to know the doc pretty well. You do when you're bleeding a man—you get a pretty fair idea of what goes on in his head, and what he's most likely to do if certain things should happen. So I knew the doc pretty well.

"I knew for instance, that he had never told his wife the truth about his past; that he had stalled her with some lie about being born in West Virginia. That was fine—for me! Then I knew that he kept a gun in his desk, and I knew why. It was kept there for the purpose of killing himself if the truth ever came out about his diploma. He figured that if, at the first hint of exposure, he wiped himself out, the authorities, out of respect for the good reputation he had built up, would hush things up.

"And his wife—even if she herself learned the truth—would be spared the shame of a public scandal. I can't see myself dying just to spare some woman's feeling, but the doc was a funny guy in some ways—and he was nutty about his wife.

"That's the way I had him figured out, and that's the way things turned out.

"My plan might sound complicated, but it was simple enough. I got hold of the real Esteps—it took a lot of hunting, but I found them at last. I brought the woman to San Francisco, and told the man to stay away.

"Everything would have gone fine if he had done what I told him; but he was afraid that Edna and I were going to double-cross him, so he came here to keep an eye on us. But I didn't know that until you put the finger on him for me.

"I brought Edna here and, without telling her any more than she had to know; drilled her until she was letter-perfect in her part.

"A couple days before she came I had gone to see the doc, and had demanded a hundred thousand cool smacks. He laughed at me, and I left, pretending to be as hot as hell.

"As soon as Edna arrived, I sent her to call on him. She asked him to perform an illegal operation on her daughter. He, of course, refused. Then she pleaded with him, loud enough for the nurse or whoever else was in the reception-room to hear. And when she raised her voice she was careful to stick to words that could be interpreted the way we wanted them to. She ran off her end to perfection, leaving in tears.

"Then I sprung my other trick! I had a fellow—a fellow who's a whiz at that kind of stuff—make me a plate: an imitation of newspaper printing. It was all worded like the real article, and said that the state authorities were investigating information that a prominent surgeon in San Francisco was practicing under a license secured by false credentials. This plate measured four and an eighth by six and three-quarter inches. If you'll look at the first inside page of the *Evening Times* any day in the week you'll see a photograph just that size.

"On the day after Edna's call, I bought a copy of the first edition of the *Times*—on the street at ten in the morning. I had this scratche friend of mine remove the photograph with acid, and print this fake article in its place.

"That evening I substituted a 'home edition' outer sheet for the one that had come with the paper we had cooked up, and made a switch as soon as the doc's newsboy made his delivery. There was nothing to that part of it. The kid just tossed the paper into the vestibule. It's simply a case of duck into the doorway, trade papers, and go on, leaving the loaded one for the doc to read."

I was trying not to look too interested, but my ears were cocked for every word. At the start, I had been prepared for a string of lies. But I knew now that he was telling me the truth! Every syllable was a boast; he was half-drunk with appreciation of his own cleverness—the cleverness with which he had planned and carried out his program of treachery and murder.

I knew that he was telling the truth, and I suspected that he was telling more of it than he had intended. He was fairly bloated with vanity—the vanity that fills the crook almost invariably after a little success, and makes him ripe for the pen.

His eyes glistened, and his little mouth smiled triumphantly around the words that continued to roll out of it.

"The doc read the paper, all right—and shot himself. But first he wrote and mailed a note—to me. I didn't figure on his wife's being accused of killing him. That was plain luck.

"I figured that the fake piece in the paper would be overlooked in the excitement. Edna would then go forward, claiming to be his first wife; and his shooting himself after her first call, with what the nurse had overheard, would make his death seem a confession that Edna *was* his wife.

"I was sure that she would stand up under any sort of an investigation. Nobody knew anything about the doc's real past; except what he had told them, which would be found false.

"Edna had really married a Dr Humbert Estep in Philadelphia in '96; and the twenty-seven years that had passed since then would do a lot to hide the fact that that Dr Humbert Estep wasn't this Dr Humbert Estep.

"All I wanted to do was convince the doc's real wife and her lawyers that she wasn't really his wife at all. And we did that! Everybody took it for granted that Edna was the legal wife.

"The next play would have been for Edna and the real wife to have reached some sort of an agreement about the estate, whereby Edna would have got the bulk—or at least half—of it; and nothing would have been made public.

"If worst came to worst, we were prepared to go to court. We were sitting pretty! But I'd have been satisfied with half the estate. It would have come to a few hundred thousand at the least, and that would have been plenty for me—even deducting the twenty thousand I had promised Edna.

"But when the police grabbed the doc's wife and charged her with his murder, I saw my way into the whole roll. All I had to do was sit tight and wait until they convicted her. Then the court would turn the entire pile over to Edna.

"I had the only evidence that would free the doc's wife: the note he had written me. But I couldn't—even if I had wanted to—have turned it in without exposing my hand. When he read that fake piece in the paper, he tore it out, wrote his message to me across the face of it, and sent it to me. So the note is a dead give-away. However, I didn't have any intention of publishing it, anyhow.

"Up to this point everything had gone like a dream. All I had to do was wait until it was time to cash in on my brains. And that's the time that the real Humbert Estep picked out to mess up the works.

"He shaved his mustache off, put on some old clothes, and came snooping around to see that Edna and I didn't run out on him. As if he could have stopped us! After you put the finger on him for me, I brought him up here.

"I intended salving him along until I could find a place to keep him until all the cards had been played. That's what I was going to hire you for—to take care of him.

"But we got to talking, and wrangling, and I had to knock him down. He didn't get up, and I found that he was dead. His neck was broken. There was nothing to do but take him out to the park and leave him.

"I didn't tell Edna. She didn't have a lot of use for him, as far as I could see, but you can't tell how women will take things. Anyhow, she'll stick, now that it's done. She's on the up and up all the time. And if she should talk, she can't do a lot of damage. She only knows her own part of the lay.

"All this long-winded story is so you'll know just exactly what you're up against. Maybe you think you can dig up the proof of these things I have told you. You can this far. You can prove that Edna wasn't the doc's wife. You can prove that I've been blackmailing him. But you can't prove that the doc's wife didn't *believe* that Edna was his real wife! It's her word against Edna's and mine.

"We'll swear that we had convinced her of it, which will give her a motive. You can't prove that the phoney news article I told you about ever existed. It'll sound like a hop-head's dream to a jury.

"You can't tie last night's murder on me—I've got an alibi that will knock your hat off! I can prove that I left here with a friend of mine who was drunk, and that I took him to his hotel and put him to bed, with the help of a night clerk and a bellboy. And what have you got against that? The word of two private detectives. Who'll believe you?

"You can convict me of conspiracy to defraud, or something—maybe. But, regardless of that, you can't free Mrs Estep without my help.

"Turn me loose and I'll give you the letter the doc wrote me. It's the goods, right enough! In his own handwriting, written across the face of the fake newspaper story—which ought to fit the torn place in the paper that the police are supposed to be holding—and he wrote that he was going to kill himself, in words almost that plain."

That would turn the trick—there was no doubt of it. And I believed Ledwich's story. The more I thought it over the better I liked it. It fit into the facts everywhere. But I wasn't enthusiastic about giving this big crook his liberty.

"Don't make me laugh!" I said. "I'm going to put you away and free Mrs Estep—both."

"Go ahead and try it! You're up against it without the letter; and you don't think a man with brains enough to plan a job like this one would be foolish enough to leave the note where it could be found, do you?"

I wasn't especially impressed with the difficulty of convicting this Ledwich and freeing the dead man's widow. His scheme—that cold-blooded zigzag of treachery for everybody he had dealt with, including his latest accomplice, Edna Estep—wasn't as airtight as he thought it. A week in which to run out a few lines in the East, and—But a week was just what I didn't have!

Vance Richmond's words were running through my head: "But another day of imprisonment—two days, or perhaps even two hours—and she won't need anybody to clear her. Death will have done it!"

If I was going to do Mrs Estep any good, I had to move quick. Law or no law, her life was in my fat hands. This man before me—his eyes bright and hopeful now and his mouth anxiously pursed—was thief, blackmailer, double-crosser, and at least twice a murderer. I hated to let him walk out. But there was the woman dying in a hospital....

XII

Keeping my eye on Ledwich, I went to the telephone, and got Vance Richmond on the wire at his residence.

"How is Mrs Estep?" I asked.

"Weaker! I talked with the doctor half an hour ago, and he says—"

I cut in on him; I didn't want to listen to the details.

"Get over to the hospital, and be where I can reach you by phone. I may have news for you before the night is over."

"What—Is there a chance? Are you—"

I didn't promise him anything. I hung up the receiver and spoke to Ledwich. "I'll do this much for you. Slip me the note, and I'll give you your gun and put you out the back door. There's a bull on the corner out front, and I can't take you past him."

He was on his feet, beaming.

"Your word on it?" he demanded.

"Yes—get going!"

He went past me to the phone, gave a number (which I made a note of) and then spoke hurriedly into the instrument.

"This is Shuler. Put a boy in a taxi with that envelope I gave you to hold for me, and send him out here right away."

He gave his address, said "Yes" twice and hung up.

There was nothing surprising about his unquestioning acceptance of my word. He couldn't afford to doubt that I'd play fair with him. And, also, all successful bunko men come in time to believe that the world—except for themselves—is populated by a race of human sheep who may be trusted to conduct themselves with true sheep-like docility.

Ten minutes later the door-bell rang. We answered it together, and Ledwich took a large envelope from a messenger boy, while I memorized the number on the boy's cap. Then we went back to the front room.

Ledwich slit the envelope and passed its contents to me: a piece of rough-torn newspaper. Across the face of the fake article he had told me about was written a message in a jerky hand.

> "I wouldn't have suspected you, Ledwich, of such profound stupidity. My last thought will be—this bullet that ends my life also ends your years of leisure. You'll have to go to work now.
>
> ESTEP."

The doctor had died game!

I took the envelope from the big man, put the death note in it, and put them in my pocket. Then I went to a front window, flattening a cheek against the glass until I could see O'Gar, dimly outlined in the night, patiently standing where I had left him hours before.

"The city dick is still on the corner," I told Ledwich. "Here's your gat"—holding out the gun I had shot from his fingers a little while back—"take it, and blow through the back door. Remember, that's all I'm offering you—the gun and a fair start. If you play square with me, I'll not do anything to help find you—unless I have to keep myself in the clear."

"Fair enough!"

He grabbed the gun, broke it to see that it was still loaded, and wheeled toward the rear of the flat. At the door he pulled up, hesitated, and faced me again. I kept him covered with my automatic.

"Will you do me one favor I didn't put in the bargain?" he asked.

"What is it?"

"That note of the doc's is in an envelope with my handwriting and maybe my finger-prints on it. Let me put it in a fresh envelope, will you? I don't want to leave any broader trail behind than I have to."

With my left hand—my right being busy with the gun—I fumbled for the envelope and tossed it to him. He took a plain envelope from the table, wiped it carefully with his handkerchief, put the note in it, taking care not to touch it with the balls of his fingers, and passed it back to me; and I put it in my pocket.

I had a hard time to keep from grinning in his face.

That fumbling with the handkerchief told me that the envelope in my pocket was empty, that the death-note was in

Ledwich's possession—though I hadn't seen it pass there. He had worked one of his bunko tricks upon me.

"Beat it!" I snapped, to keep from laughing in his face.

He spun on his heel. His feet pounded against the floor. A door slammed in the rear.

I tore into the envelope he had given me. I needed to be sure he had double-crossed me.

The envelope was empty.

Our agreement was wiped out.

I sprang to the front window, threw it wide open, and leaned out. O'Gar saw me immediately—clearer than I could see him. I swung my arm in a wide gesture toward the rear of the house. O'Gar set out for the alley on the run. I dashed back through Ledwich's flat to the kitchen, and stuck my head out of an already open window.

I could see Ledwich against the white-washed fence—throwing the back gate open, plunging through it into the alley.

O'Gar's squat bulk appeared under a light at the end of the alley.

Ledwich's revolver was in his hand. O'Gar's wasn't—not quite.

Ledwich's gun swung up—the hammer clicked.

O'Gar's gun coughed fire.

Ledwich fell with a slow revolving motion over against the white fence, gasped once or twice, and went down in a pile.

I walked slowly down the stairs to join O'Gar; slowly, because it isn't a nice thing to look at a man you've deliberately sent to his death. Not even if it's the surest way of saving an innocent life, and if the man who dies is a Jake Ledwich—altogether treacherous.

"How come?" O'Gar asked, when I came into the alley, where he stood looking down at the dead man.

"He got out on me," I said simply.

"He must've."

I stooped and searched the dead man's pockets until I found the suicide note, still crumpled in the handkerchief. O'Gar was examining the dead man's revolver.

"Look it!" he exclaimed. "Maybe this ain't my lucky day! He snapped at me once, and his gun missed fire. No wonder! Somebody must've been using an ax on it—the firing pin's broke clean off!"

"Is that so?" I asked; just as if I hadn't discovered, when I first picked the revolver up, that the bullet which had knocked it out of Ledwich's hand had made it harmless.

BLACK MASK, MARCH 1, 1924

FROM THE AUTHOR OF "ZIGZAGS OF TREACHERY"

I'll have another story riding your way in a day or two; one for the customers who don't like their sleuths to do too much brain-work.

The four rules for shadowing that I gave in "Zigzags" are the first and last words on the subject. There are no other tricks to learn. Follow them, and, once you get the hang of it, shadowing is the easiest of detective work, except, perhaps, to an extremely nervous man. You simply saunter along somewhere within sight of your subject; and, barring bad breaks, the only thing that can make you lose him is over-anxiety on your own part.

Even a clever criminal may be shadowed for weeks without suspecting it. I know one operative who shadowed a forger—a wily old hand—for more than three months without arousing his suspicion. I myself trailed one for six weeks, riding trains and making half a dozen small towns with him; and I'm not exactly inconspicuous—standing an inch or so over six feet.

Another thing: a detective may shadow a man for days and in the end have but the haziest idea of the man's features. Tricks of carriage, ways of wearing clothes, general outline, individual mannerisms—all as seen from the rear—are much more important to the shadow than faces. They can be recognized at a greater distance, and do not necessitate getting in front of his subject at any time.

Back—and it's only a couple years back—in the days before I decided that there was more fun in writing about man hunting than in that hunting, I wasn't especially fond of shadowing, though I had plenty of it to do. But I worked under one superintendent who needed only the flimsiest of excuses to desert his desk and get out on the street behind some suspect.

Sincerely,
DASHIELL HAMMETT
San Francisco, Cal.

9

ONE HOUR

BLACK MASK, APRIL 1, 1924

Like all of Mr Hammett's detective stories, this tale starts with a very ordinary police case, and just as you think you have it all figured out, it takes several unexpected turns and ends up with a bang.

I

"This is Mr Chrostwaite," Vance Richmond said.

Chrostwaite, wedged between the arms of one of the attorney's large chairs, grunted what was perhaps meant for an acknowledgment of the introduction. I grunted back at him, and found myself a chair.

He was a big balloon of a man—this Chrostwaite—in a green plaid suit that didn't make him look any smaller than he was. His tie was a gaudy thing, mostly of yellow, with a big diamond set in the center of it, and there were more stones on his pudgy hands. Spongy fat blurred his features, making it impossible for his round purplish face to ever hold any other expression than the discontented hoggishness that was habitual to it. He reeked of gin.

"Mr Chrostwaite is the Pacific Coast agent for the Mutual Fire Extinguisher Manufacturing Company," Vance Richmond began, as soon as I had got myself seated. "His office is on Kearny Street, near California. Yesterday, at about two-forty-five in the afternoon, he went to his office, leaving his machine—a Hudson touring car—standing in front, with the engine running. Ten minutes later, he came out. The car was gone."

I looked at Chrostwaite. He was looking at his fat knees, showing not the least interest in what his attorney was saying. I looked quickly back at Vance Richmond; his clean gray face and lean figure were downright beautiful beside his bloated client.

"A man named Newhouse," the lawyer was saying, "who was the proprietor of a printing establishment on California Street, just around the corner from Mr Chrostwaite's office, was run down and killed by Mr Chrostwaite's car at the corner of Clay and Kearny Streets, five minutes after Mr Chrostwaite had left the car to go into his office. The police found the car shortly afterward, only a block away from the scene of the accident—on Montgomery near Clay.

"The thing is fairly obvious. Some one stole the car immediately after Mr Chrostwaite left it; and in driving rapidly away, ran down Newhouse; and then, in fright, abandoned the car. But here is Mr Chrostwaite's position; three nights ago, while driving perhaps a little recklessly out—"

"Drunk," Chrostwaite said, not looking up from his plaid knees; and though his voice was hoarse, husky—it was the hoarseness of a whisky-burnt throat—there was no emotion in his voice.

"While driving perhaps a little recklessly out Van Ness Avenue," Vance Richmond went on, ignoring the interruption,

"Mr Chrostwaite knocked a pedestrian down. The man wasn't badly hurt, and he is being compensated very generously for his injuries. But we are to appear in court next Monday to face a charge of reckless driving, and I am afraid that this accident of yesterday, in which the printer was killed, may hurt us.

"No one thinks that Mr Chrostwaite was in his car when it killed the printer—we have a world of evidence that he wasn't. But I am afraid that the printer's death may be made a weapon against us when we appear on the Van Ness Avenue charge. Being an attorney, I know just how much capital the prosecuting attorney—if he so chooses—can make out of the really insignificant fact that the same car that knocked down the man on Van Ness Avenue killed another man yesterday. And, being an attorney, I know how likely the prosecuting attorney is to so choose. And he can handle it in such a way that we will be given little or no opportunity to tell our side.

"The worst that can happen, of course, is that, instead of the usual fine, Mr Chrostwaite will be sent to the city jail for thirty or sixty days. That is bad enough, however, and that is what we wish to—"

Chrostwaite spoke again, still regarding his knees.

"Damned nuisance!" he said.

"That is what we wish to avoid," the attorney continued. "We are willing to pay a stiff fine, and expect to, for the accident on Van Ness Avenue was clearly Mr Chrostwaite's fault. But we—"

"Drunk as a lord!" Chrostwaite said.

"But we don't want to have this other accident, with which we had nothing to do, given a false weight in connection with the slighter accident. What we want, then, is to find the man or men who stole the car and ran down John Newhouse. If they are apprehended before we go to court, we won't be in danger of suffering for their act. Think you can find them before Monday?"

"I'll try," I promised; "though it isn't—"

The human balloon interrupted me by heaving himself to his feet, fumbling with his fat jeweled fingers for his watch.

"Three o'clock," he said. "Got a game of golf for three-thirty." He picked up his hat and gloves from the desk. "Find 'em, will you? Damned nuisance going to jail!"

And he waddled out.

II

From the attorney's office, I went down to the Hall of Justice, and, after hunting around a few minutes, found a policeman who had arrived at the corner of Clay and Kearny Streets a few seconds after Newhouse had been knocked down.

"I was just leaving the Hall when I seen a bus scoot around the corner at Clay Street," this patrolman—a big sandy-haired man named Coffee—told me. "Then I seen people gathering around, so I went up there and found this John Newhouse stretched out. He was already dead. Half a dozen people had seen him hit, and one of 'em had got the license number of the car that done it. We found the car standing empty just around the corner on Montgomery Street, pointing north. They was two fellows in the car when it hit Newhouse, but nobody saw what they looked like. Nobody was in it when we found it."

"In what direction was Newhouse walking?"

"North along Kearny Street, and he was about three-quarters across Clay when he was knocked. The car was coming north on Kearny, too, and turned east on Clay. It mightn't have been all the fault of the fellows in the car—according to them that seen the accident. Newhouse was walking across the street looking at a piece of paper in his hand. I found a piece of foreign money—paper money—in his hand, and I guess that's what he was looking at. The lieutenant tells me it was Dutch money—a hundred florin note, he says."

"Found out anything about the men in the car?"

"Nothing! We lined up everybody we could find in the neighborhood of California and Kearny Streets—where the car was stolen from—and around Clay and Montgomery Streets—where it was left at. But nobody remembered seeing the fellows getting in it or getting out of it. The man that owns the car wasn't driving it—it was stole all right, I guess. At first I thought maybe they was something shady about the accident. This John Newhouse had a two-or three-day-old black eye on him. But we run that out and found that he had a attack of heart trouble or something a couple days ago, and fell, fetching his eye up against a chair. He'd been home sick for three days—just left his house half an hour or so before the accident."

"Where'd he live?"

"On Sacramento Street—way out. I got his address here somewhere."

He turned over the pages of a grimy memoranda book, and I got the dead man's house number, and the names and addresses of the witnesses to the accident that Coffee had questioned.

That exhausted the policeman's information, so I left him.

III

My next play was to canvass the vicinity of where the car had been stolen and where it had been deserted, and then interview the witnesses. The fact that the police had fruitlessly gone over this ground made it unlikely that I would find anything of value; but I couldn't skip these things on that account. Ninety-nine per cent of detective work is a patient collecting of details—and your details must be got as nearly first-hand as possible, regardless of who else has worked the territory before you.

Before starting on this angle, however, I decided to run around to the dead man's printing establishment—only three blocks from the Hall of Justice—and see if any of his employees had heard anything that might help me.

Newhouse's establishment occupied the ground floor of a small building on California, between Kearny and Montgomery. A small office was partitioned off in front, with a connecting doorway leading to the press-room in the rear.

The only occupant of the small office, when I came in from the street, was a short, stocky, worried-looking blond man of forty or thereabouts, who sat at the desk in his shirt-sleeves, checking off figures in a ledger, against others on a batch of papers before him.

I introduced myself, telling him that I was a Continental Detective Agency operative, interested in Newhouse's death. He told me his name was Ben Soules, and that he was Newhouse's foreman. We shook hands, and then he waved me to a chair across the desk; pushed back the papers and book upon which he had been working, and scratched his head disgustedly with the pencil in his hand.

"This is awful!" he said. "What with one thing and another, we're heels over head in work, and I got to fool with these books that I don't know anything at all about, and—"

He broke off to pick up the telephone, which had jingled.

"Yes.... This is Soules.... We're working on them now... I'll give 'em to you by Monday noon at the least.... I know we promised them for yesterday, but... I know! I know! But the boss's death set us back. Explain that to Mr Chrostwaite. And... And I'll promise you that we'll give them to you Monday morning, sure!"

Soules slapped the receiver irritably on its hook and looked at me.

"You'd think that since it was his own car that killed the boss, he'd have decency enough not to squawk over the delay!"

"Chrostwaite?"

"Yes—that was one of his clerks. We're printing some leaflets for him—promised to have 'em ready yesterday—but between the boss's death and having a couple new hands to break in, we're behind with everything. I been here eight years, and this is the first time we ever fell down on an order—and every damned customer is yelling his head off. If we were like most printers they'd be used to waiting; but we've been too good to them. But this Chrostwaite! You'd think he'd have some decency, seeing that his car killed the boss!"

I nodded sympathetically, slid a cigar across the desk, and waited until it was burning in Soules' mouth before I asked:

"You said something about having a couple new hands to break in. How come?"

"Yes. Mr Newhouse fired two of our printers last week—Fincher and Key. He found that they belonged to the I. W. W., so he gave them their time."

"Any trouble with them, or anything against them except that they were Wobblies?"

"No—they were pretty good workers."

"Any trouble with them after he fired them?" I asked.

"No real trouble, though they were pretty hot. They made red speeches all over the place before they left."

"Remember what day that was?"

"Wednesday of last week, I think. Yes, Wednesday, because I hired two new men on Thursday."

"How many men do you work?"

"Three, besides myself."

"Was Mr Newhouse sick very often?"

"Not sick enough to stay away very often, though every now and then his heart would go back on him, and he'd have to stay in bed for a week or ten days. He wasn't what you could call real well at any time. He never did anything but the office work—I run the shop."

"When was he taken sick this last time?"

"Mrs Newhouse called up Tuesday morning and said he had had another spell, and wouldn't be down for a few days. He came in yesterday—which was Thursday—for about ten minutes in the afternoon, and said he would be back on the job this morning. He was killed just after he left."

"How did he look—very sick?"

"Not so bad. He never looked well, of course, but I couldn't see much difference from usual yesterday. This last spell hadn't been as bad as most, I reckon—he was usually laid up for a week or more."

"Did he say where he was going when he left? The reason I ask is that, living out on Sacramento Street, he would naturally have taken a car at that street if he had been going home, whereas he was run down on Clay Street."

"He said he was going up to Portsmouth Square to sit in the sun for half an hour or so. He had been cooped up indoors for two or three days, he said, and he wanted some sunshine before he went back home."

"He had a piece of foreign money in his hand when he was hit. Know anything about it?"

"Yes. He got it here. One of our customers—a man named Van Pelt—came in to pay for some work we had done yesterday afternoon while the boss was here. When Van Pelt pulled out his wallet to pay his bill, this piece of Holland money—I don't know what you call it—was among the bills. I think he said it was worth something like thirty-eight dollars. Anyway, the boss took it, giving Van Pelt his change. The boss said he wanted to show the Holland money to his boys—and he could have it changed back into American money later."

"Who is this Van Pelt?"

"He's a Hollander—is planning to open a tobacco importing business here in a month or two. I don't know much about him outside of that."

"Where's his home, or office?"

"His office is on Bush Street, near Sansome."

"Did he know that Newhouse had been sick?"

"I don't think so. The boss didn't look much different from usual."

"What's this Van Pelt's full name?"

"Hendrik Van Pelt."

"What does he look like?"

Before Soules could answer, three evenly spaced buzzes sounded above the rattle and whirring of the presses in the back of the shop.

I slid the muzzle of my gun—I had been holding it in my lap for five minutes—far enough over the edge of the desk for Ben Soules to see it.

"Put both of your hands on top of the desk," I said.

He put them there.

The press-room door was directly behind him, so that, facing him across the desk, I could look over his shoulder at it. His stocky body served to screen my gun from the view of whoever came through the door, in response to Soules' signal.

I didn't have long to wait.

Three men—black with ink—came to the door, and through it into the little office. They strolled in careless and casual, laughing and joking to one another.

But one of them licked his lips as he stepped through the door. Another's eyes showed white circles all around the irises. The third was the best actor—but he held his shoulders a trifle too stiffly to fit his otherwise careless carriage.

"Stop right there!" I barked at them when the last one was inside the office—and I brought my gun up where they could sec it.

They stopped as if they had all been mounted on the same pair of legs.

I kicked my chair back, and stood up.

I didn't like my position at all. The office was entirely too small for me. I had a gun, true enough, and whatever weapons may have been distributed among these other men were out of sight. But these four men were too close to me; and a gun isn't a thing of miracles. It's a mechanical contraption that is capable of just so much and no more.

If these men decided to jump me, I could down just one of them before the other three were upon me. I knew it, and they knew it.

"Put your hands up," I ordered, "and turn around!"

None of them moved to obey. One of the inked men grinned wickedly; Soules shook his head slowly; the other two stood and looked at me.

I was more or less stumped. You can't shoot a man just because he refuses to obey an order—even if he is a criminal. If they had turned around for me, I could have lined them up against the wall, and, being behind them, have held them safe while I used the telephone.

But that hadn't worked.

My next thought was to back across the office to the street door, keeping them covered, and then either stand in the door and yell for help, or take them into the street, where I could handle them. But I put that thought away as quickly as it came to me.

These four men were going to jump me—there was no doubt of that. All that was needed was a spark of any sort to explode them into action. They were standing stiff-legged and tense, waiting for some move on my part. If I took a step backward—the battle would be on.

We were close enough for any of the four to have reached out and touched me. One of them I could shoot before I was smothered—one out of four. That meant that each of them had only one chance out of four of being the victim—low enough odds for any but the most cowardly of men.

I grinned what was supposed to be a confident grin—because I was up against it hard—and reached for the telephone: I had to do something! Then I cursed myself! I had merely changed the signal for the onslaught. It would come now when I picked up the receiver.

But I couldn't back down again—that, too, would be a signal—I had to go through with it.

The perspiration trickled across my temples from under my hat as I drew the phone closer with my left hand.

The street door opened! An exclamation of surprise came from behind me.

I spoke rapidly, without taking my eyes from the four men in front of me.

"Quick! The phone! The police!"

With the arrival of this unknown person—one of Newhouse's customers, probably—I figured I had the edge again. Even if he took no active part beyond calling the police in, the enemy would have to split to take care of him—and that would give me a chance to pot at least two of them before I was knocked over. Two out of four—each of them had an even chance of being dropped—which *is* enough to give even a nervy man cause for thinking a bit before he jumps.

"Hurry!" I urged the newcomer.

"Yes! Yes!" he said—and in the blurred sound of the "s" there was evidence of foreign birth.

Keyed up as I was, I didn't need any more warning than that.

I threw myself sidewise—a blind tumbling away from the spot where I stood. But I wasn't quite quick enough.

The blow that came from behind didn't hit me fairly, but I got enough of it to fold up my legs as if the knees were hinged with paper—and I slammed into a heap on the floor....

Something dark crashed toward me. I caught it with both hands. It may have been a foot kicking at my face. I wrung it as a washerwoman wrings a towel.

Down my spine ran jar after jar. Perhaps somebody was beating me over the head. I don't know. My head wasn't alive. The blow that had knocked me down had numbed me all over. My eyes were no good. Shadows swam to and fro in front of them—that was all. I struck, gouged, tore at the shadows. Sometimes I found nothing. Sometimes I found things that felt like parts of bodies. Then I would hammer at them, tear at them. My gun was gone.

My hearing was no better than my sight—or not so good. There wasn't a sound in the world. I moved in a silence that was more complete than any silence I had ever known. I was a ghost fighting ghosts.

I found presently that my feet were under me again, though some squirming thing was on my back, and kept me from standing upright. A hot, damp thing like a hand was across my face.

I put my teeth into it. I snapped my head back as far as it would go. Maybe it smashed into the face it was meant for. I don't know. Anyhow the squirming thing was no longer on my back.

Dimly I realized that I was being buffeted about by blows that I was too numb to feel. Ceaselessly, with head and shoulders and elbows and fists and knees and feet, I struck at the shadows that were around me....

Suddenly I could see again—not clearly—but the shadows were taking on colors; and my ears came back a little, so that grunts and growls and curses and the impact of blows sounded in them. My straining gaze rested upon a brass cuspidor six inches or so in front of my eyes. I knew then that I was down on the floor again.

As I twisted about to hurl a foot into a soft body above me, something that was like a burn, but wasn't a burn, ran down one leg—a knife. The sting of it brought consciousness back into me with a rush.

I grabbed the brass cuspidor and used it to club a way to my feet—to club a clear space in front of me. Men were hurling themselves upon me. I swung the cuspidor high and flung it over their heads, through the frosted glass door into California Street.

Then we fought some more.

But you can't throw a brass cuspidor through a glass door into California Street between Montgomery and Kearny without attracting attention—it's too near the heart of daytime San Francisco. So presently—when I was on the floor again with six or eight hundred pounds of flesh hammering my face into the boards—we were pulled apart, and I was dug out of the bottom of the pile by a squad of policemen.

Big sandy-haired Coffee was one of them, but it took a lot of arguing to convince him that I was the Continental operative who had talked to him a little while before.

"Man! Man!" he said, when I finally convinced him. "Them lads sure—God! have worked you over! You got a face on you like a wet geranium!"

I didn't laugh. It wasn't funny.

I looked out of the one eye, which was working just now, at the five men lined up across the office—Soules, the three inky printers, and the man with the blurred "s," who had started the slaughter by tapping me on the back of the head.

He was a rather tall man of thirty or so, with a round ruddy face that wore a few bruises now. He had been, apparently, rather well-dressed in expensive black clothing, but he was torn and ragged now. I knew who he was without asking—Hendrik Van Pelt.

"Well, man, what's the answer?" Coffee was asking me.

By holding one side of my jaw firmly with one hand I found that I could talk without too much pain.

"This is the crowd that ran down Newhouse," I said, "and it wasn't an accident. I wouldn't mind having a few more of the details myself, but I was jumped before I got around to all of them. Newhouse had a hundred-florin note in his hand when he was run down, and he was walking in the direction of police headquarters—was only half a block away from the Hall of Justice.

"Soules tells me that Newhouse said he was going up to Portsmouth Square to sit in the sun. But Soules didn't seem to know that Newhouse was wearing a black eye—the one you told me you had investigated. If Soules didn't see the shiner, then it's a good bet that Soules didn't see Newhouse's face that day!

"Newhouse was walking from his printing shop toward police headquarters with a piece of foreign paper money in his hand—remember that!

"He had frequent spells of sickness, which, according to friend Soules, always before kept him at home for a week or ten days at a time. This time he was laid up for only two and a half days.

"Soules tells me that the shop is three days behind with its orders, and he says that's the first time in eight years they've ever been behind. He blames Newhouse's death—which only happened yesterday. Apparently, Newhouse's previous sick spells never delayed things—why should this last spell?

"Two printers were fired last week, and two new ones hired the very next day—pretty quick work. The car with which Newhouse was run down was taken from just around the corner, and was deserted within quick walking distance of the shop. It was left facing north, which is pretty good evidence that its occupants went south after they got out. Ordinary car thieves wouldn't have circled back in the direction from which they came.

"Here's my guess: This Van Pelt is a Dutchman, and he had some plates for phoney hundred-florin notes. He hunted around until he found a printer who would go in with him.

He found Soules, the foreman of a shop whose proprietor was now and then at home for a week or more at a time with a bad heart. One of the printers under Soules was willing to go in with them. Maybe the other two turned the offer down. Maybe Soules didn't ask them at all. Anyhow; they were discharged, and two friends of Soules were given their places.

"Our friends then got everything ready, and waited for Newhouse's heart to flop again. It did—Monday night. As soon as his wife called up next morning and said he was sick, these birds started running off their counterfeits. That's why they fell behind with their regular work. But this spell of Newhouse's was lighter than usual. He was up and moving around within two days, and yesterday afternoon he came down here for a few minutes.

"He must have walked in while all of our friends were extremely busy in some far corner. He must have spotted some of the phoney money, immediately sized up the situation, grabbed one bill to show the police, and started out for police headquarters—no doubt thinking he had not been seen by our friends here.

"They must have got a glimpse of him as he was leaving, however. Two of them followed him out. They couldn't, afoot, safely knock him over within a block or two of the Hall of Justice. But, turning the corner, they found Chrostwaite's car standing there with idling engine. That solved their getaway problem. They got in the car and went on after Newhouse. I suppose the original plan was to shoot him—but he crossed Clay Street with his eyes fastened upon the phoney money in his hand. That gave them a golden chance. They piled the car into him. It was sure death, they knew—his bum heart would finish the job if the actual collision didn't kill him. Then they deserted the car and came back here.

"There are a lot of loose ends to be gathered in—but this pipe-dream I've just told you fits in with all the facts we know—and

I'll bet a month's salary I'm not far off anywhere. There ought to be a three-day crop of Dutch notes cached somewhere! You people—"

I suppose I'd have gone on talking forever—in the giddy, head-swimming intoxication of utter exhaustion that filled me—if the big sandy-haired patrolman hadn't shut me off by putting a big hand across my mouth.

"Be quiet, man," he said, lifting me out of the chair, and spreading me flat on my back on the desk. "I'll have an ambulance here in a second for you."

The office was swirling around in front of my one open eye—the yellow ceiling swung down toward me, rose again, disappeared, came back in odd shapes. I turned my head to one side to avoid it, and my glance rested upon the white dial of a spinning clock.

Presently the dial came to rest, and I read it—four o'clock.

I remembered that Chrostwaite had broken up our conference in Vance Richmond's office at three, and I had started to work.

"One full hour!" I tried to tell Coffee before I went to sleep.

The police wound up the job while I was lying on my back in bed. In Van Pelt's office on Bush Street they found a great bale of hundred-florin notes. Van Pelt, they learned, had considerable reputation in Europe as a high-class counterfeiter. One of the printers came through, stating that Van Pelt and Soules were the two who followed Newhouse out of the shop, and killed him.

Section Two: The Cody Years

CONTENTS

1

THE HOUSE IN TURK STREET

BLACK MASK, APRIL 15, 1924

We wouldn't consider an issue complete without one of Mr Hammett's stories in it, and after you've read this tale, you'll understand why.

I had been told that the man for whom I was hunting lived in a certain Turk Street block, but my informant hadn't been able to give me his house number. Thus it came about that late one rainy afternoon I was canvassing this certain block, ringing each bell, and reciting a myth that went like this:

"I'm from the law office of Wellington and Berkeley. One of our clients—an elderly lady—was thrown from the rear platform of a street car last week and severely injured. Among those who witnessed the accident, was a young man whose name we don't know. But we have been told that he lives in this neighborhood." Then I would describe the man I wanted, and wind up: "Do you know of anyone who looks like that?"

All down one side of the block the answers were:

"No,"

"No,"

"No."

I crossed the street and started to work the other side. The first house: "No."

The second: "No."

The third. The fourth.

The fifth—

No one came to the door in answer to my first ring. After a while, I rang again. I had just decided that no one was at home, when the knob turned slowly and a little old woman opened the door. She was a very fragile little old woman, with a piece of gray knitting in one hand, and faded eyes that twinkled pleasantly behind gold-rimmed spectacles. She wore a stiffly starched apron over a black dress and there was white lace at her throat.

"Good evening," she said in a thin friendly voice. "I hope you didn't mind waiting. I always have to peep out to see who's here before I open the door—an old woman's timidity."

She laughed with a little gurgling sound in her throat.

"Sorry to disturb you," I apologized. "But—"

"Won't you come in, please?"

"No; I just want a little information. I won't take much of your time."

"I wish you would come in," she said, and then added with mock severity, "I'm sure my tea is getting cold."

She took my damp hat and coat, and I followed her down a narrow hall to a dim room, where a man got up as we entered. He was old too, and stout, with a thin white beard that fell upon a white vest that was as stiffly starched as the woman's apron.

"Thomas," the little fragile woman told him; "this is Mr—"

"Tracy," I said, because that was the name I had given the other residents of the block; but I came as near blushing when I said it, as I have in fifteen years. These folks weren't made to be lied to.

Their name, I learned, was Quarre; and they were an affectionate old couple. She called him "Thomas" every time she spoke to him, rolling the name around in her mouth as if she liked the taste of it. He called her "my dear" just as frequently, and twice he got up to adjust a cushion more comfortably to her frail back.

I had to drink a cup of tea with them and eat some little spiced cookies before I could get them to listen to a question. Then Mrs Quarre made little sympathetic clicking sounds with her tongue and teeth, while I told about the elderly lady who had fallen off a street car. The old man rumbled in his beard that it was "a damn shame," and gave me a fat and oily cigar. I had to assure them that the fictitious elderly lady was being taken care of and was coming along nicely—I was afraid they were going to insist upon being taken to see her.

Finally I got away from the accident itself, and described the man I wanted. "Thomas," Mrs Quarre said; "isn't that the young man who lives in the house with the railing—the one who always looks so worried?"

The old man stroked his snowy beard and pondered.

"But, my dear," he rumbled at last; "hasn't he got dark hair?"

She beamed upon her husband and then upon me.

"Thomas is so observant," she said with pride. "I had forgotten; but the young man I spoke of does have dark hair, so he couldn't be the one who saw the accident at all."

The old man then suggested that one who lived in the block below might be my man. They discussed this one at some length before they decided that he was too tall and too old. Mrs Quarre suggested another. They discussed that one, and voted against him. Thomas offered a candidate; he was weighed and discarded. They chattered on:

"But don't you think, Thomas... Yes, my dear, but... Of course you're right, Thomas, but..."

Two old folks enjoying a chance contact with the world that they had dropped out of.

Darkness settled. The old man turned on a light in a tall lamp that threw a soft yellow circle upon us, and left the rest of the room dim. The room was a large one, and heavy with the thick hangings and bulky horse-hair furniture of a generation ago. I burned the cigar the old man had given me, and slumped comfortably down in my chair, letting them run on, putting in a word or two whenever they turned to me. I didn't expect to get any information here; but I was comfortable, and the cigar was a good one. Time enough to go out into the drizzle when I had finished my smoke.

Something cold touched the nape of my neck.

"Stand up!"

I didn't stand up: I couldn't. I was paralyzed. I sat and blinked at the Quarres.

And looking at them, I knew that something cold *couldn't* be against the back of my neck; a harsh voice *couldn't* have ordered me to stand up. It wasn't possible!

Mrs Quarre still sat primly upright against the cushions her husband had adjusted to her back; her eyes still twinkled with friendliness behind her glasses; her hands were still motionless in her lap, crossed at the wrists over the piece of knitting. The old man still stroked his white beard, and let cigar smoke drift unhurriedly from his nostrils.

They would go on talking about the young men in the neighborhood who might be the man I wanted. Nothing had happened. I had dozed.

"Get up!"

The cold thing against my neck jabbed deep into the flesh.

I stood up.

"Frisk him," the harsh voice came from behind.

The old man carefully laid his cigar down, came to me, and ran his hands over my body. Satisfied that I was unarmed, he emptied my pockets, dropping the contents upon the chair that I had just left.

Mrs Quarre was pouring herself some more tea.

"Thomas," she said; "you've overlooked that little watch pocket in the trousers."

He found nothing there.

"That's all," he told the man behind me, and returned to his chair and cigar.

"Turn around, you!" the harsh voice ordered.

I turned and faced a tall, gaunt, raw-boned man of about my own age, which is thirty-five. He had an ugly face—hollow-cheeked, bony, and spattered with big pale freckles. His eyes were of a watery blue, and his nose and chin stuck out abruptly.

"Know me?" he asked.

"No."

"You're a liar!"

I didn't argue the point: he was holding a level gun in one big freckled hand.

"You're going to know me pretty well before you're through with me," this big ugly man threatened. "You're going to—"

"Hook!" a voice came from a portiéred doorway—the doorway through which the ugly man had no doubt crept up behind me. "Hook, come here!"

The voice was feminine—young, clear, and musical.

"What do you want?" the ugly man called over his shoulder.

"*He's* here."

"All right!" He turned to Thomas Quarre. "Keep this joker safe."

From somewhere among his whiskers, his coat, and his stiff white vest, the old man brought out a big black revolver, which he handled with no signs of either weakness or unfamiliarity.

The ugly man swept up the things that had been taken from my pockets, and carried them through the portiéres with him.

Mrs Quarre smiled brightly up at me.

"Do sit down, Mr Tracy," she said.

I sat.

Through the portiéres a new voice came from the next room; a drawling baritone voice whose accent was unmistakably British; cultured British.

"What's up, Hook?" this voice was asking.

The harsh voice of the ugly man:

"Plenty's up, I'm telling you! They're onto us! I started out a while ago; and as soon as I got to the street, I seen a man I knowed on the other side. He was pointed out to me in Philly five-six years ago. I don't know his name, but I remembered his mug—he's a Continental Detective Agency man. I came back in right away, and me and Elvira watched him out of the window. He went to every house on the other side of the street, asking questions or something. Then he came over and started to give this side a whirl, and after a while he rings the bell. I tell the old woman and her husband to get him in, stall him along, and see what he says for himself. He's got a song and dance about looking for a guy what seen an old woman bumped by a street car—but that's the bunk! He's gunning for us. There ain't nothing else to it. I went in and stuck him up just now. I meant to wait till you come, but I was scared he'd get nervous and beat it. Here's his stuff if you want to give it the once-over."

The British voice:

"You shouldn't have shown yourself to him. The others could have taken care of him."

Hook:

"What's the diff? Chances is he knows us all anyway. But supposing he didn't, what diff does it make?"

The drawling British voice:

"It may make a deal of difference. It was stupid."

Hook, blustering:

"Stupid, huh? You're always bellyaching about other people being stupid. To hell with you, I say! If you don't like my style, to hell with you! Who does all the work? Who's the guy that swings all the jobs? Huh? Where—"

The young feminine voice:

"Now, Hook, for God's sake don't make that speech again. I've listened to it until I know it by heart!"

A rustle of papers, and the British voice:

"I say, Hook, you're correct about his being a detective. Here is an identification card among his things."

The Quarres were listening to the conversation in the next room with as much interest as I, but Thomas Quarre's eyes never left me, and his fat fingers never relaxed about the gun in his lap. His wife sipped tea, with her head cocked on one side in the listening attitude of a bird.

Except for the weapon in the old man's lap, there was not a thing to persuade the eye that melodrama was in the room; the Quarres were in every other detail still the pleasant old couple who had given me tea and expressed sympathy for the elderly lady who had been injured.

The feminine voice from the next room:

"Well, what's to be done? What's our play?"

Hook:

"That's easy to answer. We're going to knock this sleuth off, first thing!"

The feminine voice:

"And put our necks in the noose?"

Hook, scornfully:

"As if they ain't there if we don't! You don't think this guy ain't after us for the L.A. job, do you?"

The British voice:

"You're an ass, Hook, and a quite hopeless one. Suppose this chap is interested in the Los Angeles affair, as is probable; what then? He is a Continental operative. Is it likely that his organization doesn't know where he is? Don't you think they know he was coming up here? And don't they know as much about us—chances are—as he does? There's no use killing him. That would only make matters worse. The thing to do is to tie him up and leave him here. His associates will hardly come looking for him until tomorrow—and that will give us all night to manage our disappearance."

My gratitude went out to the British voice! Somebody was in my favor, at least to the extent of letting me live. I hadn't been feeling very cheerful these last few minutes. Somehow, the fact that I couldn't see these people who were deciding whether I was to live or die, made my plight seem all the more desperate. I felt better now, though far from gay; I had confidence in the drawling British voice; it was the voice of a man who habitually carries his point.

Hook, bellowing:

"Let me tell you something, brother: that guy's going to be knocked off! That's flat! I'm taking no chances. You can jaw all you want to about it, but I'm looking out for my own neck and it'll be a lot safer with that guy where he can't talk. That's flat. He's going to be knocked off!"

The feminine voice, disgustedly:

"Aw, Hook, be reasonable!"

The British voice, still drawling, but dead cold:

"There's no use reasoning with you, Hook, you've the instincts and the intellect of a troglodyte. There is only one sort of language that you understand; and I'm going to talk that language to you, my son. If you are tempted to do anything silly between now and the time of our departure, just say this to yourself two or three times: 'If he dies, I die. If he dies, I die.' Say it as if it were out of the Bible—because it's that true."

There followed a long space of silence, with a tenseness that made my not particularly sensitive scalp tingle. Beyond the portiere, I knew, two men were matching glances in a battle of wills, which might any instant become a physical struggle, and my chances of living were tied up in that battle.

When, at last, a voice cut the silence, I jumped as if a gun had been fired; though the voice was low and smooth enough.

It was the British voice, confidently victorious, and I breathed again.

"We'll get the old people away first," the voice was saying. "You take charge of our guest, Hook. Tie him up neatly. But remember—no foolishness. Don't waste time questioning him—he'll lie. Tie him up while I get the bonds, and we'll be gone in less than half an hour."

The portiéres parted and Hook came into the room—a scowling Hook whose freckles had a greenish tinge against the sallowness of his face. He pointed a revolver at me, and spoke to the Quarres:

"He wants you."

They got up and went into the next room, and for a while an indistinguishable buzzing of whispers came from that room.

Hook, meanwhile, had stepped back to the doorway, still menacing me with his revolver; and pulled loose the plush ropes that were around the heavy curtains. Then he came around behind me, and tied me securely to the high-backed chair; my arms to the chair's arms, my legs to the chair's legs, my body to the chair's back and seat; and he wound up by gagging me with the corner of a cushion that was too well-stuffed for my comfort. The ugly man was unnecessarily rough throughout; but I was a lamb. He wanted an excuse for drilling me, and I wanted above all else that he should have no excuse.

As he finished lashing me into place, and stepped back to scowl at me, I heard the street door close softly, and then light footsteps ran back and forth overhead.

Hook looked in the direction of those footsteps, and his little watery blue eyes grew cunning.

"Elvira!" he called softly.

The portiéres bulged as if someone had touched them, and the musical feminine voice came through.

"What?"

"Come here."

"I'd better not. He wouldn't—"

"Damn him!" Hook flared up. "Come here!"

She came into the room and into the circle of light from the tall lamp; a girl in her early twenties, slender and lithe, and dressed for the street, except that she carried her hat in one hand. A white face beneath a bobbed mass of flame-colored hair. Smoke-gray eyes that were set too far apart for trustworthiness—though not for beauty—laughed at me; and her red mouth laughed at me, exposing the edges of little sharp animal-teeth. She was beautiful; as beautiful as the devil, and twice as dangerous.

She laughed at me—a fat man all trussed up with red plush rope, and with the corner of a green cushion in my mouth—and she turned to the ugly man.

"What do you want?"

He spoke in an undertone, with a furtive glance at the ceiling, above which soft steps still padded back and forth.

"What say we shake him?"

Her smoke-gray eyes lost their merriment and became hard and calculating.

"There's a hundred thousand he's holding—a third of it's mine. You don't think I'm going to take a Mickey Finn on that, do you?"

"Course not! Supposing we get the hundred grand?"

"How?"

"Leave it to me, kid; leave it to me! If I swing it, will you go with me? You know I'll be good to you."

She smiled contemptuously, I thought—but he seemed to like it.

"You're whooping right you'll be good to me," she said. "But listen, Hook: we couldn't get away with it—not unless you *get him.* I know him! I'm not running away with anything that belongs to him unless he is fixed so that he can't come after it."

Hook moistened his lips and looked around the room at nothing. Apparently he didn't like the thought of tangling with the owner of the British drawl. But his desire for the girl was too strong for his fear of the other man.

"I'll do it!" he blurted. "I'll get him! Do you mean it, kid? If I get him, you'll go with me?"

She held out her hand.

"It's a bet," she said, and he believed her.

His ugly face grew warm and red and utterly happy, and he took a deep breath and straightened his shoulders. In his place, I might have believed her myself—all of us have fallen for that sort of thing at one time or another—but sitting tied up on the side-lines, I knew that he'd have been better off playing with a gallon of nitro than with this baby. She was dangerous! There was a rough time ahead for this Hook!

"This is the lay—" Hook began, and stopped, tongue-tied.

A step had sounded in the next room.

Immediately the British voice came through the portieres, and there was an edge of exasperation to the drawl now:

"This is really too much! I can't"—he said *reahly* and *cawnt*—"leave for a moment without having things done all wrong. Now just what got into you, Elvira, that you must go in and exhibit yourself to our detective friend?"

Fear flashed into her smoke-gray eyes, and out again, and she spoke airily:

"Don't be altogether yellow," she said. "Your precious neck can get along all right without so much guarding."

The portières parted, and I twisted my head around as far as I could get it for my first look at this man who was responsible for my still being alive. I saw a short fat man, hatted and coated for the street, and carrying a tan traveling bag in one hand.

Then his face came into the yellow circle of light, and I saw that it was a Chinese face. A short fat Chinese, immaculately clothed in garments that were as British as his accent.

"It isn't a matter of color," he told the girl—and I understood now the full sting of her jibe; "it's simply a matter of ordinary wisdom."

His face was a round yellow mask, and his voice was the same emotionless drawl that I had heard before; but I knew that he was as surely under the girl's sway as the ugly man—or he wouldn't have let her taunt bring him into the room. But I doubted that she'd find this Anglicized oriental as easily handled as Hook.

"There was no particular need," the Chinese was still talking, "for this chap to have seen any of us." He looked at me now for the first time, with little opaque eyes that were like two black seeds. "It's quite possible that he didn't know any of us, even by description. This showing ourselves to him is the most arrant sort of nonsense."

"Aw, hell, Tai!" Hook blustered. "Quit your bellyaching, will you? What's the diff? I'll knock him off, and that takes care of that!"

The Chinese set down his tan bag and shook his head.

"There will be no killing," he drawled, "or there will be quite a bit of killing. You don't mistake my meaning, do you, Hook?"

Hook didn't. His Adam's apple ran up and down with the effort of his swallowing, and behind the cushion that was choking me, I thanked the yellow man again.

Then this red-haired she-devil put her spoon in the dish.

"Hook's always offering to do things that he has no intention of doing," she told the Chinese.

Hook's ugly face blazed red at this reminder of his promise to *get* the Chinese, and he swallowed again, and his eyes looked as if nothing would have suited him better than an opportunity to crawl under something. But the girl had him; her influence was stronger than his cowardice.

He suddenly stepped close to the Chinese, and from his advantage of a full head in height scowled down into the round yellow face that was as expressionless as a clock without hands.

"Tai," the ugly man snarled; "you're done. I'm sick and tired of all this dog you put on—acting like you was a king or something. I've took all the lip I'm going to take from a Chink! I'm going to—"

He faltered, and his words faded away into silence. Tai looked up at him with eyes that were as hard and black and inhuman as two pieces of coal. Hook's lips twitched and he flinched away a little.

I stopped sweating. The yellow man had won again. But I had forgotten the red-haired she-devil.

She laughed now—a mocking laugh that must have been like a knife to the ugly man.

A bellow came from deep in his chest, and he hurled one big fist into the round blank face of the yellow man.

The force of the punch carried Tai all the way across the room, and threw him on his side in one corner.

But he had twisted his body around to face the ugly man even as he went hurtling across the room—a gun was in his hand before he went down—and he was speaking before his legs had settled upon the floor—and his voice was a cultured British drawl.

"Later," he was saying; "we will settle this thing that is between us. Just now you will drop your pistol and stand very still while I get up."

Hook's revolver—only half out of his pocket when the oriental had covered him—thudded to the rug. He stood rigidly still while Tai got to his feet, and Hook's breath came out noisily, and each freckle stood ghastily out against the dirty scared white of his face.

I looked at the girl. There was contempt in the eyes with which she looked at Hook, but no disappointment.

Then I made a discovery: *something had changed in the room near her!*

I shut my eyes and tried to picture that part of the room as it had been before the two men had clashed. Opening my eyes suddenly, I had the answer.

On the table beside the girl had been a book and some magazines. They were gone now. Not two feet from the girl was the tan bag that Tai had brought into the room. Suppose the bag had held the bonds from the Los Angeles job that they had mentioned. It probably had. What then? It probably now held the book and magazines that had been on the table! The girl had stirred up the trouble between the two men to distract their attention while she made a switch. Where would the loot be, then? I didn't know, but I suspected that it was too bulky to be on the girl's slender person.

Just beyond the table was a couch, with a wide red cover that went all the way down to the floor. I looked from the couch to the girl. She was watching me, and her eyes twinkled with a flash of mirth as they met mine coming from the couch. The couch it was!

By now the Chinese had pocketed Hook's revolver, and was talking to him:

"If I hadn't a dislike for murder, and if I didn't think that you will perhaps be of some value to Elvira and me in effecting our departure, I should certainly relieve us of the handicap of your stupidity now. But I'll give you one more chance. I would suggest, however, that you think carefully before you give way to any more of your violent impulses." He turned to the girl. "Have you been putting foolish ideas in our Hook's head?"

She laughed.

"Nobody could put any kind in it."

"Perhaps you're right," he said, and then came over to test the lashings about my arms and body.

Finding them satisfactory, he picked up the tan bag, and held out the gun he had taken from the ugly man a few minutes before.

"Here's your revolver, Hook, now try to be sensible. We may as well go now. The old man and his wife will do as they were told. They are on their way to a city that we needn't mention by name in front of our friend here, to wait for us and their share of the bonds. Needless to say, they will wait a long while—they are out of it now. But between ourselves there must be no more treachery. If we're to get clear, we must help each other."

According to the best dramatic rules, these folks should have made sarcastic speeches to me before they left, but they didn't. They passed me without even a farewell look, and went out of sight into the darkness of the hall.

Suddenly the Chinese was in the room again, running tiptoe—an open knife in one hand, a gun in the other. This was the man I had been thanking for saving my life!

He bent over me.

The knife moved on my right side, and the rope that held that arm slackened its grip. I breathed again, and my heart went back to beating.

"Hook will be back," Tai whispered, and was gone.

On the carpet, three feet in front of me, lay a revolver.

The street door closed, and I was alone in the house for a while.

You may believe that I spent that while struggling with the red plush ropes that bound me. Tai had cut one length, loosening my right arm somewhat and giving my body more play, but I was far from free. And his whispered "Hook will be back" was all the spur I needed to throw my strength against my bonds.

I understood now why the Chinese had insisted so strongly upon my life being spared. I was the weapon with which Hook was to be removed. The Chinese figured that Hook would make some excuse as soon as they reached the street, slip back into the house, knock me off, and rejoin his confederates. If he didn't do it on his own initiative, I suppose the Chinese would suggest it.

So he had put a gun within reach—in case I could get loose—and had loosened my ropes as much as he could, not to have me free before he himself got away.

This thinking was a side-issue. I didn't let it slow up my efforts to get loose. The *why* wasn't important to me just now—the important thing was to have that revolver in my hand when the ugly man came into this room again.

Just as the front door opened, I got my right arm completely free, and plucked the strangling cushion from my mouth. The rest of my body was still held by the ropes—held loosely—but held. There was no time for more.

I threw myself, chair and all, forward, breaking the fall with my free arm. The carpet was thick. I went down on my face, with the heavy chair atop me, all doubled up any which way; but my right arm was free of the tangle, and my right hand grasped the gun.

My left side—the wrong side—was toward the hall door. I twisted and squirmed and wrestled under the bulky piece of furniture that sat on my back.

An inch—two inches—six inches, I twisted. Another inch. Feet were at the hall door. Another inch.

The dim light hit upon a man hurrying into the room—a glint of metal in his hand.

I fired.

He caught both hands to his belly, bent double, and slid out across the carpet.

That was over. But that was far from being all. I wrenched at the plush ropes that held me, while my mind tried to sketch what lay ahead.

The girl had switched the bonds, hiding them under the couch—there was no question of that. She had intended coming back for them before I had time to get free. But Hook had come back first, and she would have to change her plan. What more likely than that she would now tell the Chinese that Hook had made the switch? What then? There was only one answer: Tai would come back for the bonds—both of them would come. Tai knew that I was armed now, but they had said that the bonds represented a hundred thousand dollars. That would be enough to bring them back!

I kicked the last rope loose and scrambled to the couch. The bonds were beneath it: four thick bundles of Liberty Bonds, done up with heavy rubber bands. I tucked them under one arm, and went over to the man who was dying near the door. His gun was under one of his legs, I pulled it out, stepped over him, and went into the dark hall.

Then I stopped to consider.

The girl and the Chinese would split to tackle me. One would come in the front door and the other in the rear. That would be the safest way for them to handle me. My play, obviously, was to wait just inside one of those doors for them. It would be foolish for me to leave the house. That's exactly what they would be expecting at first—and they would be lying in ambush.

Decidedly, my play was to lie low within sight of this front door and wait until one of them came through it—as one of them surely would, when they had tired of waiting for me to come out.

Toward the street door, the hall was lighted with the glow that filtered through the glass from the street lights. The stairway leading to the second-storey threw a triangular shadow across part of the hall—a shadow that was black enough for any purpose. I crouched low in this three-cornered slice of night, and waited.

I had two guns: the one the Chinese had given me, and the one I had taken from Hook. I had fired one shot; that would leave me eleven still to use—unless one of the weapons had been used since it was loaded. I broke the gun Tai had given me, and in the dark ran my fingers across the back of the cylinder. My fingers touched *one* shell—under the hammer. Tai had taken no chances; he had given me one bullet—the bullet with which I had dropped Hook.

I put that gun down on the floor, and examined the one I had taken from Hook. It was *empty*. The Chinese had taken no chances at all! He had emptied Hook's gun before returning it to him after their quarrel.

I was in a hole! Alone, unarmed, in a strange house that would presently hold two who were hunting me—and that one of them was a woman didn't soothe me any—she was none the less deadly on that account.

For a moment I was tempted to make a dash for it; the thought of being out in the street again was pleasant; but I put the idea away. That would be foolishness, and plenty of it. Then I remembered the bonds under my arm. They would have to be my weapon; and if they were to serve me, they would have to be concealed.

I slipped out of my triangular shadow and went up the stairs. Thanks to the street lights, the upstairs rooms were not too dark for me to move around. Around and around I went through the rooms, hunting for a place to hide the Liberty Bonds.

But when suddenly a window rattled, as if from the draught created by the opening of an outside door somewhere, I still had the loot in my hands.

There was nothing to do now but to chuck them out of a window and trust to luck. I grabbed a pillow from a bed, stripped off the white case, and dumped the bonds into it. Then I leaned out of an already open window and looked down into the night, searching for a desirable dumping place: I didn't want the bonds to land on an ash-can or a pile of bottles, or anything that would make a racket.

And, looking out of the window, I found a better hiding-place. The window opened into a narrow court, on the other side of which was a house of the same sort as the one I was in. That house was of the same height as this one, with a flat tin roof that sloped down the other way. The roof wasn't far from me—not too far to chuck the pillow-case. I chucked it. It disappeared over the edge of the roof and crackled softly on the tin.

If I had been a movie actor or something of the sort, I suppose I'd have followed the bonds; I suppose I'd have jumped from the sill, caught the edge of the roof with my fingers, swung a while, and then pulled myself up and away. But dangling in spaee doesn't appeal to me; I preferred to face the Chinese and the redhead.

Then I did another not at all heroic thing. I turned on all the lights in the room, lighted a cigarette (we all like to pose a little now and then), and sat down on the bed to await my capture. I might have stalked my enemies through the dark house, and possibly have nabbed them; but most likely I would simply have succeeded in getting myself shot. And I don't like to be shot.

The girl found me.

She came creeping up the hall, an automatic in each hand, hesitated for an instant outside the door, and then came in on the jump. And when she saw me sitting peacefully on the side of the bed, her eyes snapped scornfully at me, as if I had done something mean. I suppose she thought I should have given her an opportunity to put lead in me.

"I got him, Tai," she called, and the Chinese joined us.

"What did Hook do with the bonds?" he asked point blank.

I grinned into his round yellow face and led my ace.

"Why don't you ask the girl?"

His face showed nothing, but I imagined that his fat body stiffened a little within its fashionable British clothing. That encouraged me, and I went on with my little lie that was meant to stir things up.

"Haven't you rapped to it," I asked; "that they were fixing up to ditch you?"

"You dirty liar!" the girl screamed, and took a step toward me.

Tai halted her with an imperative gesture. He stared through her with his opaque black eyes, and as he stared the blood slid out of her face. She had this fat yellow man on her string, right enough, but he wasn't exactly a harmless toy.

"So that's how it is?" he said slowly, to no one in particular. "So that's how it is?" Then to me: "Where did they put the bonds?"

The girl went close to him and her words came out tumbling over each other:

"Here's the truth of it, Tai, so help me God! I switched the stuff myself. Hook wasn't in it. I was going to run out on both of you. I stuck them under the couch downstairs, but they're not there now. That's the God's truth!"

He was eager to believe her, and her words had the ring of truth to them. And I knew that—in love with her as he was—he'd more readily forgive her treachery with the bonds than he would forgive her for planning to run off with Hook; so I made haste to stir things up again. The old timer who said "*Divide to conquer*" or something of the sort, knew what he was talking about.

"Part of that is right enough," I said. "She did stick the bonds under the couch—but Hook was in on it. They fixed it up between them while you were upstairs. He was to pick a fight with you, and during the argument she was to make the switch, and that is exactly what they did."

I had him!

As she wheeled savagely toward me, he stuck the muzzle of an automatic in her side—a smart jab that checked the angry words she was hurling at me.

"I'll take your guns, Elvira," he said, and took them.

There was a purring deadliness in his voice that made her surrender them without a word.

"Where are the bonds now ?" he asked me.

I grinned.

"I'm not with you, Tai. I'm against you."

He studied me with his little eyes that were like black seeds for a while, and I studied him; and I hoped that his studying was as fruitless as mine.

"I don't like violence," he said slowly, "and I believe you are a sensible person. Let us traffic, my friend."

"You name it," I suggested.

"Gladly! As a basis for our bargaining, we will stipulate that you have hidden the bonds where they cannot be found by anyone else; and that I have you completely in my power, as the shilling shockers used to have it."

"Reasonable enough," I said, "go on."

"The situation, then, is what gamblers call a standoff. Neither of us has the advantage. As a detective, you want us; but we have you. As thieves, we want the bonds; but you have them. I offer you the girl in exchange for the bonds, and that seems to me an equitable offer. It will give me the bonds and a chance to get away. It will give you no small degree of success in your task as a detective. Hook is dead. You will have the girl. All that will remain is to find me and the bonds again—by no means a hopeless task. You will have turned a defeat into more than half of a victory, with an excellent chance to make it a complete one."

"How do I know that you'll give me the girl?" He shrugged.

"Naturally, there can be no guarantee. But, knowing that she planned to desert me for the swine who lies dead below, you can't imagine that my feelings for her are the most friendly. Too, if I take her with me, she will want a share in the loot."

I turned the lay-out over in my mind, and looked at it from this side and that and the other.

"This is the way it looks to me," I told him at last. "You aren't a killer. I'll come through alive no matter what happens. All right; why should I swap? You and the girl will be easier to find again than the bonds, and they are the most important part of the job anyway. I'll hold on to them, and take my chances on finding you folks again. Yes, I'm playing it safe."

And I meant it, for the time being, at least.

"No, I'm not a killer," he said, very softly; and he smiled the first smile I had seen on his face. It wasn't a pleasant smile: and there was something in it that made you want to shudder. "But I am other things, perhaps, of which you haven't thought. But this talking is to no purpose. Elvira!"

The girl, who had been standing a little to one side, watching us, came obediently forward.

"You will find sheets in one of the bureau drawers," he told her. "tear one or two of them into strips strong enough to tie up your friend securely."

The girl went to the bureau. I wrinkled my head, trying to find a not too disagreeable answer to the question in my mind. The answer that came first wasn't nice: *torture.*

Then a faint sound brought us all into tense motionlessness.

The room we were in had two doors: one leading into the hall, the other into another bedroom. It was through the hall door that the faint sound had come—the sound of creeping feet.

Swiftly, silently, Tai moved backward to a position from which he could watch the hall door without losing sight of the girl and me—and the gun poised like a live thing in his fat hand was all the warning we needed to make no noise.

The faint sound again, just outside the door.

The gun in Tai's hand seemed to quiver with eagerness.

Through the other door—the door that gave to the next room—popped Mrs Quarre, an enormous cocked revolver in her thin hand.

"Let go it, you nasty heathen," she screeched.

Tai dropped his pistol before he turned to face her, and he held his hands up high—all of which was very wise.

Thomas Quarre came through the hall door then; he also held a cocked revolver—the mate of his wife's—though, in front of his bulk, his didn't look so enormously large.

I looked at the old woman again, and found little of the friendly fragile one who had poured tea and chatted about the neighbors. This was a witch if there ever was one—a witch of the blackest, most malignant sort. Her little faded eyes were sharp with ferocity, her withered lips were taut in a wolfish snarl, and her thin body fairly quivered with hate.

"I knew it," she was shrilling. "I told Tom as soon as we got far enough away to think things over. I knew it was a frame-up! I knew this supposed detective was a pal of yours! I knew it was just a scheme to beat Thomas and me out of our shares! Well, I'll show you, you yellow monkey! And the rest of you too! I'll show the whole caboodle of you! Where are them bonds? Where are they?"

The Chinese had recovered his poise, if he had ever lost it.

"Our stout friend can tell you perhaps," he said. "I was about to extract the information from him when you so—ah—dramatically arrived."

"Thomas, for goodness' sakes don't stand there dreaming," she snapped at her husband, who to all appearances was still the same mild old man who had given me an excellent cigar. "Tie up this Chinaman! I don't trust him an inch, and I won't feel easy until he's tied up. Tie him, up, and then we'll see what's to be done."

I got up from my seat on the side of the bed, and moved cautiously to a spot that I thought would be out of the line of fire if the thing I expected happened.

Tai had dropped the gun that had been in his hand, but he hadn't been searched. The Chinese are a thorough people; if one of them carries a gun at all, he usually carries two or three or more. (I remember picking up one in Oakland during the last tong war, who had five on him—one under each armpit, one on each hip, and one in his waistband.) One gun had been taken from Tai, and if they tried to truss him up without frisking him, there was likely to be fireworks. So I moved off to one side.

Fat Thomas Quarre went phlegmatically up to the Chinese to carry out his wife's orders—and bungled the job perfectly.

He put his bulk between Tai and the old woman's gun.

Tai's hands moved.

An automatic was in each.

Once more Tai ran true to racial form. When a Chinese shoots, he keeps on shooting until his gun is empty.

When I yanked Tai over backward by his fat throat, and slammed him to the floor, his guns were still barking metal; and they clicked empty as I got a knee on one of his arms. I didn't take any chances. I worked on his throat until his eyes and tongue told me that he was out of things for a while.

Then I looked around.

Thomas Quarre was huddled against the bed, plainly dead, with three round holes in his starched white vest—holes that were brown from the closeness of the gun that had put them there.

Across the room, Mrs Quarre lay on her back. Her clothes had somehow settled in place around her fragile body, and death had given her once more the gentle friendly look she had worn when I first saw her. One thin hand was on her bosom, covering, I found later, the two bulletholes that were there.

The red-haired girl Elvira was gone.

Presently Tai stirred, and, after taking another gun from his clothes, I helped him sit up. He stroked his bruised throat with one fat hand, and looked coolly around the room.

"So this is how it came out?" he said.

"Uh-huh!"

"Where's Elvira?"

"Got away—for the time being."

He shrugged.

"Well, you can call it a decidedly successful operation. The Quarres and Hook dead; the bonds and I in your hands."

"Not so bad," I admitted, "but will you do me a favor?"

"If I may."

"Tell me what the hell this is all about!"

"All about?" he asked.

"Exactly! From what you people have let me overhear, I gather that you pulled some sort of job in Los Angeles that netted you a hundred-thousand-dollars' worth of Liberty Bonds; but I can't remember any recent job of that size down there."

"Why, that's preposterous!" he said with what, for him, was almost wild-eyed amazement. "Preposterous! Of course you know all about it!"

"I do not! I was trying to find a young fellow named Fisher who left his Tacoma home in anger a week or two ago. His father wants him found on the quiet, so that he can come down and try to talk him into going home again. I was told that I might find Fisher in this block of Turk Street, and that's what brought me here."

He didn't believe me. He never believed me. He went to the gallows thinking me a liar.

When I got out into the street again (and Turk Street was a lovely place when I came free into it after my evening in that house!) I bought a newspaper that told me most of what I wanted to know.

A boy of twenty—a messenger in the employ of a Los Angeles stock and bond house—had disappeared two days before, while on his way to a bank with a wad of Liberty Bonds. That same night this boy and a slender girl with bobbed red hair had registered at a hotel in Fresno as *J. M. Riordan and wife.* The next morning the boy had been found in his room—murdered. The girl was gone. The bonds were gone.

That much the paper told me. During the next few days, digging up a little here and a little there, I succeeded in piecing together most of the story.

The Chinese—whose full name was Tai Choon Tau—had been the brains of the mob. Their game had been a variation of the always-reliable badger game. Tai selected the victims, and he must have been a good judge of humans, for he seems never to have picked a bloomer. He would pick out some youth who was messenger or runner for a banker or broker—one who carried either cash or negotiable securities in large quantities around the city.

The girl Elvira would then *make* this lad, get him all fussed up over her—which shouldn't have been very hard for her—and then lead him gently around to running away with her and whatever he could grab in the way of his employer's bonds or currency.

Wherever they spent the first night of their flight, there Hook would appear—foaming at the mouth and loaded for bear. The girl would plead and tear her hair and so forth, trying to keep Hook—in his role of irate husband—from butchering the youth. Finally she would succeed, and in the end the youth would find himself without either girl or the fruits of his thievery.

Sometimes he had surrendered to the police. Two we found had committed suicide. The Los Angeles lad had been built of tougher stuff than the others. He had put up a fight, and Hook had had to kill him. You can measure the girl's skill in her end of the game by the fact that not one of the half dozen youths who had been trimmed had said the least thing to implicate her; and some of them had gone to great trouble to keep her out of it.

The house in Turk Street had been the mob's retreat, and, that it might be always a safe one, they had not worked their game in San Francisco. Hook and the girl were supposed by the neighbors to be the Quarres' son and daughter—and Tai was the Chinese cook. The Quarres' benign and respectable appearances had also come in handy when the mob had securities to be disposed of.

The Chinese went to the gallows. We threw out the widest and finest-meshed of dragnets for the red-haired girl; and we turned up girls with bobbed red hair by the scores. But the girl Elvira was not among them.

I promised myself that some day...

2

THE GIRL WITH SILVER EYES

BLACK MASK, JUNE 1924

Mr Hammett has written some lively and unusual tales about his realistic detective from the Continental Detective Agency, whose name has never been disclosed; but for action, shrewd detective-work, sheer interest, and surprise, his latest, herewith, surpasses them all.

COMPLETE DETECTIVE NOVELETTE

I

A bell jangled me into wakefulness. I rolled to the edge of my bed and reached for the telephone. The neat voice of the Old Man—the Continental Detective Agency's San Francisco manager—came to my ears:

"Sorry to disturb you, but you'll have to go up to the Glenton Apartments on Leavenworth Street. A man named Burke Pangburn, who lives there, phoned me a few minutes ago asking to have someone sent up to see him at once. He seemed rather excited. Will you take care of it? See what he wants."

I said I would and, yawning, stretching and cursing Pangburn—whoever he was—got my fat body out of pajamas and into street clothes.

The man who had disturbed my Sunday morning sleep—I found when I reached the Glenton—was a slim, white-faced person of about twenty-five, with big brown eyes that were red-rimmed just now from either sleeplessness or crying, or both. His long brown hair was rumpled when he opened the door to admit me; and he wore a mauve dressing-robe spotted with big jade parrots over wine-colored silk pajamas.

The room into which he led me resembled an auctioneer's establishment just before the sale—or maybe one of these alley tea-rooms. Fat blue vases, crooked red vases, lanky yellow vases, vases of various shapes and colors; marble statuettes, ebony statuettes, statuettes of any material; lanterns, lamps and candlesticks; draperies, hangings and rugs of all sorts; odds and ends of furniture that were all somehow queerly designed; peculiar pictures hung here and there in unexpected places. A hard room to feel comfortable in.

"My fiancée," he began immediately in a high-pitched voice that was within a notch of hysteria, "has disappeared! Something has happened to her! Foul play of some horrible sort! I want you to find her—to save her from this terrible thing that..."

I followed him this far and then gave it up. A jumble of words came out of his mouth—"spirited away... mysterious something... lured into a trap"—but they were too disconnected for me to make anything out of them. So I stopped trying to understand him, and waited for him to babble himself empty of words.

I have heard ordinarily reasonable men, under stress of excitement, run on even more crazily than this wild-eyed youth; but his dress—the parroted robe and gay pajamas—and his surroundings—this deliriously furnished room—gave him too theatrical a setting; made his words sound utterly unreal.

He himself, when normal, should have been a rather nice-looking lad: his features were well spaced and, though his mouth and chin were a little uncertain, his broad forehead was good. But standing there listening to the occasional melodramatic phrase that I could pick out of the jumbled noises he was throwing at me, I thought that instead of parrots on his robe he should have had cuckoos.

Presently he ran out of language and was holding his long, thin hands out to me in an appealing gesture, saying,

"Will you?" over and over. "Will you? Will you?"

I nodded soothingly, and noticed that tears were on his thin cheeks.

"Suppose we begin at the beginning," I suggested, sitting down carefully on a carved bench affair that didn't look any too strong.

"Yes! Yes!" He was standing legs apart in front of me, running his fingers through his hair. "The beginning. I had a letter from her every day until—"

"That's not the beginning," I objected. "Who is she? What is she?"

"She's Jeanne Delano!" he exclaimed in surprise at my ignorance. "And she is my fiancée. And now she is gone, and I know that—"

The phrases "*victim of foul play*,"

"*into a trap*" and so on began to flow hysterically out again.

Finally I got him quieted down and, sandwiched in between occasional emotional outbursts, got a story out of him that amounted to this:

This Burke Pangburn was a poet. About two months before, he had received a note from a Jeanne Delano—forwarded from his publishers—praising his latest book of rhymes. Jeanne Delano happened to live in San Francisco, too, though she hadn't known that he did. He had answered her note, and had received another. After a little of this they met. If she really was as beautiful as he claimed, then he wasn't to be blamed for falling in love with her. But whether or not she was really beautiful, he thought she was, and he had fallen hard.

This Delano girl had been living in San Francisco for only a little while, and when the poet met her she was living alone in an Ashbury Avenue apartment. He did not know where she came from or anything about her former life. He suspected—from certain indefinite suggestions and peculiarities of conduct which he couldn't put in words—that there was a cloud of some sort hanging over the girl; that neither her past nor her present were free from difficulties. But he hadn't the least idea what those difficulties might be. He hadn't cared. He knew absolutely nothing about her, except that she was beautiful, and he loved her, and she had promised to marry him.

Then, on the third of the month—exactly twenty-one days before this Sunday morning—the girl had suddenly left San Francisco. He had received a note from her, by messenger.

This note, which he showed me after I had insisted point blank on seeing it, read:

> "*Burke love:*
>
> *Have just received a wire, and must go East on next train. Tried to get you on the phone, but couldn't. Will write you as soon as I know what my address will be. If anything.* (These two words were erased and could be read only with great difficulty.) *Love me until I'm back with you forever.*
>
> *Your Jeanne.*"

Nine days later he had received another letter from her, from Baltimore, Maryland. This one, which I had a still harder time getting a look at, read:

"Dearest Poet:

It seems like two years since I have seen you, and I have a fear that it's going to be between one and two months before I see you again.

I can't tell you now, beloved, about what brought me here. There are things that can't be written. But as soon as I'm back with you, I shall tell you the whole wretched story.

If anything should happen—I mean to me—you'll go on loving me forever, won't you, beloved? But that's foolish. Nothing is going to happen. I'm just off the train, and tired from traveling.

Tomorrow I shall write you a long, long letter to make up for this.

My address here is 215 N. Stricker St. Please, Mister, at least one letter a day! Your own

Jeanne"

For nine days he had had a letter from her each day—with two on Monday to make up for the none on Sunday—and then her letters had stopped. And the daily letters he had sent to the address she gave—215 N. Stricker Street—had begun to come back to him, marked "Not known."

He had sent a telegram, and the telegraph company had informed him that its Baltimore office had been unable to find a Jeanne Delano at the North Stricker Street address.

For three days he had waited, expecting hourly to hear from the girl, and no word had come. Then he had bought a ticket for Baltimore.

"But," he wound up, "I was afraid to go. I know she's in some sort of trouble—I can feel that—but I'm a silly poet. I can't deal with mysteries. Either I would find nothing at all or, if by luck I did stumble on the right track, the probabilities are that I would only muddle things; add fresh complications, perhaps endanger her life still further. I can't go blundering at it in that fashion, without knowing whether I am helping or harming her. It's a task for an expert in that sort of thing. So I thought of your agency. You'll be careful, won't you? It may be—

I don't know—that she won't want assistance. It may be that you can help her without her knowing anything about it. You are accustomed to that sort of thing; you can do it, can't you?"

II

I turned the job over and over in my mind before answering him. The two great bugaboos of a reputable detective agency are the persons who bring in a crooked plan or a piece of divorce work all dressed up in the garb of a legitimate operation, and the irresponsible person who is laboring under wild and fanciful delusions—who wants a dream run out.

This poet—sitting opposite me now twining his long, white fingers nervously together—was, I thought, sincere; but I wasn't so sure of his sanity.

"Mr Pangburn," I said after a while, "I'd like to handle this thing for you, but I'm not sure that I can. The Continental is rather strict, and, while I believe this thing is on the level, still I am only a hired man and have to go by the rules. Now if you could give us the endorsement of some firm or person of standing—a reputable lawyer, for instance, or any legally responsible party—we'd be glad to go ahead with the work. Otherwise, I am afraid—"

"But I know she's in danger!" he broke out. "I know that—And I can't be advertising her plight—airing her affairs—to everyone."

"I'm sorry, but I can't touch it unless you can give me some such endorsement." I stood up. "But you can find plenty of detective agencies that aren't so particular."

His mouth worked like a small boy's, and he caught his lower lip between his teeth. For a moment I thought he was going to burst into tears. But instead he said slowly:

"I dare say you are right. Suppose I refer you to my brother-in-law, Roy Axford. Will his word be sufficient?"

"Yes."

Roy Axford—R. F. Axford—was a mining man who had a finger in at least half of the big business enterprises of the Pacific Coast; and his word on anything was commonly considered good enough for anybody.

"If you can get in touch with him now," I said, "and arrange for me to see him today, I can get started without much delay."

Pangburn crossed the room and dug a telephone out from among a heap of his ornaments. Within a minute or two he was talking to someone whom he called "Rita."

"Is Roy home?... Will he be home this afternoon?... No, you can give him a message for me, though... Tell him I'm sending a gentleman up to see him this afternoon on a personal matter—personal with me—and that I'll be very grateful if he'll do what I want... Yes... You'll find out, Rita... It isn't a thing to talk about over the phone... Yes, thanks!"

He pushed the telephone back into its hiding place and turned to me.

"He'll be at home until two o'clock. Tell him what I told you and if he seems doubtful, have him call me up. You'll have to tell him the whole thing; he doesn't know anything at all about Miss Delano."

"All right. Before I go, I want a description of her."

"She's beautiful!" he exclaimed. "The most beautiful woman in the world!"

That would look nice on a reward circular.

"That isn't exactly what I want," I told him. "How old is she?"

"Twenty-two."

"Height?"

"About five feet eight inches, or possibly nine."

"Slender, medium or plump?"

"She's inclined toward slenderness, but she—"

There was a note of enthusiasm in his voice that made me fear he was about to make a speech, so I cut him off with another question.

"What color hair?"

"Brown—so dark that it's almost black—and it's soft and thick and—"

"Yes, yes. Long or bobbed?"

"Long and thick and—"

"What color eyes?"

"You've seen shadows on polished silver when—"

I wrote down *gray eyes* and hurried on with the interrogation.

"Complexion?"

"Perfect!"

"Uh-huh. But is it light, or dark, or florid, or sallow; or what?"

"Fair."

"Face oval, or square, or long and thin, or what shape?"

"Oval."

"What shaped nose? Large, small, turned-up—"

"Small and regular!" There was a touch of indignation in his voice.

"How did she dress? Fashionably? And did she favor bright or quiet colors?"

"Beaut—" And then as I opened my mouth to head him off he came down to earth with:

"Very quietly—usually dark blues and browns."

"What jewelry did she wear?"

"I've never seen her wear any."

"Any scars, or moles?" The horrified look on his white face urged me on to give him a full shot. "Or warts, or deformities that you know?"

He was speechless, but he managed to shake his head.

"Have you a photograph of her?"

"Yes, I'll show you."

He bounded to his feet, wound his way through the room's excessive furnishings and out through a curtained doorway. Immediately he was back with a large photograph in a carved ivory frame. It was one of these artistic photographs—a thing of shadows and hazy outlines—not much good for identification purposes. She was beautiful—right enough—but that meant nothing; that's the purpose of an artistic photograph.

"This the only one you have?"

"Yes."

"I'll have to borrow it, but I'll get it back to you as soon as I have my copies made."

"No! No!" he protested against having his lady love's face given to a lot of gumshoes. "That would be terrible!"

I finally got it, but it cost me more words than I like to waste on an incidental.

"I want to borrow a couple of her letters, or something in her writing, too," I said.

"For what?"

"To have photostatic copies made. Handwriting specimens come in handy—give you something to go over hotel registers with. Then, even if going under fictitious names, people now and then write notes and make memorandums."

We had another battle, out of which I came with three envelopes and two meaningless sheets of paper, all bearing the girl's angular writing.

"She have much money?" I asked, when the disputed photograph and handwriting specimens were safely tucked away in my pocket.

"I don't know. It's not the sort of thing that one would pry into. She wasn't poor; that is, she didn't have to practice any petty economies; but I haven't the faintest idea either as to the amount of her income or its source. She had an account at the Golden Gate Trust Company, but naturally I don't know anything about its size."

"Many friends here?"

"That's another thing I don't know. I think she knew a few people here, but I don't know who they were. You see, when we were together we never talked about anything but ourselves. You know what I mean: there was nothing we were interested in but each other. We were simply—"

"Can't you even make a guess at where she came from, who she was?"

"No. Those things didn't matter to me. She was Jeanne Delano, and that was enough for me."

"Did you and she ever have any financial interests in common? I mean, was there ever any transaction in money or other valuables in which both of you were interested?"

What I meant, of course, was had she got into him for a loan, or had she sold him something, or got money out of him in any other way.

He jumped to his feet, and his face went fog-gray. Then he sat down again—slumped down—and blushed scarlet.

"Pardon me," he said thickly. "You didn't know her, and of course you must look at the thing from all angles. No, there was nothing like that. I'm afraid you are going to waste time if you are going to work on the theory that she was an adventuress. There was nothing like that! She was a girl with something terrible hanging over her; something that called her to Baltimore suddenly; something that has taken her away from me. Money? What could money have to do with it? I love her!"

III

R. F. Axford received me in an office-like room in his Russian Hill residence: a big blond man, whose forty-eight or nine years had not blurred the outlines of an athlete's body. A big, full-blooded man with the manner of one whose self-confidence is complete and not altogether unjustified.

"What's our Burke been up to now?" he asked amusedly when I told him who I was. His voice was a pleasant vibrant bass.

I didn't give him all the details.

"He was engaged to marry a Jeanne Delano, who went East about three weeks ago and then suddenly disappeared. He knows very little about her; thinks something has happened to her; and wants her found."

"Again?" His shrewd blue eyes twinkled. "And to a Jeanne this time! She's the fifth within a year, to my knowledge, and no doubt I missed one or two who were current while I was in Hawaii. But where do I come in?"

"I asked him for responsible endorsement. I think he's all right, but he isn't, in the strictest sense, a responsible person. He referred me to you."

"You're right about his not being, in the strictest sense, a responsible person." The big man screwed up his eyes and mouth in thought for a moment. Then: "Do you think that something has really happened to the girl? Or is Burke imagining things?"

"I don't know. I thought it was a dream at first. But in a couple of her letters there are hints that something was wrong."

"You might go ahead and find her then," Axford said. "I don't suppose any harm will come from letting him have his Jeanne back. It will at least give him something to think about for a while."

"I have your word for it then, Mr Axford, that there will be no scandal or anything of the sort connected with the affair?"

"Assuredly! Burke is all right, you know: It's simply that he is spoiled. He has been in rather delicate health all his life; and then he has an income that suffices to keep him modestly, with a little over to bring out books of verse and buy doo-daws for his rooms. He takes himself a little too solemnly—is too much the poet—but he's sound at bottom."

"I'll go ahead with it, then," I said, getting up. "By the way, the girl has an account at the Golden Gate Trust Company, and I'd like to find out as much about it as possible, especially where her money came from. Clement, the cashier, is a model of caution when it comes to giving out information about depositors. If you could put in a word for me it would make my way smoother."

"Be glad to."

He wrote a couple of lines across the back of a card and gave it to me; and, promising to call on him if I needed further assistance, I left.

IV

I telephoned Pangburn that his brother-in-law had given the job his approval. I sent a wire to the agency's Baltimore branch, giving what information I had. Then I went up to Ashbury Avenue, to the apartment house in which the girl had lived.

The manager—an immense Mrs Clute in rustling black—knew little, if any more about the girl than Pangburn. The girl had lived there for two and a half months; she had had occasional callers, but Pangburn was the only one that the manager could describe to me. The girl had given up the apartment on the third of the month, saying that she had been called East, and she had asked the manager to hold her mail until she sent her new address. Ten days later Mrs Clute had received a card from the girl instructing her to forward her mail to 215 N. Stricker Street, Baltimore, Maryland. There had been no mail to forward.

The single thing of importance that I learned at the apartment house was that the girl's two trunks had been taken away by a green transfer truck. Green was the color used by one of the city's largest transfer companies.

I went then to the office of this transfer company, and found a friendly clerk on duty. (A detective, if he is wise, takes pains to make and keep as many friends as possible among transfer company, express company and railroad employees.) I left the office with a memorandum of the transfer company's check numbers and the Ferry baggage-room to which the two trunks had been taken.

At the Ferry Building, with this information, it didn't take me many minutes to learn that the trunks had been checked to Baltimore. I sent another wire to the Baltimore branch, giving the railroad check numbers.

Sunday was well into night by this time, so I knocked off and went home.

V

Half an hour before the Golden Gate Trust Company opened for business the next morning I was inside, talking to Clement, the cashier. All the traditional caution and conservatism of bankers rolled together wouldn't be one-two-three to the amount usually displayed by this plump, white-haired old man. But one look at Axford's card, with "*Please give the bearer all possible assistance*" inked across the back of it, made Clement even eager to help me.

"You have, or have had, an account here in the name of Jeanne Delano," I said. "I'd like to know as much as possible about it: to whom she drew checks, and to what amounts; but especially all you can tell me about where her money came from."

He stabbed one of the pearl buttons on his desk with a pink finger, and a lad with polished yellow hair oozed silently into the room. The cashier scribbled with a pencil on a piece of paper and gave it to the noiseless youth, who disappeared. Presently he was back, laying a handful of papers on the cashier's desk.

Clement looked through the papers and then up at me.

"Miss Delano was introduced here by Mr Burke Pangburn on the sixth of last month, and opened an account with eight hundred and fifty dollars in cash. She made the following deposits after that: four hundred dollars on the tenth; two hundred and fifty on the twenty-first; three hundred on the twenty-sixth; two hundred on the thirtieth; and twenty thousand dollars on the second of this month. All of these deposits except the last were made with cash. The last one was a check—which I have here."

He handed it to me: a Golden Gate Trust Company check.

PAY TO THE ORDER OF JEANNE DELANO,
TWENTY THOUSAND DOLLARS.
(SIGNED) BURKE PANGBURN.

It was dated the second of the month.

"Burke Pangburn!" I exclaimed, a little stupidly. "Was it usual for him to draw checks to that amount?"

"I think not. But we shall see."

He stabbed the pearl button again, ran his pencil across another slip of paper, and the youth with the polished yellow hair made a noiseless entrance, exit, entrance, and exit.

The cashier looked through the fresh batch of papers that had been brought to him.

"On the first of the month, Mr Pangburn deposited twenty thousand dollars—a check against Mr Axford's account here."

"Now how about Miss Delano's withdrawals?" I asked.

He picked up the papers that had to do with her account again.

"Her statement and canceled checks for last month haven't been delivered to her yet. Everything is here. A check for eighty-five dollars to the order of H. K. Clute on the fifteenth of last month; one 'to cash' for three hundred dollars on the twentieth, and another of the same kind for one hundred dollars on the twenty-fifth. Both of these checks were apparently cashed here by her. On the third of this month she closed out her account, with a check to her own order for twenty-one thousand, five hundred and fifteen dollars."

"And that check?"

"Was cashed here by her."

I lighted a cigarette, and let these figures drift around in my head. None of them—except those that were fixed to Pangburn's and Axford's signatures—seemed to be of any value to me. The Clute check—the only one the girl had drawn in anyone else's favor—had almost certainly been for rent.

"This is the way of it," I summed up aloud. "On the first of the month, Pangburn deposited Axford's check for twenty thousand dollars. The next day he gave a check to that amount to Miss Delano, which she deposited. On the following day she closed her account, taking between twenty-one and twenty-two thousand dollars in currency."

"Exactly," the cashier said.

VI

Before going up to the Glenton Apartments to find out why Pangburn hadn't come clean with me about the twenty thousand dollars, I dropped in at the agency, to see if any word had come from Baltimore. One of the clerks had just finished decoding a telegram.

It read:

> "Baggage arrived Mt. Royal Station on eighth. Taken away same day. Unable to trace. 215 North Stricker Street is Baltimore Orphan Asylum. Girl not known there. Continuing our efforts to find her."

The Old Man came in from luncheon as I was leaving. I went back into his office with him for a couple of minutes.

"Did you see Pangburn?" he asked.

"Yes. I'm working on his job now—but I think it's a bust."

"What is it?"

"Pangburn is R. F. Axford's brother-in-law. He met a girl a couple of months ago, and fell for her. She sizes up as a worker. He doesn't know anything about her. The first of the month he got twenty thousand dollars from his brother-in-law and passed it over to the girl. She blew, telling him she had been called to Baltimore, and giving him a phoney address that turns out to be an orphan asylum. She sent her trunks to Baltimore, and sent him some letters from there—but a friend could have taken care of the baggage and could have remailed her letters for her. Of course, she would have needed a ticket to check the trunks on, but in a twenty-thousand-dollar game that would be a small expense. Pangburn held out on me; he didn't tell me a word about the money. Ashamed of being easy pickings, I reckon. I'm going to the bat with him on it now."

The Old Man smiled his mild smile that might mean anything, and I left.

VII

Ten minutes of ringing Pangburn's bell brought no answer. The elevator boy told me he thought Pangburn hadn't been in all night. I put a note in his box and went down to the railroad company's offices, where I arranged to be notified if an unused Baltimore-San Francisco ticket was turned in for redemption.

That done, I went up to the *Chronicle* office and searched the files for weather conditions during the past month, making a memorandum of four dates upon which it had rained steadily day and night. I carried my memorandum to the offices of the three largest taxicab companies.

That was a trick that had worked well for me before. The girl's apartment was some distance from the street car line, and I was counting upon her having gone out—or having had a caller—on one of those rainy dates. In either case, it was very likely that she—or her caller—had left in a taxi in preference to walking through the rain to the car line. The taxicab companies' daily records would show any calls from her address, and the fares' destinations.

The ideal trick, of course, would have been to have the records searched for the full extent of the girl's occupancy of the apartment; but no taxicab company would stand for having that amount of work thrust upon them, unless it was a matter of life and death. It was difficult enough for me to persuade them to turn clerks loose on the four days I had selected.

I called up Pangburn again after I left the last taxicab office, but he was not at home. I called up Axford's residence, thinking that the poet might have spent the night there, but was told that he had not.

Late that afternoon I got my copies of the girl's photograph and handwriting, and put one of each in the mail for Baltimore. Then I went around to the three taxicab companies' offices and got my reports. Two of them had nothing for me. The third's records showed two calls from the girl's apartment.

On one rainy afternoon a taxi had been called, and one passenger had been taken to the Glenton Apartments. That passenger, obviously, was either the girl or Pangburn. At half-past twelve one night another call had come in, and this passenger had been taken to the Marquis Hotel.

The driver who had answered this second call remembered it indistinctly when I questioned him, but he thought that his fare had been a man. I let the matter rest there for the time; the Marquis isn't a large hotel as San Francisco hotels go, but it is too large to make canvassing its guests for the one I wanted practicable.

I spent the evening trying to reach Pangburn, with no success. At eleven o'clock I called up Axford, and asked him if he had any idea where I might find his brother-in-law.

"Haven't seen him for several days," the millionaire said. "He was supposed to come up for dinner last night, but didn't. My wife tried to reach him by phone a couple times today, but couldn't."

VIII

The next morning I called Pangburn's apartment before I got out of bed, and got no answer. Then I telephoned Axford and made an appointment for ten o'clock at his office.

"I don't know what he's up to now," Axford said good-naturedly when I told him that Pangburn had apparently been away from his apartment since Sunday, "and I suppose there's small chance of guessing. Our Burke is nothing if not erratic. How are you progressing with your search for the damsel in distress?"

"Far enough to convince me that she isn't in a whole lot of distress. She got twenty thousand dollars from your brother-in-law the day before she vanished."

"Twenty thousand dollars from Burke? She must be a wonderful girl! But wherever did he get that much money?"

"From you."

Axford's muscular body straightened in his chair.

"From me?"

"Yes—your check."

"He did not."

There was nothing argumentative in his voice; it simply stated a fact.

"You didn't give him a check for twenty thousand dollars on the first of the month?"

"No."

"Then," I suggested, "perhaps we'd better take a run over to the Golden Gate Trust Company."

Ten minutes later we were in Clement's office.

"I'd like to see my cancelled checks," Axford told the cashier.

The youth with the polished yellow hair brought them in presently—a thick wad of them—and Axford ran rapidly through them until he found the one he wanted. He studied that one for a long while, and when he looked up at me he shook his head slowly but with finality.

"I've never seen it before."

Clement mopped his head with a white handkerchief, and tried to pretend that he wasn't burning up with curiosity and fears that his bank had been gypped.

The millionaire turned the check over and looked at the endorsement.

"Deposited by Burke," he said in the voice of one who talks while he thinks of something entirely different, "on the first."

"Could we talk to the teller who took in the twenty-thousand-dollar check that Miss Delano deposited?" I asked Clement.

He pressed one of his desk's pearl buttons with a fumbling pink finger, and in a minute or two a little sallow man with a hairless hèad came in.

"Do you remember taking a check for twenty thousand from Miss Jeanne Delano a few weeks ago?" I asked him.

"Yes, sir! Yes, sir! Perfectly."

"Just what do you remember about it?"

"Well, sir, Miss Delano came to my window with Mr Burke Pangburn. It was his check. I thought it was a large check for him to be drawing, but the book-keepers said he had enough money in his account to cover it. They stood there—Miss Delano and Mr Pangburn—talking and laughing while I entered the deposit in her book, and then they left, and that was all."

"This check," Axford said slowly, after the teller had gone back to his cage, "is a forgery. But I shall make it good, of course. That ends the matter, Mr Clement, and there must be no more to-do about it."

"Certainly, Mr Axford. Certainly."

Clement was all enormously relieved smiles and head-noddings, with this twenty-thousand-dollar load lifted from his bank's shoulders.

Axford and I left the bank then and got into his coupé, in which we had come from his office. But he did not immediately start the engine. He sat for a while staring at the traffic of Montgomery Street with unseeing eyes.

"I want you to find Burke," he said presently, and there was no emotion of any sort in his bass voice. "I want you to find him without risking the least whisper of scandal. If my wife knew of all this—She mustn't know. She thinks her brother is a choice morsel. I want you to find him for me. The girl doesn't matter any more, but I suppose that where you find one you will find the other. I'm not interested in the money, and I don't want you to make any special attempt to recover that; it could hardly be done, I'm afraid, without publicity. I want you to find Burke before he does something else."

"If you want to avoid the wrong kind of publicity," I said, "your best bet is to spread the right kind first. Let's advertise him as missing, fill the papers up with his pictures and so forth. They'll play him up strong. He's your brother-in-law and he's a poet. We can say that he has been ill—you told me that he had been in delicate health all his life—and that we fear he has dropped dead somewhere or is suffering under some mental derangement. There will be no necessity of mentioning the girl or the money, and our explanation may keep people—especially your wife—from guessing the truth when the fact that he is missing leaks out. It's bound to leak out somehow."

He didn't like my idea at first, but I finally won him over.

We went up to Pangburn's apartment then, easily securing admittance on Axford's explanation that we had an engagement with him and would wait there for him. I went through the rooms inch by inch, prying into each hole and hollow and crack; reading everything that was written anywhere, even down to his manuscripts; and I found nothing that threw any light on his disappearance.

I helped myself to his photographs—pocketing five of the dozen or more that were there. Axford did not think that any of the poet's bags or trunks were missing from the packroom. I did not find his Golden Gate Trust Company deposit book.

I spent the rest of the day loading the newspapers up with what we wished them to have; and they gave my ex-client one grand spread: first-page stuff with photographs and all possible trimmings. Anyone in San Francisco who didn't know that Burke Pangburn—brother-in-law of R. F. Axford and author of *Sandpatches and Other Verse*—was missing, either couldn't read or wouldn't.

IX

This advertising brought results. By the following morning, reports were rolling in from all directions, from dozens of people who had seen the missing poet in dozens of places. A few of these reports looked promising—or at least possible—but the majority were ridiculous on their faces.

I came back to the agency from running out one that had—until run out—looked good, to find a note on my desk asking me to call up Axford.

"Can you come down to my office now?" he asked when I got him on the wire.

There was a lad of twenty-one or – two with Axford when I was ushered into his office: a narrow-chested, dandified lad of the sporting clerk type.

"This is Mr Fall, one of my employees," Axford told me. "He says he saw Burke Sunday night."

"Where?" I asked Fall.

"Going into a roadhouse near Halfmoon Bay."

"Sure it was him?"

"Absolutely! I've seen him come in here to Mr Axford's office to know him. It was him all right."

"How'd you come to see him?"

"I was coming up from further down the shore with some friends, and we stopped in at the roadhouse to get something to eat. As we were leaving, a car drove up and Mr Pangburn and a girl or woman—

I didn't notice her particularly—got out and went inside. I didn't think anything of it until I saw in the paper last night that he hadn't been seen since Sunday. So then I thought to myself that—"

"What roadhouse was this?" I cut in, not being interested in his mental processes.

"The White Shack."

"About what time?"

"Somewhere between eleven-thirty and midnight, I guess."

"He see you?"

"No. I was already in our car when he drove up. I don't think he'd know me anyway."

"What did the woman look like?"

"I don't know. I didn't see her face, and I can't remember how she was dressed or even if she was short or tall."

That was all Fall could tell me.

We shooed him out of the office, and I used Axford's telephone to call up "Wop" Healey's dive in North Beach and leave word that when "Porky" Grout came in he was to call up "Jack." That was a standing arrangement by which I got word to Porky whenever I wanted to see him, without giving anybody a chance to tumble to the connection between us.

"Know the White Shack?" I asked Axford, when I was through phoning.

"I know where it is, but I don't know anything about it."

"Well, it's a tough hole. Run by 'Tin-Star' Joplin, an ex-yegg who invested his winnings in the place when Prohibition made the roadhouse game good. He makes more money now than he ever heard of in his piking safe-ripping days. Retailing liquor is a sideline with him; his real profit comes from acting as a relay station for the booze that comes through Halfmoon Bay for points beyond; and the dope is that half the booze put ashore by the Pacific rum fleet is put ashore in Halfmoon Bay.

"The White Shack is a tough hole, and it's no place for your brother-in-law to be hanging around. I can't go down there myself without stirring things up; Joplin and I are old friends. But I've got a man I can put in there for a few nights. Pangburn may be a regular visitor, or he may even be staying there. He wouldn't be the first one Joplin had ever let hide-out there. I'll put this man of mine in the place for a week, anyway, and see what he can find."

"It's all in your hands," Axford said. "Find Burke without scandal—that's all I ask."

X

From Axford's office I went straight to my rooms, left the outer door unlocked, and sat down to wait for Porky Grout. I had waited an hour and a half when he pushed the door open and came in.

" 'Lo! How's tricks?"

He swaggered to a chair, leaned back in it, put his feet on the table and reached for a pack of cigarettes that lay there.

That was Porky Grout. A pasty-faced man in his thirties, neither large nor small, always dressed flashily—even if sometimes dirtily—and trying to hide an enormous cowardice behind a swaggering carriage, a blustering habit of speech, and an exaggerated pretense of self-assurance.

But I had known him for three years; so now I crossed the room and pushed his feet roughly off the table, almost sending him over backward.

"What's the idea?" He came to his feet, crouching and snarling. "Where do you get that stuff? Do you want a smack in the—"

I took a step toward him. He sprang away, across the room.

"Aw, I didn't mean nothin'. I was only kiddin'!"

"Shut up and sit down," I advised him.

I had known this Porky Grout for three years, and had been using him for nearly that long, and I didn't know a single thing that could be said in his favor. He was a coward. He was a liar. He was a thief, and a hophead. He was a traitor to his kind and, if not watched, to his employers. A nice bird to deal with! But detecting is a hard business, and you use whatever tools come to hand. This Porky was an effective tool if handled right, which meant keeping your hand on his throat all the time and checking up every piece of information he brought in.

His cowardice was—for my purpose—his greatest asset. It was notorious throughout the criminal Coast; and though nobody—crook or not—could possibly think him a man to be trusted, nevertheless he was not actually distrusted. Most of his fellows thought him too much the coward to be dangerous; they thought he would be afraid to betray them; afraid of the summary vengeance that crookdom visits upon the squealer. But they didn't take into account Porky's gift for convincing himself that he was a lion-hearted fellow, when no danger was near. So he went freely where he desired and where I sent him, and brought me otherwise unobtainable bits of information upon matters in which I was interested.

For nearly three years I had used him with considerable success, paying him well, and keeping him under my heel. *Informant* was the polite word that designated him in my reports; the underworld has even less lovely names than the common *stool-pigeon* to denote his kind.

"I have a job for you," I told him, now that he was seated again, with his feet on the floor.

His loose mouth twitched up at the left corner, pushing that eye into a knowing squint.

"I thought so."

He always says something like that.

"I want you to go down to Halfmoon Bay and stick around Tin-Star Joplin's joint for a few nights. Here are two photos"—sliding one of Pangburn and one of the girl across the table. "Their names and descriptions are written on the backs. I want to know if either of them shows up down there, what they're doing, and where they're hanging out. It may be that Tin-Star is covering them up."

Porky was looking knowingly from one picture to the other.

"I think I know this guy," he said out of the corner of his mouth that twitches.

That's another thing about Porky. You can't mention a name or give a description that won't bring that same remark, even though you make them up.

"Here's some money." I slid some bills across the table. "If you're down there more than a couple of nights, I'll get some more to you. Keep in touch with me, either over this phone or the undercover one at the office. And—remember this—lay off the stuff! If I come down there and find you all snowed up, I promise that I'll tip Joplin off to you."

He had finished counting the money by now—there wasn't a whole lot to count—and he threw it contemptuously back on the table.

"Save that for newspapers," he sneered. "How am I goin' to get anywheres if I can't spend no money in the joint?"

"That's plenty for a couple of days' expenses; you'll probably knock back half of it. If you stay longer than a couple of days, I'll get more to you. And you get your pay when the job is done, and not before."

He shook his head and got up.

"I'm tired of pikin' along with you. You can turn your own jobs. I'm through!"

"If you don't get down to Halfmoon Bay tonight, you *are* through," I assured him, letting him get out of the threat whatever he liked.

After a little while, of course, he took the money and left. The dispute over expense money was simply a preliminary that went with every job I sent him out on.

XI

After Porky had cleared out, I leaned back in my chair and burned half a dozen Fatimas over the job. The girl had gone first with the twenty thousand dollars, and then the poet had gone; and both had gone, whether permanently or not, to the White Shack. On its face, the job was an obvious affair. The girl had given Pangburn the *work* to the extent of having him forge a check against his brother-in-law's account; and then, after various moves whose value I couldn't determine at the time, they had gone into hiding together.

There were two loose ends to be taken care of. One of them—the finding of the confederate who had mailed the letters to Pangburn and who had taken care of the girl's baggage—was in the Baltimore branch's hands. The other was: Who had ridden in the taxicab that I had traced from the girl's apartment to the Marquis Hotel?

That might not have any bearing upon the job, or it might. Suppose I could find a connection between the Marquis Hotel and the White Shack. That would make a completed chain of some sort. I searched the back of the telephone directory and found the roadhouse number. Then I went up to the Marquis Hotel.

The girl on duty at the hotel switchboard, when I got there, was one with whom I had done business before.

"Who's been calling Halfmoon Bay numbers?" I asked her.

"My God!" She leaned back in her chair and ran a pink hand gently over the front of her rigidly waved red hair. "I got enough to do without remembering every call that goes through. This ain't a boarding-house. We have more'n one call a week."

"You don't have many Halfmoon Bay calls," I insisted, leaning an elbow on the counter and letting a folded five-spot peep out between the fingers of one hand. "You ought to remember any you've had lately."

"I'll see," she sighed, as if willing to do her best on a hopeless task.

She ran through her tickets.

"Here's one—from room 522, a couple weeks ago."

"What number was called?"

"Halfmoon Bay 51."

That was the roadhouse number. I passed over the five-spot.

"Is 522 a permanent guest?"

"Yes. Mr Kilcourse. He's been here three or four months."

"What is he?"

"I don't know. A perfect gentleman, if you ask me."

"That's nice. What does he look like?"

"Tall and elegant."

"Be yourself," I pleaded. "What does he look like?"

"He's a young man, but his hair is turning gray. He's dark and handsome. Looks like a movie actor."

"Bull Montana?" I asked, as I moved off toward the desk.

The key to 522 was in its place in the rack. I sat down where I could keep an eye on it. Perhaps an hour later a clerk took it out and gave it to a man who did look somewhat like an actor. He was a man of thirty or so, with dark skin, and dark hair that showed gray around the ears. He stood a good six feet of fashionably dressed slenderness.

Carrying the key, he disappeared into an elevator.

I called up the agency then and asked the Old Man to send Dick Foley over. Ten minutes later Dick arrived. He's a little shrimp of a Canadian—there isn't a hundred and ten pounds of him—who is the smoothest shadow I've ever seen, and I've seen most of them.

"I have a bird in here I want tailed," I told Dick. "His name is Kilcourse and he's in room 522. Stick around outside, and I'll give you the spot on him."

I went back to the lobby and waited some more.

At eight o'clock Kilcourse came down and left the hotel. I went after him for half a block—far enough to turn him over to Dick—and then went home, so that I would be within reach of a telephone if Porky Grout tried to get in touch with me. No call came from him that night.

XII

When I arrived at the agency the next morning, Dick was waiting for me.

"What luck?" I asked.

"Damndest!" The little Canadian talks like a telegram when his peace of mind is disturbed, and just now he was decidedly peevish. "Took me two blocks. Shook me. Only taxi in sight."

"Think he made you?"

"No. Wise head. Playing safe."

"Try him again, then. Better have a car handy, in case he tries the same trick again."

My telephone jingled as Dick was going out. It was Porky Grout, talking over the agency's unlisted line.

"Turn up anything?" I asked.

"Plenty," he bragged.

"Good! Are you in town?"

"Yes."

"I'll meet you in my rooms in twenty minutes," I said.

The pasty-faced informant was fairly bloated with pride in himself when he came through the door I had left unlocked for him. His swagger was almost a cake-walk; and the side of his mouth that twitches was twisted into a knowing leer that would have fit a Solomon.

"I knocked it over for you, kid," he boasted. "Nothin' to it—for me! I went down there and talked to ever'body that knowed anything, seen ever'thing there was to see, and put the X-ray on the whole dump. I made a—"

"Uh-huh," I interrupted. "Congratulations and so forth. But just what did you turn up?"

"Now' le'me tell you." He raised a dirty hand in a traffic-cop sort of gesture, and blew a stream of cigarette smoke at the ceiling. "Don't crowd me. I'll give you all the dope."

"Sure," I said. "I know. You're great, and I'm lucky to have you to knock off my jobs for me, and all that! But is Pangburn down there?"

"I'm gettin' around to that. I went down there and—"

"Did you see Pangburn?"

"As I was sayin', I went down there and—"

"Porky," I said, "I don't give a damn what you did! Did you see Pangburn?"

"Yes. I seen him."

"Fine! Now what did you see?"

"He's camping down there with Tin-Star. Him and the broad that you give me a picture of are both there. She's been there a month. I didn't see her, but one of the waiters told me about her. I seen Pangburn myself. They don't show themselves much—stick back in Tin-Star's part of the joint—where he lives—most of the time. Pangburn's been there since Sunday. I went down there and—"

"Learn who the girl is? Or anything about what they're up to?"

"No. I went down there and—"

"All right! *Went down there* again tonight. Call me up as soon as you know positively Pangburn is there—that he hasn't gone out. Don't make any mistakes. I don't want to come down there and scare them up on a false alarm. Use the agency's undercover line, and just tell whoever answers that you won't be in town until late. That'll mean that Pangburn is there; and it'll let you call up from Joplin's without giving the play away."

"I got to have more dough," he said, as he got up. "It costs—"

"I'll file your application," I promised. "Now beat it, and let me hear from you tonight, the minute you're sure Pangburn is there."

Then I went up to Axford's office.

"I think I have a line on him," I told the millionaire. "I hope to have him where you can talk to him tonight. My man says he was at the White Shack last night, and is probably living there. If he's there tonight, I'll take you down, if you want."

"Why can't we go now?"

"No. The place is too dead in the daytime for my man to hang around without making himself conspicuous, and I don't want to take any chances on either you or me showing ourselves there until we're sure we're coming face to face with Pangburn."

"What do you want me to do then?"

"Have a fast car ready tonight, and be ready to start as soon as I get word to you."

"Righto. I'll be at home after five-thirty. Phone me as soon as you're ready to go, and I'll pick you up."

XIII

At nine-thirty that evening I was sitting beside Axford on the front seat of a powerfully engined foreign car, and we were roaring down a road that led to Halfmoon Bay. Porky's telephone call had come.

Neither of us talked much during that ride, and the imported monster under us made it a rather short ride. Axford sat comfortable and relaxed at the wheel, but I noticed for the first time that he had a rather heavy jaw.

The White Shack is a large building, square-built, of imitation stone. It is set away back from the road, and is approached by two curving driveways, which, together, make a semi-circle whose diameter is the public road. The center of this semicircle is occupied by sheds under which Joplin's patrons stow their cars, and here and there around the sheds are flower-beds and clumps of shrubbery.

We were still going at a fair clip when we turned into one end of this semi-circular driveway, and—Axford slammed on his brakes, and the big machine threw us into the windshield as it jolted into an abrupt stop—barely in time to avoid smashing into a cluster of people who had suddenly loomed up before us.

In the glow from our headlights faces stood sharply out; white, horrified faces, furtive faces, faces that were callously curious. Below the faces, white arms and shoulders showed, and bright gowns and jewelry, against the duller background of masculine clothing.

This was the first impression I got, and then, by the time I had removed my face from the windshield, I realized that this cluster of people had a core, a thing about which it centered. I stood up, trying to look over the crowd's heads, but I could see nothing.

Jumping down to the driveway, I pushed through the crowd.

Face down on the white gravel a man sprawled—a thin man in dark clothes—and just above his collar, where the head and neck join, was a hole. I knelt to peer into his face.

Then I pushed through the crowd again, back to where Axford was just getting out of the car, the engine of which was still running.

"Pangburn is dead—shot!"

XIV

Methodically, Axford took off his gloves, folded them and put them in a pocket. Then he nodded his understanding of what I had told him, and walked toward where the crowd stood around the dead poet. I looked after him until he had vanished in the throng. Then I went winding through the outskirts of the crowd, hunting for Porky Grout.

I found him standing on the porch, leaning against a pillar. I passed where he could see me, and went on around to the side of the roadhouse that afforded most shadow.

In the shadows Porky joined me. The night wasn't cool, but his teeth were chattering.

"Who got him?" I demanded.

"I don't know," he whined, and that was the first thing of which I had ever known him to confess complete ignorance. "I was inside, keepin' an eye on the others."

"What others?"

"Tin-Star, and some guy I never seen before, and the broad. I didn't think the kid was going out. He didn't have no hat."

"What *do* you know about it?"

"A little while after I phoned you, the girl and Pangburn came out from Joplin's part of the joint and sat down at a table around on the other side of the porch, where it's fairly dark. They eat for a while and then this other guy comes over and sits down with 'em. I don't know his name, but I think I've saw him around town. He's a tall guy, all rung up in fancy rags."

That would be Kilcourse.

"They talk for a while and then Joplin joins 'em. They sit around the table laughin' and talkin' for maybe a quarter of a hour. Then Pangburn gets up and goes indoors. I got a table that I can watch 'em from, and the place is crowded, and I'm afraid I'll lose my table if I leave it, so I don't follow the kid. He ain't got no hat; I figure he ain't goin' nowhere. But he must of gone through the house and out front, because pretty soon there's a noise that I thought was a auto backfire, and then the sound of a car gettin' away quick. And then some guy squawks that there's a dead man outside. Ever'body runs out here, and it's Pangburn."

"You dead sure that Joplin, Kilcourse and the girl were all at the table when Pangburn was killed?"

"Absolutely," Porky said, "if this dark guy's name is Kilcourse."

"Where are they now?"

"Back in Joplin's hang-out. They went up there as soon as they seen Pangburn had been croaked."

I had no illusions about Porky. I knew he was capable of selling me out and furnishing the poet's murderer with an alibi. But there was this about it: if Joplin, Kilcourse or the girl had fixed him, and had fixed my informant, then it was hopeless for me to try to prove that they weren't on the rear porch when the shot was fired. Joplin had a crowd of hangers-on who would swear to anything he told them without batting an eye. There would be a dozen supposed witnesses to their presence on the rear porch.

Thus the only thing for me to do was to take it for granted that Porky was coming clean with me.

"Have you seen Dick Foley?" I asked, since Dick had been shadowing Kilcourse.

"No."

"Hunt around and see if you can find him. Tell him I've gone up to talk to Joplin, and tell him to come on up. Then you can stick around where I can get hold of you if I want you."

I went in through a French window, crossed an empty dance-floor and went up the stairs that led to Tin-Star Joplin's living quarters in the rear second story. I knew the way, having been up there before. Joplin and I were old friends.

I was going up now to give him and his friends a shake-down on the off-chance that some good might come of it, though

I knew that I had nothing on any of them. I could have tied something on the girl, of course, but not without advertising the fact that the dead poet had forged his brother-in-law's signature to a check. And that was no go.

"Come in," a heavy, familiar voice called when I rapped on Joplin's living-room door.

I pushed the door open and went in.

Tin-Star Joplin was standing in the middle of the floor: a big-bodied ex-yegg with inordinately thick shoulders and an expressionless horse face. Beyond him Kilcourse sat dangling one leg from the corner of a table, alertness hiding behind an amused half-smile on his handsome dark face. On the other side of a room a girl whom I knew for Jeanne Delano sat on the arm of a big leather chair. And the poet hadn't exaggerated when he told me she was beautiful.

"You!" Joplin grunted disgustedly as soon as he recognized me. "What the hell do *you* want?"

"What've you got?"

My mind wasn't on this sort of repartee, however; I was studying the girl. There was something vaguely familiar about her—but I couldn't place her. Perhaps I hadn't seen her before; perhaps much looking at the picture Pangburn had given me was responsible for my feeling of recognition. Pictures will do that.

Meanwhile, Joplin had said:

"Time to waste is one thing I ain't got."

And I had said:

"If you'd saved up all the time different judges have given you, you'd have plenty."

I had seen the girl somewhere before. She was a slender girl in a glistening blue gown that exhibited a generous spread of front, back and arms that were worth showing. She had a mass of dark brown hair above an oval face of the color that pink ought to be. Her eyes were wide-set and of a gray shade that wasn't altogether unlike the shadows on polished silver that the poet had compared them to.

I studied the girl, and she looked back at me with level eyes, and still I couldn't place her. Kilcourse still sat dangling a leg from the table corner.

Joplin grew impatient.

"Will you stop gandering at the girl, and tell me what you want of me?" he growled.

The girl smiled then, a mocking smile that bared the edges of razor-sharp little animal teeth. And with the smile I knew her!

Her hair and skin had fooled me. The last time I had seen her—the only time I had seen her before—her face had been marble-white, and her hair had been short and the color of fire. She and an older woman and three men and I had played hide-and-seek one evening in a house in Turk Street over a matter of the murder of a bank messenger and the theft of a hundred thousand dollars' worth of Liberty Bonds. Through her intriguing three of her accomplices had died that evening, and the fourth—the Chinese—had eventually gone to the gallows at Folsom prison. Her name had been Elvira then, and since her escape from the house that night we had been fruitlessly hunting her from border to border, and beyond.

Recognition must have shown in my eyes in spite of the effort I made to keep them blank, for, swift as a snake, she had left the arm of the chair and was coming forward, her eyes more steel than silver.

I put my gun in sight.

Joplin took a half-step toward me.

"What's the idea?" he barked.

Kilcourse slid off the table, and one of his thin dark hands hovered over his necktie.

"This is the idea," I told them. "I want the girl for a murder a couple months back, and maybe—I'm not sure—for tonight's. Anyway, I'm—"

The snapping of a light-switch behind me, and the room went black.

I moved, not caring where I went so long as I got away from where I had been when the lights went out.

My back touched a wall and I stopped, crouching low.

"Quick, kid!" A hoarse whisper that came from where I thought the door should be.

But both of the room's doors, I thought, were closed, and could hardly be opened without showing gray rectangles. People moved in the blackness, but none got between me and the lighter square of windows.

Something clicked softly in front of me—too thin a click for the cocking of a gun—but it could have been the opening of a spring-knife, and I remembered that Tin-Star Joplin had a fondness for that weapon.

"Let's go! Let's go!" A harsh whisper that cut through the dark like a blow.

Sounds of motion, muffled, indistinguishable... one sound not far away...

Abruptly a strong hand clamped one of my shoulders, a hard-muscled body strained against me. I stabbed out with my gun, and heard a grunt.

The hand moved up my shoulder toward my throat.

I snapped up a knee, and heard another grunt.

A burning point ran down my side.

I stabbed again with my gun—pulled it back until the muzzle was clear of the soft obstacle that had stopped it, and squeezed the trigger.

The crash of the shot. Joplin's voice in my ear—a curiously matter-of-fact voice:

"God damn! That got me."

XV

I spun away from him then, toward where I saw the dim yellow of an open door. I had heard no sounds of departure. I had been too busy. But I knew that Joplin had tied into me while the others made their get-away.

Nobody was in sight as I jumped, slid, tumbled down the steps—any number at a time. A waiter got in my path as I plunged toward the dance-floor. I don't know whether his interference was intentional or not. I didn't ask. I slammed the flat of my gun in his face and went on. Once I jumped a leg that came out to trip me; and at the outer door I had to smear another face.

Then I was out in the semi-circular driveway, from one end of which a red tail-light was turning east into the county road.

While I sprinted for Axford's car I noticed that Pangburn's body had been removed. A few people still stood around the spot where he had lain, and they gaped at me now with open mouths.

The car was as Axford had left it, with idling engine. I swung it through a flower-bed and pointed it east on the public road. Five minutes later I picked up the red point of a tail-light again.

The car under me had more power than I would ever need, more than I would have known how to handle. I don't know how fast the one ahead was going, but I closed in as if it had been standing still.

A mile and a half, or perhaps two—

Suddenly a man was in the road ahead—a little beyond the reach of my lights. The lights caught him, and I saw that it was Porky Grout!

Porky Grout standing facing me in the middle of the road, the dull metal of an automatic in each hand.

The guns in his hands seemed to glow dimly red and then go dark in the glare of my headlights—glow and then go dark, like two bulbs in an automatic electric sign.

The windshield fell apart around me.

Porky Grout—the informant whose name was a synonym for cowardice the full length of the Pacific Coast—stood in the center of the road shooting at a metal comet that rushed down upon him...

I didn't see the end.

I confess frankly that I shut my eyes when his set white face showed close over my radiator. The metal monster under me trembled—not very much—and the road ahead was empty except for the fleeing red light. My windshield was gone. The wind tore at my uncovered hair and brought tears to my squinted-up eyes.

Presently I found that I was talking to myself, saying, "That was Porky. That was Porky." It was an amazing fact. It was no surprise that he had double-crossed me. That was to be expected. And for him to have crept up the stairs behind me and turned off the lights wasn't astonishing. But for him to have stood straight up and died—

An orange streak from the car ahead cut off my wonderment. The bullet didn't come near me—it isn't easy to shoot accurately from one moving car into another—but at the pace I was going it wouldn't be long before I was close enough for good shooting.

I turned on the searchlight above the dashboard. It didn't quite reach the car ahead, but it enabled me to see that the girl was driving, while Kilcourse sat screwed around beside her, facing me. The car was a yellow roadster.

I eased up a little. In a duel with Kilcourse here I would have been at a disadvantage, since I would have had to drive as well as shoot. My best play seemed to be to hold my distance until we reached a town, as we inevitably must. It wasn't midnight yet. There would be people on the streets of any town, and policemen. Then I could close in with a better chance of coming off on top.

A few miles of this and my prey tumbled to my plan. The yellow roadster slowed down, wavered, and came to rest with its length across the road. Kilcourse and the girl were out immediately and crouching in the road on the far side of their barricade.

I was tempted to dive pell-mell into them, but it was a weak temptation, and when its short life had passed I put on the brakes and stopped. Then I fiddled with my searchlight until it bore full upon the roadster.

A flash came from somewhere near the roadster's wheels, and the searchlight shook violently, but the glass wasn't touched. It would be their first target, of course, and...

Crouching in my car, waiting for the bullet that would smash the lense, I took off my shoes and overcoat.

The third bullet ruined the light.

I switched off the other lights, jumped to the road, and when I stopped running I was squatting down against the near side of the yellow roadster. As easy and safe a trick as can be imagined.

The girl and Kilcourse had been looking into the glare of a powerful light. When that light suddenly died, and the weaker ones around it went, too, they were left in pitch unseeing blackness, which must last for the minute or longer that their eyes would need to readjust themselves to the gray-black of the night. My stockinged feet had made no sound on the macadam road, and now there was only a roadster between us; and I knew it and they didn't.

From near the radiator Kilcourse spoke softly:

"I'm going to try to knock him off from the ditch. Take a shot at him now and then to keep him busy."

"I can't see him," the girl protested.

"Your eyes'll be all right in a second. Take a shot at the car anyway."

I moved toward the radiator as the girl's pistol barked at the empty touring car.

Kilcourse, on hands and knees, was working his way toward the ditch that ran along the south side of the road. I gathered my legs under me, intent upon a spring and a blow with my gun upon the back of his head. I didn't want to kill him, but I wanted to put him out of the way quick. I'd have the girl to take care of, and she was at least as dangerous as he.

As I tensed for the spring, Kilcourse, guided perhaps by some instinct of the hunted, turned his head and saw me—saw a threatening shadow.

Instead of jumping I fired.

I didn't look to see whether I had hit him or not. At that range there was little likelihood of missing. I bent double and slipped back to the rear of the roadster, keeping on my side of it.

Then I waited.

The girl did what I would perhaps have done in her place. She didn't shoot or move toward the place the shot had come from. She thought I had forestalled Kilcourse in using the ditch and that my next play would be to circle around behind her. To offset this, she moved around the rear of the roadster, so that she could ambush me from the side nearest Axford's car.

Thus it was that she came creeping around the corner and poked her delicately chiseled nose plunk into the muzzle of the gun that I held ready for her.

She gave a little scream.

Women aren't always reasonable: they are prone to disregard trifles like guns held upon them. So I grabbed her gun-hand, which was fortunate for me. As my hand closed around the weapon, she pulled the trigger, catching a chunk of my forefinger between hammer and frame. I twisted the gun out of her hand; released my finger.

But she wasn't done yet.

With me standing there holding a gun not four inches from her body, she turned and bolted off toward where a clump of trees made a jet-black blot to the north.

When I recovered from my surprise at this amateurish procedure, I stuck both her gun and mine in my pockets, and set out after her, tearing the soles of my feet at every step.

She was trying to get over a wire fence when I caught her.

XVI

"Stop playing, will you?" I said crossly, as I set the fingers of my left hand around her wrist and started to lead her back to the roadster. "This is a serious business. Don't be so childish!"

"You are hurting my arm."

I knew I wasn't hurting her arm, and I knew this girl for the direct cause of four, or perhaps five, deaths; yet I loosened my grip on her wrist until it wasn't much more than a friendly clasp. She went back willingly enough to the roadster, where, still holding her wrist, I switched on the lights.

Kilcourse lay just beneath the headlight's glare, huddled on his face, with one knee drawn up under him.

I put the girl squarely in the line of light.

"Now stand there," I said, "and behave. The first break you make, I'm going to shoot a leg out from under you," and I meant it.

I found Kilcourse's gun, pocketed it, and knelt beside him.

He was dead, with a bullet-hole above his collar-bone.

"Is he—" her mouth trembled.

"Yes."

She looked down at him, and shivered a little.

"Poor Fag," she whispered.

I've gone on record as saying that this girl was beautiful, and, standing there in the dazzling white of the headlights, she was more than that. She was a thing to start crazy thoughts even in the head of an unimaginative middle-aged thief catcher. She was—Anyhow; I suppose that is why I scowled at her and said:

"Yes, poor Fag, and poor Hook, and poor Tai, and poor kid of a Los Angeles bank messenger, and poor Burke," calling the roll, so far as I knew it, of men who had died loving her.

She didn't flare up. Her big gray eyes lifted, and she looked at me with a gaze that I couldn't fathom, and her lovely oval face under the mass of brown hair—which I knew was phoney—was sad.

"I suppose you do think—" she began.

But I had had enough of this; I was uncomfortable along the spine.

"Come on," I said. "We'll leave Kilcourse and the roadster here for the present."

She said nothing, but went with me to Axford's big machine, and sat in silence while I laced my shoes. I found a robe on the back seat and gave it to her.

"Better wrap this around your shoulders. The windshield is gone. It'll be cool."

She followed my suggestion without a word, but when I had edged our vehicle around the rear of the roadster, and had straightened out in the road again, going east, she laid a hand on my arm.

"Aren't we going back to the White Shack?"

"No. Redwood City—the county jail."

A mile perhaps, during which, without looking at her, I knew she was studying my rather lumpy profile. Then her hand was on my forearm again and she was leaning toward me so that her breath was warm against my cheek.

"Will you stop for a minute? There's something—some things I want to tell you."

I brought the car to a halt in a cleared space of hard soil off to one side of the road, and screwed myself a little around in the seat to face her more directly.

"Before you start," I told her, "I want you to understand that we stay here for just so long as you talk about the Pangburn affair. When you get off on any other line—then we finish our trip to Redwood City."

"Aren't you even interested in the Los Angeles affair?"

"No. That's closed. You and Hook Riordan and Tai Choon Tau and the Quarres were equally responsible for the messenger's death, even if Hook did the actual killing. Hook and the Quarres passed out the night we had our party in Turk Street. Tai was hanged last month. Now I've got you. We had enough evidence to swing the Chinese, and we've even more against you. That is done—finished—completed. If you want to tell me anything about Pangburn's death, I'll listen. Otherwise—"

I reached for the self-starter.

A pressure of her fingers on my arm stopped me.

"I do want to tell you about it," she said earnestly. "I want you to know the truth about it. You'll take me to Redwood City, I know. Don't think that I expect—that I have any foolish hopes. But I'd like you to know the truth about this thing. I don't know why I should care especially what you think, but—"

Her voice dwindled off to nothing.

XVII

Then she began to talk very rapidly—as people talk when they fear interruptions before their stories are told—and she sat leaning slightly forward, so that her beautiful oval face was very close to mine.

"After I ran out of the Turk Street house that night—while you were struggling with Tai—my intention was to get away from San Francisco. I had a couple of thousand dollars, enough to carry me any place. Then I thought that going away would be what you people would expect me to do, and that the safest thing for me to do would be to stay right here. It isn't hard for a woman to change her appearance. I had bobbed red hair, white skin, and wore gay clothes. I simply dyed my hair, bought these transformations to make it look long, put color on my face, and bought some dark clothes. Then I took an apartment on Ashbury Avenue under the name of Jeanne Delano, and I was an altogether different person.

"But, while I knew I was perfectly safe from recognition anywhere, I felt more comfortable staying indoors for a while, and, to pass the time, I read a good deal. That's how I happened to run across Burke's book. Do you read poetry?"

I shook my head. An automobile going toward Halfmoon Bay came into sight just then—the first one we'd seen since we left the White Shack. She waited until it had passed before she went on, still talking rapidly.

"Burke wasn't a genius, of course, but there was something about some of his things that—something that got inside me. I wrote him a little note, telling him how much I had enjoyed these things, and sent it to his publishers. A few days later I had a note from Burke, and I learned that he lived in San Francisco. I hadn't known that.

"We exchanged several notes, and then he asked if he could call, and we met. I don't know whether I was in love with him or not, even at first. I did like him, and, between the ardor of his love for me and the flattery of having a fairly well-known poet for a suitor, I really thought that I loved him. I promised to marry him.

"I hadn't told him anything about myself, though now I know that it wouldn't have made any difference to him. But I was afraid to tell him the truth, and I wouldn't lie to him, so I told him nothing.

"Then Fag Kilcourse saw me one day on the street, and knew me in spite of my new hair, complexion and clothes. Fag hadn't much brains, but he had eyes that could see through anything. I don't blame Fag. He acted according to his code. He came up to my apartment, having followed me home; and I told him that I was going to marry Burke and be a respectable housewife. That was dumb of me. Fag was square. If I had told him that I was ribbing Burke up for a trimming, Fag would have let me alone, would have kept his hands off. But when I told him that I was through with the graft, had 'gone queer,' that made me his meat. You know how crooks are: everyone in the world is either a fellow crook or a prospective victim. So if I was no longer a crook, then Fag considered me fair game.

"He learned about Burke's family connections, and then he put it up to me—twenty thousand dollars, or he'd turn me up. He knew about the Los Angeles job, and he knew how badly I was wanted. I was up against it then. I knew I couldn't hide from Fag or run away from him. I told Burke I had to have twenty thousand dollars. I didn't think he had that much, but I thought he could get it. Three days later he gave me a check for it. I didn't know at the time how he had raised it, but it wouldn't have mattered if I had known. I had to have it.

"But that night he told me where he got the money; that he had forged his brother-in-law's signature. He told me because, after thinking it over, he was afraid that when the forgery was discovered I would be caught with him and considered equally guilty. I'm rotten in spots, but I wasn't rotten enough to let him put himself in the pen for me, without knowing what it was all about. I told him the whole story. He didn't bat an eye. He insisted that the money be paid Kilcourse, so that I would be safe, and began to plan for my further safety.

"Burke was confident that his brother-in-law wouldn't send him over for forgery, but, to be on the safe side, he insisted that I move and change my name again and lay low until we knew how Axford was going to take it. But that night, after he had gone, I made some plans of my own. I did like Burke—I liked him too much to let him be the goat without trying to save him, and I didn't have a great deal of faith in Axford's kindness. This was the second of the month. Barring accidents, Axford wouldn't discover the forgery until he got his cancelled checks early the following month. That gave me practically a month to work in.

"The next day I drew all my money out of the bank, and sent Burke a letter, saying that I had been called to Baltimore, and I laid a clear trail to Baltimore, with baggage and letters and all, which a pal there took care of for me. Then I went down to Joplin's and got him to put me up. I let Fag know I was there, and when he came down I told him I expected to have the money for him in a day or two.

"He came down nearly every day after that, and I stalled him from day to day, and each time it got easier. But my time was getting short. Pretty soon Burke's letters would be coming back from the phoney address I had given him, and I wanted to be on hand to keep him from doing anything foolish. And I didn't want to get in touch with him until I could give him the twenty thousand, so he could square the forgery before Axford learned of it from his cancelled checks.

"Fag was getting easier and easier to handle, but I still didn't have him where I wanted him. He wasn't willing to give up the twenty thousand dollars—which I was, of course, holding all this time—unless I'd promise to stick with him for good. And I still thought I was in love with Burke, and I didn't want to tie myself up with Fag, even for a little while.

"Then Burke saw me on the street one Sunday night. I was careless, and drove into the city in Joplin's roadster—the one back there. And, as luck would have it, Burke saw me. I told him the truth, the whole truth. And he told me that he had just hired a private detective to find me. He was like a child in some ways: it hadn't occurred to him that the sleuth would dig up anything about the money. But I knew the forged check would be found in a day or two at the most. I knew it!

"When I told Burke that he went to pieces. All his faith in his brother-in-law's forgiveness went. I couldn't leave him the way he was. He'd have babbled the whole thing to the first person he met. So I brought him back to Joplin's with me. My idea was to hold him there for a few days, until we could see how things were going. If nothing appeared in the papers about the check, then we could take it for granted that Axford had hushed the matter up, and Burke could go home and try to square himself. On the other hand, if the papers got the whole story, then Burke would have to look for a permanent hiding-place, and so would I.

"Tuesday evening's and Wednesday morning's papers were full of the news of his disappearance, but nothing was said about the check. That looked good, but we waited another day for good measure. Fag Kilcourse was in on the game by this time, of course, and I had had to pass over the twenty thousand dollars, but I still had hopes of getting it—or most of it—back, so I continued to string him along. I had a hard time keeping him off Burke, though, because he had begun to think he had some sort of right to me, and jealousy made him wicked. But I got Tin-Star to throw a scare into him, and I thought Burke was safe.

"Tonight one of Tin-Star's men came up and told us that a man named Porky Grout, who had been hanging around the place for a couple of nights, had made a couple of cracks that might mean he was interested in us. Grout was pointed out to me, and I took a chance on showing myself in the public part of the place, and sat at a table close to his. He was plain rat—as I guess you know—and in less than five minutes I had him at my table, and half an hour later I knew that he had tipped you off that Burke and I were in the White Shack. He didn't tell me all this right out, but he told me more than enough for me to guess the rest.

"I went up and told the others. Fag was for killing both Grout and Burke right away. But I talked him out of it. That wouldn't help us any, and I had Grout where he would jump in the ocean for me. I thought I had Fag convinced, but—We finally decided that Burke and I would take the roadster and leave, and that when you got here Porky Grout was to pretend he was hopped up, and point out a man and a woman—any who happened to be handy—as the ones he had taken for us. I stopped to get a cloak and gloves, and Burke went on out to the car alone—and Fag shot him. I didn't know he was going to! I wouldn't have let him! Please believe that! I wasn't as much in love with Burke as I had thought, but please believe that after all he had done for me I wouldn't have let them hurt him!

"After that it was a case of stick with the others whether I liked it or not, and I stuck. We ribbed Grout to tell you that all three of us were on the back porch when Burke was killed, and we had any number of others primed with the same story. Then you came up and recognized me. Just my luck that it had to be you—the only detective in San Francisco who knew me!

"You know the rest: how Porky Grout came up behind you and turned off the lights, and Joplin held you while we ran for the car; and then, when you closed in on us, Grout offered to stand you off while we got clear, and now..."

XVIII

Her voice died, and she shivered a little. The robe I had given her had fallen away from her white shoulders. Whether or not it was because she was so close against my shoulder, I shivered, too. And my fingers, fumbling in my pocket for a cigarette, brought it out twisted and mashed.

"That's all there is to the part you promised to listen to," she said softly, her face turned half away. "I wanted you to know. You're a hard man, but somehow I—"

I cleared my throat, and the hand that held the mangled cigarette was suddenly steady.

"Now don't be crude, sister," I said. "Your work has been too smooth so far to be spoiled by rough stuff now."

She laughed—a brief laugh that was bitter and reckless and just a little weary, and she thrust her face still closer to mine, and the gray eyes were soft and placid.

"Little fat detective whose name I don't know"—her voice had a tired huskiness in it, and a tired mockery—"you think I am playing a part, don't you? You think I am playing for liberty. Perhaps I am. I certainly would take it if it were offered me. But—Men have thought me beautiful, and I have played with them. Women are like that. Men have loved me and, doing what I liked with them, I have found men contemptible. And then comes this little fat detective whose name I don't know, and he acts as if I were a hag—an old squaw. Can I help then being piqued into some sort of feeling for him? Women are like that. Am I so homely that any man has a right to look at me without even interest? Am I ugly?"

I shook my head.

"You're quite pretty," I said, struggling to keep my voice as casual as the words.

"You beast!" she spat, and then her smile grew gentle again. "And yet it is because of that attitude that I sit here and turn myself inside out for you. If you were to take me in your arms and hold me close to the chest that I am already leaning against, and if you were to tell me that there is no jail ahead for me just now, I would be glad, of course. But, though for a while you might hold me, you would then be only one of the men with which I am familiar: men who love and are used and are succeeded by other men. But because you do none of these things, because you are a wooden block of a man, I find myself wanting you. Would I tell you this, little fat detective, if I were playing a game?"

I grunted noncommittally, and forcibly restrained my tongue from running out to moisten my dry lips.

"I'm going to this jail tonight if you are the same hard man who has goaded me into whining love into his uncaring ears, but before that, can't I have one whole-hearted assurance that you think me a little more than 'quite pretty'? Or at least a hint that if I were not a prisoner your pulse might beat a little faster when I touch you? I'm going to this jail for a long while—perhaps to the gallows. Can't I take my vanity there not quite in tatters to keep me company? Can't you do some slight thing to keep me from the afterthought of having bleated all this out to a man who was simply bored?"

Her lids had come down half over the silver-gray eves; her head had tilted back so far that a little pulse showed throbbing in her white throat; her lips were motionless over slightly parted teeth, as the last word had left them. My fingers went deep into the soft white flesh of her shoulders. Her head went further back, her eyes closed, one hand came up to my shoulder.

"You're beautiful as all hell!" I shouted crazily into her face, and flung her against the door.

It seemed an hour that I fumbled with starter and gears before I had the car back in the road and thundering toward the San Mateo County jail. The girl had straightened herself up in the seat again, and sat huddled within the robe I had given her. I squinted straight ahead into the wind that tore at my hair and face, and the absence of the windshield took my thoughts back to Porky Grout.

Porky Grout, whose yellowness was notorious from Seattle to San Diego, standing rigidly in the path of a charging metal monster, with an inadequate pistol in each hand. She had done that to Porky Grout—this woman beside me! She had done that to Porky Grout, and he hadn't even been human! A slimy reptile whose highest thought had been a skinful of dope had gone grimly to death that she might get away—she—this woman whose shoulders I had gripped, whose mouth had been close under mine!

I let the car out another notch, holding the road somehow.

We went through a town: a scurrying of pedestrians for safety, surprised faces staring at us, street lights glistening on the moisture the wind had whipped from my eyes. I passed blindly by the road I wanted, circled back to it, and we were out in the country again.

XIX

At the foot of a long, shallow hill I applied the brakes and we snapped to motionlessness.

I thrust my face close to the girl's.

"Furthermore, you are a liar!" I knew I was shouting foolishly, but I was powerless to lower my voice. "Pangburn never put Axford's name on that check. He never knew anything about it. You got in with him because you knew his brother-in-law was a millionaire. You pumped him, finding out everything he knew about his brother-in-law's account at the Golden Gate Trust. You stole Pangburn's bank book—it wasn't in his room when I searched it—and deposited the forged Axford check to his credit, knowing that under those circumstances the check wouldn't be questioned. The next day you took Pangburn into the bank, saying you were going to make a deposit. You took him in because with him standing beside you the check to which *his* signature had been forged wouldn't be questioned. You knew that, being a gentleman, he'd take pains not to see what you were depositing.

"Then you framed the Baltimore trip. He told the truth to me—the truth so far as he knew it. Then you met him Sunday night—maybe accidentally, maybe not. Anyway, you took him down to Joplin's, giving him some wild yarn that he would swallow and that would persuade him to stay there for a few days. That wasn't hard, since he didn't know anything about either of the twenty-thousand-dollar checks. You and your pal Kilcourse knew that if Pangburn disappeared nobody would ever know that he hadn't forged the Axford check, and nobody would ever suspect that the second check was phoney. You'd have killed him quietly, but when Porky tipped you off that I was on my way down you had to move quick—so you shot him down. That's the truth of it!" I yelled.

All this while she had watched me with wide gray eyes that were calm and tender, but now they clouded a little and a pucker of pain drew her brows together.

I yanked my head away and got the car in motion.

Just before we swept into Redwood City one of her hands came up to my forearm, rested there for a second, patted the arm twice, and withdrew.

I didn't look at her, nor, I think, did she look at me, while she was being booked. She gave her name as Jeanne Delano, and refused to make any statement until she had seen an attorney. It all took a very few minutes.

As she was being led away, she stopped and asked if she might speak privately with me.

We went together to a far corner of the room.

She put her mouth close to my ear so that her breath was warm again on my cheek, as it had been in the car, and whispered the vilest epithet of which the English language is capable.

Then she walked out to her cell.

BLACK MASK, JUNE 1924

"THE GIRL WITH THE SILVER EYES"

Many thanks for the check for "The Girl with the Silver Eyes."

Taken in a lump, the story is pure fiction, but most of its details are based on things that I've either run into myself or got second hand from other detectives. For instance, *"Tin-Star" Joplin's* roadhouse is in California, though not near Halfmoon Bay, and he is exactly as I have set him down. *"Porky" Grout's* original died of tuberculosis in Butte, Montana, two or three years ago. (Some day I'm going to do a psychological study of a stool-pigeon. They're an interesting lot: almost without exception more cowardly even than the ordinary crook, yet they follow the most dangerous calling in the criminal world; for not only is their own world against them, but the detectives who use them seldom hesitate to sacrifice them if anything is gained thereby.) *Jeanne Delano* is partly real, but mostly "made up." (It may be that the Redwood City jail will fail to hold her.) *Fag Kilcourse* has perhaps a half a dozen originals: he isn't an unusual type.

I simply shook these people up together, added a few more to round out the cast of characters, and siced my little fat detective on 'em.

Sincerely yours,
DASHIELL HAMMETT.
San Francisco, Calif.

3

WOMEN, POLITICS AND MURDER

BLACK MASK, SEPTEMBER 1924

Mr Hammett's San Francisco detective is on the job again, working on a mystery the solution of which is so simple that you'll be ashamed of yourself for not figuring it out. And take our word for it, you won't come within a thousand miles of the explanation—yet this is the most realistic and probable story in the issue.

I

A plump maid with bold green eyes and a loose, full-lipped mouth led me up two flights of steps and into an elaborately furnished boudoir, where a woman in black sat at a window. She was a thin woman of a little more than thirty, this murdered man's widow, and her face was white and haggard.

"You are from the Continental Detective Agency?" she asked before I was two steps inside the room.

"Yes."

"I want you to find my husband's murderer." Her voice was shrill, and her dark eyes had wild lights in them. "The police have done nothing. Four days, and they have done nothing. They say it was a robber, but they haven't found him. They haven't found anything!"

"But, Mrs Gilmore," I began, not exactly tickled to death with this explosion, "you must— "

"I know! I know!" she broke in. "But they have done nothing, I tell you—nothing. I don't believe they've made the slightest effort. I don't believe they want to find h-him!"

"Him?" I asked, because she had started to say *her*. "You think it was a man?"

She bit her lip and looked away from me, out of the window to where San Francisco Bay, the distance making toys of its boats, was blue under the early afternoon sun.

"I don't know," she said hesitantly; "it might have— "

Her face spun toward me—a twitching face—and it seemed impossible that anyone could talk so fast, hurl words out so rapidly one after the other.

"I'll tell you. You can judge for yourself. Bernard wasn't faithful to me. There was a woman who calls herself Cara Kenbrook. She wasn't the first. But I learned about her last month. We quarreled. Bernard promised to give her up. Maybe he didn't. But if he did, I wouldn't put it past her—A woman like that would do anything—anything. And down in my heart I really believe she did it!"

"And you think the police don't want to arrest her?"

"I didn't mean exactly that. I'm all unstrung, and likely to say anything. Bernard was mixed up in politics, you know; and if the police found, or thought, that politics had anything to do with his death, they might—

I don't know just what I mean. I'm a nervous, broken woman, and full of crazy notions." She stretched a thin hand out to me. "Straighten this tangle out for me! Find the person who killed Bernard!"

I nodded with empty assurance, still not any too pleased with my client.

"Do you know this Kenbrook woman?" I asked.

"I've seen her on the street, and that's enough to know what sort of person she is!"

"Did you tell the police about her?"

"No-o." She looked out of the window again, and then, as I waited, she added, defensively:

"The police detectives who came to see me acted as if they thought I might have killed Bernard. I was afraid to tell them that I had cause for jealousy. Maybe I shouldn't have kept quiet about that woman, but I didn't think she had done it until afterward, when the police failed to find the murderer. Then I began to think she had done it; but I couldn't make myself go to the police and tell them that I had withheld information. I knew what they'd think. So I—You can twist it around so it'll look as if I hadn't known about the woman, can't you?"

"Possibly. Now as I understand it, your husband was shot on Pine Street, between Leavenworth and Jones, at about three o'clock Tuesday morning. That right?"

"Yes."

"Where was he going?"

"Coming home, I suppose; but I don't know where he had been. Nobody knows. The police haven't found out, if they have tried. He told me Monday evening that he had a business engagement. He was a building contractor, you know. He went out at about half-past eleven, saying he would probably be gone four or five hours."

"Wasn't that an unusual hour to be keeping a business engagement?"

"Not for Bernard. He often had men come to the house at midnight."

"Can you make any guess at all where he was going that night?"

She shook her head with emphasis.

"No. I knew nothing at all about his business affairs, and even the men in his office don't seem to know where he went that night."

That wasn't unlikely. Most of the B. F. Gilmore Construction Company's work had been on city and state contracts, and it isn't altogether unheard-of for secret conferences to go with that kind of work. Your politician-contractor doesn't always move in the open.

"How about enemies?" I asked.

"I don't know anybody that hated him enough to kill him."

"Where does this Kenbrook woman live, do you know?"

"Yes—in the Garford Apartments on Bush Street."

"Nothing you've forgotten to tell me, is there?" I asked, stressing the *me* a little.

"No, I've told you everything I know—every single thing."

II

Walking over to California Street, I shook down my memory for what I had heard here and there of Bernard Gilmore. I could remember a few things—the opposition papers had been in the habit of exposing him every election year—but none of them got me anywhere. I had known him by sight: a boisterous, red-faced man who had hammered his way up from hod-carrier to the ownership of a half-a-million-dollar business and a pretty place in local politics. "A roughneck with a manicure," somebody had called him; a man with a lot of enemies and more friends; a big, good-natured, hard-hitting rowdy.

Odds and ends of a dozen graft scandals in which he had been mixed up, without anybody ever really getting anything on him, flitted through my head as I rode downtown on the too-small outside seat of a cable-car. Then there had been some talk of a bootlegging syndicate of which he was supposed to be the head...

I left the car at Kearny Street and walked over to the Hall of Justice. In the detectives' assembly-room I found O'Gar, the detective-sergeant in charge of the Homicide Detail: a squat man of fifty who goes in for wide-brimmed hats of the movie-sheriff sort, but whose little blue eyes and bullet head aren't handicapped by the trick headgear.

"I want some dope on the Gilmore killing," I told him.

"So do I," he came back. "But if you'll come along I'll tell you what little I know while I'm eating. I ain't had lunch yet."

Safe from eavesdroppers in the clatter of a Sutter Street lunch-room, the detective-sergeant leaned over his clam chowder and told me what he knew about the murder, which wasn't much.

"One of the boys, Kelly, was walking his beat early Tuesday morning, coming down the Jones Street hill from California Street to Pine. It was about three o'clock—no fog or nothing—a clear night. Kelly's within maybe twenty feet of Pine Street when he hears a shot. He whisks around the corner, and there's a man dying on the north sidewalk of Pine Street, halfway between Jones and Leavenworth. Nobody else is in sight. Kelly runs up to the man and finds it's Gilmore. Gilmore dies before he can say a word. The doctors say he was knocked down and then shot; because there's a bruise on his forehead, and the bullet slanted upward in his chest. See what I mean? He was lying on his back when the bullet hit him, with his feet pointing toward the gun it came from. It was a .38."

"Any money on him?"

O'Gar fed himself two spoons of chowder and nodded.

"Six hundred smacks, a coupla diamonds and a watch. Nothing touched."

"What was he doing on Pine Street at that time in the morning?"

"Damned if I know, brother. Chances are he was going home, but we can't find out where he'd been. Don't even know what direction he was walking in when he was knocked over. He was lying across the sidewalk with his feet to the curb; but that don't mean nothing—he could of turned around three or four times after he was hit."

"All apartment buildings in that block, aren't there?"

"Uh-huh. There's an alley or two running off from the south side; but Kelly says he could see the mouths of both alleys when the shot was fired—before he turned the corner—and nobody got away through them."

"Reckon somebody who lives in that block did the shooting?" I asked.

O'Gar tilted his bowl, scooped up the last drops of the chowder, put them in his mouth, and grunted.

"May be. But we got nothing to show that Gilmore knew anybody in that block."

"Many people gather around afterward?"

"A few. There's always people on the street to come running if anything happens. But Kelly says there wasn't anybody that looked wrong—just the ordinary night crowd. The boys gave the neighborhood a combing, but didn't turn up anything."

"Any cars around?"

"Kelly says there wasn't, that he didn't see any, and couldn't have missed seeing it if there'd been one."

"What do you think?" I asked.

He got to his feet, glaring at me.

"I don't think," he said disagreeably; "I'm a police detective."

I knew by that that somebody had been panning him for not finding the murderer.

"I have a line on a woman," I told him. "Want to come along and talk to her with me?"

"I want to," he growled, "but I can't. I got to be in court this afternoon—in half an hour."

III

In the vestibule of the Garford Apartments, I pressed the button tagged Miss Cara Kenbrook several times before the door clicked open. Then I mounted a flight of stairs and walked down a hall to her door. It was opened presently by a tall girl of twenty-three or -four in a black and white crepe dress.

"Miss Cara Kenbrook?"

"Yes."

I gave her a card—one of those that tell the truth about me.

"I'd like to ask you a few questions; may I come in?"

"Do."

Languidly she stepped aside for me to enter, closed the door behind me, and led me back into a living-room that was littered with newspapers, cigarettes in all stages of consumption from unlighted freshness to cold ash, and miscellaneous articles of feminine clothing. She made room for me on a chair by dumping off a pair of pink silk stockings and a hat, and herself sat on some magazines that occupied another chair.

"I'm interested in Bernard Gilmore's death," I said, watching her face.

It wasn't a beautiful face, although it should have been. Everything was there—perfect features; smooth, white skin; big, almost enormous, brown eyes—but the eyes were dead-dull, and the face was as empty of expression as a china door-knob, and what I said didn't change it.

"Bernard Gilmore," she said without interest. "Oh, yes."

"You and he were pretty close friends, weren't you?" I asked, puzzled by her blankness.

"We had been—yes."

"What do you mean by *had been?*'

She pushed back a lock of her short-cut brown hair with a lazy hand.

"I gave him the air last week," she said casually, as if speaking of something that had happened years ago.

"When was the last time you saw him?"

"Last week—Monday, I think—a week before he was killed."

"Was that the time when you broke off with him?"

"Yes."

"Have a row, or part friends?"

"Not exactly either. I just told him that I was through with him."

"How did he take it?"

"It didn't break his heart. I guess he'd heard the same thing before."

"Where were you the night he was killed?"

"At the Coffee Cup, eating and dancing with friends until about one o'clock. Then I came home and went to bed."

"Why did you split with Gilmore?"

"Couldn't stand his wife."

"Huh?"

"She was a nuisance." This without the faintest glint of either annoyance or humor. "She came here one night and raised a racket; so I told Bernie that if he couldn't keep her away from me he'd have to find another playmate."

"Have you any idea who might have killed him?" I asked.

"Not unless it was his wife—these excitable women are always doing silly things."

"If you had given her husband up, what reason would she have for killing him, do you think?"

"I'm sure I don't know," she replied with complete indifference. "But I'm not the only girl that Bernie ever looked at."

"Think there were others, do you? Know anything, or are you just guessing?"

"I don't know any names," she said, "but I'm not just guessing."

I let that go at that and switched back to Mrs Gilmore, wondering if this girl could be full of dope.

"What happened the night his wife came here?"

"Nothing but that. She followed Bernie here, rang the bell, rushed past me when I opened the door, and began to cry and call Bernie names. Then she started on me, and I told him that if he didn't take her away I'd hurt her, so he took her home."

Admitting I was licked for the time, I got up and moved to the door. I couldn't do anything with this baby just now. I didn't think she was telling the whole truth, but on the other hand it wasn't reasonable to believe that anybody would lie so woodenly—with so little effort to be plausible.

"I may be back later," I said as she let me out.

"All right."

Her manner didn't even suggest that she hoped I wouldn't.

IV

From this unsatisfactory interview I went to the scene of the killing, only a few blocks away, to get a look at the neighborhood. I found the block just as I had remembered it and as O'Gar had described it: lined on both sides by apartment buildings, with two blind alleys—one of which was dignified with a name, Touchard Street—running from the south side.

The murder was four days old; I didn't waste any time snooping around the vicinity; but, after strolling the length of the block, boarded a Hyde Street car, transferred at California Street, and went up to see Mrs Gilmore again. I was curious to know why she hadn't told me about her call on Cara Kenbrook.

The same plump maid who had admitted me earlier in the afternoon opened the door.

"Mrs Gilmore is not at home," she said. "But I think she'll be back in half an hour or so."

"I'll wait," I decided.

The maid took me into the library, an immense room on the second floor, with barely enough books in it to give it that name. She switched on a light—the windows were too heavily curtained to let in much daylight—crossed to the door, stopped, moved over to straighten some books on a shelf, looked at me with a half-questioning, half-inviting look in her green eyes, started for the door again, and halted.

By that time I knew she wanted to say something, and needed encouragement. I leaned back in my chair and grinned at her, and decided I had made a mistake—the smile into which her slack lips curved held more coquetry than anything else. She came over to me, walking with an exaggerated swing of the hips, and stood close in front of me.

"What's on your mind?" I asked.

"Suppose—suppose a person knew something that nobody else knew; what would it be worth to them?"

"That," I stalled, "would depend on how valuable it was."

"Suppose I knew who killed the boss?" She bent her face close down to mine, and spoke in a husky whisper. "What would that be worth?"

"The newspapers say that one of Gilmore's clubs has offered a thousand-dollar reward. You'd get that."

Her green eyes went greedy, and then suspicious.

"If *you* didn't."

I shrugged. I knew she'd go through with it—whatever it was—now; so I didn't even explain to her that the Continental doesn't touch rewards, and doesn't let its hired men touch them.

"I'll give you my word," I said; "but you'll have to use your own judgment about trusting me."

She licked her lips.

"You're a good fellow, I guess. I wouldn't tell the police, because I know they'd beat me out of the money. But you look like I can trust you." She leered into my face. "I used to have a gentleman friend who was the very image of you, and he was the grandest—"

"Better speak your piece before somebody comes in," I suggested.

She shot a look at the door, cleared her throat, licked her loose mouth again, and dropped on one knee beside my chair.

"I was coming home late Monday night—the night the boss was killed—and was standing in the shadows saying good night to my friend, when the boss came out of the house and walked down the street. And he had hardly got to the corner, when she—Mrs Gilmore—came out, and went down the street after him. Not trying to catch up with him, you understand; but following him. What do you think of that?"

"What do *you* think of it?"

"*I* think that she finally woke up to the fact that all of her Bernie's dates didn't have anything to do with the building business."

"Do you know that they didn't?"

"Do I know it? I knew that man! He liked 'em—liked 'em all." She smiled into my face, a smile that suggested all evil. "I found *that* out soon after I first came here."

"Do you know when Mrs Gilmore came back that night—what time?"

"Yes," she said; "at half-past three."

"Sure?"

"Absolutely! After I got undressed I got a blanket and sat at the head of the front stairs. My room's in the rear of the top floor. I wanted to see if they came home together, and if there was a fight. After she came in alone I went back to my room, and it was just twenty-five minutes to four then. I looked at my alarm clock."

"Did you see her when she came in?"

"Just the top of her head and shoulders when she turned toward her room at the landing."

"What's your name?" I asked.

"Lina Best."

"All right, Lina," I told her. "If this is the goods I'll see that you collect on it. Keep your eyes open, and if anything else turns up you can get in touch with me at the Continental office. Now you'd better beat it, so nobody will know we've had our heads together."

Alone in the library, I cocked an eye at the ceiling and considered the information Lina Best had given me. But I soon gave that up—no use trying to guess at things that will work out for themselves in a while. I found a book, and spent the next half-hour reading about a sweet young she-chump and a big strong he-chump and all their troubles.

Then Mrs Gilmore came in, apparently straight from the street.

I got up and closed the doors behind her, while she watched me with wide eyes.

"Mrs Gilmore," I said, when I faced her again, "why didn't you tell me that you followed your husband the night he was killed?"

"That's a lie!" she cried; but there was no truth in her voice. "That's a lie!"

"Don't you think you're making a mistake?" I urged. "Don't you think you'd better tell me the whole thing?"

She opened her mouth, but only a dry sobbing sound came out; and she began to sway with a hysterical rocking motion, the fingers of one black-gloved hand plucking at her lower lip, twisting and pulling it.

I stepped to her side and set her down in the chair I had been sitting in, making foolish clucking sounds—meant to soothe her—with my tongue. A disagreeable ten minutes—

and gradually she pulled herself together; her eyes lost their glassiness, and she stopped clawing at her mouth.

"I did follow him." It was a hoarse whisper, barely audible.

Then she was out of the chair, kneeling, with arms held up to me, and her voice was a thin scream.

"But I didn't kill him! I didn't! Please believe that I didn't!"

I picked her up and put her back in the chair.

"I didn't say you did. Just tell me what did happen."

"I didn't believe him when he said he had a business engagement," she moaned. "I didn't trust him. He had lied to me before. I followed him to see if he went to that woman's rooms."

"Did he?"

"No. He went into an apartment house on Pine Street, in the block where he was killed. I don't know exactly which house it was—I was too far behind him to make sure. But I saw him go up the steps and into one—near the middle of the block."

"And then what did you do?"

"I waited, hiding in a dark doorway across the street. I knew the woman's apartment was on Bush Street, but I thought she might have moved, or be meeting him here. I waited a long time, shivering and trembling. It was chilly and I was frightened—afraid somebody would come into the vestibule where I was. But I made myself stay I wanted to see if he came out alone, or if that woman came out. I had a right to do it—he had deceived me before.

"It was terrible, horrible—crouching there in the dark—cold and scared. Then—it must have been about half-past two—I couldn't stand it any longer. I decided to telephone the woman's apartment and find out if she were home. I went down to an all-night lunch-room on Ellis Street and called her up."

"Was she home?"

"No! I tried for fifteen minutes, or maybe longer, but nobody answered the phone. So I *knew* she was in that Pine Street building."

"And what did you do then?"

"I went back there, determined to wait until he came out. I walked up Jones Street. When I was between Bush and Pine I heard a shot. I thought it was a noise made by an automobile then, but now I know that it was the shot that killed Bernie.

"When I reached the corner of Pine and Jones, I could see a policeman bending over Bernie on the sidewalk, and I saw people gathering around. I didn't know then that it was Bernie lying on the sidewalk. In the dark and at that distance I couldn't even see whether it was a man or a woman.

"I was afraid that Bernard would come out to see what was going on, or look out of a window, and discover me; so I didn't go down that way. I was afraid to stay in the neighborhood now, for fear the police would ask me what I was doing loitering in the street at three in the morning—and have it come out that I had been following my husband. So I kept on walking up Jones Street, to California, and then straight home."

"And then what?" I led her on.

"Then I went to bed. I didn't go to sleep—lay there worrying over Bernie; but still not thinking it was he I had seen lying in the street. At nine o'clock that morning two police detectives came and told me Bernie had been killed. They questioned me so sharply that I was afraid to tell them the whole truth. If they had known I had reason for being jealous, and had followed my husband that night, they would have accused me of shooting him. And what could I have done? Everybody would have thought me guilty.

"So I didn't say anything about the woman. I thought they'd find the murderer, and then everything would be all right. I didn't think *she* had done it then, or I would have told you the whole thing the first time you were here. But four days went by without the police finding the murderer, and I began to think they suspected *me!* It was terrible! I couldn't go to them and confess that I had lied to them, and I was sure that the woman had killed him and that the police had failed to suspect her because I hadn't told them about her.

"So I employed you. But I was afraid to tell even you the whole truth. I thought that if I just told you there had been another woman and who she was, you could do the rest without having to know that I had followed Bernie that night. I was afraid *you* would think I had killed him, and would turn me over to the police if I told you everything. And now you *do* believe it! And you'll have me arrested! And they'll hang me! I know it! I know it!"

She began to rock crazily from side to side in her chair.

"Sh-h-h," I soothed her. "You're not arrested yet. Sh-h-h."

I didn't know what to make of her story. The trouble with these nervous, hysterical women is that you can't possibly tell when they're lying and when telling the truth unless you have outside evidence—half of the time they themselves don't know.

"When you heard the shot," I went on when she had quieted down a bit, "you were walking north on Jones, between Bush and Pine? You could see the corner of Pine and Jones?"

"Yes—clearly."

"See anybody?"

"No—not until I reached the corner and looked down Pine Street. Then I saw a policeman bending over Bernie, and two men walking toward them."

"Where were the two men?"

"On Pine Street east of Jones. They didn't have hats on—as if they had come out of a house when they heard the shot."

"Any automobiles in sight either before or after you heard the shot?"

"I didn't see or hear any."

"I have some more questions, Mrs Gilmore," I said; "but I'm in a hurry now. Please don't go out until you hear from me again."

"I won't," she promised; "but—"

I didn't have any answers for anybody's questions, so I ducked my head and left the library.

Near the street door Lina Best appeared out of a shadow, her eyes bright and inquisitive.

"Stick around," I said without any meaning at all, stepped around her, and went on out into the street.

V

I returned then to the Garford Apartments, walking, because I had a lot of things to arrange in my mind before I faced Cara Kenbrook again. And, even though I walked slowly, they weren't all exactly filed in alphabetical order when I got there. She had changed the black and white dress for a plush-like gown of bright green, but her empty doll's face hadn't changed.

"Some more questions," I explained when she opened her door.

She admitted me without word or gesture, and led me back into the room where we had talked before.

"Miss Kenbrook," I asked, standing beside the chair she had offered me, "why did you tell me you were home in bed when Gilmore was killed?"

"Because it's so." Without the flicker of a lash.

"And you wouldn't answer the doorbell?"

I had to twist the facts to make my point. Mrs Gilmore had phoned, but I couldn't afford to give this girl a chance to shunt the blame for her failure to answer off on central.

She hesitated for a split second.

"No—because I didn't hear it."

One cool article, this baby! I couldn't figure her. I didn't know then, and I don't know now, whether she was the owner of the world's best poker face or was just naturally stupid. But whichever she was, she was thoroughly and completely it!

I stopped trying to guess, and got on with my probing.

"And you wouldn't answer the phone either?"

"It didn't ring—or not enough to awaken me."

I chuckled—an artificial chuckle—because central could have been ringing the wrong number. However...

"Miss Kenbrook," I lied, "your phone rang at 2:30 and at 2:40 that morning. And your doorbell rang almost continually from about 2:50 until after 3:00."

"Perhaps," she said; "but I wonder who'd be trying to get me at that hour."

"You didn't hear either?"

"No."

"But you were here?"

"Yes—who was it?" carelessly.

"Get your hat," I bluffed, "and I'll show them to you down at headquarters."

She glanced down at the green gown and walked toward an open bedroom door.

"I suppose I'd better get a cloak, too," she said.

"Yes," I advised her; "and bring your toothbrush."

She turned around then and looked at me, and for a moment it seemed that some sort of expression—surprise maybe—was about to come into her big brown eyes; but none actually came. The eyes stayed dull and empty.

"You mean you're arresting me?"

"Not exactly. But if you stick to your story about being home in bed at 3:00 last Tuesday morning I can promise you you *will* be arrested. If I were you I'd think up another story while we're riding down to the Hall of Justice."

She left the doorway slowly and came back into the room, as far as a chair that stood between us, put her hands on its back, and leaned over it to look at me. For perhaps a minute neither of us spoke—just stood there staring at each other, while I tried to keep my face as expressionless as hers.

"Do you really think," she asked at last, "that I wasn't here when Bernie was killed?"

"I'm a busy man, Miss Kenbrook." I put all the certainty I could fake into my voice. "If you want to stick to your funny story, it's all right with me. But please don't expect me to stand here and argue about it. Get your hat and cloak."

She shrugged, and came around the chair on which she had been leaning.

"I suppose you *do* know something," she said, sitting down. "Well, it's tough on Stan, but women and children first."

My ears twitched at the name *Stan*, but I didn't interrupt her.

"I *was* in the Coffee Cup until one o'clock," she was saying, her voice still flat and emotionless. "And I *did* come home afterward. I'd been drinking *vino* all evening, and it always makes me blue. So after I came home I got to worrying over things. Since Bernie and I split finances haven't been so good. I took stock that night—or morning—and found only four dollars in my purse. The rent was due, and the world looked pretty damned blue.

"Half-lit on Dago wine as I was, I decided to run over and see Stan, tell him all my troubles, and make a touch. Stan is a good egg and he's always willing to go the limit for me. Sober, I wouldn't have gone to see him at three in the morning; but it seemed a perfectly sensible thing to do at the time.

"It's only a few minutes' walk from here to Stan's. I went down Bush Street to Leavenworth, and up Leavenworth to Pine. I was in the middle of that last block when Bernie was shot—I heard it. And when I turned the corner into Pine Street I saw a copper bending over a man on the pavement right in front of Stan's. I hesitated for a couple of minutes, standing in the shadow of a pole, until three or four men had gathered around the man on the sidewalk. Then I went over.

"It was Bernie. And just as I got there I heard the copper tell one of the men that he had been shot. It was an awful shock to me. You know how things like that will hit you!"

I nodded; though God knows there was nothing in this girl's face, manner, or voice to suggest shock. She might have been talking about the weather.

"Dumfounded, not knowing what to do," she went on, "I didn't even stop. I went on, passing as close to Bernie as I am to you now, and rang Stan's bell. He let me in. He had been half-undressed when I rang. His rooms are in the rear of the building, and he hadn't heard the shot, he said. He didn't know Bernie had been killed until I told him. It sort of knocked the wind out of him. He said Bernie had been there—in Stan's rooms—since midnight, and had just left.

"Stan asked me what I was doing there, and I told him my tale of woe. That was the first time Stan knew that Bernie and I were so thick. I met Bernie through Stan, but Stan didn't know we had got so chummy.

"Stan was worried for fear it would come out that Bernie had been to see him that night, because it would make a lot of trouble for him—some sort of shady deal they had on, I guess. So he didn't go out to see Bernie. That's about all there is to it. I got some money from Stan, and stayed in his rooms until the police had cleared out of the neighborhood; because neither of us wanted to get mixed up in anything. Then I came home. That's straight—on the level."

"Why didn't you get this off your chest before?" I demanded, knowing the answer.

It came.

"I was afraid. Suppose I told about Bernie throwing me down, and said I was close to him—a block or so away—when he was killed, and was half-full of vino? The first thing everybody would have said was that I had shot him! I'd lie about it still if I thought you'd believe me."

"So Bernie was the one who broke off, and not you?"

"Oh, yes," she said lightly.

VI

I lit a Fatima and breathed smoke in silence for a while, and the girl sat placidly watching me.

Here I had two women—neither normal. Mrs Gilmore was hysterical, abnormally nervous. This girl was dull, subnormal. One was the dead man's wife; the other his mistress; and each with reason for believing she had been thrown down for the other. Liars, both; and both finally confessing that they had been near the scene of the crime at the time of the crime, though neither admitted seeing the other. Both, by their own accounts, had been at that time even further from normal than usual—Mrs Gilmore filled with jealousy; Cara Kenbrook half-drunk.

What was the answer? Either could have killed Gilmore; but hardly both—unless they had formed some sort of crazy partnership, and in that event—Suddenly all the facts I had gathered—true and false—clicked together in my head. I had the answer—the one simple, satisfying answer!

I grinned at the girl, and set about filling in the gaps in my solution.

"Who is Stan?" I asked.

"Stanley Tennant—he has something to do with the city."

Stanley Tennant. I knew him by reputation, a—

A key rattled in the hall door.

The hall door opened and closed, and a man's footsteps came toward the open doorway of the room in which we were. A tall, broad-shouldered man in tweeds filled the doorway—a ruddy-faced man of thirty-five or so, whose appearance of athletic blond wholesomeness was marred by close-set eyes of an indistinct blue.

Seeing me, he stopped—a step inside the room.

"Hello, Stan!" the girl said lightly. "This gentleman is from the Continental Detective Agency. I've just emptied myself to him about Bernie. Tried to stall him at first, but it was no good."

The man's vague eyes switched back and forth between the girl and me. Around the pale irises his eyeballs were pink.

He straightened his shoulders and smiled too jovially.

"And what conclusion have you come to?" he inquired.

The girl answered for me.

"I've already had *my* invitation to take a ride."

Tennant bent forward. With an unbroken swing of his arms, he swept a chair up from the floor into my face. Not much force behind it, but quick.

I went back against the wall, fending off the chair with both arms—threw it aside—and looked into the muzzle of a nickeled revolver.

A table drawer stood open—the drawer from which he had grabbed the gun while I was busy with the chair. The revolver, I noticed, was of .38 caliber.

"Now," his voice was thick, like a drunk's, "turn around."

I turned my back to him, felt a hand moving over my body, and my gun was taken away.

"All right," he said, and I faced him again.

He stepped back to the girl's side, still holding the nickel-plated revolver on me. My own gun wasn't in sight—in his pocket perhaps. He was breathing noisily, and his eyeballs had gone from pink to red. His face, too, was red, with veins bulging in the forehead.

"You know me?" he snapped.

"Yes, I know you. You're Stanley Tennant, assistant city engineer, and your record is none too lovely." I chattered away on the theory that conversation is always somehow to the advantage of the man who is looking into the gun. "You're supposed to be the lad who supplied the regiment of well-trained witnesses who turned last year's investigation of graft charges against the engineer's office into a comedy. Yes, Mr Tennant, I know you. You're the answer to why Gilmore was so lucky in landing city contracts with bids only a few dollars beneath his competitors'. Yes, Mr Tennant, I know you. You're the bright boy who—"

I had a lot more to tell him, but he cut me off.

"That will do out of you!" he yelled. "Unless you want me to knock a corner off your head with this gun."

Then he addressed the girl, not taking his eyes from me.

"Get up, Cara."

She got out of her chair and stood beside him. His gun was in his right hand, and that side was toward her. He moved around to the other side.

The fingers of his left hand hooked themselves inside of the girl's green gown where it was cut low over the swell of her breasts. His gun never wavered from me. He jerked his left hand, ripping her gown down to the waistline.

"*He* did that, Cara," Tennant said.

She nodded.

His fingers slid inside of the flesh-colored undergarment that was now exposed, and he tore that as he had torn the gown.

"*He* did that."

She nodded again.

His bloodshot eyes darted little measuring glances at her face—swift glances that never kept his eyes from me for the flash of time I would have needed to tie into him.

Then—eyes and gun on me—he smashed his left fist into the girl's blank white face.

One whimper—low and not drawn out—came from her as she went down in a huddle against the wall. Her face—well, there wasn't *much* change in it. She looked dumbly up at Tennant from where she had fallen.

"*He* did that," Tennant was saying.

She nodded, got up from the floor, and returned to her chair.

"Here's our story." The man talked rapidly, his eyes alert on me. "Gilmore was never in my rooms in his life, Cara, and neither were you. The night he was killed you were home shortly after one o'clock, and stayed there. You were sick—probably from the wine you had been drinking—and called a doctor. His name is Howard. I'll see that he's fixed. He got here at 2:30 and stayed until 3:30.

"Today, this gumshoe, learning that you had been intimate with Gilmore, came here to question you. He knew you hadn't killed Gilmore, but he made certain suggestions to you—you can play them up as strong as you like; maybe say that he's been annoying you for months—and when you turned him down he threatened to frame you.

"You refused to have anything to do with him, and he grabbed you, tearing your clothes, and bruising your face when you resisted. I happened to come along then, having an engagement with you, and heard you scream. Your front door was unlocked, so I rushed in, pulled this fellow away, and disarmed him. Then we held him until the police—whom we will phone for—came. Got that?"

"Yes, Stan."

"Good! Now listen: When the police get here this fellow will spill all he knows, of course, and the chances are that all three of us will be taken in. That's why I want you to know what's what right now. I ought to have enough pull to get you and me out on bail tonight, or, if worst comes to worst, to see that my lawyer gets to me tonight—so I can arrange for the witnesses we'll need. Also I ought to be able to fix it so our little fat friend will be held for a day or two, and not allowed to see anybody until late tomorrow—which will give us a good start on him. I don't know how much he knows, but between your story and the stories of a couple of other smart little ladies I had in mind, I'll fix him up with a rep that will keep any jury in the world from ever believing him about anything."

"How do you like that?" he asked me, triumphantly.

"You big clown," I laughed at him, "I think it's funny!"

But I didn't really think so. In spite of what I thought I knew about Gilmore's murder—in spite of my simple, satisfactory solution—something was crawling up my back, my knees felt jerky, and my hands were wet with sweat. I had had people try to frame me before—no detective stays in the business long without having it happen—but I had never got used to it. There's a peculiar deadliness about the thing—especially if you know how erratic juries can be—that makes your flesh crawl, no matter how safe your judgment tells you are.

"Phone the police," Tennant told the girl; "and for God's sake keep your story straight!"

As he tried to impress that necessity on the girl his eyes left me.

I was perhaps five feet from him and his level gun.

A jump—not straight at him—off to one side—put me close.

The gun roared under my arm. I was surprised not to feel the bullet. It seemed that he *must* have hit me.

There wasn't a second shot.

I looped my right fist over as I jumped. It landed when I landed. It took him too high—up on the cheekbone—but it rocked him back a couple of steps.

I didn't know what had happened to his gun. It wasn't in his hand any more. I didn't stop to look for it. I was busy, crowding him back—not letting him set himself—staying close to him—driving at him with both hands.

He was a head taller than I, and had longer arms, but he wasn't any heavier or stronger. I suppose he hit me now and then as I hammered him across the room. He must have. But I didn't feel anything.

I worked him into a corner. Jammed him back in a corner with his legs cramped under him—which didn't give him much leverage to hit from. I got my left arm around his body, holding him where I wanted him. And I began to throw my right fist into him.

I liked that. His belly was flabby, and it got softer every time I hit it. I hit it often.

He was chopping at my face, but by digging my nose into his chest and holding it there I kept my beauty from being altogether ruined. Meanwhile I threw my right fist into him.

Then I became aware that Cara Kenbrook was moving around behind me; and I remembered the revolver that had fallen somewhere when I had charged Tennant. I didn't like that; but there was nothing I could do about it—except put more weight in my punches. My own gun, I thought, was in one of his pockets. But neither of us had time to hunt for it now.

Tennant's knees sagged the next time I hit him.

Once more, I said to myself, and then I'll step back, let him have one on the button, and watch him fall.

But I didn't get that far.

Something that I knew was the missing revolver struck me on the top of the head. An ineffectual blow—not clean enough to stun me—but it took the steam out of my punches.

Another.

They weren't hard, these taps, but to hurt a skull with a hunk of metal you don't have to hit it hard.

I tried to twist away from the next bump, and failed. Not only failed, but let Tennant wiggle away from me.

That was the end.

I wheeled on the girl just in time to take another rap on the head, and then one of Tennant's fists took me over the ear.

I went down in one of those falls that get pugs called quitters—my eyes were open, my mind was alive, but my legs and arms wouldn't lift me up from the floor.

Tennant took my own gun out of a pocket, and with it held on me, sat down in a Morris chair, to gasp for the air I had pounded out of him. The girl sat in another chair; and I, finding I could manage it, sat up in the middle of the floor and looked at them.

Tennant spoke, still panting.

"This is fine—all the signs of a struggle we need to make our story good!"

"If they don't believe you were in a fight," I suggested sourly, pressing my aching head with both hands, "you can strip and show them your little tummy."

"And you can show them this!"

He leaned down and split my lip with a punch that spread me on my back.

Anger brought my legs to life. I got up on them. Tennant moved around behind the Morris chair. My black gun was steady in his hand.

"Go easy," he warned me. "My story will work if I have to kill you—maybe work better."

That was sense. I stood still.

"Phone the police, Cara," he ordered.

She went out of the room, closing the door behind her; and all I could hear of her talk was a broken murmur.

VII

Ten minutes later three uniformed policemen arrived. All three knew Tennant, and they treated him with respect. Tennant reeled off the story he and the girl had cooked up, with a few changes to take care of the shot that had been fired from the nickeled gun and our rough-house. She nodded her head vigorously whenever a policeman looked at her. Tennant turned both guns over to the white-haired sergeant in charge.

I didn't argue, didn't deny anything, but told the sergeant:

"I'm working with Detective-Sergeant O'Gar on a job. I want to talk to him over the phone and then I want you to take all three of us down to the detective bureau."

Tennant objected to that, of course; not because he expected to gain anything, but on the off-chance that he might. The white-haired sergeant looked from one of us to the other in puzzlement. Me, with my skinned face and split lip; Tennant, with a red lump under one eye where my first wallop had landed; and the girl, with most of the clothes above the waistline ripped off and a bruised cheek.

"It has a queer look, this thing," the sergeant decided aloud; "and I shouldn't wonder but what the detective bureau was the place for the lot of you."

One of the patrolmen went into the hall with me, and I got O'Gar on the phone at his home. It was nearly ten o'clock by now, and he was preparing for bed.

"Cleaning up the Gilmore murder," I told him. "Meet me at the Hall. Will you get hold of Kelly, the patrolman who found Gilmore, and bring him down there? I want him to look at some people."

"I will that," O'Gar promised, and I hung up.

The "wagon" in which the three policemen had answered Cara Kenbrook's call carried us down to the Hall of Justice, where we all went into the captain of detectives' office. McTighe, a lieutenant, was on duty.

I knew McTighe, and we were on pretty good terms; but I wasn't an influence in local politics, and Tennant was. I don't mean that McTighe would have knowingly helped Tennant frame me; but with me stacked up against the assistant city engineer, I knew who would get the benefit of any doubt there might be.

My head was thumping and roaring just now, with knots all over it where the girl had beaned me. I sat down, kept quiet, and nursed my head while Tennant and Cara Kenbrook, with a lot of details that they had not wasted on the uniformed men, told their tale and showed their injuries.

Tennant was talking—describing the terrible scene that had met his eyes when, drawn by the girl's screams, he had rushed into her apartment—when O'Gar came into the office. He recognized Tennant with a lifted eyebrow; and came over to sit beside me.

"What the hell is all this?" he muttered.

"A lovely mess," I whispered back. "Listen—in that nickel gun on the desk there's an empty shell. Get it for me."

He scratched his head doubtfully, listened to the next few words of Tennant's yarn, glanced at me out of the corner of his eye, and then went over to the desk and picked up the revolver.

McTighe looked at him—a sharp, questioning look.

"Something on the Gilmore killing," the detective-sergeant said, breaking the gun.

The lieutenant started to speak, changed his mind, and O'Gar brought the shell over and handed it to me.

"Thanks," I said, putting it in my pocket. "Now listen to my friend there. It's a good act, if you like it."

Tennant was winding up his history.

"...Naturally a man who tried a thing like that on an unprotected woman would be yellow; so it wasn't very hard to handle him after I got his gun away from him. I hit him a couple of times, and he quit—begging me to stop, getting down on his knees. Then we called the police."

McTighe looked at me with eyes that were cold and hard. Tennant had made a believer of him, and not only of him—the police-sergeant and his two men were glowering at me. I suspected that even O'Gar—with whom I had been through a dozen storms—would have been half-convinced if the engineer hadn't added the neat touches about my kneeling.

"Well, what have *you* got to say?" McTighe challenged me in a tone which suggested that it didn't make much difference what I said.

"I've got nothing to say about this dream," I said shortly. "I'm interested in the Gilmore murder—not in this stuff." I turned to O'Gar. "Is the patrolman here?"

The detective-sergeant went to the door, and called: "Oh, Kelly!"

Kelly came in—a big, straight-standing man, with iron-gray hair and an intelligent fat face.

"You found Gilmore's body?" I asked.

"I did."

I pointed at Cara Kenbrook.

"Ever see her before?"

His gray eyes studied her carefully;

"Not that I remember," he answered.

"Did she come up the street while you were looking at Gilmore, and go into the house he was lying in front of?"

"She did not."

I took out the empty shell O'Gar had got for me, and chucked it down on the desk in front of the patrolman.

"Kelly," I asked, *"why did you kill Gilmore?'*

Kelly's right hand went under his coat-tail at his hip.

I jumped for him.

Somebody grabbed me by the neck. Somebody else piled on my back. McTighe aimed a big fist at my face, but it missed. My legs had been suddenly kicked from under me, and I went down hard with men all over me.

When I was yanked to my feet again, big Kelly stood straight up by the desk, weighing his service revolver in his hand. His clear eyes met mine, and he laid the weapon on the desk. Then he unfastened his shield and put it with the gun.

"It was an accident," he said simply.

By this time the birds who had been manhandling me woke up to the fact that maybe they were missing part of the play—that maybe I wasn't a maniac. Hands dropped off me; and presently everybody was listening to Kelly.

He told his story with unhurried evenness, his eyes never wavering or clouding. A deliberate man, though unlucky.

"I was walkin' my beat that night, an' as I turned the corner of Jones into Pine I saw a man jump back from the steps of a buildin' into the vestibule. A burglar, I thought, an' cat-footed it down there. It was a dark vestibule, an' deep, an' I saw-somethin' that looked like a man in it, but I wasn't sure.

"'Come out o' there!' I called, but there was no answer. I took my gun in my hand an' started up the steps. I saw him move just then, comin' out. An' then my foot slipped. It was worn smooth, the bottom step, an' my foot slipped. I fell forward, the gun went off, an' the bullet hit him. He had come out a ways by then, an' when the bullet hit him he toppled over frontwise, tumblin' down the steps onto the sidewalk.

"When I looked at him I saw it was Gilmore. I knew him to say 'howdy' to, an' he knew me—which is why he must o' ducked out of sight when he saw me comin' around the corner. He didn't want me to see him comin' out of a buildin' where I knew Mr Tennant lived, I suppose, thinkin' I'd put two an' two together, an' maybe talk.

"I don't say that I did the right thing by lyin', but it didn't hurt anybody. It was an accident; but he was a man with a lot of friends up in high places, an'—accident or no—I stood a good chance of bein' broke, an' maybe sent over for a while. So I told my story the way you people know it. I couldn't say I'd seen anything suspicious without maybe puttin' the blame on some innocent party, an' I didn't want that. I'd made up my mind that if anybody was arrested for the murder, an' things looked bad for them, I'd come out an' say I'd done it. Home, you'll find a confession all written out—written out in case somethin' happened to me—so nobody else'd ever be blamed.

"That's why I had to say I'd never seen the lady here. I did see her—saw her go into the buildin' that night—the buildin' Gilmore had come out of. But I couldn't say so without makin' it look bad for her; so I lied. I could have thought up a better story if I'd had more time, I don't doubt; but I had to think quick. Anyways, I'm glad it's all over."

VIII

Kelly and the other uniformed policeman had left the office, which now held McTighe, O'Gar, Cara Kenbrook, Tennant and me. Tennant had crossed to my side, and was apologizing.

"I hope you'll let me square myself for this evening's work. But you know how it is when somebody you care for is in a jam. I'd have killed you if I had thought it would help Cara—on the level. Why didn't you tell us that you didn't suspect her?"

"But I did suspect the pair of you," I said. "It looked as if Kelly had to be the guilty one; but you people carried on so much that I began to feel doubtful. For a while it was funny—you thinking she had done it, and she thinking you had, though I suppose each had sworn to his or her innocence. But after a time it stopped being funny. You carried it too far."

"How did you rap to Kelly?" O'Gar, at my shoulder, asked.

"Miss Kenbrook was walking north on Leavenworth—and was half-way between Bush and Pine—when the shot was fired. She saw nobody, no cars, until she rounded the corner. Mrs Gilmore, walking north on Jones, was about the same distance away when *she* heard the shot, and she saw nobody until she reached Pine Street. If Kelly had been telling the truth, she would have seen him on Jones Street. He said he didn't turn the corner until after the shot was fired.

"Either of the women could have killed Gilmore, but hardly both; and I doubted that either could have shot him and got away without running into Kelly or the other. Suppose both of them were telling the truth—what then? Kelly must have been lying! He was the logical suspect anyway—the nearest known person to the murdered man when the shot was fired.

"To back all this up, he had let Miss Kenbrook go into the apartment building at 3:00 in the morning, in front of which a man had just been killed, without questioning her or mentioning her in his report. That looked as if he *knew* who had done the killing. So I took a chance with the empty shell trick, it being a good bet that he would have thrown his away, and would think that—"

McTighe's heavy voice interrupted my explanation.

"How about this assault charge?" he asked, and had the decency to avoid my eye when I turned toward him with the others.

Tennant cleared his throat.

"Er—ah—in view of the way things have turned out, and knowing that Miss Kenbrook doesn't want the disagreeable publicity that would accompany an affair of this sort, why, I'd suggest that we drop the whole thing." He smiled brightly from McTighe to me. "You know nothing has gone on the records yet."

"Make the big heap play his hand out," O'Gar growled in my ear. "Don't let him drop it."

"Of course if Miss Kenbrook doesn't want to press the charge," McTighe was saying, watching me out of the tail of his eye, "I suppose—"

"If everybody understands that the whole thing was a plant," I said, "and if the policemen who heard the story are brought in here now and told by Tennant and Miss Kenbrook that it was all a lie—then I'm willing to let it go at that. Otherwise, I won't stand for a hush-up."

"You're a damned fool!" O'Gar whispered. "Put the screws on them!"

But I shook my head. I didn't see any sense in making a lot of trouble for myself just to make some for somebody else—and suppose Tennant *proved* his story...

So the policemen were found, and brought into the office again, and told the truth.

And presently Tennant, the girl, and I were walking together like three old friends through the corridors toward the door, Tennant still asking me to let him make amends for the evening's work.

"You've *pot* to get me do something!" he insisted. "It's only right!"

His hand dipped into his coat, and came out with a thick bill-fold.

"Here," he said; "let me—"

We were going, at that happy moment, down the stone vestibule steps that led to Kearny Street—six or seven steps there are.

"No," I said; "let me—"

He was on the next to the top step, when I reached up and let go.

He settled in a rather limp pile at the bottom.

Leaving his empty-faced lady love to watch over him, I strolled up through Portsmouth Square toward a restaurant where the steaks come thick.

4

THE GOLDEN HORSESHOE

BLACK MASK, NOVEMBER 1924

In our recent voting contest for favorite BLACK MASK *authors, Dashiell Hammett received thousands of votes because of his series of stories of the adventures of his San Francisco detective. He has created one of the most convincing and realistic characters in all detective fiction. The story, herewith, is one of his best to date. We know you'll enjoy it to the last word.*

A COMPLETE NOVELETTE

I

"I haven't anything very exciting to offer you this time," Vance Richmond said as we shook hands. "I want you to find a man for me—a man who is not a criminal."

There was an apology in his voice. The last couple of jobs this lean, gray-faced attorney had thrown my way had run to gun-play and other forms of rioting, and I suppose he thought anything less than that would put me to sleep. Was a time when he might have been right—when I was a young sprout of twenty or so, newly attached to the Continental Detective Agency. But the fifteen years that had slid by since then had dulled my appetite for rough stuff. I don't mean that I shuddered whenever I considered the possibility of some bird taking a poke at me; but I didn't call that day a total loss in which nobody tried to puncture my short, fat carcass.

"The man I want found," the lawyer went on, as we sat down, "is an English architect named Norman Ashcraft. He is a man of about thirty-seven, five feet ten inches tall, well built, and fair-skinned, with light hair and blue eyes. Four years ago he was a typical specimen of the clean-cut blond Britisher. He may not be like that now—those four years have been rather hard ones for him, I imagine.

"I want to find him for Mrs Ashcraft, his wife. I know your agency's rule against meddling with family affairs, but I can assure you that no matter how things turn out there will be no divorce proceedings in which you will be involved.

"Here is the story. Four years ago the Ashcrafts were living together in England, in Bristol. It seems that Mrs Ashcraft is of a very jealous disposition, and he was rather high-strung. Furthermore, he had only what money he earned at his profession, while she had inherited quite a bit from her parents. Ashcraft was rather foolishly sensitive about being the husband of a wealthy woman—was inclined to go out of his way to show that he was not dependent upon her money, that he wouldn't be influenced by it. Foolish, of course, but just the sort of attitude a man of his temperament would assume. One night she accused him of paying too much attention to another woman. They quarreled, and he packed up and left.

"She was repentant within a week—especially repentant since she had learned that her suspicion had had no foundation outside of her own jealousy—and she tried to find him. But he was gone. It became manifest that he had left England.

She had him searched for in Europe, in Canada, in Australia, and in the United States. She succeeded in tracing him from Bristol to New York, and then to Detroit, where he had been arrested and fined for disturbing the peace in a drunken row of some sort. After that he dropped out of sight until he bobbed up in Seattle ten months later."

The attorney hunted through the papers on his desk and found a memorandum.

"On May 23, 1923, he shot and killed a burglar in his room in a hotel there. The Seattle police seem to have suspected that there was something funny about the shooting, but had nothing to hold Ashcraft on. The man he killed was undoubtedly a burglar. Then Ashcraft disappeared again, and nothing was heard of him until just about a year ago. Mrs Ashcraft had advertisements inserted in the personal columns of papers in the principal American cities.

"One day she received a letter from him, from San Francisco. It was a very formal letter, and simply requested her to stop advertising. Although he was through with the name Norman Ashcraft, he wrote, he disliked seeing it published in every newspaper he read.

"She mailed a letter to him at the General Delivery window here, and used another advertisement to tell him about it. He answered it, rather caustically. She wrote him again, asking him to come home. He refused, though he seemed less bitter toward her. They exchanged several letters, and she learned that he had become a drug addict, and what was left of his pride would not let him return to her until he looked—and was at least somewhat like—his former self. She persuaded him to accept enough money from her to straighten himself out. She sent him this money each month, in care of General Delivery, here.

"Meanwhile she closed up her affairs in England—she had no close relatives to hold her there—and came to San Francisco, to be on hand when her husband was ready to return to her. A year has gone. She still sends him money each month. She still waits for him to come back to her. He has repeatedly refused to see her, and his letters are evasive—filled with accounts of the struggle he is having, making headway against the drug one month, slipping back the next.

"She suspects by now, of course, that he has no intention of ever coming back to her; that he does not intend giving up the drug; that he is simply using her as a source of income. I have urged her to discontinue the monthly allowance for a while. That would at least bring about an interview, I think, and she could learn definitely what to expect. But she will not do that. You see, she blames herself for his present condition. She thinks her foolish flare of jealousy is responsible for his plight, and she is afraid to do anything that might either hurt him *or* induce him *to* hurt himself further. Her mind is unchangeably made up in that respect. She wants him back, wants him straightened out; but if he will not come, then she is content to continue the payments for the rest of his life. But she wants to know what she is to expect. She wants to end this devilish uncertainty in which she has been living.

"What we want, then, is for you to find Ashcraft. We want to know whether there is any likelihood of his ever becoming a man again, or whether he is gone beyond redemption. There is your job. Find him, learn whatever you can about him, and then, after we know something, we will decide whether it is wiser to force an interview between them—in hopes that she will be able to influence him—or not."

"I'll try it," I said. "When does Mrs Ashcraft send him his monthly allowance?"

"On the first of each month."

"Today is the twenty-eighth. That'll give me three days to wind up a job I have on hand. Got a photo of him?"

"Unfortunately, no. In her anger immediately after their row, Mrs Ashcraft destroyed everything she had that would remind her of him. But I don't think a photograph would be of any great help at the post office. Without consulting me, Mrs Ashcraft watched for her husband there on several occasions, and did not see him. It is more than likely that he has someone else call for his mail."

I got up and reached for my hat.

"See you around the second of the month," I said, as I left the office.

II

On the afternoon of the first, I went down to the post office and got hold of Lusk, the inspector in charge of the division at the time.

"I've got a line on a scratcher from up north," I told Lusk, "who is supposed to be getting his mail at the window. Will you fix it up so I can get a spot on him?"

Post office inspectors are all tied up with rules and regulations that forbid their giving assistance to private detectives except on certain criminal matters. But a friendly inspector doesn't have to put you through the third degree. You lie to him—so that he will have an alibi in case there's a kick-back—and whether he thinks you're lying or not doesn't matter.

So presently I was downstairs again, loitering within sight of the A to D window, with the clerk at the window instructed to give me the office when Ashcraft's mail was called for. There was no mail for him there at the time. Mrs Ashcraft's letter would hardly get to the clerks that afternoon, but I was taking no chances. I stayed on the job until the windows closed at eight o'clock, and then went home.

At a few minutes after ten the next morning I got my action. One of the clerks gave me the signal. A small man in a blue suit and a soft gray hat was walking away from the window with an envelope in his hand. A man of perhaps forty years, though he looked older. His face was pasty, his feet dragged, and, although his clothes were fairly new, they needed brushing and pressing.

He came straight to the desk in front of which I stood fiddling with some papers. Out of the tail of my eye I saw that he had not opened the envelope in his hand—was not going to open it. He took a large envelope from his pocket, and I got just enough of a glimpse of its front to see that it was already stamped and addressed. I twisted my neck out of joint trying to read the address, but failed. He kept the addressed side against his body, put the letter he had got from the window in it, and licked the flap backward, so that there was no possible way for anybody to see the front of the envelope. Then he rubbed the flap down carefully and turned toward the mailing slots. I went after him. There was nothing to do but to pull the always reliable stumble.

I overtook him, stepped close and faked a fall on the marble floor, bumping into him, grabbing him as if to regain my balance. It went rotten. In the middle of my stunt my foot really did slip, and we went down on the floor like a pair of wrestlers, with him under me. To botch the trick thoroughly, he fell with the envelope pinned under him.

I scrambled up, yanked him to his feet, mumbled an apology and almost had to push him out of the way to beat him to the envelope that lay face down on the floor. I had to turn it over as I handed it to him in order to get the address:

Mr Edward Bohannon,
Golden Horseshoe Cafe,
Tijuana, Baja California,
Mexico.

I had the address, but I had tipped my mitt. There was no way in God's world for this little man in blue to miss knowing that I had been trying to get that address.

I dusted myself off while he put his envelope through a slot. He didn't come back past me, but went on down toward the Mission Street exit. I couldn't let him get away with what he knew. I didn't want Ashcraft tipped off before I got to him. I would have to try another trick as ancient as the one the slippery floor had bungled for me. I set out after the little man again.

Just as I reached his side he turned his head to see if he was being followed.

"Hello, Micky!" I hailed him. "How's everything in Chi?"

"You got me wrong." He spoke out of the side of his gray-lipped mouth, not stopping. "I don't know nothin' about Chi."

His eyes were pale blue, with needle point pupils—the eyes of a heroin or morphine user.

"Quit stalling." I walked along at his side. We had left the building by this time and were going down Mission Street. "You fell off the rattler only this morning."

He stopped on the sidewalk and faced me.

"Me? Who do you think I am?"

"You're Micky Parker. The Dutchman gave us the rap that you were headed here. They got him—if you don't already know it."

"You're cuckoo," he sneered. "I don't know what the hell you're talkin' about!"

That was nothing—neither did I. I raised my right hand in my overcoat pocket.

"Now I'll tell one," I growled at him. "And keep your hands away from your clothes or I'll let the guts out of you."

He flinched away from my bulging pocket.

"Hey, listen, brother!" he begged. "You got me wrong—on the level. My name ain't Micky Parker, an' I ain't been in Chi in six years. I been here in Frisco for a solid year, an' that's the truth."

"You got to show me."

"I can do it," he exclaimed, all eagerness. "You come down the drag with me, an' I'll show you. My name's Ryan, an' I been livin' aroun' the corner here on Sixth Street for six or eight months."

"Ryan?" I asked.

"Yes—John Ryan."

I chalked that up against him. Of course there have been Ryans christened John, but not enough of them to account for the number of times that name appears in criminal records. I don't suppose there are three old-time yeggs in the country who haven't used the name at least once; it's the John Smith of yeggdom.

This particular John Ryan led me around to a house on Sixth Street, where the landlady—a rough-hewn woman of fifty, with bare arms that were haired and muscled like the village smithy's—assured me that her tenant had to her positive knowledge been in San Francisco for months, and that she remembered seeing him at least once a day for a couple of weeks back. If I had been really suspicious that this Ryan was my mythical Micky Parker from Chicago, I wouldn't have taken the woman's word for it, but as it was I pretended to be satisfied.

That seemed to be all right then. Mr Ryan had been led astray, had been convinced that I had mistaken him for another crook, and that I was not interested in the Ashcraft letter. I would be safe—reasonably safe—in letting the situation go as it stood. But loose ends worry me. And you can't always count on people doing and thinking what you want. This bird was a hophead, and he had given me a phoney-sounding name, so...

"What do you do for a living?" I asked him.

"I ain't been doin' nothin' for a coupla months," he pattered, "but I expec' to open a lunch room with a fella nex' week."

"Let's go up to your room," I suggested. "I want to talk to you."

He wasn't enthusiastic, but he took me up. He had two rooms and a kitchen on the third floor. They were dirty, foul-smelling rooms. I dangled a leg from the corner of a table and waved him into a squeaky rocking chair in front of me. His pasty face and dopey eyes were uneasy.

"Where's Ashcraft?" I threw at him. He jerked, and then looked at the floor.

"I don't know what you're talkin' about," he mumbled.

"You'd better figure it out," I advised him, "or there's a nice cool cell down in the booby-hutch that will be wrapped around you."

"You ain't got nothin' on me."

"What of that? How'd you like to do a thirty or a sixty on a vag charge?"

"Vag, hell!" he snarled, looking up at me. "I got five hundred smacks in my kick. Does that look like you can vag me?"

I grinned down at him.

"You know better than that, Ryan. A pocketful of money'll get you nothing in California. You've got no job. You can't show where your money comes from. You're made to order for the vag law."

I had this bird figured as a dope peddler. If he was—or was anything else off color that might come to light when he was vagged—the chances were that he would be willing to sell Ashcraft out to save himself; especially since, so far as I knew, Ashcraft wasn't on the wrong side of the criminal law.

"If I were you," I went on while he stared at the floor and thought, "I'd be a nice, obliging fellow and do my talking now. You're—"

He twisted sidewise in his chair and one of his hands went behind him.

I kicked him out of his chair.

The table slipped under me or I would have stretched him. As it was, the foot that I aimed at his jaw took him on the chest and carried him over backward, with the rocking-chair piled on top of him. I pulled the chair off and took his gun—a cheap nickel-plated .32. Then I went back to my seat on the corner of the table.

He had only that one flash of fight in him. He got up sniveling.

"I'll tell you. I don't want no trouble, an' it ain't nothin' to me. I didn't know there was nothin' wrong. This Ashcraft told me he was jus' stringin' his wife along. He give me ten bucks a throw to get his letter ever' month an' send it to him in Tijuana. I knowed him here, an' when he went south six months ago—he's got a girl down there—I promised I'd do it for him. I knowed it was money—he said it was his 'alimony'—but I didn't know there was nothin' wrong."

"What sort of a hombre is this Ashcraft? What's his graft?"

"I don't know. He could be a con man—he's got a good front. He's a Englishman, an' mostly goes by the name of Ed Bohannon. He hits the hop. I don't use it myself"—that was a good one—"but you know how it is in a burg like this, a man runs into all kinds of people. I don't know nothin' about what he's up to. I jus' send the money ever' month an' get my ten."

That was all I could get out of him. He couldn't—or wouldn't—tell me where Ashcraft had lived in San Francisco or who he had mobbed up with. However, I had learned that Bohannon was Ashcraft, and not another go-between, and that was something.

Ryan squawked his head off when he found that I was going to vag him anyway. For a moment it looked like I would have to kick him loose from his backbone again.

"You said you'd spring me if I talked," he wailed.

"I did not. But if I had—when a gent flashes a rod on me I figure it cancels any agreement we might have had. Come on."

I couldn't afford to let him run around loose until I got in touch with Ashcraft. He would have been sending a telegram before I was three blocks away, and my quarry would be on his merry way to points north, east, south and west.

It was a good hunch I played in nabbing Ryan. When he was finger-printed at the Hall of Justice he turned out to be one Fred Rooney, alias "Jamocha," a peddler and smuggler who had crushed out of the Federal Prison at Leavenworth, leaving eight years of a tenner still unserved.

"Will you sew him up for a couple of days?" I asked the captain of the city jail. "I've got work to do that will go smoother if he can't get any word out for a while."

"Sure," the captain promised. "The federal people won't take him off our hands for two or three days. I'll keep him air-tight till then."

III

From the jail I went up to Vance Richmond's office and turned my news over to him.

"Ashcraft is getting his mail in Tijuana. He's living down there under the name of Ed Bohannon, and maybe has a woman there. I've just thrown one of his friends—the one who handled the mail and an escaped con—in the cooler."

"Was that necessary?" Richmond asked. "We don't want to work any hardships. We're really trying to help Ashcraft, you know."

"I could have spared this bird," I admitted. "But what for? He was all wrong. If Ashcraft can be brought back to his wife, he's better off with some of his shady friends out of the way. If he can't, what's the difference? Anyway, we've got one line on him safely stowed away where we can find it when we want it."

The attorney shrugged, and reached for the telephone.

He called a number. "Is Mrs Ashcraft there?... This is Mr Richmond... No, we haven't exactly found him, but I think we know where he is... Yes... In about fifteen minutes."

He put down the telephone and stood up.

"We'll run up to Mrs Ashcraft's house and see her."

Fifteen minutes later we were getting out of Richmond's car in Jackson Street near Gough. The house was a three-story white stone building, set behind a carefully sodded little lawn with an iron railing around it.

Mrs Ashcraft received us in a drawing-room on the second floor. A tall woman of less than thirty, slimly beautiful in a gray dress. Clear was the word that best fits her; it described the blue of her eyes, the pink-white of her skin, and the light brown of her hair.

Richmond introduced me to her, and then I told her what I had learned, omitting the part about the woman in Tijuana. Nor did I tell her that the chances were her husband was a crook nowadays.

"Mr Ashcraft is in Tijuana, I have been told. He left San Francisco about six months ago. His mail is being forwarded to him in care of a cafe there, under the name of Edward Bohannon."

Her eyes lighted up happily, but she didn't throw a fit. She wasn't that sort. She addressed the attorney.

"Shall I go down? Or will you?"

Richmond shook his head.

"Neither. You certainly shouldn't go, and I cannot—not at present. I must be in Eureka by the day after tomorrow, and shall have to spend several days there." He turned to me. "You'll have to go. You can no doubt handle it better than I could. You will know what to do and how to do it. There are no definite instructions I can give you. Your course will have to depend on Mr Ashcraft's attitude and condition. Mrs Ashcraft doesn't wish to force herself on him, but neither does she wish to leave anything undone that might help him."

Mrs Ashcraft held a strong, slender hand out to me.

"You will do whatever you think wisest."

It was partly a question, partly an expression of confidence.

"I will," I promised.

I liked this Mrs Ashcraft.

IV

Tijuana hadn't changed much in the two years I had been away. Still the same six or seven hundred feet of dusty and dingy street running between two almost solid rows of saloons,—perhaps thirty-five of them to a row,—with dirtier side streets taking care of the dives that couldn't find room on the main street.

The automobile that had brought me down from San Diego dumped me into the center of the town early in the afternoon, and the day's business was just getting under way. That is, there were only two or three drunks wandering around among the dogs and loafing Mexicans in the street, although there was already a bustle of potential drunks moving from one saloon to the next. But this was nothing like the crowd that would be here the following week, when the season's racing started.

In the middle of the next block I saw a big gilded horseshoe. I went down the street and into the saloon behind the sign. It was a fair sample of the local joint. A bar on your left as you came in, running half the length of the building, with three or four slot machines on one end. Across from the bar, against the right-hand wall, a dance floor that ran from the front wall to a raised platform, where a greasy orchestra was now preparing to go to work. Behind the orchestra was a row of low stalls or booths, with open fronts and a table and two benches apiece. Opposite them, in the space between the bar and the rear of the building, a man with a hair-lip was shaking pills out of a keno goose.

It was early in the day, and there were only a few buyers present, so the girls whose business it is to speed the sale of drinks charged down on me in a flock.

"Buy me a drink? Let's have a little drink? Buy a drink, honey?"

I shooed them away—no easy job—and caught a bartender's eye. He was a beefy, red-faced Irishman, with sorrel hair plastered down in two curls that hid what little forehead he had.

"I want to see Ed Bohannon," I told him confidentially.

He turned blank fish-green eyes on me.

"I don't know no Ed Bohannon."

Taking out a piece of paper and a pencil I scribbled, *Jamocha is copped,* and slid the paper over to the bartender.

"If a man who says he's Ed Bohannon asks for that, will you give it to him?"

"I guess so."

"Good," I said. "I'll hang around a while."

I walked down the room and sat at a table in one of the stalls. A lanky girl who had done something to her hair that made it purple was camped beside me before I had settled in my seat.

"Buy me a little drink?" she asked.

The face she made at me was probably meant for a smile. Whatever it was, it beat me. I was afraid she'd do it again, so I surrendered.

"Yes," I said, and ordered a bottle of beer for myself from the waiter who was already hanging over my shoulder.

The beer wasn't bad, for green beer; but at four bits a bottle it wasn't anything to write home about. This Tijuana happens to be in Mexico—by about a mile—but it's an American town, run by Americans, who sell American artificial booze at American prices. If you know your way around the United States you can find lots of places—especially near the Canadian line—where good booze can be bought for less than you are soaked for poison in Tijuana.

The purple-haired woman at my side downed her shot of whiskey, and was opening her mouth to suggest that we have another drink,—hustlers down there don't waste any time at all,—when a voice spoke from behind me.

"Cora, Frank wants you."

Cora scowled, looking over my shoulder.

Then she made that damned face at me again, said "All right, Kewpie. Will you take care of my friend here?" and left me.

Kewpie slid into the seat beside me. She was a little chunky girl of perhaps eighteen—not a day more than that. Just a kid. Her short hair was brown and curly over a round, boyish face with laughing, impudent eyes. Rather a cute little trick.

I bought her a drink and got another bottle of beer.

"What's on your mind?" I asked her.

"Hooch." She grinned at me—a grin that was as boyish as the straight look of her brown eyes. "Gallons of it."

"And besides that?"

I knew this switching of girls on me hadn't been purposeless.

"I hear you're looking for a friend of mine," Kewpie said.

"That might be. What friends have you got?"

"Well, there's Ed Bohannon for one. You know Ed?"

I shook my head.

"No—not yet."

"But you're looking for him?"

"Uh-huh."

"Maybe I could tell you how to find him, if I knew you were all right."

"It doesn't make any difference to me," I said carelessly. "I've a few more minutes to waste, and if he doesn't show up by then it's all one to me."

She cuddled against my shoulder.

"What's the racket? Maybe I could get word to Ed."

I stuck a cigarette in her mouth, one in my own, and lit them.

"Let it go," I bluffed. "This Ed of yours seems to be as exclusive as all hell. Well, it's no skin off *my* face. I'll buy you another drink and then trot along."

She jumped up.

"Wait a minute. I'll see if I can get him. What's your name?"

"Parker will do as well as any other," I said, the name I had used on Ryan popping first into my mind.

"You wait," she called back as she moved toward the back door. "I think I can find him."

"I think so too," I agreed.

Ten minutes went by, and a man came to my table from the front of the establishment. He was a blond Englishman of less than forty, with all the marks of the gentleman gone to pot on him. Not altogether on the rocks yet, but you could see evidence of the downhill slide plainly in the dullness of his blue eyes, in the pouches under his eyes, in the blurred lines around his mouth and the mouth's looseness, and in the grayish tint of his skin. He was still fairly attractive in appearance—enough of his former wholesomeness remained for that.

He sat down facing me across the table.

"You're looking for me?"

There was only a hint of the Britisher in his accent.

"You're Ed Bohannon?"

He nodded.

"Jamocha was picked up a couple of days ago," I told him, "and ought to be riding back to the Kansas big house by now. He got word out for me to give you the rap. He knew I was heading this way."

"How did they come to get him?"

His blue eyes were suspicious on my face.

"Don't know," I said. "Maybe they picked him up on a circular."

He frowned at the table and traced a meaningless design with a finger in a puddle of beer. Then he looked sharply at me again.

"Did he tell you anything else?"

"*He* didn't tell me anything. He got word out to me by somebody's mouthpiece. I didn't see him."

"You're staying down here a while?"

"Yes, for two or three days," I said. "I've got something on the fire."

He stood up and smiled, and held out his hand.

"Thanks for the tip, Parker," he said. "If you'll take a walk with me I'll give you something real to drink."

I didn't have anything against that. He led me out of the Golden Horseshoe and down a side street to an adobe house set out where the town fringed off into the desert. In the front room he waved me to a chair and went into the next room.

"What do you fancy?" he called through the door. "Rye, gin, tequila, Scotch—"

"The last one wins," I interrupted his catalog.

He brought in a bottle of Black and White, a siphon and some glasses, and we settled down to drinking. When that bottle was empty there was another to take its place. We drank and talked, drank and talked, and each of us pretended to be drunker than he really was—though before long we were both as full as a pair of goats.

It was a drinking contest pure and simple. He was trying to drink me into a pulp—a pulp that would easily give up all of its secrets—and I was trying the same game on him. Neither of us made much progress. Neither he nor I was young enough in the world to blab much when we were drunk that wouldn't have come out if we had been sober. Few grown men do, unless they get to boasting, or are very skillfully handled. All that afternoon we faced each other over the table in the center of the room, drank and entertained each other.

"Y' know," he was saying somewhere along toward dark, "I've been a damn' ass. Got a wife—the nicesh woman in the worl'. Wantsh me t' come back to her, an' all tha' short of thing. Yet I hang around here, lappin' up this shtuff—hittin' the pipe—when I could be shomebody. Arc—architec', y' un'ershtand—good one, too. But I got in rut—got mixsh up with theshe people. C-can't sheem to break 'way. Goin' to, though—no spoofin'. Goin' back to li'l wife, nicesh woman in the worl'. Don't you shay anything t' Kewpie. She'd raishe hell 'f she knew I wash goin' t' shake her. Nishe girl, K-kewpie, but tough. S-shtick a bloomin' knife in me. Good job, too! But I'm goin' back to wife. Breakin' 'way from p-pipe an' ever'thing. Look at me. D' I look like a hop-head? Course not! Curin' m'self, tha's why. I'll show you—take a smoke now—show you I can take it or leave it alone."

Pulling himself dizzily up out of his chair, he wandered into the next room, bawling a song at the top of his voice:

"A dimber mort with a quarter-stone slum,
A-bubbin' of max with her cove—
A bingo fen in a crack-o'-dawn drum,
A-waitin' for—"

He came staggering into the room again carrying an elaborate opium layout—all silver and ebony—on a silver tray. He put it on the table and flourished a pipe at me.

"Have a li'l rear on me, Parker."

I told him I'd stick to the Scotch.

"Give y' shot of C. F y'd rather have it," he invited me.

I declined the cocaine, so he sprawled himself comfortably on the floor beside the table, rolled and cooked a pill, and our party went on—with him smoking his hop and me punishing the liquor—each of us still talking for the other's benefit, and trying to get the other to talk for our own.

I was holding down a lovely package by the time Kewpie came in, at midnight.

"Looks like you folks are enjoying yourselves," she laughed, leaning down to kiss the Englishman's rumpled hair as she stepped over him.

She perched herself on the table and reached for the Scotch.

"Everything's lovely," I assured her, though probably I didn't say it that clear.

I was fighting a battle with myself just about then. I had an idea that I wanted to dance. Down in Yucatan, four or five months before—hunting for a lad who had done wrong by the bank that employed him—I had seen some natives dance the *naual.* And that naual dance was the one thing in the world I wanted to do just then. (I was carrying a beautiful bun!) But I knew that if I sat still—as I had been sitting all evening—I could keep my cargo in hand, while it wasn't going to take much moving around to knock me over.

I don't remember whether I finally conquered the desire to dance or not. I remember Kewpie sitting on the table, grinning her boy's grin at me, and saying:

"You ought to stay oiled all the time, Shorty; it improves you."

I don't know whether I made any answer to that or not. Shortly afterward, I know, I spread myself beside the Englishman on the floor and went to sleep.

V

The next two days were pretty much like the first one. Ashcraft and I were together twenty-four hours each of the days, and usually the girl was with us, and the only time we weren't drinking was when we were sleeping off what we had been drinking. We spent most of those three days in either the adobe house or the Golden Horseshoe, but we found time to take in most of the other joints in town now and then. I had only a hazy idea of some of the things that went on around me, though I don't think I missed anything entirely. On the second day someone added a first name to the alias I had given the girl—and thereafter I was "Painless" Parker to Tijuana, and still am to some of them. I don't know who christened me, or why.

Ashcraft and I were as thick as thieves, on the surface, but neither of us ever lost his distrust of the other, no matter how drunk we got—and we got plenty drunk. He went up against his mud-pipe regularly. I don't think the girl used the stuff, but she had a pretty capacity for hard liquor. I would go to sleep not knowing whether I was going to wake up or not; but I had nothing on me to give me away, so I figured that I was safe unless I talked myself into a jam. I didn't worry much,—bedtime usually caught me in a state that made worry impossible.

Three days of this, and then, sobering up, I was riding back to San Francisco, making a list of what I knew and guessed about Norman Ashcraft, alias Ed Bohannon.

The list went something like this:

(1) He suspected, if he didn't know, that I had come down to see him on his wife's account: he had been too smooth and had entertained me too well for me to doubt that; (2) he apparently had decided to return to his wife, though there was no guarantee that he would actually do so; (3) he was not incurably addicted to drugs; he merely smoked opium and, regardless of what the Sunday supplements say, an opium smoker is little, if any; worse off than a tobacco smoker; (4) he might pull himself together under his wife's influence, but it was doubtful: physically he hadn't gone to the dogs, but he had had his taste of the gutter and seemed to like it; (5) the girl Kewpie was crazily in love with him, while he liked her, but wasn't turning himself inside out over her.

A good night's sleep on the train between Los Angeles and San Francisco set me down in the Third and Townsend Street station with nearly normal head and stomach and not too many kinks in my nerves. I put away a breakfast that was composed of more food than I had eaten in three days, and went up to Vance Richmond's office.

"Mr Richmond is still in Eureka," his stenographer told me. "I don't expect him back until the first of the week."

"Can you get him on the phone for me?"

She could, and did.

Without mentioning any names, I told the attorney what I knew and guessed.

"I see," he said. "Suppose you go out to Mrs A's house and tell her. I will write her tonight, and I probably shall be back in the city by the day after tomorrow. I think we can safely delay action until then."

I caught a street car, transferred at Van Ness Avenue, and went out to Mrs Ashcraft's house. Nothing happened when I rang the bell. I rang it several times before I noticed that there were two morning newspapers in the vestibule. I looked at the dates—this morning's and yesterday morning's.

An old man in faded overalls was watering the lawn next door.

"Do you know if the people who live here have gone away?" I called to him.

"I don't guess so. The back door's open, I seen this mornin'."

He returned his attention to his hose, and then stopped to scratch his chin.

"They may of gone," he said slowly. "Come to think on it, I ain't seen any of 'em for—I don't remember seein' any of 'em yesterday."

I left the front steps and went around the house, climbed the low fence in back and went up the back steps. The kitchen door stood about a foot open. Nobody was visible in the kitchen, but there was a sound of running water.

I knocked on the door with my knuckles, loudly. There was no answering sound. I pushed the door open and went in. The sound of water came from the sink. I looked in the sink.

Under a thin stream of water running from one of the faucets lay a carving knife with nearly a foot of keen blade. The knife was clean, but the back of the porcelain sink—where water had splashed with only small, scattered drops—was freckled with red-brown spots. I scraped one of them with a finger-nail—dried blood.

Except for the sink, I could see nothing out of order in the kitchen. I opened a pantry door. Everything seemed all right there. Across the room another door led to the front of the house. I opened the door and went into a passageway. Not enough light came from the kitchen to illuminate the passageway. I fumbled in the dusk for the light-button that I knew should be there. I stepped on something soft.

Pulling my foot back, I felt in my pocket for matches, and struck one. In front of me, his head and shoulders on the floor, his hips and legs on the lower steps of a flight of stairs, lay a Filipino boy in his underclothes.

He was dead. One eye was cut, and his throat was gashed straight across, close up under his chin. I could see the killing without even shutting my eyes. At the top of the stairs—the killer's left hand dashing into the Filipino's face—thumb-nail gouging into eye—pushing the brown face back—tightening the brown throat for the knife's edge—the slash—and the shove down the steps.

The light from my second match showed me the button. I clicked on the lights, buttoned my coat, and went up the steps. Dried blood darkened them here and there, and at the second-floor landing the wall paper was stained with a big blot. At the head of the stairs I found another light-button, and pressed it.

I walked down the hall, poked my head into two rooms that seemed in order, and then turned a corner—and pulled up with a jerk, barely in time to miss stumbling over a woman who lay there.

She was huddled on the floor, face down, with knees drawn up under her and both hands clasped to her stomach. She wore a nightgown, and her hair was in a braid down her back.

I put a finger on the back of her neck. Stone-cold.

Kneeling on the floor—to avoid the necessity of turning her over—I looked at her face. She was the maid who had admitted Richmond and me four days ago.

I stood up again and looked around. The maid's head was almost touching a closed door. I stepped around her and pushed the door open. A bedroom, and not the maid's. It was an expensively dainty bedroom in cream and gray, with French prints on the walls. Nothing in the room was disarranged except the bed. The bed clothes were rumpled and tangled, and piled high in the center of the bed—in a pile that was too large...

Leaning over the bed, I began to draw the covers off. The second piece came away stained with blood. I yanked the rest off.

Mrs Ashcraft was dead there.

Her body was drawn up in a little heap, from which her head hung crookedly, dangling from a neck that had been cut clean through to the bone. Her face was marked with four deep scratches from temple to chin. One sleeve had been torn from the jacket of her blue silk pajamas. Bedding and pajamas were soggy with the blood that the clothing piled over her had kept from drying.

I put the blanket over her again, edged past the dead woman in the hall, and went down the front stairs, switching on more lights, hunting for the telephone. Near the foot of the stairs I found it. I called the police detective bureau first, and then Vance Richmond's office.

"Get word to Mr Richmond that Mrs Ashcraft has been murdered," I told his stenographer. "I'm at her house, and he can get in touch with me here any time during the next two or three hours."

Then I went out of the front door and sat on the top step, smoking a cigarette while I waited for the police.

I felt rotten. I've seen dead people in larger quantities than three in my time, and I've seen some that were hacked up pretty badly; but this thing had fallen on me while my nerves were ragged from three days of boozing.

The police automobile swung around the corner and began disgorging men before I had finished my first cigarette. O'Gar, the detective-sergeant in charge of the Homicide Detail, was the first man up the steps.

"Hullo," he greeted me. "What have you got hold of this time?"

I was glad to see him. This squat, bulletheaded sergeant is as good a man as the department has, and he and I have always been lucky when we tied up together.

"I found three bodies in there before I quit looking," I told him as I led him indoors. "Maybe a regular detective like you—with a badge and everything—can find more."

"You didn't do bad—for a lad," he said.

My wooziness had passed. I was eager to get to work. These people lying dead around the house were merely counters in a game again—or almost. I remembered the feel of Mrs Ashcraft's slim hand in mine, but I stuck that memory in the back of my mind. You hear now and then of detectives who have not become callous, who have not lost what you might call the human touch. I always feel sorry for them, and wonder why they don't chuck their jobs and find another line of work that wouldn't be so hard on their emotions. A sleuth who doesn't grow a tough shell is in for a gay life—day in and day out poking his nose into one kind of woe or another.

I showed the Filipino to O'Gar first, and then the two women. We didn't find any more. Detail work occupied all of us—O'Gar, the eight men under him, and me—for the next few hours. The house had to be gone over from roof to cellar. The neighbors had to be grilled. The employment agencies through which the servants had been hired had to be examined. Relatives and friends of the Filipino and the maid had to be traced and questioned. Newsboys, mail carriers, grocers' delivery men, laundrymen, had to be found, questioned and, when necessary, investigated.

When the bulk of the reports were in, O'Gar and I sneaked away from the others—especially away from the newspaper men, who were all over the place by now—and locked ourselves in the library.

"Night before last, huh? Wednesday night?" O'Gar grunted when we were comfortable in a couple of leather chairs, burning tobacco.

I nodded. The report of the doctor who had examined the bodies, the presence of the two newspapers in the vestibule, and the fact that neither neighbor, grocer nor butcher had seen any of them since Wednesday, combined to make Wednesday night—or early Thursday morning—the correct date.

"I'd say the killer cracked the back door," O'Gar went on, staring at the ceiling through smoke, "picked up the carving knife in the kitchen, and went upstairs. Maybe he went straight to Mrs Ashcraft's room—maybe not. But after a bit he went in there. The torn sleeve and the scratches on her face mean that there was a tussle. The Filipino and the maid heard the noise—heard her scream maybe—and rushed to her room to find out what was the matter. The maid most likely got there just as the killer was coming out—and got hers. I guess the Filipino saw him then and ran. The killer caught him at the head of the back stairs—and finished him. Then he went down to the kitchen, washed his hands, dropped the knife, and blew."

"So far, so good," I agreed; "but I notice you skip lightly over the question of who he was and why he killed."

He pushed his hat back and scratched his bullet head.

"Don't crowd me," he rumbled; "I'll get around to that. There seem to be just three guesses to take your pick from. We know that nobody else lived in the house outside of the three that were killed. So the killer was either a maniac who did the job for the fun of it, a burglar who was discovered and ran wild, or somebody who had a reason for bumping off Mrs Ashcraft, and then had to kill the two servants when they discovered him.

"Taking the knife from the kitchen would make the burglar guess look like a bum one. And, besides, we're pretty sure nothing was stolen. A good prowler would bring his own weapon with him if he wanted one. But the hell of it is that there are a lot of bum prowlers in the world—half-wits who would be likely to pick up a knife in the kitchen, go to pieces when the house woke up, slash everybody in sight, and then beat it without turning anything over.

"So it could have been a prowler; but my personal guess is that the job was done by somebody who wanted to wipe out Mrs Ashcraft."

"Not so bad," I applauded. "Now listen to this: Mrs Ashcraft has a husband in Tijuana, a mild sort of hop-head who is mixed up with a bunch of thugs. She was trying to persuade him to come back to her. He has a girl down there who is young, goofy over him, and a bad actor—one tough youngster. He was planning to run out on the girl and come back home."

"So-o-o?" O'Gar said softly.

"But," I continued, "I was with both him and the girl, in Tijuana, night before last—when this killing was done."

"So-o?"

A knock on the door interrupted our talk. It was a policeman to tell me that I was wanted on the phone. I went down to the first floor, and Vance Richmond's voice came over the wire.

"What is it? Miss Henry delivered your message, but she couldn't give me any details."

I told him the whole thing.

"I'll leave for the city tonight," he said when I had finished. "You go ahead and do whatever you want. You're to have a free hand."

"Right," I replied. "I'll probably be out of town when you get back. You can reach me through the agency if you want to get in touch with me. I'm going to wire Ashcraft to come up—in your name."

After Richmond had hung up, I called the city jail and asked the captain if John Ryan, alias Fred Rooney, alias Jamocha, was still there.

"No. Federal officers left for Leavenworth with him and two other prisoners yesterday morning."

Up in the library again, I told O'Gar hurriedly:

"I'm catching the evening train south, betting my marbles that the job was made in Tijuana. I'm wiring Ashcraft to come up. I want to get him away from the Mexican town for a day or two, and if he's up here you can keep an eye on him. I'll give you a description of him, and you can pick him up at Vance Richmond's office. He'll probably connect there first thing."

Half an hour of the little time I had left I spent writing and sending three telegrams. The first was to Ashcraft.

> "Edward Bohannon,
> Golden Horseshoe Cafe,
> Tijuana, Mexico.
>
> *Mrs Ashcraft is dead. Can you come immediately?*
> *Vance Richmond"*

The other two were in code. One went to the Continental Detective Agency's Kansas City branch, asking that an operative be sent to Leavenworth to question Jamocha. The other requested the Los Angeles branch to have a man meet me in San Diego the next day.

Then I dashed out to my rooms for a bagful of clean clothes, and went to sleep riding south again.

VI

San Diego was gay and packed when I got off the train early the next afternoon—filled with the crowd that the first Saturday of the racing season across the border had drawn. Movie folk from Los Angeles, farmers from the Imperial Valley, sailors from the Pacific Fleet, gamblers, tourists, grifters, and even regular people, from everywhere. I lunched, registered and left my bag at a hotel, and went up to the U.S. Grant Hotel to pick up the Los Angeles operative I had wired for.

I found him in the lobby—a freckle-faced youngster of twenty-two or so, whose bright gray eyes were busy just now with a racing program, which he held in a hand that had a finger bandaged with adhesive tape. I passed him and stopped at the cigar stand, where I bought a package of cigarettes and straightened out an imaginary dent in my hat. Then I went out to the street again. The bandaged finger and the business with the hat were our introductions. Somebody invented those tricks back before the Civil War, but they still worked smoothly, so their antiquity was no reason for discarding them.

I strolled up Fourth Street, getting away from Broadway—San Diego's main stem—and the operative caught up with me. His name was Gorman, and he turned out to be a pretty good lad. I gave him the lay.

"You're to go down to Tijuana and take a plant on the Golden Horseshoe Café. There's a little chunk of a girl hustling drinks in there—short curly brown hair; brown eyes; round face; rather large red mouth; square shoulders. You can't miss her; she's a nice-looking kid of about eighteen, called Kewpie. She's the target for your eye. Keep away from her. Don't try to rope her. I'll give you an hour's start. Then I'm coming down to talk to her. I want to know what she does right after I leave, and what she does for the next few days. You can get in touch with me at the"—I gave him the name of my hotel and my room number—"each night. Don't give me a tumble anywhere else. I'll most likely be in and out of the Golden Horseshoe often."

We parted, and I went down to the plaza and sat on a bench under the palms for an hour. Then I went up to the corner and fought for a seat on a Tijuana stage.

Fifteen or more miles of dusty riding—packed five in a seat meant for three—a momentary halt at the Immigration Station on the line, and I was climbing out of the stage at the entrance to the race track. The ponies had been running for some time, but the turnstiles were still spinning a steady stream of customers into the track. I turned my back on the gate and went over to the row of jitneys in front of the Monte Carlo—the big wooden casino—got into one, and was driven over to the Old Town.

The Old Town had a deserted look. Nearly everybody was over watching the dogs do their stuff. Gorman's freckled face showed over a drink of mescal when I entered the Golden Horseshoe. I hoped he had a good constitution. He needed one if he was going to do his sleuthing on a distilled cactus diet.

The welcome I got from the Horseshoers was just like a homecoming. Even the bartender with the plastered-down curls gave me a grin.

"Where's Kewpie?" I asked.

"Brother-in-lawing, Ed?" a big Swede girl leered at me. "I'll see if I can find her for you."

Kewpie came through the back door just then.

"Hello, Painless!" She climbed all over me, hugging me, rubbing her face against mine, and the Lord knows what all. "Down for another swell souse?"

"No," I said, leading her back toward the stalls. "Business this time. Where's Ed?"

"Up north. His wife kicked off and he's gone to collect the remains."

"That makes you sorry?"

She showed her big white teeth in a boy's smile of pure happiness.

"You bet! It's tough on me that papa has come into a lot of sugar."

I looked at her out of the corner of my eyes—a glance that was supposed to be wise.

"And you think Ed's going to bring the jack back to you?"

Her eyes snapped darkly at me.

"What's eating you?" she demanded.

I smiled knowingly.

"One of two things is going to happen," I predicted. "Ed's going to ditch you—he was figuring on that, anyway—or he's going to need every brownie he can scrape up to keep his neck from being—"

"You God-damned liar!"

Her right shoulder was to me, touching my left. Her left hand flashed down under her short skirt. I pushed her shoulder forward, twisting her body sharply away from me. The knife her left hand had whipped up from her leg jabbed deep into the underside of the table. A thick-bladed knife, I noticed, balanced for accurate throwing.

She kicked backward, driving one of her sharp heels into my ankle. I slid my left arm around behind her and pinned her elbow to her side just as she freed the knife from the table.

"What th' hell's all 'is?"

I looked up.

Across the table a man stood glaring at me—legs apart, fists on hips. He was a big man, and ugly. A tall, raw-boned man with wide shoulders, out of which a long, skinny yellow neck rose to support a little round head. His eyes were black shoe-buttons stuck close together at the top of a little mashed nose. His mouth looked as if it had been torn in his face, and it was stretched in a snarl now, baring a double row of crooked brown teeth.

"Where d' yuh get 'at stuff?" this lovely person roared at me.

He was too tough to reason with.

"If you're a waiter," I told him, "bring me a bottle of beer and something for the kid. If you're not a waiter—sneak."

He leaned over the table and I gathered my feet in. It looked like I was going to need them to move around on.

"I'll bring yuh a—"

The girl wriggled out of my hands and shut him up.

"Mine's liquor," she said sharply.

He snarled, looked from one of us to the other, showed me his dirty teeth again, and wandered away.

"Who's your friend?"

"You'll do well to lay off him," she advised me, not answering my question.

Then she slid her knife back in its hiding place under her skirt and twisted around to face me.

"Now what's all this about Ed being in trouble?"

"You read about the killing in the papers?"

"Yes."

"You oughtn't need a map, then," I said. "Ed's only out is to put the job on you. But I doubt if he can get away with that. If he can't, he's nailed."

"You're crazy!" she exclaimed. "You weren't too drunk to know that both of us were here with you when the killing was done."

"I'm not crazy enough to think that proves anything," I corrected her. "But I am crazy enough to expect to go back to San Francisco wearing the killer on my wrist."

She laughed at me. I laughed back and stood up.

"See you some more," I said as I strolled toward the door.

I returned to San Diego and sent a wire to Los Angeles, asking for another operative. Then I got something to eat and spent the evening lying across the bed in my hotel room smoking and scheming and waiting for Gorman.

It was late when he arrived, and he smelled of mescal from San Diego to St. Louis and back, but his head seemed level enough.

"Looked like I was going to have to shoot you loose from the place for a moment," he grinned. "Between the twist flashing the pick and the big guy loosening a sap in his pocket, it looked like action was coming."

"You let me alone," I ordered. "Your job is to see what goes on, and that's all. If I get carved, you can mention it in your report, but that's your limit. What did you turn up?"

"After you blew, the girl and the big guy put their noodles together. They seemed kind of agitated—all agog, you might say. He slid out, so I dropped the girl and slid along behind him. He came to town and got a wire off. I couldn't crowd him close enough to see who it was to. Then he went back to the joint. Things were normal when I knocked off."

"Who is the big guy? Did you learn?"

"He's no sweet dream, from what I hear. 'Gooseneck' Flinn is the name on his calling cards. He's bouncer and general utility man for the joint. I saw him in action against a couple of gobs, and he's nobody's meat—as pretty a double throw-out as I've ever seen."

So this Gooseneck party was the Golden Horseshoe's clean-up man, and he hadn't been in sight during my three-day spree? I couldn't possibly have been so drunk that I'd forget his ugliness. And it had been on one of those three days that Mrs Ashcraft and her servants had been killed.

"I wired your office for another op," I told Gorman. "He's to connect with you. Turn the girl over to him, and you camp on Gooseneck's trail. I think we're going to hang three killings on him, so watch your step. I'll be in to stir things up a little more tomorrow; but remember, no matter what happens, everybody plays his own game. Don't ball things up trying to help me."

"Aye, aye, Cap," and he went off to get some sleep.

The next afternoon I spent at the race track, fooling around with the bangtails while I waited for night. The track was jammed with the usual Sunday crowd. I ran into any number of old acquaintances, some of them on my side of the game, some on the other, and some neutral. One of the second lot was "Trick-hat" Schultz. At our last meeting—a copper was leading him out of a Philadelphia court room toward a fifteen-year bit—he had promised to open me up from my eyebrows to my ankles the next time he saw me. He greeted me this afternoon with an eight inch smile, bought me a shot of what they sell for gin under the grandstand, and gave me a tip on a horse named Beeswax. I'm not foolish enough to play anybody's tips, so I didn't play this one. Beeswax ran so far ahead of the others that it looked like he and his competitors were in separate races, and he paid twenty-something to one. So Trick-hat had his revenge after all.

After the last race, I got something to eat at the Sunset Inn, and then drifted over to the big casino—the other end of the same building. A thousand or more people of all sorts were jostling one another there, fighting to go up against poker, craps, chuck-a-luck, wheels of fortune, roulette and twenty-one with whatever money the race track had left or given them. I didn't buck any of the games. My playtime was over. I walked around through the crowd looking for my men.

I spotted the first one—a sunburned man who was plainly a farm hand in his Sunday clothes. He was pushing toward the door, and his face held that peculiar emptiness which belongs to the gambler who has gone broke before the end of the game. It's a look of regret that is not so much for the loss of the money as for the necessity of quitting.

I got between the farm hand and the door.

"Clean you?" I asked sympathetically when he reached me.

A sheepish sort of nod.

"How'd you like to pick up five bucks for a few minutes' work?" I tempted him.

He would like it, but what was the work?

"I want you to go over to the Old Town with me and look at a man. Then you get your pay. There are no strings to it."

That didn't exactly satisfy him, but five bucks are five bucks; and he could drop out any time he didn't like the looks of things. He decided to try it.

I put the farm hand over by a door, and went after another—a little, plump man with round, optimistic eyes and a weak mouth. He was willing to earn five dollars in the simple and easy manner I had outlined. The next man I braced was a little too timid to take a chance on a blind game. Then I got a Filipino—glorious in a fawncolored suit, with a coat split to the neck and pants whose belled bottoms would have held a keg apiece—and a stocky young Greek who was probably either a waiter or a barber.

Four men were enough. My quartet pleased me immensely. They didn't look too intelligent for my purpose, and they didn't look like thugs or sharpers. I put them in a jitney and took them over to the Old Town.

"Now this is it," I coached them when we had arrived. "I'm going into the Golden Horseshoe Cafe, around the corner. Give me two or three minutes, and then come in and buy yourselves a drink." I gave the farm hand a five-dollar bill. "You pay for the drinks with that—it isn't part of your wages. There's a tall, broad-shouldered man with a long, yellow neck and a small ugly face in there. You can't miss him. I want you all to take a good look at him without letting him get wise. When you're sure you'd know him again anywhere, give me the nod, and come back here and you get your money. Be careful when you give me the nod. I don't want anybody in there to find out that you know me."

It sounded queer to them, but there was the promise of five dollars apiece, and there were the games back in the casino, where five dollars might buy a man into a streak of luck that—write the rest of it yourself. They asked questions, which I refused to answer, but they stuck.

Gooseneck was behind the bar, helping out the bartenders, when I entered the place. They needed help. The joint bulged with customers. The dance floor looked like a mob scene. Thirsts were lined up four deep at the bar. A shotgun wouldn't have sounded above the din: men and women laughing, roaring and cursing; bottles and glasses rattling and banging; and louder and more disagreeable than any of those noises was the noise of the sweating orchestra. Turmoil, uproar, stink—a Tijuana joint on Sunday night.

I couldn't find Gorman's freckled face in the crowd, but I picked out the hatchet-sharp white face of Hooper, another Los Angeles operative, who, I knew then, had been sent down in response to my second telegram. Kewpie was farther down the bar, drinking with a little man whose meek face had the devil-may-care expression of a model husband on a tear. She nodded at me, but didn't leave her client.

Gooseneck gave me a scowl and the bottle of beer I had ordered. Presently my four hired men came in. They did their parts beautifully!

First they peered through the smoke, looking from face to face, and hastily avoiding eyes that met theirs. A little of this, and one of them, the Filipino, saw the man I had described, behind the bar. He jumped a foot in the excitement of his discovery, and then, finding Gooseneck glaring at him, turned his back and fidgeted. The three others spotted Gooseneck now, and sneaked looks at him that were as conspicuously furtive as a set of false whiskers. Gooseneck glowered at them.

The Filipino turned around, looked at me, ducked his head sharply, and bolted for the street. The three who were left shot their drinks down their gullets and tried to catch my eye. I was reading a sign high on the wall behind the bar:

ONLY GENUINE PRE-WAR AMERICAN AND BRITISH WHISKEYS SERVED HERE

I was trying to count how many lies could be found in those nine words, and had reached four, with promise of more, when one of my confederates, the Greek, cleared his throat with the noise of a gasoline engine's backfire. Gooseneck was edging down the bar, a bungstarter in one hand, his face purple.

I looked at my assistants. Their nods wouldn't have been so terrible had they come one at a time; but they were taking no chances on my looking away again before they could get their reports in. The three heads bobbed together—a signal that nobody within twenty feet could, or did, miss—and they scooted out of the door, away from the long-necked man and his bungstarter.

I emptied my glass of beer, sauntered out of the saloon and around the corner. They were clustered where I had told them to wait.

"We'd know him! We'd know him!" they chorused.

"That's fine," I praised them. "You did great. I think you're all natural-born gumshoes. Here's your pay. Now if I were you boys, I think I'd sort of avoid that place after this; because, in spite of the clever way you covered yourselves up—and you did nobly!—he might possibly suspect something. There's no use taking chances, anyway."

They grabbed their wages and were gone before I had finished my speech. I returned to the Golden Horseshoe—to be on hand in case one of them should decide to sell me out and come back there to spill the deal to Gooseneck.

Kewpie had left her model husband, and met me at the door. She stuck an arm through mine and led me toward the rear of the building. I noticed that Gooseneck was gone from behind the bar. I wondered if he was out gunning for my four ex-employees.

"Business looks good," I chattered as we pushed through the crowd. "You know, I had a tip on Beeswax this afternoon, and wouldn't play the pup." I made two or three more aimless cracks of that sort—just because I knew the girl's mind was full of something else. She paid no attention to anything I said.

But when we had dropped down in front of a vacant table, she asked:

"Who were your friends?"

"What friends?"

"The four jobbies who were at the bar when you were there a few minutes ago."

"Too hard for me, sister." I shook my head. "There were slews of men there. Oh, yes! I know who you mean! Those four gents who seemed kind of smitten with Gooseneck's looks. I wonder what attracted them to him—besides his beauty."

She grabbed my arm with both hands.

"So help me God, Painless," she swore, "if you tie anything on Ed, I'll kill you!"

Her brown eyes were big and damp. She was a hard and wise little baby—had rubbed the world's sharp corners with both shoulders—but she was only a kid, and she was worried sick over this man of hers. However, the business of a sleuth is to catch criminals, not to sympathize with their ladyloves.

I patted her hands.

"I could give you some good advice," I said as I stood up, "but you wouldn't listen to it, so I'll save my breath. It won't do any harm to tell you to keep an eye on Gooseneck, though—he's shifty."

There wasn't any special meaning to that speech, except that it might tangle things up a little more. One way of finding what's at the bottom of either a cup of coffee or a situation is to keep stirring it up until whatever is on the bottom comes to the surface. I had been playing that system thus far on this affair.

Hooper came into my room in the San Diego hotel at a little before two the next morning.

"Gooseneck disappeared, with Gorman tailing him, immediately after your first visit," he said. "After your second visit, the girl went around to adobe house on the edge of town, and she was still there when I knocked off. The place was dark."

Gorman didn't show up.

VII

A bellhop with a telegram roused me at ten o'clock in the morning. The telegram was from Mexicali:

> "DROVE HERE LAST NIGHT HOLED UP WITH FRIENDS SENT TWO WIRES.
>
> GORMAN."

That was good news. The long-necked man had fallen for my play, had taken my four busted gamblers for four witnesses, had taken their nods for identifications. Gooseneck was the lad who had done the actual killing, and Gooseneck was in flight.

I had shed my pajamas and was reaching for my union suit when the boy came back with another wire. This one was from O'Gar, through the agency:

"ASHCRAFT DISAPPEARED YESTERDAY"

I used the telephone to get Hooper out of bed.

"Get down to Tijuana," I told him. "Stick up the house where you left the girl last night, unless you run across her at the Golden Horseshoe. Stay there until she shows. Stay with her until she connects with a big blond Englishman, and then switch to him. He's a man of less than forty, tall, with blue eyes and yellow hair. Don't let him shake you—he's the big boy in this party just now. I'll be down. If the Englishman and I stay together and the girl leaves us, take her, but otherwise stick to him."

I dressed, put down some breakfast and caught a stage for the Mexican town. The boy driving the stage made fair time, but you would have thought we were standing still to see a maroon roadster pass us near Palm City. Ashcraft was driving the roadster.

The roadster was empty, standing in front of the adobe house, when I saw it again. Up in the next block, Hooper was doing an imitation of a drunk, talking to two Indians in the uniforms of the Mexican Army.

I knocked on the door of the adobe house.

Kewpie's voice: "Who is it?"

"Me—Painless. Just heard that Ed is back."

"Oh!" she exclaimed. A pause. "Come in."

I pushed the door open and went in. The Englishman sat tilted back in a chair, his right elbow on the table, his right hand in his coat pocket—if there was a gun in that pocket it was pointing at me.

"Hello," he said. "I hear you've been making guesses about me."

"Call 'em anything you like." I pushed a chair over to within a couple of feet of him, and sat down. "But don't let's kid each other. You had Gooseneck knock your wife off so you could get what she had. The mistake you made was in picking a sap like Gooseneck to do the turn—a sap who went on a killing spree and then lost his nerve. Going to read and write just because three or four witnesses put the finger on him! And only going as far as Mexicali! That's a fine place to pick! I suppose he was so scared that the five-or six-hour ride over the hills seemed like a trip to the end of the world!"

The man's face told me nothing. He eased himself around in his chair an inch or two, which would have brought the gun in his pocket—if a gun *was* there—in line with my thick middle. The girl was somewhere behind me, fidgeting around. I was afraid of her. She was crazily in love with this man in front of me, and I had seen the blade she wore on one leg. I imagined her fingers itching for it now. The man and his gun didn't worry me much. He was not rattlebrained, and he wasn't likely to bump me off either in panic or for the fun of it.

I kept my chin going.

"You aren't a sap, Ed, and neither am I. I want to take you riding north with bracelets on, but I'm in no hurry. What I mean is, I'm not going to stand up and trade lead with you. This is all in my daily grind. It isn't a matter of life or death with me. If I can't take you today, I'm willing to wait until tomorrow. I'll get you in the end, unless somebody beats me to you—and that won't break my heart. There's a rod between my vest and my belly. If you'll have Kewpie get it out, we'll be all set for the talk I want to make."

He nodded slowly, not taking his eyes from me. The girl came close to my back. One of her hands came over my shoulder, went under my vest, and my old black gun left me. Before she stepped away she laid the point of her knife against the nape of my neck for an instant—a gentle reminder. I managed not to squirm or jump.

"Good," I said when she gave my gun to the Englishman, who pocketed it with his left hand. "Now here's my proposition. You and Kewpie ride across the border with me—so we won't have to fool with extradition papers—and I'll have you locked up. We'll do our fighting in court. I'm not absolutely certain that I can tie the killings on either of you, and if I flop, you'll be free. If I make the grade—as I hope to—you'll swing, of course. But there's always a good chance of beating the courts—especially if you're guilty—and that's the only chance you have that's worth a damn.

"What's the sense of scooting? Spending the rest of your life dodging bulls? Only to be nabbed finally—or bumped off trying to get away? You'll maybe save your neck, but what of the money your wife left? That money is what you are in the game for—it's what you had your wife killed for. Stand trial and you've a chance to collect it. Run—and you kiss it goodbye. Are you going to ditch it—throw it away just because your cat's-paw bungled the deal? Or are you going to stick to the finish—win everything or lose everything?"

A lot of these boys who make cracks about not being taken alive have been wooed into peaceful surrender with that kind of talk. But my game just now was to persuade Ed and his girl to bolt. If they let me throw them in the can I might be able to convict one of them, but my chances weren't any too large. It depended on how things turned out later. It depended on whether I could prove that Gooseneck had been in San Francisco on the night of the killings, and I imagined that he would be well supplied with all sorts of proof to the contrary. We had not been able to find a single finger-print of the killer's in Mrs Ashcraft's house. And if I *could* convince a jury that he was in San Francisco at the time, then I would have to show that he had done the killing. And after that I would have the toughest part of the job still ahead of me—to prove that he had done the killing for one of these two, and not on his own account. I had an idea that when we picked Gooseneck up and put the screws to him he would talk. But that was only an idea.

What I was working for was to make this pair dust out. I didn't care where they went or what they did, so long as they scooted. I'd trust to luck and my own head to get profit out of their scrambling—I was still trying to stir things up.

The Englishman was thinking hard. I knew I had him worried, chiefly through what I had said about Gooseneck Flinn. If I had pulled the moth-eaten stuff—said that Gooseneck had been picked up and had squealed—this Englishman would have put me down as a liar; but the little I had said was bothering him.

He bit his lip and frowned. Then he shook himself and chuckled.

"You're balmy, Painless," he said. "But you—"

I don't know what he was going to say—whether I was going to win or lose.

The front door slammed open, and Gooseneck Flinn came into the room.

His clothes were white with dust. His face was thrust forward to the full length of his long, yellow neck.

His shoe-button eyes focused on me. His hands turned over. That's all you could see. They simply turned over—and there was a heavy revolver in each.

"Your paws on the table, Ed," he snarled.

Ed's gun—if that is what he had in his pocket—was blocked from a shot at the man in the doorway by a corner of the table. He took his hand out of his pocket, empty, and laid both palms down on the table-top.

"Stay where y'r at!" Gooseneck barked at the girl.

She was standing on the other side of the room. The knife with which she had pricked the back of my neck was not in sight.

Gooseneck glared at me for nearly a minute, but when he spoke it was to Ed and Kewpie.

"So this is what y' wired me to come back for, huh? A trap! Me the goat for yur! I'll be y'r goat! I'm goin' to speak my piece, an' then I'm goin' out o' here if I have to smoke my way through the whole damn Mex army! I killed y'r wife all right—an' her help, too. Killed 'em for the thousand bucks—"

The girl took a step toward him, screaming:

"Shut up, damn you!"

Her mouth was twisting and working like a child's, and there was water in her eyes.

"Shut up, yourself!" Gooseneck roared back at her, and his thumb raised the hammer of the gun that threatened her. "I'm doin' the talkin'. I killed her for—"

Kewpie bent forward. Her left hand went under the hem of her skirt. The hand came up—empty. The flash from Gooseneck's gun lit on a flying steel blade.

The girl spun back across the room—hammered back by the bullets that tore through her chest. Her back hit the wall. She pitched forward to the floor.

Gooseneck stopped shooting and tried to speak. The brown haft of the girl's knife stuck out of his yellow throat. He couldn't get his words past the blade. He dropped one gun and tried to take hold of the protruding haft. Halfway up to it his hand came, and dropped. He went down slowly—to his knees—hands and knees—rolled over on his side—and lay still.

I jumped for the Englishman. The revolver Gooseneck had dropped turned under my foot, spilling me sidewise. My hand brushed the Englishman's coat, but he twisted away from me, and got his guns out.

His eyes were hard and cold and his mouth was shut until you could hardly see the slit of it. He backed slowly across the floor, while I lay still where I had tumbled. He didn't make a speech. A moment of hesitation in the doorway. The door jerked open and shut. He was gone.

I scooped up the gun that had thrown me, sprang to Gooseneck's side, tore the other gun out of his dead hand, and plunged into the street. The maroon roadster was trailing a cloud of dust into the desert behind it. Thirty feet from me stood a dirt-caked black touring car. That would be the one in which Gooseneck had driven back from Mexicali.

I jumped for it, climbed in, brought it to life, and pointed it at the dust-cloud ahead.

VIII

The car under me, I discovered, was surprisingly well engined for its battered looks—its motor was so good that I knew it was a border-runner's car. I nursed it along, not pushing it. There were still four or five hours of daylight left, and while there was any light at all I couldn't miss the cloud of dust from the fleeing roadster.

I didn't know whether we were following a road or not. Sometimes the ground under me looked like one, but mostly it didn't differ much from the rest of the desert. For half an hour or more the dust-cloud ahead and I held our respective positions, and then I found that I was gaining.

The going was roughening. Any road that we might originally have been using had petered out. I opened up a little, though the jars it cost me were vicious. But if I was going to avoid playing Indian among the rocks and cactus, I would have to get within striking distance of my man before he deserted his car and started a game of hide and seek on foot. I'm a city man. I have done my share of work in the open spaces, but I don't like it. My taste in playgrounds runs more to alleys, backyards and cellars than to canyons, mesas and arroyos.

I missed a boulder that would have smashed me up—missed it by a hair—and looked ahead again to see that the maroon roadster was no longer stirring up the grit. It had stopped.

The roadster was empty. I kept on.

From behind the roadster a pistol snapped at me, three times. It would have taken good shooting to plug me at that instant. I was bounding and bouncing around in my seat like a pellet of quicksilver in a nervous man's palm.

He fired again from the shelter of his car, and then dashed for a narrow arroyo—a sharp-edged, ten-foot crack in the earth—off to the left. On the brink, he wheeled to snap another cap at me—and jumped down out of sight.

I twisted the wheel in my hands, jammed on the brakes and slid the black touring car to the spot where I had seen him last. The edge of the arroyo was crumbling under my front wheels. I released the brake. Tumbled out. Shoved.

The car plunged down into the gully after him.

Sprawled on my belly, one of Gooseneck's guns in each hand, I wormed my head over the edge. On all fours, the Englishman was scrambling out of the way of the car. The car was mangled, but still sputtering. One of the man's fists was bunched around a gun—mine.

"Drop it and stand up, Ed!" I yelled.

Snake-quick, he flung himself around in a sitting position on the arroyo bottom, swung his gun up—and I smashed his forearm with my second shot.

He was holding the wounded arm with his left hand when I slid down beside him, picked up the gun he had dropped, and frisked him to see if he had any more.

He grinned at me.

"You know," he drawled, "I fancy your true name isn't Painless Parker at all. You don't act like it."

Twisting a handkerchief into a tourniquet of a sort, I knotted it around his wounded arm, which was bleeding.

"Let's go upstairs and talk," I suggested, and helped him up the steep side of the gully.

We climbed into his roadster.

"Out of gas," he said. "We've got a nice walk ahead of us."

"We'll get a lift. I had a man watching your house, and another one shadowing Gooseneck. They'll be coming out after me, I reckon. Meanwhile, we have time for a nice heart-to-heart talk."

"Go ahead, talk your head off," he invited; "but don't expect me to add much to the conversation. You've got nothing on me." (I'd like to have a dollar, or even a nickel, for every time I've heard that remark!) "You saw Kewpie bump Gooseneck off to keep him from peaching on her."

"So that's your play?" I inquired. "The girl hired Gooseneck to kill your wife—out of jealousy—when she learned that you were planning to shake her and return to your own world?"

"Exactly."

"Not bad, Ed, but there's one rough spot in it."

"Yes?"

"Yes," I repeated. "You are not Ashcraft!"

He jumped, and then laughed.

"Now your enthusiasm is getting the better of your judgment," he kidded me. "Could I have deceived another man's wife? Don't you think her lawyer, Richmond, made me prove my identity?"

"Well, I'll tell you, Ed, I think I'm a smarter baby than either of them. Suppose you had a lot of stuff that belonged to Ashcraft—papers, letters, things in his handwriting? If you were even a fair hand with a pen, you could have fooled his wife. She thought her husband had had four tough years and had become a hophead. That would account for irregularities in his writing. And I don't imagine you ever got very familiar in your letters—not enough so to risk any missteps. As for the lawyer—his making you identify yourself was only a matter of form. It never occurred to him that you weren't Ashcraft. Identification is easy, anyway. Give me a week and I'll prove that I'm the Sultan of Turkey."

He shook his head sadly.

"That comes from riding around in the sun." I went on.

"At first your game was to bleed Mrs Ashcraft for an allowance—to take the cure. But after she closed out her affairs in England and came here, you decided to wipe her out and take everything. You knew she was an orphan and had no close relatives to come butting in. You knew it wasn't likely that there were many people in America who could say you were not Ashcraft. Now if you want to you can do your stalling for just as long as it takes us to send a photograph of you to England—to be shown to the people that knew him there. But you understand that you will do your stalling in the can, so I don't see what it will get you."

"Where do you think Ashcraft would be while I was spending his money?"

There were only two possible guesses. I took the more reasonable one.

"Dead."

I imagined his mouth tightened a little, so I took another shot, and added:

"Up north."

That got to him, though he didn't get excited. But his eyes became thoughtful behind his smile. The United States is all "up north" from Tijuana, but it was even betting that he thought I meant Seattle, where the last record of Ashcraft had come from.

"You may be right, of course," he drawled. "But even at that, I don't see just how you expect to hang me. Can you prove that Kewpie didn't think I was Ashcraft? Can you prove that she knew why Mrs Ashcraft was sending me money? Can you prove that she knew anything about my game? I rather think not. There are still any number of reasons for her to have been jealous of this other woman.

"I'll do my bit for fraud, Painless, but you're not going to swing me. The only two who could possibly tie anything on me are dead behind us. Maybe one of them told you something. What of it? You know damned well that you won't be allowed to testify to it in court. What someone who is now dead may have told you—unless the person it affects was present—isn't evidence, and you know it."

"You may get away with it," I admitted. "Juries are funny, and I don't mind telling you that I'd be happier if I knew a few things about those murders that I don't know. Do you mind telling me about the ins and outs of your switch with Ashcraft—in Seattle?"

He squinted his blue eyes at me.

"You're a puzzling chap, Painless," he said. "I can't tell whether you know everything, or are just sharp-shooting." He puckered his lips and then shrugged. "I'll tell you. It won't matter greatly. I'm due to go over for this impersonation, so a confession to a little additional larceny won't matter."

IX

"The hotel-sneak used to be my lay," the Englishman said after a pause. "I came to the States after England and the Continent got uncomfortable. I was rather good at it. I had the proper manner—the front. I could do the gentleman without sweating over it, you know. In fact there was a day, not so long ago, when I wasn't 'Liverpool Ed.' But you don't want to hear me brag about the select blood that flows through these veins.

"To get back to our knitting: I had rather a successful tour on my first American voyage. I visited most of the better hotels between New York and Seattle, and profited nicely. Then, one night in a Seattle hotel, I worked the tarred and put myself into a room on the fourth floor. I had hardly closed the door behind me before another key was rattling in it. The room was night-dark. I risked a flash from my light, picked out a closet door, and got behind it just in time.

"The clothes closet was empty; rather a stroke of luck, since there was nothing in it for the room's occupant to come for. He—it was a man—had switched on the lights by then.

"He began pacing the floor. He paced it for three solid hours—up and down, up and down, up and down—while I stood behind the closet door with my gun in my hand, in case he should pull it open. For three solid hours he paced that damned floor. Then he sat down and I heard a pen scratching on paper. Ten minutes of that and he was back at his pacing; but he kept it up for only a few minutes this time. I heard the latches of a valise click. And a shot!

"I bounded out of my retreat. He was stretched on the floor, with a hole in the side of his head. A bad break for me, and no mistake! I could hear excited voices in the corridor. I stepped over the dead chap, found the letter he had been writing on the writing-desk. It was addressed to Mrs Norman Ashcraft, at a Wine Street number in Bristol, England. I tore it open. He had written that he was going to kill himself, and it was signed Norman. I felt better. A murder couldn't be made out of it.

"Nevertheless, I was here in this room with a flashlight, skeleton keys, and a gun—to say nothing of a handful of jewelry that I had picked up on the next floor. Somebody was knocking on the door.

"'Get the police!' I called through the door, playing for time.

"Then I turned to the man who had let me in for all this. I would have pegged him for a fellow Britisher even if I hadn't seen the address on his letter. There are thousands of us on the same order—blond, fairly tall, well set up. I took the only chance there was. His hat and topcoat were on a chair where he had tossed them. I put them on and dropped my hat beside him. Kneeling, I emptied his pockets, and my own, gave him all my stuff, pouched all of his. Then I traded guns with him and opened the door.

"What I had in mind was that the first arrivals might not know him by sight, or not well enough to recognize him immediately. That would give me several seconds to arrange my disappearance in. But when I opened the door I found that my idea wouldn't work out as I had planned. The house detective was there, and a policeman, and I knew I was licked. There would be little chance of sneaking away from them. But I played my hand out. I told them I had come up to my room and found this chap on the floor going through my belongings. I had seized him, and in the struggle had shot him.

"Minutes went by like hours, and nobody denounced me. People were calling me Mr Ashcraft. My impersonation was succeeding. It had me gasping then, but after I learned more about Ashcraft it wasn't so surprising. He had arrived at the hotel only that afternoon, and no one had seen him except in his hat and coat—the hat and coat I was wearing. We were of the same size and type—typical blond Englishmen.

"Then I got another surprise. When the detective examined the dead man's clothes he found that the maker's labels had been ripped out. When I got a look at his diary, later, I found the explanation of that. He had been tossing mental coins with himself, alternating between a determination to kill himself, and another to change his name and make a new place for himself in the world—putting his old life behind him. It was while he was considering the second plan that he had removed the markers from all of his clothing.

"But I didn't know that while I stood there among those people. All I knew was that miracles were happening. I met the miracles half-way, not turning a hair, accepting everything as a matter of course. I think the police smelled something wrong, but they couldn't put their hands on it. There was the dead man on the floor, with a prowler's outfit in his pockets, a pocketful of stolen jewelry, and the labels gone from his clothes—a burglar's trick. And there I was—a well-to-do Englishman whom the hotel people recognized as the room's rightful occupant.

"I had to talk small just then, but after I went through the dead man's stuff I knew him inside and outside, backward and forward. He had nearly a bushel of papers, and a diary that had everything he had ever done or thought in it. I put in the first night studying those things—memorizing them—and practicing his signature. Among the other things I had taken from his pockets were fifteen hundred dollars' worth of traveler's checks, and I wanted to be able to get them cashed in the morning.

"I stayed in Seattle for three days—as Norman Ashcraft. I had tumbled into something rich and I wasn't going to throw it away. The letter to his wife would keep me from being charged with murder if anything slipped, and I knew I was safer seeing the thing through than running. When the excitement had quieted down I packed up and came down to San Francisco, resuming my own name—Edward Bohannon. But I held on to all of Ashcraft's property, because I had learned from it that his wife had money, and I knew I could get some of it if I played my cards right.

"She saved me the trouble of figuring out a deal for myself. I ran across one of her advertisements in the *Examiner*, answered it, and—here we are."

I looked toward Tijuana. A cloud of yellow dust showed in a notch between two low hills. That would be the machine in which Gorman and Hooper were tracking me. Hooper would have seen me set out after the Englishman, would have waited for Gorman to arrive in the car in which he had followed Gooseneck from Mexicali—Gorman would have had to stay some distance in the rear—and then both of the operatives would have picked up my trail.

I turned to the Englishman.

"But you didn't have Mrs Ashcraft killed?"

He shook his head.

"You'll never prove it."

"Maybe not," I admitted.

I took a package of cigarettes out of my pocket and put two of them on the seat between us.

"Suppose we play a game. This is just for my own satisfaction. It won't tie anybody to anything—won't prove anything. If you did a certain thing, pick up the cigarette that is nearer me. If you didn't do that thing, pick up the one nearer you. Will you play?"

"No, I won't," he said emphatically. "I don't like your game. But I do want a cigarette."

He reached out his uninjured arm and picked up the cigarette nearer *me*.

"Thanks, Ed," I said. "Now I hate to tell you this, but I'm going to swing you."

"You're balmy, my son."

"You're thinking of the San Francisco job, Ed," I explained. "I'm talking about Seattle. You, a hotel sneak-thief, were discovered in a room with a man who had just died with a bullet in his head. What do you think a jury will make out of that, Ed?"

He laughed at me. And then something went wrong with the laugh. It faded into a sickly grin.

"Of course you did," I said. "When you started to work out your plan to inherit all of Mrs Ashcraft's wealth by having her killed, the first thing you did was to destroy that suicide letter of her husband's. No matter how carefully you guarded it, there was always a chance that somebody would stumble into it and knock your game on the head. It had served its purpose—you wouldn't need it. It would be foolish to take a chance on it turning up.

"I can't put you up for the murders you engineered in San Francisco; but I can sock you with the one you didn't do in Seattle—so justice won't be cheated. You're going to Seattle, Ed, to hang for Ashcraft's suicide."

And he did.

5

WHO KILLED BOB TEAL?

TRUE DETECTIVE MAGAZINE, NOVEMBER 1924

Operative Teal went out to shadow a thief, who didn't even know he was suspected. Seven hours after Teal left his agency's office, he was found—shot to death. Whose hand cut him down?

"Teal was killed last night."

The Old Man—the Continental Detective Agency's San Francisco manager—spoke without looking at me. His voice was as mild as his smile, and gave no indication of the turmoil that was seething in his mind.

If I kept quiet, waiting for the Old Man to go on, it wasn't because the news didn't mean anything to me. I had been fond of Bob Teal—we all had. He had come to the agency fresh from college two years before; and if ever a man had the makings of a crack detective in him, this slender, broad-shouldered lad had. Two years is little enough time in which to pick up the first principles of sleuthing, but Bob Teal, with his quick eye, cool nerve, balanced head, and whole-hearted interest in the work, was already well along the way to expertness. I had an almost fatherly interest in him, since I had given him most of his early training.

The Old Man didn't look at me as he went on. He was talking to the open window at his elbow.

"He was shot with a .32, twice, through the heart. He was shot behind a row of signboards on the vacant lot on the northwest corner of Hyde and Eddy Streets, at about ten last night. His body was found by a patrolman a little after eleven. The gun was found about fifteen feet away. I have seen him and I have gone over the ground myself. The rain last night wiped out any leads the ground may have held, but from the condition of Teal's clothing and the position in which he was found, I would say that there was no struggle, and that he was shot where he was found, and not carried there afterward. He was lying behind the signboards, about thirty feet from the sidewalk, and his hands were empty. The gun was held close enough to him to singe the breast of his coat. Apparently no one either saw or heard the shooting. The rain and wind would have kept pedestrians off the street, and would have deadened the reports of a .32, which are not especially loud, anyway."

The Old Man's pencil began to tap the desk, its gentle clicking setting my nerves on edge. Presently it stopped, and the Old Man went on:

"Teal was shadowing a Herbert Whitacre—had been shadowing him for three days. Whitacre is one of the partners in the firm Ogburn & Whitacre, farm-development engineers. They have options on a large area of land in several of the new irrigation districts. Ogburn handles the sales end, while Whitacre looks after the rest of the business, including the book-keeping.

"Last week Ogburn discovered that his partner had been making false entries. The books show certain payments made on the land, and Ogburn learned that these payments had not been made. He estimates that the amount of Whitacre's thefts may be anywhere from $150,000 to $250,000. He came in to see me three days ago and told me all this, and wanted to have Whitacre shadowed in an endeavor to learn what he has done with the stolen money. Their firm is still a partnership, and a partner cannot be prosecuted for stealing from the partnership, of course. Thus, Ogburn could not have his partner arrested, but he hoped to find the money, and then recover it through civil action. Also he was afraid that Whitacre might disappear.

"I sent Teal out to shadow Whitacre, who supposedly didn't know that his partner suspected him. Now I am sending you out to find Whitacre. I'm determined to find him and convict him if I have to let all regular business go and put every man I have on this job for a year. You can get Teal's reports from the clerks. Keep in touch with me."

All that, from the Old Man, was more than an ordinary man's oath written in blood.

In the clerical office I got the two reports Bob had turned in. There was none for the last day, of course, as he would not have written that until after he had quit work for the night. The first of these two reports had already been copied and a copy sent to Ogburn; a typist was working on the other now.

In his reports Bob had described Whitacre as a man of about thirty-seven, with brown hair and eyes, a nervous manner, a smooth-shaven, medium-complexioned face, and rather small feet. He was about five feet eight inches tall, weighed about a hundred and fifty pounds, and dressed fashionably, though quietly. He lived with his wife in an apartment on Gough Street. They had no children. Ogburn had given Bob a description of Mrs Whitacre: a short, plump, blond woman of something less than thirty.

Those who remember this affair will know that the city, the detective agency, and the people involved all had names different from the ones I have given them. But they will know also that I have kept the facts true. Names of some sort are essential to clearness, and when the use of the real names might cause embarrassment, or pain even, pseudonyms are the most satisfactory alternative.

In shadowing Whitacre, Bob had learned nothing that seemed to be of any value in finding the stolen money. Whitacre had gone about his usual business, apparently, and Bob had seen him do nothing downright suspicious. But Whitacre had seemed very nervous, had often stopped to look around, obviously suspecting that he was being shadowed without being sure of it. On several occasions Bob had had to drop him to avoid being recognized. On one of these occasions, while waiting in the vicinity of Whitacre's residence for him to return, Bob had seen Mrs Whitacre—or a woman who fit the description Ogburn had given—leave in a taxicab. Bob had not tried to follow her, but he had made a memorandum of the taxi's license number.

These two reports read and practically memorized, I left the agency and went down to Ogburn & Whitacre's suite in the Packard Building. A stenographer ushered me into a tastefully furnished office, where Ogburn sat at a desk signing mail. He offered me a chair. I introduced myself to him: a medium-sized man of perhaps thirty-five, with sleek brown hair and the cleft chin that is associated in my mind with orators, lawyers, and salesmen.

"Oh, yes!" he said, pushing aside the mail, his mobile, intelligent face lighting up. "Has Mr Teal found anything?"

"Mr Teal was shot and killed last night."

He looked at me blankly for a moment out of wide brown eyes, and then repeated: "Killed?"

"Yes," I replied, and told him what little I knew about it.

"You don't think—" he began when I had finished, and then stopped. "You don't think Herb would have done that?"

"What do you think?"

"I don't think Herb would commit murder! He's been jumpy the last few days, and I was beginning to think he suspected I had discovered his thefts, but I don't believe he would have gone that far, even if he knew Mr Teal was following him. I honestly don't!"

"Suppose," I suggested, "that sometime yesterday Teal found where he had put the stolen money, and then Whitacre learned that Teal knew it. Don't you think that under those circumstances Whitacre might have killed him?"

"Perhaps," he said slowly, "but I'd hate to think so. In a moment of panic Herb might—but I really don't think he would."

"When did you see him last?"

"Yesterday. We were here in the office together most of the day. He left for home a few minutes before six. But I talked with him over the phone later. He called me up at home at a little after seven, and said he was coming down to see me, wanted to tell me something. I thought he was going to confess his dishonesty, and that maybe we would be able to straighten out this miserable affair. But he didn't show up; changed his mind, I suppose. His wife called up at about ten. She wanted him to bring something from downtown when he went home, but of course he was not there. I staid in all evening waiting for him, but he didn't—"

He stuttered, stopped talking, and his face drained white.

"My God. I'm wiped out!" he said faintly, as if the thought of his own position had just come to him. "Herb gone, money gone, three years' work gone for nothing! And I'm legally responsible for every cent he stole. God!"

He looked at me with eyes that pleaded for a contradiction, but I couldn't do anything except assure him that everything possible would be done to find both Whitacre and the money. I left him trying frantically to get his attorney on the telephone.

From Ogburn's office I went up to Whitacre's apartment. As I turned the corner below into Gough Street I saw a big, hulking man going up the apartment house steps, and recognized him as George Dean. Hurrying to join him, I regretted that he had been assigned to the job instead of some other member of the Police Detective Homicide Detail. Dean isn't a bad sort, but he isn't so satisfactory to work with as some of the others; that is, you can never be sure that he isn't holding out some important detail so that George Dean would shine as the clever sleuth in the end. Working with a man of that sort, you're bound to fall into the same habit—which doesn't make for teamwork.

I arrived in the vestibule as Dean pressed Whitacre's bell-button.

"Hello," I said. "You in on this?"

"Uh-huh. What d'you know?"

"Nothing. I just got it."

The front door clicked open, and we went together up to the Whitacre's apartment on the third floor. A plump, blond woman in a light blue house-dress opened the apartment door. She was rather pretty in a thick-featured, stolid way.

"Mrs Whitacre?" Dean inquired.

"Yes."

"Is Mr Whitacre in?"

"No. He went to Los Angeles this morning," she said, and her face was truthful.

"Know where we can get in touch with him there?"

"Perhaps at the Ambassador, but I think he'll be back by tomorrow or the next day."

Dean showed her his badge.

"We want to ask you a few questions," he told her, and with no appearance of astonishment she opened the door wide for us to enter. She led us into a blue and cream living-room, where we found a chair apiece. She sat facing us on a big blue settle.

"Where was your husband last night?" Dean asked.

"Home. Why?" Her round blue eyes were faintly curious.

"Home all night?"

"Yes, it was a rotten rainy night. Why?" She looked from Dean to me.

Dean's glance met mine, and I nodded an answer to the question that I read there.

"Mrs Whitacre," he said bluntly, "I have a warrant for your husband's arrest."

"A warrant? For what?"

"Murder."

"Murder?" It was a stifled scream.

"Exactly, an' last night."

"But—but I told you he was—"

"And Ogburn told me," I interrupted leaning forward, "that you called up his apartment last night, asking if your husband was there."

She looked at me blankly for a dozen seconds; and then she laughed, the clear laugh of one who has been the victim of some slight joke.

"You win," she said, and there was neither shame nor humiliation in either face or voice. "Now listen"—the amusement had left her—

"I don't know what Herb has done, or how I stand, and I oughtn't to talk until I see a lawyer. But I like to dodge all the trouble I can. If you folks will tell me what's what, on your word of honor, I'll maybe tell you what I know, if anything. What I mean is, if talking will make things any easier for me, if you can show me it will, maybe I'll talk—provided I know anything."

That seemed fair enough, if a little surprising. Apparently this plump woman who could lie with every semblance of candor, and laugh when she was tripped up, wasn't interested in anything much beyond her own comfort.

"You tell it," Dean said to me.

I shot it out all in a lump.

"Your husband had been cooking the books for some time, and got into his partner for something like $200,000 before Ogburn got wise to it. Then he had your husband shadowed, trying to find the money. Last night your husband took the man who was shadowing him over on a lot and shot him."

Her face puckered thoughtfully. Mechanically she reached for a package of a popular brand of cigarettes that lay on a table behind the settle, and proffered them to Dean and me. We shook our heads. She put a cigarette in her mouth, scratched a match on the sole of her slipper, lit the cigarette, and stared at the burning end. Finally she shrugged, her face cleared, and she looked up at us.

"I'm going to talk," she said. "I never got any of the money, and I'd be a chump to make a goat of myself for Herb. He was all right, but if he's run out and left me flat, there's no use of me making a lot of trouble for myself over it. Here goes: I'm not Mrs Whitacre, except on the register. My name is Mae Landis. Maybe there is a real Mrs Whitacre, and maybe not. I don't know. Herb and I have been living together here for over a year.

"About a month ago he began to get jumpy, nervous, even worse than usual. He said he had business worries. Then a couple of days ago I discovered that his pistol was gone from the drawer where it had been kept ever since we came here, and that he was carrying it. I asked him: 'What's the idea?' He said he thought he was being followed, and asked me if I'd seen anybody hanging around the neighborhood as if watching our place. I told him no; I thought he was nutty.

"Night before last he told me that he was in trouble, and might have to go away, and that he couldn't take me with him, but would give me enough money to take care of me for a while. He seemed excited, packed his bags so they'd be ready if he needed them in a hurry, and burned up all his photos and a lot of letters and papers. His bags are still in the bedroom, if you want to go through them. When he didn't come home last night I had a hunch that he had beat it without his bags and without saying a word to me, much less giving me any money—leaving me with only twenty dollars to my name and not even much that I could hock, and with the rent due in four days."

"When did you see him last?"

"About eight o'clock last night. He told me he was going down to Mr Ogburn's apartment to talk some business over with him, but he didn't go there. I know that. I ran out of cigarettes—I like Elixir Russians, and I can't get them uptown here—so I called up Mr Ogburn's to ask Herb to bring some home with him when he came, and Mr Ogburn said he hadn't been there."

"How long have you known Whitacre?" I asked.

"Couple of years. I guess. I think I met him first at one of the Beach resorts."

"Has he got any people?"

"Not that I know of. I don't know a whole lot about him. Oh, yes! I do know that he served three tears in prison in Oregon for forgery. He told me that one night when he was lushed up. He served them under the name of Barber, or Barbee, or something like that. He said he was walking the straight and narrow now;"

Dean produced a small automatic pistol, fairly new-looking in spite of the mud that clung to it, and handed it to the woman.

"Ever see that?"

She nodded her blond head.

"Yep! That's Herb's, or its twin."

Dean pocketed the gun again, and we stood up.

"Where do I stand now?" she asked. "You're not going to lock me up as a witness or anything, are you?"

"Not just now," Dean assured her. "Stick around where we can find you if we want you, and you won't be bothered. Got any idea which direction Whitacre'd be likely to go in?"

"No."

"We'd like to give the place the once-over. Mind?"

"Go ahead," she invited. "Take it apart if you want to. I'm coming all the way with you people."

We very nearly did take the place apart, but we found not a thing of value. Whitacre, when he had burned the things that might have given him away, had made a clean job of it.

"Did he ever have any pictures taken by a professional photographer?" I asked just before we left.

"Not that I know of."

"Will you let us know if you hear anything or remember anything else that might help?"

"Sure," she said heartily; "sure."

Dean and I rode down in the elevator in silence, and walked out into Gough Street.

"What do you think of all that?" I asked when we were outside.

"She's a lil, huh?" He grinned. "I wonder how much she knows. She identified the gun an' gave us that dope about the forgery sentence up north, but we'd of found out them things anyway. If she was wise she'd tell us everything she knew we'd find out, an' that would make her other stuff go over stronger. Think she's dumb or wise?"

"We won't guess," I said. "We'll slap a shadow on her and cover her mail. I have the number of a taxi she used a couple days ago. We'll look that up too."

At a corner drug store I telephoned the Old Man, asking him to detail a couple of the boys to keep Mae Landis and her apartment under surveillance night and day; also to have the Post Office Department let us know if she got any mail that might have been addressed by Whitacre. I told the Old Man

I would see Ogburn and get some specimens of the fugitive's writing for comparison with the woman's mail.

Then Dean and I set about tracing the taxi in which Bob Teal had seen the woman ride away. Half an hour in the taxi company's office gave us the information that she had been driven to a number on Greenwich Street. We went to the Greenwich Street address.

It was a ramshackle building, divided into apartments or flats of a dismal and dingy sort. We found the landlady in the basement: a gaunt woman in soiled gray, with a hard, thin-lipped mouth and pale, suspicious eyes. She was rocking vigorously in a creaking chair and sewing on a pair of overalls, while three dirty kids tussled with a mongrel puppy up and down the room.

Dean showed his badge, and told her that we wanted to speak to her in privacy. She got up to chase the kids and their dog out, and then stood with hands on hips facing us.

"Well, what do you want?" she demanded sourly.

"Want to get a line on your tenants," Dean said. "Tell us about them."

"Tell you about them?" She had a voice that would have been harsh enough even if she hadn't been in such a peevish mood. "What do you think I got to say about 'em? What do you think I am? I'm a woman that minds her own business! Nobody can't say that I don't run a respectable—"

This was getting us nowhere.

"Who lives in number one?" I asked.

"The Auds—two old folks and their grandchildren. If you know anything against them, it's more'n them that has lived with 'em for ten years does!"

"Who lives in number two?"

"Mrs Codman and her boys, Frank and Fred. They been here three years, and—"

I carried her from apartment to apartment, until finally we reached a second-floor one that didn't bring quite so harsh an indictment of my stupidity for suspecting its occupants of whatever it was that I suspected them of.

"The Quirks live there." She merely glowered now, whereas she had had a snippy manner before. "And they're decent people, if you ask me!"

"How long have they been here?"

"Six months or more."

"What does he do for a living?"

"I don't know." Sullenly. "Travels maybe."

"How many in the family?"

"Just him and her, and they're nice quiet people, too."

"What does he look like?"

"Like an ordinary man. I ain't a detective. I don't go 'round snoopin' into folks' faces to see what they look like, and prying into their business. I ain't—"

"How old a man is he?"

"Maybe between thirty-five and forty, if he ain't younger or older."

"Large or small?"

"He ain't as short as you, and he ain't as tall as this feller with you," glaring scornfully from my short stoutness to Dean's big bulk, "and he ain't as fat as neither of you."

"Mustache?"

"No."

"Light hair?"

"No." Triumphantly: "Dark."

"Dark eyes, too?"

"I guess so."

Dean, standing off to one side, looked over the woman's shoulder at me. His lips framed the name: "Whitacre."

"Now how about Mrs Quirk—what does she look like?" I went on.

"She's got light hair, is short and chunky, and maybe under thirty."

Dean and I nodded our satisfaction at each other; that sounded like Mae Landis, right enough.

"Are they home much?" I continued.

"I don't know," the gaunt woman snarled sullenly, and I knew she did know, so I waited, looking at her, and presently she added grudgingly: "I think they're away a lot, but I ain't sure."

"I know," I ventured, "they are home very seldom, and then only in the daytime—and you know it."

She didn't deny it, so I asked: "Are they in now?"

"I don't think so, but they might be."

"Let's take a look at the joint," I suggested to Dean.

He nodded and told the woman: "Take us up to their apartment an' unlock the door for us."

"I won't!" she said with sharp emphasis. "You got no right goin' into folks' homes unless you got a search-warrant. You got one?"

"We got nothin'," Dean grinned at her, "but we can get plenty if you want to put us to the trouble. You run this house; you can go into any of the flats any time you want, an' you can take us in. Take us up, an' we'll lay off you: but if you're going to put us to a lot of trouble, then you'll take your chances of bein' tied up with the Quirks, an' maybe sharin' a cell with 'em. Think that over."

She thought it over, and then, grumbling and growling with each step, took us up to the Quirks' apartment. She made sure they weren't at home, then admitted us.

The apartment consisted of three rooms, a bath, and a kitchen, furnished in the shabby fashion that the ramshackle exterior of the building had prepared us for. In these rooms we found a few articles of masculine and feminine clothing, toilet accessories, and so on. But the place had none of the marks of a permanent abode; there were no pictures, no cushions, none of the dozens of odds and ends of personal belongings that are usually found in homes. The kitchen had the appearance of long disuse; the interiors of the coffee, tea, spice, and flour containers were clean.

Two things we found that meant something: A handful of Elixer Russian cigarettes on a table; and a new box of .32 cartridges—ten of which were missing—in a dresser drawer.

All through our searching the landlady hovered over us, her pale eyes sharp and curious; but now we chased her out, telling her that, law or no law, we were taking charge of the apartment.

"This was or is a hide-out for Whitacre and his woman all right," Dean said when we were alone. "The only question is whether he intended to lay low here or whether it was just a place where he made preparations for his getaway. I reckon the best thing is to have the Captain put a man in here night and day until we turn up Brother Whitacre."

"That's safest," I agreed, and he went to the telephone in the front room to arrange it.

After Dean was through phoning, I called up the Old Man to see if anything new had developed.

"Nothing new," he told me. "How are you coming along?"

"Nicely. Maybe I'll have news for you this evening."

"Did you get those specimens of Whitacre's writing from Ogburn? Or shall I have someone else take care of it?"

"I'll get them this evening," I promised.

I wasted ten minutes trying to reach Ogburn at his office before I looked at my watch and saw that it was after six o'clock. I found his residence listed in the telephone directory, and called him there.

"Have you anything in Whitacre's writing at home?" I asked. "I want to get a couple of samples—would like to get them this evening, though if necessary I can wait until tomorrow."

"I think I have some of his letters here. If you come over now I'll give them to you."

"Be with you in fifteen minutes," I told him.

"I'm going down to Ogburn's," I told Dean, "to get some of Whitacre's scribbling while you're waiting for your man to come from Headquarters to take charge of this place. I'll meet you at the States as soon as you can get away. We'll eat there, and make our plans for the night."

"Uh-huh," he grunted, making himself comfortable in one chair, with his feet on another, as I let myself out.

Ogburn was dressing when I reached his apartment, and had his collar and tie in his hand when he came to the door to let me in.

"I found quite a few of Herb's letters," he said as we walked back to his bedroom.

I looked through the fifteen or more letters that lay on a table, selecting the ones I wanted, while Ogburn went on with his dressing.

"How are you progressing?" he asked presently.

"So-so. Heard anything that might help?"

"No, but just a few minutes ago I happened to remember that Herb used to go over to the Mills Building quite frequently. I've seen him going in and out often, but never thought anything of it. I don't know whether it is of any importance or—"

I jumped out of my chair.

"That does it!" I cried. "Can I use your phone?"

"Certainly. It's in the hallway, near the door." He looked at me in surprise. "It's a slot phone; have you a nickel in change?"

"Yes." I was going through the bedroom door.

"The switch is near the door," he called after me, "if you want a light. Do you think—"

But I didn't stop to listen to his questions. I was making for the telephone, searching my pockets for a nickel. And, fumbling hurriedly with the nickel, I muffed it—not entirely by accident, for I had a hunch that I wanted to work out. The nickel rolled away down the carpeted hallway. I switched on the light, recovered the nickel, and called the "Quirks' " number. I'm glad I played that hunch.

Dean was still there.

"That joint's dead," I sang. "Take the landlady down to Headquarters, and grab the Landis woman, too. I'll meet you there—at Headquarters."

"You mean it?" he rumbled.

"Almost," I said, and hung up the receiver.

I switched off the hall light and, whistling a little tune to myself, walked back to the room where I had left Ogburn. The door was not quite closed. I walked straight up to it, kicked it open with one foot, and jumped back, hugging the wall.

Two shots—so close together that they were almost one—crashed.

Flat against the wall, I pounded my feet against the floor and wainscot, and let out a medley of shrieks and groans that would have done credit to a carnival wild-man.

A moment later Ogburn appeared in the doorway, a revolver in his hand, his face wolfish. He was determined to kill me. It was my life or his, so—I slammed my gun down on the sleek, brown top of his head.

When he opened his eyes, two policemen were lifting him into the back of a patrol-wagon.

I found Dean in the detectives' assembly-room in the Hall of Justice.

"The landlady identifies Mae Landis as Mrs Quirk," he said. "Now what?"

"Where is she now?"

"One of the policewomen is holding both of them in the Captain's office."

"Ogburn is over in the Pawnshop Detail office," I told him. "Let's take the landlady in for a look at him."

Ogburn sat leaning forward, holding his head in his hands and staring sullenly at the feet of the uniformed man who guarded him, when we took the gaunt landlady in to see him.

"Ever see him before?" I asked her.

"Yes"–reluctantly—"that's Mr Quirk."

Ogburn didn't look up, and he paid not the least attention to any of us.

After we had told the landlady that she could go home, Dean led me back to a far corner of the assembly-room, where we could talk without disturbance.

"Now spill it!" he burst out. "How come all the startling developments, as the newspaper boys call 'em?"

"Well, first-off, I knew that the question *Who killed Bob Teal?* could have only one answer. Bob wasn't a boob! He might possibly have let a man he was trailing lure him behind a row of billboards on a dark night, but he would have gone prepared for trouble. He wouldn't have died with empty hands, from a gun that was close enough to scorch his coat. The murderer *had* to be somebody Bob trusted, so it couldn't be Whitacre. Now Bob was a conscientious sort of lad, and he wouldn't have stopped shadowing Whitacre to go over and talk with some friend. There was only one man who could have persuaded him to drop Whitacre for a while, and that one man was the one he was working for—Ogburn.

"If I hadn't known Bob, I might have thought he had hidden behind the billboards to watch Whitacre; but Bob wasn't an amateur. He knew better than to pull any of that spectacular gumshoe stuff. So there was nothing to it but Ogburn!

"With that to go on, the rest was ducksoup. All the stuff Mae Landis gave us—identifying the gun as Whitacre's, and giving Ogburn an alibi by saying she had talked to him on the phone at ten o'clock—only convinced me that she and Ogburn were working together. When the landlady described 'Quirk' for us, I was fairly certain of it. Her description would fit either Whitacre or Ogburn, but there was no sense to Whitacre's having the apartment on Greenwich Street, while if Ogburn and the Landis woman were thick, they'd need a meeting-place of some sort. The rest of the box of cartridges there helped some too.

"Then tonight I put on a little act in Ogburn's apartment, chasing a nickel along the floor and finding traces of dried mud that had escaped the cleaning-up he no doubt gave the carpet and clothes after he came home from walking through the lot in the rain. We'll let the experts decide whether it *could* be mud from the lot on which Bob was killed, and the jury can decide whether it *is*.

"There are a few more odds and ends—like the gun. The Landis woman said Whitacre had had it for more than a year, but in spite of being muddy it looks fairly new to me. We'll send the serial number to the factory, and find when it was turned out.

"For motive, just now all I'm sure of is the woman, which should be enough. But I think that when Ogburn & Whitacre's books are audited, and their finances sifted, we'll find something there. What I'm banking on strong is that Whitacre will come in, now that he is cleared of the murder charge."

And that is exactly what happened.

Next day Herbert Whitacre walked into Police Headquarters at Sacramento and surrendered.

Neither Ogburn nor Mae Landis ever told what they knew, but with Whitacre's testimony, supported by what we were able to pick up here and there, we went into court when the time came and convinced the jury that the facts were these:

Ogburn and Whitacre had opened their farm development business as a plain swindle. They had options on a lot of land, and they planned to sell as many shares in their enterprise as possible before the time came to exercise their options. Then they intended packing up their bags and disappearing. Whitacre hadn't much nerve, and he had a clear remembrance of the three years he had served in prison for forgery; so, to bolster his courage, Ogburn had told his partner that he had a friend in the Post Office Department in Washington, D.C., who would tip him off the instant any official suspicion was aroused.

The two partners made a neat little pile out of their venture, Ogburn taking charge of the money until the time came for the split-up. Meanwhile Ogburn and Mae Landis—Whitacre's supposed wife—had become intimate, and had rented the apartment on Greenwich Street, meeting there afternoons when Whitacre was busy at the office, and when Ogburn was supposed to be out hunting fresh victims. In this apartment Ogburn and the woman had hatched their little scheme, whereby they were to get rid of Whitacre, keep all the loot, and clear Ogburn of criminal complicity in the affairs of Ogburn & Whitacre.

Ogburn had come into the Continental Office and told his little tale of his partner's dishonesty, engaging Bob Teal to shadow him. Then he had told Whitacre that he had received a tip from his friend in Washington that an investigation was about to be made. The two partners planned to leave town on their separate ways the following week. The next night Mae Landis told Whitacre she had seen a man loitering in the neighborhood, apparently watching the building in which they lived. Whitacre—thinking Bob a Post Office Inspector—had gone completely to pieces, and it had taken the combined efforts of the woman and his partner—apparently working separately—to keep him from bolting immediately. They had persuaded him to stick it out another few days.

On the night of the murder, Ogburn, pretending skepticism of Whitacre's story about being followed, had met Whitacre for the purpose of learning if he really was being shadowed. They had walked the streets in the rain for an hour. Then Ogburn, convinced, had announced his intention of going back and talking to the supposed Post Office Inspector, to see if he could be bribed. Whitacre had refused to accompany his partner, but had agreed to wait for him in a dark doorway.

Ogburn had taken Bob Teal over behind the billboards on some pretext, and had murdered him. Then he had hurried back to his partner, crying: "My God! He grabbed me and I shot him. We'll have to leave!"

Whitacre, in blind panic, had left San Francisco without stopping for his bags or even notifying Mae Landis. Ogburn was supposed to leave by another route. They were to meet in Oklahoma City ten days later, where Ogburn—after getting the loot out of the Los Angeles banks, where he had deposited it under various names—was to give Whitacre his share, and then they were to part for good.

In Sacramento next day Whitacre had read the newspapers, and had understood what had been done to him. He had done all the book-keeping; all the false entries in Ogburn & Whitacre's books were in his writing. Mae Landis had revealed his former criminal record, and had fastened the ownership of the gun—really Ogburn's—upon him. He was framed completely! He hadn't a chance of clearing himself.

He had known that his story would sound like a far-fetched and flimsy lie; he had a criminal record. For him to have surrendered and told the truth would have been merely to get himself laughed at.

As it turned out, Ogburn went to the gallows, Mae Landis is now serving a fifteen-year sentence, and Whitacre, in return for his testimony and restitution of the loot, was not prosecuted for his share in the land swindle.

6

MIKE, ALEC OR RUFUS

BLACK MASK, JANUARY 1925

Mr Hammett and his hard-boiled sleuth are too well known to BLACK MASK *readers to need much of an introduction. That the following story is as interesting and surprising as any which Mr Hammett has yet written, is all we need to say to arouse your interest.*

I don't know whether Jacob Coplin was tall or short. All of him I ever got a look at was his round head—naked scalp and wrinkled face, both of them the color and texture of Manila paper—propped up on white pillows in a big four-poster bed. The rest of him was buried under a thick pile of bedding.

Besides he and I in the room that first time, there were his wife, a roly-poly woman with lines in a plump white face like scratches in ivory; his daughter Phyllis, a smart little Jewess of the popular-member-of-the-younger-set type; and the maid who had opened the door for me, a big-boned blonde girl in apron and cap.

I had introduced myself as a representative of the North American Casualty Company's San Francisco office, which

I was in a way. There was no immediate profit in admitting I was a Continental Detective Agency sleuth, just now in the casualty company's hire, so I held back that part.

"I want a list of the stuff you lost," I told Coplin; "but first—"

"Stuff?" Coplin's yellow sphere of a skull bobbed off the pillows, and he wailed to the ceiling: "A hundred thousand dollars if a nickel, and he calls it *stuff!*"

Mrs Coplin pushed her husband's head down on the pillows again with a short-fingered fat hand.

"Now, Jakie, don'd ged excited," she soothed him.

Phyllis Coplin's dark eyes twinkled, and she winked one of them at me.

The man in bed turned his face to me again, smiled a bit shamefacedly, and chuckled.

"Well, if you people want to call your seventy-five-thousand-dollar loss *stuff*, I guess I can stand it for twenty-five thousand."

"So it adds up to a hundred thousand?" I asked.

"Yes. None of them were insured to their full value, and some weren't insured at all."

That was very usual. I don't remember ever having anybody admit that anything stolen from them was insured to the hilt—always it was half, or, at most, three-quarters covered by the policy.

"Suppose you tell me exactly what happened," I suggested, and added, to head off another speech that usually comes: "I know you've already told the police the whole thing, but I'll have to have it from you."

"Well, we were getting dressed to go to the Bauers' last night. I brought my wife's and daughter's jewelry—the valuable pieces—home with me from the safe-deposit box. I had just got my coat on, and had called to them to hurry up with their dressing when the door-bell rang."

"What time was this?"

"Just about half past eight. I went out of this room into the sitting-room across the passageway, and was putting some cigars in my case when Hilda"—nodding at the blonde maid—"came walking into the room, backwards. I started to ask her if she had gone crazy, walking around backwards, when I saw the robber. He—"

"Just a moment." I turned to the maid. "What happened when you answered the bell?"

"Why, I opened the door, of course, and this man was standing there, and he had a revolver in his hand, and he stuck it against my—my stomach, and pushed me back into the room where Mr Coplin was, and he shot Mr Coplin, and—"

"When I saw him and the revolver in his hand," Coplin took the story away from his servant; "it gave me a fright, sort of, and I let my cigar case slip out of my hand. Trying to catch it again—no sense in ruining good cigars even if you are being robbed—he must have thought I was trying to get a gun or something. Anyway he shot me in the leg. My wife and Phyllis came running in when they heard the shot, and he pointed the revolver at them, took all their jewels, and had them empty my pockets. Then he made them drag me back into Phyllis's room, into the closet, and he locked us all in there. And, mind you, he don't say a word all this time, not a word—just makes motions with his gun and his left hand."

"How bad did he bang your leg?"

"Depends on whether you want to believe me or the doctor. He says it's nothing much. Just a scratch, he says, but it's my leg that's shot, not his!"

"Did he say anything when you opened the door?" I asked the maid.

"No, sir."

"Did any of you hear him say anything while he was here?"

None of them had.

"What happened after he locked you in the closet?"

"Nothing that we knew about," Coplin said; "until McBirney and a policeman came and let us out."

"Who's McBirney?"

"The janitor."

"How'd he happen along with a policeman?"

"He heard the shot, and came upstairs just as the robber was starting down after leaving here. The robber turned around and ran upstairs, then, into an apartment on the seventh floor, and stayed there—keeping the woman who lives there, a Miss Eveleth, quiet with his revolver—until he got a chance to sneak out and get away. He knocked her unconscious before he left, and—and that's all. McBirney called the police right after he saw the robber, but they got here too late to be any good."

"How long were you in the closet?"

"Ten minutes—maybe fifteen."

"What sort of looking man was the robber?"

"Short and thin and—"

"How short?"

"About your height, or maybe shorter."

"About five feet five or six, say? What would he weigh?"

"Oh, I don't know—maybe a hundred and fifteen or twenty. He was kind of puny."

"How old?"

"Not more than twenty-two or three."

"Oh, Papa," Phyllis objected; "he was thirty, or near it!"

"What do you think?" I asked Mrs Coplin.

"Twenty-five, I'll say."

"And you?" to the maid.

"I don't know exactly, sir; but he wasn't very old."

"Light or dark?"

"He was light," Coplin said. "He needed a shave, and his beard was yellowish."

"More of a light brown," Phyllis amended.

"Maybe, but it was light."

"What color eyes?"

"I don't know. He had a cap pulled down over them. They looked dark, but that might have been because they were in the shadow."

"How would you describe the part of his face you could see?"

"Pale, and kind of weak looking—small chin. But you couldn't see much of his face: he had his coat collar turned up and his cap pulled down."

"How was he dressed?"

"A blue cap pulled down over his eyes, a blue suit, black shoes, and black gloves—silk ones."

"Shabby or neat?"

"Kind of cheap looking clothes, needing pressing, awfully wrinkled."

"What sort of gun?"

Phyllis Coplin put in her word ahead of her father.

"Papa and Hilda keep calling it a revolver, but it was an automatic—a .38."

"Would you folks know him if you saw him again?"

"Yes," they agreed.

I cleared a space on the bedside table and got out a pencil and sheet of paper.

"I want a list of what he got, with as thorough a description of each piece as possible, and the price you paid for it, where you bought it, and when."

I got the list half an hour later.

"Do you know the number of Miss Eveleth's apartment?" I asked as I reached for my hat.

"702, two floors above."

I went up there and rang the bell. The door was opened by a girl of twenty-something, whose nose was hidden under adhesive tape. She had nice clear hazel eyes, dark hair, and outdoor athletics written all over her.

"Miss Eveleth?"

"Yes."

"I'm from the insurance company that insured the Coplin's jewelry, and I'm looking for information about the robbery."

She touched her bandaged nose and smiled ruefully.

"This is some of my information."

"How did it happen?"

"A penalty of femininity—I forgot to mind my own business. But what you want, I suppose, is what I know about the scoundrel. The doorbell rang a few minutes before nine last night, and when I opened the door he was here. As soon as I got the door open he jabbed a pistol at me, and said:

"'Inside, kid!'

"I let him in with no hesitancy at all: I was quite instantaneous about it, and he kicked the door to behind him.

"'Where's the fire-escape?' he asked.

"The fire-escape doesn't come to any of my windows, and I told him so, but he wouldn't take my word for it. He drove me ahead of him to each of the windows; but of course he didn't find his fire-escape, and he got peevish about it, as if it were my fault. I didn't like some of the things he called me, and he was such a little half-portion of a man, so I tried to take him in hand. But—well, man is still the dominant male so far as I'm concerned. In plain American, he busted me in the nose and left me where I fell. I was dazed, though not quite all the way out, and when I got up he had gone. I ran out into the corridor then, and found some policemen on the stairs. I sobbed out my pathetic little tale to them, and they told me of the Coplin robbery. Two of them came back here with me and searched the apartment. I hadn't seen him actually leave, and they thought he might be foxy enough or desperate enough to jump into a closet and stay there until the coast was clear. But they didn't find him here."

"How long do you think it was after he knocked you down that you ran out into the corridor?"

"Oh, it couldn't have been five minutes. Perhaps only half that time."

"What did Mr Robber look like?"

"Small, not quite so large as I; with a couple of days' growth of light hair on his face; dressed in shabby blue clothes, with black cloth gloves."

"How old?"

"Not very. His beard was thin, patchy, and he had a boyish face."

"Notice his eyes?"

"Blue. His hair, where it showed under the edge of his cap was a very light yellow, almost white."

"What sort of voice?"

"Very deep bass, though he may have been putting that on."

"Know him if you'd see him again?"

"Yes, indeed!" She put a gentle finger on her bandaged nose. "My nose would know, as the ads say, anyway!"

From Miss Eveleth's apartment I went down to the office on the first floor, where I found McBirney, the janitor, and his wife, who managed the apartment building. She was a scrawny little woman with the angular mouth and nose of a nagger; he was big, broad-shouldered; with sandy hair and mustache; good-humored, shiftless red face; and genial eyes of a pale and watery-blue.

He drawled out what he knew of the looting.

"I was a-fixin' a spigot on the fourth floor when I heard the shot. I went up to see what was the matter, an' just as I got far enough up the front stairs to see the Coplins' door, the fella came out. We seen each other at the same time, an' he aims his gun at me. There's a lot o' things I might of done, but what I did do was to duck down an' get my head out o' range. I heard him run upstairs, an' I got up just in time to see him make the turn between the fifth and sixth floors.

"I didn't go after him. I didn't have a gun or nothin', an' I figured we had him cooped. A man could get out o' this buildin' to the roof of the next from the fourth floor, an' maybe from the fifth, but not from any above that; an' the Coplins' apartment is on the fifth. I figured we had this fella. I could stand in front of the elevator an' watch both the front an' back stairs; an' I rang for the elevator, an' told Ambrose, the elevator-boy, to give the alarm an' run outside an' keep his eye on the fire-escape until the police came.

"The missus came up with my gun in a minute or two, an' told me that Martinez—Ambrose's brother, who takes care of the switchboard an' the front door—was callin' the police. I could see both stairs plain, an' the fella didn't come down them; an' it wasn't more 'n a few minutes before the police—a whole pack of 'em—came from the Richmond Station. Then we let the Coplins out of the closet where they were, an' started to search the buildin'. An' then Miss Eveleth came runnin' down the stairs, her face an' dress all bloody an' told about him bein' in her apartment; so we were pretty sure we'd land him. But we didn't. We searched every apartment in the buildin', but didn't find hide nor hair of him."

"Of course you didn't!" Mrs McBirney said unpleasantly. "But if you had—"

"I know," the janitor said with the indulgent air of one who has learned to take his pannings as an ordinary part of married life; "if I'd been a hero an' grabbed him, an' got myself all mussed up. Well, I ain't foolish like old man Coplin, gettin' himself plugged in the foot, or Blanche Eveleth, gettin' her nose busted. I'm a sensible man that knows when he's licked; an' I ain't jumpin' at no guns!"

"No! You're not doing anything that—"

This Mr and Mrs stuff wasn't getting me anywhere, so I cut in with a question to the woman.

"Who is the newest tenant you have?"

"Mr and Mrs Jerald; they came the day before yesterday."

"What apartment?"

"704—next door to Miss Eveleth."

"Who are these Jeralds?"

"They come from Boston. He told me he came out here to open a branch of a manufacturing company. He's a man of at least fifty, thin and dyspeptic looking."

"Just him and his wife?"

"Yes. She's poorly too—been in a sanatorium for a year or two."

"Who's the next newest tenant?"

"Mr Heaton, in 535. He's been here a couple of weeks; but he's down in Los Angeles right now. He went away three days ago, and said he would be gone for ten or twelve days."

"What does he look like, and what does he do?"

"He's with a theatrical agency, and he's kind of fat and red-faced."

"Who's the next newest?"

"Miss Eveleth. She's been here about a month."

"And the next?"

"The Wageners, in 923. They've been here going on two months."

"What are they?"

"He's a retired real estate agent. The others are his wife and son Jack—a boy of maybe nineteen. I see him with Phyllis Coplin a lot."

"How long have the Coplins been here?"

"It'll be two years next month."

I turned from Mrs McBirney to her husband.

"Did the police search all these people's apartments?"

"Yeah," he said. "We went into every room, every alcove an' every closet from cellar to roof."

"Did you get a good look at the robber?"

"Yeah. There's a light in the hall outside of the Coplins' door, an' it was shinin' full on his face when I saw him."

"Could he have been one of your tenants?"

"No, he couldn't."

"Know him if you saw him again?"

"You bet."

"What did he look like?"

"A little runt; a light-complected youngster of twenty-three or four in an old blue suit."

"Can I get hold of Ambrose and Martinez—the elevator and door boys who were on duty last night—now?"

The janitor looked at his watch.

"Yeah. They ought to be on the job now. They come on at two."

I went out into the lobby and found them together, matching nickels. They were brothers: slim, bright-eyed Filipino boys. They didn't add much to my dope.

Ambrose had come down to the lobby and told his brother to call the police as soon as McBirney had given him his orders, and then he had beat it out the back door to take a plant on the fire-escapes. The fire-escapes ran down the back and one side wall. By standing a little off from the corner of those walls, the Filipino had been able to keep his eyes on both of them, as well as on the back door.

There was plenty of illumination, he said, and he could see both fire-escapes all the way to the roof, and he had seen nobody on them.

Martinez had given the police a rap on the phone, and had then watched the front door and the foot of the front stairs. He had seen nothing.

Neither of them had seen anyone in the building either before or after the Coplins were turned for their jewels who fit the robber's description.

I had just finished questioning the Filipinos when the street door opened and two men came in. I knew one of them: Bill Garren, a police detective on the Pawn Shop Detail. The other was a small blond youth all flossy in pleated pants, short, square-shouldered coat, and patent-leather shoes with fawn spats to match his hat and gloves. His face wore a sullen pout. He didn't seem to like being with Garren.

"What are you up to around here?" the detective hailed me.

"The Coplin doings for the insurance company," I explained.

"Getting anywhere?" he wanted to know.

"About ready to make a pinch," I said, not altogether in earnest and not altogether joking.

"The more the merrier," he grinned. "I've already made mine." Nodding at the dressy youth. "Come on upstairs with us."

The three of us got into the elevator, and Ambrose carried us to the fifth floor. Before pressing the Coplins' bell, Garren gave me what he had.

"This lad tried to soak a ring in a Third Street shop a little while ago—an emerald and diamond ring that looks like one of the Coplin lot. He's doing the clam now; he hasn't said a word—yet. I'm going to show him to these people; then I'm going to take him down to the Hall of Justice and get words out of him—words that fit together in nice sentences and everything!"

The prisoner looked sullenly at the floor and paid no attention to this threat. Garren rang the bell, and the maid Hilda opened the door. Her eyes widened when she saw the dressy boy, but she didn't say anything as she led us into the sitting-room, where Mrs Coplin and her daughter were. They looked up at us.

"Hello, Jack!" Phyllis greeted the prisoner.

"'Lo, Phyl," he mumbled, not looking at her.

"Among friends, huh? Well, what's the answer?" Garren demanded of the girl.

She put her chin in the air, and although her face turned red, she looked haughtily at the police detective.

"Would you mind removing your hat?" she asked.

Bill isn't a bad bimbo, but he hasn't any meekness. He answered her by tilting his hat over one eye and turning to her mother.

"Ever see this lad before?"

"Why, cerdainly!" Mrs Coplin exclaimed. "Thad's Mr Wagener who lives upsdairs."

"Well," said Bill; "Mr Wagener was picked up in a hock-shop trying to get rid of this ring." He fished a gaudy green and white ring from his pocket. "Know it?"

"Cerdainly!" Mrs Coplin said, looking at the ring. "Id belongs to my Phyllis, and the robber—" Her mouth dropped open as she began to understand. "How could Mr Wagener—?"

"Yes, how?" Bill repeated.

The girl stepped between Garren and me, turning her back on him to face me.

"I can explain everything," she announced.

That sounded too much like a movie sub-title to be very promising, but—

"Go ahead," I encouraged her.

"I found that ring in the passageway near the front door after the excitement was over. The robber must have dropped it. I didn't say anything to Papa and Mama about it, because I thought nobody would ever know the difference, and it was insured, so I thought I might as well sell it and be that much money in. I asked Jack last night if he could sell it for me, and he said he knew just how to go about it. He didn't have anything to do with it outside of that; but I did think he'd have sense enough not to try to pawn it right away!"

She looked scornfully at her accomplice.

"See what you've done!" she accused him.

He fidgeted and pouted at his feet.

"Ha! Ha! Ha!" Bill Garren said sourly. "That's a nifty! Did you ever hear the one about the two Irishmen that got in the Y.W.C.A. by mistake?"

She didn't say whether she had heard it or not.

"Mrs Coplin," I asked; "making allowances for the different clothes, and the unshaven face, could this lad have been the robber?"

She shook her head with emphasis.

"No! He could nod be id!"

"Set your prize down, Bill," I suggested; "and let's go over in a corner and whisper things at each other."

"Right."

He dragged a heavy chair to the center of the floor, sat Wagener on it, anchored him there with handcuffs,—not exactly necessary, but Bill was grouchy at not getting his prisoner identified as the robber,—and then he and I stepped out into the passageway. We could keep an eye on the sitting-room from there without having our low-voiced conversation overheard.

"This is simple!" I whispered into his big red ear. "There are only five ways to figure the lay. First: Wagener stole the stuff for the Coplins. Second: the Coplins framed the robbery themselves, and got Wagener to peddle it. Third: Wagener and the girl engineered the deal without the old folks being in on it. Fourth: Wagener pulled it on his own hook and the girl is covering him up. Fifth: she told us the truth. None of them explain why your little playmate should have been dumb enough to flash the ring downtown this morning; but that can't be explained by any system. Which of the five do you favor?"

"I like 'em all," he grumbled. "But what I like most is that I've got this baby right—got him trying to pass a hot ring. That suits me fine. You do the guessing. I don't ask for any more than I've got."

That wasn't so foolish.

"It doesn't irritate me any either," I agreed. "The way it stands the insurance company can welch on the policies; but I'd like to smoke it out a little further, far enough to put away anybody who has been trying to run a hooligan on the North American. We'll clean up all we can on this kid, stow him in the can, and then see what further damage we can do."

"All right," Garren said. "Suppose you get hold of the janitor and that Eveleth woman while I'm showing the boy to old man Coplin, and getting the maid's opinion."

I nodded and went out into the corridor, leaving the door unlocked behind me. I took the elevator to the seventh floor, and told Ambrose to get hold of McBirney and send him to the Coplins' apartment. Then I rang Blanche Eveleth's bell.

"Can you come downstairs for a minute or two?" I asked her. "We've a prize who might be your friend of last night."

"Will I?" She started toward the stairs with me. "And if he's the right one, can I pay him back for my battered beauty?"

"You can," I promised. "Go as far as you like, so you don't maul him too badly to stand trial."

I took her into the Coplins' apartment without ringing the bell, and found everybody in Jacob Coplin's bedroom. A look at Garren's glum face told me that neither the old man nor the maid had given him a nod on the prisoner.

I put the finger on Jack Wagener. Disappointment came into Blanche Eveleth's eyes.

"You're wrong," she said. "That's not he."

Garren scowled at her. It was a pipe that if the Coplins were tied up with young Wagener, they wouldn't identify him as the robber. Bill had been counting on that identification coming from the two outsiders,—Blanche Eveleth and the janitor,—and now one of them had flopped.

The other one rang the bell just then, and the maid brought him into the room.

I pointed at Jack Wagener, who stood beside Garren, staring sullenly at the floor.

"Know him, McBirney?"

"Yeah. Mr Wagener's son Jack."

"Is he the man who shooed you away with a gun last night?"

McBirney's watery eyes popped in surprise.

"No," he said with decision, and began to look doubtful.

"In an old suit, cap pulled down, needing a shave—could it have been him?"

"No-o-o," the janitor drawled; "I don't think so, though it—You know, now that I come to think about it, there was something familiar about that fella, an' maybe—By cracky, I think maybe you're right—though I couldn't exactly say for sure."

"That'll do!" Garren grunted in disgust.

An identification of the sort the janitor was giving isn't worth a damn one way or the other. Even positive and immediate identifications aren't always the goods. A lot of people who don't know any better—and some who do, or should—have given circumstantial evidence a bad name. It is misleading sometimes. But for genuine, undiluted, pre-war untrustworthiness, it can't come within gunshot of human testimony. Take any man you like—unless he is the one in a hundred thousand with a mind trained to keep things straight, and not always even then—get him excited, show him something, give him a few hours to think it over and talk it over, and then ask him about it. It's dollars to marks that you'll have a hard time finding any connection between what he saw and what he says he saw. Like this McBirney—another hour, and he'd be ready to gamble his life on Jack Wagener's being the robber.

Garren wrapped his fingers around the boy's arm and started for the door.

"Where to, Bill?" I asked.

"Up to talk to his people. Coming along?"

"Stick around a while," I invited. "I'm going to put on a party. But first, tell me, did the coppers who came here when the alarm was turned in do a good job?"

"I didn't see it," the police detective said. "I didn't get here until the fireworks were pretty well over, but I understand the boys did all that could be expected of them."

I turned to Jacob Coplin. I did my talking to him chiefly because we—his wife and daughter, the maid, the janitor, Blanche Eveleth, Garren and his prisoner, and I—were grouped around the old man's bed, and by looking at him I could get at least a one-eyed view of everybody else.

"Somebody has been kidding me somewhere," I began my speech. "If all the things I've been told about this job are right, then so is Prohibition. Your stories don't fit together, not even almost. Take the bird who stuck you up. He seems to have been pretty well acquainted with your affairs. It might be luck that he hit your apartment at a time when all of your jewelry was on hand, instead of another apartment, or your apartment at another time. But I don't like luck. I'd rather figure that he knew what he was doing. He nicked you for your pretties, and then he galloped up to Miss Eveleth's apartment. He may have been about to go downstairs when he ran into McBirney, or he may not. Anyway, he went upstairs, into Miss Eveleth's apartment, looking for a fire-escape. Funny, huh? He knew enough about the place to make a push-over out of the stick-up, but he didn't know there were no fire-escapes on Miss Eveleth's side of the building.

"He didn't speak to you or to McBirney, but he talked to Miss Eveleth, in a bass voice. A very, very deep voice. Funny, huh? From Miss Eveleth's apartment he vanished with every exit watched. The police must have been here before he left her apartment, and they would have blocked the outlets first thing, whether McBirney and Ambrose had already done that or not. But he got away. Funny, huh? He wore a wrinkled suit, which might have been taken from a bundle just before he went to work, and he was a small man. Miss Eveleth isn't a small woman, but she would be a small man. A guy with a suspicious disposition would almost think Blanche Eveleth was the robber."

Jacob Coplin, his wife, young Wagener, the janitor and the maid were gaping at me. Garren was sizing up the Eveleth girl with narrowed eyes, while she glared white-hot at me. Phyllis Coplin was looking at me with a contemptuous sort of pity for my feeble-mindedness.

Bill Garren finished his inspection of the girl and nodded slowly.

"She could get away with it," he gave his opinion; "indoors and if she kept her mouth shut."

"Exactly," I said.

"Exactly my eye!" Phyllis Coplin exploded. "Do you two correspondence-school detectives think we wouldn't know the difference between a man and a woman dressed in man's clothes? He had a day or two's growth of hair on his face—real hair, if you know what I mean. Do you think he could have fooled us with false whiskers? This happened, you know; it's not in a play!"

The others stopped gaping, and heads bobbed up and down.

"Phyllis is right," Jacob Coplin backed up his offspring; "he was a man—no woman dressed like one."

His wife, the maid, and the janitor nodded vigorous indorsements.

But I'm a bullheaded sort of bird when it comes to going where the evidence leads. I spun to face Blanche Eveleth.

"Can you add anything to the occasion?" I asked her.

She smiled very sweetly at me and shook her head.

"All right, bum," I said. "You're pinched. Let's go."

Then it seemed she could add something to the occasion. She had something to say, quite a few things to say, and they were all about me. They weren't nice things. In anger her voice was shrill, and just now she was madder than you'd think anybody could get on short notice. I was sorry for that. This job had run along peacefully and gently so far, hadn't been marred by any rough stuff, had been almost ladylike in every particular; and I had hoped it would go that way to the end. But the more she screamed at me the nastier she got. She didn't have any words I hadn't heard before, but she fitted them together in combinations that were new to me. I stood as much of it as I could.

Then I knocked her over with a punch in the mouth.

"Here! Here!" Bill Garren yelled, grabbing my arm.

"Save your strength, Bill," I advised him, shaking his hand off and going over to yank the Eveleth person up from the floor. "Your gallantry does you credit, and all the like of that, but I think you'll find Blanche's real name is Mike or Alec or Rufus."

I hauled her or him—which ever you *like*—to his or her feet and asked it:

"Feel like telling us about it?"

For answer I got a snarl.

"All right," I said to the others; "in the absence of authoritative information I'll give you my dope. If Blanche Eveleth could have been the robber except for the beard and the difficulty of a woman passing for a man, why couldn't the robber have been Blanche Eveleth before and after the robbery by using a—what do you call it—strong depilatory on his face, and a wig? It's hard for a woman to masquerade as a man, but there are lots of men who can get away with the feminine role. Couldn't this bird, after renting his apartment as Blanche Eveleth and getting everything lined up, have stayed in his apartment for a couple of days letting his beard grow? Come down and knock the job over? Beat it upstairs, get the hair off his face, and get into his female rig in, say, fifteen minutes? My guess is that he could. And he had fifteen minutes. I don't know about the smashed nose. Maybe he stumbled going up the stairs and had to twist his plans to account for it; or maybe he smacked himself intentionally."

My guesses weren't far off, though his name was Fred—Frederick Agnew Rudd. He was known in Toronto, having done a stretch in the Ontario Reformatory as a boy of nineteen, caught shop-lifting in his she-makeup. He wouldn't come through, and we never turned up his gun or the blue suit, cap, and black gloves, although we found a cavity in his mattress where he had stuffed them out of the police's sight until later that night, when he could get rid of them. The Coplin sparklers came to light piece by piece when we had plumbers take apart the drains and radiators in apartment 702.

7

THE WHOSIS KID

BLACK MASK, MARCH 1925

We have talked so many times of Mr Hammett's "shrewd, canny sleuth," his "hard-boiled detective," etc., that we're at the end of our rope for words to introduce him to new readers... Well, he is a shrewd, canny, hard-boiled sleuth, and this is an exciting tale.

A COMPLETE DETECTIVE NOVELETTE

I

It started in Boston, back in 1917. I ran into Lew Maher on the Tremont street sidewalk of the Touraine Hotel one afternoon, and we stopped to swap a few minutes' gossip in the snow.

I was telling him something or other when he cut in with:

"Sneak a look at this kid coming up the street. The one with the dark cap."

Looking, I saw a gangling youth of eighteen or so; pasty and pimply face, sullen mouth, dull hazel eyes, thick, shapeless nose. He passed the city sleuth and me without attention, and

I noticed his ears. They weren't the battered ears of a pug, and they weren't conspicuously deformed, but their rims curved in and out in a peculiar crinkled fashion.

At the corner he went out of sight, turning down Boylston street toward Washington.

"There's a lad that will make a name for his-self if he ain't nabbed or rocked off too soon," Lew predicted. "Better put him on your list. The Whosis Kid. You'll be looking for him some one of these days."

"What's his racket?"

"Stick-up, gunman. He's got the makings of a good one. He can shoot, and he's plain crazy. He ain't hampered by nothing like imagination or fear of consequences. I wish he was. It's these careful, sensible birds that are easiest caught. I'd swear the Kid was in on a coupla jobs that were turned in Brookline last month. But I can't fit him to 'em. I'm going to clamp him some day, though—and that's a promise."

Lew never kept his promise. A prowler killed him in an Audubon Road residence a month later.

A week or two after this conversation I left the Boston branch of the Continental Detective Agency to try army life. When the war was over I returned to the agency payroll in Chicago, stayed there for a couple of years, and got transferred to San Francisco.

So, all in all, it was nearly eight years later that I found myself sitting behind the Whosis Kid's crinkled ears at the Dreamland Rink.

Friday night is fight night at the Steiner Street house. This particular one was my first idle evening in several weeks. I had gone up to the rink, fitted myself to a hard wooden chair not too far from the ring, and settled down to watch the boys throw gloves at one another. The show was about a quarter done when I picked out this pair of odd and somehow familiar ears two rows ahead of me.

I didn't place them right away. I couldn't see their owner's face. He was watching Kid Cipriani and Bunny Keogh assault each other. I missed most of that fight. But during the brief wait before the next pair of boys went on, the Whosis Kid turned his head to say something to the man beside him. I saw his face and knew him.

He hadn't changed much, and he hadn't improved any. His eyes were duller and his mouth more wickedly sullen than I had remembered them. His face was as pasty as ever, if not so pimply.

He was directly between me and the ring. Now that I knew him, I didn't have to pass up the rest of the card. I could watch the boys over his head without being afraid he would get out on me.

So far as I knew, the Whosis Kid wasn't wanted anywhere—not by the Continental, anyway—and if he had been a pickpocket, or a con man, or a member of any of the criminal trades in which we are only occasionally interested, I would have let him alone. But stick-ups are always in demand. The Continental's most important clients are insurance companies of one sort or another, and robbery policies make up a good percentage of the insurance business these days.

When the Whosis Kid left in the middle of the main event—along with nearly half of the spectators, not caring what happened to either of the muscle-bound heavies who were putting on a room-mate act in the ring—I went with him.

He was alone. It was the simplest sort of shadowing. The streets were filled with departing fight fans. The Kid walked down to Fillmore street, took on a stack of wheats, bacon and coffee at a lunch room, and caught a No. 22 car.

He—and likewise I—transferred to a No. 5 car at McAllister street, dropped off at Polk, walked north one block, turned back west for a block and a fraction, and went up the front stairs of a dingy light-housekeeping room establishment that occupied the second and third floors over a repair shop on the south side of Golden Gate avenue, between Van Ness and Franklin.

That put a wrinkle in my forehead. If he had left the street car at either Van Ness or Franklin, he would have saved himself a block of walking. He had ridden down to Polk and walked back. For the exercise, maybe.

I loafed across the street for a short while, to see what—if anything—happened to the front windows. None that had been dark before the Kid went in lighted up now. Apparently he didn't have a front room—unless he was a very cautious young man. I knew he hadn't tumbled to my shadowing. There wasn't a chance of that. Conditions had been too favorable to me.

The front of the building giving me no information, I strolled down Van Ness avenue to look at the rear. The building ran through to Redwood street, a narrow back street that split the block in half. Four back windows were lighted, but they told me nothing. There was a back door. It seemed to belong to the repair shop. I doubted that the occupants of the upstairs rooms could use it.

On my way home to my bed and alarm clock, I dropped in at the office, to leave a note for the Old Man:

> *Tailing the Whosis Kid, stick-up, 25-27, 155, 5 foot 11 inches, sallow, br. hair, hzl. eyes, thick nose, crooked ears. Origin Boston. Anything on him? Will be vicinity Golden Gate and Van Ness.*

II

Eight o'clock the next morning found me a block below the house in which the Kid had gone, waiting for him to appear. A steady, soaking rain was falling, but I didn't mind that. I was closed up inside a black coupé, a type of car whose tamely respectable appearance makes it the ideal one for city work. This part of Golden Gate avenue is lined with automobile repair shops, second hand automobile dealers, and the like. There are always dozens of cars standing idle to the block. Although I stayed there all day, I didn't have to worry over my being too noticeable.

That was just as well. For nine solid, end-to-end hours I sat there and listened to the rain on the roof, and waited for the Whosis Kid, with not a glimpse of him, and nothing to eat except Fatimas. I wasn't any too sure he hadn't slipped me. I didn't know that he lived in this place I was watching. He could have gone to his home after I had gone to mine. However, in this detective business pessimistic guesses of that sort are always bothering you, if you let them. I stayed parked, with my eye on the dingy door into which my meat had gone the night before.

At a little after five that evening, Tommy Howd, our pug-nosed office boy, found me and gave me a memorandum from the Old Man:

> *Whosis Kid known to Boston branch as robbery-suspect, but have nothing definite on him. Real name believed to be Arthur Cory or Carey. May have been implicated in Tunnicliffe jewelry robbery in Boston last month. Employee killed, $60,000 unset stones taken.*
>
> *No description of two bandits. Boston branch thinks this angle worth running out. They authorize surveillance.*

After I had read this memorandum, I gave it back to the boy,—there's no wisdom in carrying around a pocketful of stuff relating to your job,—and asked him:

"Will you call up the Old Man and ask him to send somebody up to relieve me while I get a bite of food? I haven't chewed since breakfast."

"Swell chance!" Tommy said. "Everybody's busy. Hasn't been an op in all day. I don't see why you fellas don't carry a hunk or two of chocolate in your pockets to—"

"You've been reading about Arctic explorers," I accused him. "If a man's starving he'll eat anything, but when he's just ordinarily hungry he doesn't want to clutter up his stomach with a lot of candy. Scout around and see if you can pick me up a couple of sandwiches and a bottle of milk."

He scowled at me, and then his fourteen-year-old face grew cunning.

"I tell you what," he suggested. "You tell me what this fella looks like, and which building he's in, and I'll watch while you go get a decent meal. Huh? Steak, and French fried potatoes, and pie, and coffee."

Tommy has dreams of being left on the job in some such circumstance, of having everything break for him while he's there, and of rounding up regiments of desperadoes all by himself. I don't think he'd muff a good chance at that, and I'd be willing to give him a whack at it. But the Old Man would scalp me if he knew I turned a child loose among a lot of thugs.

So I shook my head.

"This guy wears four guns and carries an ax, Tommy. He'd eat you up."

"Aw, applesauce! You ops are all the time trying to make out nobody else could do your work. These crooks can't be such tough mugs—or they wouldn't let you catch 'em!"

There was some truth in that, so I put Tommy out of the coupé into the rain.

"One tongue sandwich, one ham, one bottle of milk. And make it sudden."

But I wasn't there when he came back with the food. He had barely gone out of sight when the Whosis Kid, his overcoat collar turned up against the rain that was driving down in close-packed earnest just now, came out of the rooming-house doorway.

He turned south on Van Ness.

When the coupé got me to the corner he was not in sight. He couldn't have reached McAllister street. Unless he had gone into a building, Redwood street—the narrow one that split the block—was my best bet. I drove up Golden Gate avenue another block, turned south, and reached the corner of Franklin and Redwood just in time to see my man ducking into the back door of an apartment building that fronted on McAllister street.

I drove on slowly, thinking.

The building in which the Kid had spent the night and this building into which he had just gone had their rears on the same back street, on opposite sides, a little more than half a block apart. If the Kid's room was in the rear of his building, and he had a pair of strong glasses, he could keep a pretty sharp eye on all the windows—and probably much of the interiors—of the rooms on that side of the McAllister street building.

Last night he had ridden a block out of his way. Having seen him sneak into the back door just now, my guess was that he had not wished to leave the street car where he could be seen from this building. Either of his more convenient points of departure from the car would have been in sight of this building. This would add up to the fact that the Kid was watching someone in this building, and did not want them to be watching him.

He had now gone calling through the back door. That wasn't difficult to explain. The front door was locked, but the back door—as in most large buildings—probably was open all day. Unless the Kid ran into a janitor or someone of the sort, he could get in with no trouble. The Kid's call was furtive, whether his host was at home or not.

I didn't know what it was all about, but that didn't bother me especially. My immediate problem was to get to the best place from which to pick up the Kid when he came out.

If he left by the back door, the next block of Redwood street—between Franklin and Gough—was the place for me and my coupé. But he hadn't promised me he would leave that way. It was more likely that he would use the front door. He would attract less attention walking boldly out the front of the building than sneaking out the back. My best bet was the corner of McAllister and Van Ness. From there I could watch the front door as well as one end of Redwood street.

I slid the coupé down to that corner and waited.

Half an hour passed. Three quarters.

The Whosis Kid came down the front steps and walked toward me, buttoning his overcoat and turning up the collar as he walked, his head bent against the slant of the rain.

A curtained black Cadillac touring car came from behind me, a car I thought had been parked down near the City Hall when I took my plant here.

It curved around my coupé, slid with chainless recklessness in to the curb, skidded out again, picking up speed somehow on the wet paving.

A curtain whipped loose in the rain.

Out of the opening came pale fire-streaks. The bitter voice of a small-caliber pistol. Seven times.

The Whosis Kid's wet hat floated off his head—a slow balloon-like rising.

There was nothing slow about the Kid's moving.

Plunging, in a twisting swirl of coat-skirts, he flung into a shop vestibule.

The Cadillac reached the next corner, made a dizzy sliding turn, and was gone up Franklin street. I pointed the coupé at it.

Passing the vestibule into which the Kid had plunged, I got a one-eyed view of him, on his knees, still trying to get a dark gun untangled from his overcoat. Excited faces were in the doorway behind him. There was no excitement in the street. People are too accustomed to automobile noises nowadays to pay much attention to the racket of anything less than a six-inch gun.

By the time I reached Franklin street, the Cadillac had gained another block on me. It was spinning to the left, up Eddy street.

I paralleled it on Turk street, and saw it again when I reached the two open blocks of Jefferson Square. Its speed was decreasing. Five or six blocks further, and it crossed ahead of me—on Steiner street—close enough for me to read the license plate. Its pace was moderate now. Confident that they had made a clean getaway, its occupants didn't want to get in trouble through speeding. I slid into their wake, three blocks behind.

Not having been in sight during the early blocks of the flight, I wasn't afraid that they would suspect my interest in them now.

Out on Haight street near the park panhandle, the Cadillac stopped to discharge a passenger. A small man—short and slender—with cream-white face around dark eyes and a tiny black mustache. There was something foreign in the cut of his dark coat and the shape of his gray hat. He carried a walking-stick.

The Cadillac went on out Haight street with-out giving me a look at the other occupants. Tossing a mental nickel, I stuck to the man afoot. The chances always are against you being able to trace a suspicious car by its license number, but there is a slim chance.

My man went into a drug store on the corner and used the telephone. I don't know what else he did in there, if anything. Presently a taxicab arrived. He got in and was driven to the Marquis Hotel. A clerk gave him the key to room 761. I dropped him when he stepped into an elevator.

III

At the Marquis I am among friends.

I found Duran, the house copper, on the mezzanine floor, and asked him:

"Who is 761?"

Duran is a white-haired old-timer who looks, talks, and acts like the president of an exceptionally strong bank. He used to be captain of detectives in one of the larger Middle Western cities. Once he tried too hard to get a confession out of a safe-ripper, and killed him. The newspapers didn't like Duran. They used that accident to howl him out of his job.

"761?" he repeated in his grandfatherly manner. "That is Mr Maurois, I believe. Are you especially interested in him?"

"I have hopes," I admitted. "What do you know about him?"

"Not a great deal. He has been here perhaps two weeks. We shall go down and see what we can learn."

We went to the desk, the switchboard, the captain of bellhops, and upstairs to question a couple of chambermaids. The occupant of 761 had arrived two weeks ago, had registered as *Edouard Maurois, Dijon, France,* had frequent telephone calls, no mail, no visitors, kept irregular hours and tipped freely. Whatever business he was in or had was not known to the hotel people.

"What is the occasion of your interest in him, if I may ask?" Duran inquired after we had accumulated these facts. He talks like that.

"I don't exactly know yet," I replied truthfully. "He just connected with a bird who is wrong, but this Maurois may be all right himself. I'll give you a rap the minute I get anything solid on him."

I couldn't afford to tell Duran I had seen his guest snapping caps at a gunman under the eyes of the City Hall in daylight. The Marquis Hotel goes in for respectability. They would have shoved the Frenchman out in the streets. It wouldn't help me to have him scared up.

"Please do," Duran said. "You owe us something for our help, you know, so please don't withhold any information that might save us unpleasant notoriety."

"I won't," I promised. "Now will you do me another favor? I haven't had my teeth in anything except my mouth since seven-thirty this morning. Will you keep an eye on the elevators, and let me know if Maurois goes out? I'll be in the grill, near the door."

"Certainly."

On my way to the grillroom I stopped at the telephone booths and called up the office. I gave the night office man the Cadillac's license number.

"Look it up on the list and see whom it belongs to."

The answer was: "H. J. Paterson, San Pablo, issued for a Buick roadster."

That about wound up that angle. We could look up Paterson, but it was safe betting it wouldn't get us anything. License plates, once they get started in crooked ways, are about as easy to trace as Liberty Bonds.

All day I had been building up hunger. I took it into the grillroom and turned it loose. Between bites I turned the day's events over in my mind. I didn't think hard enough to spoil my appetite. There wasn't that much to think about.

The Whosis Kid lived in a joint from which some of the McAllister street apartments could be watched. He visited the apartment building furtively. Leaving, he was shot at, from a car that must have been waiting somewhere in the vicinity. Had the Frenchman's companion in the Cadillac—or his companions, if more than one—been the occupant of the apartment the Kid had visited? Had they expected him to visit it? Had they tricked him into visiting it, planning to shoot him down as he was leaving? Or were they watching the front while the Kid watched the rear? If so, had either known that the other was watching? And who lived there?

I couldn't answer any of these riddles. All I knew was that the Frenchman and his companions didn't seem to like the Whosis Kid.

Even the sort of meal I put away doesn't take forever to eat. When I finished it, I went out to the lobby again.

Passing the switchboard, one of the girls—the one whose red hair looks as if it had been poured into its waves and hardened—gave me a nod.

I stopped to see what she wanted.

"Your friend just had a call," she told me.

"You get it?"

"Yes. A man is waiting for him at Kearny and Broadway. Told him to hurry."

"How long ago?"

"None. They're just through talking."

"Any names?"

"No."

"Thanks."

I went on to where Duran was stalling with an eye on the elevators.

"Shown yet?" I asked.

"No."

"Good. The redhead on the switchboard just told me he had a phone call to meet a man at Kearny and Broadway. I think I'll beat him to it."

Around the corner from the hotel, I climbed into my coupé and drove down to the Frenchman's corner.

The Cadillac he had used that afternoon was already there, with a new license plate. I passed it and took a look at its one occupant—a thickset man of forty-something with a cap pulled low over his eyes. All I could see of his features was a wide mouth slanting over a heavy chin.

I put the coupé in a vacant space down the street a way. I didn't have to wait long for the Frenchman. He came around the corner afoot and got into the Cadillac. The man with the big chin drove. They went slowly up Broadway. I followed.

IV

We didn't go far, and when we came to rest again, the Cadillac was placed conveniently for its occupants to watch the Venetian Cafe, one of the gaudiest of the Italian restaurants that fill this part of town.

Two hours went by.

I had an idea that the Whosis Kid was eating at the Venetian. When he left, the fireworks would break out, continuing the celebration from where it had broken off that afternoon on McAllister street. I hoped the Kid's gun wouldn't get caught in his coat this time. But don't think I meant to give him a helping hand in his two-against-one fight.

This party had the shape of a war between gunmen. It would be a private one as far as I was concerned. My hope was that by hovering on the fringes until somebody won, I could pick up a little profit for the Continental, in the form of a wanted crook or two among the survivors.

My guess at the Frenchman's quarry was wrong. It wasn't the Whosis Kid. It was a man and a woman. I didn't see their faces. The light was behind them. They didn't waste any time between the Venetian's door and their taxicab.

The man was big—tall, wide, and thick. The woman looked small at his side. I couldn't go by that. Anything weighing less than a ton would have seemed tiny beside him.

As the taxicab pulled away from the cafe, the Cadillac went after it. I ran in the Cadillac's wake.

It was a short chase.

The taxicab turned into a dark block on the edge of Chinatown. The Cadillac jumped to its side, bearing it over to the curb.

A noise of brakes, shouting voices, broken glass. A woman's scream. Figures moving in the scant space between touring car and taxicab. Both cars rocking. Grunts. Thuds. Oaths.

A man's voice: "Hey! You can't do that! Nix! Nix!"

It was a stupid voice.

I had slowed down until the coupé was barely moving toward this tussle ahead. Peering through the rain and darkness, I tried to pick out a detail or so as I approached, but I could see little.

I was within twenty feet when the curbward door of the taxicab banged open. A woman bounced out. She landed on her knees on the sidewalk, jumped to her feet, and darted up the street.

Putting the coupé closer to the curb, I let the door swing open. My side windows were spattered with rain. I wanted to get a look at the woman when she passed. If she should take the open door for an invitation, I didn't mind talking to her.

She accepted the invitation, hurrying as directly to the car as if she had expected me to be waiting for her. Her face was a small oval above a fur collar.

"Help me!" she gasped. "Take me from here—quickly."

There was a suggestion of foreignness too slight to be called an accent.

"How about—?"

I shut my mouth. The thing she was jabbing me in the body with was a snub-nosed automatic.

"Sure! Get in," I urged her.

She bent her head to enter. I looped an arm over her neck, throwing her down across my lap. She squirmed and twisted—a small-boned, hard-fleshed body with strength in it.

I wrenched the gun out of her hand and pushed her back on the seat beside me.

Her fingers dug into my arms.

"Quick! Quick! Ah, please, quickly! Take me—"

"What about your friend?" I asked.

"Not him! He is of the others! Please, quickly!"

A man filled the open coupé door—the big-chinned man who had driven the Cadillac.

His hand seized the fur at the woman's throat.

She tried to scream—made the gurgling sound of a man with a slit throat. I smacked his chin with the gun I had taken from her.

He tried to fall into the coupé. I pushed him out.

Before his head had hit the sidewalk, I had the door closed, and was twisting the coupé around in the street.

We rode away. Two shots sounded just as we turned the first corner. I don't know whether they were fired at us or not. I turned other corners. The Cadillac did not appear again.

So far, so good. I had started with the Whosis Kid, dropped him to take Maurois, and now let him go to see who this woman was. I didn't know what this confusion was all about, but I seemed to be learning *who* it was all about.

"Where to?" I asked presently.

"To home," she said, and gave me an address.

I pointed the coupé at it with no reluctance at all. It was the McAllister street apartments the Whosis Kid had visited earlier in the evening.

We didn't waste any time getting there. My companion might know it or might not, but I knew that all the other players in this game knew that address. I wanted to get there before the Frenchman and Big Chin.

Neither of us said anything during the ride. She crouched close to me, shivering. I was looking ahead, planning how I was to land an invitation into her apartment. I was sorry I hadn't held on to her gun. I had let it fall when I pushed Big Chin out of the car. It would have been an excuse for a later call if she didn't invite me in.

I needn't have worried. She didn't invite me. She insisted that I go in with her. She was scared stiff.

"You will not leave me?" she pleaded as we drove up McAllister street. "I am in complete terror. You cannot go from me! If you will not come in, I will stay with you."

I was willing enough to go in, but I didn't want to leave the coupé where it would advertise me.

"We'll ride around the corner and park the car," I told her, "and then I'll go in with you."

I drove around the block, with an eye in each direction for the Cadillac. Neither eye found it. I left the coupé on Franklin street and we returned to the McAllister street building.

She had me almost running through the rain that had lightened now to a drizzle.

The hand with which she tried to fit a key to the front door was a shaky, inaccurate hand. I took the key and opened the door. We rode to the third floor in an automatic elevator, seeing no one. I unlocked the door to which she led me, near the rear of the building.

Holding my arm, with one hand, she reached inside and snapped on the lights in the passageway.

I didn't know what she was waiting for, until she cried:

"Frana! Frana! Ah, Frana!"

The muffled yapping of a small dog replied. The dog did not appear.

She grabbed me with both arms, trying to crawl up my damp coat-front.

"They are here!" she cried in the thin dry voice of utter terror. "They are here!"

V

"Is anybody supposed to be here?" I asked, putting her around to one side, where she wouldn't be between me and the two doors across the passageway.

"No! Just my little dog Frana, but—"

I slid my gun half out of my pocket and back again, to make sure it wouldn't catch if I needed it, and used my other hand to get rid of the woman's arms.

"You stay here. I'll see if you've got company."

Moving to the nearest door, I heard a seven-year-old voice—Lew Maher's—saying: *"He can shoot and he's plain crazy. He ain't hampered by nothing like imagination or fear of consequences."*

With my left hand I turned the first door's knob. With my left foot I kicked it open.

Nothing happened.

I put a hand around the frame, found the button, switched on the lights.

A sitting-room, all orderly.

Through an open door on the far side of the room came the muffled yapping of Frana. It was louder now and more excited. I moved to the doorway. What I could see of the next room, in the light from this, seemed peaceful and unoccupied enough. I went into it and switched on the lights.

The dog's voice came through a closed door. I crossed to it, pulled it open. A dark fluffy dog jumped snapping at my leg. I grabbed it where its fur was thickest and lifted it squirming and snarling. The light hit it. It was purple—purple as a grape! Dyed purple!

Carrying this yapping, yelping artificial hound a little away from my body with my left hand, I moved on to the next room—a bedroom. It was vacant. Its closet hid nobody. I found the kitchen and bathroom. Empty. No one was in the apartment. The purple pup had been imprisoned by the Whosis Kid earlier in the day.

Passing through the second room on my way back to the woman with her dog and my report, I saw a slitted envelope lying face-down on a table. I turned it over. The stationery of a fashionable store, it was addressed to Mrs Inés Almad, here.

The party seemed to be getting international. Maurois was French; the Whosis Kid was Boston American; the dog had a Bohemian name (at least I remember nabbing a Czech forger a few months before whose first name was Frana); and Inés, I imagine, was either Spanish or Portuguese. I didn't know what Almad was, but she was undoubtedly foreign, and not, I thought, French.

I returned to her. She hadn't moved an inch.

"Everything seems to be all right," I told her. "The dog got himself caught in a closet."

"There is no one here?"

"No one."

She took the dog in both hands, kissing its fluffy stained head, crooning affectionate words to it in a language that made no sense to me.

"Do your friends—the people you had your row with tonight—know where you live?" I asked.

I knew they did. I wanted to see what she knew.

She dropped the dog as if she had forgotten it, and her brows puckered.

"I do not know that," she said slowly. "Yet it may be. If they do—"

She shuddered, spun on her heel, and pushed the hall door violently shut.

"They may have been here this afternoon," she went on. "Frana has made himself prisoner in closets before, but I fear everything. I am coward-like. But there is none here now?"

"No one," I assured her again.

We went into the sitting-room. I got my first good look at her when she shed her hat and dark cape.

She was a trifle under medium height, a dark-skinned woman of thirty in a vivid orange gown. She was dark as an Indian, with bare-brown shoulders round and sloping, tiny feet and hands, her fingers heavy with rings. Her nose was thin and curved, her mouth full-lipped and red, her eyes—long and thickly lashed—were of an extraordinary narrowness. They were dark eyes, but nothing of their color could be seen through the thin slits that separated the lids. Two dark gleams through veiling lashes. Her black hair was disarranged just now in fluffy silk puffs. A rope of pearls hung down on her dark chest. Earrings of black iron—in a peculiar clublike design—swung beside her cheeks.

Altogether, she was an odd trick. But I wouldn't want to be quoted as saying that she wasn't beautiful—in a wild way.

She was shaking and shivering as she got rid of her hat and cloak. White teeth held her lower lip as she crossed the room to turn on an electric heater. I took advantage of this opportunity to shift my gun from my overcoat pocket to my pants. Then I took off the coat.

Leaving the room for a second, she returned with a brown-filled quart bottle and two tumblers on a bronze tray, which she put on a little table near the heater.

The first tumbler she filled to within half an inch of its rim. I stopped her when she had the other nearly half full.

"That'll do fine for me," I said.

It was brandy, and not at all hard to get down. She shot her tumblerful into her throat as if she needed it, shook her bare shoulders, and sighed in a satisfied way.

"You will think, certainly, I am lunatic," she smiled at me. "Flinging myself on you, a stranger in the street, demanding of you time and troubles."

"No," I lied seriously. "I think you're pretty level-headed for a woman who, no doubt, isn't used to this sort of stuff."

She was pulling a little upholstered bench closer to the electric heater, within reach of the table that held the brandy. She sat down now, with an inviting nod at the bench's empty half.

The purple dog jumped into her lap. She pushed it out. It started to return. She kicked it sharply in the side with the pointed toe of her slipper. It yelped and crawled under a chair across the room.

I avoided the window by going the long way around the room. The window was curtained, but not thickly enough to hide all of the room from the Whosis Kid—if he happened to be sitting at his window just now with a pair of field-glasses to his eyes.

"But I am not level-headed, really," the woman was saying as I dropped beside her. "I am coward-like, terribly. And even becoming accustomed—It is my husband, or he who was my husband. I should tell you. Your gallantry deserves the explanation, and I do not wish you should think a thing that is not so."

I tried to look trusting and credulous. I expected to disbelieve everything she said.

"He is most crazily jealous," she went on in her low-pitched, soft voice, with a peculiar way of saying words that just missed being marked enough to be called a foreign accent. "He is an old man, and incredibly wicked. These men he has sent to me! A woman there was once—tonight's men are not first. I don't know what—what they mean. To kill me, perhaps—to maim, to disfigure—I do not know."

"And the man in the taxi with you was one of them?" I asked. "I was driving down the street behind you when you were attacked, and I could see there was a man with you. He was one of them?"

"Yes! I did not know it, but it must have been that he was. He does not defend me. A pretense, that is all."

"Ever try sicking the cops on this hubby of yours?"

"It is what?"

"Ever notify the police?"

"Yes, but"—she shrugged her brown shoulders—"I would as well have kept quiet, or better. In Buffalo it was, and they—they bound my husband to keep the peace, I think you call it. A thousand dollars! Poof! What is that to him in his jealousy? And I—I cannot stand the things the newspapers say—the jesting of them. I must leave Buffalo. Yes, once I do try sicking the cops on him. But not more."

"Buffalo?" I explored a little. "I lived there for a while—on Crescent avenue."

"Oh, yes. That is out by the Delaware Park."

That was right enough. But her knowing something about Buffalo didn't prove anything about the rest of her story.

VI

She poured more brandy. By speaking quick I held my drink down to a size suitable for a man who has work to do. Hers was as large as before. We drank, and she offered me cigarettes in a lacquered box—slender cigarettes, hand-rolled in black paper.

I didn't stay with mine long. It tasted, smelt and scorched like gunpowder.

"You don't like my cigarettes?"

"I'm an old-fashioned man," I apologized, rubbing its fire out in a bronze dish, fishing in my pocket for my own deck. "Tobacco's as far as I've got. What's in these fireworks?"

She laughed. She had a pleasant laugh, with a sort of coo in it.

"I am so very sorry. So many people do not like them. I have a Hindu incense mixed with the tobacco."

I didn't say anything to that. It was what you would expect of a woman who would dye her dog purple.

The dog moved under its chair just then, scratching the floor with its nails.

The brown woman was in my arms, in my lap, her arms wrapped around my neck. Close-up, opened by terror, her eyes weren't dark at all. They were gray-green. The blackness was in the shadow from her heavy lashes.

"It's only the dog," I assured her, sliding her back on her own part of the bench. "It's only the dog wriggling around under the chair."

"Ah!" she blew her breath out with enormous relief.

Then we had to have another shot of brandy.

"You see, I am most awfully the coward," she said when the third dose of liquor was in her. "But, ah, I have had so much trouble. It is a wonder that I am not insane."

I could have told her she wasn't far enough from it to do much bragging, but I nodded with what was meant for sympathy.

She lit another cigarette to replace the one she had dropped in her excitement. Her eyes became normal black slits again.

"I do not think it is nice"—there was a suggestion of a dimple in her brown cheek when she smiled like that—"that I throw myself into the arms of a man even whose name I do not know, or anything of him."

"That's easy to fix. My name is Young," I lied; "and I can let you have a case of Scotch at a price that will astonish you. I think maybe I could stand it if you call me Jerry. Most of the ladies I let sit in my lap do."

"Jerry Young," she repeated, as if to herself. "That is a nice name. And you are the bootlegger?"

"Not *the*," I corrected her; "just *a*. This is San Francisco."

The going got tough after that.

Everything else about this brown woman was all wrong, but her fright was real. She was scared stiff. And she didn't intend being left alone this night. She meant to keep me there—to massage any more chins that stuck themselves at her. Her idea—she being that sort—was that I would be most surely held with affection. So she must turn herself loose on me. She wasn't hampered by any pruderies or puritanisms at all.

I also have an idea. Mine is that when the last gong rings I'm going to be leading this baby and some of her playmates to the city prison. That is an excellent reason—among a dozen others I could think of—why I shouldn't get mushy with her.

I was willing enough to camp there with her until something happened. That apartment looked like the scene of the next action. But I had to cover up my own game. I couldn't let her know she was only a minor figure in it. I had to pretend there was nothing behind my willingness to stay but a desire to protect her. Another man might have got by with a chivalrous, knight-errant, protector-of-womanhood-without-personal-interest attitude. But I don't look, and can't easily act, like that kind of person. I had to hold her off without letting her guess that my interest wasn't personal. It was no cinch. She was too damned direct, and she had too much brandy in her.

I didn't kid myself that my beauty and personality were responsible for any of her warmth. I was a thick-armed male with big fists. She was in a jam. She spelled my name P-r-o-t-e-c-t-i-o-n. I was something to be put between her and trouble.

Another complication: I am neither young enough nor old enough to get feverish over every woman who doesn't make me think being blind isn't so bad. I'm at that middle point around forty where a man puts other feminine qualities—amiability, for one—above beauty on his list. This brown woman annoyed me. She was too sure of herself. Her work was rough. She was trying to handle me as if I were a farmer boy. But in spite of all this, I'm constructed mostly of human ingredients. This woman got more than a stand-off when faces and bodies were dealt. I didn't like her. I hoped to throw her in the can before I was through. But I'd be a liar if I didn't admit that she had me stirred up inside—between her cuddling against me, giving me the come-on, and the brandy I had drunk.

The going was tough—no fooling.

A couple of times I was tempted to bolt. Once I looked at my watch—2:06. She put a ring-heavy brown hand on the timepiece and pushed it down to my pocket.

"Please, Jerry!" the earnestness in her voice was real. "You cannot go. You cannot leave me here. I will not have it so. I will go also, through the streets following. You cannot leave me to be murdered here!"

I settled down again.

A few minutes later a bell rang sharply.

She went to pieces immediately. She piled over on me, strangling me with her bare arms. I pried them loose enough to let me talk.

"What bell is that?"

"The street door. Do not heed it."

I patted her shoulder.

"Be a good girl and answer it. Let's see who it is."

Her arms tightened.

"No! No! No! They have come!"

The bell rang again.

"Answer it," I insisted.

Her face was flat against my coat, her nose digging into my chest.

"No! No!"

"All right," I said. "I'll answer it myself."

I untangled myself from her, got up and went into the passageway. She followed me. I tried again to persuade her to do the talking. She would not, although she didn't object to my talking. I would have liked it better if whoever was downstairs didn't learn that the woman wasn't alone. But she was too stubborn in her refusal for me to do anything with her.

"Well?" I said into the speaking-tube.

"Who the hell are you?" a harsh, deep-chested voice asked. "What do you want?"

"I want to talk to Inés."

"Speak your piece to me," I suggested, "and I'll tell her about it."

The woman, holding one of my arms, had an ear close to the tube.

"Billie, it is," she whispered. "Tell him that he goes away."

"You're to go away," I passed the message on.

"Yeah?" the voice grew harsher and deeper. "Will you open the door, or will I bust it in?"

There wasn't a bit of playfulness in the question. Without consulting the woman, I put a finger on the button that unlocks the street door.

"Welcome," I said into the tube.

"He's coming up," I explained to the woman. "Shall I stand behind the door and tap him on the skull when he comes in? Or do you want to talk to him first?"

"Do not strike him!" she exclaimed. "It is Billie."

That suited me. I hadn't intended putting the slug to him—not until I knew who and what he was, anyway. I had wanted to see what she would say.

VII

Billie wasn't long getting up to us. I opened the door when he rang, the woman standing beside me. He didn't wait for an invitation. He was through the doorway before I had the door half opened. He glared at me. There was plenty of him!

A big, red-faced, red-haired bale of a man—big in any direction you measured him—and none of him was fat. The skin was off his nose, one cheek was clawed, the other swollen.

His hatless head was a tangled mass of red hair. One pocket had been ripped out of his coat, and a button dangled on the end of a six-inch ribbon of torn cloth.

This was the big heaver who had been in the taxicab with the woman.

"Who's this mutt?" he demanded, moving his big paws toward me.

I knew the woman was a goof. It wouldn't have surprised me if she had tried to feed me to the battered giant. But she didn't. She put a hand on one of his and soothed him.

"Do not be nasty, Billie. He is a friend. Without him I would not this night have escaped."

He scowled. Then his face straightened out and he caught her hand in both of his.

"So you got away it's all right," he said huskily. "I'd a done better if we'd been outside. There wasn't no room in that taxi for me to turn around. And one of them guys crowned me."

That was funny. This big clown was apologizing for getting mangled up protecting a woman who had scooted, leaving him to get out as well as he could.

The woman led him into the sitting-room, I tagging along behind. They sat on the bench. I picked out a chair that wasn't in line with the window the Whosis Kid ought to be watching.

"What did happen, Billie?" She touched his grooved cheek and skinned nose with her fingertips. "You are hurt."

He grinned with a sort of shamefaced delight. I saw that what I had taken for a swelling in one cheek was only a big hunk of chewing tobacco.

"I don't know all that happened," he said. "One of 'em crowned me, and I didn't wake up till a coupla hours afterwards. The taxi driver didn't give me no help in the fight, but he was a right guy and knowed where his money would come from. He didn't holler or nothing. He took me around to a doc that wouldn't squawk, and the doc straightened me out, and then I come up here."

"Did you see each one of those men?" she asked.

"Sure! I seen 'em, and felt 'em, and maybe tasted 'em."

"They were how many?"

"Just two of 'em. A little fella with a trick tickler, and a husky with a big chin on him."

"There was no other? There was not a younger man, tall and thin?"

That could be the Whosis Kid. She thought he and the Frenchman were working together?

Billie shook his shaggy, banged-up head.

"Nope. They was only two of 'em."

She frowned and chewed her lip.

Billie looked sidewise at me—a look that said "Beat it."

The woman caught the glance. She twisted around on the bench to put a hand on his head.

"Poor Billie," she cooed; "his head most cruelly hurt saving me, and now, when he should be at his home giving it rest, I keep him here talking. You go, Billie, and when it is morning and your poor head is better, you will telephone to me?"

His red face got dark. He glowered at me.

Laughing, she slapped him lightly on the cheek that bulged around his cud of tobacco.

"Do not become jealous of Jerry. Jerry is enamored of one yellow and white lady somewhere, and to her he is most faithful. Not even the smallest liking has he for dark women." She smiled a challenge at me. "Is it not so, Jerry?"

"No," I denied. "And, besides, all women are dark."

Billie shifted his chew to the scratched cheek and bunched his shoulders.

"What the hell kind of a crack is that to be making?" he rumbled.

"That means nothing it should not, Billie," she laughed at him. "It is only an epigram."

"Yeah?" Billie was sour and truculent. I was beginning to think he didn't like me. "Well, tell your little fat friend to keep his smart wheezes to himself. I don't like 'em."

That was plain enough. Billie wanted an argument. The woman, who held him securely enough to have steered him off, simply laughed again. There was no profit in trying to find the reason behind any of her actions. She was a nut. Maybe she thought that since we weren't sociable enough for her to keep both on hand, she'd let us tangle, and hold on to the one who rubbed the other out of the picture.

Anyway, a row was coming. Ordinarily I am inclined to peace. The day is past when I'll fight for the fun of it. But I've been in too many rumpuses to mind them much. Usually nothing very bad happens to you, even if you lose. I wasn't going to back down just because this big stiff was meatier than I. I've always been lucky against the large sizes. He had been banged up earlier in the evening. That would cut down his steam some. I wanted to hang around this apartment a little longer, if it could be managed. If Billie wanted to tussle—and it looked as if he did—he could.

It was easy to meet him half-way: anything I said would be used against me.

I grinned at his red face, and suggested to the woman, solemnly:

"I think if you'd dip him in blueing he'd come out the same color as the other pup."

As silly as that was, it served. Billie reared up on his feet and curled his paws into fists.

"Me and you'll take a walk," he decided; "out where there's space enough."

I got up, pushed my chair back with a foot, and quoted "Red" Burns to him: "If you're close enough, there's room enough."

He wasn't a man you had to talk to much. We went around and around.

It was fists at first. He started it by throwing his right at my head. I went in under it and gave him all I had in a right and left to the belly. He swallowed his chew of tobacco. But he didn't bend. Few big men are as strong as they look. Billie was.

He didn't know anything at all. His idea of a fight was to stand up and throw fists at your head—right, left, right, left. His fists were as large as wastebaskets. They wheezed through the air. But always at the head—the easiest part to get out of the way.

There was room enough for me to go in and out. I did that. I hammered his belly. I thumped his heart. I mauled his belly again. Every time I hit him he grew an inch, gained a pound and picked up another horsepower. I don't fool when I hit, but nothing I did to this human mountain—not even making him swallow his hunk of tobacco—had any visible effect on him.

I've always had a reasonable amount of pride in my ability to sock. It was disappointing to have this big heaver take the best I could give him without a grunt. But I wasn't discouraged. He couldn't stand it forever. I settled down to make a steady job of it.

Twice he clipped me. Once on the shoulder. A big fist spun me half around. He didn't know what to do next. He came in on the wrong side. I made him miss, and got clear. The other time he caught me on the forehead. A chair kept me from going down. The smack hurt me. It must have hurt him more. A skull is tougher than a knuckle. I got out of his way when he closed in, and let him have something to remember on the back of his neck.

The woman's dusky face showed over Billie's shoulder as he straightened up. Her eyes were shiny behind their heavy lashes, and her mouth was open to let white teeth gleam through.

Billie got tired of the boxing after that, and turned the set-to into a wrestling match, with trimmings. I would rather have kept on with the fists. But I couldn't help myself. It was his party. He grabbed one of my wrists, yanked, and we thudded chest to chest.

He didn't know any more about this than he had about that. He didn't have to. He was big enough and strong enough to play with me.

I was underneath when we tumbled down on the floor and began rolling around. I did my best. It wasn't anything. Three times I put a scissors on him. His body was too big for my short legs to clamp around. He chucked me off as if he were amusing the baby. There was no use at all in trying to do things to his legs. No hold known to man could have held them. His arms were almost as strong. I quit trying.

Nothing I knew was any good against this monster. He was out of my range. I was satisfied to spend all that was left of my strength trying to keep him from crippling me—and waiting for a chance to out-smart him.

He threw me around a lot. Then my chance came.

I was flat on my back, with everything but one or two of my most centrally located intestines squeezed out. Kneeling astride me, he brought his big hands up to my throat and fastened them there.

That's how much he didn't know!

You can't choke a man that way—not if his hands are loose and he knows a hand is stronger than a finger.

I laughed in his purple face and brought my own hands up. Each of them picked one of his little fingers out of my flesh. It wasn't a dream at that. I was all in, and he wasn't. But no man's little finger is stronger than another's hand. I twisted them back. They broke together.

He yelped. I grabbed the next—the ring fingers.

One of them snapped. The other was ready to pop when he let go.

Jerking up, I butted him in the face. I twisted from between his knees. We came on our feet together.

The doorbell rang.

VIII

Fight interest went out of the woman's face. Fear came in. Her fingers picked at her mouth.

"Ask who's there," I told her.

"Who—who is there?"

Her voice was flat and dry.

"Mrs Keil," came from the corridor, the words sharp with indignation. "You will have to stop this noise immediately! The tenants are complaining—and no wonder! A pretty hour to be entertaining company and carrying on so!"

"The landlady," the dark woman whispered. Aloud: "I am sorry, Mrs Keil. There will not be more noises."

Something like a sniff came through the door, and the sound of dimming footsteps.

Inés Almad frowned reproachfully at Billie.

"You should not have done this," she blamed him.

He looked humble, and at the floor, and at me. Looking at me, the purple began to flow back into his face.

"I'm sorry," he mumbled. "I told this fella we ought to take a walk. We'll do it now, and there won't be no more noise here."

"Billie!" her voice was sharp. She was reading the law to him. "You will go out and have attention for your hurts. If you have not won these fights, because of that am I to be left here alone to be murdered?"

The big man shuffled his feet, avoided her gaze and looked utterly miserable. But he shook his head stubbornly.

"I can't do it, Inés," he said. "Me and this guy has got to finish it. He busted my fingers, and I got to bust his jaw'."

"Billie!"

She stamped one small foot and looked imperiously at him. He looked as if he'd like to roll over on his back and hold his paws in the air. But he stood his ground.

"I got to," he repeated. "There ain't no way out of it."

Anger left her face. She smiled very tenderly at him.

"Dear old Billie," she murmured, and crossed the room to a secretary in a corner.

When she turned, an automatic pistol was in her hand. Its one eye looked at Billie.

"Now, *lechón*" she purred, "go out!"

The red man wasn't a quick thinker. It took a full minute for him to realize that this woman he loved was driving him away with a gun. The big dummy might have known that his three broken fingers had disqualified him. It took another minute for him to get his legs in motion. He went toward the door in slow bewilderment, still only half believing this thing was really happening.

The woman followed him step by step. I went ahead to open the door.

I turned the knob. The door came in, pushing me back against the opposite wall.

In the doorway stood Edouard Maurois and the man I had swatted on the chin. Each had a gun.

I looked at Inés Almad, wondering what turn her craziness would take in the face of this situation. She wasn't so crazy as I had thought. Her scream and the thud of her gun on the floor sounded together.

"Ah!" the Frenchman was saying. "The gentlemen were leaving? May we detain them?"

The man with the big chin—it was larger than ever now with the marks of my tap—was less polite.

"Back up, you birds!" he ordered, stooping for the gun the woman had dropped.

I still was holding the doorknob. I rattled it a little as I took my hand away—enough to cover up the click of the lock as I pushed the button that left it unlatched. If I needed help, and it came, I wanted as few locks as possible between me and it.

Then—Billie, the woman and I walking backward—we all paraded into the sitting-room. Maurois and his companion both wore souvenirs of the row in the taxicab. One of the Frenchman's eyes was bruised and closed—a beautiful shiner. His clothes were rumpled and dirty. He wore them jauntily in spite of that, and he still had his walking stick, crooked under the arm that didn't hold his gun.

Big Chin held us with his own gun and the woman's while Maurois ran his hand over Billie's and my clothes, to see if we were armed. He found my gun and pocketed it. Billie had no weapons.

"Can I trouble you to step back against the wall?" Maurois asked when he was through.

We stepped back as if it was no trouble at all. I found my shoulder against one of the window curtains. I pressed it against the frame, and turned far enough to drag the curtain clear of a foot or more of pane.

If the Whosis Kid was watching, he should have had a clear view of the Frenchman—the man who had shot at him earlier in the evening. I was putting it up to the Kid. The corridor door was unlocked. If the Kid could get into the building—no great trick—he had a clear path. I didn't know where he fit in, but I wanted him to join us, and I hoped he wouldn't disappoint me. If everybody got together here, maybe whatever was going on would come out where I could see it and understand it.

Meanwhile, I kept as much of myself as possible out of the window. The Kid might decide to throw lead from across the alley.

Maurois was facing Inés. Big Chin's guns were on Billie and me.

"I do not *comprends* ze *anglais* ver' good," the Frenchman was mocking the woman. "So it is when you say you meet wit' me, I t'ink you say in New Orleans. I do not know you say San Francisc'. I am ver' sorry to make ze mistake. I am mos' sorry zat I keep you wait. But now I am here. You have ze share for me?"

"I have not." She held her hands out in an empty gesture. "The Kid took those—everything from me."

"What?" Maurois dropped his taunting smile and his vaudeville accent. His one open eye flashed angrily. "How could he, unless—?"

"He suspected us, Edouard." Her mouth trembled with earnestness. Her eyes pleaded for belief. She was lying. "He had me followed. The day after I am there he comes. He takes all. I am afraid to wait for you. I fear your unbelief. You would not—"

"*C'est incroyable!*" Maurois was very excited over it. "I was on the first train south after our—our theatricals. Could the Kid have been on that train without my knowing it? *Non!* And how else could he have reached you before I? You are playing with me, *ma petite* Inés. That you did join the Kid, I do not doubt. But not in New Orleans. You did not go there. You came here to San Francisco."

"Edouard!" she protested, fingering his sleeve with one brown hand, the other holding her throat as if she were having trouble getting the words out. "You cannot think that thing! Do not those weeks in Boston say it is not possible? For one like the Kid—or like any other—am I to betray you? You know me not more than to think I am like that?"

She was an actress. She was appealing, and pathetic, and anything else you like—including dangerous.

The Frenchman took his sleeve away from her and stepped back a step. White lines ringed his mouth below his tiny mustache, and his jaw muscles bulged. His one good eye was worried. She had got to him, though not quite enough to upset him altogether. But the game was young yet.

"I do not know what to think," he said slowly. "If I have been wrong—I must find the Kid first. Then I will learn the truth."

"You don't have to look no further, brother. I'm right among you!"

The Whosis Kid stood in the passageway door. A black revolver was in each of his hands. Their hammers were up.

IX

It was a pretty tableau.

There is the Whosis Kid in the door—a lean lad in his twenties, all the more wicked-looking because his face is weak and slack-jawed and dull-eyed. The cocked guns in his hands are pointing at everybody or at nobody, depending on how you look at them.

There is the brown woman, her cheeks pinched in her two fists, her eyes open until their green-grayishness shows. The fright I had seen in her face before was nothing to the fright that is there now.

There is the Frenchman—whirled doorward at the Kid's first word—his gun on the Kid, his cane still under his arm, his face a tense white blot.

There is Big Chin, his body twisted half around, his face over one shoulder to look at the door, with one of his guns following his face around.

There is Billie—a big, battered statue of a man who hasn't said a word since Inés Almad started to gun him out of the apartment.

And, last, here I am—not feeling so comfortable as I would home in bed, but not actually hysterical either. I wasn't altogether dissatisfied with the shape things were taking.

Something was going to happen in these rooms. But I wasn't friendly enough to any present to care especially what happened to whom. For myself, I counted on coming through all in one piece. Few men *get* killed. Most of those who meet sudden ends *get themselves* killed. I've had twenty years of experience at dodging that. I can count on being one of the survivors of whatever blow-up there is. And I hope to take most of the other survivors for a ride.

But right now the situation belonged to the men with guns—the Whosis Kid, Maurois and Big Chin.

The Kid spoke first. He had a whining voice that came disagreeably through his thick nose.

"This don't look nothing like Chi to me, but, anyways, we're all here."

"Chicago!" Maurois exclaimed. "You did not go to Chicago!"

The Kid sneered at him.

"Did you? Did she? What would I be going there for? You think me and her run out on you, don't you? Well, we would of if she hadn't put the two X's to me the same as she done to you, and the same as the three of us done to the boob."

"That may be," the Frenchman replied; "but you do not expect me to believe that you and Inés are not friends? Didn't I see you leaving here this afternoon?"

"You seen me, all right," the Kid agreed; "but if my rod hadn't of got snagged in my dogger you wouldn't have seen nothing else. But I ain't got nothing against you now. I thought you and her had ditched me, just as you think me and her done you. I know different now, from what I heard while I was getting in here. She twisted the pair of us, Frenchy, just like we twisted the boob. Ain't you got it yet?"

Maurois shook his head slowly.

What put an edge to this conversation was that both men were talking over their guns.

"Listen," the Kid asked impatiently. "We was to meet up in Chi for a three-way split, wasn't we?"

The Frenchman nodded.

"But she tells me," the Kid went on, "she'll connect with me in St. Louis, counting you out; and she ribs you up to meet her in New Orleans, ducking me. And then she gyps the pair of us by running out here to Frisco with the stuff.

"We're a couple of suckers, Frenchy, and there ain't no use of us getting hot at each other. There's enough of it for a fat two-way cut. What I say is let's forget what's done, and me and you make it fifty-fifty. Understand, I ain't begging you. I'm making a proposition. If you don't like it, to hell with you! You know me. You never seen the day I wouldn't shoot it out with you or anybody else. Take your pick!"

The Frenchman didn't say anything for a while. He was converted, but he didn't want to weaken his hand by coming in too soon. I don't know whether he believed the Kid's words or not, but he believed the Kid's guns. You can get a bullet out of a cocked revolver a lot quicker than out of a hammerless automatic. The Kid had the bulge there. And the Kid had him licked because the Kid had the look of one who doesn't give a damn what happens next.

Finally Maurois looked a question at Big Chin. Big Chin moistened his lips, but said nothing.

Maurois looked at the Kid again, and nodded his head.

"You are right," he said. "We will do that."

"Good!" The Kid did not move from his door. "Now who are these plugs?"

"These two"—Maurois nodded at Billie and me—"are friends of our Inés. This"—indicating Big Chin—"is a confrere of mine."

"You mean he's in with you? That's all right with me." The Kid spoke crisply. "But, you understand, his cut comes out of yours. I get half, and no trimming."

The Frenchman frowned, but he nodded in agreement.

"Half is yours, if we find it."

"Don't get no headache over that," the Kid advised him. "It's here and we'll get it."

He put one of his guns away and came into the room, the other gun hanging loosely at his side. When he walked across the room to face the woman, he managed it so that Big Chin and Maurois were never behind him.

"Where's the stuff?" he demanded.

Inés Almad wet her red mouth with her tongue and let her mouth droop a little and looked softly at the Kid, and made her play.

"One of us is as bad as are the others, Kid. We all—each of us tried to get for ourselves everything. You and Edouard have put aside what is past. Am I more wrong than you? I have them, true, but I have not them here. Until tomorrow will you wait? I will get them. We will divide them among us three, as it was to have been. Shall we not do that?"

"Not any!" The Kid's voice had finality in it.

"Is that just?" she pleaded, letting her chin quiver a bit. "Is there a treachery of which I am guilty that also you and Edouard are not? Do you—?"

"That ain't the idea at all," the Kid told her. "Me and Frenchy are in a fix where we got to work together to get anywhere. So we're together. With you it's different. We don't need you. We can take the stuff away from you. You're out! Where's the stuff?"

"Not here! Am I foolish sufficient to leave them here where so easily you could find them? You *do* need my help to find them. Without me you cannot—"

"You're silly! I might flop for that if I didn't know you. But I know you're too damned greedy to let 'em get far away from you. And you're yellower than you're greedy. If you're smacked a couple of times, you'll kick in. And don't think I got any objections to smacking you over!"

She cowered back from his upraised hand.

The Frenchman spoke quickly.

"We should search the rooms first, Kid. If we don't find them there, then we can decide what to do next."

The Whosis Kid laughed sneeringly at Maurois.

"All right. But, get this, I'm not going out of here without that stuff—not if I have to take this rat apart. My way's quicker, but we'll hunt first if you want to. Your con-whatever-you-call-him can keep these plugs tucked in while me and you upset the joint."

They went to work. The Kid put away his gun and brought out a long-bladed spring-knife. The Frenchman unscrewed the lower two-thirds of his cane, baring a foot and a half of swordblade.

No cursory search, theirs. They took the room we were in first. They gutted it thoroughly, carved it to the bone. Furniture and pictures were taken apart. Upholstering gave up its stuffing. Floor coverings were cut. Suspicious lengths of wallpaper were scraped loose. They worked slowly. Neither would let the other get behind him. The Kid would not turn his back on Big Chin.

The sitting-room wrecked, they went into the next room, leaving the woman, Billie and me standing among the litter. Big Chin and his two guns watched over us.

As soon as the Frenchman and the Kid were out of sight, the woman tried her stuff out on our guardian. She had a lot of confidence in her power with men, I'll say that for her.

For a while she worked her eyes on Big Chin, and then, very softly:

"Can I—?"

"You can't!" Big Chin was loud and gruff. "Shut up!"

The Whosis Kid appeared at the door.

"If nobody don't say nothing maybe nobody won't get hurt," he snarled, and went back to his work.

The woman valued herself too highly to be easily discouraged. She didn't put anything in words again, but she looked things at Big Chin—things that had him sweating and blushing. He was a simple man. I didn't think she'd get anywhere. If there had been no one present but the two of them, she might have put Big Chin over the jumps; but he wouldn't be likely to let her get to him with a couple of birds standing there watching the show:

Once a sharp yelp told us that the purple Frana—who had fled rearward when Maurois and Big Chin arrived—had got in trouble with the searchers. There was only that one yelp, and it stopped with a suddenness that suggested trouble for the dog.

The two men spent nearly an hour in the other rooms. They didn't find anything. Their hands, when they joined us again, held nothing but the cutlery.

X

"I said to you it was not here," Inés told them triumphantly. "Now will you—?"

"You can't tell me nothing I'll believe." The Kid snapped his knife shut and dropped it in his pocket. "I still think it's here."

He caught her wrist, and held his other hand, palm up, under her nose.

"You can put 'em in my hand, or I'll take 'em."

"They are not here! I swear it!"

His mouth lifted at the corner in a savage grimace.

"Liar!"

He twisted her arm roughly, forcing her to her knees. His free hand went to the shoulder-strap of her orange gown.

"I'll damn soon find out," he promised.

Billie came to life.

"Hey!" he protested, his chest heaving in and out. "You can't do that!"

"Wait, Kid!" Maurois—putting his sword-cane together again—called. "Let us see if there is not another way."

The Whosis Kid let go of the woman and took three slow steps back from her. His eyes were dead circles without any color you could name—the dull eyes of the man whose nerves quit functioning in the face of excitement. His bony hands pushed his coat aside a little and rested where his vest bulged over the sharp corners of his hip-bones.

"Let's me and you get this right, Frenchy," he said in his whining voice. "Are you with me or her?"

"You, most certainly, but—"

"All right. Then *be* with me! Don't be trying to gum every play I make. I'm going to frisk this dolly, and don't think I ain't. What are you going to do about it?"

The Frenchman pursed his mouth until his little black mustache snuggled against the tip of his nose. He puckered his eyebrows and looked thoughtfully out of his one good eye. But he wasn't going to do anything at all about it, and he knew he wasn't. Finally he shrugged.

"You are right," he surrendered. "She should be searched."

The Kid grunted contemptuous disgust at him and went toward the woman again.

She sprang away from him, to me. Her arms clamped around my neck in the habit they seemed to have.

"Jerry!" she screamed in my face. "You will not allow him! Jerry, please not!"

I didn't say anything.

I didn't think it was exactly genteel of the Kid to frisk her, but there were several reasons why I didn't try to stop him. First, I didn't want to do anything to delay the unearthing of this "stuff" there had been so much talk about. Second, I'm no Galahad. This woman had picked her playmates, and was largely responsible for this angle of their game. If they played rough, she'd have to make the best of it. And, a good strong third, Big Chin was prodding me in the side with a gunmuzzle to remind me that I couldn't do anything if I wanted to—except get myself slaughtered.

The Kid dragged Inés away. I let her go.

He pulled her over to what was left of the bench by the electric heater, and called the Frenchman there with a jerk of his head.

"You hold her while I go through her," he said.

She filled her lungs with air. Before she could turn it loose in a shriek, the Kid's long fingers had fit themselves to her throat.

"One chirp out of you and I'll tie a knot in your neck," he threatened.

She let the air wheeze out of her nose.

Billie shuffled his feet. I turned my head to look at him. He was puffing through his mouth. Sweat polished his forehead under his matted red hair. I hoped he wasn't going to turn his wolf loose until the "stuff" came to the surface. If he would wait a while I might join him.

He wouldn't wait. He went into action when—Maurois holding her—the Kid started to undress the woman.

He took a step toward them. Big Chin tried to wave him back with a gun. Billie didn't even see it. His eyes were red on the three by the bench.

"Hey, you can't do that!" he rumbled. "You can't do that!"

"No?" The Kid looked up from his work. "Watch me."

"Billie!" the woman urged the big man on in his foolishness.

Billie charged.

Big Chin let him go, playing safe by swinging both guns on me. The Whosis Kid slid out of the plunging giant's path. Maurois hurled the girl straight at Billie—and got his gun out.

Billie and Inés thumped together in a swaying tangle.

The Kid spun behind the big man. One of the Kid's hands came out of his pocket with the spring-knife. The knife clicked open as Billie regained his balance.

The Kid jumped close.

He knew knives. None of your clumsy downward strokes with the blade sticking out the bottom of his fist.

Thumb and crooked forefinger guided blade. He struck upward. Under Billie's shoulder. Once. Deep.

Billie pitched forward, smashing the woman to the floor under him. He rolled off her and was dead on his back among the furniture-stuffing. Dead, he seemed larger than ever, seemed to fill the room.

The Whosis Kid wiped his knife clean on a piece of carpet, snapped it shut, and dropped it back in his pocket. He did this with his left hand. His right was close to his hip. He did not look at the knife. His eyes were on Maurois.

But if he expected the Frenchman to squawk, he was disappointed. Maurois' little mustache twitched, and his face was white and strained, but:

"We'd better hurry with what we have to do, and get out of here," he suggested.

The woman sat up beside the dead man, whimpering. Her face was ashy under her dark skin. She was licked. A shaking hand fumbled beneath her clothes. It brought out a little flat silk bag.

Maurois—nearer than the Kid—took it. It was sewed too securely for his fingers to open. He held it while the Kid ripped it with his knife. The Frenchman poured part of the contents out in one cupped hand.

Diamonds. Pearls. A few colored stones among them.

XI

Big Chin blew' his breath out in a faint whistle. His eyes were bright on the sparkling stones. So were the eyes of Maurois, the woman, and the Kid.

Big Chin's inattention was a temptation. I could reach his jaw. I could knock him over. The strength Billie had mauled out of me had nearly all come back by now. I could knock Big Chin over and have at least one of his guns by the time the Kid and Maurois got set. It was time for me to do something. I had let these comedians run the show long enough. The stuff had come to light. If I let the party break up there was no telling when, if ever, I could round up these folks again.

But I put the temptation away and made myself wait a bit longer. No use going off half-cocked. With a gun in my hand, facing the Kid and Maurois, I still would have less than an even break. That's not enough. The idea in this detective business is to catch crooks, not to put on heroics.

Maurois was pouring the stones back in the bag when I looked at him again. He started to put the bag in his pocket. The Whosis Kid stopped him with a hand on his arm.

"I'll pack 'em."

Maurois' eyebrows went up.

"There's two of you and one of me," the Kid explained. "I trust you, and all the like of that, but just the same I'm carrying my own share."

"But—"

The doorbell interrupted Maurois' protest.

The Kid spun to the girl.

"You do the talking—and no wise breaks!"

She got up from the floor and went to the passageway.

"Who is there?" she called.

The landlady's voice, stern and wrathful:

"Another sound, Mrs Almad, and I shall call the police. This is disgraceful!"

I wondered what she would have thought if she had opened the unlocked door and taken a look at her apartment—furniture whittled and gutted; a dead man—the noise of whose dying had brought her up here this second time—lying in the middle of the litter.

I wondered—I took a chance.

"Aw, go jump down the sewer!" I told her.

A gasp, and we heard no more from her. I hoped she was speeding her injured feelings to the telephone. I might need the police she had mentioned.

The Kid's gun was out. For a while it was a toss-up. I would lie down beside Billie, or I wouldn't. If I could have been knifed quietly, I would have gone. But nobody was behind me. The Kid knew I wouldn't stand still and quiet while he carved me. He didn't want any more racket than necessary, now that the jewels were on hand.

"Keep your clam shut or I'll shut it for you!" was the worst I got out of it.

The Kid turned to the Frenchman again. The Frenchman had used the time spent in this side-play to pocket the gems.

"Either we divvy here and now, or I carry the stuff," the Kid announced. "There's two of you to see I don't take a Micky Finn on you."

"But, Kid, we cannot stay here! Is not the landlady even now calling the police? We will go elsewhere to divide. Why cannot you trust me when you are with me?"

Two steps put the Kid between the door and both Maurois and Big Chin. One of the Kid's hands held the gun he had flashed on me. The other was conveniently placed to his other gun.

"Nothing stirring!" he said through his nose. "My cut of them stones don't go out of here in nobody else's kick. If you want to split 'em here, good enough. If you don't, I'll do the carrying. That's flat!"

"But the police!"

"You worry about them. I'm taking one thing at a time, and it's the stones right now."

A vein came out blue in the Frenchman's forehead. His small body was rigid. He was trying to collect enough courage to swap shots with the Kid. He knew, and the Kid knew, that one of them was going to have all the stuff when the curtain came down. They had started off by double-crossing each other. They weren't likely to change their habits. One would have the stones in the end. The other would have nothing—except maybe a burial.

Big Chin didn't count. He was too simple a thug to last long in his present company. If he had known anything, he would have used one of his guns on each of them right now. Instead, he continued to cover me, trying to watch them out of the tail of his eye.

The woman stood near the door, where she had gone to talk to the landlady. She was staring at the Frenchman and the Kid. I wasted precious minutes that seemed to run into hours trying to catch her eye. I finally got it.

I looked at the light-switch, only a foot from her. I looked at her. I looked at the switch again. At her. At the switch.

She got me. Her hand crept sidewise along the wall.

I looked at the two principal players in this button-button game.

The Kid's eyes were dead—and deadly—circles. Maurois' one open eye was watery. He couldn't make the grade. He put a hand in his pocket and brought out the silk bag.

The woman's brown finger topped the light button. God knows she was nothing to gamble on, but I had no choice. I had to be in motion when the lights went. Big Chin would pump metal. I had to trust Inés not to balk. If she did, my name was Denis.

Her nail whitened.

I went for Maurois.

Darkness—streaked with orange and blue—filled with noise.

My arms had Maurois. We crashed down on dead Billie. I twisted around, kicking the Frenchman's face. Loosened one arm. Caught one of his. His other hand gouged at my face. That told me the bag was in the one I held. Clawing fingers tore my mouth. I put my teeth in them and kept them there. One of my knees was on his face. I put my weight on it. My teeth still held his hand. Both of my hands were free to get the bag.

Not nice, this work, but effective.

The room was the inside of a black drum on which a giant was beating the long roll. Four guns worked together in a prolonged throbbing roar.

Maurois' fingernails dug into my tongue. I had to open my mouth—let his hand escape. One of my hands found the bag. He wouldn't let go. I screwed his thumb. He cried out. I had the bag.

I tried to leave him then. He grabbed my legs. I kicked at him—missed. He shuddered twice—and stopped moving. A flying bullet had hit him, I took it. Rolling over to the floor, snuggling close to him, I ran a hand over him. A hard bulge came under my hand. I put my hand in his pocket and took back my gun.

On hands and knees—one fist around my gun, the other clutching the silk sack of jewels—I turned to where the door to the next room should have been. A foot wrong, I corrected my course. As I went through the door, the racket in the room behind me stopped.

XII

Huddled close to the wall inside the door, I stowed the silk bag away, and regretted that I hadn't stayed plastered to the floor behind the Frenchman. This room was dark. It hadn't been dark when the woman switched off the sitting-room lights. Every room in the apartment had been lighted then. All were dark now. Not knowing who had darkened them, I didn't like it.

No sounds came from the room I had quit.

The rustle of gently falling rain came from an open window that I couldn't see, off to one side.

Another sound came from behind me. The muffled tattoo of teeth on teeth.

That cheered me. Inés the scary, of course. She had left the sitting-room in the dark and put out the rest of the lights. Maybe nobody else was behind me.

Breathing quietly through wide-open mouth, I waited. I couldn't hunt for the woman in the dark without making noises. Maurois and the Kid had strewn furniture and parts of furniture everywhere. I wished I knew if she was holding a gun. I didn't want to have her spraying me.

Not knowing, I waited where I was.

Her teeth clicked on for minutes.

Something moved in the sitting-room. A gun thundered.

"Inés!" I hissed toward the chattering teeth.

No answer. Furniture scraped in the sitting-room. Two guns went off together. A groaning broke out.

"I've got the stuff," I whispered under cover of the groaning.

That brought an answer.

"Jerry! Ah, come here to me!"

The groans went on, but fainter, in the other room. I crawled toward the woman's voice. I went on hands and knees, bumping as carefully as possible against things. I couldn't see anything. Midway, I put a hand down on a soggy bundle of fur—the late purple Frana. I went on.

Inés touched my shoulder with an eager hand.

"Give them to me," were her first words.

I grinned at her in the dark, patted her hand, found her head, and put my mouth to her ear.

"Let's get back in the bedroom," I breathed, paying no attention to her request for the loot. "The Kid will be coming." I didn't doubt that he had bested Big Chin. "We can handle him better in the bedroom."

I wanted to receive him in a room with only one door.

She led me—both of us on hands and knees—to the bedroom. I did what thinking seemed necessary as we crawled. The Kid couldn't know yet how the Frenchman and I had come out. If he guessed, he would guess that the Frenchman had survived. He would be likely to put me in the chump class with Billie, and think the Frenchman could handle me. The chances were that he had got Big Chin, and knew it by now. It was black as black in the sitting-room, but he must know by now that he was the only living thing there.

He blocked the only exit from the apartment. He would think, then, that Inés and Maurois were still alive in it, with the spoils. What would he do about it? There was no pretense of partnership now; That had gone with the lights. The Kid was after the stones. The Kid was after them alone.

I'm no wizard at guessing the other guy's next move. But my idea was that the Kid would be on his way after us, soon. He knew—he must know—that the police were coming; but I had him doped as crazy enough to disregard the police until they appeared. He'd figure that there would be only a couple of them—prepared for nothing more violent than a drinking-party. He could handle them—or he would think he could. Meanwhile, he would come after the stones.

The woman and I reached the bedroom, the room farthest back in the apartment, a room with only one door. I heard her fumbling with the door, trying to close it. I couldn't see, but I got my foot in the way.

"Leave it open," I whispered.

I didn't want to shut the Kid out. I wanted to take him in.

On my belly, I crawled back to the door, felt for my watch, and propped it on the sill, in the angle between door and frame. I wriggled back from it until I was six or eight feet away, looking diagonally across the open doorway at the watch's luminous dial.

The phosphorescent numbers could not be seen from the other side of the door. They faced me. Anybody who came through the door—unless he jumped—must, if only for a split-second, put some part of himself between me and the watch.

On my belly, my gun cocked, its butt steady on the floor, I waited for the faint light to be blotted out.

I waited a time. Pessimism: perhaps he wasn't coming; perhaps I would have to go after him; perhaps he would run out, and I would lose him after all my trouble.

Inés, beside me, breathed quaveringly in my ear, and shivered.

"Don't touch me," I growled at her as she tried to cuddle against me.

She was shaking my arm.

Glass broke in the next room.

Silence.

The luminous patches on the watch burnt my eyes. I couldn't afford to blink. A foot could pass the dial while I was blinking. I couldn't afford to blink, but I had to blink. I blinked. I couldn't tell whether something had passed the watch or not. I had to blink again. Tried to hold my eyes stiffly opened. Failed. I almost shot at the third blink. I could have sworn something had gone between me and the watch.

The Kid, whatever he was up to, made no sound.

The dark woman began to sob beside me. Throat noises that could guide bullets.

I lumped her with my eyes and cursed the lot—not aloud, but from the heart.

My eyes smarted. Moisture filmed them. I blinked it away, losing sight of the watch for precious instants. The butt of my gun was slimy with my hand's sweat. I was thoroughly uncomfortable, inside and out.

Gunpowder burned at my face.

A screaming maniac of a woman was crawling all over me.

My bullet hit nothing lower than the ceiling.

I flung, maybe kicked, the woman off, and snaked backward. She moaned somewhere to one side. I couldn't see the Kid—couldn't hear him. The watch was visible again, farther away. A rustling.

The watch vanished.

I fired at it.

Two points of light near the floor gave out fire and thunder.

My gun-barrel as close to the floor as I could hold it, I fired between those points. Twice.

Twin flames struck at me again.

My right hand went numb. My left took the gun. I sped two more bullets on their way. That left one in my gun.

I don't know what I did with it. My head filled up with funny notions. There wasn't any room. There wasn't any darkness. There wasn't anything...

I opened my eyes in dim light. I was on my back. Beside me the dark woman knelt, shivering and sniffling. Her hands were busy—in my clothes.

One of them came out of my vest with the jewel-bag.

Coming to life, I grabbed her arm. She squealed as if I were a stirring corpse. I got the bag again.

"Give them back, Jerry," she wailed, trying frantically to pull my fingers loose. "They are my things. Give them!"

Sitting up, I looked around.

Beside me lay a shattered bedside lamp, whose fall—caused by carelessness with my feet, or one of the Kid's bullets—

had KO'd me. Across the room, face down, arms spread in a crucified posture, the Whosis Kid sprawled. He was dead.

From the front of the apartment—almost indistinguishable from the throbbing in my head—came the pounding of heavy blows. The police were kicking down the unlocked door.

The woman went quiet. I whipped my head around. The knife stung my cheek—put a slit in the lapel of my coat. I took it away from her.

There was no sense to this. The police were already here. I humored her, pretending a sudden coming to full consciousness.

"Oh, it's you!" I said. "Here they are."

I handed her the silk bag of jewels just as the first policeman came into the room.

XIII

I didn't see Inés again before she was taken back East to be hit with a life-sentence in the Massachusetts big house. Neither of the policemen who crashed into her apartment that night knew me. The woman and I were separated before I ran into anyone who did know me, which gave me an opportunity to arrange that she would not be tipped off to my identity. The most difficult part of the performance was to keep myself out of the newspapers, since I had to tell the coroner's jury about the deaths of Billie, Big Chin, Maurois and the Whosis Kid. But I managed it. So far as I know, the dark woman still thinks I am Jerry Young, the bootlegger.

The Old Man talked to her before she left San Francisco. Fitting together what he got from her and what the Boston branch got, the history runs like this:

A Boston jeweler named Tunnicliffe had a trusted employee named Binder. Binder fell in with a dark woman named

Inés Almad. The dark woman, in turn, had a couple of shifty friends—a Frenchman named Maurois, and a native of Boston whose name was either Carey or Cory, but who was better known as the Whosis Kid. Out of that sort of combination almost anything was more than likely to come.

What came was a scheme. The faithful Binder—part of whose duties it was to open the shop in the morning and close it at night—was to pick out the richest of the unset stones bought for the holiday trade, carry them off with him one evening, and turn them over to Inés. She was to turn them into money.

To cover up Binder's theft, the Whosis Kid and the Frenchman were to rob the jeweler's shop immediately after the door was opened the following morning. Binder and the porter—who would not notice the absence of the most valuable pieces from the stock—would be the only ones in the shop. The robbers would take whatever they could get. In addition to their pickings, they were to be paid two hundred and fifty dollars apiece, and in case either was caught later, Binder could be counted on not to identify them.

That was the scheme as Binder knew it. There were angles he didn't suspect.

Between Inés, Maurois and the Kid there was another agreement. She was to leave for Chicago with the stones as soon as Binder gave them to her, and wait there for Maurois and the Kid. She and the Frenchman would have been satisfied to run off and let Binder hold the sack. The Whosis Kid insisted that the hold-up go through as planned, and that the foolish Binder be killed. Binder knew too much about them, the Kid said, and he would squawk his head off as soon as he learned he had been double-crossed.

The Kid had his way, and he had shot Binder.

Then had come the sweet mess of quadruple and sextuple crossing that had led all three into calamity: the woman's private agreements with the Kid and Maurois—to meet one in

St. Louis and the other in New Orleans—and her flight alone with the loot to San Francisco.

Billie was an innocent bystander—or almost. A lumber-handler Inés had run into somewhere, and picked up as a sort of cushion against the rough spots along the rocky road she traveled.

8

THE SCORCHED FACE

BLACK MASK, MAY 1925

Here's another realistic detective tale by Mr Hammett, formerly of the Pinkerton's. It has a ring of truth in it that makes you forget that you are only reading and not actually following the San Francisco sleuth around.

A NOVELETTE OF THE CONTINENTAL SLEUTH

I

"We expected them home yesterday," Alfred Banbrock wound up his story. "When they had not come by this morning, my wife telephoned Mrs Walden. Mrs Walden said they had not been down there—had not been expected, in fact."

"On the face of it, then," I suggested, "it seems that your daughters went away of their own accord, and are staying away on their own accord?"

Banbrock nodded gravely. Tired muscles sagged in his fleshy face.

"It would seem so," he agreed. "That is why I came to your agency for help instead of going to the police."

"Have they ever disappeared before?"

"No. If you read the papers and magazines, you've no doubt seen hints that the younger generation is given to irregularity. My daughters came and went pretty much as they pleased. But, though I can't say I ever knew what they were up to, we always knew where they were in a general way."

"Can you think of any reason for their going away like this?"

He shook his weary head.

"Any recent quarrels?" I probed.

"N—" He changed it to: "Yes—although I didn't attach any importance to it, and wouldn't have recalled it if you hadn't jogged my memory. It was Thursday evening—the evening before they went away."

"And it was about—?"

"Money, of course. We never disagreed over anything else. I gave each of my daughters an adequate allowance—perhaps a very liberal one. Nor did I keep them strictly within it. There were few months in which they didn't exceed it. Thursday evening they asked for an amount of money even more than usual in excess of what two girls should need. I wouldn't give it to them, though I finally did give them a somewhat smaller amount. We didn't exactly quarrel—not in the strict sense of the word—but there was a certain lack of friendliness between us."

"And it was after this disagreement that they said they were going down to Mrs Walden's, in Monterey, for the week-end?"

"Possibly. I'm not sure of that point. I don't think I heard of it until the next morning, but they may have told my wife before that. I shall ask her if you wish."

"And you know of no other possible reason for their running away?"

"None. I can't think that our dispute over money—by no means an unusual one—had anything to do with it."

"What does their mother think?"

"Their mother is dead," Banbrock corrected me. "My wife is their stepmother. She is only two years older than Myra, my older daughter. She is as much at sea as I."

"Did your daughters and their stepmother get along all right together?"

"Yes! Yes! Excellently! If there was a division in the family, I usually found them standing together against me."

"Your daughters left Friday afternoon?"

"At noon, or a few minutes after. They were going to drive down."

"The car, of course, is still missing?"

"Naturally."

"What was it?"

"A Locomobile, with a special cabriolet body. Black."

"You can give me the license and engine numbers?"

"I think so."

He turned in his chair to the big roll-top desk that hid a quarter of one office wall, fumbled with papers in a compartment, and read the numbers over his shoulder to me. I put them on the back of an envelope.

"I'm going to have this car put on the police department list of stolen machines," I told him. "It can be done without mentioning your daughters. The police bulletin might find the car for us. That would help us find your daughters."

"Very well," he agreed, "if it can be done without disagreeable publicity. As I told you at first, I don't want any more advertising than is absolutely necessary—unless it becomes likely that harm has come to the girls."

I nodded understanding, and got up.

"I want to go out and talk to your wife," I said. "Is she home now?"

"Yes, I think so. I'll phone her and tell her you are coming."

II

In a big limestone fortress on top a hill in Sea Cliff, looking down on ocean and bay, I had my talk with Mrs Banbrock. She was a tall dark girl of not more than twenty-two years, inclined to plumpness.

She couldn't tell me anything her husband hadn't at least mentioned, but she could give me finer details.

I got descriptions of the two girls:

Myra—20 years old; 5 feet 8 inches; 150 pounds; athletic; brisk, almost masculine manner and carriage; bobbed brown hair; brown eyes; medium complexion; square face, with large chin and short nose; scar over left ear, concealed by hair; fond of horses and all outdoor sports. When she left the house she wore a blue and green wool dress, small blue hat, short black seal coat, and black slippers.

Ruth—18 years; 5 feet 4 inches; 105 pounds; brown eyes; brown bobbed hair; medium complexion; small oval face; quiet, timid, inclined to lean on her more forceful sister. When last seen she had worn a tobacco-brown coat trimmed with brown fur over a gray silk dress, and a wide brown hat.

I got two photographs of each girl, and an additional snapshot of Myra standing in front of the cabriolet. I got a list of the things they had taken with them—such things as would naturally be taken on a week-end visit. What I valued most of what I got was a list of their friends, relatives, and other acquaintances, so far as Mrs Banbrock knew them.

"Did they mention Mrs Walden's invitation before their quarrel with Mr Banbrock?" I asked, when I had my lists stowed away.

"I don't think so," Mrs Banbrock said thoughtfully. "I didn't connect the two things at all. They didn't really quarrel with their father, you know. It wasn't harsh enough to be called a quarrel."

"Did you see them when they left?"

"Assuredly! They left at about half-past twelve Friday afternoon. They kissed me as usual when they went, and there was certainly nothing in their manner to suggest anything out of the ordinary."

"You've no idea at all where they might have gone?"

"None."

"Can't even make a guess?"

"I can't. Among the names and addresses I have given you are some of friends and relatives of the girls in other cities. They may have gone to one of those. Do you think we should—?"

"I'll take care of that," I promised. "Could you pick out one or two of them as the most likely places for the girls to have gone?"

She wouldn't try it.

"No," she said positively, "I could not."

From this interview I went back to the agency, and put the agency machinery in motion; arranging to have operatives from some of the Continental's other branches call on the out-of-town names on my list; having the missing Locomobile put on the police department list; turning one photograph of each girl over to a photographer to be copied.

That done, I set out to talk to the persons on the list Mrs Banbrock had given me. My first call was on a Constance Delee, in an apartment building on Post Street. I saw a maid. The maid said Miss Delee was out of town. She wouldn't tell me where her mistress was, or when she would be back.

From there I went up on Van Ness Avenue and found a Wayne Ferris in an automobile salesroom: a sleek-haired young man whose very nice manners and clothes completely hid anything else—brains for instance—he might have had. He was very willing to help me, and he knew nothing. It took him a long time to tell me so. A nice boy.

Another blank: "Mrs Scott is in Honolulu."

In a real estate office on Montgomery Street I found my next one—another sleek, stylish, smooth-haired young man with nice manners and nice clothes. His name was Raymond Elwood. I would have thought him a no more distant relative of Ferris than cousin if I hadn't known that the world—especially the dancing, teaing world—was full of their sort. I learned nothing from him.

Then I drew some more blanks: "Out of town,"

"Shopping,"

"I don't know where you can find him."

I found one more of the Banbrock girls' friends before I called it a day. Her name was Mrs Stewart Correll. She lived in Presidio Terrace, not far from the Banbrocks. She was a small woman, or girl, of about Mrs Banbrock's age. A little fluffy blonde person with wide eyes of that particular blue which always looks honest and candid no matter what is going on behind it.

"I haven't seen either Ruth or Myra for two weeks or more," she said in answer to my question.

"At that time—the last time you saw them—did either say anything about going away?"

"No."

Her eyes were wide and frank. A little muscle twitched in her upper lip.

"And you've no idea where they might have gone?"

"No."

Her fingers were rolling her lace handkerchief into a little ball.

"Have you heard from them since you last saw them?"

"No."

She moistened her mouth before she said it.

"Will you give me the names and addresses of all the people you know who were also known by the Banbrock girls?"

"Why—? Is there—?"

"There's a chance that some of them may have seen them more recently than you," I explained. "Or may even have seen them since Friday."

Without enthusiasm, she gave me a dozen names. All were already on my list. Twice she hesitated as if about to speak a name she did not want to speak. Her eyes stayed on mine, wide and honest. Her fingers, no longer balling the handkerchief, picked at the cloth of her skirt.

I didn't pretend to believe her. But my feet weren't solidly enough on the ground for me to put her on the grill. I gave her a promise before I left, one that she could get a threat out of if she liked.

"Thanks, very much," I said. "I know it's hard to remember things exactly. If I run across anything that will help your memory, I'll be back to let you know about it."

"Wha—? Yes, do!" she said.

Walking away from the house, I turned my head to look back just before I passed out of sight. A curtain swung into place at a second-floor window. The street lights weren't bright enough for me to be sure the curtain had swung in front of a blonde head.

My watch told me it was nine-thirty: too late to line up any more of the girls' friends. I went home, wrote my report for the day, and turned in, thinking more about Mrs Correll than about the girls.

She seemed worth an investigation.

III

Some telegraphic reports were in when I got to the office the next morning. None was of any value. Investigation of the names and addresses in other cities had revealed nothing. An investigation in Monterey had established reasonably—which is about as well as anything is ever established in the detecting business—that the girls had not been there recently; that the Locomobile had not been there.

The early editions of the afternoon papers were on the street when I went out to get some breakfast before taking up the grind where I had dropped it the previous night. I bought a paper to prop behind my grapefruit.

It spoiled my breakfast for me.

BANKER'S WIFE SUICIDE

> Mrs Stewart Correll, wife of the vice-president of the Golden Gate Trust Company, was found dead early this morning by her maid in her bedroom, in her home in Presidio Terrace. A bottle believed to have contained poison was on the floor beside the bed.
>
> The dead woman's husband could give no reason for his wife's suicide. He said she had not seemed depressed or...

I gave my eggs and toast a quick play, put my coffee down in a lump, and got going.

At the Correll residence I had to do a lot of talking before I could get to Correll. He was a tall, slim man of less than thirty-five, with a sallow, nervous face and blue eyes that fidgeted.

"I'm sorry to disturb you at a time like this," I apologized when I had finally insisted my way into his presence. "I won't take up more of your time than necessary. I am an operative of the Continental Detective Agency. I have been trying to find Ruth and Myra Banbrock, who disappeared several days ago. You know them, I think."

"Yes," he said without interest. "I know them."

"You knew they had disappeared?"

"No." His eyes switched from a chair to a rug. "Why should I?"

"Have you seen either of them recently?" I asked, ignoring his question.

"Last week—Wednesday, I think. They were just leaving—standing at the door talking to my wife—when I came home from the bank."

"Didn't your wife say anything to you about their vanishing?"

"No. Really, I can't tell you anything about the Misses Banbrock. If you'll excuse me—"

"Just a moment longer," I said. "I wouldn't have bothered you if it hadn't been necessary. I was here last night, to question Mrs Correll. She seemed nervous. My impression was that some of her answers to my questions were—uh—evasive. I want—"

He was up out of his chair. His face was red in front of mine.

"You!" he cried. "I can thank you for—"

"Now, Mr Correll," I tried to quiet him, "there's no use—"

But he had himself all worked up.

"You drove my wife to her death," he accused me. "You killed her with your damned prying—with your bulldozing threats; with your—"

That was silly. I felt sorry for this young man whose wife had killed herself. Apart from that, I had work to do. I tightened the screws.

"We won't argue, Correll," I told him. "The point is that I came here to see if your wife could tell me anything about the Banbrocks. She told me less than the truth. Later, she committed suicide. I want to know why. Come through for me, and I'll do what I can to keep the papers and the public from linking her death with the girls' disappearance."

"Linking her death with their disappearance?" he exclaimed. "That's absurd!"

"Maybe—but the connection is there!" I hammered away at him. I felt sorry for him, but I had work to do. "It's there. If you'll give it to me, maybe it won't have to be advertised. I'm going to get it, though. You give it to me—or I'll go after it out in the open."

For a moment I thought he was going to take a poke at me. I wouldn't have blamed him. His body stiffened—then sagged, and he dropped back into his chair. His eyes fidgeted away from mine.

"There's nothing I can tell," he mumbled. "When her maid went to her room to call her this morning, she was dead. There was no message, no reason, nothing."

"Did you see her last night?"

"No. I was not home for dinner. I came in late and went straight to my own room, not wanting to disturb her. I hadn't seen her since I left the house that morning."

"Did she seem disturbed or worried then?"

"No."

"Why do you think she did it?"

"My God, man, I don't know! I've thought and thought, but I don't know!"

"Health?"

"She seemed well. She was never ill, never complained."

"Any recent quarrels?"

"We never quarreled—never in the year and a half we have been married!"

"Financial trouble?"

He shook his head without speaking or looking up from the floor.

"Any other worry?"

He shook his head again.

"Did the maid notice anything peculiar in her behavior last night?"

"Nothing."

"Have you looked through her things—for papers, letters?"

"Yes—and found nothing." He raised his head to look at me. "The only thing"—he spoke very slowly—"there was a little pile of ashes in the grate in her room, as if she had burned papers, or letters."

Correl held nothing more for me—nothing I could get out of him, anyway.

The girl at the front gate in Alfred Banbrock's Shoreman's Building suite told me he was *in conference.* I sent my name in. He came out of conference to take me into his private office. His tired face was full of questions.

I didn't keep him waiting for the answers. He was a grown man. I didn't edge around the bad news.

"Things have taken a bad break," I said as soon as we were locked in together. "I think we'll have to go to the police and newspapers for help. A Mrs Correll, a friend of your daughters, lied to me when I questioned her yesterday. Last night she committed suicide."

"Irma Correll? Suicide?"

"You knew her?"

"Yes! Intimately! She was—that is, she was a close friend of my wife and daughters. She killed herself?"

"Yes. Poison. Last night. Where does she fit in with your daughters' disappearance?"

"Where?" he repeated. "I don't know. Must she fit in?"

"I think she must. She told me she hadn't seen your daughters for a couple of weeks. Her husband told me just now that they were talking to her when he came home from the bank last Wednesday afternoon. She seemed nervous when I questioned her. She killed herself shortly afterward. There's hardly a doubt that she fits in somewhere."

"And that means—?"

"That means," I finished for him, "that your daughters may be perfectly safe, but that we can't afford to gamble on that possibility."

"You think harm has come to them?"

"I don't think anything," I evaded, "except that with a death tied up closely with their going, we can't afford to play around."

Banbrock got his attorney on the phone—a pink-faced, white-haired old boy named Norwall, who had the reputation of knowing more about corporations than all the Morgans, but who hadn't the least idea as to what police procedure was all about—and told him to meet us at the Hall of Justice.

We spent an hour and a half there, getting the police turned loose on the affair, and giving the newspapers what we wanted them to have. That was plenty of dope on the girls, plenty of photographs and so forth; but nothing about the connection between them and Mrs Correll. Of course we let the police in on that angle.

IV

After Banbrock and his attorney had gone away together, I went back to the detectives' assembly room to chew over the job with Pat Reddy, the police sleuth assigned to it.

Pat was the youngest member of the detective bureau—a big blond Irishman who went in for the spectacular in his lazy way.

A couple of years ago he was a new copper, pounding his feet in harness on a hillside beat. One night he tagged an automobile that was parked in front of a fireplug. The owner came out just then and gave him an argument. She was Althea Wallach, only and spoiled daughter of the owner of the Wallach Coffee Company—a slim, reckless youngster with hot eyes. She must have told Pat plenty. He took her over to the station and dumped her in a cell.

Old Wallach, so the story goes, showed up the next morning with a full head of steam and half the lawyers in San Francisco. But Pat made his charge stick, and the girl was fined. Old Wallach did everything but take a punch at Pat in the corridor afterward. Pat grinned his sleepy grin at the coffee importer, and drawled:

"You better lay off me—or I'll stop drinking your coffee."

That crack got into most of the newspapers in the country, and even into a Broadway show.

But Pat didn't stop with the snappy comeback. Three days later he and Althea Wallach went over to Alameda and got themselves married. I was in on that part. I happened to be on the ferry they took, and they dragged me along to see the deed done.

Old Wallach immediately disowned his daughter, but that didn't seem to worry anybody else. Pat went on pounding his beat, but, now that he was conspicuous, it wasn't long before his qualities were noticed. He was boosted into the detective bureau. Old Wallach relented before he died, and left Althea both of his millions.

Pat took the afternoon off to go to the funeral, and went back to work that night, catching a wagonload of gunmen. He kept on working. I don't know what his wife did with her money, but Pat didn't even improve the quality of his cigars—though he should have. He lived now in the Wallach mansion, true enough, and now and then on rainy mornings he would be driven down to the Hall in a Hispano-Suiza brougham; but there was no difference in him beyond that.

That was the big blond Irishman who sat across a desk from me in the assembly room and fumigated me with something shaped like a cigar.

He took the cigar-like thing out of his mouth presently, and spoke through the fumes.

"This Correll woman you think's tied up with the Banbrocks—she was stuck-up a couple of months back and nicked for eight hundred dollars. Know that?"

I hadn't known it.

"Lose anything besides cash?" I asked.

"No."

"You believe it?"

He grinned.

"That's the point," he said. "We didn't catch the bird who did it. With women who lose things that way—especially money—it's always a question whether it's a hold-up or a hold-out."

He teased some more poison-gas out of the cigar-thing, and added:

"The hold-up might have been on the level, though. What are you figuring on doing now?"

"Let's go up to the agency and see if anything new has turned up. Then I'd like to talk to Mrs Banbrock again. Maybe she can tell us something about the Correll woman."

At the office I found that reports had come in on the rest of the out-of-town names and addresses. Apparently none of these people knew anything about the girls' whereabouts. Reddy and I went on up to Sea Cliff to the Banbrock home.

Banbrock had telephoned the news of Mrs Correll's death to his wife, and she had read the papers. She told us she could think of no reason for the suicide. She could imagine no possible connection between the suicide and her stepdaughters' vanishing.

"Mrs Correll seemed as nearly contented and happy as usual the last time I saw her, two or three weeks ago," Mrs Banbrock said. "Of course she was by nature inclined to be dissatisfied with things, but not to the extent of doing a thing like this."

"Do you know of any trouble between her and her husband?"

"No. So far as I know, they were happy, though—"

She broke off. Hesitancy, embarrassment showed in her dark eyes.

"Though?" I repeated.

"If I don't tell you now, you'll think I am hiding something," she said, flushing, and laughing a little laugh that held more nervousness than amusement. "It hasn't any bearing, but I was always just a little jealous of Irma. She and my husband were—well, everyone thought they would marry. That was a little before he and I married. I never let it show, and I dare say it was a foolish idea, but I always had a suspicion that Irma married Stewart more in pique than for any other reason, and that she was still fond of Alfred—Mr Banbrock."

"Was there anything definite to make you think that?"

"No, nothing—really! I never thoroughly believed it. It was just a sort of vague feeling. Cattiness, no doubt, more than anything else."

It was getting along toward evening when Pat and I left the Banbrock house. Before we knocked off for the day, I called up the Old Man—the Continental's San Francisco branch manager, and therefore my boss—and asked him to sic an operative on Irma Correll's past.

I took a look at the morning papers—thanks to their custom of appearing almost as soon as the sun is out of sight—before I went to bed. They had given our job a good spread. All the facts except those having to do with the Correll angle were there, plus photographs, and the usual assortment of guesses and similar garbage.

The following morning I went after the friends of the missing girls to whom I had not yet talked. I found some of them, and got nothing of value from them. Late in the morning I telephoned the office to see if anything new had turned up.

It had.

"We've just had a call from the sheriff's office at Martinez," the Old Man told me. "An Italian grape-grower near Knob

Valley picked up a charred photograph a couple of days ago, and recognized it as Ruth Banbrock when he saw her picture in this morning's paper. Will you get up there? A deputy sheriff and the Italian are waiting for you in the Knob Valley marshal's office."

"I'm on my way," I said.

At the ferry building I used the four minutes before my boat left trying to get Pat Reddy on the phone, with no success.

Knob Valley is a town of less than a thousand people, a dreary, dirty town in Contra Costa county. A San Francisco-Sacramento local set me down there while the afternoon was still young.

I knew the marshal slightly—Tom Orth. I found two men in the office with him. Orth introduced us. Abner Paget, a gawky man of forty-something, with a slack chin, scrawny face, and pale intelligent eyes, was the deputy sheriff. Gio Cereghino, the Italian grape-grower, was a small, nut-brown man with strong yellow teeth that showed in an everlasting smile under his black mustache, and soft brown eyes.

Paget showed me the photograph. A scorched piece of paper the size of a half-dollar, apparently all that had not been burned of the original picture. It was Ruth Banbrock's face. There was little room for doubting that. She had a peculiarly excited—almost drunken—look, and her eyes were larger than in the other pictures of her I had seen. But it was her face.

"He says he found it day 'fore yesterday," Paget explained dryly, nodding at the Italian. "The wind blew it against his foot when he was walkin' up a piece of road near his place. He picked it up an' stuck it in his pocket, he says, for no special reason, I guess, except maybe that guineas like pictures."

He paused to regard the Italian meditatively. The Italian nodded his head in vigorous affirmation.

"Anyways," the deputy sheriff went on, "he was in town this mornin', an' seen the pictures in the papers from Frisco. So he come in here an' told Tom about it. Tom an' me decided the best thing was to phone your agency—since the papers said you was workin' on it."

I looked at the Italian.

Paget, reading my mind, explained:

"Cereghino lives over in the hills. Got a grape-ranch there. Been around here five or six years, an' ain't killed nobody that I know of."

"Remember the place where you found the picture?" I asked the Italian.

His grin broadened under his mustache, and his head went up and down.

"For sure, I remember that place."

"Let's go there," I suggested to Paget.

"Right. Comin' along, Tom?"

The marshal said he couldn't. He had something to do in town. Cereghino, Paget and I went out and got into a dusty Ford that the deputy sheriff drove.

We rode for nearly an hour, along a county road that bent up the slope of Mount Diablo. After a while, at a word from the Italian, we left the county road for a dustier and ruttier one.

A mile of this one.

"This place," Cereghino said.

Paget stopped the Ford. We got out in a clearing. The trees and bushes that had crowded the road retreated here for twenty feet or so on either side, leaving a little dusty circle in the woods.

"About this place," the Italian was saying. "I think by this stump. But between that bend ahead and that one behind, I know for sure."

V

Paget was a countryman. I am not. I waited for him to move.

He looked around the clearing, slowly, standing still between the Italian and me. His pale eyes lighted presently. He went around the Ford to the far side of the clearing. Cereghino and I followed.

Near the fringe of brush at the edge of the clearing, the scrawny deputy stopped to grunt at the ground. The wheel-marks of an automobile were there. A car had turned around here.

Paget went on into the woods. The Italian kept close to his heels. I brought up the rear. Paget was following some sort of track. I couldn't see it, either because he and the Italian blotted it out ahead of me, or because I'm a shine Indian.

We went back quite a way.

Paget stopped. The Italian stopped.

Paget said, "Uh-huh," as if he had found an expected thing.

The Italian said something with the name of God in it.

I trampled a bush, coming beside them to see what they saw.

I saw it.

At the base of a tree, on her side, her knees drawn up close to her body, a girl was dead.

She wasn't nice to see. Birds had been at her.

A tobacco-brown coat was half on, half off her shoulders. I knew she was Ruth Banbrock before I turned her over to look at the side of her face the ground had saved from the birds.

Cereghino stood watching me while I examined the girl. His face was mournful in a calm way. The deputy sheriff paid little attention to the body. He was off in the brush, moving around, looking at the ground.

He came back as I finished my examination.

"Shot," I told him, "once in the right temple. Before that, I think, there was a fight. There are marks on the arm that was under her body. There's nothing on her—no jewelry, money—nothing."

"That goes," Paget said. "Two women got out of the car back in the clearin', an' came here. Could've been three women—if the others carried this one. Can't make out how many went back. One of 'em was larger than this one. There was a scuffle here. Find the gun?"

"No," I said.

"Neither did I. It went away in the car, then. There's what's left of a fire over there." He ducked his head to the left. "Paper an' rags burnt. Not enough left to do us any good. I reckon the photo Cereghino found blew away from the fire. Late Friday, I'd put it, or maybe Saturday mornin'... No nearer than that."

I took the deputy sheriff's word for it. He seemed to know his stuff.

"Come here. I'll show you somethin'," he said, and led me over to a little black pile of ashes.

He hadn't anything to show me. He wanted to talk to me away from the Italian's ears.

"I think the guinea's all right," he said, "but I reckon I'd best hold him a while to make sure. This is some way from his place, an' he stuttered a little bit too much tellin' me how he happened to be passin' here. Course, that don't mean nothin' much. All these guineas peddle *vino*, an' I guess that's what brought him out this way. I'll hold him a day or two, anyways."

"Good," I agreed. "This is your country, and you know the people. Can you visit around and see what you can pick up? Whether anybody saw anything? Saw a Locomobile cabriolet? Or anything else? You can get more than I could."

"I'll do that," he promised.

"All right. Then I'll go back to San Francisco now. I suppose you'll want to camp here with the body?"

"Yeah. You drive the Ford back to Knob Valley, an' tell Tom what's what. He'll come or send out. I'll keep the guinea here with me."

Waiting for the next west-bound train out of Knob Valley, I got the office on the telephone. The Old Man was out. I told my story to one of the office men and asked him to get the news to the Old Man as soon as he could.

Everybody was in the office when I got back to San Francisco. Alfred Banbrock, his face a pink-gray that was deader than solid gray could have been. His pink and white old lawyer. Pat Reddy, sprawled on his spine with his feet on another chair. The Old Man, with his gentle eyes behind gold spectacles and his mild smile, hiding the fact that fifty years of sleuthing had left him without any feelings at all on any subject. (Whitey Clayton used to say the Old Man could spit icicles in August.)

Nobody said anything when I came in. I said my say as briefly as possible.

"Then the other woman—the woman who killed Ruth was—?"

Banbrock didn't finish his question. Nobody answered it.

"We don't know what happened," I said after a while. "Your daughter and someone we don't know may have gone there. Your daughter may have been dead before she was taken there. She may have—"

"But Myra!" Banbrock was pulling at his collar with a finger inside. "Where is Myra?"

I couldn't answer that, nor could any of the others.

"You are going up to Knob Valley now?" I asked him.

"Yes, at once. You will come with me?"

I wasn't sorry I could not.

"No. There are things to be done here. I'll give you a note to the marshal. I want you to look carefully at the piece of your daughter's photograph the Italian found—to see if you remember it."

Banbrock and the lawyer left.

VI

Reddy lit one of his awful cigars. "We found the car," the Old Man said.

"Where?"

"In Sacramento. It was left in a garage there either late Friday night or early Saturday. Foley has gone up to investigate it. And Reddy has uncovered a new angle."

Pat nodded through his smoke.

"A hock-shop dealer came in this morning," Pat said, "and told us that Myra Banbrock and another girl came to his joint last week and hocked a lot of stuff. They gave him phoney names, but he swears one of them was Myra. He recognized her picture as soon as he saw it in the paper. Her companion wasn't Ruth. It was a little blonde."

"Mrs Correll?"

"Uh-huh. The shark can't swear to that, but I think that's the answer. Some of the jewelry was Myra's, some Ruth's, and some we don't know; I mean we can't prove it belonged to Mrs Correll—though we will."

"When did all this happen?"

"They soaked the stuff Monday before they went away."

"Have you seen Correll?"

"Uh-huh," Pat said. "I did a lot of talking to him, but the answers weren't worth much. He says he don't know whether any of her jewelry is gone or not, and doesn't care. It was hers, he says, and she could do anything she wanted with it. He was kind of disagreeable. I got along a little better with one of the maids. She says some of Mrs Correll's pretties disappeared last week. Mrs Correll said she had lent them to a friend. I'm going to show the stuff the hock-shop has to the maid tomorrow, to see if she can identify it. She didn't know anything else—except that Mrs Correll was out of the picture for a while on Friday—the day the Banbrock girls went away."

"What do you mean, out of the picture?" I asked.

"She went out late in the morning and didn't show up until somewhere around three the next morning. She and Correll had a row over it, but she wouldn't tell him where she had been."

I liked that. It could mean something.

"And," Pat went on, "Correll has just remembered that his wife had an uncle who went crazy in Pittsburgh in 1902, and that she had a morbid fear of going crazy herself, and that she had often said she would kill herself if she thought she was going crazy. Wasn't it nice of him to remember those things at last? To account for her death?"

"It was," I agreed, "but it doesn't get us anywhere. It doesn't even prove that he knows anything. Now my guess is—"

"To hell with your guess," Pat said, getting up and pushing his hat in place. "Your guesses all sound like a lot of static to me. I'm going home, eat my dinner, read my Bible, and go to bed."

I suppose he did. Anyway, he left us.

We all might as well have spent the next three days in bed for all the profit that came out of our running around. No place we visited, nobody we questioned, added to our knowledge. We were in a blind alley.

We learned that the Locomobile was left in Sacramento by Myra Banbrock, and not by anyone else, but we didn't learn where she went afterward. We learned that some of the jewelry in the pawnshop was Mrs Correll's. The Locomobile was brought back from Sacramento. Mrs Correll was buried. Ruth Banbrock was buried. The newspapers found other mysteries. Reddy and I dug and dug, and all we brought up was dirt.

The following Monday brought me close to the end of my rope. There seemed nothing more to do but sit back and hope that the circulars with which we had plastered North America would bring results. Reddy had already been called off and put to running out fresher trails. I hung on because Banbrock wanted me to keep at it so long as there was the shadow of anything to keep at. But by Monday I had worked myself out.

Before going to Banbrock's office to tell him I was licked, I dropped in at the Hall of Justice to hold a wake over the job with Pat Reddy. He was crouched over his desk, writing a report on some other job.

"Hello!" he greeted me, pushing his report away and smearing it with ashes from his cigar. "How do the Banbrock doings?"

"They don't," I admitted. "It doesn't seem possible, with the stack-up what it is, that we should have come to a dead stop! It's there for us, if we can find it. The need of money before both the Banbrock and the Correll calamities: Mrs Correll's suicide after I had questioned her about the girls; her burning things before she died and the burning of things immediately before or after Ruth Banbrock's death."

"Maybe the trouble is," Pat suggested, "that you're not such a good sleuth."

"Maybe."

We smoked in silence for a minute or two after that insult.

"You understand," Pat said presently, "there doesn't have to be any connection between the Banbrock death and disappearance and the Correll death."

"Maybe not. But there has to be a connection between the Banbrock death and the Banbrock disappearance. There was a connection—in a pawnshop—between the Banbrock and Correll actions before these things. If there is that connection, then—"

I broke off, all full of ideas.

"What's the matter?" Pat asked. "Swallow your gum?"

"Listen!" I let myself get almost enthusiastic. "We've got what happened to three women hooked up together. If we could tie up some more in the same string—I want the names and addresses of all the women and girls in San Francisco who have committed suicide, been murdered, or have disappeared within the past year."

"You think this is a wholesale deal?"

"I think the more we can tie up together, the more lines we'll have to run out. And they can't all lead nowhere. Let's get our list, Pat!"

We spent all the afternoon and most of the night getting it. Its size would have embarrassed the Chamber of Commerce. It looked like a hunk of the telephone book. Things happen in a city in a year. The section devoted to strayed wives and daughters was the largest; suicides next; and even the smallest division—murders—wasn't any too short.

We could check off most of the names against what the police department had already learned of them and their motives, weeding out those positively accounted for in a manner nowise connected with our present interest. The remainder we split into two classes; those of unlikely connection, and those of more possible connection. Even then, the second list was longer than I had expected, or hoped.

There were six suicides in it, three murders, and twenty-one disappearances.

Reddy had other work to do. I put the list in my pocket and went calling.

VII

For four days I ground at the list. I hunted, found, questioned, and investigated friends and relatives of the women and girls on my list. My questions all hit in the same direction. Had she been acquainted with Myra Banbrock? Ruth? Mrs Correll? Had she been in need of money before her death or disappearance?

Had she destroyed anything before her death or disappearance? Had she known any of the other women on my list?

Three times I drew yeses.

Sylvia Varney, a girl of twenty, who had killed herself on November 5th, had drawn six hundred dollars from the bank the week before her death. No one in her family could say what she had done with the money. A friend of Sylvia Varney's—Ada Youngman, a married woman of twenty-five or -six—had disappeared on December 2nd, and was still gone. The Varney girl had been at Mrs Youngman's home an hour before she—the Varney girl—killed herself.

Mrs Dorothy Sawdon, a young widow, had shot herself on the night of January 13th. No trace was found of either the money her husband had left her or the funds of a club whose treasurer she was. A bulky letter her maid remembered having given her that afternoon was never found.

These three women's connection with the Banbrock-Correll affair was sketchy enough. None of them had done anything that isn't done by nine out of ten women who kill themselves or run away. But the troubles of all three had come to a head within the past few months—and all three were women of about the same financial and social position as Mrs Correll and the Banbrocks.

Finishing my list with no fresh leads, I came back to these three.

I had the names and addresses of sixty-two friends of the Banbrock girls. I set about getting the same sort of catalogue on the three women I was trying to bring into the game. I didn't have to do all the digging myself. Fortunately, there were two or three operatives in the office with nothing else to do just then.

We got something.

Mrs Sawdon had known Raymond Elwood. Sylvia Varney had known Raymond Elwood. There was nothing to show Mrs

Youngman had known him, but it was likely she had. She and the Varney girl had been thick.

I had already interviewed this Raymond Elwood in connection with the Banbrock girls, but had paid no especial attention to him. I had considered him just one of the sleek-headed, high-polished young men of whom there was quite a few listed.

I went back at him, all interest now; the results were promising.

He had, as I have said, a real estate office on Montgomery Street. We were unable to find a single client he had ever served, or any signs of one's existence. He had an apartment out in the Sunset District, where he lived alone. His local record seemed to go back no farther than ten months, though we couldn't find its definite starting point. Apparently he had no relatives in San Francisco. He belonged to a couple of fashionable clubs. He was vaguely supposed to be "well connected in the East." He spent money.

I couldn't shadow Elwood, having too recently interviewed him. Dick Foley did. Elwood was seldom in his office during the first three days Dick tailed him. He was seldom in the financial district. He visited his clubs, he danced and tead and so forth, and each of those three days he visited a house on Telegraph Hill.

The first afternoon Dick had him, Elwood went to the Telegraph Hill house with a tall fair girl from Burlingame. The second day—in the evening—with a plump young woman who came out of a house out on Broadway. The third evening with a very young girl who seemed to live in the same building as he.

Usually Elwood and his companion spent from three to four hours in the house on Telegraph Hill. Other people—all apparently well-to-do—went in and out of the house while it was under Dick's eye.

I climbed Telegraph Hill to give the house the up-and-down. It was a large house—a big frame house painted egg-yellow. It hung dizzily on a shoulder of the hill, a shoulder that was sharp where rock had been quarried away. The house seemed about to go skiing down on the roofs far below.

It had no immediate neighbors. The approach was screened by bushes and trees.

I gave that section of the hill a good strong play, calling at all the houses within shooting distance of the yellow one. Nobody knew anything about it, or about its occupants. The folks on the Hill aren't a curious lot—perhaps because most of them have something to hide on their own account.

My climbing uphill and downhill got me nothing until I succeeded in learning who owned the yellow house. The owner was an estate whose affairs were in the hands of the West Coast Trust Company.

I took my investigations to the trust company, with some satisfaction. The house had been leased eight months ago by Raymond Elwood, acting for a client named T. F. Maxwell.

We couldn't find Maxwell. We couldn't find anybody who knew Maxwell. We couldn't find any evidence that Maxwell was anything but a name.

One of the operatives went up to the yellow house on the hill, and rang the bell for half an hour with no result. We didn't try that again, not wanting to stir things up at this stage.

I made another trip up the hill, house-hunting. I couldn't find a place as near the yellow house as I would have liked, but I succeeded in renting a three-room flat from which the approach to it could be watched.

Dick and I camped in the flat—with Pat Reddy, when he wasn't off on other duties—and watched machines turn into the screened path that led to the egg-tinted house. Afternoon and night there were machines. Most of them carried women. We saw no one we could place as a resident of the house.

Elwood came daily, once alone, the other time with women whose faces we couldn't see from our window.

We shadowed some of the visitors away. They were without exception reasonably well off financially, and some were socially prominent. We didn't go up against any of them with talk. Even a carefully planned pretext is as likely as not to tip your mitt when you're up against a blind game.

Three days of this—and our break came.

It was early evening, just dark. Pat Reddy had phoned that he had been up on a job for two days and a night, and was going to sleep the clock around. Dick and I were sitting at the window of our flat, watching automobiles turn toward the yellow house, writing down their license numbers as they passed through the blue-white patch of light an arc-lamp put in the road just beyond our window.

A woman came climbing the hill, afoot. She was a tall woman, strongly built. A dark veil, not thick enough to advertise the fact that she wore it to hide her features, nevertheless did hide them. Her way was up the hill, past our flat, on the other side of the roadway.

A night-wind from the Pacific was creaking a grocer's sign down below, swaying the arc-light above. The wind caught the woman as she passed out of our building's sheltered area. Coat and skirts tangled. She put her back to the wind, a hand to her hat. Her veil whipped out straight from her face.

Her face was a face from a photograph—Myra Banbrock's face.

Dick made her with me.

"Our Baby!" he cried, bouncing to his feet.

"Wait," I said. "She's going into the joint on the edge of the hill. Let her go. We'll go after her when she's inside. That's our excuse for frisking the joint."

I went into the next room, where our telephone was, and called Pat Reddy's number.

"She didn't go in," Dick called from the window. "She went past the path."

"After her!" I ordered. "There's no sense to that! What's the matter with her?" I felt sort of indignant about it. "She's got to go in! Tail her. I'll find you after I get Pat."

Dick went.

Pat's wife answered the telephone. I told her who I was.

"Will you shake Pat out of the covers and send him up here? He knows where I am. Tell him I want him in a hurry."

"I will," she promised. "I'll have him there in ten minutes—wherever it is."

Outdoors, I went up the road, hunting for Dick and Myra Banbrock. Neither was in sight. Passing the bushes that masked the yellow house, I went on, circling down a stony path to the left. No sign of either.

I turned back in time to see Dick going into our flat. I followed.

"She's in," he said when I joined him. "She went up the road, cut across through some bushes, came back to the edge of the cliff, and slid feet-first through a cellar window."

That was nice. The crazier the people you are sleuthing act, as a rule, the nearer you are to an ending of your troubles.

Reddy arrived within a minute or two of the time his wife had promised. He came in buttoning his clothes.

"What the hell did you tell Althea?" he growled at me. "She gave me an overcoat to put over my pajamas, dumped the rest of my clothes in the car, and I had to get in them on the way over."

"I'll cry with you after awhile," I dismissed his troubles. "Myra Banbrock just went into the joint through a cellar window. Elwood has been there an hour. Let's knock it off."

Pat is deliberate.

"We ought to have papers, even at that," he stalled.

"Sure," I agreed, "but you can get them fixed up afterward. That's what you're here for. Contra Costa county wants her—maybe to try her for murder. That's all the excuse we need to get into the joint. We go there for her. If we happen to run into anything else—well and good."

Pat finished buttoning his vest.

"Oh, all right!" he said sourly. "Have it your way. But if you get me smashed for searching a house without authority, you'll have to give me a job with your law-breaking agency."

"I will." I turned to Foley. "You'll have to stay outside, Dick. Keep your eye on the getaway. Don't bother anybody else, but if the Banbrock girl gets out, stay behind her."

"I expected it," Dick howled. "Any time there's any fun I can count on being stuck off somewhere on a street corner!"

VIII

Pat Reddy and I went straight up the bush-hidden path to the yellow house's front door, and rang the bell.

A big black man in a red fez, red silk jacket over red-striped silk shirt, red zouave pants and red slippers, opened the door. He filled the opening, framed in the black of the hall behind him.

"Is Mr Maxwell home?" I asked.

The black man shook his head and said words in a language I don't know.

"Mr Elwood, then?"

Another shaking of the head. More strange language.

"Let's see whoever is home then," I insisted.

Out of the jumble of words that meant nothing to me, I picked three in garbled English, which I thought were "master," "not," and "home."

The door began to close. I put a foot against it.

Pat flashed his buzzer.

Though the black man had poor English, he had knowledge of police badges.

One of his feet stamped on the floor behind him. A gong boomed deafeningly in the rear of the house.

The black man bent his weight to the door.

My weight on the foot that blocked the door, I leaned sidewise, swaying to the negro.

Slamming from the hip, I put my fist in the middle of him.

Reddy hit the door and we went into the hall.

"'Fore God, Fat Shorty," the black man gasped in good black Virginian, "you done hurt me!"

Reddy and I went by him, down the hall whose bounds were lost in darkness.

The bottom of a flight of steps stopped my feet.

A gun went off upstairs. It seemed to point at us. We didn't get the bullets.

A babel of voices—women screaming, men shouting—came and went upstairs; came and went as if a door was being opened and shut.

"Up, my boy!" Reddy yelped in my ear.

We went up the stairs. We didn't find the man who had shot at us.

At the head of the stairs, a door was locked. Reddy's bulk forced it.

We came into a bluish light. A large room, all purple and gold. Confusion of overturned furniture and rumpled rugs. A gray slipper lay near a far door. A green silk gown was in the center of the floor. No person was there.

I raced Pat to the curtained door beyond the slipper. The door was not locked. Reddy yanked it wide.

A room with three girls and a man crouching in a corner, fear in their faces. Neither of them was Myra Banbrock, or Raymond Elwood, or anyone we knew.

Our glances went away from them after the first quick look.

The open door across the room grabbed our attention.

The door gave to a small room.

The room was chaos.

A small room, packed and tangled with bodies. Live bodies, seething, writhing. The room was a funnel into which men and women had been poured. They boiled noisily toward the one small window that was the funnel's outlet. Men and women, youths and girls, screaming, struggling, squirming, fighting. Some had no clothes.

"We'll get through and block the window!" Pat yelled in my ear.

"Like hell—" I began, but he was gone ahead into the confusion.

I went after him.

I didn't mean to block the window. I meant to save Pat from his foolishness. No five men could have fought through that boiling turmoil of maniacs. No ten men could have turned them from the window.

Pat—big as he is—was down when I got to him. A half dressed girl—a child—was driving at his face with sharp high-heels. Hands, feet, were tearing him apart.

I cleared him with a play of gun-barrel on shins and wrists—dragged him back.

"Myra's not there!" I yelled into his ear as I helped him up. "Elwood's not there!"

I wasn't sure, but I hadn't seen them, and I doubted that they would be in this mess. These savages, boiling again to the window, with no attention for us, whoever they were, weren't insiders. They were the mob, and the principals shouldn't be among them.

"We'll try the other rooms," I yelled again. "We don't want these." Pat rubbed the back of his hand across his torn face and laughed.

"It's a cinch I don't want 'em any more," he said.

We went back to the head of the stairs the way we had come. We saw no one. The man and girls who had been in the next room were gone.

At the head of the stairs we paused. There was no noise behind us except the now fainter babel of the lunatics fighting for their exit.

A door shut sharply downstairs.

A body came out of nowhere, hit my back, flattened me to the landing.

The feel of silk was on my cheek. A brawny hand was fumbling at my throat.

I bent my wrist until my gun, upside down, lay against my cheek. Praying for my ear, I squeezed.

My cheek took fire. My head was a roaring thing, about to burst.

The silk slid away.

Pat hauled me upright.

We started down the stairs.

Swish!

A thing came past my face, stirring my bared hair.

A thousand pieces of glass, china, plaster, exploded upward at my feet.

I tilted head and gun together.

A negro's red-silk arms were still spread over the balustrade above.

I sent him two bullets. Pat sent him two.

The negro teetered over the rail.

He came down on us, arms out-flung—a dead man's swan-dive.

We scurried down the stairs from under him.

He shook the house when he landed, but we weren't watching him then.

The smooth sleek head of Raymond Elwood took our attention.

In the light from above, it showed for a furtive split-second around the newel-post at the foot of the stairs. Showed and vanished.

Pat Reddy, closer to the rail than I, went over it in a one-hand vault down into the blackness below.

I made the foot of the stairs in two jumps, jerked myself around with a hand on the newel, and plunged into the suddenly noisy dark of the hall.

A wall I couldn't see hit me. Caroming off the opposite wall, I spun into a room whose curtained grayness was the light of day after the hall.

IX

Pat Reddy stood with one hand on a chair-back, holding his belly with the other. His face was mouse-colored under its blood. His eyes were glass agonies. He had the look of a man who had been kicked.

The grin he tried failed. He nodded toward the rear of the house. I went back.

In a little passageway I found Raymond Elwood.

He was sobbing and pulling frantically at a locked door. His face was the hard white of utter terror.

I measured the distance between us.

He turned as I jumped.

I put everything I had in the downswing of my gun-barrel—

A ton of meat and bone crashed into my back.

I went over against the wall, breathless, giddy, sick.

Red-silk arms that ended in brown hands locked around me.

I wondered if there was a whole regiment of these gaudy negroes—or if I was colliding with the same one over and over.

This one didn't let me do much thinking.

He was big. He was strong. He didn't mean any good.

My gun-arm was flat at my side, straight down. I tried a shot at one of the negro's feet. Missed. Tried again. He moved his feet. I wriggled around, half facing him.

Elwood piled on my other side.

The negro bent me backward, folding my spine on itself like an accordion.

I fought to hold my knees stiff. Too much weight was hanging on me. My knees sagged. My body curved back.

Pat Reddy, swaying in the doorway, shone over the negro's shoulder like the Angel Gabriel.

Gray pain was in Pat's face, but his eyes were clear. His right hand held a gun. His left was getting a blackjack out of his hip pocket.

He swung the sap down on the negro's shaven skull.

The black man wheeled away from me, shaking his head.

Pat hit him once more before the negro closed with him—hit him full in the face, but couldn't beat him off.

Twisting my freed gun-hand up, I drilled Elwood neatly through the chest, and let him slide down me to the floor.

The negro had Pat against the wall, bothering him a lot. His broad red back was a target.

But I had used five of the six bullets in my gun. I had more in my pocket, but reloading takes time.

I stepped out of Elwood's feeble hands, and went to work with the flat of my gun on the negro. There was a roll of fat where his skull and neck fit together. The third time I hit it, he flopped, taking Pat with him.

I rolled him off. The blond police detective—not very blond now—got up.

At the other end of the passageway, an open door showed an empty kitchen.

Pat and I went to the door that Elwood had been playing with. It was a solid piece of carpentering, and neatly fastened.

Yoking ourselves together, we began to beat the door with our combined three hundred and seventy or eighty pounds.

It shook, but held. We hit it again. Wood we couldn't see tore.

Again.

The door popped away from us. We went through—down a flight of steps—rolling, snowballing down—until a cement floor stopped us.

Pat came back to life first.

"You're a hell of an acrobat," he said. "Get off my neck!"

I stood up. He stood up. We seemed to be dividing the evening between falling on the floor and getting up from the floor.

A light-switch was at my shoulder. I turned it on.

If I looked anything like Pat, we were a fine pair of nightmares. He was all raw meat and dirt, with not enough clothes left to hide much of either.

I didn't like his looks, so I looked around the basement in which we stood. To the rear was a furnace, coal-bins and a woodpile. To the front was a hallway and rooms, after the manner of the upstairs.

The first door we tried was locked, but not strongly. We smashed through it into a photographer's dark-room.

The second door was unlocked, and put us in a chemical laboratory: retorts, tubes, burners and a small still. There was a little round iron stove in the middle of the room. No one was there.

We went out into the hallway and to the third door, not so cheerfully. This cellar looked like a bloomer. We were wasting our time here, when we should have stayed upstairs. I tried the door.

It was firm beyond trembling.

We smacked it with our weight, together, experimentally. It didn't shake.

"Wait."

Pat went to the woodpile in the rear and came back with an axe.

He swung the axe against the door, flaking out a hunk of wood. Silvery points of light sparkled in the hole. The other side of the door was an iron or steel plate.

Pat put the axe down and leaned on the helve. "You write the next prescription," he said.

I didn't have anything to suggest, except:

"I'll camp here. You beat it upstairs, and see if any of your coppers have shown up. This is a God-forsaken hole, but somebody may have sent in an alarm. See if you can find another way into this room—a window, maybe—or man-power enough to get us in through this door."

Pat turned toward the steps.

A sound stopped him—the clicking of bolts on the other side of the iron-lined door.

A jump put Pat on one side of the frame. A step put me on the other.

Slowly the door moved in. Too slowly.

I kicked it open.

Pat and I went into the room on top of my kick.

His shoulder hit the woman. I managed to catch her before she fell.

Pat took her gun. I steadied her back on her feet.

Her face was a pale blank square.

She was Myra Banbrock, but she now had none of the masculinity that had been in her photographs and description.

Steadying her with one arm—which also served to block her arms—

I looked around the room.

A small cube of a room whose walls were brown-painted metal. On the floor lay a queer little dead man.

A little man in tight-fitting black velvet and silk. Black velvet blouse and breeches, black silk stockings and skull cap, black patent leather pumps. His face was small and old and bony, but smooth as stone, without line or wrinkle.

A hole was in his blouse, where it fit high under his chin. The hole bled very slowly. The floor around him showed it had been bleeding faster a little while ago.

Beyond him, a safe was open. Papers were on the floor in front of it, as if the safe had been tilted to spill them out.

The girl moved against my arm.

"You killed him?" I asked.

"Yes," too faint to have been heard a yard away.

"Why?"

She shook her short brown hair out of her eyes with a tired jerk of her head.

"Does it make any difference?" she asked. "I did kill him."

"It might make a difference," I told her, taking my arm away, and going over to shut the door. People talk more freely in a room with a closed door. "I happen to be in your father's employ. Mr Reddy is a police detective. Of course, neither of us can smash any laws, but if you'll tell us what's what, maybe we can help you."

"My father's employ?" she questioned.

"Yes. When you and your sister disappeared, he engaged me to find you. We found your sister, and—"

Life came into her face and eyes and voice.

"I didn't kill Ruth!" she cried. "The papers lied! I didn't kill her! I didn't know she had the revolver. I didn't know it! We were going away to hide from—from everything. We stopped in the woods to burn the—those things. That's the first time I knew she had the revolver. We had talked about suicide at first, but I had persuaded her—thought I had persuaded her—not to. I tried to take the revolver away from her, but I couldn't. She shot herself while I was trying to get it away. I tried to stop her. I didn't kill her!"

This was getting somewhere.

"And then?" I encouraged her.

"And then I went to Sacramento and left the car there, and came back to San Francisco. Ruth told me she had written Raymond Elwood a letter. She told me that before I persuaded her not to kill herself—the first time. I tried to get the letter from Raymond. She had written him she was going to kill herself. I tried to get the letter, but Raymond said he had given it to Hador.

"So I came here this evening to get it. I had just found it when there was a lot of noise upstairs. Then Hador came in and found me. He bolted the door. And—and I shot him with the revolver that was in the safe. I—I shot him when he turned around, before he could say anything. It had to be that way, or I couldn't."

"You mean you shot him without being threatened or attacked by him?" Pat asked.

"Yes. I was afraid of him, afraid to let him speak. I hated him! I couldn't help it. It had to be that way. If he had talked I couldn't have shot him. He—he wouldn't have let me!"

"Who was this Hador?" I asked.

She looked away from Pat and me, at the walls, at the ceiling, at the queer little dead man on the floor.

X

"He was a—" She cleared her throat, and started again, staring down at her feet. "Raymond Elwood brought us here the first time. We thought it was funny. But Hador was a devil. He told you things and you believed them. You couldn't help it.

He told you *everythin'* and you believed it. Perhaps we were drugged. There was always a warm bluish wine. It must have been drugged. We couldn't have done those things if it hadn't. Nobody would—He called himself a priest—a priest of Alzoa. He taught a freeing of the spirit from the flesh by—"

Her voice broke huskily. She shuddered.

"It was horrible!" she went on presently in the silence Pat and I had left for her. "But you believed him. That is the whole thing. You can't understand it unless you understand that. The things he taught could not be so. But he said they were, and you *believed* they were. Or maybe—I don't know—maybe you pretended you believed them, because you were crazy and drugs were in your blood. We came back again and again, for weeks, months, before the disgust that had to come drove us away.

"We stopped coming, Ruth and I—and Irma. And then we found out what he was. He demanded money, more money than we had been paying while we believed—or pretended belief—in his cult. We couldn't give him the money he demanded. I told him we wouldn't. He sent us photographs—of us—taken during the—the times here. They were—*pictures—you—couldn't—explain*. And they were true! We knew them true! What could we do? He said he would send copies to our father, every friend, everyone we knew—unless we paid.

"What could we do—except pay? We got the money somehow. We gave him money—more—more—more. And then we had no more—could get no more. We didn't know what to do! There was nothing to do, except—Ruth and Irma wanted to kill themselves. I thought of that, too. But I persuaded Ruth not to. I said we'd go away. I'd take her away—keep her safe. And then—then—this!"

She stopped talking, went on staring at her feet.

I looked again at the little dead man on the floor, weird in his black cap and clothes. No more blood came from his throat.

It wasn't hard to put the pieces together. This dead Hador, self-ordained priest of something or other, staging orgies under the alias of religious ceremonies. Elwood, his confederate, bringing women of family and wealth to him. A room lighted for photography, with a concealed camera. Contributions from his converts so long as they were faithful to the cult. Blackmail—with the help of the photographs—afterward.

I looked from Hador to Pat Reddy. He was scowling at the dead man. No sound came from outside the room.

"You have the letter your sister wrote Elwood?" I asked the girl.

Her hand flashed to her bosom, and crinkled paper there.

"Yes."

"It says plainly she meant to kill herself?"

"Yes."

"That ought to square her with Contra Costa county," I said to Pat.

He nodded his battered head.

"It ought to," he agreed. "It's not likely that they could prove murder on her even without that letter. With it, they'll not take her into court. That's a safe bet. Another is that she won't have any trouble over this shooting. She'll come out of court free, and thanked in the bargain."

Myra Banbrock flinched away from Pat as if he had hit her in the face.

I was her father's hired man just now. I saw her side of the affair.

I lit a cigarette and studied what I could see of Pat's face through blood and grime. Pat is a right guy.

"Listen, Pat," I wheedled him, though with a voice that was as if I were not trying to wheedle him at all. "Miss Banbrock can go into court and come out free and thanked, as you say. But to do it, she's got to use everything she knows. She's got to have all the evidence there is. She's got to use all those photographs Hador took—or all we can find of them.

"Some of those pictures have sent women to suicide, Pat—at least two that we know; If Miss Banbrock goes into court, we've got to make the photographs of God knows how many other women public property. We've got to advertise things that will put Miss Banbrock—and you can't say how many other women and girls—in a position that at least two women have killed themselves to escape."

Pat scowled at me and rubbed his dirty chin with a dirtier thumb.

I took a deep breath and made my play.

"Pat, you and I came here to question Raymond Elwood, having traced him here. Maybe we suspected him of being tied up with the mob that knocked over the St. Louis bank last month. Maybe we suspected him of handling the stuff that was taken from the mail cars in that stick-up near Denver week before last. Anyway, we were after him, knowing that he had a lot of money that came from nowhere, and a real estate office that did no real estate business.

"We came here to question him in connection with one of these jobs I've mentioned. We were jumped by a couple of the shines upstairs when they found we were sleuths. The rest of it grew out of that. This religious cult business was just something we ran into, and didn't interest us especially. So far as we knew, all these folks jumped us just through friendship for the man we were trying to question. Hador was one of them, and, tussling with you, you shot him with his own gun, which, of course, is the one Miss Banbrock found in the safe."

Reddy didn't seem to like my suggestion at all. The eyes with which he regarded me were decidedly sour.

"You're goofy," he accused me. "What'll that get anybody? That won't keep Miss Banbrock out of it. She's here, isn't she, and the rest of it will come out like thread off a spool."

"But Miss Banbrock *wasn't* here," I explained. "Maybe the upstairs is full of coppers by now. Maybe not. Anyway, you're going to take Miss Banbrock out of here and turn her over to Dick Foley, who will take her home. She's got nothing to do with this party. Tomorrow she, and her father's lawyer, and I, will all go up to Martinez and make a deal with the prosecuting attorney of Contra Costa county. We'll show him how Ruth killed herself. If somebody happens to connect the Elwood who I hope is dead upstairs with the Elwood who knew the girls and Mrs Correll, what of it? If we keep out of court—as we'll do by convincing the Contra Costa people they can't possibly convict her of her sister's murder—we'll keep out of the newspapers—and out of trouble."

Pat hung fire, thumb still to chin.

"Remember," I urged him, "it's not only Miss Banbrock we're doing this for. It's a couple of dead ones, and a flock of live ones, who certainly got mixed up with Hador of their own accords, but who don't stop being human beings on that account."

Pat shook his head stubbornly.

"I'm sorry," I told the girl with faked hopelessness. "I've done all I can, but it's a lot to ask of Reddy. I don't know that I blame him for being afraid to take a chance on—"

Pat is Irish.

"Don't be so damned quick to fly oft'," he snapped at me, cutting short my hypocrisy. "But why do I have to be the one that shot this Hador? Why not you?"

I had him!

"Because," I explained, "you're a bull and I'm not. There'll be less chance of a slip-up if he was shot by a bona fide, star-wearing, flat-footed officer of the peace. I killed most of those birds upstairs. You ought to do something to show you were here."

That was only part of the truth. My idea was that if Pat took the credit, he couldn't very well ease himself out afterward, no matter what happened. Pat's a right guy, and I'd trust him anywhere—but you can trust a man just as easily if you have him sewed up.

Pat grumbled and shook his head, but:

"I'm ruining myself, I don't doubt," he growled, "but I'll do it, this once."

"Attaboy!" I went over to pick up the girl's hat from the corner in which it lay. "I'll wait here until you come back from turning her over to Dick." I gave the girl her hat and orders together. "You go to your home with the man Reddy turns you over to. Stay there until I come, which will be as soon as I can make it. Don't tell anybody anything, except that I told you to keep quiet. That includes your father. Tell him I told you not to tell him even where you saw me. Got it?"

"Yes, and I—"

Gratitude is nice to think about afterward, but it takes time when there's work to be done.

"Get going, Pat!"

They went.

XI

As soon as I was alone with the dead man I stepped over him and knelt in front of the safe, pushing letters and papers away, hunting for photographs. None was in sight. One compartment of the safe was locked.

I frisked the corpse. No key. The locked compartment wasn't very strong, but neither am I the best safe-burglar in the West. It took me a while to get into it.

What I wanted was there. A thick sheaf of negatives. A stack of prints—half a hundred of them.

I started to run through them, hunting for the Banbrock girls' pictures. I wanted to have them pocketed before Pat came back. I didn't know how much farther he would let me go.

Luck was against me—and the time I had wasted getting into the compartment. He was back before I had got past the sixth print in the stack. Those six had been—pretty bad.

"Well, that's done," Pat growled at me as he came into the room. "Dick's got her. Elwood is dead, and so is the only one of the negroes I saw upstairs. Everybody else seems to have beat it. No bulls have shown—so I put in a call for a wagonful."

I stood up, holding the sheaf of negatives in one hand, the prints in the other.

"What's all that?" he asked.

I went after him again.

"Photographs. You've just done me a big favor, Pat, and I'm not hoggish enough to ask another. But I'm going to put something in front of you, Pat. I'll give you the lay, and you can name it.

"These"—I waved the pictures at him—"are Hador's meal-tickets—the photos he was either collecting on or planning to collect on. They're photographs of people, Pat, mostly women and girls, and some of them are pretty rotten.

"If tomorrow's papers say that a flock of photos were found in this house after the fireworks, there's going to be a fat suicide-list in the next day's papers, and a fatter list of disappearances. If the papers say nothing about the photos, the lists may be a little smaller, but not much. Some of the people whose pictures are here know they are here. They will expect the police to come hunting for them. We know this much about the photographs—two women have killed themselves to get away from them. This is an armful of stuff that can dynamite a lot of people, Pat, and a lot of families—no matter which of those two ways the papers read.

"But, suppose, Pat, the papers say that just before you shot Hador he succeeded in burning a lot of pictures and papers, burning them beyond recognition. Isn't it likely, then, that there won't be any suicides? That some of the disappearances of recent months may clear themselves up? There she is, Pat—you name it."

Looking back, it seems to me I had come a lot nearer being eloquent than ever before in my life.

But Pat didn't applaud.

He cursed me. He cursed me thoroughly, bitterly, and with an amount of feeling that told me I had won another point in my little game. He called me more things than I ever listened to before from a man who was built of meat and bone, and who therefore could be smacked.

When he was through, we carried the papers and photographs and a small book of addresses we found in the safe into the next room, and fed them to the little round iron stove there. The last of them was ash before we heard the police overhead.

"That's absolutely all!" Pat declared when we got up from our work. "Don't ever ask me to do anything else for you if you live to be a thousand."

"That's absolutely all," I echoed.

I like Pat. He is a right guy. The sixth photograph in the stack had been of his wife—the coffee importer's reckless, hot-eyed daughter.

9

CORKSCREW

BLACK MASK, SEPTEMBER 1925

A STORY OF THE CONTINENTAL SLEUTH

I

Boiling like a coffee pot before we were five miles out of Filmer, the automobile stage carried me south into the shimmering heat, blinding sunlight, and bitter white dust of the Arizona desert.

I was the only passenger. The driver felt as little like talking as I. All morning we rode through cactus-spiked, sage-studded oven-country, without conversation, except when the driver cursed the necessity of stopping to feed his clattering machine more water. The car crept through soft sifting sand; wound between steep-walled red mesas; dipped into dry arroyas where clumps of dusty mesquite were like white lace in the glare; and skirted sharp-edged barrancos.

All these things were hot. All of them tried to get rid of their heat by throwing it on the car. My fat melted in the heat. The heat dried my perspiration before I could feel its moisture. The dazzling light scorched my eyeballs; puckered my lids; cooked my mouth. Alkali stung my nose; was gritty between my teeth.

It was a nice ride! I understood why the natives were a hard lot. A morning like this would put any man in a mood to kill his brother, and would fry his brother into not caring whether he was killed.

The sun climbed up in the brazen sky. The higher it got, the larger and hotter it got. I wondered how much hotter it would have to get to explode the cartridges in the gun under my arm. Not that it mattered—if it got any hotter, we would all blow up anyway. Car, desert, chauffeur and I would all bang out of existence in one explosive flash. I didn't care if we did!

That was my frame of mind as we pushed up a long slope, topped a sharp ridge, and slid down into Corkscrew.

Corkscrew wouldn't have been impressive at any time. It especially wasn't this white-hot Sunday afternoon. One sandy street following the crooked edge of the Tirabuzon Cañon, from which, by translation, the town took its name. A town, it was called, but village would have been flattery: fifteen or eighteen shabby buildings slumped along the irregular street, with tumbledown shacks leaning against them, squatting close to them, and trying to sneak away from them.

That was Corkscrew. One look at it, and I believed all I had heard about it!

In the street, four dusty automobiles cooked. Between two buildings I could see a corral where half a dozen horses bunched their dejection under a shed. No person was in sight. Even the stage driver, carrying a limp and apparently empty mail sack, had vanished into a building labelled "Adderly's Emporium."

Gathering up my two gray-powdered bags, I climbed out and crossed the road to where a weather-washed sign, on which Cañon House was barely visible, hung over the door of a two-storey, iron-roofed, adobe house.

I crossed the wide, unpainted and unpeopled porch, and pushed a door open with my foot, going into a dining-room, where a dozen men and a woman sat eating at oilcloth-covered tables. In one corner of the room, was a cashier's desk; and, on the wall behind it, a key-rack. Between rack and desk, a pudgy man whose few remaining hairs were the exact shade of his sallow skin, sat on a stool, and pretended he didn't see me.

"A room and a lot of water," I said, dropping my bags, and reaching for the glass that sat on top of a cooler in the corner.

"You can have your room," the sallow man growled, "but water won't do you no good. You won't no sooner drink and wash, than you'll be thirsty and dirty all over again. Where in hell is that register?"

He couldn't find it, so he pushed an old envelope across the desk at me.

"Register on the back of that. Be with us a spell?"

"Most likely."

A chair upset behind me.

I turned around as a lanky man with enormous red ears reared himself upright with the help of his hands on the table—one of them flat in the plate of ham and eggs he had been eating.

"Ladiesh an' gentsh," he solemnly declaimed, "th' time hash came for yuh t' give up y'r evil waysh an' git out y'r knittin'. Th' law' hash came to Orilla County!"

The drunk bowed to me, upset his ham and eggs, and sat down again. The other diners applauded with thump of knives and forks on tables and dishes.

I looked them over while they looked me over. A miscellaneous assortment: weather-beaten horsemen, clumsily muscled laborers, men with the pasty complexions of night workers. The one woman in the room didn't belong to Arizona. She was a thin girl of maybe twenty-five, with too-bright dark eyes, dark, short hair, and a sharp prettiness that was the mark of a larger settlement than this. You've seen her, or her sisters, in the larger cities, in the places that get going after the theaters let out.

The man with her was range country—a slim lad in the early twenties, not very tall, with pale blue eyes that were startling in so dark-tanned a face. His features were a bit too perfect in their clean-cut regularity.

"So you're the new deputy sheriff?" the sallow man questioned the back of my head.

Somebody had kept my secret right out in the open! There was no use trying to cover up.

"Yes." I hid my annoyance under a grin that took in him and the diners. "But I'll trade my star right now for that room and water we were talking about."

He took me through the dining-room and upstairs to a board-walled room in the rear second floor, said, "This is it," and left me.

I did what I could with the water in a pitcher on the washstand to free myself from the white grime I had accumulated. Then I dug a gray shirt and a suit of whipcords out of my bags, and bolstered my gun under my left shoulder, where it wouldn't be a secret.

In each side pocket of my coat I stowed a new .32 automatic—small, snub-nosed affairs that weren't much better than toys. Their smallness let me carry them where they'd be close to my hands without advertising the fact that the gun under my shoulder wasn't all my arsenal.

The dining-room was empty when I went downstairs again. The sallow pessimist who ran the place stuck his head out of a door.

"Any chance of getting something to eat?" I asked.

"Hardly any," jerking his head toward a sign that said:

"Meals 6 to 8 A.M., 12 to 2 and 5 to 7 P.M."

"You can grub up at the Jew's—if you ain't particular," he added sourly.

I went out, across the porch that was too hot for idlers, and into the street that was empty for the same reason. Huddled against the wall of a large one-storey adobe building, which had Border Palace painted all across its front, I found the Jew's.

It was a small shack—three wooden walls stuck against the adobe wall of the Border Palace—jammed with a lunch counter, eight stools, a stove, a handful of cooking implements, half the flies in the world, an iron cot behind a half-drawn burlap curtain, and the proprietor. The interior had once been painted white. It was a smoky grease-color now, except where homemade signs said:

"Meals At All Hours. No Credit" and gave the prices of various foods. These signs were a fly-specked yellow-gray.

The proprietor wasn't a Jew—an Armenian or something of the sort, I thought. He was a small man, old, scrawny, dark-skinned, wrinkled and cheerful.

"You the new sheriff?" he asked, and when he grinned I saw he had no teeth.

"Deputy," I admitted, "and hungry. I'll eat anything you've got that won't bite back, and that won't take long to get ready."

"Sure!" He turned to his stove and began banging pans around. "We need sheriffs," he said over his shoulder. "Sure, we need them!"

"Somebody been picking on you?"

He showed his empty gums in another grin.

"Nobody pick on me—I tell you that!" He flourished a stringy hand at a sugar barrel under the shelves behind his counter. "I fix them decidedly!"

A shotgun butt stuck out of the barrel. I pulled it out: a double-barrel shotgun with the barrels sawed off short: a mean weapon close up.

I slid it back into its resting place as the old man began thumping dishes down in front of me.

II

The food inside me and a cigarette burning, I went out into the crooked street again. From the Border Palace came the clicking of pool balls. I followed the sound through the door.

In a large room, four men were leaning over a couple of pool tables, while five or six more watched them from chairs along the wall. On one side of the room was an oak bar, with nobody behind it. Through an open door in the rear came the sound of shuffling cards.

A big man whose paunch was dressed in a white vest, over a shirt in the bosom of which a diamond sparkled, came toward me; his triple chinned red face expanding into the professionally jovial smile of a confidence man.

"I'm Bardell," he greeted me, stretching out a fat and shiny-nailed hand on which more diamonds glittered. "This is my joint. I'm glad to know you, sheriff! By God, we need you, and I hope you can spend a lot of your time here. These waddies"—and he chuckled, nodding at the pool players—"cut up rough on me sometimes, and I'm glad there's going to be somebody around who can handle them."

I let him pump my hand up and down.

"Let me make you known to the boys," he went on, turning with one arm across my shoulders. "These are Circle H. A. R. riders"—waving some of his rings at the pool players—"except this Milk River hombre, who, being a peeler, kind of looks down on ordinary hands."

The Milk River hombre was the slender youth who had sat beside the girl in the Cañon House dining-room. His companions were young—though not quite so young as he—

sun-marked, wind-marked, pigeon-toed in high-heeled boots. Buck Small was sandy and pop-eyed; Smith was sandy and short; Dunne was a rangy Irishman.

The men watching the game were mostly laborers from the Orilla Colony, or hands from some of the smaller ranches in the neighborhood. There were two exceptions: Chick Orr, short, thick-bodied, heavy-armed, with the shapeless nose, battered ears, gold front teeth and gnarled hands of a pugilist; and Gyp Rainey, a slack-chinned, ratty individual whose whole front spelled cocaine.

Conducted by Bardell, I went into the back room to meet the poker players. There were only four of them. The other six card tables, the keno outfit, and the dice table were idle.

One of the players was the big-eared drunk who had made the welcoming speech at the hotel. Slim Vogel was the name. He was a Circle H. A. R. hand, as was Red Wheelan, who sat beside him. Both of them were full of hooch. The third player was a quiet, middle-aged man named Keefe. Number four was Mark Nisbet, a pale, slim man. Gambler was written all over him, from his heavy-lidded brown eyes to the slender sureness of his white fingers.

Nisbet and Vogel didn't seem to be getting along so good.

It was Nisbet's deal, and the pot had already been opened. Vogel, who had twice as many chips as anybody else, threw away two cards.

"I want both of 'em of'n th' top—this time!" and he didn't say it nicely.

Nisbet dealt the cards, with nothing in his appearance to show he had heard the crack. Red Wheelan took three cards. Keefe was out. Nisbet drew one. Wheelan bet. Nisbet stayed. Vogel raised. Wheelan stayed. Nisbet raised. Vogel bumped it again. Wheelan dropped out. Nisbet raised once more.

"I'm bettin' you took *your* draw of'n th' top, too," Vogel snarled across the table at Nisbet, and tilted the pot again.

Nisbet called. He had aces over kings. The cowpuncher had three nines.

Vogel laughed noisily as he raked in the chips.

"'F I could keep a sheriff behind you t' watch you all th' time, I'd do somethin' for myself!"

Nisbet pretended to be busy straightening his chips. I sympathized with him. He had played his hand rotten—but how else can you play against a drunk?

"How d'you like our little town?" Red Wheelan asked me.

"I haven't seen much of it yet," I stalled. "The hotel, the lunch-counter—they're all I've seen outside of here."

Wheelan laughed.

"So you met the Jew? That's Slim's friend!"

Everybody except Nisbet laughed, including Slim Vogel.

"Slim tried to beat the Jew out of two bits worth of Java and sinkers once. He says he forgot to pay for 'em, but it's more likely he sneaked out. Anyways, the next day, here comes the Jew, stirring dust into the ranch, a shotgun under his arm. He'd lugged that instrument of destruction fifteen miles across the desert, on foot, to collect his two bits. He collected, too! He took his little two bits away from Slim right there between the corral and the bunkhouse—at the cannon's mouth, as you might say!"

Slim Vogel grinned ruefully and scratched one of his big ears.

"The old son-of-a-gun done came after me just like I was a damned thief! 'F he'd of been a man I'd of seen him in hell 'fore I'd of gave it to him. But what can y' do with an old buzzard that ain't even got no teeth to bite you with?"

His bleary eyes went back to the table, and the laughter went out of them. The laugh on his loose lips changed to a sneer.

"Let's play," he growled, glaring at Nisbet. "It's a honest man's deal this time!"

Bardell and I went back to the front of the building, where the cowboys were still knocking the balls around. I sat in one of the chairs against the wall, and let them talk around me. The conversation wasn't exactly fluent. Anybody could tell there was a stranger present.

My first job was to get over that.

"Got any idea," I asked nobody in particular, "where I could pick up a horse? One that can run pretty good, but that isn't too tricky for a bum rider to sit."

The Milk River hombre was playing the seven ball in a side pocket. He made the shot, and his pale eyes looked at the pocket into which the ball had gone for a couple of seconds before he straightened up. Lanky Dunne was looking fixedly at nothing, his mouth puckered a bit. Buck Small's pop-eyes were intent on the tip of his cue.

"You might get one at Echlin's stable," Milk River said slowly, meeting my gaze with guileless blue eyes; "though it ain't likely he's got anything that'll live long if you hurry it. I tell you what—Peery, out to the ranch, has got a buckskin that'd just fit you. He won't want to let him go, but if you took some real money along and flapped it in his face, maybe you could deal. He does need money."

"You're not steering me into a horse I can't handle, are you?" I asked.

The pale eyes went blank.

"I ain't steering you into nothing whatsomever, Mister," he said. "You asked for information. I give it to you. But I don't mind telling you that anybody that can stay in a rocking chair can sit that buckskin."

"That's fine. I'll go out tomorrow."

Milk River put his cue down, frowning.

"Come to think of it, Peery's going down to the lower camp tomorrow. I tell you—if you got nothing else to do, we'll mosey out there right now. It's Sunday, and we'll be sure of catching him."

"Good," I said, and stood up.

"You boys going home?" Milk River asked his companions.

"Yeah," Smith spoke casually. "We gotta roll out early in the mornin', so I s'pose we'd ought to be shakin' along out there. I'll see if Slim an' Red are ready."

They weren't. Vogel's disagreeable voice came through the open door.

"I'm camped right here! I got this reptile on th' run, an' it's only a matter o' time 'fore he'll have t' take a chance on pullin' 'em of'n th' bottom t' save his hide. An' that's exac'ly what I'm awaitin' for! Th' first time he gets fancy, I'm goin't' open him up from his Adam's apple plumb down to his ankles!"

Smith returned to us.

"Slim an' Red are gonna play 'em a while. They'll git a lift out when they git enough."

Milk River, Smith, Dunne, Small and I went out of the Border Palace.

III

Three steps from the door, a stooped, white-mustached man in a collarless stiff-bosomed shirt swooped down on me, as if he had been lying in wait.

"My name's Adderly" he introduced himself, holding out one hand toward me while flicking the other at Adderly's Emporium. "Got a minute or two to spare? I'd like to make you acquainted with some of the folks."

The Circle H. A. R. men were walking slowly toward one of the machines in the street.

"Can you wait a couple of minutes?" I called after them.

Milk River looked back over his shoulder.

"Yes. We got to gas and water the flivver. Take your time."

Adderly led me toward his store, talking as he walked.

"Some of the better element is at my house—danged near all the better element. The folks who'll back you up if you'll put the fear of God in Corkscrew. We're tired and sick of this perpetual hell-raising."

We went through his store, across a yard, and into his house. There were a dozen or more people in his living-room.

The Reverend Dierks—a gangling, emaciated man with a tight mouth in a long, thin face—made a speech at me. He called me brother, he told me what a wicked place Corkscrew was, and he told me he and his friends were prepared to swear out warrants for the arrest of various men who had committed sixty-some crimes during the past two years.

He had a list of them, with names, dates, and hours, which he read to me. Everybody I had met that day—except those here—was on that list at least once, along with a lot of names I didn't know. The crimes ranged from murder to intoxication and the use of profane language.

"If you'll let me have that list, I'll study it," I promised.

He gave it to me, but he wasn't to be put off with promises.

"To refrain even for an hour from punishing wickedness is to be a partner to that wickedness, brother. You have been inside that house of sin operated by Bardell. You have heard the Sabbath desecrated with the sound of pool-balls. You have smelled the foul odor of illegal rum on men's breaths!

"Strike now, brother! Let it not be said that you condoned evil from your first day in Corkscrew! You have seen men whose garments did not conceal the deadly weapons under them! In that list is the black record of many months' unatoned sinfulness. Strike now, brother, for the Lord and righteousness! Go into those hells and do your duty as an officer of the law and a Christian!"

This was a minister; I didn't like to laugh.

I looked at the others. They were sitting—men and women—on the edges of their chairs. On their faces were the same expressions you see around a prize ring just before the gong rings.

Mrs Echlin, the livery man's wife, an angular-faced, angular-bodied woman, caught my gaze with her pebble-hard eyes.

"And that brazen scarlet woman who calls herself Senora Gaia—and the three hussies who pretend they're her daughters! You ain't much of a deputy sheriff if you leave 'em in that house of theirs one night longer—to poison the manhood of Orilla County!"

The others nodded vigorously. Echlin's eyes had lit up at his wife's words, and he licked his lips as he nodded.

Miss Janey, school teacher, false-toothed, sour-faced, put in her part:

"And even worse than those—those creatures, is that Clio Landes! Worse, because at least those—those hussies"—she looked down, managed a blush, looked out of the corners of her eyes at the minister—"those hussies are at least openly what they are. While she—who knows how bad she really is?"

"I don't know about her," Adderly began, but his wife shut him up.

"I do!" she snapped. She was a large, mustached woman whose corsets made knobs and points in her shiny black dress. "Miss Janey is perfectly right. That woman is worse than the rest!"

"Is this Clio Landes person on your list?" I asked, not remembering it.

"No, brother, she is not," the Reverend Dierks said regretfully. "But only because she is more subtle than the others. Corkscrew would indeed be better without her—a woman of obviously low moral standards, with no visible means of support, associating with our worst element."

"I'm glad to have met you folks," I said as I folded the list and put it in my pocket. "And I'm glad to know you'll back me up."

I edged toward the door, hoping to get away without much more talk. Not a chance. The Reverend Dierks followed me up.

"You will strike now, brother? You will carry God's war immediately into blind tiger and brothel and gambling hell?"

The others were on their feet now, closing in.

"I'll have to look things over first," I stalled.

"Brother, are you evading your duty? Are you procrastinating in the face of Satan? If you are the man I hope you are, you will march now, with the decent citizens of Corkscrew at your heels, to wipe from the face of our town the sin that blackens it!"

So that was it. I was to lead one of these vice-crusading mobs. I wondered how many of these crusaders would be standing behind me if one of the devil's representatives took a shot at me. The minister maybe—his thin face was grimly pugnacious. But I couldn't imagine what good he'd be in a row. The others would scatter at the first sign of trouble.

I stopped playing politics and said my say.

"I'm glad to have your support," I said, "but there isn't going to be any wholesale raiding—not for a while, anyway. Later, I'll try to get around to the bootleggers and gamblers and similar small fry, though I'm not foolish enough to think I can put them all out of business. Just now, so long as they don't cut up too rough, I don't expect to bother them. I haven't the time.

"This list you've given me—I'll do what I think ought to be done after I've examined it, but I'm not going to worry a lot over a batch of petty misdemeanors that happened a year ago. I'm starting from scratch. What happens from now on is what interests me. See you later."

And I left.

The cowboys' car was standing in front of the store when I came out.

"I've been meeting the better element," I explained as I found a place in it between Milk River and Buck Small.

Milk River's brown face wrinkled around his eyes.

"Then you know what kind of riff-raff we are," he said.

IV

Dunne driving, the car carried us out of Corkscrew at the street's southern end, and then west along the sandy and rocky bottom of a shallow draw. The sand was deep and the rocks were numerous; we didn't make very good time. An hour and a half of jolting, sweltering and smothering in this draw, and we climbed up out of it and crossed to a larger and greener draw, where the mesquite grew in small trees and bees zizzed among wild flowers.

Around a bend in this draw the Circle H. A. R. buildings sat. We got out of the automobile under a low shed, where another car already stood. A heavily muscled, heavily boned man came around a white-washed building toward us. His face was square and dark. His close-clipped mustache and deep-set small eyes were dark.

This, I learned, was Peery, who bossed the ranch for the owner, who lived in the East.

"He wants a nice, mild horse," Milk River told Peery, "and we thought maybe you might sell him that Rollo horse of yours. That's the nicest, mildest horse I ever heard tell of."

Peery tilted his high-crowned sombrero back on his head and rocked on his heels.

"What was you figuring on paying for this here horse?"

"If it suits me," I said, "I'm willing to pay what it takes to buy him."

"That ain't so bad," he said. "S'pose one of you boys dab a rope on that buckskin and bring him around for the gent to look at."

Smith and Dunne set out together, pretending they weren't going eagerly.

"Where's Red and Slim?" Peery asked.

"Stayin' in a while," Small told him. "Slim's a million ahead in a poker game."

Presently the two cowhands came back, riding, with the buckskin between them, already saddled and bridled. I noticed each of them had a rope on him. He was a loose-jointed pony of an unripe lemon color, with a sad, drooping, Roman-nosed head.

"There he is," Peery said. "Try him out and we'll talk dinero. I warn you, I ain't so damned anxious to get rid of him that I'll let him go for nothing. But you try him first—trot him down the draw a little ways and back. He's downright sweet."

I chucked away my cigarette and went over to the buckskin. He cocked one mournful eye at me, twitched one ear, and went on looking sadly at the ground. Dunne and Smith took their lines off him, and I got into the saddle.

Rollo stood still under me until the other horses had left his side.

Then he showed me what he had.

He went straight up in the air—and hung there long enough to turn around before he came down. He stood on his front feet and then on his hind ones, and then he got off all of them again.

I didn't like this, but it wasn't a surprise. I had known I was a lamb being led to the slaughter. This was the third time it had happened to me. I might as well get it over with. A city man in range country is bound to find himself sitting on a disagreeable bone sooner or later. I'm a city man. I can sit any street car or taxicab in the world, and I can even ride a horse if he'll cooperate. But when the horse doesn't want to stay under me—the horse wins.

Rollo was going to win. I wasn't foolish enough to waste strength fighting him.

So the next time he traded ends, I went away from him, holding myself limp, so the tumble wouldn't ruin me.

Smith had caught the yellow pony, and was holding its head, when I took my knees off my forehead and stood up.

Peery, squatting on his heels, was frowning at me. Milk River was looking at Rollo with what was supposed to be a look of utter amazement.

"Now whatever did you do to Rollo to make him act thataway?" Peery asked me.

"Maybe he was only fooling," I suggested. "I'll try him again."

Once more Rollo stood still and sad until I was securely up on him. Then he went into convulsions under me—convulsions that lasted until I piled on my neck and one shoulder in a clump of brush.

I stood up, rubbing my left shoulder, which had hit a rock. Smith was holding the buckskin. The faces of all five men were serious and solemn—too serious and solemn.

"Maybe he don't like you," Buck Small gave his opinion.

"Might be," I admitted as I climbed into the saddle for the third time.

The lemon-tinted devil was getting warmed up by now, was beginning to take pride in his work. He let me stay aboard longer than before, so he could slam me off harder.

I was sick when I hit the ground in front of Peery and Milk River. It took me a little while to get up, and I had to stand still for a moment, until I could feel the ground under my feet.

"Hold him a couple of seconds—" I began.

Peery's big frame stood in front of me.

"That's enough," he said. "I ain't going to have you killed on my hands."

I shook my head violently, trying to clear it, so I could see him better.

"Get out of my way," I growled. "I like this. I want more of it."

"You don't top my pony no more," he grow led back at me. "He ain't used to playing so rough. You're liable to hurt him, falling off carelessly like that."

I tried to get past him. He barred my way with a thick arm. I drove my right fist at his dark face.

He went back, busy trying to keep his feet under him.

I went over and hoisted myself up on Rollo.

I had the buckskin's confidence by this time. We were old friends. He didn't mind showing me his secret stuff. He did things no horse could possibly do. Looking down, I was surprised not to see his kidneys and liver—because I knew damned well he was turning himself inside out.

I landed in the same clump of brush that had got me once before.

I couldn't see much when I got up—only the yellow of Rollo.

I heard Peery's bass voice, protesting to somebody:

"No, let the damned fool kill himself if he wants to."

I heaved myself wearily into the saddle again.

For a while I thought Rollo had had enough. He was a well-behaved animal under me. That was fine. I had ridden him at last.

Nonsense! He was fooling.

He put his nose in the sand. He put it in the sky. And, using his head for a base, he wagged his body as a puppy would wag its tail.

I went away from him—and stayed where I landed.

I didn't know whether I could have got up again if I had wanted to. But I didn't want to. I closed my eyes and rested. If I hadn't done what I had set out to do, I was willing to fail.

Small, Dunne and Milk River carried me indoors and spread me on a bunk.

"I don't think that horse would be much good to me," I told them. "Maybe I'd better look at another."

"You don't want to get discouraged like that," Small advised me.

"You better lay still and rest, fella," Milk River said. "You're liable to fall apart if you start moving around."

I took his advice.

V

When I woke up it was morning, and Milk River was prodding me with a finger.

"You figuring on getting up for breakfast, or would you like it brung to you?"

I moved cautiously until I found I was all in one piece.

"I can crawl that far."

He sat down on a bunk across the room and rolled a cigarette while I put on my shoes—the only things, except my hat, I hadn't slept in. He had something to say, so I gave him time, lacing my shoes slowly.

Presently he said it:

"I always had the idea that nobody that couldn't sit a horse some couldn't amount to nothing much. I ain't so sure now. You can't ride any, and never will. You don't seem to have the least notion what to do after you get in the middle of the animal! But, still and all, a hombre that'll let a bronc dirty him up three times and running and then ties into a gent who tries to keep him from making it permanent, ain't exactly hay wire."

He lit his cigarette, and broke the match in half.

"I got a sorrel horse you can have for a hundred dollars. He don't take no interest in handling cows, but he's all horse, and he ain't mean."

I went into my money-belt—slid five twenties over into his lap.

"Better look at him first," he objected.

"You've seen him," I yawned, standing up. "Where's that breakfast you were bragging about?"

Six men were eating in the chuck-shack when we came in. Three of them were hands I hadn't seen before. Neither Peery, Wheelan, nor Vogel was there. Milk River introduced me to the strangers as the high-diving deputy sheriff, and, between bites of the food the one-eyed Chinese cook put on the table, the meal was devoted almost exclusively to wise cracks about my riding ability.

That suited me. I was sore and stiff, but my bruises weren't wasted. I had bought myself a place of some sort in this desert community, and maybe even a friend or two. In less than a day I had accomplished what, by milder means, would have taken weeks, or months. These cowhands were kidding me just about as they would have kidded each other.

We were following the smoke of our cigarettes outdoors when running hoofs brought a swirl of dust up the draw.

Red Wheelan slid off his horse and staggered out of the sand-cloud.

"Slim's dead!" he said thickly.

Half a dozen voices shot questions at him. He stood swaying, trying to answer them. He was drunk as a lord!

"Nisbet shot him. I heard about it when I woke up this mornin'. He was shot early this mornin'—in front of Bardell's. I left 'em aroun' midnight last night, an' went down to Gaia's. I heard about it this mornin'. I went after Nisbet, but"—he looked down sheepishly at his empty belt—"Bardell took m' gun away."

He swayed again. I caught him, steadying him.

"Horses!" Peery bawled over my shoulder. "We're going to town!"

I let go of Wheelan and turned around.

"We're going to town," I repeated, "but no foolishness when we get there. This is my job, and if I want any help I'll tell you."

Peery's eyes met mine.

"Slim belonged to us," he said.

"And whoever killed Slim belongs to me," I said.

That was all on the subject, but I didn't think I had made the point stick.

VI

An hour later we were dismounting in front of the Border Palace, going indoors.

A long, thin, blanket-wrapped body lay on two tables that had been pushed together. Half the citizens of Corkscrew were there. Behind the bar, Chick Orr's battered face showed, hard and watchful. Gyp Rainey was sitting in a corner, rolling a cigarette with shaky fingers that sprinkled the floor with tobacco crumbs. Beside him, paying no attention to anything, not even looking up at our arrival, Mark Nisbet sat.

"By God, I'm glad to see you!" Bardell was telling me, his fat face not quite so red as it had been the day before. "This thing of having men killed at my front door has got to stop, and you're the man to stop it!"

I noticed that the Circle H. A. R. men had not followed me into the center of the room, but had stopped in a loose semicircle just inside the street door.

I lifted a flap of the blanket and looked at the dead man. A small hole was in his forehead, over his right eye.

"Has a doctor seen him?" I asked.

"Yes," Bardell said. "Doc Haley saw him, but couldn't do anything. He must have been dead before he fell."

"Can you send for Haley?"

"I reckon I can." Bardell called to Gyp Rainey, "Run across the street and tell Doc Haley that the deputy sheriff wants to talk to him."

Gyp went gingerly through the cowboys grouped at the door and vanished.

I didn't like this public stuff. I'd rather do my questioning on the side. But to try that here would probably call for a showdown with Peery and his men, and I wasn't quite ready for that.

"What do you know about the killing, Bardell?" I began.

"Nothing," he said emphatically, and then went on to tell me what he knew. "Nisbet and I were in the back room, counting the day's receipts. Chick was straightening the bar up. Nobody else was in here. It was about half-past one this morning, maybe.

"We heard the shot—right out front, and all run out there, of course. Chick was closest, so he got there first. Slim was laying in the street—dead."

"And what happened after that?"

"Nothing. We brought him in here. Adderly and Doc Haley—who lives right across the street—and the Jew next door had heard the shot, too, and they came out and—and that's all there was to it."

I turned to Gyp.

He spit in a cuspidor and hunched his shoulders.

"Bardell's give it all to you."

"Didn't see anything before or after except what Bardell has said?"

"Nothin'."

"Don't know who shot him?"

"Nope."

I saw Adderly's white mustache near the front of the room, and I put him on the stand next. He couldn't contribute anything. He had heard the shot, had jumped out of bed, put on pants and shoes, and had arrived in time to see Chick kneeling beside the dead man. He hadn't seen anything Bardell hadn't mentioned.

Dr Haley had not arrived by the time I was through with Adderly, and I wasn't ready to open on Nisbet yet. Nobody else there seemed to know anything.

"Be back in a minute," I said, and went through the cowboys at the door to the street.

The Jew was giving his joint a much-needed cleaning.

"Good work," I praised him; "it needed it."

He climbed down from the counter on which he had been standing to reach the ceiling. The walls and floor were already comparatively clean.

"I not think it was so dirty," he grinned, showing his empty gums, "but when the sheriff come in to eat and make faces at my place, what am I going to do but clean him up?"

"Know anything about the killing last night?"

"Sure, I know. I am in my bed, and I hear that shot. I jump out of my bed, grab that shotgun, and run to the door. There is that Slim Vogel in the street, and that Chick Orr on his knees alongside him. I stick my head out. There is Mr Bardell and that Nisbet standing in their door.

"Mr Bardell say, 'How is he, Chick?'

"That Chick Orr, he say, 'He's dead enough.'

"That Nisbet, he does not say anything, but he turn around and go back into the place. And then comes the doctor and Mr Adderly, and I go out, and after the doctor looks at him and says he is dead, we carry him into Mr Bardell's place and put him on those tables."

That was all the Jew knew. I returned to the Border Palace. Dr Haley—a fussy little man whose nervous fingers played with his lips—was there.

The sound of the shot had awakened him, he said, but he had seen nothing beyond what the others had already told me. The bullet was a .38. Death had been instantaneous.

So much for that.

I sat on a corner of a pool table, facing Mark Nisbet. Feet shuffled on the floor behind me and I could feel tension making.

"What can you tell me, Nisbet?" I asked.

He didn't look up from the floor. No muscle moved in his face except those that shaped his mouth to his words.

"Nothing that is likely to help," he said, picking his words slowly and carefully. "You were in the afternoon and saw Slim, Wheelan, Keefe and I playing. Well, the game went on like that. He won a lot of money—or he seemed to think it was a lot—as long as we played poker. But Keefe left before midnight, and Wheelan shortly after. Nobody else came in the game, so we were kind of short-handed for poker. We quit it and played some high-card. I cleaned Vogel—got his last nickel. It was about one o'clock when he left, say half an hour before he was shot."

"You and Vogel get along pretty well?"

The gambler's eyes switched up to mine, turned to the floor again.

"You know better than that. You heard him riding me ragged. Well, he kept that up—maybe was a little rawer toward the last."

"And you let him ride?"

"I did just that. I make my living out of cards, not out of picking fights."

"There was no trouble over the table, then?"

"I didn't say that. There was trouble. He made a break for his gun after I cleaned him."

"And you?"

"I shaded him on the draw—took his gun—unloaded it—gave it back to him—told him to beat it. He went."

"No shooting in here?"

"Not a shot."

"And you didn't see him again until after he had been killed?"

"That's right."

I got down from my perch on the table and walked over to Nisbet, holding out one hand.

"Let me look at your gun."

He slid it swiftly out of his clothes—butt-first—into my hand. A .38 S. & W., loaded in all six chambers.

"Don't lose it," I said as I handed it back to him, "I may want it later."

A roar from Peery turned me around. As I turned I let my hands go into my coat pockets to rest on the .32 toys.

Peery's right hand was near his neck, within striking distance of the gun I knew he had under his vest. Spread out behind him, his men were as ready for action as he. Their hands hovered close to the bulges that showed where their weapons were packed.

"Maybe that's a deputy sheriff's idea of what had ought to be done," Peery was bellowing, "but it ain't mine! That skunk killed Slim. Slim went out of here toting too much money. That skunk shot him down without even giving him a chance to go for his iron, and took his dirty money back. If you think we're going to stand for "

"Maybe somebody's got some evidence I haven't heard," I cut in. "The way it stands, I haven't got enough to convict Nisbet, and I don't see any sense in arresting a man just because it looks as if he might have done a thing."

"Evidence be damned! Facts are facts, and you know this—"

"The first fact for you to study," I interrupted him again, "is that I'm running this show—running it my own way. Got anything against that?"

"Plenty!"

A worn .45 appeared in his fist. Guns blossomed in the hands of the men behind him.

I got between Peery's gun and Nisbet, feeling ashamed of the little popping noise my .32s were going to make compared with the roar of the guns facing me.

"What I'd like"—Milk River had stepped away from his fellows, and was leaning his elbows on the bar, facing them, a gun in each hand, a purring quality in his drawling voice—"would be for whosoever wants to swap lead with our high-diving deputy to wait his turn. One at a time is my idea. I don't like this idea of crowding him."

Peery's face went purple.

"What I don't like," he bellowed at the boy, "is a yellow puppy that'll throw down the men he rides with!"

Milk River's dark face flushed, but his voice was still a purring drawl.

"Mister jigger, what you don't like and what you do like are so damned similar to me that I can't tell 'em apart. And you don't want to forget that I ain't one of your rannies. I got a contract to gentle some horses for you at ten dollars per gentle. Outside of that, you and yours are strangers to me."

The excitement was over. The action that had been brewing had been talked to death by now.

"Your contract expired just about a minute and a half ago," Peery was telling Milk River. "You can show up at the Circle H. A. R. just once more—that's when you come for whatever stuff you left behind you. You're through!"

He pushed his square-jawed face at me.

"And you needn't think all the bets are in!"

He spun on his heel, and his hands trailed him out to their horses.

VII

Milk River and I were sitting in my room in the Cañon House an hour later, talking. I had sent word to the county seat that the coroner had a job down here, and had found a place to stow Vogel's body until he came.

"Can you tell me who spread the grand news that I was a deputy sheriff?" I asked Milk River, who was making a cigarette while I lit one of the Fatimas he had refused. "It was supposed to be a secret."

"Was it? Nobody would of thought it. Our Mr Turney didn't do nothing else for two days but run around telling folks what was going to happen when the new deputy come. He sure laid out a reputation for you! According to his way of telling it, you was the toughest, hardest, strongest, fastest, sharpest, biggest, wisest and meanest man west of the Mississippi River."

"Who is this Turney?"

"You mean you don't know him? From the way he talked, I took it you and him ate off the same plate."

"Never even heard any rumors about him. Who is he?"

"He's the gent that bosses the Orilla County Company outfit up the way."

So my client's local manager was the boy who had tipped my mitt!

"Got anything special to do the next few days?" I asked.

"Nothing downright special."

"I've got a place on the payroll for a man who knows this country and can chaperon me around it."

He poured a mouthful of gray smoke at the ceiling.

"I'd have to know what the play was before I'd set in," he said slowly. "You ain't a regular deputy, and you don't belong in this country. It ain't none of my business, but I wouldn't want to tie in with a blind game."

That was sensible enough.

"I'll spread it out for you," I offered. "I'm a private detective—the San Francisco branch of the Continental Detective Agency. The stockholders of the Orilla Colony Company sent me down here. They've spent a lot of money irrigating and developing their land, and now they're about ready to start selling it.

"According to them, the combination of heat and water makes it ideal farm land—as good as the Imperial Valley. Nevertheless, there doesn't seem to be any great rush of customers. What's the matter, so the stockholders figure, is that you original inhabitants of this end of the state are such a hard lot that peaceful farmers don't want to come among you.

"It's no secret from anybody that both borders of this United States are sprinkled with sections that are as lawless now as they ever were in the old days. There's too much money in running immigrants over the line, and it's too easy, not to have attracted a lot of gentlemen who don't care how they get their money. With only 450 immigration inspectors divided between the two borders, the government hasn't been able to do much. The official guess is that some 135,000 foreigners were run into the country last year through back and side doors. Compared to this graft, rum-running—even dope-running—is kid stuff!

"Because this end of Orilla County isn't railroaded or telephoned up, it has got to be one of the chief smuggling sections, and therefore, according to these men who hired me, full of assorted thugs. On another job a couple of months ago, I happened to run into a smuggling game, and knocked it over. The Orilla Colony people thought I could do the same thing for them down here. So hither I come to make this part of Arizona nice and lady-like.

"I stopped over at the county seat and got myself sworn in as deputy sheriff, in case the official standing came in handy. The sheriff said he didn't have a deputy down here and hadn't the money to hire one, so he was glad to sign me on. But we thought it was a secret—until I got here."

"I think you're going to have one hell of a lot of fun," Milk River grinned at me, "so I reckon I'll take that job you was offering. But I ain't going to be no deputy myself. I'll play around with you, but I don't want to tie myself up, so I'll have to enforce no laws I don't like. If you want to have me hanging around you sort of loose and individual-like, I'm with you."

"It's a bargain. Now what can you tell me that I ought to know?"

He blew more smoke at the ceiling.

"Well, you needn't bother none about the Circle H. A. R. They're plenty tough, but they ain't running nothing over the line."

"That's all right as far as it goes," I agreed, "but my job is to clean out trouble-makers, and from what I've seen of them they come under that heading."

"You're going to have one hell of a lot of fun," Milk River repeated. "Of course they're troublesome! But how could Peery raise cows down here if he didn't get hisself a crew that's a match for the gunmen your Orilla Colony people don't like? And you know how cowhands are. Set 'em down in a hard neighborhood and they're hellbent on proving to everybody that they're just as tough as the next one—and tougher."

"I've nothing against them—if they behave. Now about these border-running folks?"

"I reckon Bardell's your big meat. Whether you'll ever get anything on him is another thing—something for you to work up a lather over. Next to him—Big 'Nacio. You ain't seen him yet? A big, black-whiskered Mex that's got a rancho down the cañon—four-five mile this side of the line. Anything that comes over the line comes through that rancho. But proving that's another item for you to beat your head about."

"He and Bardell work together?"

"Uh-huh—I reckon he works for Bardell. Another thing you got to include in your tally is that these foreign gents who buy their way across the line don't always—nor even mostly—wind up where they want to. It ain't nothing unusual these days to find some bones out in the desert beside what was a grave until the coyotes opened it. And the buzzards are getting fat! If the immigrant's got anything worth taking on him, or if a couple of government men happen to be nosing around, or if anything happens to make the smuggling gents nervous, they usually drop their customer and dig him in where he falls."

The racket of the dinner-bell downstairs cut off our conference at this point.

VIII

There were only eight or ten diners in the dining-room. None of Peery's men was there. Milk River and I sat at a table back in one corner of the room. Our meal was about half eaten when the dark-eyed girl I had seen the previous day came in.

She came straight to our table. I stood up to learn her name was Clio Landes. She was the girl the better element wanted floated. She gave me a flashing smile, a strong, thin hand, and sat down.

"I hear you've lost your job again, you big bum," she laughed at Milk River.

I had known she didn't belong to Arizona. Her voice was New York.

"If that's all you heard, I'm still way ahead of you," Milk River grinned back at her. "I gone and got me another job—riding herd on law and order."

Something that could have been worry flashed into her dark eyes, and out again.

"You might just as well start looking for another hired man right away," she advised me. "He never kept a job longer than a few days in his life."

From the distance came the sound of a shot.

I went on eating.

Clio Landes said:

"Don't you coppers get excited over things like that?"

"The first rule," I told her, "is never to let anything interfere with your meals, if you can help it."

An overalled man came in from the street.

"Nisbet's been killed down in Bardell's!" he yelled.

To Bardell's Border Palace Milk River and I went, half the diners running ahead of us, with half the town.

We found Nisbet in the back room, stretched out on the floor, dead. A hole that a .45 could have made was in his chest, which the men around him had bared.

Bardell's fingers gripped my arm.

"Never give him a chance, the dogs!" he cried thickly. "Cold murder!"

"He say anything before he died?"

"No. He was dead when we got to him."

"Who shot him?"

"One of the Circle H. A. R., you can bet your neck on that!"

"Didn't anybody see it?"

"Nobody here admits they saw it."

"How did it happen?"

"Mark was out front. Me and Chick and five or six of these men were there. Mark came back here. Just as he stepped through the door—bang!"

Bardell shook his fist at the open window.

I crossed to the window and looked out. A five-foot strip of rocky ground lay between the building and the sharp edge of the Tirabuzon Cañon. A close-twisted rope was tight around a small knob of rock at the cañon's edge.

I pointed at the rope. Bardell swore savagely.

"If I'd of seen that we'd of got him! We didn't think anybody could get down there, and didn't look very close. We ran up and down the ledge, looking between buildings."

We went outside, where I lay on my belly and looked down into the cañon. The rope—one end fastened to the knob—ran straight down the rock wall for twenty feet, and disappeared among the trees and bushes of a narrow shelf that ran along the wall there. Once on that shelf, a man could find ample cover to shield his retreat.

"What do you think?" I asked Milk River, who lay beside me.

"A clean getaway."

I stood up, pulling up the rope. A rope such as any one of a hundred cowhands might have owned, in no way distinguishable from any other to my eyes. I handed it to Milk River.

"It don't mean nothing to me. Might be anybody's," he said.

"The ground tell you anything?"

He shook his head again.

"You go down into the cañon and see what you can pick up," I told him. "I'll ride out to the Circle H. A. R. If you don't find anything, ride out that way."

I went back indoors, for further questioning. Of the seven men who had been in Bardell's place at the time of the shooting, three seemed to be fairly trustworthy. The testimony of those three agreed with Bardell's in every detail.

"Didn't you say you were going out to see Peery?" Bardell asked.

"Yes."

"Chick, get horses! Me and you'll ride out there with the deputy, and as many of you other men as want to go. He'll need guns behind him!"

"Nothing doing!" I stopped Chick. "I'm going by myself. This posse stuff is out of my line."

Bardell scowled, but he nodded his head in agreement.

"You're running it," he said. "I'd like to go out there with you, but if you want to play it different, I'm gambling you're right."

IX

In the livery stable, where we had put our horses, I found Milk River saddling them, and we rode out of town together.

Half a mile out, we split. He turned to the left, down a trail that led into the cañon, calling over his shoulder to me:

"If you get through out there sooner than you think, you can maybe pick me up by following the draw the ranch-house is in down to the cañon. Don't be too hard on the boys!"

I turned into the draw that led toward the Circle H. A. R., the long-legged, long-bodied horse Milk River had sold me carrying me along easily and swiftly. It was too soon after midday for riding to be pleasant. Heat waves boiled out of the draw-bottom, the sun hurt my eyes, dust caked my throat. That same dust rose behind me in a cloud that advertised me to half the state, notwithstanding that I was riding below the landscape.

Crossing from this draw into the larger one the Circle H. A. R. occupied, I found Peery waiting for me.

He didn't say anything, didn't move a hand. He just sat his horse and watched me approach. Two .45s were bolstered on his legs.

I came alongside and held out the lariat I had taken from the rear of the Border Palace. As I held it out I noticed that no rope decorated his saddle.

"Know anything about this?" I asked.

He looked at the rope, but made no move to take it.

"Looks like one of those things hombres use to drag steers around with."

"Can't fool you, can I?" I grunted. "Ever see this particular one before?"

He took a minute or more to think up an answer to that.

"Yeah," finally. "Fact is, I lost that same rope somewheres between here and town this morning."

"Know where I found it?"

"Don't hardly make no difference." He reached for it. "The main thing is you found it."

"It might make a difference," I said, moving the rope out of his reach. "I found it strung down the cañon wall, behind Bardell's, where you could slide down it after you potted Nisbet."

His hands went to his guns. I turned so he could see the shape of one of the pocketed automatics I was holding.

"Don't do anything you'll be sorry for," I advised him.

"Shall I gun this la-ad now?" Dunne's brogue rolled from behind me, "or will we wait a bit?"

I looked around to see him standing behind a boulder, a .30-30 rifle held on me. Above other rocks, other heads and other weapons showed.

I took my hand out of my pocket and put it on my saddle horn.

Peery spoke past me to the others.

"He tells me Nisbet's been shot."

"Now ain't that provokin'?" Buck Small grieved. "I hope it didn't hurt him none."

"Dead," I supplied.

"Whoever could 'a' done th' like o' that?" Dunne wanted to know.

"It wasn't Santa Claus," I gave my opinion.

"Got anything else to tell me?" Peery demanded.

"Isn't that enough?"

"Yeah. Now if I was you, I'd ride right back to Corkscrew and go to bed."

"You mean you don't want to go back with me?"

"Not any. If you want to try and take me, now—"

I didn't want to try, and I said so.

"Then there's nothing keeping you here," he pointed out.

I grinned at him and his friends, pulled the sorrel around, and started back the way I had come.

A few miles down, I swung off to the south again, found the lower end of the Circle H. A. R. draw, and followed it down into the Tirabuzon Cañon. Then I started to work up toward the point where the rope had been let down.

The cañon deserved its name—a rough and stony, tree and bush-choked, winding gutter across the face of Arizona. But it was nicely green and cool compared to most of the rest of the State.

I hadn't gone far when I ran into Milk River, leading his horse toward me. He shook his head.

"Not a damned thing! I can cut sign with the rest of 'em, but there's too many rocky ridges here."

I dismounted. We sat under a tree and smoked some tobacco. "How 'd you come out?" he wanted to know.

"So-so. The rope is Peery's, but he didn't want to come along with me. I figure we can find him when we want him, so I didn't insist. It would have been kind of uncomfortable."

He looked at me out of the end of his pale eyes.

"A hombre might guess," he said slowly, "that you was playing the Circle H. A. R. against Bardell's crew, encouraging each side to eat up the other, and save you the trouble."

"You could be either right or wrong. Do you think that'd be a dumb play?"

"I don't know. I reckon not—if you're making it, and if you're sure you're strong enough to take hold when you have to."

X

Night was coming on when Milk River and I turned into Corkscrew's crooked street. It was too late for the Cañon House's dining-room, so we got down in front of the Jews shack.

Chick Orr was standing in the Border Palace doorway. He turned his hammered mug to call something over his shoulder. Bardell appeared beside him, looked at me with a question in his eyes, and the pair of them stepped out into the street.

"What result?" Bardell asked.

"No visible ones."

"You didn't make the pinch?" Chick Orr demanded, incredulously.

"That's right. I invited a man to ride back with me, but he said no."

The ex-pug looked me up and down and spit on the ground at my feet.

"Ain't you a swell mornin'-glory?" he snarled. "I got a great mind to smack you down, you shine elbow, you!"

"Go ahead," I invited him. "I don't mind skinning a knuckle on you."

His little eyes brightened. Stepping in, he let an open hand go at my face. I took my face out of the way, and turned my back, taking off coat and shoulder-holster.

"Hold these, Milk River. And make the spectators behave while I take this pork-and-beaner for a romp."

Corkscrew came running as Chick and I faced each other. We were pretty much alike in size and age, but his fat was softer than mine, I thought. He had been a professional. I had battled around a little, but there was no doubt that he had me shaded on smartness. To offset that, his hands were lumpy and battered, while mine weren't. And he was—or had been—used to gloves, while bare knuckles was more in my line.

Popular belief has it that you can do more damage with bare hands than with gloves, but, as usual, popular belief is wrong. The chief value of gloves is the protection they give your hands. Jaw-bones are tougher than finger-bones, and after you've pasted a tough face for a while with bare knuckles you find your hands aren't holding up very well, that you can't get the proper snap into your punches. If you don't believe me, look up the records. You'll find that knock-outs began to come quicker as soon as the boys in the profession began to pad their fists.

So I figured I hadn't anything to fear from this Chick Orr—or not a whole lot. I was in better shape, had stronger hands, and wasn't handicapped with boxing-glove training. I wasn't altogether right in my calculations.

He crouched, waiting for me to come to him. I went, trying to play the boob, faking a right swing for a lead.

Not so good! He stepped outside instead of in. The left I chucked at him went wide. He rapped me on the cheek-bone.

I stopped trying to out-smart him. His left hand played a three-note tune on my face before I could get in to him.

I smacked both hands into his body, and felt happy when the flesh folded softly around them. He got away quicker than I could follow, and shook me up with a sock on the jaw.

He left-handed me some more—in the eye, in the nose. His right scraped my forehead, and I was in again.

Left, right, left, I dug into his middle. He slashed me across the face with forearm and fist, and got clear.

He fed me some more lefts, splitting my lip, spreading my nose, stinging my face from forehead to chin. And when I finally got past that left hand I walked into a right uppercut that came up from his ankle to click on my jaw with a shock that threw me back half a dozen steps.

Keeping after me, he swarmed all over me. The evening air was full of fists. I pushed my feet into the ground and stopped the hurricane with a couple of pokes just above where his shirt ran into his pants.

He copped me with his right again—but not so hard. I laughed at him, remembering that something had clicked in his hand when he landed that uppercut, and plowed into him, hammering at him with both hands.

He got away again—cut me up with his left. I smothered his left arm with my right, hung on to it, and whaled him with my own left, keeping them low. His right banged into me. I let it bang. It was dead.

He nailed me once more before the fight ended—with a high straight left that smoked as it came. I managed to keep my feet under me, and the rest of it wasn't so bad. He chopped me a lot more, but his steam was gone.

He went down after a while, from an accumulation of punches rather than from any especial one, and couldn't get up.

His face didn't have a mark on it that I was responsible for. Mine must have looked as if it had been run through a grinder.

"Maybe I ought to wash up before we eat," I said to Milk River as I took my coat and gun.

"Hell, yes!" he agreed, staring at my face.

A plump man in a Palm Beach suit got in front of me, taking my attention.

"I am Mr Turney of the Orilla Colony Company," he introduced himself. "Am I to understand that you have not made an arrest since you have been here?"

This was the bird who had advertised me! I didn't like that, and I didn't like his round, aggressive face.

"Yes," I confessed.

"There have been two murders in two days," he ran on, "concerning which you have done nothing, though in each case the evidence seems clear enough. Do you think that is satisfactory? Do you think you are performing the duties for which you were employed?"

I didn't say anything.

"Let me tell you that it is not at all satisfactory," he supplied the answers to his own questions. "Neither is it satisfactory that you should have employed this man"—stabbing a plump finger in Milk River's direction—"who is notoriously one of the most lawless men in the county. I want you to understand clearly that unless there is a distinct improvement in your work—unless you show some disposition to do the things you were engaged to do—that engagement will be terminated!"

"Who'd you say you are?" I asked, when he had talked himself out.

"Mr Turney, general superintendent of the Orilla Colony."

"So? Well, Mr General Superintendent Turney, your owners forgot to tell me anything about you when they employed me. So I don't know you at all. Any time you've got anything to say to me, you turn it over to your owners, and if it's important enough, maybe they'll pass it on to me."

He puffed himself up.

"I shall certainly inform them that you have been extremely remiss in your duty, however proficient you may be in street brawls!"

"Will you put a postscript on for me," I called after him as he walked away. "Tell 'em I'm kind of busy just now and can't use any advice—no matter who it comes from."

Milk River and I went ten steps toward the Cañon House, and came face to face with the Reverend Dierks, Miss Janey, and old Adderly. None of them looked at me with anything you could call pleasure.

"You should be ashamed of yourself!" Miss Janey ground out between her false teeth. "Fighting in the street—you who are supposed to keep the peace!"

"As a deputy sheriff you're terrible," Adderly put in. "There's been more trouble here since you came than there ever was before!"

"I must say, brother, that I am deeply disappointed in your actions as a representative of the law!" was the minister's contribution.

I didn't like to say, "Go to hell!" to a group that included a minister and a woman, and I couldn't think of anything else, so, with Milk River making a poor job of holding in his laughter, I stepped around the better element, and we went on to the Cañon House.

Vickers, the sallow, pudgy proprietor, was at the door.

"If you think I got towels to mop up the blood from every hombre that gets himself beat up, you're mistaken," he growled at me. "And I don't want no sheets torn up for bandages, neither!"

"I never seen such a disagreeable cuss as you are," Milk River insisted as we climbed the stairs. "Seems like you can't get along with nobody. Don't you never make no friends?"

"Only with saps!"

I did what I could with water and adhesive tape to reclaim my face, but the result was a long way from beauty. Milk River sat on the bed and grinned and watched me.

"How does a fellow go about winning a fight he gets the worst of?" he inquired.

"It's a gift," was the only answer I could think up.

"You're a lot gifted. That Chick give you more gifts than a Christmas tree could hold."

XI

My patching finished, we went down to the Jew's for food. Three eaters were sitting at the counter. I had to exchange comments on the battle with them while I ate.

We were interrupted by the running of horses in the street. A dozen or more men went past the door, and we could hear them pulling up sharply, dismounting, in front of Bardell's.

Milk River leaned sidewise until his mouth was close to my ear.

"Big 'Nacio's crew from down the cañon. You better hold on tight, chief, or they'll shake the town from under you."

We finished our meal and went out to the street.

In the glow from the big lamp over Bardell's door a Mexican lounged against the wall. A big black-bearded man, his clothes gay with silver buttons, two white-handled guns bolstered low on his thighs, the holsters tied down.

"Will you take the horses over to the stable?" I asked Milk River. "I'm going up and lie across the bed and grow strength again."

He looked at me curiously, and went over to where we had left the ponies.

I stopped in front of the bearded Mexican, and pointed with my cigarette at his guns.

"You're supposed to take those things off when you come to town," I said pleasantly. "Matter of fact, you're not supposed to bring 'em in at all, but I'm not inquisitive enough to look under a man's coat for them. You can't wear them out in the open, though."

Beard and mustache parted to show a smiling curve of yellow teeth.

"Mebbe if *el senor jerife* no lak t'ese t'ings, he lak try take t'em 'way?"

"No. *You* put 'em away."

His smile spread.

"I lak t'em here. I wear t'em here."

"You do what I tell you," I said, still pleasantly, and left him, going back to the Jew's shack.

Leaning over the counter, I picked the sawed-off shotgun out of its nest.

"Can I borrow this? I want to make a believer out of a guy."

"Yes, sir, sure! You help yourself!"

I cocked both barrels before I stepped outdoors.

The big Mexican wasn't in sight. I found him inside, telling his friends about it. Some of his friends were Mexican, some

American, some God knows what. All wore guns. All had the look of thugs.

The big Mexican turned when his friends gaped past him at me. His hands dropped to his guns as he turned, but he didn't draw.

"I don't know what's in this cannon," I told the truth, centering the riot gun on the company, "maybe pieces of barbed wire and dynamite shavings. We'll find out if you birds don't start piling your guns on the bar right away—because I'll sure-God splash you with it!"

They piled their weapons on the bar. I didn't blame them. This thing in my hands would have mangled them plenty!

"After this, when you come to Corkscrew, put your guns out of sight."

Fat Bardell pushed through them, putting joviality back on his face.

"Will you tuck these guns away until your customers are ready to leave town?" I asked him.

"Yes! Yes! Be glad to!" he exclaimed when he had got over his surprise.

I returned the shotgun to its owner and went up to the Cañon House.

A door just a room or two from mine opened as I walked down the hall. Chick Orr came out, saying:

"Don't do nothin' I wouldn't do," over his shoulder.

I saw Clio Landes standing inside the door.

Chick turned from the door, saw me, and stopped, scowling at me.

"You can't fight worth a damn!" he said. "All you know is how to hit!"

"That's right."

He rubbed a swollen hand over his belly.

"I never could learn to take 'em down there. That's what beat me in the profesh."

I tried to look sympathetic, while he studied my face carefully.

"I messed you up, for a fact." His scowl curved up in a gold-toothed grin. The grin went away. The scowl came back. "Don't pick no more fights with me—I might hurt you!"

He poked me in the ribs with a thumb, and went on past me, down the stairs.

The girl's door was closed when I passed it. In my room, I dug out my fountain pen and paper, and had three words of my report written when a knock sounded on my door.

"Come in," I called, having left the door unlocked for Milk River.

Clio Landes pushed the door open.

"Busy?"

"No. Come in and make yourself comfortable. Milk River will be along in a few minutes."

I switched over to the bed, giving her my only chair.

"You're not foxing Milk River, are you?" she asked point-blank.

"No. I got nothing to hang on him. He's right so far as I'm concerned. Why?"

"Nothing, only I thought there might be a caper or two you were trying to cop him for. You're not fooling me, you know! These hicks think you're a bust, but I know different."

"Thanks for those few kind words. But don't be press-agenting my wisdom around. I've had enough advertising. What are you doing out here in the sticks?"

"Lunger!" She tapped her chest. "A croaker told me I'd last longer out here. Like a boob, I fell for it. Living out here isn't any different from dying in the big city."

"How long have you been away from the noise?"

"Three years—a couple up in Colorado, and then this hole. Seem like three centuries."

"I was back there on a job in April," I led her on, "for two or three weeks."

"You were?"

It was just as if I'd said I had been to heaven. She began to shoot questions at me: was this still so-and-so? Was that still thus?

We had quite a little gabfest, and I found I knew some of her friends. A couple of them were high-class swindlers, one was a bootleg magnate, and the rest were a mixture of bookies, conmen, and the like. When I was living in New York, back before the war, I had spent quite a few of my evenings in Dick Malloy's Briar Patch, a cabaret on Seventh Avenue, near where the Ringside opened later. This girl had been one of the Briar Patch's regular customers a few years after my time there.

I couldn't find out what her grift was. She talked a blend of thieves' slang and high-school English, and didn't say much about herself.

We were getting along fine when Milk River came in.

"My friends still in town?" I asked.

"Yes. I hear 'em bubbling around down in Bardell's. I hear you've been makin' yourself more unpopular."

"What now?"

"Your friends among the better element don't seem to think a whole lot of that trick of yours of giving Big 'Nacio's guns, and his hombres', to Bardell to keep. The general opinion seems to be you took the guns out of their right hands and put 'em back in the left."

"I only took 'em to show that I could," I explained. "I didn't want 'em. They would have got more anyway. I think I'll go down and show myself to 'em. I won't be long."

The Border Palace was noisy and busy. None of Big 'Nacio's friends paid any attention to me. Bardell came across the room to tell me:

"I'm glad you backed the boys down. Saved me a lot of trouble, maybe."

I nodded and went out, around to the livery stable, where I found the night man hugging a little iron stove in the office.

"Got anybody who can ride to Filmer with a message tonight?"

"Maybe I can find somebody," he said without enthusiasm.

"Give him a good horse and send him up to the hotel as soon as you can," I requested.

I sat on the edge of the Cañon House porch until a long-legged lad of eighteen or so arrived on a pinto pony and asked for the deputy sheriff. I left the shadow I had been sitting in, and went down into the street, where I could talk to the boy without having an audience.

"Th' old man said yuh wanted to send somethin' to Filmer."

"Can you head out of here toward Filmer, and then cross over to the Circle H. A. R.?"

"Yes, suh, I c'n do that."

"Well, that's what I want. When you get there, tell Peery that Big 'Nacio and his men are in town, and might be riding that way before morning. And don't let the information get out to anybody else."

"I'll do jus' that, suh."

"This is yours, I'll pay the stable bill later." I slid a bill into his hand. "Get going."

Up in my room again, I found Milk River and the girl sitting around a bottle of liquor. I gave my oath of office the laugh to the extent of three drinks. We talked and smoked a while, and then the party broke up. Milk River told me he had the room next to mine.

I added another word to the report I had started, decided I needed sleep more than the client needed the report, and went to bed.

XII

Milk River's knuckles on the door brought me out of bed to shiver in the cold of five-something in the morning.

"This isn't a farm!" I grumbled at him as I let him in. "You're in the city now. You're supposed to sleep until the sun comes up."

"The eye of the law ain't never supposed to sleep," he grinned at me, his teeth clicking together, because he hadn't any more clothes on than I. "Fisher, who's got a ranch out that-away, sent a man in to tell you that there's a battle going on out at the Circle H. A. R. He hit my door instead of yours. Do we ride out that-away, chief?"

"We do. Hunt up some rifles, water, and the horses. I'll be down at the Jew's, ordering breakfast and getting some lunch wrapped up."

Forty minutes later Milk River and I were out of Corkscrew.

The morning warmed as we rode, the sun making long violet pictures on the desert, raising the dew in a softening mist. The mesquite was fragrant, and even the sand—which would be as nice as a dusty stove-top later—had a fresh, pleasant odor. There was nothing to hear but the creaking of leather, the occasional clink of metal, and the plop-plop of the horses' feet on hard ground, which changed to a shff-shff when we struck loose sand.

The battle seemed to be over, unless the battlers had run out of bullets and were going at it hand to hand.

Up over the ranch buildings, as we approached, three blue spots that were buzzards circled, and a moving animal showed against the sky for an instant on a distant ridge.

"A bronc that ought to have a rider and ain't," Milk River pronounced it.

Farther along, we passed a bullet-riddled Mexican sombrero, and then the sun sparkled on a handful of empty brass cartridges.

One of the ranch buildings was a charred black pile. Nearby another one of the men I had disarmed in Bardell's lay dead on his back.

A bandaged head poked around a building-corner, and its owner stepped out, his right arm in a sling, a revolver in his left. Behind him trotted the one-eyed Chinese cook, swinging a cleaver.

Milk River recognized the bandaged man.

"Howdy, Red! Been quarreling?"

"Some. We took all th' advantage we could of th' warnin' you sent out, an' when Big 'Nacio an' his herd showed up just 'fore daylight, we Injuned them all over the county. I stopped a couple o' slugs, so I stayed to home whilst th' rest o' th' boys followed 'em south. 'F you listen sharp, you can hear a pop now an' then."

"Do we follow 'em, or head 'em?" Milk River asked me.

"Can we head 'em?"

"Might. If Big 'Nacio's running, he'll circle back to his rancho along about dark. If we cut into the cañon and slide along down, maybe we can be there first. He won't make much speed having to fight of Peery and the boys as he goes."

"We'll try it."

Milk River leading, we went past the ranch buildings, and on down the draw; going into the cañon at the point where I had entered it the previous day. After a while the footing got better, and we made better time.

The sun climbed high enough to let its rays down on us, and the comparative coolness in which we had been riding went away. At noon we stopped to rest the horses, eat a couple of sandwiches, and smoke a bit. Then we went on.

Presently the sun passed, began to crawl down on our right, and shadows grew in the cañon. The welcome shade had reached the east wall when Milk River, in front, stopped.

"Around this next bend it is."

We dismounted, took a drink apiece, blew the sand off our rifles, and went forward afoot, toward a clump of bushes that covered the crooked cañon's next twist.

Beyond the bend, the floor of the cañon ran downhill into a round saucer. The saucer's sides sloped gently up to the desert floor. In the middle of the saucer, four low adobe buildings sat. In spite of their exposure to the desert sun, they looked somehow damp and dark. From one of them a thin plume of bluish smoke rose. Water ran out of a rock-bordered hole in one sloping cañon-wall, disappearing in a thin stream that curved behind one of the buildings.

No man, no animal was in sight.

"I'm going to prospect down there," Milk River said, handing me his hat and rifle.

"Right," I agreed. "I'll cover you, but if anything breaks, you'd better get out of the way. I'm not the most dependable rifle-shot in the world!"

For the first part of his trip Milk River had plenty of cover. He went ahead rapidly. The screening plants grew fewer. His pace fell off. Flat on the ground, he squirmed from clump to boulder, from hummock to bush.

Thirty feet from the nearest building, he ran out of places to hide. I thought he would scout the buildings from that point, and then come back. Instead, he jumped up and sprinted to the shelter of the nearest building.

Nothing happened. He crouched against the wall for several long minutes, and then began to work his way toward the rear.

A hatless Mexican came around the corner.

I couldn't make out his features, but I saw his body stiffen.

His hand went to his waist.

Milk River's gun flashed.

The Mexican dropped. The bright steel of his knife glittered high over Milk River's head, and rang when it landed on a stone.

Milk River went out of my sight around the building. When I saw him again he was charging at the black doorway of the second building.

Fire-streaks came out of the door to meet him.

I did what I could with the two rifles—laying a barrage ahead of him—pumping lead at the open door, as fast as I could get it out. I emptied the second rifle just as he got too close to the door for me to risk another shot.

Dropping the rifle, I ran back to my horse, and rode to my crazy assistant's assistance.

He didn't need any. It was all over when I arrived.

He was driving another Mexican and Gyp Rainey out of the building with the nozzles of his guns.

"This is the crop," he greeted me. "Leastways, I couldn't find no more."

"What are you doing here?" I asked Rainey.

But the hop-head didn't want to talk. He looked sullenly at the ground and made no reply.

"We'll tie 'em up," I decided, "and then look around."

Milk River did most of the tying, having had more experience with ropes.

He trussed them back to back on the ground, and we went exploring.

XIII

Except for plenty of guns of all sizes and more than plenty of ammunition to fit, we didn't find anything very exciting until we came to a heavy door—barred and padlocked—set half in the foundation of the principal building, half in the mound on which the building sat.

I found a broken piece of rusty pick, and knocked the padlock off with it. Then we took the bar off and swung the door open.

Men came eagerly toward us out of an unventilated, unlighted cellar. Seven men who talked a medley of languages as they came.

We used our guns to stop them.

Their jabbering went high, excited.

"Quiet!" I yelled at them.

They knew what I meant, even if they didn't understand the word. The babel stopped and we looked them over. All seven seemed to be foreigners—and a hard-looking gang of cutthroats. A short Jap with a scar from ear to ear; three Slavs, one bearded, barrel-bodied, red-eyed, the other two bullet-headed, cunning-faced; a swarthy husky who was unmistakably a Greek; a bow-legged man whose probable nationality I couldn't guess; and a pale fat man whose china-blue eyes and puckered red mouth were probably Teutonic.

Milk River and I tried them out with English first, and then with what Spanish we could scrape up between us. Both attempts brought a lot of jabbering from them, but nothing in either of those languages.

"Got anything else?" I asked Milk River.

"Chinook is all that's left."

That wouldn't help much. I tried to remember some of the words we used to think were French in the A. E. F.

"*Que désirez-vous?*" brought a bright smile to the fat face of the blue-eyed man.

I caught "*Nous allons à les États-Unis*" before the speed with which he threw the words at me confused me beyond recognizing anything else.

That was funny. Big 'Nacio hadn't let these birds know that they were already in the United States. I suppose he could manage them better if they thought they were still in Mexico.

"*Montrez-moi votrepasse-port.*"

That brought a sputtering protest from Blue Eyes. They had been told no passports were necessary. It was because they had been refused passports that they were paying to be smuggled in.

"Quand etes-vous tenu ici?"

Hier meant yesterday, regardless of what the other things he put in his answer were. Big 'Nacio had come straight to Corkscrew after bringing these men across the border and sticking them in his cellar, then.

We locked the immigrants in their cellar again, putting Rainey and the Mexican in with them. Rainey howled like a wolf when I took his hypodermic needle and his coke away from him.

"Sneak up and take a look at the country," I told Milk River, "while I plant the man you killed."

By the time he came back I had the dead Mexican arranged to suit me: slumped down in a chair a little off from the front door of the principal building, his back against the wall, a sombrero tilted down over his face.

"There's dust kicking up some ways off," Milk River reported. "Wouldn't surprise me none if we got our company along towards dark."

Darkness had been solid for an hour when they came.

By then, fed and rested, we were ready for them. A light was burning in the house. Milk River was in there, tinkling a mandolin. Light came out of the open front door to show the dead Mexican dimly—a statue of a sleeper. Beyond him, around the corner except for my eyes and forehead, I lay close to the wall.

We could hear our company long before we could see them. Two horses—but they made enough noise for ten—coming lickety-split down to the lighted door.

Big 'Nacio, in front, was out of the saddle and had one foot in the doorway before his horse's front feet—thrown high by the violence with which the big man had pulled him up—hit the ground again. The second rider was close behind him.

The bearded man saw the corpse. He jumped at it, swinging his quirt, roaring:

"*Arriba, piojo!*"

The mandolin's tinkling stopped.

I scrambled up.

Big 'Nacio's whiskers went down in surprise.

His quirt caught a button of the dead man's clothes, tangled there, the loop on its other end holding one of Big 'Nacio's wrists.

His other hand went to his thigh.

My gun had been in my hand for an hour. I was close. I had leisure to pick my target. When his hand touched his gun-butt, I put a bullet through hand and thigh.

As he fell, I saw Milk River knock the second man down with a clout of gun-barrel on back of his head.

"Seems like we team-up pretty good," the sunburned boy said as he stooped to take the enemy's weapons from them.

The bearded man's bellowing oaths made conversation difficult.

"I'll put this one you beaned in the cooler," I said. "Watch 'Nacio, and we'll patch him up when I come back."

I dragged the unconscious man halfway to the cellar door before he came to. I goaded him the rest of the way with my gun, shooed him indoors, shooed the other prisoners away from the door, and closed and barred it again.

The bearded man had stopped howling when I returned.

"Anybody riding after you?" I asked, as I knelt beside him and began cutting his pants away with my pocket knife.

For answer to that I got a lot of information about myself, my habits, my ancestors. None of it happened to be the truth, but it was colorful.

"Maybe we'd better put a hobble on his tongue," Milk River suggested.

"No. Let him cry!" I spoke to the bearded man again. "If I were you, I'd answer that question. If it happens that the Circle H. A. R. riders trail you here and take us unawares, it's a gut that you're in for a lynching. *Ahorcar*, understand?"

He hadn't thought of that.

"*Si, si.* T'at Peery an' hees hombres. T'ey *segtiir—mucho rapidez!*"

"Any of your men left, besides you and this other?"

"No! *S'ingunP'*

"Suppose you build as much fire as you can out here in front while I'm stopping this egg's bleeding, Milk River."

The lad looked disappointed.

"Ain't we going to bushw'ack them waddies none?"

"Not unless we have to."

By the time I had put a couple of tourniquets on the Mexican, Milk River had a roaring fire lighting the buildings and most of the saucer in which they sat. I had intended stowing 'Nacio and Milk River indoors, in case I couldn't make Peery talk sense. But there wasn't time. I had just started to explain my plan to Milk River when Peery's bass voice came from outside the ring of light.

"Put 'em up, everybody!"

XIV

"Easy!" I cautioned Milk River, and stood up. But I didn't raise my hands.

"The excitement's over," I called. "Come on down."

Ten minutes passed. Peery rode into the light. His square-jawed face was grime-streaked and grim. His horse was muddy lather all over. His guns were in his hands.

Behind him rode Dunne—as dirty, as grim, as ready with his firearms.

Nobody followed Dunne. The others were spread around us in the darkness, then.

Peery leaned over his pony's head to look at Big 'Nacio, who was lying breathlessly still on the ground.

"Dead?"

"No—a slug through hand and leg. I've got some of his friends under lock and key indoors."

Mad red rims showed around Peery's eyes in the firelight.

"You can keep the others," he said harshly. "This hombre will do us."

I didn't misunderstand him.

"I'm keeping all of them."

"I ain't got a damned bit of confidence in you," Peery growled down at me. "You ain't done nothing since you been here, and it ain't likely you ever will. I'm making sure that this Big 'Nacio's riding stops right here. I'm taking care of him myself."

"Nothing stirring!"

"How you figuring on keeping me from taking him?" he laughed viciously at me. "You don't think me and Irish are alone, do you? If you don't believe you're corralled, make a play!"

I believed him, but—

"That doesn't make any difference. If I were a grub-line rider, or a desert rat, or any lone guy with no connections, you'd rub me out quick enough. But I'm not, and you know I'm not. I'm counting on that. You've got to kill me to take 'Nacio. That's flat! I don't think you want him bad enough to go that far. Right or wrong, I'm playing it that way."

He stared at me for a while. Then his knees urged his horse toward the Mexican, 'Nacio sat up and began pleading with me to save him.

Slowly I raised my right hand to my shoulder-holstered gun.

"Drop it!" Peery ordered, both his guns close to my head.

I grinned at him, took my gun out slowly, slowly turned it until it was level between his two.

We held that pose long enough to work up a good sweat apiece. It wasn't restful!

A queer light flickered in his red-rimmed eyes.

I didn't guess what was coming until too late.

His left-hand gun swung away from me—exploded.

A hole opened in the top of Big 'Nacio's head. He pitched over on his side.

The grinning Milk River shot Peery out of the saddle.

I was under Peery's right-hand gun when it went off. I was scrambling under his rearing horse's feet.

Dunne's revolvers coughed.

"Inside!" I yelled to Milk River, and put two bullets into Dunne's pony.

Rifle bullets sang every which way across, around, under, over us.

Inside the lighted doorway Milk River hugged the floor, spouting fire and lead from both hands.

Dunne's horse was down. Dunne got up—caught both hands to his face—went down beside his horse.

Milk River turned off the fireworks long enough for me to dash over him into the house.

While I smashed the lamp chimney, blew out the flame, he slammed the door.

Bullets made music on door and wall.

"Did I do right, shooting that jigger?" Milk River asked.

"Good work!" I lied.

There was no use bellyaching over what was done, but I hadn't wanted Peery dead. Dunne's death was unnecessary, too. The proper place for guns is after talk has failed, and I hadn't run out of words by any means when this brown-skinned lad had gone into action.

The bullets stopped punching holes in our door.

"The boys have got their heads together," Milk River guessed. "They can't have a hell of a lot of caps left if they've been snapping them at 'Nacio since early morning."

I found a white handkerchief in my pocket and began stuffing one corner in a rifle muzzle.

"What's for that?" Milk River asked.

"Talk." I moved to the door. "And you're to hold your hand until I'm through."

"I never seen such a hombre for making talk," he complained.

I opened the door a cautious crack. Nothing happened. I eased the rifle through the crack and waved it in the light of the still burning fire. Nothing happened. I opened the door and stepped out.

"Send somebody down to talk!" I yelled at the outer darkness.

A voice I didn't recognize cursed bitterly, and began a threat: "We'll give yuh—"

It broke off in silence.

Metal glinted off to one side.

Buck Small, his bulging eyes dark-circled, a smear of blood on one cheek, came into the light.

"What are you people figuring on doing?" I asked.

He looked sullenly at me.

"We're figurin' on gettin' that Milk River party. We ain't got nothin' against you. You're doin' what you're paid to do. But Milk River hadn't ought of killed Peery!"

Milk River bounced stiff-legged out of the door.

"Any time you want any part of me, you pop-eyed this-and-that, all you got to do is name it!"

Small's hands curved toward his bolstered guns.

"Cut it!" I growled at Milk River, getting in front of him, pushing him back to the door. "I've got work to do. I can't waste time watching you boys cut up. This is no time to be bragging about what a desperate guy you are!"

I finally got rid of him, and faced Small again.

"You boys want to take a tumble to yourselves, Buck. The wild and woolly days are over. You're in the clear so far. 'Nacio jumped you, and you did what was right when you massacred his riders all over the desert. But you've got no right to fool with my prisoners. Peery wouldn't understand that. And if we hadn't shot him, he'd have swung later!

"For Milk River's end of it: he doesn't owe you anything. He dropped Peery under your guns—dropped him with less than an even break! You people had the cards stacked against us. Milk River took a chance you or I wouldn't have taken. You've got nothing to howl about.

"I've got ten prisoners in there, and I've got a lot of guns, and stuff to put in 'em. If you make me do it, I'm going to deal out the guns to my prisoners and let 'em fight. I'd rather lose every damned one of them that way than let you take one of 'em away from me!

"All that you boys can get out of fighting us is a lot of grief—whether you win or lose. This end of Orilla County has been left to itself longer than most of the Southwest. But those days are over. Outside money has come into it; outside people are coming. You can't buck it! Men tried that in the old days, and failed. Will you talk it over with the others?"

"Yeah," and he went away in the darkness.

I went indoors.

"I think they'll be sensible," I told Milk River, "but you can't tell. So maybe you better hunt around and see if you can find a way through the floor to our basement hoosegow, because I meant what I said about giving guns to our captives."

Twenty minutes later Buck Small was back.

"You win," he said. "We want to take Peery and Dunne with us."

XV

Nothing ever looked better to me than my bed in the Cañon House the next—Wednesday—night. My grandstand play with the yellow horse, my fight with Chick Orr, the unaccustomed riding I had been doing—these things had filled me fuller of aches than Orilla County was of sand.

Our ten prisoners were resting in an old outdoor store-room of Adderly's, guarded by volunteers from among the better element, under the supervision of Milk River. They would be safe there, I thought, until the immigration inspectors—to whom I had sent word—could come for them. Most of Big 'Nacio's men had been killed in the fight with the Circle H. A. R. hands, and I didn't think Bardell could collect men enough to try to open my prison.

The Circle H. A. R. riders would behave reasonably well from now on, I thought. There were two angles still open, but the end of my job in Corkscrew wasn't far away. So I wasn't dissatisfied with myself as I got stiffly out of my clothes and climbed into bed for the sleep I had earned.

Did I get it? No.

I was just comfortably bedded down when somebody began thumping on my door.

It was fussy little Dr Haley.

"I was called into your temporary prison a few minutes ago to look at Rainey," the doctor said. "He tried to escape, and broke his arm in a fight with one of the guards. That isn't serious, but the man's condition is. He should be given some cocaine. I don't think it is safe to leave him without the drug any longer. I would have given him an injection, but Milk River stopped me, saying you had given orders that nothing was to be done without instructions from you."

"Is he really in bad shape?"

"Yes."

"I'll go down and talk to him," I said, reluctantly starting to dress again. "I gave him a shot now and then on the way up from the rancho—enough to keep him from falling down on us. But I want to get some information out of him now, and he gets no more until he'll talk. Maybe he's ripe now."

We could hear Rainey's howling before we reached the jail.

Milk River was squatting on his heels outside the door, talking to one of the guards.

"He's going to throw a joe on you, chief, if you don't give him a pill," Milk River told me. "I got him tied up now, so's he can't pull the splints off his arm. He's plumb crazy!"

The doctor and I went inside, the guard holding a lantern high at the door so we could see.

In one corner of the room, Gyp Rainey sat in the chair to which Milk River had tied him. Froth was in the corners of his mouth. He was writhing with cramps. The other prisoners were trying to get some sleep, their blankets spread on the floor as far from Rainey as they could get.

"For Christ's sake give me a shot!" Rainey whined at me.

"Give me a hand, Doctor, and we'll carry him out."

We lifted him, chair and all, and carried him outside.

"Now stop your bawling and listen to me," I ordered. "You shot Nisbet. I want the straight story of it. The straight story will bring you a shot, and nothing else will."

"I didn't kill him!" he screamed. "I didn't! Before God, I didn't!"

"That's a lie. You stole Peery's rope while the rest of us were in Bardell's place Monday morning, talking over Slim's death. You tied the rope where it would look like the murderer had made a getaway down the cañon. Then you stood at the window until Nisbet came into the back room—and you shot him. Nobody went down that rope—or Milk River would have found some sign. Will you come through?"

He wouldn't. He screamed and cursed and pleaded and denied knowledge of the murder.

"Back you go!" I said.

Dr Haley put a hand on my arm.

"I don't want you to think I am interfering, but I really must warn you that what you're doing is dangerous. It is my belief, and my duty to advise you, that you are endangering this man's life by refusing him some of the drug."

"I know it, Doctor, but I'll have to risk it. He's not so far gone, or he wouldn't be lying. When the sharp edge of the drug-hunger hits him, he'll talk!"

Gyp Rainey stowed away again, I went back to my room. But not to bed.

Clio Landes was waiting for me, sitting there—I had left the door unlocked—with a bottle of whisky. She was about three-quarters lit up—one of those melancholy lushes.

She was a poor, sick, lonely, homesick girl, far away from her world. She dosed herself with alcohol, remembered her dead parents, sad bits of her childhood and unfortunate slices of her past, and cried over them. She poured out all her hopes and fears to me—including her liking for Milk River, who was a good kid even if he had never been within two thousand miles of Forty-second Street and Broadway.

The talk always came back to that: New York, New York, New York.

It was close to four o'clock Thursday morning when the whisky finally answered my prayers, and she went to sleep on my shoulder.

I picked her up and carried her down the hall to her own room. Just as I reached her door, fat Bardell came up the stairs.

"More work for the sheriff," he commented jovially, and went on.

I took her slippers off, tucked her in bed, opened the window, and went out, locking the door behind me and chucking the key over the transom.

After that I slept.

XVI

The sun was high and the room was hot when I woke to the familiar sound of someone knocking on the door. This time it was one of the volunteer guards—the long-legged boy who had carried the warning to Peery Monday night.

"Gyp wants t' see yuh." The boy's face was haggard. "He wants yuh more'n I ever seen a man want anything."

Rainey was a wreck when I got to him.

"I killed him! I killed him!" he shrieked at me. "Bardell knowed the Circle H. A. R. would hit back f'r Slim's killin'. He made me kill Nisbet an' stack th' deal agin Peery so's it'd be up t' you t' go up agin 'em. He'd tried it before an' got th' worst of it!

"Gimme a shot! That's th' God's truth! I stoled th' rope, planted it, an' shot Nisbet wit' Bardell's gun when Bardell sent him back there! Th' gun's under th' tin-can dump in back o' Adderly's. Gimme th' shot! Gimme it!"

"Where's Milk River?" I asked the long-legged boy.

"Sleepin', I reckon. He left along about day-light."

"All right, Gyp! Hold it until the doc gets here. I'll send him right over!"

I found Dr Haley in his house. A minute later he was carrying a charge over to the hypo.

The Border Palace didn't open until noon. Its doors were locked. I went up the street to the Cañon House. Milk River came out just as I stepped up on the porch.

"Hello, young fellow," I greeted him. "Got any idea which room your friend Bardell reposes in?"

He looked at me as if he had never seen me before.

"S'pose you find out for yourself. I'm through doing your chores. You can find yourself a new wet nurse, Mister, or you can go to hell!"

The odor of whisky came out with the words, but he wasn't drunk enough for that to be the whole explanation.

"What's the matter with you?" I asked.

"What's the matter is I think you're a lousy—"

I didn't let it get any farther than that.

His right hand whipped to his side as I stepped in.

I jammed him between the wall and my hip before he could draw, and got one of my hands on each of his arms.

"You may be a curly wolf with your rod," I growled, shaking him, a lot more peeved than if he had been a stranger, "but if you try any of your monkey business on me, I'll turn you over my knee!"

Clio Landes' thin fingers dug into my arm.

"Stop it!" she cried. "Stop it! Why don't you behave?" to Milk River; and to me: "He's sore over something this morning. He doesn't mean what he says!"

I was sore myself.

"I mean what I said," I insisted.

But I took my hands off him, and went indoors. Inside the door I ran into sallow Vickers, who was hurrying to see what the rumpus was about.

"What room is Bardell's?"

"214. Why?"

I went on past him and upstairs.

My gun in one hand, I used the other to knock on Bardell's door.

"Who is it?" came through.

I told him.

"What do you want?"

I said I wanted to talk to him.

He kept me waiting for a couple of minutes before he opened. He was half-dressed. All his clothes below the waist were on. Above, he had a coat on over his undershirt, and one of his hands was in his coat pocket.

His eyes jumped big when they lit on my gun.

"You're arrested for Nisbet's murder!" I informed him. "Take your hand out of your pocket."

He tried to look as if he thought I was kidding him.

"For Nisbet's murder?"

"Uh-huh. Rainey came through. Take your hand out of your pocket."

"You're arresting me on the say-so of a hophead?"

"Uh-huh. Take your hand out of your pocket."

"You're—"

"Take your hand out of your pocket."

His eyes moved from mine to look past my head, a flash of triumph burning in them.

I beat him to the first shot by a hairline, since he had wasted time waiting for me to fall for that ancient trick.

His bullet cut my neck.

Mine took him where his undershirt was tight over his fat chest.

He fell, tugging at his pocket, trying to get the gun out for another shot.

I could have jumped him, but he was going to die anyhow. That first bullet had got his lungs. I put another into him.

The hall filled with people.

"Get the doctor!" I called to them.

But Bardell didn't need him. He was dead before I had the words out of my mouth.

Chick Orr came through the crowd, into the room.

I stood up, sticking my gun back in its holster.

"I've got nothing on you, Chick, yet," I said slowly. "You know better than I do whether there is anything to get or not. If I were you, I'd drift out of Corkscrew without wasting too much time packing up."

The ex-pug squinted his eyes at me, rubbed his chin, and made a clucking sound in his mouth.

His gold teeth showed in a grin.

"'F anybody asks for me, you tell 'em I'm off on a tour," and he pushed out through the crowd again.

When the doctor came, I took him up the hall to my room, where he patched my neck. The wound wasn't much, but my neck is fleshy, and it bled a lot—all over me, in fact.

After he had finished, I got fresh clothes from my bag and undressed. But when I went to wash, I found the doctor had used all my water. Getting into coat, pants and shoes, I went down to the kitchen for more.

The hall was empty when I came upstairs again, except for Clio Landes.

She went past me without looking at me—deliberately not looking at me.

I washed, dressed, and strapped on my gun. One more angle to be cleaned up, and I would be through. I didn't think I'd need the .32 toys any more, so I put them away. One more angle, and I was done. I was pleased with the idea of getting away from Corkscrew. I didn't like the place, had never liked it, liked it less than ever since Milk River's break.

I was thinking about him when I stepped out of the hotel—to see him standing across the street.

I didn't give him a tumble, but turned toward the lower end of the street.

One step. A bullet kicked up dirt at my feet.

I stopped.

"Go for it, fat boy!" Milk River yelled. "It's me or you!"

I turned slowly to face him, looking for an out. But there wasn't any.

His eyes were insane-lighted slits. His face was a ghastly savage mask. He was beyond reasoning with.

"Put it away!" I ordered, though I knew the words were wasted.

"It's me or you!" he repeated, and put another bullet into the ground in front of me. "Warm your iron!"

I stopped looking for an out. Blood thickened in my head, and things began to look queer. I could feel my neck thickening. I hoped I wasn't going to get too mad to shoot straight.

I went for my gun.

He gave me an even break.

His gun swung down to me as mine straightened to him.

We pulled triggers together.

Flame jumped at me.

I smacked the ground—my right side all numb.

He was staring at me—bewildered. I stopped staring at him, and looked at my gun—the gun that had only clicked when I pulled the trigger!

When I looked up again, he was coming toward me, slowly, his gun hanging at his side.

"Played it safe, huh?" I raised my gun so he could see the broken firing-pin. "Serves me right for leaving it on the bed when I went downstairs for water."

Milk River dropped his gun—grabbed mine.

Clio Landes came running from the hotel to him.

"You're not—?"

Milk River stuck my gun in her face.

"You done that?"

"I was afraid he—" she began.

"You!"

With the back of an open hand, Milk River struck the girl's mouth.

He dropped down beside me, his face a boy's face. A tear fell hot on my hand.

"Chief, I didn't—"

"That's all right," I assured him, and I meant it.

I missed whatever else he said. The numbness was leaving my side, and the feeling that came in its place wasn't pleasant. Everything stirred inside me...

XVII

I was in bed when I came to. Dr Haley was doing disagreeable things to my side. Behind him, Milk River held a basin in unsteady hands.

"Milk River," I whispered, because that was the best I could do in the way of talk.

He bent his ear to me.

"Get the Jew. He killed Vogel. Careful—gun on him. Talk self-defense—maybe confess. Lock him up with others."

Sweet sleep again.

Night, dim lamplight was in the room when I opened my eyes again. Clio Landes sat beside my bed, staring at the floor, woebegone.

"Good evening," I managed.

I was sorry I had said anything.

She cried all over me and kept me busy assuring her she had been forgiven for the trickery with my gun. I don't know how many times I forgave her. It got to be a damned nuisance. No sooner would I say that everything was all right than she'd begin all over again to ask me to forgive her.

"I was so afraid you'd kill him, because he's only a kid, and somebody had told him a lot of things about you and me, and I knew how crazy he was, and he's only a kid, and I was so afraid you'd kill him," and so on and so on.

Half an hour of this had me woozy with fever.

"And now he won't talk to me, won't even look at me, won't let me come in here when he's here. And nothing will ever make things right again, and I was so afraid you'd kill him, because he's only a boy, and..."

I had to shut my eyes and pretend I had passed out to shut her up.

I must have slept some, because when I looked around again it was day, and Milk River was in the chair.

He stood up, not looking at me, his head hanging.

"I'll be moving on, Chief, now that you're coming around all right. I want you to know, though, that if I'd knowed what that—done to your gun I wouldn't never have throwed down on you."

"What was the matter with you, anyhow?" I growled at him.

His face got beet-color and he shuffled his feet.

"Crazy, I reckon," he mumbled. "I had a couple of drinks, and then Bardell filled me full of stuff about you and her, and that you was playing me for a Chinaman. And—and I just went plumb loco, I reckon."

"Any of it left in your system?"

"Hell, no, chief! I'd give a leg if none of it had never happened!"

"Then suppose you stop this foolishness and sit down and talk sense. Are you and the girl still on the outs?"

They were, most emphatically, most profanely.

"You're a big boob!" I told him. "She's a stranger out here, and homesick for her New York. I could talk her language and knew the people she knew. That's all there was—"

"But that ain't the big point, chief! Any woman that would pull a—"

"Bunk! It was a shabby trick, right enough. But a woman who'll pull a trick like that for you when you are in a jam is worth a million an ounce, and you'd know it if you had anything to know anything with. Now you run out and find this Clio person, and bring her back with you, and no nonsense!"

He pretended he was going reluctantly. But I heard her voice when he knocked on her door. And they let me lay there in my bed of pain for one solid hour before they remembered me. They came in walking so close together that they were stumbling over each other's feet.

"Now let's talk business," I grumbled. "What day is this?"

"Monday."

"Did you get the Jew?"

"I done that thing," Milk River said, dividing the one chair with the girl. "He's over to the county seat now—went over with the others. He swallowed that self-defense bait, and told me all about it. How'd you ever figure it out, chief?"

"Figure what out?"

"That the Jew killed poor old Slim. He says Slim come in there that night, woke him up, ate a dollar and ten cents' worth of grub on him, and then dared him to try and collect. In the argument that follows, Slim goes for his gun, and the Jew gets scared and shoots him—after which Slim obligingly staggers out o' doors to die. I can see all that clear enough, but how'd you hit on it?"

"I oughtn't give away my professional secrets, but I will this once. The Jew was cleaning house when I went in to ask him for what he knew about the killing, and he had scrubbed his floor before he started on the ceiling. If that meant anything at all, it meant that he had had to scrub his floor, and was making the cleaning general to cover it up. So maybe Slim had bled some on that floor.

"Starting from that point, the rest came easily enough. Slim leaving the Border Palace in a wicked frame of mind, broke after his earlier winning, humiliated by Nisbet's triumph in the gun-pulling, soured further by the stuff he had been drinking all day. Red Wheelan had reminded him that afternoon of the time the Jew had followed him to the ranch to collect two bits. What more likely than he'd carry his meanness into the Jew's shack? That Slim hadn't been shot with the shotgun didn't mean anything. I never had any faith in that shotgun from the first. If the Jew had been depending on that for his protection, he wouldn't have put it in plain sight, and under a shelf, where it wasn't easy to get out. I figured the shotgun was there for moral effect, and he'd have another one stowed out of sight for use.

"Another point you folks missed was that Nisbet seemed to be telling a straight story—not at all the sort of tale he'd have told if he were guilty. Bardell's and Chick's weren't so good, but the chances are they really thought Nisbet had killed Slim, and were trying to cover him up."

Milk River grinned at me, pulling the girl closer with the one arm that was around her.

"You ain't so downright dumb," he said. "Clio done warned me the first time she seen you that I'd best not try to run no sandies on you."

A far-away look came into his pale eyes.

"Think of all them folks that were killed and maimed and jailed—all over a dollar and ten cents. It's a good thing Slim didn't eat five dollars' worth of grub. He'd of depopulated the State of Arizona complete!"

10

DEAD YELLOW WOMEN

BLACK MASK, NOVEMBER 1925

She was sitting straight and stiff in one of the Old Man's chairs when he called me into his office—a tall girl of perhaps twenty-four, broad-shouldered, deep-bosomed, in mannish gray clothes. That she was Oriental showed only in the black shine of her bobbed hair, in the pale yellow of her unpowdered skin, and in the fold of her upper lids at the outer eye-corners, half hidden by the dark rims of her spectacles. But there was no slant to her eyes, her nose was almost aquiline, and she had more chin than Mongolians usually have. She was modern Chinese-American from the flat heels of her tan shoes to the crown of her untrimmed felt hat.

I knew her before the Old Man introduced me. The San Francisco papers had been full of her affairs for a couple of days. They had printed photographs and diagrams, interviews, editorials, and more or less expert opinions from various sources. They had gone back to 1912 to remember the stubborn fight of the local Chinese—mostly from Fokien and Kwangtung, where democratic ideas and hatred of Manchus go together—to have her father kept out of the United States, to which he had scooted when the Manchu rule flopped. The papers had recalled the excitement in Chinatown when Shan Fang was allowed to land—insulting placards had been hung in the streets, an unpleasant reception had been planned.

But Shan Fang had fooled the Cantonese. Chinatown had never seen him. He had taken his daughter and his gold—presumably the accumulated profits of a life-time of provincial misrule—down to San Mateo County, where he had built what the papers described as a palace on the edge of the Pacific. There he had lived and died in a manner suitable to a *Ta Jen* and a millionaire.

So much for the father. For the daughter—this young woman who was coolly studying me as I sat down across the table from her: she had been ten-year-old Ai Ho, a very Chinese little girl, when her father had brought her to California. All that was Oriental of her now were the features I have mentioned and the money her father had left her. Her name, translated into English, had become Water Lily, and then, by another step, Lillian. It was as Lillian Shan that she had attended an eastern university, acquired several degrees, won a tennis championship of some sort in 1919, and published a book on the nature and significance of fetishes, whatever all that is or are.

Since her father's death, in 1921, she had lived with her four Chinese servants in the house on the shore, where she had written her first book and was now at work on another. A couple of weeks ago, she had found herself stumped, so she said—had run into a blind alley. There was, she said, a certain old cabalistic manuscript in the Arsenal Library in Paris that she believed would solve her troubles for her. So she had packed some clothes and, accompanied by her maid, a Chinese woman named Wang Ma, had taken a train for New York, leaving the three other servants to take care of the house during her absence. The decision to go to France for a look at the manuscript had been formed one morning—she was on the train before dark.

On the train between Chicago and New York, the key to the problem that had puzzled her suddenly popped into her head. Without pausing even for a night's rest in New York, she had turned around and headed back for San Francisco. At the ferry here she had tried to telephone her chauffeur to bring a car for her. No answer. A taxicab had carried her and her maid to her house. She rang the door-bell to no effect.

When her key was in the lock the door had been suddenly opened by a young Chinese man—a stranger to her. He had refused her admittance until she told him who she was. He mumbled an unintelligible explanation as she and the maid went into the hall.

Both of them were neatly bundled up in some curtains.

Two hours later Lillian Shan got herself loose—in a linen closet on the second floor. Switching on the light, she started to untie the maid. She stopped. Wang Ma was dead. The rope around her neck had been drawn too tight.

Lillian Shan went out into the empty house and telephoned the sheriff's office in Redwood City.

Two deputy sheriffs had come to the house, had listened to her story, had poked around, and had found another Chinese body—another strangled woman—buried in the cellar. Apparently she had been dead a week or a week and a half; the dampness of the ground made more positive dating impossible. Lillian Shan identified her as another of her servants—Wan Lan, the cook.

The other servants—Hoo Lun and Yin Hung—had vanished. Of the several hundred thousand dollars' worth of furnishings old Shan Fang had put into the house during his life, not a nickel's worth had been removed. There were no signs of a struggle. Everything was in order. The closest neighboring house was nearly half a mile away. The neighbors had seen nothing, knew nothing.

That's the story the newspapers had hung headlines over, and that's the story this girl, sitting very erect in her chair, speaking with businesslike briskness, shaping each word as exactly as if it were printed in black type, told the Old Man and me.

"I am not at all satisfied with the effort the San Mateo County authorities have made to apprehend the murderer or murderers," she wound up. "I wish to engage your agency."

The Old Man tapped the table with the point of his inevitable long yellow pencil and nodded at me.

"Have you any idea of your own on the murders, Miss Shan?" I asked.

"I have not."

"What *do you* know about the servants—the missing ones as well as the dead?"

"I really know little or nothing about them." She didn't seem very interested. "Wang Ma was the most recent of them to come to the house, and she has been with me for nearly seven years. My father employed them, and I suppose he knew something about them."

"Don't you know where they came from? Whether they have relatives? Whether they have friends? What they did when they weren't working?"

"No," she said. "I did not pry into their lives."

"The two who disappeared—what do they look like?"

"Hoo Lun is an old man, quite white-haired and thin and stooped. He did the housework. Yin Hung, who was my chauffeur and gardener, is younger, about thirty years old, I think. He is quite short, even for a Cantonese, but sturdy. His nose has been broken at some time and not set properly. It is very flat, with a pronounced bend in the bridge."

"Do you think this pair, or either of them, could have killed the women?"

"I do not think they did."

"The young Chinese—the stranger who let you in the house—what did he look like?"

"He was quite slender, and not more than twenty or twenty-one years old, with large gold fillings in his front teeth. I think he was quite dark."

"Will you tell me exactly why you are dissatisfied with what the sheriff is doing, Miss Shan?"

"In the first place, I am not sure they are competent. The ones I saw certainly did not impress me with their brilliance."

"And in the second place?"

"Really," she asked coldly, "is it necessary to go into all my mental processes?"

"It is."

She looked at the Old Man, who smiled at her with his polite, meaningless smile—a mask through which you can read nothing.

For a moment she hung fire. Then: "I don't think they are looking in very likely places. They seem to spend the greater part of their time in the vicinity of the house. It is absurd to think the murderers are going to return."

I turned that over in my mind.

"Miss Shan," I asked, "don't you think they suspect you?"

Her dark eyes burned through her glasses at me and, if possible, she made herself more rigidly straight in her chair.

"Preposterous!"

"That isn't the point," I insisted. "Do they?"

"I am not able to penetrate the police mind," she came back. "Do *you?*"

"I don't know anything about this job but what I've read and what you've just told me. I need more foundation than that to suspect anybody. But I can understand why the sheriff's office would be a little doubtful. You left in a hurry. They've got your word for why you went and why you came back, and your word is all. The woman found in the cellar could have been killed just before you left as well as just after. Wang Ma, who could have told things, is dead. The other servants are missing. Nothing was stolen. That's plenty to make the sheriff think about you!"

"Do you suspect me?" she asked again.

"No," I said truthfully. "But that proves nothing."

She spoke to the Old Man, with a chin-tilting motion, as if she were talking over my head.

"Do you wish to undertake this work for me?"

"We shall be very glad to do what we can," he said, and then to me, after they had talked terms and while she was writing a check, "you handle it. Use what men you need."

"I want to go out to the house first and look the place over," I said.

Lillian Shan was putting away her checkbook.

"Very well. I am returning home now. I will drive you down."

It was a restful ride. Neither the girl nor I wasted energy on conversation. My client and I didn't seem to like each other very much. She drove well.

II

The Shan house was a big brownstone affair, set among sodded lawns. The place was hedged shoulder-high on three sides. The fourth boundary was the ocean, where it came in to make a notch in the shore-line between two small rocky points.

The house was full of hangings, rugs, pictures, and so on—a mixture of things American, European and Asiatic. I didn't spend much time inside. After a look at the linen-closet, at the still open cellar grave, and at the pale, thick-featured Danish woman who was taking care of the house until Lillian Shan could get a new corps of servants, I went outdoors again. I poked around the lawns for a few minutes, stuck my head in the garage, where two cars, besides the one in which we had come from town, stood, and then went off to waste the rest of the afternoon talking to the girl's neighbors. None of them knew anything. Since we were on opposite sides of the game, I didn't hunt up the sheriff's men.

By twilight I was back in the city, going into the apartment building in which I lived during my first year in San Francisco. I found the lad I wanted in his cubby-hole room, getting his small body into a cerise silk shirt that was something to look at. Cipriano was the bright-faced Filipino boy who looked after the building's front door in the daytime. At night, like all the Filipinos in San Francisco, he could be found down on Kearny Street, just below Chinatown, except when he was in a Chinese gambling-house passing his money over to the yellow brothers.

I had once, half-joking, promised to give the lad a fling at gumshoeing if the opportunity ever came. I thought I could use him now.

"Come in, sir!"

He was dragging a chair out of a corner for me, bowing and smiling. Whatever else the Spaniards do for the people they rule, they make them polite.

"What's doing in Chinatown these days?" I asked as he went on with his dressing.

He gave me a white-toothed smile.

"I take eleven bucks out of bean-game last night."

"And you're getting ready to take it back tonight?"

"Not all of 'em, sir! Five bucks I spend for this shirt."

"That's the stuff," I applauded his wisdom in investing part of his fan-tan profits. "What else is doing down there?"

"Nothing unusual, sir. You want to find something?"

"Yeah. Hear any talk about the killings down the country last week? The two Chinese women?"

"No, sir. Chinaboy don't talk much about things like that. Not like us Americans. I read about those things in newspapers, but I have not heard."

"Many strangers in Chinatown nowadays?"

"All the time there's strangers, sir. But I guess maybe some new Chinaboys are there. Maybe not, though."

"How would you like to do a little work for me?"

"Yes, sir! Yes, sir! Yes, sir!" He said it oftener than that, but that will give you the idea. While he was saying it he was down on his knees, dragging a valise from under the bed. Out of the valise he took a pair of brass knuckles and a shiny revolver.

"Here! I want some information. I don't want you to knock anybody off for me."

"I don't knock 'em," he assured me, stuffing his weapons in his hip pockets. "Just carry these—maybe I need 'em."

I let it go at that. If he wanted to make himself bow-legged carrying a ton of iron it was all right with me.

"Here's what I want. Two of the servants ducked out of the house down there." I described Yin Hung and Hoo Lun. "I want to find them. I want to find what anybody in Chinatown knows about the killings. I want to find who the dead women's friends and relatives are, where they came from, and the same thing for the two men. I want to know about those strange Chinese—where they hang out, where they sleep, what they're up to.

"Now, don't try to get all this in a night. You'll be doing fine if you get any of it in a week. Here's twenty dollars. Five of it is your night's pay. You can use the other to carry you around. Don't be foolish and poke your nose into a lot of grief. Take it easy and see what you can turn up for me. I'll drop in tomorrow."

From the Filipino's room I went to the office. Everybody except Fiske, the night man, was gone, but Fiske thought the Old Man would drop in for a few minutes later in the night.

I smoked, pretended to listen to Fiske's report on all the jokes that were at the Orpheum that week, and grouched over my job. I was too well known to get anything on the quiet in Chinatown. I wasn't sure Cipriano was going to be much help. I needed somebody who was in right down there.

This line of thinking brought me around to "Dummy" Uhl. Uhl was a dummerer who had lost his store. Five years before, he had been sitting on the world. Any day on which his sad face, his package of pins, and his *I am deaf and dumb* sign didn't take twenty dollars out of the office buildings along his route was a rotten day. His big card was his ability to play the statue when skeptical people yelled or made sudden noises behind him. When the Dummy was right, a gun off beside his ear wouldn't make him twitch an eye-lid. But too much heroin broke his nerves until a whisper was enough to make him jump. He put away his pins and his sign—another man whose social life had ruined him.

Since then Dummy had become an errand boy for whoever would stake him to the price of his necessary nose-candy. He slept somewhere in Chinatown, and he didn't care especially how he played the game. I had used him to get me some information on a window-smashing six months before. I decided to try him again.

I called "Loop" Pigatti's place—a dive down on Pacific Street, where Chinatown fringes into the Latin Quarter. Loop is a tough citizen, who runs a tough hole, and who minds his own business, which is making his dive show a profit. Everybody looks alike to Loop. Whether you're a yegg, stool-pigeon, detective, or settlement worker, you get an even break out of Loop and nothing else. But you can be sure that, unless it's something that might hurt his business, anything you tell Loop will get no further. And anything he tells you is more than likely to be right.

He answered the phone himself.

"Can you get hold of Dummy Uhl for me?" I asked after I had told him who I was.

"Maybe."

"Thanks. I'd like to see him tonight."

"You got nothin' on him?"

"No, Loop, and I don't expect to. I want him to get something for me."

"All right. Where d'you want him?"

"Send him up to my joint. I'll wait there for him."

"If he'll come," Loop promised and hung up.

I left word with Fiske to have the Old Man call me up when he came in, and then I went up to my rooms to wait for my informant.

He came in a little after ten—a short, stocky, pasty-faced man of forty or so, with mousecolored hair streaked with yellow-white.

"Loop says y'got sumpin' f'r me."

"Yes," I said, waving him to a chair, and closing the door. "I'm buying news."

He fumbled with his hat, started to spit on the floor, changed his mind, licked his lips, and looked up at me.

"What kind o' news? I don't know nothin'."

I was puzzled. The Dummy's yellowish eyes should have showed the pinpoint pupils of the heroin addict. They didn't. The pupils were normal. That didn't mean he was off the stuff—he had put cocaine into them to distend them to normal. The puzzle was—why? He wasn't usually particular enough about his appearance to go to that trouble.

"Did you hear about the Chinese killings down the shore last week?" I asked him.

"No."

"Well," I said, paying no attention to the denial, "I'm hunting for the pair of yellow men who ducked out—Hoo Lun and Yin Hung. Know anything about them?"

"No."

"It's worth a couple of hundred dollars to you to find either of them for me. It's worth another couple hundred to find out about the killings for me. It's worth another to find the slim Chinese youngster with gold teeth who opened the door for the Shan girl and her maid."

"I don't know nothin' about them things," he said.

But he said it automatically while his mind was busy counting up the hundreds I had dangled before him. I suppose his dope-addled brains made the total somewhere in the thousands. He jumped up.

"I'll see what I c'n do. S'pose you slip me a hundred now, on account."

I didn't see that.

"You get it when you deliver."

We had to argue that point, but finally he went off grumbling and growling to get me my news.

I went back to the office. The Old Man hadn't come in yet. It was nearly midnight when he arrived.

"I'm using Dummy Uhl again," I told him, "and I've put a Filipino boy down there too. I've got another scheme, but I don't know anybody to handle it. I think if we offered the missing chauffeur and house-man jobs in some out-of-the-way place up the country, perhaps they'd fall for it. Do you know anybody who could pull it for us?"

"Exactly what have you in mind?"

"It must be somebody who has a house out in the country, the farther the better, the more secluded the better. They would phone one of the Chinese employment offices that they needed three servants—cook, house-man, and chauffeur. We throw in the cook for good measure, to cover the game. It's got to be air-tight on the other end, and, if we're going to catch our fish, we have to give 'em time to investigate. So whoever does it must have some servants, and must put up a bluff—

I mean in his own neighborhood—that they are leaving, and the servants must be in on it. And we've got to wait a couple of days, so our friends here will have time to investigate. I think we'd better use Fong Yick's employment agency, on Washington Street.

"Whoever does it could phone Fong Yick tomorrow morning, and say he'd be in Thursday morning to look the applicants over. This is Monday—that'll be long enough. Our helper gets at the employment office at ten Thursday morning. Miss Shan and I arrive in a taxicab ten minutes later, when he'll be in the middle of questioning the applicants. I'll slide out of the taxi into Fong Yick's, grab anybody that looks like one of our missing servants. Miss Shan will come in a minute or two behind me and check me up—so there won't be any false-arrest mix-ups."

The Old Man nodded approval.

"Very well," he said. "I think I can arrange it. I will let you know tomorrow."

I went home to bed. Thus ended the first day.

III

At nine the next morning, Tuesday, I was talking to Cipriano in the lobby of the apartment building that employs him. His eyes were black drops of ink in white saucers. He thought he had got something.

"Yes, sir! Strange Chinaboys are in town, some of them. They sleep in a house on Waverly Place—on the western side, four houses from the house of Jair Quon, where I sometimes play dice. And there is more—I talk to a white man who knows they are hatchet-men from Portland and Eureka and Sacramento. They are Hip Sing men—a tong war starts—pretty soon, maybe."

"Do these birds look like gunmen to you?"

Cipriano scratched his head.

"No, sir, maybe not. But a fellow can shoot sometimes if he don't look like it. This man tells me they are Hip Sing men."

"Who was this white man?"

"I don't know the name, but he lives there. A short man—snow-bird."

"Gray hair, yellowish eyes?"

"Yes, sir."

That, as likely as not, would be Dummy Uhl. One of my men was stringing the other. The tong stuff hadn't sounded right to me anyhow. Once in a while they mix things, but usually they are blamed for somebody else's crimes. Most wholesale killings in Chinatown are the result of family or clan feuds—such as the ones the "Four Brothers" used to stage.

"This house where you think the strangers are living—know anything about it?"

"No, sir. But maybe you could go through there to the house of Chang Li Ching on other street—Spofford Alley."

"So? And who is this Chang Li Ching?"

"I don't know, sir. But he is there. Nobody sees him, but all Chinaboys say he is great man."

"So? And his house is in Spofford Alley?"

"Yes, sir, a house with red door and red steps. You find it easy, but better not fool with Chang Li Ching."

I didn't know whether that was advice or just a general remark.

"A big gun, huh?" I probed.

But my Filipino didn't really know anything about this Chang Li Ching. He was basing his opinion of the Chinese's greatness on the attitude of his fellow countrymen when they mentioned him.

"Learn anything about the two Chinese men?" I asked after I had fixed this point.

"No, sir, but I will—you bet!"

I praised him for what he had done, told him to try it again that night, and went back to my rooms to wait for Dummy Uhl, who had promised to come there at ten-thirty. It was not quite ten when I got there, so I used some of my spare time to call up the office. The Old Man said Dick Foley—our shadow ace—was idle, so I borrowed him. Then I fixed my gun and sat down to wait for my stool-pigeon.

He rang the bell at eleven o'clock. He came in frowning tremendously.

"I don't know what t' hell to make of it, kid," he spoke importantly over the cigarette he was rolling. "There's sumpin' makin' down there, an' that's a fact. Things ain't been anyways quiet since the Japs began buyin' stores in the Chink streets, an' maybe that's got sumpin' to do with it. But there ain't no strange Chinks in town—not a damn one! I got a hunch your men have gone down to L.A., but I expec' t' know f'r certain tonight. I got a Chink ribbed up t' get the dope; 'f I was you, I'd put a watch on the boats at San Pedro. Maybe those fellas'll swap papers wit' a coupla Chink sailors that'd like t' stay here."

"And there are no strangers in town?"

"Not any."

"Dummy," I said bitterly, "you're a liar, and you're a boob, and I've been playing you for a sucker. You were in on that killing, and so were your friends, and I'm going to throw you in the can, and your friends on top of you!"

I put my gun in sight, close to his scared-gray face.

"Keep yourself still while I do my phoning!"

Reaching for the telephone with my free hand, I kept one eye on the Dummy.

It wasn't enough. My gun was too close to him.

He yanked it out of my hand. I jumped for him.

The gun turned in his fingers. I grabbed it—too late. It went off, its muzzle less than a foot from where I'm thickest. Fire stung my body.

Clutching the gun with both hands I folded down to the floor. Dummy went away from there, leaving the door open behind him.

One hand on my burning belly, I crossed to the window and waved an arm at Dick Foley, stalling on a corner down the street. Then I went to the bathroom and looked to my wound. A blank cartridge does hurt if you catch it close up!

My vest and shirt and union suit were ruined, and I had a nasty scorch on my body. I greased it, taped a cushion over it, changed my clothes, loaded the gun again, and went down to the office to wait for word from Dick. The first trick in the game looked like mine. Heroin or no heroin, Dummy Uhl would not have jumped me if my guess—based on the trouble he was taking to make his eyes look right and the lie he had sprung on me about there being no strangers in Chinatown—hadn't hit close to the mark.

Dick wasn't long in joining me.

"Good pickings!" he said when he came in. The little Canadian talks like a thrifty man's telegram. "Beat it for phone. Called Hotel Irvington. Booth—couldn't get anything but number. Ought to be enough. Then Chinatown. Dived in cellar west side Waverly Place. Couldn't stick close enough to spot place. Afraid to take chance hanging around. How do you like it?"

"I like it all right. Let's look up 'The Whistler's' record."

A file clerk got it for us—a bulky envelope the size of a brief case, crammed with memoranda, clippings and letters. The gentleman's biography, as we had it, ran like this:

Neil Conyers, alias The Whistler, was born in Philadelphia—out on Whiskey Hill—in 1883. In '94, at the age of eleven, he was picked up by the Washington police. He had gone there to join Coxey's Army. They sent him home. In '98 he was arrested in his home town for stabbing another lad in a row over an election-night bonfire. This time he was released in his parents' custody. In 1901 the Philadelphia police grabbed him again, charging him with being the head of the first organized automobile-stealing ring. He was released without trial, for lack of evidence. But the district attorney lost his job in the resultant scandal. In 1908 Conyers appeared on the Pacific Coast—at Seattle, Portland, San Francisco, and Los Angeles—in company with a con-man known as "Duster" Hughes. Hughes was shot and killed the following year by a man whom he'd swindled in a fake airplane manufacturing deal. Conyers was arrested on the same deal. Two juries disagreed and he was turned loose. In 1910 the Post Office Department's famous raid on get-rich-quick promoters caught him. Again there wasn't enough evidence against him to put him away. In 1915 the law scored on him for the first time. He went to San Quentin for buncoing some visitors to the Panama-Pacific International Exposition. He stayed there for three years. In 1919 he and a Jap named Hasegawa nicked the Japanese colony of Seattle for $20,000, Conyers posing as an American who had held a commission in the Japanese army during that late war. He had a counterfeit medal of the Order of the Rising Sun which the emperor was supposed to have pinned on him. When the game fell through, Hasegawa's family made good the $20,000—Conyers got out of it with a good profit and not even any disagreeable publicity. The thing had been hushed. He returned to San Francisco after that, bought the Hotel Irvington, and had been living there now for five years without anybody being able to add another word to his criminal record. He was up to something, but nobody could learn what. There wasn't a chance in the world of getting a detective into his hotel as a guest. Apparently the joint was always without vacant rooms. It was as exclusive as the Pacific-Union Club.

This, then, was the proprietor of the hotel Dummy Uhl had got on the phone before diving into his hole in Chinatown.

I had never seen Conyers. Neither had Dick. There were a couple of photographs in his envelope. One was the profile and full-face photograph of the local police, taken when he had been picked up on the charge that led him to San Quentin. The other was a group picture: all rung up in evening clothes, with the phoney Japanese medal on his chest, he stood among half a dozen of the Seattle Japs he had trimmed—a flashlight picture taken while he was leading them to the slaughter.

These pictures showed him to be a big bird, fleshy, pompous-looking, with a heavy, square chin and shrewd eyes.

"Think you could pick him up?" I asked Dick.

"Sure."

"Suppose you go up there and see if you can get a room or apartment somewhere in the neighborhood—one you can watch the hotel from. Maybe you'll get a chance to tail him around now and then."

I put the pictures in my pocket, in case they'd come in handy, dumped the rest of the stuff back in its envelope, and went into the Old Man's office.

"I arranged that employment office stratagem," he said. "A Frank Paul, who has a ranch out beyond Martinez, will be in Fong Tick's establishment at ten Thursday morning, carrying out his part."

"That's fine! I'm going calling in Chinatown now. If you don't hear from me for a couple of days, will you ask the street-cleaners to watch what they're sweeping up?"

He said he would.

IV

San Francisco's Chinatown jumps out of the shopping district at California Street and runs north to the Latin Quarter—a strip two blocks wide by six long. Before the fire nearly twenty-five thousand Chinese lived in those dozen blocks. I don't suppose the population is a third of that now.

Grant Avenue, the main street and spine of this strip, is for most of its length a street of gaudy shops catering to the tourist trade and flashy chopsuey houses, where the racket of American jazz orchestras drowns the occasional squeak of a Chinese flute. Farther out, there isn't so much paint and gilt, and you can catch the proper Chinese smell of spices and vinegar and dried things. If you leave the main thoroughfares and show places and start poking around in alleys and dark corners, and nothing happens to you, the chances are you'll find some interesting things—though you won't like some of them.

However, I wasn't poking around as I turned off Grant Avenue at Clay Street, and went up to Spofford Alley, hunting for the house with red steps and red door, which Cipriano had said was Chang Li Ching's. I did pause for a few seconds to look up Waverly Place when I passed it. The Filipino had told me the strange Chinese were living there, and that he thought their house might lead through to Chang Li Ching's; and Dick Foley had shadowed Dummy Uhl there.

But I couldn't guess which was the important house. Four doors from Jair Quon's gambling house, Cipriano had said, but I didn't know where Jair Quon's was. Waverly Place was a picture of peace and quiet just now. A fat Chinese was stacking crates of green vegetables in front of a grocery. Half a dozen small yellow boys were playing at marbles in the middle of the street. On the other side, a blond young man in tweeds was climbing the six steps from a cellar to the street, a painted Chinese woman's face showing for an instant before she closed the door behind him. Up the street a truck was unloading rolls of paper in front of one of the Chinese newspaper plants. A shabby guide was bringing four sightseers out of the Temple of the Queen of Heaven—a joss house over the Sue Hing headquarters.

I went on up to Spofford Alley and found my house with no difficulty at all. It was a shabby building with steps and door the color of dried blood, its windows solidly shuttered with thick, tight-nailed planking. What made it stand out from its neighbors was that its ground floor wasn't a shop or place of business. Purely residential buildings are rare in Chinatown: almost always the street floor is given to business, with the living quarters in cellar or upper storeys.

I went up the three steps and tapped the red door with my knuckles.

Nothing happened.

I hit it again, harder. Still nothing. I tried it again, and this time was rewarded by the sounds of scraping and clicking inside.

At least two minutes of this scraping and clicking, and the door swung open—a bare four inches.

One slanting eye and a slice of wrinkled brown face looked out of the crack at me, above the heavy chain that held the door.

"Whata wan'?"

"I want to see Chang Li Ching."

"No savvy. Maybe closs stleet."

"Bunk! You fix your little door and run back and tell Chang Li Ching I want to see him."

"No can do! No savvy Chang."

"You tell him I'm here," I said, turning my back on the door. I sat down on the top step, and added, without looking around, "I'll wait."

While I got my cigarettes out there was silence behind me. Then the door closed softly and the scraping and clicking broke out behind it. I smoked a cigarette and another and let time go by, trying to look like I had all the patience there was. I hoped this yellow man wasn't going to make a chump of me by letting me sit there until I got tired of it.

Chinese passed up and down the alley, scuffling along in American shoes that can never be made to fit them. Some of them looked curiously at me, some gave me no attention at all. An hour went to waste, and a few minutes, and then the familiar scraping and clicking disturbed the door.

The chain rattled as the door swung open. I wouldn't turn my head.

"Go 'way! No catch 'em Chang!"

I said nothing. If he wasn't going to let me in he would have let me sit there without further attention.

A pause.

"What a wan'?"

"I want to sec Chang Li Ching," I said without looking around.

Another pause, ended by the banging of the chain against the door-frame.

"All light."

I chucked my cigarette into the street, got up and stepped into the house. In the dimness I could make out a few pieces of cheap and battered furniture. I had to wait while the Chinese put four arm-thick bars across the door and padlocked them there. Then he nodded at me and scuffled across the floor, a small, bent man with hairless yellow-head and a neck like a piece of rope.

Out of this room, he led me into another, darker still, into a hallway, and down a flight of rickety steps. The odors of musty clothing and damp earth were strong. We walked through the dark across a dirt floor for a while, turned to the left, and cement was under my feet. We turned twice more in the dark, and then climbed a flight of unplaned wooden steps into a hall that was fairly light with the glow from shaded electric lights.

In this hall my guide unlocked a door, and we crossed a room where cones of incense burned, and where, in the light of an oil lamp, little red tables with cups of tea stood in front of wooden panels, marked with Chinese characters in gold paint, which hung on the walls. A door on the opposite side of this room let us into pitch blackness, where I had to hold the tail of my guide's loose made-to-order blue coat.

So far he hadn't once looked back at me since our tour began, and neither of us had said anything. This running upstairs and downstairs, turning to the right and turning to the left, seemed harmless enough. If he got any fun out of confusing me, he was welcome. I was confused enough now, so far as the directions were concerned. I hadn't the least idea where I might be. But that didn't disturb me so much. If I was going to be cut down, a knowledge of my geographical position wouldn't make it any more pleasant. If I was going to come out all right, one place was still as good as another.

We did a lot more of the winding around, we did some stair-climbing and some stair-descending, and the rest of the foolishness. I figured I'd been indoors nearly half an hour by now, and I had seen nobody but my guide.

Then I saw something else.

We were going down a long, narrow hall that had brown-painted doors close together on either side. All these doors were closed—secretive-looking in the dim light. Abreast of one of them, a glint of dull metal caught my eye—a dark ring in the door's center.

I went to the floor.

Going down as if I'd been knocked, I missed the flash. But I heard the roar, smelled the powder.

My guide spun around, twisting out of one slipper. In each of his hands was an automatic as big as a coal scuttle. Even while trying to get my own gun out I wondered how so puny a man could have concealed so much machinery on him.

The big guns in the little man's hands flamed at me. Chinese-fashion, he was emptying them—crash! crash! crash!

I thought he was missing me until I had my finger tight on my trigger. Then I woke up in time to hold my fire.

He wasn't shooting at me. He was pouring metal into the door behind me—the door from which I had been shot at.

I rolled away from it, across the hall.

The scrawny little man stepped closer and finished his bombardment. His slugs shredded the wood as if it had been paper. His guns clicked empty.

The door swung open, pushed by the wreck of a man who was trying to hold himself up by clinging to the sliding panel in the door's center.

Dummy Uhl—all the middle of him gone—slid down to the floor and made more of a puddle than a pile there.

The hall filled with yellow men, black guns sticking out like briars in a blackberry patch.

I got up. My guide dropped his guns to his side and sang out a guttural solo. Chinese began to disappear through various doors, except four who began gathering up what twenty bullets had left of Dummy Uhl.

The stringy old boy tucked his empty guns away and came down the hall to me, one hand held out toward my gun.

"You give 'em," he said politely.

I gave 'em. He could have had my pants.

My gun stowed away in his shirt-bosom, he looked casually at what the four Chinese were carrying away, and then at me.

"No like 'em fella, huh?" he asked.

"Not so much," I admitted.

"All light. I take you."

Our two-man parade got under way again. The ring-around-the-rosy game went on for another flight of stairs and some right and left turns, and then my guide stopped before a door and scratched it with his finger-nails.

V

The door was opened by another Chinese. But this one was none of your Cantonese runts. He was a big meat-eating wrestler—bull-throated, mountain-shouldered, gorilla-armed, leather skinned. The god that made him had plenty of material, and gave it time to harden.

Holding back the curtain that covered the door, he stepped to one side. I went in, and found his twin standing on the other side of the door.

The room was large and cubical, its doors and windows—if any—hidden behind velvet hangings of green and blue and silver. In a big black chair, elaborately carved, behind an inlaid black table, sat an old Chinese man. His face was round and plump and shrewd, with a straggle of thin white whiskers on his chin. A dark, close-fitting cap was on his head; a purple robe, tight around his neck, showed its sable lining at the bottom, where it had fallen back in a fold over his blue satin trousers.

He did not get up from his chair, but smiled mildly over his whiskers and bent his head almost to the tea things on the table.

"It was only the inability to believe that one of your excellency's heaven-born splendor would waste his costly time on so mean a clod that kept the least of your slaves from running down to prostrate himself at your noble feet as soon as he heard the Father of Detectives was at his unworthy door."

That came out smoothly in English that was a lot clearer than my own. I kept my face straight, waiting.

"If the Terror of Evildoers will honor one of my deplorable chairs by resting his divine body on it, I can assure him the chair shall be burned afterward, so no lesser being may use it. Or will the Prince of Thief-catchers permit me to send a servant to his palace for a chair worthy of him?"

I went slowly to a chair, trying to arrange words in my mind. This old joker was spoofing me with an exaggeration—a burlesque—of the well-known Chinese politeness. I'm not hard to get along with: I'll play anybody's game up to a certain point.

"It's only because I'm weak-kneed with awe of the mighty Chang Li Ching that I dare to sit down," I explained, letting myself down on the chair, and turning my head to notice that the giants who had stood beside the door were gone.

I had a hunch they had gone no farther than the other side of the velvet hangings that hid the door.

"If it were not that the King of Finders-out"—he was at it again—"knows everything, I should marvel that he had heard my lowly name."

"Heard it? Who hasn't?" I kidded back. "Isn't the word *change*, in English, derived from Chang? Change, meaning alter, is what happens to the wisest man's opinions after he has heard the wisdom of Chang Li Ching!" I tried to get away from this vaudeville stuff, which was a strain on my head. "Thanks for having your man save my life back there in the passage."

He spreads his hands out over the table.

"It was only because I feared the Emperor of Hawkshaws would find the odor of such low blood distasteful to his elegant nostrils that the foul one who disturbed your excellency was struck down quickly. If I have erred, and you would have chosen that he be cut to pieces inch by inch, I can only offer to torture one of my sons in his place."

"Let the boy live," I said carelessly, and turned to business. "I wouldn't have bothered you except that I am so ignorant that only the help of your great wisdom could ever bring me up to normal."

"Does one ask the way of a blind man?" the old duller asked, cocking his head to one side. "Can a star, however willing, help the moon? If it pleases the Grandfather of Bloodhounds to flatter Chang Li Ching into thinking he can add to the great one's knowledge, who is Chang to thwart his master by refusing to make himself ridiculous?"

I took that to mean he was willing to listen to my questions.

"What I'd like to know is, who killed Lillian Shan's servants, Wang Ma and Wan Lan?"

He played with a thin strand of his white beard, twisting it in a pale, small finger.

"Does the stag-hunter look at the hare?" he wanted to know. "And when so mighty a hunter pretends to concern himself with the death of servants, can Chang think anything except that it pleases the great one to conceal his real object? Yet it may be, because the dead were servants and not girdle-wearers, that the Lord of Snares thought the lowly Chang Li Ching, insignificant one of the Hundred Names, might have knowledge of them. Do not rats know the way of rats?"

He kept this stuff up for some minutes, while I sat and listened and studied his round, shrewd yellow mask of a face, and hoped that something clear would come of it all. Nothing did.

"My ignorance is even greater than I had arrogantly supposed," he brought his speech to an end. "This simple question you put is beyond the power of my muddled mind. I do not know who killed Wang Ma and Wan Lan."

I grinned at him, and put another question:

"Where can I find Hoo Lun and Yin Hung?"

"Again I must grovel in my ignorance," he murmured, "only consoling myself with the thought that the Master of Mysteries knows the answers to his questions, and is pleased to conceal his infallibly accomplished purpose from Chang."

And that was as far as I got.

There were more crazy compliments, more bowing and scraping, more assurances of eternal reverence and love, and then I was following my rope-necked guide through winding, dark halls, across dim rooms, and up and down rickety stairs again.

At the street door—after he had taken down the bars—he slid my gun out of his shirt and handed it to me. I squelched the impulse to look at it then and there to see if anything had been done to it. Instead I stuck it in my pocket and stepped through the door.

"Thanks for the killing upstairs," I said.

The Chinese grunted, bowed, and closed the door.

I went up to Stockton Street, and turned toward the office, walking along slowly, punishing my brains.

First, there was Dummy Uhl's death to think over. Had it been arranged before-hand: to punish him for bungling that morning and, at the same time, to impress me? And how? And why? Or was it supposed to put me under obligations to the Chinese? And, if so, why? Or was it just one of those complicated tricks the Chinese like? I put the subject away and pointed my thoughts at the little plump yellow man in the purple robe.

I liked him. He had humor, brains, nerve, everything. To jam him in a cell would be a trick you'd want to write home about. He was my idea of a man worth working against.

But I didn't kid myself into thinking I had anything on him. Dummy Uhl had given me a connection between The Whistler's Hotel Irvington and Chang Li Ching. Dummy Uhl had gone into action when I accused him of being mixed up in the Shan killings. That much I had—and that was all, except that Chang had said nothing to show he wasn't interested in the Shan troubles.

In this light, the chances were that Dummy's death had not been a planned performance. It was more likely that he had seen me coming, had tried to wipe me out, and had been knocked off by my guide because he was interfering with the audience Chang had granted me. Dummy couldn't have had a very valuable life in the Chinese's eye—or in anybody else's.

I wasn't at all dissatisfied with the day's work so far. I hadn't done anything brilliant, but I had got a look at my destination, or thought I had. If I was butting my head against a stone wall, I at least knew where the wall was and had seen the man who owned it.

In the office, a message from Dick Foley was waiting for me. He had rented a front apartment up the street from the Irvington and had put in a couple of hours trailing The Whistler.

The Whistler had spent half an hour in "Big Fat" Thomson's place on Market Street, talking to the proprietor and some of the sure-thing gamblers who congregate there. Then he had taxi-cabbed out to an apartment house on O'Farrell Street—the Glenway—where he had rung one of the bells. Getting no answer, he had let himself into the building with a key. An hour later he had come out and returned to his hotel. Dick hadn't been able to determine which bell he had rung, or which apartment he had visited.

I got Lillian Shan on the telephone.

"Will you be in this evening?" I asked. "I've something I want o go into with you, and I can't give it to you over the wire."

"I will be at home until seven-thirty."

"All right, I'll be down."

t was seven-fifteen when the car I had hired put me down er front door. She opened the door for me. The Danish an who was filling in until new servants were employed l there only in the daytime, returning to her own home—a ack from the shore—at night.

evening gown Lillian Shan wore was severe enough, ggested that if she would throw away her glasses and do g for herself, she might not be so unfeminine looking he took me upstairs, to the library, where a clean-cut lad of twenty-something in evening clothes got up from a chair as we came in—a well-set up boy with fair hair and skin.

His name, I learned when we were introduced, was Garthorne. The girl seemed willing enough to hold our conference in his presence. I wasn't. After I had done everything but insist point-blank on seeing her alone, she excused herself—calling him Jack—and took me out into another room.

By then I was a bit impatient.

"Who's that?" I demanded.

She put her eyebrows up for me.

"Mr John Garthorne," she said.

"How well do you know him?"

"May I ask why you are so interested?"

"You may. Mr John Garthorne is all wrong, I think."

"Wrong?"

I had another idea.

"Where does he live?"

She gave me an O'Farrell Street number.

"The Glenway Apartments?"

"I think so." She was looking at me without any affectation at all. "Will you please explain?"

"One more question and I will. Do you know a Chinese named Chang Li Ching?"

"No."

"All right. I'll tell you about Garthorne. So far I've run into two angles on this trouble of yours. One of them has to do with this Chang Li Ching in Chinatown, and one with an ex-convict named Conyers. This John Garthorne was in Chinatown today. I saw him coming out of a cellar that probably connects with Chang Li Ching's house. The ex-convict Conyers visited the building where Garthorne lives, early this afternoon."

Her mouth popped open and then shut.

"That is absurd!" she snapped. "I have known Mr Garthorne for some time, and—"

"Exactly how long?"

"A long—several months."

"Where'd you meet him?"

"Through a girl I knew at college."

"What does he do for a living?"

She stood stiff and silent.

"Listen, Miss Shan," I said. "Garthorne may be all right, but I've got to look him up. If he's in the clear there'll be no harm done. I want to know what you know about him."

I got it, little by little. He was, or she thought he was, the youngest son of a prominent Richmond, Virginia, family, in disgrace just now because of some sort of boyish prank. He had come to San Francisco four months ago, to wait until his father's anger cooled. Meanwhile his mother kept him in money, leaving him without the necessity of toiling during his exile. He had brought a letter of introduction from one of Lillian Shan's schoolmates. Lillian Shan had, I gathered, a lot of liking for him.

"You're going out with him tonight?" I asked when I had got this.

"Yes."

"In his car or yours?"

She frowned, but she answered my question.

"In his. We are going to drive down to Half Moon for dinner."

"I'll need a key, then, because I am coming back here after you have gone."

"You're what?"

"I'm coming back here. I'll ask you not to say anything about my more or less unworthy suspicions to him, but my honest opinion is that he's drawing you away for the evening. So if the engine breaks down on the way back, just pretend you see nothing unusual in it."

That worried her, but she wouldn't admit I might be right. I got the key, though, and then I told her of my employment agency scheme that needed her assistance, and she promised to be at the office at half past nine Thursday morning.

I didn't see Garthorne again before I left the house.

VI

In my hired car again, I had the driver take me to the nearest village, where I bought a plug of chewing tobacco, a flashlight, and a box of cartridges at the general store. My gun is a .38 Special, but I had to take the shorter, weaker cartridges, because the storekeeper didn't keep the specials in stock.

My purchases in my pocket, we started back toward the Shan house again. Two bends in the road this side of it, I stopped the car, paid the chauffeur, and sent him on his way, finishing the trip afoot.

The house was dark all around.

Letting myself in as quietly as possible, and going easy with the flashlight, I gave the interior a combing from cellar to roof. I was the only occupant. In the kitchen, I looted the icebox for a bite or two, which I washed down with milk. I could have used some coffee, but coffee is too fragrant.

The luncheon done, I made myself comfortable on a chair in the passageway between the kitchen and the rest of the house. On one side of the passageway, steps led down to the basement. On the other, steps led upstairs. With every door in the house except the outer ones open, the passageway was the center of things so far as hearing noises was concerned.

An hour went by—quietly except for the passing of cars on the road a hundred yards away and the washing of the Pacific down in the little cove. I chewed on my plug of tobacco—a substitute for cigarettes—and tried to count up the hours of my life I'd spent like this, sitting or standing around waiting for something to happen.

The telephone rang.

I let it ring. It might be Lillian Shan needing help, but I couldn't take a chance. It was too likely to be some egg trying to find out if anybody was in the house.

Another half hour went by with a breeze springing up from the ocean, rustling trees outside.

A noise came that was neither wind nor surf nor passing car.

Something clicked somewhere.

It was at a window, but I didn't know which.

I got rid of my chew, got gun and flashlight out.

It sounded again, harshly.

Somebody was giving a window a strong play—too strong. The catch rattled, and something clicked against the pane. It was a stall. Whoever he was, he could have smashed the glass with less noise than he was making.

I stood up, but I didn't leave the passageway. The window noise was a fake to draw the attention of anyone who might be in the house. I turned my back on it, trying to see into the kitchen.

The kitchen was too black to see anything.

I saw nothing there. I heard nothing there.

Damp air blew on me from the kitchen.

That was something to worry about. I had company, and he was slicker than I. He could open doors or windows under my nose. That wasn't so good.

Weight on rubber heels, I backed away from my chair until the frame of the cellar door touched my shoulder. I wasn't sure I was going to like this party. I like an even break or better, and this didn't look like one.

So when a thin line of light danced out of the kitchen to hit the chair in the passageway, I was three steps cellar-ward, my back flat against the stair-wall.

The light fixed itself on the chair for a couple of seconds, and then began to dart around the passageway, through it into the room beyond. I could see nothing but the light.

Fresh sounds came to me—the purr of automobile engines close to the house on the road side, the soft padding of feet on the back porch, on the kitchen linoleum, quite a few feet. An odor came to me—an unmistakable odor—the smell of unwashed Chinese.

Then I lost track of these things. I had plenty to occupy me close up.

The proprietor of the flashlight was at the head of the cellar steps. I had ruined my eyes watching the light: I couldn't see him.

The first thin ray he sent downstairs missed me by an inch—which gave me time to make a map there in the dark. If he was of medium size, holding the light in his left hand, a gun in his right, and exposing as little of himself as possible—his noodle should have been a foot and a half above the beginning of the light-beam, the same distance behind it, six inches to the left—my left.

The light swung sideways and hit one of my legs.

I swung the barrel of my gun at the point I had marked X in the night.

His gun-fire cooked my cheek. One of his arms tried to take me with him. I twisted away and let him dive alone into the cellar, showing me a flash of gold teeth as he went past.

The house was full of "Ah yahs" and pattering feet.

I had to move—or I'd be pushed.

Downstairs might be a trap. I went up to the passageway again.

The passageway was solid and alive with stinking bodies. Hands and teeth began to take my clothes away from me. I knew damned well I had declared myself in on something!

I was one of a struggling, tearing, grunting and groaning mob of invisibles. An eddy of them swept me toward the kitchen. Hitting, kicking, butting, I went along.

A high-pitched voice was screaming Chinese orders.

My shoulder scraped the door-frame as I was carried into the kitchen, fighting as best I could against enemies I couldn't see, afraid to use the gun I still gripped.

I was only one part of the mad scramble. The flash of my gun might have made me the center of it. These lunatics were fighting panic now: I didn't want to show them something tangible to tear apart.

I went along with them, cracking everything that got in my way, and being cracked back. A bucket got between my feet.

I crashed down, upsetting my neighbors, rolled over a body, felt a foot on my face, squirmed from under it, and came to rest in a corner, still tangled up with the galvanized bucket.

Thank God for that bucket!

I wanted these people to go away. I didn't care who or what they were. If they'd depart in peace I'd forgive their sins.

I put my gun inside the bucket and squeezed the trigger. I got the worst of the racket, but there was enough to go around. It sounded like a crump going off.

I cut loose in the bucket again, and had another idea. Two fingers of my left hand in my mouth, I whistled as shrill as I could while I emptied the gun.

It was a sweet racket!

When my gun had run out of bullets and my lungs out of air, I was alone. I was glad to be alone. I knew why men go off and live in caves by themselves. And I didn't blame them!

Sitting there alone in the dark, I reloaded my gun.

On hands and knees I found my way to the open kitchen door, and peeped out into the blackness that told me nothing. The surf made guzzling sounds in the cove. From the other side of the house came the noise of cars. I hoped it was my friends going away.

I shut the door, locked it, and turned on the kitchen light.

The place wasn't as badly upset as I had expected. Some pans and dishes were down and a chair had been broken, and the place smelled of unwashed bodies. But that was all—except a blue cotton sleeve in the middle of the floor, a straw sandal near the passageway door, and a handful of short black hairs, a bit blood-smeared, beside the sandal.

In the cellar I did not find the man I had sent down there. An open door showed how he had left me. His flashlight was there, and my own, and some of his blood.

Upstairs again, I went through the front of the house. The front door was open. Rugs had been rumpled. A blue vase was broken on the floor. A table was pushed out of place, and a couple of chairs had been upset. I found an old and greasy brown felt hat that had neither sweat-band nor hat-band. I found a grimy photograph of President Coolidge—apparently cut from a Chinese newspaper—and six wheat-straw cigarette papers.

I found nothing upstairs to show that any of my guests had gone up there.

It was half past two in the morning when I heard a car drive up to the front door. I peeped out of Lillian Shan's bedroom window, on the second floor. She was saying good-night to Jack Garthorne.

I went back to the library to wait for her.

"Nothing happened?" were her first words, and they sounded more like a prayer than anything else.

"It did," I told her, "and I suppose you had your breakdown."

For a moment I thought she was going to lie to me, but she nodded, and dropped into a chair, not as erect as usual.

"I had a lot of company," I said, "but I can't say I found out much about them. The fact is, I bit off more than I could chew, and had to be satisfied with chasing them out."

"You didn't call the sheriff's office?" There was something strange about the tone in which she put the question.

"No—I don't want Garthorne arrested yet."

That shook the dejection out of her. She was up, tall and straight in front of me, and cold.

"I'd rather not go into that again," she said.

That was all right with me, but:

"You didn't say anything to him, I hope."

"Say anything to him?" She seemed amazed. "Do you think I would insult him by repeating your guesses—your absurd guesses?"

"That's fine," I applauded her silence if not her opinion of my theories. "Now, I'm going to stay here tonight. There isn't a chance in a hundred of anything happening, but I'll play it safe."

She didn't seem very enthusiastic about that, but she finally went off to bed.

Nothing happened between then and sun-up, of course. I left the house as soon as daylight came and gave the grounds the once-over. Footprints were all over the place, from water's edge to driveway. Along the driveway some of the sod was cut where machines had been turned carelessly.

Borrowing one of the cars from the garage, I was back in San Francisco before the morning was far gone.

In the office, I asked the Old Man to put an operative behind Jack Garthorne; to have the old hat, flashlight, sandal and the rest of my souvenirs put under the microscope and searched for finger prints, foot prints, tooth-prints or what have you; and to have our Richmond branch look up the Garthornes. Then I went up to see my Filipino assistant.

He was gloomy.

"What's the matter?" I asked. "Somebody knock you over?"

"Oh, no, sir!" he protested. "But maybe I am not so good a detective. I try to follow one fella, and he turns a corner and he is gone."

"Who was he, and what was he up to?"

"I do not know, sir. There is four automobiles with men getting out of them into that cellar of which I tell you the strange Chinese live. After they are gone in, one man comes out. He wears his hat down over bandage on his upper face, and he walks away rapidly. I try to follow him, but he turns that corner, and where is he?"

"What time did all this happen?"

"Twelve o'clock, maybe."

"Could it have been later than that, or earlier?"

"Yes, sir."

My visitors, no doubt, and the man Cipriano had tried to shadow could have been the one I swatted. The Filipino hadn't thought to get the license numbers of the automobiles. He didn't know whether they had been driven by white men or Chinese, or even what make cars they were.

"You've done fine," I assured him. "Try it again tonight. Take it easy, and you'll get there."

From him I went to a telephone and called the Hall of Justice. Dummy Uhl's death had not been reported, I learned.

Twenty minutes later I was skinning my knuckles on Chang Li Ching's front door.

VII

The little old Chinese with the rope neck didn't open for me this time. Instead, a young Chinese with a smallpox-pitted face and a wide grin.

"You wanna see Chang Li Ching," he said before I could speak, and stepped back for me to enter.

I went in and waited while he replaced all the bars and locks. We went to Chang by a shorter route than before, but it was still far from direct. For a while I amused myself trying to map the route in my head as he went along, but it was too complicated, so I gave it up.

The velvet-hung room was empty when my guide showed me in, bowed, grinned, and left me. I sat down in a chair near the table and waited.

Chang Li Ching didn't put on the theatricals for me by materializing silently, or anything of the sort. I heard his soft slippers on the floor before he parted the hangings and came in. He was alone, his white whiskers ruffled in a smile that was grandfatherly.

"The Scatterer of Hordes honors my poor residence again," he greeted me, and went on at great length with the same sort of nonsense that I'd had to listen to on my first visit.

The Scatterer of Hordes part was cool enough—if it was a reference to last night's doings.

"Not knowing who he was until too late, I beaned one of your servants last night," I said when he had run out of flowers for the time. "I know there's nothing I can do to square myself for such a terrible act, but I hope you'll let me cut my throat and bleed to death in one of your garbage cans as a sort of apology."

A little sighing noise that could have been a smothered chuckle disturbed the old man's lips, and the purple cap twitched on his round head.

"The Disperser of Marauders knows all things," he murmured blandly, "even to the value of noise in driving away demons. If he says the man he struck was Chang Li Ching's servant, who is Chang to deny it?"

I tried him with my other barrel.

"I don't know much—not even why the police haven't yet heard of the death of the man who was killed here yesterday."

One of his hands made little curls in his white beard.

"I had not heard of the death," he said.

I could guess what was coming, but I wanted to take a look at it.

"You might ask the man who brought me here yesterday," I suggested.

Chang Li Ching picked up a little padded stick from the table and struck a tasseled gong that hung at his shoulder.

Across the room the hangings parted to admit the pock-marked Chinese who had brought me in.

"Did death honor our hovel yesterday?" Chang asked in English.

"No, *Ta Jen*" the pock-marked one said.

"It was the nobleman who guided me here yesterday," I explained, "not this son of an emperor."

Chang imitated surprise.

"Who welcomed the King of Spies yesterday?" he asked the man at the door.

"I bring 'em, *Ta Jen.*"

I grinned at the pock-marked man, he grinned back, and Chang smiled benevolently.

"An excellent jest," he said.

It was.

The pock-marked man bowed and started to duck back through the hangings. Loose shoes rattled on the boards behind him. He spun around. One of the big wrestlers I had seen the previous day loomed above him. The wrestler's eyes were bright with excitement, and grunted Chinese syllables poured out of his mouth. The pock-marked one talked back. Chang Li Ching silenced them with a sharp command. All this was in Chinese—out of my reach.

"Will the Grand Duke of Manhunters permit his servant to depart for a moment to attend to his distressing domestic affairs?"

"Sure."

Chang bowed with his hands together, and spoke to the wrestler.

"You will remain here to see that the great one is not disturbed and that any wishes he expresses are gratified."

The wrestler bowed and stood aside for Chang to pass through the door with the pockmarked man. The hangings swung over the door behind them.

I didn't waste any language on the man at the door, but got a cigarette going and waited for Chang to come back. The cigarette was half gone when a shot sounded in the building, not far away.

The giant at the door scowled.

Another shot sounded, and running feet thumped in the hall. The pock-marked man's face came through the hangings. He poured grunts at the wrestler. The wrestler scowled at me and protested. The other insisted.

The wrestler scowled at me again, rumbled, "You wait," and was gone with the other.

I finished my cigarette to the tune of muffled struggle-sounds that seemed to come from the floor below. There were two more shots, far apart. Feet ran past the door of the room I was in. Perhaps ten minutes had gone since I had been left alone.

I found I wasn't alone.

Across the room from the door, the hangings that covered the wall were disturbed. The blue, green and silver velvet bulged out an inch and settled back in place.

The disturbance happened the second time perhaps ten feet farther along the wall. No movement for a while, and then a tremor in the far corner.

Somebody was creeping along between hangings and wall.

I let them creep, still slumping in my chair with idle hands. If the bulge meant trouble, action on my part would only bring it that much quicker.

I traced the disturbance down the length of that wall and halfway across the other, to where I knew the door was. Then I lost it for some time. I had just decided that the creeper had gone through the door when the curtains opened and the creeper stepped out.

She wasn't four and a half feet high—a living ornament from somebody's shelf. Her face was a tiny oval of painted beauty, its perfection emphasized by the lacquer-black hair that was flat and glossy around her temples. Gold earrings swung beside her smooth cheeks, a jade butterfly was in her hair. A lavender jacket, glittering with white stones, covered her from under her chin to her knees. Lavender stockings showed under her short lavender trousers, and her bound small feet were in slippers of the same color, shaped like kittens, with yellow stones for eyes and aigrettes for whiskers.

The point of all this our-young-ladies'-fashion stuff is that she was impossibly dainty. But there she was—neither a carving nor a painting, but a living small woman with fear in her black eyes and nervous, tiny fingers worrying the silk at her bosom.

Twice as she came toward me—hurrying with the awkward, quick step of the foot-bound Chinese woman—her head twisted around for a look at the hangings over the door.

I was on my feet by now, going to meet her.

Her English wasn't much. Most of what she babbled at me I missed, though I thought "yung hel-lup" might have been meant for "You help?"

I nodded, catching her under the elbows as she stumbled against me.

She gave me some more language that didn't make the situation any clearer—unless "sul-lay-vee gull" meant slave-girl and "tak-ka wah" meant take away.

"You want me to get you out of here?" I asked.

Her head, close under my chin, went up and down, and her red flower of a mouth shaped a smile that made all the other smiles I could remember look like leers.

She did some more talking. I got nothing out of it. Taking one of her elbows out of my hand, she pushed up her sleeve, baring a forearm that an artist had spent a life-time carving out of ivory. On it were five finger-shaped bruises ending in cuts where the nails had punctured the flesh.

She let the sleeve fall over it again, and gave me more words. They didn't mean anything to me, but they tinkled prettily.

"All right," I said, sliding my gun out. "If you want to go, we'll go."

Both her hands went to the gun, pushing it down, and she talked excitedly into my face, winding up with a flicking of one hand across her collar—a pantomime of a throat being cut.

I shook my head from side to side and urged her toward the door.

She balked, fright large in her eyes.

One of her hands went to my watch-pocket. I let her take the watch out.

She put the tiny tip of one pointed finger over the twelve and then circled the dial three times.

I thought I got that. Thirty-six hours from noon would be midnight of the following night—Thursday.

"Yes," I said.

She shot a look at the door and led me to the table where the tea things were. With a finger dipped in cold tea she began to draw on the table's inlaid top. Two parallel lines I took for a street. Another pair crossed them. The third pair crossed the second and paralleled the first.

"Waverly Place?" I guessed.

Her face bobbed up and down, delightedly.

On what I took for the east side of Waverly Place she drew a square—perhaps a house. In the square she set what could have been a rose. I frowned at that. She erased the rose and in its place put a crooked circle, adding dots. I thought I had it. The rose had been a cabbage. This thing was a potato. The square represented the grocery store I had noticed on Waverly Place. I nodded.

Her finger crossed the street and put a square on the other side, and her face turned up to mine, begging me to understand her.

"The house across the street from the grocer's," I said slowly, and then, as she tapped my watch-pocket, I added, "at midnight tomorrow."

I don't know how much of it she caught, but she nodded her little head until her earrings were swinging like crazy pendulums.

With a quick diving motion, she caught my right hand, kissed it, and with a tottering, hoppy run vanished behind the velvet curtains.

I used my handkerchief to wipe the map off the table and was smoking in my chair when Chang Li Ching returned some twenty minutes later.

I left shortly after that, as soon as we had traded a few dizzy compliments. The pockmarked man ushered me out.

At the office there was nothing new for me. Foley hadn't been able to shadow The Whistler the night before.

I went home for the sleep I had not got last night.

VIII

At ten minutes after ten the next morning Lillian Shan and I arrived at the front door of Fong Yick's employment agency on Washington Street.

"Give me just two minutes," I told her as I climbed out. "Then come in."

"Better keep your steam up," I suggested to the driver. "We might have to slide away in a hurry."

In Fong Yick's, a lanky, gray-haired man whom I thought was the Old Man's Frank Paul was talking around a chewed cigar to half a dozen Chinese. Across the battered counter a fat Chinese was watching them boredly through immense steel-rimmed spectacles.

I looked at the half-dozen. The third from me had a crooked nose—a short, squat man.

I pushed aside the others and reached for him.

I don't know what the stuff he tried on me was—jiu jitsu, maybe, or its Chinese equivalent. Anyhow, he crouched and moved his stiffly open hands trickily.

I took hold of him here and there, and presently had him by the nape of his neck, with one of his arms bent up behind him.

Another Chinese piled on my back. The lean, gray-haired man did something to his face, and the Chinese went over in a corner and stayed there.

That was the situation when Lillian Shan came in.

I shook the flat-nosed boy at her.

"Yin Hung!" she exclaimed.

"Hoo Lun isn't one of the others?" I asked, pointing to the spectators.

She shook her head emphatically, and began jabbering Chinese at my prisoner. He jabbered back, meeting her gaze.

"What are you going to do with him?" she asked me in a voice that wasn't quite right.

"Turn him over to the police to hold for the San Mateo sheriff. Can you get anything out of him?"

"No."

I began to push him toward the door. The steel-spectacled Chinese blocked the way, one hand behind him.

"No can do," he said.

I slammed Yin Hung into him. He went back against the wall.

"Get out!" I yelled at the girl.

The gray-haired man stopped two Chinese who dashed for the door, sent them the other way—back hard against the wall.

We left the place.

There was no excitement in the street. We climbed into the taxicab and drove the block and a half to the Hall of Justice, where I yanked my prisoner out. The rancher Paul said he wouldn't go in, that he had enjoyed the party, but now had some of his own business to look after. He went on up Kearny Street afoot.

Half-out of the taxicab, Lillian Shan changed her mind.

"Unless it's necessary," she said, "I'd rather not go in either. I'll wait here for you."

"Righto," and I pushed my captive across the sidewalk and up the steps.

Inside, an interesting situation developed.

The San Francisco police weren't especially interested in Yin Hung, though willing enough, of course, to hold him for the sheriff of San Mateo County.

Yin Hung pretended he didn't know any English, and I was curious to know what sort of story he had to tell, so I hunted around in the detectives' assembly room until I found Bill Thode of the Chinatown detail, who talks the language some.

He and Yin Hung jabbered at each other for some time.

Then Bill looked at me, laughed, bit off the end of a cigar, and leaned back in his chair.

"According to the way he tells it," Bill said, "that Wan Lan woman and Lillian Shan had a row. The next day Wan Lan's not anywheres around. The Shan girl and Wang Ma, her maid, say Wan Lan has left, but Hoo Lun tells this fellow he saw Wang Ma burning some of Wan Lan's clothes.

"So Hoo Lun and this fellow think something's wrong, and the next day they're damned sure of it, because this fellow misses a spade from his garden tools. He finds it again that night, and it's still wet with damp dirt, and he says no dirt was dug up anywheres around the place—not outside of the house anyways. So him and Hoo Lun put their heads together, didn't like the result, and decided they'd better dust out before they went wherever Wan Lan had gone. That's the message."

"Where is Hoo Lun now?"

"He says he don't know."

"So Lillian Shan and Wang Ma were still in the house when this pair left?" I asked. "They hadn't started for the East yet?"

"So he says."

"Has he got any idea why Wan Lan was killed?"

"Not that I've been able to get out of him."

"Thanks, Bill! You'll notify the sheriff that you're holding him?"

"Sure."

Of course Lillian Shan and the taxicab were gone when I came out of the Hall of Justice door.

I went back into the lobby and used one of the booths to phone the office. Still no report from Dick Foley—nothing of any value—and none from the operative who was trying to shadow Jack Garthorne. A wire had come from the Richmond branch. It was to the effect that the Garthornes were a wealthy and well-known local family, that young Jack was usually in trouble, that he had slugged a Prohibition agent during a cafe raid a few months ago, that his father had taken him out of his will and chased him from the house, but that his mother was believed to be sending him money.

That fit in with what the girl had told me.

A street car carried me to the garage where I had stuck the roadster I had borrowed from the girl's garage the previous morning. I drove around to Cipriano's apartment building. He had no news of any importance for me. He had spent the night hanging around Chinatown, but had picked up nothing.

I was a little inclined toward grouchiness as I turned the roadster west, driving out through Golden Gate Park to the Ocean Boulevard. The job wasn't getting along as snappily as I wanted it to.

I let the roadster slide down the boulevard at a good clip, and the salt air blew some of my kinks away.

A bony-faced man with pinkish mustache opened the door when I rang Lillian Shan's bell. I knew him—Tucker, a deputy sheriff.

"I Hullo," he said. "What d'you want?"

"I'm hunting for her too."

"Keep on hunting," he grinned. "Don't let me stop you."

"Not here, huh?"

"Nope. The Swede woman that works for her says she was in and out half an hour before I got here, and I've been here about ten minutes now."

"Got a warrant for her?" I asked.

"You bet you! Her chauffeur squawked."

"Yes, I heard him," I said. "I'm the bright boy who gathered him in."

I spent five or ten minutes more talking to Tucker and then climbed in the roadster again.

"Will you give the agency a ring when you nab her?" I asked as I closed the door.

"You bet you."

I pointed the roadster at San Francisco again.

Just outside of Daly City a taxicab passed me, going south. Jack Garthorne's face looked through the window; I snapped on the brakes and waved my arm. The taxicab turned and came back to me. Garthorne opened the door, but did not get out.

I got down into the road and went over to him.

"There's a deputy sheriff waiting in Miss Shan's house, if that's where you're headed."

His blue eyes jumped wide, and then narrowed as he looked suspiciously at me.

"Let's go over to the side of the road and have a little talk," I invited.

He got out of the taxicab and we crossed to a couple of comfortable-looking boulders on the other side.

"Where is Lil—Miss Shan?" he asked.

"Ask The Whistler," I suggested.

This blond kid wasn't so good. It took him a long time to get his gun out. I let him go through with it.

"What do you mean?" he demanded.

I hadn't meant anything. I had just wanted to see how the remark would hit him. I kept quiet.

"Has The Whistler got her?"

"I don't think so," I admitted, though I hated to do it. "But the point is that she has had to go in hiding to keep from being hanged for the murders The Whistler framed."

"Hanged?"

"Uh-huh. The deputy waiting in her house has a warrant for her—for murder."

He put away his gun and made gurgling noises in his throat. "I'll go there! I'll tell everything I know!"

He started for his taxicab.

"Wait!" I called. "Maybe you'd better tell me what you know first. I'm working for her, you know."

He spun around and came back.

"Yes, that's right. You'll know what to do."

"Now what do you really know, if anything?" I asked when he was standing in front of me.

"I know the whole thing!" he cried. "About the deaths and the booze and—"

"Easy! Easy! There's no use wasting all that knowledge on the chauffeur."

He quieted down, and I began to pump him. I spent nearly an hour getting all of it.

IX

The history of his young life, as he told it to me, began with his departure from home after falling into disgrace through slugging the Prohi. He had come to San Francisco to wait until his father cooled off. Meanwhile his mother kept him in funds, but she didn't send him all the money a young fellow in a wild city could use.

That was the situation when he ran into The Whistler, who suggested that a chap with Garthorne's front could pick up some easy money in the rum-running game if he did what he was told to do. Garthorne was willing enough. He didn't like Prohibition—it had caused most of his troubles. Rum-running sounded romantic to him—shots in the dark, signal lights off the starboard bow, and so on.

The Whistler, it seemed, had boats and booze and waiting customers, but his landing arrangements were out of whack. He had his eye on a little cove down the shore line that was an ideal spot to land hooch. It was neither too close nor too far from San Francisco. It was sheltered on either side by rocky points, and screened from the road by a large house and high hedges. Given the use of that house, his troubles would be over. He could land his hooch in the cove, run it into the house, repack it innocently there, put it through the front door into his automobiles, and shoot it to the thirsty city.

The house, he told Garthorne, belonged to a Chinese girl named Lillian Shan, who would neither sell nor rent it. Garthorne was to make her acquaintance—The Whistler was already supplied with a letter of introduction written by a former classmate of the girl's, a classmate who had fallen a lot since university days—and try to work himself in with her to a degree of intimacy that would permit him to make her an offer for the use of the house. That is, he was to find out if she was the sort of person who could be approached with a more or less frank offer of a share in the profits of The Whistler's game.

Garthorne had gone through with his part, or the first of it, and had become fairly intimate with the girl, when she suddenly left for the East, sending him a note saying she would be gone several months. That was fine for the rum-runners. Garthorne, calling at the house, the next day, had learned that Wang Ma had gone with her mistress, and that the three other servants had been left in charge of the house.

That was all Garthorne knew first-hand. He had not taken part in the landing of the booze, though he would have liked to. But The Whistler had ordered him to stay away, so that he could continue his original part when the girl returned.

The Whistler told Garthorne he had bought the help of the three Chinese servants, but that the woman, Wan Lan, had been killed by the two men in a fight over their shares of the money. Booze had been run through the house once during Lillian Shan's absence. Her unexpected return gummed things. The house still held some of the booze. They had to grab her and Wang Ma and stick them in a closet until they got the stuff away. The strangling of Wang Ma had been accidental—a rope tied too tight.

The worst complication, however, was that another cargo was scheduled to land in the cove the following Tuesday night, and there was no way of getting word out to the boat that the place was closed. The Whistler sent for our hero and ordered him to get the girl out of the way and keep her out of the way until at least two o'clock Wednesday morning.

Garthorne had invited her to drive down to Half Moon with him for dinner that night. She had accepted. He had faked engine trouble, and had kept her away from the house until two-thirty, and The Whistler had told him later that everything had gone through without a hitch.

After this I had to guess at what Garthorne was driving at—he stuttered and stammered and let his ideas rattle looser than ever. I think it added up to this: he hadn't thought much about the ethics of his play with the girl. She had no attraction for him—too severe and serious to seem really feminine. And he had not pretended—hadn't carried on what could possibly be called a flirtation with her. Then he suddenly woke up to the fact that she wasn't as indifferent as he. That had been a shock to him—one he couldn't stand. He had seen things straight for the first time. He had thought of it before as simply a wit-matching game. Affection made it different—even though the affection was all on one side.

"I told The Whistler I was through this afternoon," he finished.

"How did he like it?"

"Not a lot. In fact, I had to hit him."

"So? And what were you planning to do next?"

"I was going to see Miss Shan, tell her the truth, and then—then

I thought I'd better lay low."

"I think you'd better. The Whistler might not like being hit."

"I won't hide now! I'll go give myself up and tell the truth."

"Forget it!" I advised him. "That's no good. You don't know enough to help her."

That wasn't exactly the truth, because he did know that the chauffeur and Hoo Lun had still been in the house the day after her departure for the East. But I didn't want him to get out of the game yet.

"If I were you," I went on, "I'd pick out a quiet hiding place and stay there until I can get word to you. Know a good place?"

"Yes," slowly. "I have a—a friend who will hide me—down near—near the Latin Quarter."

"Near the Latin Quarter?" That could be Chinatown. I did some sharp-shooting. "Waverly Place?"

He jumped.

"How did you know?"

"I'm a detective. I know everything. Ever hear of Chang Li Ching?"

"No."

I tried to keep from laughing into his puzzled face.

The first time I had seen this cut-up he was leaving a house in Waverly Place, with a Chinese woman's face showing dimly in the doorway behind him. The house had been across the street from a grocery. The Chinese girl with whom I had talked at Chang's had given me a slave-girl yarn and an invitation to that same house. Big-hearted Jack here had fallen for the same game, but he didn't know that the girl had anything to do with Chang Li Ching, didn't know that Chang existed, didn't know Chang and The Whistler were playmates. Now Jack is in trouble, and he's going to the girl to hide!

I didn't dislike this angle of the game. He was walking into a trap, but that was nothing to me—or, rather, I hoped it was going to help me.

"What's your friend's name?" I asked.

He hesitated.

"What is the name of the tiny woman whose door is across the street from the grocery?" I made myself plain.

"Hsiu Hsiu."

"All right," I encouraged him in his foolishness. "You go there. That's an excellent hiding place. Now if I want to get a Chinese boy to you with a message, how will he find you?"

"There's a flight of steps to the left as you go in. He'll have to skip the second and third steps, because they are fitted with some sort of alarm. So is the handrail. On the second floor you turn to the left again. The hall is dark. The second door to the right—on the right-hand side of the hall—lets you into a room. On the other side of the room is a closet, with a door hidden behind old clothes. There are usually people in the room the door opens into, so he'll have to wait for a chance to get through it. This room has a little balcony outside that you can get to from either of the windows. The balcony's sides are solid, so if you crouch low you can't be seen from the street or from other houses. At the other end of the balcony there are two loose floor boards. You slide down under them into a little room between walls. The trap-door there will let you down into another just like it where I'll probably be. There's another way out of the bottom room, down a flight of steps, but I've never been that way."

A fine mess! It sounded like a child's game. But even with all this frosting on the cake our young chump hadn't tumbled. He took it seriously.

"So that's how it's done!" I said. "You'd better get there as soon as you can, and stay there until my messenger gets to you. You'll know him by the cast in one of his eyes, and maybe I'd better give him a password. Haphazard—that'll be the word. The street door—is it locked?"

"No. I've never found it locked. There are forty or fifty Chinamen—or perhaps a hundred—living in that building, so I don't suppose the door is ever locked."

"Good. Beat it now."

X

At 10:15 that night I was pushing open the door opposite the grocery in Waverly Place—an hour and three-quarters early for my date with Hsiu Hsiu. At 9:55 Dick Foley had phoned that The Whistler had gone into the red-painted door on Spofford Alley.

I found the interior dark, and closed the door softly, concentrating on the childish directions Garthorne had given me. That I knew they were silly didn't help me, since I didn't know any other route.

The stairs gave me some trouble, but I got over the second and third without touching the handrail, and went on up. I found the second door in the hall, the closet in the room behind it, and the door in the closet. Light came through the cracks around it. Listening, I heard nothing.

I pushed the door open—the room was empty. A smoking oil lamp stunk there. The nearest window made no sound as I raised it. That was inartistic—a squeak would have impressed Garthorne with his danger.

I crouched low on the balcony, in accordance with instructions, and found the loose floorboards that opened up a black hole. Feet first, I went down in, slanting at an angle that made descent easy. It seemed to be a sort of slot cut diagonally through the wall. It was stuffy, and I don't like narrow holes. I went down swiftly, coming into a small room, long and narrow, as if placed inside a thick wall.

No light was there. My flashlight showed a room perhaps eighteen feet long by four wide, furnished with table, couch and two chairs. I looked under the one rug on the floor. The trapdoor was there—a crude affair that didn't pretend it was part of the floor.

Flat on my belly, I put an ear to the trapdoor. No sound. I raised it a couple of inches. Darkness and a faint murmuring of voices. I pushed the trapdoor wide, let it down easily on the floor and stuck head and shoulders into the opening, discovering then that it was a double arrangement. Another door was below, fitting no doubt in the ceiling of the room below.

Cautiously I let myself down on it. It gave under my foot. I could have pulled myself up again, but since I had disturbed it I chose to keep going.

I put both feet on it. It swung down. I dropped into light. The door snapped up over my head. I grabbed Hsiu Hsiu and clapped a hand over her tiny mouth in time to keep her quiet.

"Hello," I said to the startled Garthorne; "this is my boy's evening off, so I came myself."

"Hello," he gasped.

This room, I saw, was a duplicate of the one from which I had dropped, another cupboard between walls, though this one had an unpainted wooden door at one end.

I handed Hsiu Hsiu to Garthorne.

"Keep her quiet," I ordered, "while—"

The clicking of the door's latch silenced me. I jumped to the wall on the hinged side of the door just as it swung open—the opener hidden from me by the door.

The door opened wide, but not much wider than Jack Garthorne's blue eyes, nor than this mouth. I let the door go back against the wall and stepped out behind my balanced gun.

The queen of something stood there!

She was a tall woman, straight-bodied and proud. A butterfly-shaped headdress decked with the loot of a dozen jewelry stores exaggerated her height. Her gown was amethyst filigreed with gold above, a living rainbow below. The clothes were nothing!

She was—maybe I can make it clear this way. Hsiu Hsiu was as perfect a bit of feminine beauty as could be imagined. She was perfect! Then comes this queen of something—and Hsiu Hsiu's beauty went away. She was a candle in the sun. She was still pretty—prettier than the woman in the doorway, if it came to that—but you didn't pay any attention to her. Hsiu Hsiu was a pretty girl: this royal woman in the doorway was—I don't know the words.

"My God!" Garthorne was whispering harshly. "I never knew it!"

"What are you doing here?" I challenged the woman.

She didn't hear me. She was looking at Hsiu Hsiu as a tigress might look at an alley cat. Hsiu Hsiu was looking at her as an alley cat might look at a tigress. Sweat was on Garthorne's face and his mouth was the mouth of a sick man.

"What are you doing here?" I repeated, stepping closer to Lillian Shan.

"I am here where I belong," she said slowly, not taking her eyes from the slave-girl. "I have come back to my people."

That was a lot of bunk. I turned to the goggling Garthorne.

"Tike Hsiu Hsiu to the upper room, and keep her quiet, if you have to strangle her. I want to talk to Miss Shan."

Still dazed, he pushed the table under the trapdoor, climbed up on it, hoisted himself through the ceiling, and reached down. Hsiu Hsiu kicked and scratched, but I heaved her up to him. Then I closed the door through which Lillian Shan had come, and faced her.

"How did you get here?" I demanded.

"I went home after I left you, knowing what Yin Hung would say, because he had told me in the employment office, and when I got home—When I got home I decided to come here where I belong."

"Nonsense!" I corrected her. "When you got home you found a message there from Chang Li Ching, asking you—ordering you to come here."

She looked at me, saying nothing.

"What did Chang want?"

"He thought perhaps he could help me," she said, "and so I stayed here."

More nonsense.

"Chang told you Garthorne was in danger—had split with The Whistler."

"The Whistler?"

"You made a bargain with Chang," I accused her, paying no attention to her question. The chances were she didn't know The Whistler by that name.

She shook her head, jiggling the ornaments on her headdress.

"There was no bargain," she said, holding my gaze too steadily.

I didn't believe her. I said so.

"You gave Chang your house—or the use of it—in exchange for his promise that"—the boob were the first words I thought of, but I changed them—"Garthorne would be saved from The Whistler, and that you would be saved from the law."

She drew herself up.

"I did," she said calmly.

I caught myself weakening. This woman who looked like the queen of something wasn't easy to handle the way I wanted to handle her. I made myself remember that I knew her when she was homely as hell in mannish clothes.

"You ought to be spanked!" I growled at her. "Haven't you had enough trouble without mixing yourself now with a flock of highbinders? Did you see The Whistler?"

"There was a man up there," she said, "I don't know his name."

I hunted through my pocket and found the picture of him taken when he was sent to San Quentin.

"That is he," she told me when I showed it to her.

"A fine partner you picked," I raged. "What do you think his word on anything is worth?"

"I did not take his word for anything. I took Chang Li Ching's word."

"That's just as bad. They're mates. What was your bargain?"

She balked again, straight, stiff-necked and level-eyed. Because she was getting away from me with this Manchu princess stuff I got peevish.

"Don't be a chump all your life!" I pleaded. "You think you made a deal. They took you in! What do you think they're using your house for?"

She tried to look me down. I tried another angle of attack.

"Here, you don't mind who you make bargains with. Make one with me. I'm still one prison sentence ahead of The Whistler, so if his word is any good at all, mine ought to be highly valuable. You tell me what the deal was. If it's half-way decent, I'll promise you to crawl out of here and forget it. If you don't tell me, I'm going to empty a gun out of the first window I can find. And you'd be surprised how many cops a shot will draw in this part of town, and how fast it'll draw them."

The threat took some of the color out of her face.

"If I tell, you will promise to do nothing?"

"You missed part of it," I reminded her. "If I think the deal is half-way on the level I'll keep quiet."

She bit her lips and let her fingers twist together, and then it came.

"Chang Li Ching is one of the leaders of the anti-Japanese movement in China. Since the death of Sun Wen—or Sun Yat-Sen, as he is called in the south of China and here—the Japanese have increased their hold on the Chinese government until it is greater than it ever was. It is Sun Wen's work that Chang Li Ching and his friends are carrying on.

"With their own government against them, their immediate necessity is to arm enough patriots to resist Japanese aggression when the time comes. That is what my house is used for. Rifles and ammunition are loaded into boats there and sent out to ships lying far offshore. This man you call The Whistler is the owner of the ships that carry the arms to China."

"And the death of the servants?" I asked.

"Wan Lan was a spy for the Chinese government—for the Japanese. Wang Ma's death was an accident, I think, though she, too, was suspected of being a spy. To a patriot, the death of traitors is a necessary thing, you can understand that? Your people are like that too when your country is in danger."

"Garthorne told me a rum-running story," I said. "How about it?"

"He believed it," she said, smiling softly at the trapdoor through which he had gone. "They told him that, because they did not know him well enough to trust him. That is why they would not let him help in the loading."

One of her hands came out to rest on my arm.

"You will go away and keep silent?" she pleaded. "These things are against the law of your country, but would you not break another country's laws to save your own country's life? Have not four hundred million people the right to fight an alien race that would exploit them? Since the day of Taoukwang my country has been the plaything of more aggressive nations. Is any price too great for patriotic Chinese to pay to end that period of dishonor? You will not put yourself in the way of my people's liberty?"

"I hope they win," I said, "but you've been tricked. The only guns that have gone through your house have gone through in pockets! It would take a year to get a shipload through there. Maybe Chang is running guns to China. It's likely. But they don't go through your place.

"The night I was there coolies went through—coming in, not going out. They came from the beach, and they left in machines. Maybe The Whistler is running the guns over for Chang and bringing coolies back. He can get anything from a thousand dollars up for each one he lands. That's about the how of it. He runs the guns over for Chang, and brings his own stuff—coolies and no doubt some opium—back, getting his big profit on the return trip. There wouldn't be enough money in the guns to interest him.

"The guns would be loaded at a pier, all regular, masquerading as something else. Your house is used for the return. Chang may or may not be tied up with the coolie and opium game, but it's a cinch he'll let The Whistler do whatever he likes if only The Whistler will run his guns across. So, you see, you have been gypped!"

"But—"

"But nothing! You're helping Chang by taking part in the coolie traffic. And, my guess is, your servants were killed, not because they were spies, but because they wouldn't sell you out."

She was white-faced and unsteady on her feet. I didn't let her recover.

"Do you think Chang trusts The Whistler? Did they seem friendly?"

I knew he couldn't trust him, but I wanted something specific.

"No-o-o," she said slowly. "There was some talk about a missing boat."

That was good.

"They still together?"

"Yes."

"How do I get there?"

"Down these steps, across the cellar—straight across—and up two flights of steps on the other side. They were in a room to the right of the second-floor landing."

Thank God I had a direct set of instructions for once!

I jumped up on the table and rapped on the ceiling.

"Come on down, Garthorne, and bring your chaperon."

"Don't either of you budge out of here until I'm back," I told the boob and Lillian Shan when we were all together again. "I'm going to take Hsiu Hsiu with me. Come on, sister, I want you to talk to any bad men I meet. We go to see Chang Li Ching, you understand?" I made faces. "One yell out of you, and—" I put my fingers around her collar and pressed them lightly.

She giggled, which spoiled the effect a little.

"To Chang," I ordered, and, holding her by one shoulder, urged her toward the door.

We went down into the dark cellar, across it, found the other stairs, and started to climb them. Our progress was slow. The girl's bound feet weren't made for fast walking.

A dim light burned on the first floor, where we had to turn to go up to the second floor. We had just made the turn when footsteps sounded behind us.

I lifted the girl up two steps, out of the light, and crouched beside her, holding her still. Four Chinese in wrinkled street clothes came down the first-floor hall, passed our stairs without a glance, and started on.

Hsiu Hsiu opened her red flower of a mouth and let out a squeal that could have been heard over in Oakland.

I cursed, turned her loose, and started up the steps. The four Chinese came after me. On the landing ahead one of Chang's big wrestlers appeared—a foot of thin steel in his paw. I looked back.

Hsiu Hsiu sat on the bottom step, her head over her shoulder, experimenting with different sorts of yells and screams, enjoyment all over her laughing doll's face. One of the climbing yellow men was loosening an automatic.

My legs pushed me on up toward the man-eater at the head of the steps.

When he crouched close above me I let him have it.

My bullet cut the gullet out of him.

I patted his face with my gun as he tumbled down past me.

A hand caught one of my ankles.

Clinging to the railing, I drove my other foot back. Something stopped my foot. Nothing stopped me.

A bullet flaked some of the ceiling down as I made the head of the stairs and jumped for the door to the right.

Pulling it open, I plunged in.

The other of the big man-eaters caught me—caught my plunging hundred and eighty-some pounds as a boy would catch a rubber ball.

Across the room, Chang Li Ching ran plump fingers through his thin whiskers and smiled at me. Beside him, a man I knew for The Whistler started up from his chair, his beefy face twitching.

"The Prince of Hunters is welcome," Chang said, and added something in Chinese to the man-eater who held me.

The man-eater set me down on my feet, and turned to shut the door on my pursuers.

The Whistler sat down again, his red-veined eyes shifty on me, his bloated face empty of enjoyment.

I tucked my gun inside my clothes before I started across the room toward Chang. And crossing the room, I noticed something.

Behind The Whistler's chair the velvet hangings bulged just the least bit, not enough to have been noticed by anyone who hadn't seen them bulge before. So Chang didn't trust his confederate at all!

"I have something I want you to see," I told the old Chinese when I was standing in front of him, or, rather, in front of the table that was in front of him.

"That eye is privileged indeed which may gaze on anything brought by the Father of Avengers."

"I have heard," I said, as I put my hand in my pocket, "that all that starts for China doesn't get there."

The Whistler jumped up from his chair again, his mouth a snarl, his face a dirty pink. Chang Li Ching looked at him, and he sat down again.

I brought out the photograph of The Whistler standing in a group of Japs, the medal of the Order of the Rising Sun on his chest. Hoping Chang had not heard of the swindle and would not know the medal for a counterfeit, I dropped the photograph on the table.

The Whistler craned his neck, but could not see the picture.

Chang Li Ching looked at it for a long moment over his clasped hands, his old eyes shrewd and kindly, his face gentle. No muscle in his face moved. Nothing changed in his eyes.

The nails of his right hand slowly cut a red gash across the back of the clasped left hand.

"It is true," he said softly, "that one acquires wisdom in the company of the wise."

He unclasped his hands, picked up the photograph, and held it out to the beefy man. The Whistler seized it. His face drained gray, his eyes bulged out.

"Why, that's—" he began, and stopped, let the photograph drop to his lap, and slumped down in an attitude of defeat.

That puzzled me. I had expected to argue with him, to convince Chang that the medal was not the fake it was.

"You may have what you wish in payment for this," Chang Li Ching was saying to me.

"I want Lillian Shan and Garthorne cleared, and I want your fat friend here, and I want anybody else who was in on the killings."

Chang's eyes closed for a moment—the first sign of weariness I had seen on his round face.

"You may have them," he said.

"The bargain you made with Miss Shan is all off, of course," I pointed out. "I may need a little evidence to make sure I can hang this baby," nodding at The Whistler.

Chang smiled dreamily.

"That, I am regretful, is not possible."

"Why—?" I began, and stopped.

There was no bulge in the velvet curtain behind The Whistler now, I saw. One of the chair legs glistened in the light. A red pool spread on the floor under him. I didn't have to see his back to know he was beyond hanging.

"That's different," I said, kicking a chair over to the table. "Now we'll talk business."

I sat down and we went into conference.

XI

Two days later everything was cleared up to the satisfaction of police, press and public. The Whistler had been found in a dark street, hours dead from a cut in his back, killed in a bootlegging war, I heard. Hoo Lun was found. The gold-toothed Chinese who had opened the door for Lillian Shan was found. Five others were found. These seven, with Yin Hung, the chauffeur, eventually drew a life sentence apiece. They were The Whistler's men, and Chang sacrificed them without batting an eye. They had as little proof of Chang's complicity as I had, so they couldn't hit back, even if they knew that Chang had given me most of my evidence against them.

Nobody but the girl, Chang and I knew anything about Garthorne's part, so he was out, with liberty to spend most of his time at the girl's house.

I had no proof that I could tie on Chang, couldn't get any. Regardless of his patriotism, I'd have given my right eye to put the old boy away. That would have been something to write home about. But there hadn't been a chance of nailing him, so I had had to be content with making a bargain whereby he turned everything over to me except himself and his friends.

I don't know what happened to Hsiu Hsiu, the squealing slave-girl. She deserved to come through all right. I might have gone back to Chang's to ask about her, but I stayed away. Chang had learned that the medal in the photo was a trick one. I had a note from him:

> Greetings and Great Love to the Unveiler of Secrets:
>
> One whose patriotic fervor and inherent stupidity combined to blind him, so that he broke a valuable tool, trusts that the fortunes of worldly traffic will not again ever place his feeble wits in opposition to the irresistible will and dazzling intellect of the Emperor of Untanglers.

You can take that any way you like. But I know the man who wrote it, and I don't mind admitting that I've stopped eating in Chinese restaurants, and that if I never have to visit Chinatown again it'll be soon enough.

11

THE GUTTING OF COUFFIGNAL

BLACK MASK, DECEMBER 1925

I

Wedge-shaped couffignal is not a large island, and not far from the mainland, to which it is linked by a wooden bridge. Its western shore is a high, straight cliff that jumps abruptly up out of San Pablo Bay. From the top of this cliff the island slopes eastward, down to a smooth pebble beach that runs into the water again, where there are piers and a clubhouse and moored pleasure boats.

Couffignal's main street, paralleling the beach, has the usual bank, hotel, moving-picture theater, and stores. But it differs from most main streets of its size in that it is more carefully arranged and preserved. There are trees and hedges and strips of lawn on it, and no glaring signs. The buildings seem to belong beside one another, as if they had been designed by the same architect, and in the stores you will find goods of a quality to match the best city stores.

The intersecting streets—running between rows of neat cottages near the foot of the slope—become winding hedged roads as they climb toward the cliff. The higher these roads get, the farther apart and larger are the houses they lead to. The occupants of these higher houses are the owners and rulers of the island. Most of them are well-fed old gentlemen who, the profits they took from the world with both hands in their younger days now stowed away at safe percentages, have bought into the island colony so they may spend what is left of their lives nursing their livers and improving their golf among their kind. They admit to the island only as many storekeepers, working-people, and similar riffraff as are needed to keep them comfortably served.

That is Couffignal.

It was some time after midnight. I was sitting in a second-storey room in Couffignal's largest house, surrounded by wedding presents whose value would add up to something between fifty and a hundred thousand dollars.

Of all the work that comes to a private detective (except divorce work, which the Continental Detective Agency doesn't handle) I like weddings as little as any. Usually I manage to avoid them, but this time I hadn't been able to. Dick Foley, who had been slated for the job, had been handed a black eye by an unfriendly pickpocket the day before. That let Dick out and me in. I had come up to Couffignal—a two-hour ride from San Francisco by ferry and auto stage—that morning, and would return the next.

This had been neither better nor worse than the usual wedding detail. The ceremony had been performed in a little stone church down the hill. Then the house had begun to fill with reception guests. They had kept it filled to overflowing until some time after the bride and groom had sneaked off to their eastern train.

The world had been well represented. There had been an admiral and an earl or two from England; an ex-president of a South American country; a Danish baron; a tall young Russian princess surrounded by lesser titles, including a fat, bald, jovial and black-bearded Russian general who had talked to me for a solid hour about prize fights, in which he had a lot of interest, but not so much knowledge as was possible; an ambassador from one of the Central European countries; a justice of the Supreme Court; and a mob of people whose prominence and near prominence didn't carry labels.

In theory, a detective guarding wedding presents is supposed to make himself indistinguishable from the other guests. In practice, it never works out that way. He has to spend most of his time within sight of the booty, so he's easily spotted. Besides that, eight or ten people I recognized among the guests were clients or former clients of the agency, and so knew me. However, being known doesn't make so much difference as you might think, and everything had gone off smoothly.

A couple of the groom's friends, warmed by wine and the necessity of maintaining their reputations as cut-ups, had tried to smuggle some of the gifts out of the room where they were displayed and hide them in the piano. But I had been expecting that familiar trick, and blocked it before it had gone far enough to embarrass anybody.

Shortly after dark a wind smelling of rain began to pile storm clouds up over the bay. Those guests who lived at a distance, especially those who had water to cross, hurried off for their homes. Those who lived on the island stayed until the first raindrops began to patter down. Then they left.

The Hendrixson house quieted down. Musicians and extra servants left. The weary house servants began to disappear in the direction of their bedrooms. I found some sandwiches, a couple of books and a comfortable armchair, and took them up to the room where the presents were now hidden under gray-white sheeting.

Keith Hendrixson, the bride's grandfather—she was an orphan—put his head in at the door.

"Have you everything you need for your comfort?" he asked.

"Yes, thanks."

He said good night and went off to bed—a tall old man, slim as a boy.

The wind and the rain were hard at it when I went downstairs to give the lower windows and doors the up-and-down. Everything on the first floor was tight and secure, everything in the cellar. I went upstairs again.

Pulling my chair over by a floor lamp, I put sandwiches, books, ash-tray, gun and flashlight on a small table beside it. Then I switched off the other lights, set fire to a Fatima, sat down, wriggled my spine comfortably into the chair's padding, picked up one of the books, and prepared to make a night of it.

The book was called *The Lord of the Sea*, and had to do with a strong, tough and violent fellow named Hogarth, whose modest plan was to hold the world in one hand. There were plots and counterplots, kidnappings, murders, prison-breakings, forgeries and burglaries, diamonds large as hats and floating forts larger than Couffignal. It sounds dizzy here, but in the book it was as real as a dime.

Hogarth was still going strong when the lights went out.

II

In the dark, I got rid of the glowing end of my cigarette by grinding it in one of the sandwiches. Putting the book down, I picked up gun and flashlight, and moved away from the chair.

Listening for noises was no good. The storm was making hundreds of them. What I needed to know was why the lights had gone off. All the other lights in the house had been turned off some time ago. So the darkness of the hall told me nothing.

I waited. My job was to watch the presents. Nobody had touched them yet. There was nothing to get excited about.

Minutes went by, perhaps ten of them.

The floor swayed under my feet. The windows rattled with a violence beyond the strength of the storm. The dull boom of a heavy explosion blotted out the sounds of wind and falling water. The blast was not close at hand, but not far enough away to be off the island.

Crossing to the window, peering through the wet glass, I could see nothing. I should have seen a few misty lights far down the hill. Not being able to see them settled one point. The lights had gone out all over Couffignal, not only in the Hendrixson house.

That was better. The storm could have put the lighting system out of whack, could have been responsible for the explosion—maybe.

Staring through the black window, I had an impression of great excitement down the hill, of movement in the night. But all was too far away for me to have seen or heard even had there been lights, and all too vague to say what was moving. The impression was strong but worthless. It didn't lead anywhere. I told myself I was getting feeble-minded, and turned away from the window.

Another blast spun me back to it. This explosion sounded nearer than the first, maybe because it was stronger. Peering through the glass again, I still saw nothing. And still had the impression of things that were big moving down there.

Bare feet pattered in the hall. A voice was anxiously calling my name. Turning from the window again, I pocketed my gun and snapped on the flashlight. Keith Hendrixson, in pajamas and bathrobe, looking thinner and older than anybody could be, came into the room.

"Is it—"

"I don't think it's an earthquake," I said, since that is the first calamity your Californian thinks of. "The lights went off a little while ago. There have been a couple of explosions down the hill since the—"

I stopped. Three shots, close together, had sounded. Rifle-shots, but of the sort that only the heaviest of rifles could make. Then, sharp and small in the storm, came the report of a faraway pistol.

"What is it?" Hendrixson demanded.

"Shooting."

More feet were pattering in the halls, some bare, some shod. Excited voices whispered questions and exclamations. The butler, a solemn, solid block of a man, partly dressed, and carrying a lighted five-pronged candlestick, came in.

"Very good, Brophy," Hendrixson said as the butler put the candlestick on the table beside my sandwiches. "Will you try to learn what is the matter?"

"I have tried, sir. The telephone seems to be out of order, sir. Shall I send Oliver down to the village?"

"No-o. I don't suppose it's that serious. Do you think it is anything serious?" he asked me.

I said I didn't think so, but I was paying more attention to the outside than to him. I had heard a thin screaming that could have come from a distant woman, and a volley of small-arms shots. The racket of the storm muffled these shots, but when the heavier firing we had heard before broke out again, it was clear enough.

To have opened the window would have been to let in gallons of water without helping us to hear much clearer. I stood with an ear tilted to the pane, trying to arrive at some idea of what was happening outside.

Another sound took my attention from the window—the ringing of the doorbell. It rang loudly and persistently.

Hendrixson looked at me. I nodded.

"See who it is, Brophy," he said.

The butler went solemnly away, and came back even more solemnly.

"Princess Zhukovski," he announced.

She came running into the room—the tall Russian girl I had seen at the reception. Her eyes were wide and dark with excitement. Her face was very white and wet. Water ran in streams down her blue waterproof cape, the hood of which covered her dark hair.

"Oh, Mr Hendrixson!" She had caught one of his hands in both of hers. Her voice, with nothing foreign in its accents, was the voice of one who is excited over a delightful surprise. "The bank is being robbed, and the—what do you call him?—marshal of police has been killed!"

"What's that?" the old man exclaimed, jumping awkwardly, because water from her cape had dripped down on one of his bare feet. "Weegan killed? And the bank robbed?"

"Yes! Isn't it terrible?" She said it as if she were saying wonderful. "When the first explosion woke us, the general sent Ignati down to find out what was the matter, and he got down there just in time to see the bank blown up. Listen!"

We listened, and heard a wild outbreak of mixed gun-fire.

"That will be the general arriving!" she said. "He'll enjoy himself most wonderfully. As soon as Ignati returned with the news, the general armed every male in the household from Aleksandr Sergyeevich to Ivan the cook, and led them out happier than he's been since he took his division to East Prussia in 1914."

"And the duchess?" Hendrixson asked.

"He left her at home with me, of course, and I furtively crept out and away from her while she was trying for the first time in her life to put water in a samovar. This is not the night for one to stay at home!"

"H-m-m," Hendrixson said, his mind obviously not on her words. "And the bank!"

He looked at me. I said nothing. The racket of another volley came to us.

"Could you do anything down there?" he asked.

"Maybe, but—" I nodded at the presents under their covers.

"Oh, those!" the old man said. "I'm as much interested in the bank as in them; and, besides, we will be here."

"All right!" I was willing enough to carry my curiosity down the hill. "I'll go down. You'd better have the butler stay in here, and plant the chauffeur inside the front door. Better give them guns if you have any. Is there a raincoat I can borrow? I brought only a light overcoat with me."

Brophy found a yellow slicker that fit me. I put it on, stowed gun and flashlight conveniently under it, and found my hat while Brophy was getting and loading an automatic pistol for himself and a rifle for Oliver, the mulatto chauffeur.

Hendrixson and the princess followed me downstairs. At the door I found she wasn't exactly following me—she was going with me.

"But, Sonya!" the old man protested.

"I'm not going to be foolish, though I'd like to," she promised him. "But I'm going back to my Irinia Androvana, who will perhaps have the samovar watered by now."

"That's a sensible girl!" Hendrixson said, and let us out into the rain and the wind.

It wasn't weather to talk in. In silence we turned downhill between two rows of hedging, with the storm driving at our backs. At the first break in the hedge I stopped, nodding toward the black blot a house made.

"That is your—"

Her laugh cut me short. She caught my arm and began to urge me down the road again.

"I only told Mr Hendrixson that so he would not worry," she explained. "You do not think I am not going down to see the sights."

III

She was tall. I am short and thick. I had to look up to see her face—to see as much of it as the rain-gray night would let me see.

"You'll be soaked to the hide, running around in this rain," I objected.

"What of that? I am dressed for it."

She raised a foot to show me a heavy waterproof boot and a woolen-stockinged leg.

"There's no telling what we'll run into down there, and I've got work to do," I insisted. "I can't be looking out for you."

"I can look out for myself."

She pushed her cape aside to show me a square automatic pistol in one hand.

"You'll be in my way."

"I will not," she retorted. "You'll probably find I can help you. I'm as strong as you, and quicker, and I can shoot."

The reports of scattered shooting had punctuated our argument, but now the sound of heavier firing silenced the dozen objections to her company that I could still think of. After all, I could slip away from her in the dark if she became too much of a nuisance.

"Have it your own way," I growled, "but don't expect anything from me."

"You're so kind," she murmured as we got under way again, hurrying now, with the wind at our backs speeding us along.

Occasionally dark figures moved on the road ahead of us, but too far away to be recognizable. Presently a man passed us, running uphill—a tall man whose nightshirt hung out of his trousers, down below his coat, identifying him as a resident.

"They've finished the bank and are at Medcraft's!" he yelled as he went by.

"Medcraft is the jeweler," the girl informed me.

The sloping under our feet grew less sharp. The houses—dark but with faces vaguely visible here and there at windows—came closer together. Below, the flash of a gun could be seen now and then—orange streaks in the rain.

Our road put us into the lower end of the main street just as a staccato rat-ta-tat broke out.

I pushed the girl into the nearest doorway, and jumped in after her.

Bullets ripped through walls with the sound of hail tapping on leaves.

That was the thing I had taken for an exceptionally heavy rifle—a machine gun.

The girl had fallen back in a corner, all tangled up with something. I helped her up. The something was a boy of seventeen or so, with one leg and a crutch.

"It's the boy who delivers papers," Princess Zhukovski said, "and you've hurt him with your clumsiness."

The boy shook his head, grinning as he got up.

"No'm, I ain't hurt none, but you kind of scared me, jumping on me like that."

She had to stop and explain that she hadn't jumped on him, that she had been pushed into him by me, and that she was sorry and so was I.

"What's happening?" I asked the newsboy when I could get a word in.

"Everything," he boasted, as if some of the credit were his. "There must be a hundred of them, and they've blowed the bank wide open, and now some of 'em is in Medcraft's, and I guess they'll blow that up, too. And they killed Tom Weegan. They got a machine gun on a car in the middle of the street. That's it shooting now."

"Where's everybody—all the merry villagers?"

"Most of 'em are up behind the Hall. They can't do nothing, though, because the machine gun won't let 'em get near enough to see what they're shooting at, and that smart Bill Vincent told me to clear out, 'cause I've only got one leg, as if I couldn't shoot as good as the next one, if I only had something to shoot with!"

"That wasn't right of them," I sympathized. "But you can do something for me. You can stick here and keep your eye on this end of the street, so I'll know if they leave in this direction."

"You're not just saying that so I'll stay here out of the way, are you?"

"No," I lied. "I need somebody to watch. I was going to leave the princess here, but you'll do better."

"Yes," she backed me up, catching the idea. "This gentleman is a detective, and if you do what he asks you'll be helping more than if you were up with the others."

The machine gun was still firing, but not in our direction now;

"I'm going across the street," I told the girl.

"If you—"

"Aren't you going to join the others?"

"No. If I can get around behind the bandits while they're busy with the others, maybe I can turn a trick."

"Watch sharp now!" I ordered the boy, and the princess and I made a dash for the opposite sidewalk.

We reached it without drawing lead, sidled along a building for a few yards, and turned into an alley. From the alley's other end came the smell and wash and the dull blackness of the bay.

While we moved down this alley I composed a scheme by which I hoped to get rid of my companion, sending her off on a safe wild-goose chase. But I didn't get a chance to try it out.

The big figure of a man loomed ahead of us.

Stepping in front of the girl, I went on toward him. Under my slicker I held my gun on the middle of him.

He stood still. He was larger than he had looked at first. A big, slope-shouldered, barrelbodied husky. His hands were empty. I spotted the flashlight on his face for a split second. A flat-cheeked, thick-featured face, with high cheek-bones and a lot of ruggedness in it.

"Ignati!" the girl exclaimed over my shoulder.

He began to talk what I suppose was Russian to the girl. She laughed and replied. He shook his big head stubbornly, insisting on something. She stamped her foot and spoke sharply. He shook his head again and addressed me.

"General Pleshskev, he tell me bring Princess Sonya to home."

His English was almost as hard to understand as his Russian. His tone puzzled me. It was as if he was explaining some absolutely necessary thing that he didn't want to be blamed for, but that nevertheless he was going to do.

While the girl was speaking to him again, I guessed the answer. This big Ignati had been sent out by the general to bring the girl home, and he was going to obey his orders if he had to carry her. He was trying to avoid trouble with me by explaining the situation.

"Take her," I said, stepping aside.

The girl scowled at me, laughed.

"Very well, Ignati," she said in English, "I shall go home," and she turned on her heel and went back up the alley, the big man close behind her.

Glad to be alone, I wasted no time in moving in the opposite direction until the pebbles of the beach were under my feet. The pebbles ground harshly under my heels. I moved back to more silent ground and began to work my way as swiftly as I could up the shore toward the center of action.

The machine gun barked on. Smaller guns snapped. Three concussions, close together—bombs, hand grenades, my ears and my memory told me.

The stormy sky glared pink over a roof ahead of me and to the left. The boom of the blast beat my ear-drums. Fragments

I couldn't see fell around me. 'That, I thought, would be the jeweler's safe blowing apart.

I crept on up the shore line. The machine gun went silent. Lighter guns snapped, snapped, snapped. Another grenade went off. A man's voice shrieked pure terror.

Risking the crunch of pebbles, I turned down to the water's edge again. I had seen no dark shape on the water that could have been a boat. There had been boats moored along this beach in the afternoon. With my feet in the water of the bay I still saw no boat. The storm could have scattered them, but I didn't think it had. The island's western height shielded this shore. The wind was strong here, but not violent.

My feet sometimes on the edge of the pebbles, sometimes in the water, I went on up the shore line. Now I saw a boat. A gently bobbing black shape ahead. No light was on it. Nothing I could see moved on it. It was the only boat on that shore. That made it important.

Foot by foot, I approached.

A shadow moved between me and the dark rear of a building. I froze. The shadow, man-size, moved again, in the direction from which I was coming.

Waiting, I didn't know how nearly invisible, or how plain, I might be against my background. I couldn't risk giving myself away by trying to improve my position.

Twenty feet from me the shadow suddenly stopped.

I was seen. My gun was on the shadow;

"Come on," I called softly. "Keep coming. Let's see who you are."

The shadow hesitated, left the shelter of the building, drew nearer. I couldn't risk the flashlight. I made out dimly a handsome face, boyishly reckless, one cheek dark-stained.

"Oh, how d'you do?" the face's owner said in a musical baritone voice. "You were at the reception this afternoon."

"Yes."

"Have you seen Princess Zhukovski? You know her?"

"She went home with Ignati ten minutes or so ago."

"Excellent!" He wiped his stained cheek with a stained handkerchief, and turned to look at the boat. "That's Hendrixson's boat," he whispered. "They've got it and they've cast the others off."

"That would mean they are going to leave by water."

"Yes," he agreed, "unless—Shall we have a try at it?"

"You mean jump it?"

"Why not?" he asked. "There can't be very many aboard. God knows there are enough of them ashore. You're armed. I've a pistol."

"We'll size it up first," I decided, "so we'll know what we're jumping."

"That is wisdom," he said, and led the way back to the shelter of the buildings.

Hugging the rear walls of the buildings, we stole toward the boat.

The boat grew clearer in the night. A craft perhaps forty-five feet long, its stern to the shore, rising and falling beside a small pier. Across the stern something protruded. Something I couldn't quite make out. Leather soles scuffled now and then on the wooden deck. Presently a dark head and shoulders showed over the puzzling thing in the stern.

The Russian lad's eyes were better than mine.

"Masked," he breathed in my ear. "Something like a stocking over his head and face."

The masked man was motionless where he stood. We were motionless where we stood.

"Could you hit him from here?" the lad asked.

"Maybe, but night and rain aren't a good combination for sharpshooting. Our best bet is to sneak as close as we can, and start shooting when he spots us."

"That is wisdom," he agreed.

Discovery came with our first step forward. The man in the boat grunted. The lad at my side jumped forward. I recognized the thing in the boat's stern just in time to throw out a leg and trip the young Russian. He tumbled down, all sprawled out on the pebbles. I dropped behind him.

The machine gun in the boat's stern poured metal over our heads.

IV

"No good rushing that!" I said. "Roll out of it!"

I set the example by revolving toward the back of the building we had just left.

The man at the gun sprinkled the beach, but sprinkled it at random, his eyes no doubt spoiled for night-seeing by the flash of his gun.

Around the corner of the building, we sat up.

"You saved my life by tripping me," the lad said coolly.

"Yes. I wonder if they've moved the machine gun from the street, or if—"

The answer to that came immediately. The machine gun in the street mingled its vicious voice with the drumming of the one in the boat.

"A pair of them!" I complained. "Know anything about the layout?"

"I don't think there are more than ten or twelve of them," he said, "although it is not easy to count in the dark. The few I have seen are completely masked—like the man in the boat. They seem to have disconnected the telephone and light lines first and then to have destroyed the bridge. We attacked them while they were looting the bank, but in front they had a machine gun mounted in an automobile, and we were not equipped to combat on equal terms."

"Where are the islanders now?"

"Scattered, and most of them in hiding, I fancy, unless General Pleshskev has succeeded in rallying them again."

I frowned and beat my brains together. You can't fight machine guns and hand grenades with peaceful villagers and retired capitalists. No matter how well led and armed they are, you can't do anything with them. For that matter, how could anybody do much against a game of that toughness?

"Suppose you stick here and keep your eye on the boat," I suggested. "I'll scout around and see what's doing further up, and if I can get a few good men together, I'll try to jump the boat again, probably from the other side. But we can't count on that. The get-away will be by boat. We can count on that, and try to block it. If you lie down you can watch the boat around the corner of the building without making much of a target of yourself. I wouldn't do anything to attract attention until the break for the boat comes. Then you can do all the shooting you want."

"Excellent!" he said. "You'll probably find most of the islanders up behind the church. You can get to it by going straight up the hill until you come to an iron fence, and then follow that to the right."

"Right."

I moved off in the direction he had indicated.

At the main street I stopped to look around before venturing across. Everything was quiet there. The only man I could see was spread out face-down on the sidewalk near me.

On hands and knees I crawled to his side. He was dead. I didn't stop to examine him further, but sprang up and streaked for the other side of the street.

Nothing tried to stop me. In a doorway, Hat against a wall, I peeped out. The wind had stopped. The rain was no longer a driving deluge, but a steady down-pouring of small drops. Couffignal's main street, to my senses, was a deserted street.

I wondered if the retreat to the boat had already started. On the sidewalk, walking swiftly toward the bank, I heard the answer to that guess.

High up on the slope, almost up to the edge of the cliff, by the sound, a machine gun began to hurl out its stream of bullets.

Mixed with the racket of the machine gun were the sounds of smaller arms, and a grenade or two.

At the first crossing, I left the main street and began to run up the hill. Men were running toward me. Two of them passed, paying no attention to my shouted, "What's up now?"

The third man stopped because I grabbed him—a fat man whose breath bubbled, and whose face was fish-belly white.

"They've moved the car with the machine gun on it up behind us," he gasped when I had shouted my question into his ear again.

"What are you doing without a gun?" I asked.

"I—I dropped it."

"Where's General Pleshskev?"

"Back there somewhere. He's trying to capture the car, but he'll never do it. It's suicide! Why don't help come?"

Other men had passed us, running downhill, as we talked. I let the white-faced man go, and stopped four men who weren't running so fast as the others.

"What's happening now?" I questioned them.

"They's going through the houses up the hill," a sharp-featured man with a small mustache and a rifle said.

"Has anybody got word off the island yet?" I asked.

"Can't," another informed me. "They blew up the bridge first thing."

"Can't anybody swim?"

"Not in that wind. Young Catlan tried it and was lucky to get out again with a couple of broken ribs."

"The wind's gone down," I pointed out.

The sharp-featured man gave his rifle to one of the others and took off his coat.

"I'll try it," he promised.

"Good! Wake up the whole country, and get word through to the San Francisco police boat and to the Mare Island Navy Yard. They'll lend a hand if you tell 'em the bandits have machine guns. Tell 'em the bandits have an armed boat waiting to leave in. It's Hendrixson's."

The volunteer swimmer left.

"A boat?" two of the men asked together.

"Yes. With a machine gun on it. If we're going to do anything, it'll have to be now, while we're between them and their getaway. Get every man and every gun you can find down there. Tackle the boat from the roofs if you can. When the bandits' car comes down there, pour it into it. You'll do better from the buildings than from the street."

The three men went on downhill. I went uphill, toward the crackling of firearms ahead. The machine gun was working irregularly. It would pour out its rat-tat-tat for a second or so, and then stop for a couple of seconds. The answering fire was thin, ragged.

I met more men, learned from them that the general, with less than a dozen men, was still fighting the car. I repeated the advice I had given the other men. My informants went down to join them. I went on up.

A hundred yards farther along, what was left of the general's dozen broke out of the night, around and past me, flying downhill, with bullets hailing after them.

The road was no place for mortal man. I stumbled over two bodies, scratched myself in a dozen places getting over a hedge. On soft, wet sod I continued my uphill journey.

The machine gun on the hill stopped its clattering. The one in the boat was still at work.

The one ahead opened again, firing too high for anything near at hand to be its target. It was helping its fellow below, spraying the main street.

Before I could get closer it had stopped. I heard the car's motor racing. The car moved toward me.

Rolling into the hedge, I lay there, straining my eyes through the spaces between the stems. I had six bullets in a gun that hadn't yet been fired on this night that had seen tons of powder burned.

When I saw wheels on the lighter face of the road, I emptied my gun, holding it low.

The car went on.

I sprang out of my hiding-place.

The car was suddenly gone from the empty road.

There was a grinding sound. A crash. The noise of metal folding on itself. The tinkle of glass.

I raced toward those sounds.

V

Out of a black pile where an engine sputtered, a black figure leaped—to dash off across the soggy lawn. I cut after it, hoping that the others in the wreck were down for keeps.

I was less than fifteen feet behind the fleeing man when he cleared a hedge. I'm no sprinter, but neither was he. The wet grass made slippery going.

He stumbled while I was vaulting the hedge. When we straightened out again I was not more than ten feet behind him.

Once I clicked my gun at him, forgetting I had emptied it. Six cartridges were wrapped in a piece of paper in my vest pocket, but this was no time for loading.

I was tempted to chuck the empty gun at his head. But that was too chancy.

A building loomed ahead. My fugitive bore off to the right, to clear the corner.

To the left a heavy shotgun went off.

The running man disappeared around the house-corner.

"Sweet God!" General Pleshskev's mellow voice complained. "That with a shotgun I should miss all of a man at the distance!"

"Go round the other way!" I yelled, plunging around the corner after my quarry.

His feet thudded ahead. I could not see him. The general puffed around from the other side of the house.

"You have him?"

"No."

In front of us was a stone-faced bank, on top of which ran a path. On either side of us was a high and solid hedge.

"But, my friend," the general protested. "How could he have—?"

A pale triangle showed on the path above—a triangle that could have been a bit of shirt showing above the opening of a vest.

"Stay here and talk!" I whispered to the general, and crept forward.

"It must be that he has gone the other way," the general carried out my instructions, rambling on as if I were standing beside him, "because if he had come my way I should have seen him, and if he had raised himself over either of the hedges or the embankment, one of us would surely have seen him against..."

He talked on and on while I gained the shelter of the bank on which the path sat, while I found places for my toes in the rough stone facing.

The man on the road, trying to make himself small with his back in a bush, was looking at the talking general. He saw me when I had my feet on the path.

He jumped, and one hand went up.

I jumped, with both hands out.

A stone, turning under my foot, threw me sidewise, twisting my ankle, but saving my head from the bullet he sent at it.

My outflung left arm caught his legs as I spilled down. He came over on top of me. I kicked him once, caught his gun-arm, and had just decided to bite it when the general puffed up over the edge of the path and prodded the man off me with the muzzle of the shotgun.

When it came my turn to stand up, I found it not so good. My twisted ankle didn't like to support its share of my hundred-and-eighty-some pounds. Putting most of my weight on the other leg, I turned my flashlight on the prisoner.

"Hello, Flippo!" I exclaimed.

"Hello!" he said without joy in the recognition.

He was a roly-poly Italian youth of twenty-three or -four. I had helped send him to San Quentin four years ago for his part in a payroll stick-up. He had been out on parole for several months now.

"The prison board isn't going to like this," I told him.

"You got me wrong," he pleaded. "I ain't been doing a thing. I was up here to see some friends. And when this thing busted loose I had to hide, because I got a record, and if I'm picked up I'll be railroaded for it. And now you got me, and you think I'm in on it!"

"You're a mind reader," I assured him, and asked the general: "Where can we pack this bird away for a while, under lock and key?"

"In my house there is a lumber-room with a strong door and not a window."

"That'll do it. March, Flippo!"

General Pleshskev collared the youth, while I limped along behind them, examining Flippo's gun, which was loaded except for the one shot he had fired at me, and reloading my own.

We had caught our prisoner on the Russian's grounds, so we didn't have far to go.

The general knocked on the door and called out something in his language. Bolts clicked and grated, and the door was swung open by a heavily mustached Russian servant. Behind him the princess and a stalwart older woman stood.

We went in while the general was telling his household about the capture, and took the captive up to the lumber-room. I frisked him for his pocket-knife and matches—he had nothing else that could help him get out—locked him in and braced the door solidly with a length of board. Then we went downstairs again.

"You are injured!" the princess, seeing me limp across the floor, cried.

"Only a twisted ankle," I said. "But it does bother me some. Is there any adhesive tape around?"

"Yes," and she spoke to the mustached servant, who went out of the room and presently returned, carrying rolls of gauze and tape and a basin of steaming water.

"If you'll sit down," the princess said, taking these things from the servant.

But I shook my head and reached for the adhesive tape.

"I want cold water, because I've got to go out in the wet again. If you'll show me the bathroom, I can fix myself up in no time."

We had to argue about that, but I finally got to the bathroom, where I ran cold water on my foot and ankle, and strapped it with adhesive tape, as tight as I could without stopping the circulation altogether. Getting my wet shoe on again was a job, but when I was through I had two firm legs under me, even if one of them did hurt some.

When I rejoined the others I noticed that the sound of firing no longer came up the hill, and that the patter of rain was lighter, and a gray streak of coming daylight showed under a drawn blind.

I was buttoning my slicker when the knocker rang on the front door. Russian words came through, and the young Russian I had met on the beach came in.

"Aleksandr, you're—" the stalwart older woman screamed when she saw the blood on his cheek, and fainted.

He paid no attention to her at all, as if he was used to having her faint.

"They've gone in the boat," he told me while the girl and two men servants gathered up the woman and laid her on an ottoman.

"How many?" I asked.

"I counted ten, and I don't think I missed more than one or two, if any."

"The men I sent down there couldn't stop them?"

He shrugged.

"What would you? It takes a strong stomach to face a machine gun. Your men had been cleared out of the buildings almost before they arrived."

The woman who had fainted had revived by now and was pouring anxious questions in Russian at the lad. The princess was getting into her blue cape. The woman stopped questioning the lad and asked her something.

"It's all over," the princess said. "I am going to view the ruins."

That suggestion appealed to everybody. Five minutes later all of us, including the servants, were on our way downhill. Behind us, around us, in front of us, were other people going downhill, hurrying along in the drizzle that was very gentle now, their faces tired and excited in the bleak morning light.

Halfway down, a woman ran out of a crosspath and began to tell me something. I recognized her as one of Hendrixson's maids.

I caught some of her words.

"Presents gone... Mr Brophy murdered... Oliver..."

VI

"I'll be down later," I told the others, and set out after the maid.

She was running back to the Hendrixson house. I couldn't run, couldn't even walk fast. She and Hendrixson and more of his servants were standing on the front porch when I arrived.

"They killed Oliver and Brophy," the old man said.

"How?"

"We were in the back of the house, the rear second storey, watching the flashes of the shooting down in the village. Oliver was down here, just inside the front door, and Brophy in the room with the presents. We heard a shot in there, and immediately a man appeared in the doorway of our room, threatening us with two pistols, making us stay there for perhaps ten minutes. Then he shut and locked the door and went away. We broke the door down—and found Brophy and Oliver dead."

"Let's look at them."

The chauffeur was just inside the front door. He lay on his back, with his brown throat cut straight across the front, almost back to the vertebrae. His rifle was under him. I pulled it out and examined it. It had not been fired.

Upstairs, the butler Brophy was huddled against a leg of one of the tables on which the presents had been spread. His gun was gone. I turned him over, straightened him out, and found a bullet-hole in his chest. Around the hole his coat was charred in a large area.

Most of the presents were still here. But the most valuable pieces were gone. The others were in disorder, lying around any which way, their covers pulled off.

"What did the one you saw look like?" I asked.

"I didn't see him very well," Hendrixson said. "There was no light in our room. He was simply a dark figure against the candle burning in the hall. A large man in a black rubber raincoat, with some sort of black mask that covered his whole head and face, with small eyeholes."

"No hat?"

"No, just the mask over his entire face and head."

As we went downstairs again I gave Hendrixson a brief account of what I had seen and heard and done since I had left him. There wasn't enough of it to make a long tale.

"Do you think you can get information about the others from the one you caught?" he asked, as I prepared to go out.

"No. But I expect to bag them just the same."

Couffignal's main street was jammed with people when I limped into it again. A detachment of Marines from Mare Island was there, and men from a San Francisco police boat. Excited citizens in all degrees of partial nakedness boiled around them. A hundred voices were talking at once, recounting their personal adventures and braveries and losses and what they had seen. Such words as machine gun, bomb, bandit, car, shot, dynamite, and killed sounded again and again, in every variety of voice and tone.

The bank had been completely wrecked by the charge that had blown the vault. The jewelry store was another ruin. A grocer's across the street was serving as a field hospital. Two doctors were toiling there, patching up damaged villagers.

I recognized a familiar face under a uniform cap—Sergeant Roche of the harbor police—and pushed through the crowd to him.

"Just get here?" he asked as we shook hands. "Or were you in on it?"

"In on it."

"What do you know?"

"Everything."

"Who ever heard of a private detective that didn't," he joshed as I led him out of the mob.

"Did you people run into an empty boat out in the bay?" I asked when we were away from audiences.

"Empty boats have been floating around the bay all night," he said.

I hadn't thought of that.

"Where's your boat now?" I asked him.

"Out trying to pick up the bandits. I stayed with a couple of men to lend a hand here,"

"You're in luck," I told him. "Now sneak a look across the street. See the stout old boy with the black whiskers? Standing in front of the druggist's."

General Pleshskev stood there, with the woman who had fainted, the young Russian whose bloody cheek had made her faint, and a pale, plump man of forty-something who had been with them at the reception. A little to one side stood big Ignati, the two menservants I had seen at the house, and another who was obviously one of them. They were chatting together and watching the excited antics of a red-faced property-owner who was telling a curt lieutenant of Marines that it was his own personal private automobile that the bandits had stolen to mount their machine gun on, and what he thought should be done about it.

"Yes," said Roche, "I see your fellow with the whiskers."

"Well, he's your meat. The woman and two men with him are also your meat. And those four Russians standing to the left are some more of it. There's another missing, but I'll take care of that one. Pass the word to the lieutenant, and you can round up those babies without giving them a chance to fight back. They think they're safe as angels."

"Sure, are you?" the sergeant asked.

"Don't be silly!" I growled, as if I had never made a mistake in my life.

I had been standing on my one good prop. When I put my weight on the other to turn away from the sergeant, it stung me all the way to the hip. I pushed my back teeth together and began to work painfully through the crowd to the other side of the street.

The princess didn't seem to be among those present. My idea was that, next to the general, she was the most important member of the push. If she was at their house, and not yet suspicious, I figured I could get close enough to yank her in without a riot.

Walking was hell. My temperature rose. Sweat rolled out on me.

"Mister, they didn't none of 'em come down that way."

The one-legged newsboy was standing at my elbow. I greeted him as if he were my pay-check.

"Come on with me," I said, taking his arm. "You did fine down there, and now I want you to do something else for me."

Half a block from the main street I led him up on the porch of a small yellow cottage. The front door stood open, left that way when the occupants ran down to welcome police and Marines, no doubt. Just inside the door, beside a hall rack, was a wicker porch chair. I committed unlawful entry to the extent of dragging that chair out on the porch.

"Sit down, son," I urged the boy.

He sat, looking up at me with puzzled freckled face. I took a firm grip on his crutch and pulled it out of his hand.

"Here's five bucks for rental," I said, "and if I lose it I'll buy you one of ivory and gold."

And I put the crutch under my arm and began to propel myself up the hill.

It was my first experience with a crutch. I didn't break any records. But it was a lot better than tottering along on an unassisted bum ankle.

The hill was longer and steeper than some mountains I've seen, but the gravel walk to the Russians' house was finally under my feet.

I was still some dozen feet from the porch when Princess Zhukovski opened the door.

VII

"Oh!" she exclaimed, and then, recovering from her surprise, "your ankle is worse!"

She ran down the steps to help me climb them. As she came I noticed that something heavy was sagging and swinging in the righthand pocket of her gray flannel jacket.

With one hand under my elbow, the other arm across my back, she helped me up the steps and across the porch. That assured me she didn't think I had tumbled to the game. If she had, she wouldn't have trusted herself within reach of my hands. Why, I wondered, had she come back to the house after starting downhill with the others?

While I was wondering we went into the house, where she planted me in a large and soft leather chair.

"You must certainly be starving after your strenuous night," she said. "I will see if—"

"No, sit down." I nodded at a chair facing mine. "I want to talk to you."

She sat down, clasping her slender white hands in her lap. In neither face nor pose was there any sign of nervousness, not even of curiosity. And that was overdoing it.

"Where have you cached the plunder?" I asked.

The whiteness of her face was nothing to go by. It had been white as marble since I had first seen her. The darkness of her eyes was as natural. Nothing happened to her other features. Her voice was smoothly cool.

"I am sorry," she said. "The question doesn't convey anything to me."

"Here's the point," I explained. "I'm charging you with complicity in the gutting of Couffignal, and in the murders that went with it. And I'm asking you where the loot has been hidden."

Slowly she stood up, raised her chin, and looked at least a mile down at me.

"How dare you? How dare you speak so to me, a Zhukovski!"

"I don't care if you're one of the Smith Brothers!" Leaning forward, I had pushed my twisted ankle against a leg of the chair, and the resulting agony didn't improve my disposition. "For the purpose of this talk you are a thief and a murderer."

Her strong slender body became the body of a lean crouching animal. Her white face became the face of an enraged animal. One hand—claw now—swept to the heavy pocket of her jacket.

Then, before I could have batted an eye—though my life seemed to depend on my not batting it—the wild animal had vanished. Out of it—and now I know where the writers of the old fairy stories got their ideas—rose the princess again, cool and straight and tall.

She sat down, crossed her ankles, put an elbow on an arm of her chair, propped her chin on the back of that hand, and looked curiously into my face.

"However," she murmured, "did you chance to arrive at so strange and fanciful a theory?"

"It wasn't chance, and it's neither strange nor fanciful," I said. "Maybe it'll save time and trouble if I show you part of the score against you. Then you'll know how you stand and won't waste your brains pleading innocence."

"I should be grateful," she smiled, "very!"

I tucked my crutch in between one knee and the arm of my chair, so my hands would be free to check off my points on my fingers.

"First—whoever planned the job knew the island—not fairly well, but every inch of it. There's no need to argue about that. Second—the car on which the machine gun was mounted was local property, stolen from the owner here. So was the boat in which the bandits were supposed to have escaped. Bandits from the outside would have needed a car or a boat to bring their machine guns, explosives, and grenades here and there doesn't seem to be any reason why they shouldn't have used that car or boat instead of stealing a fresh one. Third—there wasn't the least hint of the professional bandit touch on this job. If you ask me, it was a military job from beginning to end. And the worst safe burglar in the world could have got into both the bank vault and the jeweler's safe without wrecking the buildings. Fourth—bandits from the outside wouldn't have destroyed the bridge. They might have blocked it, but they wouldn't have destroyed it. They'd have saved it in case they had to make their get-away in that direction. Fifth—bandits figuring on a get-away by boat would have cut the job short, wouldn't have spread it over the whole night. Enough racket was made here to wake up California all the way from Sacramento to Los Angeles. What you people did was to send one man out in the boat, shooting, and he didn't go far. As soon as he was at a safe distance, he went overboard, and swam back to the island. Big Ignati could have done it without turning a hair."

That exhausted my right hand. I switched over, counting on my left.

"Sixth—I met one of your party, the lad, down on the beach, and he was coming from the boat. He suggested that we jump it. We were shot at, but the man behind the gun was playing with us. He could have wiped us out in a second if he had been in earnest, but he shot over our heads. Seventh—that same lad is the only man on the island, so far as I know, who saw the departing bandits. Eighth—all of your people that I ran into were especially nice to me, the general even spending an hour talking to me at the reception this afternoon. That's a distinctive amateur crook trait. Ninth—after the machine gun car had been wrecked I chased its occupant. I lost him around this house. The Italian boy I picked up wasn't him. He couldn't have climbed up on the path without my seeing him. But he could have run around to the general's side of the house and vanished indoors there. The general liked him, and would have helped him. I know that, because the general performed a downright miracle by missing him at some six feet with a shotgun. Tenth—you called at Hendrixson's house for no other purpose than to get me away from there."

That finished the left hand. I went back to the right.

"Eleventh—Hendrixson's two servants were killed by someone they knew and trusted. Both were killed at close quarters and without firing a shot. I'd say you got Oliver to let you into the house, and were talking to him when one of your men cut his throat from behind. Then you went upstairs and probably shot the unsuspecting Brophy yourself. He wouldn't have been on his guard against you. Twelfth—but that ought to be enough, and I'm getting a sore throat from listing them."

She took her chin off her hand, took a fat white cigarette out of a thin black case, and held it in her mouth while I put a match to the end of it. She took a long pull at it—a draw that accounted for a third of its length—and blew the smoke down at her knees.

"That would be enough," she said when all these things had been done, "if it were not that you yourself know it was impossible for us to have been so engaged. Did you not see us—did not everyone see us—time and time again?"

"That's easy!" I argued. "With a couple of machine guns, a trunkful of grenades, knowing the island from top to bottom, in the darkness and in a storm, against bewildered civilians—it was duck soup. There are nine of you that I know of, including two women. Any five of you could have carried on the work, once it was started, while the others took turns appearing here and there, establishing alibis. And that is what you did. You took turns slipping out to alibi yourselves. Everywhere I went I ran into one of you. And the general! That whiskered old joker running around leading the simple citizens to battle! I'll bet he led 'em plenty! They're lucky there are any of 'em alive this morning!"

She finished her cigarette with another inhalation, dropped the stub on the rug, ground out the light with one foot, sighed wearily, put her hands on her hips, and asked:

"And now what?"

"Now I want to know where you have stowed the plunder."

The readiness of her answer surprised me.

"Under the garage, in a cellar we dug secretly there some months ago."

I didn't believe that, of course, but it turned out to be the truth.

I didn't have anything else to say. When I fumbled with my borrowed crutch, preparing to get up, she raised a hand and spoke gently:

"Wait a moment, please. I have something to suggest."

Half standing, I leaned toward her, stretching out one hand until it was close to her side.

"I want the gun," I said.

She nodded, and sat still while I plucked it from her pocket, put it in one of my own, and sat down again.

VIII

"You said a little while ago that you didn't care who I was," she began immediately. "But I want you to know. There are so many of us Russians who once were somebodies and who now are nobodies that I won't bore you with the repetition of a tale the world has grown tired of hearing. But you must remember that this weary tale is real to us who are its subjects. However, we fled from Russia with what we could carry of our property, which fortunately was enough to keep us in bearable comfort for a few years.

"In London we opened a Russian restaurant, but London was suddenly full of Russian restaurants, and ours became, instead of a means of livelihood, a source of loss. We tried teaching music and languages, and so on. In short, we hit on all the means of earning our living that other Russian exiles hit upon, and so always found ourselves in overcrowded, and thus unprofitable, fields. But what else did we know—could we do?

"I promised not to bore you. Well, always our capital shrank, and always the day approached on which we should be shabby and hungry, the day when we should become familiar to readers of your Sunday papers—charwomen who had been princesses, dukes who now were butlers. There was no place for us in the world. Outcasts easily become outlaws. Why not? Could it be said that we owed the world any fealty? Had not the world sat idly by and seen us despoiled of place and property and country?

"We planned it before we had heard of Couffignal. We could find a small settlement of the wealthy, sufficiently isolated, and, after establishing ourselves there, we would plunder it. Couffignal, when we found it, seemed to be the ideal place. We leased this house for six months, having just enough capital remaining to do that and to live properly here while our plans matured. Here we spent four months establishing ourselves, collecting our arms and our explosives, mapping our offensive, waiting for a favorable night. Last night seemed to be that night, and we had provided, we thought, against every eventuality. But we had not, of course, provided against your presence and your genius. They were simply others of the unforeseen misfortunes to which we seem eternally condemned."

She stopped, and fell to studying me with mournful large eyes that made me feel like fidgeting.

"It's no good calling me a genius," I objected. "The truth is you people botched your job from beginning to end. Your general would get a big laugh out of a man without military training who tried to lead an army. But here are you people with absolutely no criminal experience trying to swing a trick that needed the highest sort of criminal skill. Look at how you all played around with me! Amateur stuff! A professional crook with any intelligence would have either let me alone or knocked me off. No wonder you flopped! As for the rest of it—your troubles—

I can't do anything about them."

"Why?" very softly. "Why can't you?"

"Why should I?" I made it blunt.

"No one else knows what you know." She bent forward to put a white hand on my knee. "There is wealth in that cellar beneath the garage. You may have whatever you ask."

I shook my head.

"You aren't a fool!" she protested. "You know—"

"Let me straighten this out for you," I interrupted. "We'll disregard whatever honesty I happen to have, sense of loyalty to employers, and so on. You might doubt them, so we'll throw them out. Now I'm a detective because I happen to like the work. It pays me a fair salary, but I could find other jobs that would pay more. Even a hundred dollars more a month would be twelve hundred a year. Say twenty-five or thirty thousand dollars in the years between now and my sixtieth birthday.

"Now I pass up that twenty-five or thirty thousand of honest gain because I like being a detective, like the work. And liking work makes you want to do it as well as you can. Otherwise there'd be no sense to it. That's the fix I am in. I don't know anything else, don't enjoy anything else, don't want to know or enjoy anything else. You can't weigh that against any sum of money. Money is good stuff. I haven't anything against it. But in the past eighteen years I've been getting my fun out of chasing crooks and tackling puzzles, my satisfaction out of catching crooks and solving riddles. It's the only kind of sport I know anything about, and I can't imagine a pleasanter future than twenty-some years more of it. I'm not going to blow that up!"

She shook her head slowly, lowering it, so that now her dark eyes looked up at me under the thin arcs of her brows.

"You speak only of money," she said. "I said you may have whatever you ask."

That was out. I don't know where these women get their ideas.

"You're still all twisted up," I said brusquely, standing now and adjusting my borrowed crutch. "You think I'm a man and you're a woman. That's wrong. I'm a manhunter and you're something that has been running in front of me. There's nothing human about it. You might just as well expect a hound to play tiddly-winks with the fox he's caught. We're wasting time anyway. I've been thinking the police or Marines might come up here and save me a walk. You've been waiting for your mob to come back and grab me. I could have told you they were being arrested when I left them."

That shook her. She had stood up. Now she fell back a step, putting a hand behind her for steadiness, on her chair. An exclamation I didn't understand popped out of her mouth. Russian, I thought, but the next moment I knew it had been Italian.

"Put your hands up."

It was Flippo's husky voice. Flippo stood in the doorway, holding an automatic.

IX

I raised my hands as high as I could without dropping my supporting crutch, meanwhile cursing myself for having been too careless, or too vain, to keep a gun in my hand while I talked to the girl.

So this was why she had come back to the house. If she freed the Italian, she had thought, we would have no reason for suspecting that he hadn't been in on the robbery, and so we would look for the bandits among his friends. A prisoner, of course, he might have persuaded us of his innocence. She had given him the gun so he could either shoot his way clear, or, what would help her as much, get himself killed trying.

While I was arranging these thoughts in my head, Flippo had come up behind me. His empty hand passed over my body, taking away my own gun, his, and the one I had taken from the girl.

"A bargain, Flippo," I said when he had moved away from me, a little to one side, where he made one corner of a triangle whose other corners were the girl and I. "You're out on parole, with some years still to be served. I picked you up with a gun on you. That's plenty to send you back to the big house. I know you weren't in on this job. My idea is that you were up here on a smaller one of your own, but I can't prove that and don't want to. Walk out of here, alone and neutral, and I'll forget I saw you."

Little thoughtful lines grooved the boy's round, dark face.

The princess took a step toward him.

"You heard the offer I just now made him?" she asked. "Well, I make that offer to you, if you will kill him."

The thoughtful lines in the boy's face deepened.

"There's your choice, Flippo," I summed up for him. "All I can give you is freedom from San Quentin. The princess can give you a fat cut of the profits in a busted caper, with a good chance to get yourself hanged."

The girl, remembering her advantage over me, went at him hot and heavy in Italian, a language in which I know only four words. Two of them are profane and the other two obscene. I said all four.

The boy was weakening. If he had been ten years older, he'd have taken my offer and thanked me for it. But he was young and she—now that I thought of it—was beautiful. The answer wasn't hard to guess.

"But not to bump him off," he said to her, in English, for my benefit. "We'll lock him up in there where I was at."

I suspected Flippo hadn't any great prejudice against murder. It was just that he thought this one unnecessary, unless he was kidding me to make the killing easier.

The girl wasn't satisfied with his suggestion. She poured more hot Italian at him. Her game looked sure-fire, but it had a flaw. She couldn't persuade him that his chances of getting any of the loot away were good. She had to depend on her charms to swing him. And that meant she had to hold his eye.

He wasn't far from me.

She came close to him. She was singing, chanting, crooning Italian syllables into his round face.

She had him.

He shrugged. His whole face said yes. He turned—

I knocked him on the noodle with my borrowed crutch.

The crutch splintered apart. Flippo's knees bent. He stretched up to his full height. He fell on his face on the floor.

He lay there, dead-still, except for a thin worm of blood that crawled out of his hair to the rug.

A step, a tumble, a foot or so of hand-and-knee scrambling put me within reach of Flippo's gun.

The girl, jumping out of my path, was halfway to the door when I sat up with the gun in my hand.

"Stop!" I ordered.

"I shan't," she said, but she did, for the time at least. "I am going out."

"You are going out when I take you."

She laughed, a pleasant laugh, low and confident.

"I'm going out before that," she insisted good-naturedly.

I shook my head.

"How do you purpose stopping me?" she asked.

"I don't think I'll have to," I told her. "You've got too much sense to try to run while I'm holding a gun on you."

She laughed again, an amused ripple.

"I've got too much sense to stay," she corrected me. "Your crutch is broken, and you're lame. You can't catch me by running after me, then. You pretend you'll shoot me, but I don't believe you. You'd shoot me if I attacked you, of course, but I shan't do that. I shall simply walk out, and you know you won't shoot me for that. You'll wish you could, but you won't. You'll see."

Her face turned over her shoulder, her dark eyes twinkling at me, she took a step toward the door.

"Better not count on that!" I threatened.

For answer to that she gave me a cooing laugh. And took another step.

"Stop, you idiot!" I bawled at her.

Her face laughed over her shoulder at me. She walked without haste to the door, her short skirt of gray flannel shaping itself to the calf of each gray wool-stockinged leg as its mate stepped forward.

Sweat greased the gun in my hand.

When her right foot was on the doorsill, a little chuckling sound came from her throat.

"Adieu!" she said softly.

And I put a bullet in the calf of her left leg.

She sat down—plump! Utter surprise stretched her white face. It was too soon for pain.

I had never shot a woman before. I felt queer about it.

"You ought to have known I'd do it!" My voice sounded harsh and savage and like a stranger's in my ears. "Didn't I steal a crutch from a cripple?"

12

CREEPING SIAMESE

BLACK MASK, MARCH 1926

I

Standing beside the cashier's desk in the front office of the Continental Detective Agency's San Francisco branch, I was watching Porter check up my expense account when the man came in. He was a tall man, raw-boned, hard-faced. Gray clothes bagged loosely from his wide shoulders. In the late afternoon sunlight that came through partially drawn blinds, his skin showed the color of new tan shoes.

He opened the door briskly, and then hesitated, standing in the doorway, holding the door open, turning the knob back and forth with one bony hand. There was no indecision in his face. It was ugly and grim, and its expression was the expression of a man who is remembering something disagreeable.

Tommy Howd, our freckled and snub-nosed office boy, got up from his desk and went to the rail that divided the office.

"Do you—?" Tommy began, and jumped back.

The man had let go the doorknob. He crossed his long arms over his chest, each hand gripping a shoulder. His mouth stretched wide in a yawn that had nothing to do with relaxation.

His mouth clicked shut. His lips snarled back from clenched yellow teeth.

"Hell!" he grunted, full of disgust, and pitched down on the floor.

I heaved myself over the rail, stepped across his body, and went out into the corridor.

Four doors away, Agnes Braden, a plump woman of thirty-something who runs a public stenographic establishment, was going into her office.

"Miss Braden!" I called, and she turned, waiting for me to come up. "Did you see the man who just came in our office?"

"Yes." Curiosity put lights in her green eyes. "A tall man who came up in the elevator with me. Why?"

"Was he alone?"

"Yes. That is, he and I were the only ones who got off at this floor. Why?"

"Did you see anybody close to him?"

"No, though I didn't notice him in the elevator. Why?"

"Did he act funny?"

"Not that I noticed. Why?"

"Thanks. I'll drop in and tell you about it later."

I made a circuit of the corridors on our floor, finding nothing.

The raw-boned man was still on the floor when I returned to the office, but he had been turned over on his back. He was as dead as I had thought. The Old Man, who had been examining him, straightened up as I came in. Porter was at the telephone, trying to get the police. Tommy Howd's eyes were blue half-dollars in a white face.

"Nothing in the corridors," I told the Old Man. "He came up in the elevator with Agnes Braden. She says he was alone, and she saw nobody close to him."

"Quite so." The Old Man's voice and smile were as pleasantly polite as if the corpse at his feet had been a part of the pattern in the carpet. Fifty years of sleuthing have left him with no more emotion than a pawnbroker. "He seems to have been stabbed in the left breast, a rather large wound that was staunched with this piece of silk"—one of his feet poked at a rumpled ball of red cloth on the floor—"which seems to be a sarong."

Today is never Tuesday to the Old Man: it *seems* to be Tuesday.

"On his person," he went on, "I have found some nine hundred dollars in bills of various denominations, and some silver; a gold watch and a pocket knife of English manufacture; a Japanese silver coin, 50 *sen;* tobacco, pipe and matches; a Southern Pacific timetable; two handkerchiefs without laundry marks; a pencil and several sheets of blank paper; four two-cent stamps; and a key labeled *Hotel Montgomery, Room 540.*

"His clothes seem to be new. No doubt we shall learn something from them when we make a more thorough examination, which I do not care to make until the police come. Meanwhile, you had better go to the Montgomery and see what you can learn there."

In the Hotel Montgomery's lobby the first man I ran into was the one I wanted: Pederson, the house copper, a blond-mustached ex-bartender who doesn't know any more about gumshoeing than I do about saxophones, but who does know people and how to handle them, which is what his job calls for.

"Hullo!" he greeted me. "What's the score?"

"Six to one, Seattle, end of the fourth. Who's in 540, Pete?"

"They're not playing in Seattle, you chump! Portland! A man that hasn't got enough civic spirit to know where his team—"

"Stop it, Pete! I've got no time to be fooling with your childish pastimes. A man just dropped dead in our joint with one of your room-keys in his pocket—540."

Civic spirit went blooey in Pederson's face.

"540?" He stared at the ceiling. "That would be that fellow Rounds. Dropped dead, you say?"

"Dead. Tumbled down in the middle of the floor with a knife-cut in him. Who is this Rounds?"

"I couldn't tell you much off-hand. A big bony man with leathery skin. I wouldn't have noticed him excepting he was such a sour looking body."

"That's the bird. Let's look him up."

At the desk we learned that the man had arrived the day before, registering as H. R. Rounds, New York, and telling the clerk he expects to leave within three days. There was no record of mail or telephone calls for him. Nobody knew when he had gone out, since he had not left his key at the desk. Neither elevator boys nor bellhops could tell us anything.

His room didn't add much to our knowledge. His baggage consisted of one pigskin bag, battered and scarred, and covered with the marks of labels that had been scraped off. It was locked, but traveling bags locks don't amount to much. This one held us up about five minutes.

Rounds' clothes—some in the bag, some in the closet—were neither many nor expensive, but they were all new. The washable stuff was without laundry marks. Everything was of popular makes, widely advertised brands that could be bought in any city in the country. There wasn't a piece of paper with anything written on it. There wasn't an identifying tag. There wasn't anything in the room to tell where Rounds had come from or why.

Pederson was peevish about it.

"I guess if he hadn't got killed he'd of beat us out of a week's bill! These guys that don't carry anything to identify 'em, and that don't leave their keys at the desk when they go out, ain't to be trusted too much!"

We had just finished our search when a bellhop brought Detective Sergeant O'Gar, of the police department Homicide Detail, into the room.

"Been down to the agency?" I asked him.

"Yeah, just came from there."

"What's new?"

O'Gar pushed back his wide-brimmed black village-constable's hat and scratched his bullet head.

"Not a heap. The doc says he was opened with a blade at least six inches long by a couple wide, and that he couldn't of lived two hours after he got the blade—most likely not more'n one. We didn't find any news on him. What've you got here?"

"His name is Rounds. He registered here yesterday from New York. His stuff is new; and there's nothing on any of it to tell us anything except that he didn't want to leave a trail. No letters, no memoranda, nothing. No blood, no signs of a row, in the room."

O'Gar turned to Pederson.

"Any brown men been around the hotel? Hindus or the like?"

"Not that I saw," the house copper said. "I'll find out for you."

"Then the red silk was a sarong?" I asked.

"And an expensive one," the detective sergeant said. "I saw a lot of 'em the four years I was soldiering on the islands, but I never saw as good a one as that."

"Who wears them?"

"Men and women in the Philippines, Borneo, Java, Sumatra, Malay Peninsula, parts of India."

"Is it your idea that whoever did the carving advertised himself by running around in the streets in a red petticoat?"

"Don't try to be funny!" he growled at me. "They're often enough twisted or folded up into sashes or girdles. And how do I know he was knifed in the street? For that matter, how do I know he wasn't cut down in your joint?"

"We always bury our victims without saying anything about 'em. Let's go down and give Pete a hand in the search for your brown men."

That angle was empty. Any brown men who had snooped around the hotel had been too good at it to be caught.

I telephoned the Old Man, telling him what I had learned—which didn't cost me much breath—and O'Gar and I spent the rest of the evening sharp-shooting around without ever getting on the target once. We questioned taxicab drivers, questioned the three Roundses listed in the telephone book, and our ignorance was as complete when we were through as when we started.

The morning papers, on the streets at a little after eight o'clock that evening, had the story as we knew it.

At eleven o'clock O'Gar and I called it a night, separating in the direction of our respective beds.

We didn't stay apart long.

II

I opened my eyes sitting on the side of my bed in the dim light of a moon that was just coming up, with the ringing telephone in my hand.

O'Gar's voice: "1856 Broadway! On the hump!"

"1856 Broadway," I repeated, and he hung up.

I finished waking up while I phoned for a taxicab, and then wrestled my clothes on. My watch told me it was 12:55 A.M. as I went downstairs. I hadn't been fifteen minutes in bed.

1856 Broadway was a three-storey house set behind a pocket-size lawn in a row of like houses behind like lawns. The others were dark. 1856 shed light from every window, and from the open front door. A policeman stood in the vestibule.

"Hello, Mac! O'Gar here?"

"Just went in."

I walked into a brown and buff reception hall, and saw the detective sergeant going up the wide stairs.

"What's up?" I asked as I joined him.

"Don't know."

On the second floor we turned to the left, going into a library or sitting room that stretched across the front of the house.

A man in pajamas and bathrobe sat on a davenport there, with one bared leg stretched out on a chair in front of him. I recognized him when he nodded to me: Austin Richter, owner of a Market Street moving picture theater. He was a round-faced man of forty-five or so, partly bald, for whom the agency had done some work a year or so before in connection with a ticket-seller who had departed without turning in the day's receipts.

In front of Richter a thin white-haired man with doctor written all over him stood looking at Richter's leg, which was wrapped in a bandage just below the knee. Beside the doctor, a tall woman in a fur-trimmed dressing-gown stood, a roll of gauze and a pair of scissors in her hands. A husky police corporal was writing in a notebook at a long narrow table, a thick hickory walking stick laying on the bright blue table cover at his elbow.

All of them looked around at us as we came into the room. The corporal got up and came over to us.

"I knew you were handling the Rounds job, sergeant, so I thought I'd best get word to you as soon as I heard they was brown men mixed up in this."

"Good work, Flynn," O'Gar said. "What happened here?"

"Burglary, or maybe only attempted burglary. They was four of them—crashed the kitchen door."

Richter was sitting up very straight, and his blue eyes were suddenly excited, as were the brown eyes of the woman.

"I beg your pardon," he said, "but is there—you mentioned brown men in connection with another affair—is there another?"

O'Gar looked at me.

"You haven't seen the morning papers?" I asked the theater owner.

"No."

"Well, a man came into the Continental office late this afternoon, with a stab in his chest, and died there. Pressed against the wound, as if to stop the bleeding, was a sarong, which is where we got the brown men idea."

"His name?"

"Rounds, H. R. Rounds."

The name brought no recognition into Richter's eyes.

"A tall man, thin, with dark skin?" he asked. "In a gray suit?"

"All of that."

Richter twisted around to look at the woman.

"Molloy!" he exclaimed.

"Molloy!" she exclaimed.

"So you know him?"

Their faces came back toward me.

"Yes. He was here this afternoon. He left—"

Richter stopped, to turn to the woman again, questioningly.

"Yes, Austin," she said, putting gauze and scissors on the table, and sitting down beside him on the davenport. "Tell them."

He patted her hand and looked up at me again with the expression of a man who has seen a nice spot on which to lay down a heavy load.

"Sit down. It isn't a long story, but sit down." We found ourselves chairs.

"Molloy—Sam Molloy—that is his name, or the name I have always known him by. He came here this afternoon. He'd either called up the theater or gone there, and they had told him I was home. I hadn't seen him for three years. We could see—both my wife and I—that there was something the matter with him when he came in.

"When I asked him, he said he'd been stabbed, by a Siamese, on his way here. He didn't seem to think the wound amounted to much, or pretended he didn't. He wouldn't let us fix it for him, or look at it. He said he'd go to a doctor after he left, after he'd got rid of the thing. That was what he had come to me for. He wanted me to hide it, to take care of it until he came for it again.

"He didn't talk much. He was in a hurry, and suffering. I didn't ask him any questions. I couldn't refuse him anything. I couldn't question him even though he as good as told us that it was illegal as well as dangerous. He saved our lives once—more than my wife's life—down in Mexico, where we first knew him. That was in 1916. We were caught down there during the Villa troubles. Molloy was running guns over the border, and he had enough influence with the bandits to have us released when it looked as if we were done for.

"So this time, when he wanted me to do something for him, I couldn't ask him about it. I said, 'Yes,' and he gave me the package. It wasn't a large package: about the size of—well—a loaf of bread, perhaps, but quite heavy for its size. It was wrapped in brown paper. We unwrapped it after he had gone, that is, we took the paper off. But the inner wrapping was of canvas, tied with silk cord, and sealed, so we didn't open that. We put it upstairs in the pack room, under a pile of old magazines.

"Then, at about a quarter to twelve tonight—I had only been in bed a few minutes, and hadn't gone to sleep yet—I heard a noise in here. I don't own a gun, and there's nothing you could properly call a weapon in the house, but that walking stick"—indicating the hickory stick on the table—"was in a closet in our bedroom. So I got that and came in here to see what the noise was.

"Right outside the bedroom door I ran into a man. I could see him better than he could see me, because this door was open and he showed against the window. He was between me and it, and the moonlight showed him fairly clear. I hit him with the stick, but didn't knock him down. He turned and ran in here. Foolishly, not thinking that he might not be alone, I ran after him. Another man shot me in the leg just as I came through the door.

"I fell, of course. While I was getting up, two of them came in with my wife between them. There were four of them. They were medium-sized men, brown-skinned, but not so dark. I took it for granted that they were Siamese, because Molloy had spoken of Siamese. They turned on the lights here, and one of them, who seemed to be the leader, asked me:

"'Where is it?'

"His accent was pretty bad, but you could understand his words good enough. Of course I knew they were after what Molloy had left, but I pretended I didn't. They told me, or rather the leader did, that he knew it had been left here, but they called Molloy by another name—Dawson. I said I didn't know any Dawson, and nothing had been left here, and I tried to get them to tell me what they expected to find. They wouldn't, though—they just called it '*it*.'

"They talked among themselves, but of course I couldn't make out a word of what they were saving, and then three of them went out, leaving one here to guard us. He had a Luger pistol. We could hear the others moving around the house. The search must have lasted an hour. Then the one I took for the leader came in, and said something to our guard. Both of them looked quite elated.

"'It is not wise if you will leave this room for many minutes,' the leader said to me, and they left us—both of them—closing the door behind them.

"I knew they were going, but I couldn't walk on this leg. From what the doctor says, I'll be lucky if I walk on it inside of a couple of months. I didn't want my wife to go out, and perhaps run into one of them before they'd got away, but she insisted on going. She found they'd gone, and she phoned the police, and then ran up to the pack room and found Molloy's package was gone."

"And this Molloy didn't give you any hint at all as to what was in the package?" O'Gar asked when Richter had finished.

"Not a word, except that it was something the Siamese were after."

"Did he know the Siamese who stabbed him?" I asked.

"I think so," Richter said slowly, "though I am not sure he said he did."

"Do you remember his words?"

"Not exactly, I'm afraid."

"I think I remember them," Mrs Richter said. "My husband, Mr Richter, asked him, 'What's the matter, Molloy? Are you hurt, or sick?'

"Molloy gave a little laugh, putting a hand on his chest, and said, 'Nothing much. I run into a Siamese who was looking for me on my way here, and got careless and let him scratch me. But I kept my little bundle!' And he laughed again, and patted the package."

"Did he say anything else about the Siamese?"

"Not directly," she replied, "though he did tell us to watch out for any Asiatics we saw around the neighborhood. He said he wouldn't leave the package if he thought it would make trouble for us, but that there was always a chance that something would go wrong, and we'd better be careful. And he told my husband"—nodding at Richter—"that the Siamese had been dogging him for months, but now that he had a safe place for the package he was going to 'take them for a walk and forget to bring them back.' That was the way he put it."

"How much do you know about Molloy?"

"Not a great deal, I'm afraid," Richter took up the answering again. "He liked to talk about the places he had been and the things he had seen, but you couldn't get a word out of him about his own affairs. We met him first in Mexico, as I have told you, in 1916. After he saved us down there and got us away, we didn't see him again for nearly four years. He rang the bell one night, and came in for an hour or two. He was on his way to China, he said, and had a lot of business to attend to before he left the next day.

"Some months later I had a letter from him, from the Queen's Hotel in Kandy, asking me to send him a list of the importers and exporters in San Francisco. He wrote me a letter thanking me for the list, and I didn't hear from him again until he came to San Francisco for a week, about a year later. That was in 1921, I think.

"He was here for another week about a year after that, telling us that he had been in Brazil, but, as usual, not saying what he had been doing there. Some months later I had a letter from him, from Chicago, saying he would be here the following week. However, he didn't come. Instead, some time later, he wrote from Vladivostok, saying he hadn't been able to make it. Today was the first we'd heard of him since then."

"Where's his home? His people?"

"He always says he has neither. I've an idea he was born in England, though I don't know that he ever said so, or what made me think so."

"Got any more questions?" I asked O'Gar.

"No. Let's give the place the eye, and see if the Siamese left any leads behind 'em."

The eye we gave the house was thorough. We didn't split the territory between us, but went over everything together—everything from roof to cellar—every nook, drawer, corner.

The cellar did most for us: it was there, in the cold furnace, that we found the handful of black buttons and the fire-darkened garter clasps. But the upper floors hadn't been altogether worthless: in one room we had found the crumpled sales slip of an Oakland store, marked *1 table cover*, and in another room we had found no garters.

"Of course it's none of my business," I told Richter when O'Gar and I joined the others again, "but I think maybe if you plead self-defense you might get away with it."

He tried to jump up from the davenport, but his shot leg failed him.

The woman got up slowly.

"And maybe that would leave an out for you," O'Gar told her. "Why don't you try to persuade him?"

"Or maybe it would be better if you plead the self-defense," I suggested to her. "You could say that Richter ran to your help when your husband grabbed you, that your husband shot him and was turning his gun on you when you stabbed him. That would sound smooth enough."

"My husband?"

"Uh-huh, Mrs Rounds-Molloy-Dawson. Your late husband, anyway."

Richter got his mouth far enough closed to get words out of it.

"What is the meaning of this damned nonsense?" he demanded.

"Them's harsh words to come from a fellow like you," O'Gar growled at him. "If this is nonsense, what do you make of that yarn you told us about creeping Siamese and mysterious bundles, and God knows what all?"

"Don't be too hard on him," I told O'Gar. "Being around movies all the time has poisoned his idea of what sounds plausible. If it hadn't, he'd have known better than to see a Siamese in the moonlight at 11:45, when the moon was just coming up at somewhere around 12:45, when you phoned me."

Richter stood up on his one good leg.

The husky police corporal stepped close to him.

"Hadn't I better frisk him, sergeant?"

O'Gar shook his bullet head.

"Waste of time. He's got nothing on him. They cleaned the place of weapons. The chances are the lady dropped them in the bay when she rode over to Oakland to get a table cover to take the place of the sarong her husband carried away with him."

That shook the pair of them. Richter pretended he hadn't gulped, and the woman had a fight of it before she could make her eyes stay still on mine.

O'Gar struck while the iron was hot by bringing the buttons and garters clasps we had salvaged out of his pocket, and letting them trickle from one hand to another. That used up the last bit of the facts we had.

I threw a lie at them.

"Never me to knock the press, but you don't want to put too much confidence in what the papers say. For instance, a fellow might say a few pregnant words before he died, and the papers might say he didn't. A thing like that would confuse things."

The woman reared up her head and looked at O'Gar.

"May I speak to Austin alone?" she asked. "I don't mean out of your sight."

The detective sergeant scratched his head and looked at me. This letting your victims go into conference is always a ticklish business: they may decide to come clean, and then again, they may frame up a new out. On the other hand, if you don't let them, the chances are they get stubborn on you, and you can't get anything out of them. One way was as risky as another. I grinned at O'Gar and refused to make a suggestion. He could decide for himself, and, if he was wrong, I'd have him to dump the blame on. He scowled at me, and then nodded to the woman.

"You can go over into that corner and whisper together for a couple of minutes," he said, "but no foolishness."

She gave Richter the hickory stick, took his other arm, helped him hobble to a far corner, pulled a chair over there for him. He sat with his back to us. She stood behind him, leaning over his shoulder, so that both their faces were hidden from us.

O'Gar came closer to me.

"What do you think?" he muttered.

"I think they'll come through."

"That shot of yours about being Molloy's wife hit center. I missed that one. How'd you make it?"

"When she was telling us what Molloy had said about the Siamese she took pains both times she said 'my husband' to show that she meant Richter."

"So? Well—"

The whispering in the far corner had been getting louder, so that the s's had become sharp hisses. Now a clear emphatic sentence came from Richter's mouth.

"I'll be damned if I will!"

Both of them looked furtively over their shoulders, and they lowered their voices again, but not for long. The woman was apparently trying to persuade him to do something. He kept shaking his head. He put a hand on her arm. She pushed it away, and kept on whispering.

He said aloud, deliberately:

"Go ahead, if you want to be a fool. It's your neck. I didn't put the knife in him."

She jumped away from him, her eyes black blazes in a white face. O'Gar and I moved softly toward them.

"You rat!" she spat at Richter, and spun to face us.

"I killed him!" she cried. "This thing in the chair tried to and—"

Richter swung the hickory stick.

I jumped for it—missed—crashed into the back of his chair. Hickory stick, Richter, chair, and I sprawled together on the floor. The corporal helped me up. He and I picked Richter up and put him on the davenport again.

The woman's story poured out of her angry mouth:

"His name wasn't Molloy. It was Lange, Sam Lange. I married him in Providence in 1913 and went to China with him—to Canton, where he had a position with a steamship line. We didn't stay there long, because he got into some trouble through being mixed up in the revolution that year. After that we drifted around, mostly around Asia.

"We met this thing"—she pointed at the now sullenly quiet Richter—"in Singapore, in 1919, I think—right after the World War was over. His name is Holley, and Scotland Yard can tell you something about him. He had a proposition. He knew of a gem-bed in upper Burma, one of many that were hidden from the British when they took the country. He knew the natives who were working it, knew where they were hiding their gems.

"My husband went in with him, with two other men that were killed. They looted the natives' cache, and got away with a whole sackful of sapphires, topazes and even a few rubies. The two other men were killed by the natives and my husband was badly wounded.

"We didn't think he could live. We were hiding in a hut near the Yunnan border. Holley persuaded me to take the gems and run away with them. It looked as if Sam was done for, and if we stayed there long we'd be caught. I can't say that I was crazy about Sam anyway; he wasn't the kind you would be, after living with him for a while.

"So Holley and I took it and lit out. We had to use a lot of the stones to buy our way through Yunnan and Kwangsi and Kwangtung, but we made it. We got to San Francisco with enough to buy this house and the movie theater, and we've been here since. We've been honest since we came here, but I don't suppose that means am thing. We had enough money to keep us comfortable.

"Today Sam showed up. We hadn't heard of him since we left him on his back in Burma. He said he'd been caught and jailed for three years. Then he'd got away, and had spent the other three hunting for us. He was that kind. He didn't want me back, but he did want money. He wanted everything we had. Holley lost his nerve. Instead of bargaining with Sam, he lost his head and tried to shoot him.

"Sam took his gun away from him and shot him in the leg. In the scuffle Sam had dropped a knife—a kris, I think. I picked it up, but he grabbed me just as I got it. I don't know how it happened. All I saw was Sam staggering back, holding his chest with both hands—and the kris shining red in my hand.

"Sam had dropped his gun. Holley got it and was all for shooting Sam, but I wouldn't let him. It happened in this room. I don't remember whether I gave Sam the sarong we used for a cover on the table or not. Anyway, he tried to stop the blood with it. He went away then, while I kept Holley from shooting him.

"I knew Sam wouldn't go to the police, but I didn't know what he'd do. And I knew he was hurt bad. If he dropped dead somewhere, the chances are he'd be traced here. I watched from a window as he went down the street, and nobody seemed to pay any attention to him, but he looked so conspicuously wounded to me that I thought everybody would be sure to remember him if it got into the papers that he had been found dead somewhere.

"Holley was even more scared than I. We couldn't run away, because he had a shot leg. So we made up that Siamese story, and I went over to Oakland, and bought the table cover to take the place of the sarong. We had some guns and even a few oriental knives and swords here. I wrapped them up in paper, breaking the swords, and dropped them off the ferry when I went to Oakland.

"When the morning papers came out we read what had happened, and then we went ahead with what we had planned. We burned the suit Holley had worn when he was shot, and his garters—because the pants had a bullet-hole in them, and the bullet had cut one garter. We fixed a hole in his pajama-leg, unbandaged his leg,—I had fixed it as well as I could,—and washed away the clotted blood until it began to bleed again. Then I gave the alarm."

She raised both hands in a gesture of finality and made a clucking sound with her tongue.

"And there you are," she said.

"You got anything to say?" I asked Holley, who was staring at his bandaged leg.

"To my lawyer," he said without looking up.

O'Gar spoke to the corporal.

"The wagon, Flynn."

Ten minutes later we were in the street, helping Holley and the woman into a police car.

Around the corner on the other side of the street came three brown-skinned men, apparently Malay sailors. The one in the middle seemed to be drunk, and the other two were supporting him. One of them had a package that could have held a bottle under his arm.

O'Gar looked from them to me and laughed.

"We wouldn't be doing a thing to those babies right now if we had fallen for that yarn, would we?" he whispered.

"Shut up, you, you big heap!" I growled back, nodding at Holley, who was in the car by now. "If that bird sees them he'll identify 'em as his Siamese, and God knows what a jury would make of it!"

We made the puzzled driver twist the car six blocks out of his way to be sure we'd miss the brown men. It was worth it, because nothing interfered with the twenty years apiece that Holley and Mrs Lange drew.

Yellowback range available...

1. The Old Man in the Corner by Orczy, Baroness Emma
2. The Complete Max Carrados Vol 1 by Bramah, Ernest
3. The Complete Max Carrados Vol 2 by Bramah, Ernest

THE ARSÈNE LUPIN SERIES BY LEBLANC, MAURICE:

4. Arsène Lupin 1: The Extraordinary Adventures of Arsène Lupin - Gentleman Burglar
5. Arsène Lupin 2: Arsène Lupin vs. Herlock Sholmes
6. Arsène Lupin 3. The Hollow Needle
7. Arsène Lupin 4: 813
8. Arsène Lupin 5: The Crystal Stopper
9. Arsène Lupin 6: The Confessions of Arsène Lupin
10. Arsène Lupin 7: The Teeth of the Tiger
11. Arsène Lupin 8: The Shell Shard (aka The Woman of Mystery)
12. Arsène Lupin 9: The Return of Arsène Lupin (aka The Golden Triangle)
13. Arsène Lupin 10: The secret of Sarek (aka Island of Thirty Coffins)
14. Arsène Lupin 11: The Eight Strokes of the Clock
15. Arsène Lupin 12: The Secret Tomb
16. Arsène Lupin 13: The Countess of Cagliostro (aka Memoirs of Arsène Lupin)
17. Arsène Lupin (bonus book): Arsène Lupin (novelised by Edgar Jepson from LeBlanc's original play)

18. The Complete Raffles by Hornung, E. W.
19. The Mysterious Mickey Finn by Paul, Eliott
20. You Play the Black and the Red Comes Up by Hallas, Richard
21. The Mr. Moto Omnibus Vol 1 by Marquand, John P.
22. The Mr. Moto Omnibus Vol 2 by Marquand, John P.
23. The Complete Father Brown Vol 1 (with original illustrations) by Chesterton, G. K.
24. The Complete Father Brown Vol 2 (with original illustrations) by Chesterton, G. K.
25. A Peter Wimsey omnibus: Murder Must Advertise & The Nine Tailors by Sayers, Dorothy L.
26. Was it Murder? by Hilton, James
27. The Complete Just Men Volume 1 by Wallace, Edgar
28. The Complete Just Men Volume 2 by Wallace, Edgar
29. Carnacki by Hodgson, William Hope
30. Grey Mask by Wentworth, Patricia
31. The Case With Nine Solutions by Connington, J. J.
32. Murder by Matchlight by Lorac, E. C. R.
33. The Crossword Mystery by Punshon, E. R.
34. The Cask by Crofts, Freeman Wills
35. The Bells of Old Bailey by Bowers, Dorothy
36. Crime Unlimited by Hume, David
37. The A. A. Milne Mystery Omnibus (contains: The Red house and Four days' wonder) by Milne, A. A.
38. She Faded into Air by White, Ethel Lina
39. The Wheel Spins by White, Ethel Lina
40. The Spiral Staircase by White, Ethel Lina
41. Murder of a Lady by Wynne, Anthony
42. Thirteen Guests by Farjeon, J. Jefferson
43. The Daughter of Time by Tey, Josephine
44. The Man in the Queue by Tey, Josephine
45. A Shilling for Candles by Tey, Josephine
46. The Franchise Affair by Tey, Josephine
47. Tragedy at Law by Hare, Cyril
48. The Moonstone by Collins, Wilkie
49. The Woman in White by Collins, Wilkie
50. The Circular Staircase by Rinehart, Mary Roberts
51. The Benson Murder Case by Van Dine, S. S.
52. The Philip Marlowe Omnibus by Chandler, Raymond
53. Monsieur Lecoq by Gaboriau, Emile
54. Aurora Floyd by Braddon, Mary Elizabeth
55. The Big Bow Mystery by Zangwill, Israel
56. Dossier 113 (aka The Blackmailers) by Gaboriau, Emile
57. The Mystery of a Hansom Cab by Hume, Fergus
58. The W Plan by Seton, Graham
59. Inspector French's Greatest Case by Crofts, Freeman Wills

60. Mr Bowling Buys a Newspaper by Henderson, Donald
61. A Voice Like Velvet by Henderson, Donald
62. The Deductions of Colonel Gore by Brock, Lynn
63. The Rogue's Syndicate by Froest, Frank
64. The Middle Temple Murder by Fletcher, J. S.
65. The Millionaire Mystery by Hume, Fergus
66. Below the Clock by Turner, J. V.
67. The Rouletabille Omnibus: The Mystery of the Yellow Room and The Perfume of the Lady in Black by Leroux, Gaston
68. The Complete Dupin by Poe, Edgar Allan
69. The Complete Thinking Machine Vol 1 by Futrelle, Jacques
70. The Complete Thinking Machine Vol 2 by Futrelle, Jacques
71. The Complete Thinking Machine Vol 3 by Futrelle, Jacques
72. The Complete Montague Egg by Sayers, Dorothy L.
73. The Complete J. G. Reeder by Wallace, Edgar
74. The Complete Charlie Chan Vol 1 by Biggers, Earl der
75. The Complete Charlie Chan Vol 2 by Biggers, Earl der
76. The Dr Nikola Omnibus Vol 1 by Boothby, Guy
77. The Dr Nikola Omnibus Vol 2 by Boothby, Guy
78. A Prince of Swindlers: The Simon Carne collection by Boothby, Guy
79. The Slim Callaghan Omnibus by Cheyney, Peter
80. The Fu Manchu Omnibus by Rohmer, Sax
81. The Bulldog Drummond Omnibus: The Complete Peterson Rounds by Sapper
82. The Avenging Ray by Seamark
83. The Richard Chandos Omnibus by Yates, Dornford
84. The Alan Quatermain Omnibus: King Solomon's Mines & Allan Quatermain by Haggard, H. Rider
85. The 39 steps by Buchan, John
86. At The Villa Rose by Mason, A.E.W.
87. The Eye of Osiris by Freeman, R. Austin
88. The Weapons of Mystery by Hocking, Joseph
89. The House of Dr. Edwardes by Beeding, Francis
90. The Seven Secrets by Le Queux, William
91. Call Mr Fortune by Bailey, H. C.
92. The Three Taps by Knox, Ronald
93. The Girl at Central by Bonner, Geraldine
94. The Experiences of Loveday Brooke, Lady Detective by Pirkis, Catherine Louisa
95. Mary Louise by Baum, L. Frank
96. That Affair Next Door by Green, Anna Katherine
97. Dead Letter by Regester, Seeley
98. The Tragedy of Pudd'nhead Wilson by Twain, Mark
99. The Big Clock by Fearing, Kenneth
100. The Woman in the Window by Wallis, J. H.
101. The Sexton Blake Collection Vol 1 by Hal Meredeth (or many?)
102. The Complete Simon Iff Stories by Crowley, Aleister
103. The Castle of Otranto by Walpole, Horace
104. The Adventures of the Infallible Godahl by Anderson, Frederick Irving

THE COMPLETE SHERLOCK HOLMES

105. A Study In Scarlet
106. The Sign Of Four
107. The Adventures Of Sherlock Holmes
108. The Memoirs Of Sherlock Holmes
109. The Hound Of The Baskervilles
110. The Return Of Sherlock Holmes
111. His Last Bow
112. The Valley Of Fear
113. The Case-Book Of Sherlock Holmes

114. Graustark: The Story of a Love Behind a Throne by George Barr McCutcheon
115. Beverly of Graustark by George Barr McCutcheon
116. Truxton King: A Story of Graustark by George Barr McCutcheon
117. The Prince of Graustark by George Barr McCutcheon
118. The Complete Zenda Omnibus by Anthony Hope
119. The Mad king by Burroughs, Edgar Rice
120. The Fantomas Omnibus by Souvestre, Pierre

121. The Problemist by Clinton H. Stagg
122. The Dorrington Deed-Box by Morrison, Arthur
123. The Lone Wolf by Vance, L. J.
124. The Complete Martin Hewitt Collection Vol 1: Martin Hewitt, Investigator & Chronicles of Martin Hewitt by Morrison, Arthur
125. The Complete Martin Hewitt Collection Vol 2: Adventures of Martin Hewitt & The Red Triangle: Further Chronicles of Martin Hewitt by Morrison, Arthur
126. Seven Keys to Baldpate by Earl Derr Biggers
127. No Pockets in a Shroud by McCoy, Horace
128. The John Silence Collection by Blackwood, Algernon
129. Lady Molly Of Scotland Yard by Orczy, Baroness Emma
130. Skin O' My Tooth by Orczy, Baroness Emma
131. The Wrong Box by Stevenson, R. L. and Lloyd Osbourne
132. Tutt and Mr Tutt by Train, Arthur C.
133. The Clue by Wells, Carolyn
134. The Complete Trent Case Book by Bentley, E. C.
135. The Luck of the Vails by Benson, E. F.
136. The Rome Express by Griffiths, Arthur
137. The Complete Curious Mr Tarrant by C. Daly King
138. Rope and Gaslight (2-in-1 text) by Hamilton, Patrick
139. Prince Zaleski and Cumming's King Monk by Shiel, M. P.
140. The Assassination Bureau Ltd. by London, Jack
141. Introducing Clubfoot by Williams, Valentine
142. Master of Mysteries: The complete Uncle Abner collection by Post, Melville Davisson
143. The Red Redmaynes by Phillpotts, Eden
144. Thrilling Stories of the Railway by Whitechurch, Victor L.
145. The Grey Wig: Stories and Novelettes by Zangwill, Israel
146. The Lodger by Lowndes, Marie Belloc
147. The Man from Manchester by Donovan, Dick (Joyce Emerson Preston Muddock)
148. Mr. Meeson's Will by H. Rider Haggard by Haggard, H. Rider
149. Devlin the Barber by Farjeon, B. L.
150. Checkmate by Joseph Sheridan Le Fanu
151. Recollections of a Detective Police-Officer by Waters
152. The Widow Lerouge by Gaboriau, Emile
153. The Expressman and the Detective by Pinkerton, Allan
154. Zadig and Vathek by Voltaire
155. The Stillwater Tragedy by Aldrich, Thomas Bailey
156. The Memoirs of Constantine Dix by Pain, Barry
157. Ashes to Ashes by Ostrander, Isabel
158. The Jewel of Seven Stars by Stoker, Bram
159. The Thomas Love Peacock Collection by Peacock, Thomas Love

THE COMPLETE DERLETH SOLAR PONS

160. In Re: Sherlock Holmes - The Adventures of Solar Pons
161. The Memoirs of Solar Pons
162. The Return of Solar Pons
163. The Reminiscences of Solar Pons
164. The Casebook of Solar Pons
165. The Novels of Solar Pons: Terror over London and Mr. Fairlie's Final Journey
166. The Chronicles of Solar Pons
167. The Apocrypha of Solar Pons

168. The Triumphs of Eugene Valmont
169. The Female Detective by Forrester, Andrew
170. Cain's Jawbone by Torquemada
171. The Great Impersonation by Oppenheim, E. Phillips

THE DASHIELL HAMMETT COLLECTION

172. The Complete Sam Spade
173. The Complete Thin Man
174. The Complete Continental Op Vol 1
175. The Complete Continental Op Vol 2

For more details and a full list of titles visit https://www.hachetteindia.com/home/yellowbacks